D0629632

TOUGH GUYS
&
Dangerous Dames

Tough Guys

& Dangerous Dames

Edited by

Robert E. Weinberg,
Stefan Dziemianowicz
and Martin H. Greenberg

BARNES
&NOBLE
BOOKS
NEW YORK

The editors would like to thank Walker Martin
for his invaluable assistance in preparing this book.

Copyright © 1993 by Robert E. Weinberg,
Stefan R. Dziemianowicz and Martin H. Greenberg.
All rights reserved.

This edition published by Barnes & Noble, Inc.,
by arrangement with Martin H. Greenberg.

1993 Barnes & Noble Books

Book design by Charles Ziga, Ziga Design

ISBN 1-56619-011-8

Printed and bound in the United States of America

M 9 8 7 6 5 4 3 2 1

Acknowledgments

Grateful acknowledgment is made to the following for permission to reprint their copyright materials:

"The Magician Murder" by Ramon DeColta (pseudonym for Raoul F. Whitfield), copyright 1932 by Keith Alan Deutsch. All rights reserved. From THE BLACK MASK, issue 15, No. 9 (Nov. 1932); Copyright 1932 by Pro-Distributors Publishing Company, Inc. Copyright renewed © 1960 by Popular Publications, Inc. Assigned to Keith Alan Deutsch. Reprinted by special arrangement with Keith Alan Deutsch, proprietor and conservator of the respective copyrights and successor-in-interest to Popular Publications, Inc.

"Black" by Paul Cain (a.k.a. Peter Ruric; né George Sims), copyright 1932 by Keith Alan Deutsch. All rights reserved. From THE BLACK MASK, issue 15, No. 3 (May 1932); Copyright 1932 by Pro-Distributors Publishing Company, Inc. Copyright renewed © 1960 by Popular Publications, Inc. Assigned to Keith Alan Deutsch. Reprinted by special arrangement with Keith Alan Deutsch, proprietor and conservator of the respective copyrights and successor-in-interest to Popular Publications, Inc.

The title and logo BLACK MASK is the exclusive copyright of Keith Alan Deutsch.

"Sail" by Lester Dent. Copyright 1936, © 1964 by Lester Dent. From BLACK MASK. Reprinted by permission of Mrs. Norma Dent and Will Murray.

*   *   *

"The King in Yellow" by Raymond Chandler—from THE SIMPLE ART OF MURDER by Raymond Chandler. Copyright © 1950 by Raymond Chandler, © renewed 1978 by Helga Greene. Reprinted by permission of Houghton Mifflin Co. All rights reserved.

"Chains of Darkness" by Frederick Nebel. From DIME DETECTIVE MAGAZINE, July 1, 1933. Copyright 1933 by Popular Publications, Inc. Copyright renewed © 1962 and assigned to Argosy Communications, Inc. All rights reserved. Reprinted by permission of Argosy Communications, Inc.

"The Arm of Mother Manzoli" by Merle Constiner. From DIME DETECTIVE MAGAZINE, April, 1944. Copyright 1944 by Popular Publications, Inc. Copyright renewed © 1972 and assigned to Argosy Communications, Inc. All rights reserved. Reprinted by permission of Argosy Communications, Inc.

"Murder in the Red" by Norbert Davis. From DIME DETECTIVE MAGAZINE, April, 1940. Copyright 1940 by Popular Publications, Inc. Copyright renewed © 1968 and assigned to Argosy Communications, Inc. All rights reserved. Reprinted by permission of Argosy Communications, Inc.

"Brand of Kane" by Hugh B. Cave. From DIME DETECTIVE MAGAZINE, July 15, 1935. Copyright 1935 by Popular Publications, Inc. Reprinted by permission of the author.

"Two Biers for Buster" by William Campbell Gault. Copyright 1947 by Popular Publications, Inc. First published in DIME DETECTIVE. Reprinted by permission of the author.

"Mr. Sinister" by Carroll John Daly. From FLYNN'S DETECTIVE FICTION, April, 1944. Copyright 1944 by Fictioneers, Inc., a subsidiary of Popular Publications, Inc. Copyright renewed © 1972 and assigned to Argosy Communications, Inc. All rights reserved. Reprinted by permission of Argosy Communications, Inc.

"The Kid Clips a Coupon" by Erle Stanley Gardner. Copyright 1934 by Popular Publications, Inc. From DETECTIVE FICTION WEEKLY, April 21, 1934. Reprinted by permission of Curtis Brown, Ltd.

"The Lady is a Corpse!" by John D. MacDonald. Copyright 1950 by Popular Publications, Inc. From DETECTIVE TALES, September, 1950. Reprinted by permission of George Diskant and Associates, Inc.

"The Lunatic Plague" by Donald Wandrei. Copyright 1936 by Street & Smith Publications, Inc. From CLUES, August, 1936. Reprinted by permission of Helen Mary Hughesdon.

"Slack Wires" by Arthur J. Burks. Copyright 1937 by Street & Smith Publications, Inc. From CLUES, February, 1937. Reprinted by permission of Forrest J Ackerman, 2495 Glendower Ave., Hollywood, CA 90027.

"Names in the Black Book" by Robert E. Howard. Copyright 1934 by Trojan Publications. From SUPER DETECTIVE STORIES, May, 1934. Reprinted by permission of Glenn Lord.

"Power of the Puppets" by Fritz Leiber. Copyright 1942 by Better Publications. From THRILLING MYSTERY, January, 1942. Reprinted by permission of Richard Curtis Associates, Inc.

"Death is a Vampire" by Robert Bloch. Copyright 1944 by Better Publications. From THRILLING MYSTERY, Fall, 1944. Reprinted by permission of the Scott Meredith Literary Agency, Inc., 845 Third Ave., New York, NY 10022.

"I Feel Bad Killing You" by Leigh Brackett. Copyright 1944 by Fictioneers, Inc., a subsidiary of Popular Publications, Inc. Copyright renewed © 1972 and assigned to Argosy Communications, Inc. All rights reserved. Reprinted by permission of Blassingame, McCauley and Wood.

"The Case of the Frozen Corpses" by Ray Cummings. Copyright 1939 by Popular Publications, Inc. From DIME MYSTERY, January, 1939. Reprinted by permission of Forrest J Ackerman, 2495 Glendower Ave., Hollywood, CA 90027.

"Death at the Main" by Frank Gruber. Copyright 1936 by Standard Magazines, Inc. From THRILLING DETECTIVE, December, 1936. Reprinted by permission of the Scott Meredith Literary Agency, Inc., 845 Third Ave., New York, NY 10022.

Contents

INTRODUCTION

Between 1920 and 1950, America was one tough country. The landscape from New York City to Los Angeles was a single poorly-lit city street, traversed by huge black sedans with running boards and lined with gambling dens, speakeasies, and cheap boarding houses. The residents were small-time hoods perpetually muffled in fedoras and rumpled overcoats, rich thrill-seekers slumming to pique their jaded appetites, smart-aleck con men looking to make a quick buck, and painted ladies of dubious virtue. When they walked the streets it was to a background rhythm of belching .45 automatics police were powerless to stop. None of them showed their face before nightfall, and every morning, they read the obituaries like the sports page.

This is a gross exaggeration of course, but you would have had a hard time proving it to readers of pulp detective magazines. More than 200 such magazines were published in the first half of this century, and virtually all of them depicted an America overrun with criminals, seething with vice, and wallowing in moral turpitude. Here was the home of the hard-boiled detective, a character whose existence confirmed the country's social decline, and whose task it was to halt it.

Tough Guys and Dangerous Dames is a celebration of the hard-boiled detective, a true American folk hero who stood with one foot firmly planted in the imaginations of writers and the other in the reality of twentieth-century urban America. He first began appearing in stories about the time that popular fiction began reflecting the gritty facts of life in "The Roaring Twenties": racketeering, organized crime, bootlegging, police corruption, and other anti-social activities that elite nineteenth-century crime fighters might have deemed beneath their dignity. He was a man of the people who believed in democratic ideals and sought ways to circumvent the injustice of traditional systems of law enforcement. Unlike his Holmesian predecessors, who rarely soiled their fingers, the hard-boiled detective was also a man of action who was not afraid to enforce his personal code of honor with the appropriate hardware. If you didn't admire his values, you at least had to respect his body count.

The hard-boiled detective appeared under scores of names during the pulp years, and each of his avatars could be counted on to find an audience willing to follow his continuing adventures. His pervasive influence is evident from the twenty-four stories collected here from twelve representative magazines of the hard-boiled era. After the hard-boiled detective's debut in 1923, no mystery-detective magazine went untouched by his example.

The magazine that became synonymous with the hard-boiled detective was *Black Mask* (1920–1951). It hadn't been planned that way. *Black Mask* was created by H. L. Mencken and George Jean Nathan, who determined that the money they could make from a popular mystery fiction magazine would help subsidize their literary periodical *The Smart Set*. Because they interpreted "mystery" very broadly, early issues of *Black Mask* included western, adventure, and ghost stories as well as tales of crime and detection.

When *Black Mask* debuted in April 1920, its contents were nearly indistinguishable from those of other general fiction magazines at the newsstands. Then, in the June 1, 1923 issue, Carroll John Daly introduced Race Williams, the first hard-boiled detective, in his story "Knights of the Open Palm." Four months later the magazine published Peter Collinson's "Arson Plus," the first of thirty-four stories that would center around another hard-boiled detective, the Continental Op. Collinson was a pseudonym for Dashiell Hammett, the writer whom Joseph T. "Cap" Shaw would make the cornerstone of the magazine when he assumed editorial duties with the December 1926 issue.

As Shaw was to write in his introduction to *The Hard-Boiled Omnibus* in 1946, he recognized in Hammett's fiction a quality that distinguished it from the sophisticated but stodgy tales of deduction that hitherto had dominated the field: "character conflict is the main theme; the ensuing crime, or its threat, is incidental." He encouraged other writers to follow Hammett's method, for he believed that by predicating stories on "the problems inherent in human behavior," authors could wreak an infinite number of variations on the limited detective story formula.

This was borne out by the legacy of *Black Mask*, particularly during Shaw's tenure. The ten years that he managed the magazine represent the Golden Age of the hard-boiled tale. Writers whom he published included most of those who helped define the form: Dashiell Hammett, Carroll John Daly, Raymond Chandler, Horace McCoy (who would later write the *noir* classic *They Shoot Horses, Don't They?*), Erle Stanley Gardner, Norbert Davis, and Theodore Tinsely. In fact, the majority of authors in this book eventually published a story in *Black Mask*.

Raoul Whitfield was one of Shaw's most dependable writers. He published ninety stories in *Black Mask*, and was so prolific that it was necessary to publish his two dozen adventures of Filipino detective Joe Gar under the pseudonym Ramon Decolta. "The Magician Murder" (1932) is a typical Joe Gar tale that hews perfectly to Shaw's prescriptions for hard-boiled writing:

the crime is not nearly as interesting as the greedy motivations of its criminals or the inherent disrespect of the police force for private detectives.

In contrast to the exotic setting and clear motives of Whitfield's Jo Gar tales, Paul Cain (a pseudonym for screenwriter Peter Ruric) explored murky city streets and even murkier motives for the characters in his seventeen *Black Mask* stories. Cain earned a reputation as the most hard-boiled of all hard-boiled writers, not only for his terse prose style but because of the depressing bleakness of many of his plots. "Black" (1932), one of two stories about the eponymous gunman (who was never given a first name), is quintessential Cain: by the end of the story, justice has been served but it's questionable whether good has actually triumphed.

Lester Dent was one of the last writers to publish in *Black Mask* during the Shaw years. "Sail" (1936) was the first of two Dent stories featuring Oscar Sail, an operative who (like Dent himself) lived on a boat off the Florida coast. The story's opening scene, in which Sail works coolly to conceal a corpse from a snooping police officer, is more hard-boiled than anything that had appeared in the *Doc Savage* novels Dent had been writing under the Kenneth Robeson pseudonym since 1933, and a good example of how *Black Mask* gave writers a chance to flex their imaginations.

Clues Detectives Stories (1926–1943) was a more varied magazine than *Black Mask*. It debuted several years after *Black Mask* went hard-boiled, and although the hard-boiled influence eventually crept into its pages, it offered readers an unpredictable mix of traditional and non-traditional detective and crime fiction. The magazine's eclectic character was no doubt shaped by three editor and publisher changes in its first seven years. It was enhanced when Street & Smith Publications bought the magazine in 1933 and began publishing stories by writers associated with genres other than the mystery-detective field.

Donald Wandrei had distinguished himself in Street & Smith's science fiction magazine *Astounding Stories* before he began writing his tales of detective inventor I. V. Frost in the mid-1930s. Small wonder, then, that Frost is a sort of scientific Sherlock Holmes who, as Wandrei writes in "The Lunatic Plague (1936), "lived purely for the thrill of the man hunt, the pursuit of knowledge, the application of logic and science to the solution of crime." Wandrei's twist on the hard-boiled formula was to make Frost the brains of his serial adventures, and his beautiful assistant, the petite Jean Moray, the unlikely brawn.

Pulpsmith Arthur J. Burks had written nearly every type of pulp fiction, including several detective series, by the time he began writing for *Clues*. Harlan Dyce, the circus-midget turned detective in "Slack Wires" (1937) and other adventures was, like Burks's blind ex-prize fighter detective Eddie

Kelly, a forerunner of the so-called "defective detective," an unusual sub-genre of hard-boiled fiction from the late 1930s in which the heroes all had to factor their peculiar physical or medical problems into their crime-solving exploits.

Another publication full of unusual detectives was *Detective Dragnet* (1928–1949), which changed its name to *10 Detective Aces* in 1933. Exploring the more dramatic possibilities inherent in the detective story format, it ranged between stories of weird menace and often weirder heroes. Paul Chadwick's "Tarantula Bait" (1932) is one of several adventures in which criminologist Wade Hammond is tasked with unmasking the evil intelligence behind a seemingly supernatural plot. Frederick C. Davis's "The Sinister Sphere" (1933) introduced Stephen Thatcher, alias the "Moon Man," an athletic vigilante wearing a helmet made of two-way argus glass, who robbed from white collar criminals to redistribute their ill-gotten gains among the Depression-era poor in thirty-eight adventures written between 1933 and 1936.

Popular Publications' *Dime Detective* (1931–1953) was more in the *Black Mask* mold. Present in the first issue and in forty-three more issues between 1931 and 1937 was Frederick Nebel's Jack Cardigan, the longest-lived and arguably definitive "dime detective." Cardigan was the muscle behind the two-man Cosmos Agency, and in stories like "Chains of Darkness" (1933), sometimes took to violent extremes the antipathy between private detectives and police officers. Of particular importance in these stories is Cardigan's spunky assistant Patricia Seaward, one of the first women to be given more than just the frail heroine's role in hard-boiled fiction.

Raymond Chandler came to *Dime Detective* from *Black Mask* and brought with him the character type who would eventually become detective Philip Marlowe, hero of critically acclaimed novels such as *The Big Sleep* (1939), *Farewell, My Lovely* (1940), and *The Lady in the Lake* (1943). Chandler wrote only seven stories for *Dime Detective*, all of them remarkable for their portrayal of the hard-boiled detective as a natural outgrowth of his environment. "The King in Yellow" was the only story not to feature Marlowe-prototype John Dalmas, but like Dalmas, its anti-hero detective Steve Grayce seems as much a prisoner of his seedy, cut-rate milieu as the hero who rises above it.

The traditional hard-boiled dick championed by Chandler and Nebel never went out of style in *Dime Detective*, as is evident from his appearance as late as 1947 in William Campbell Gault's "Two Biers for Buster," an uncommon blend of detection and wartime intrigue. However, many *Dime Detective* authors explored less traditional pathways for developing the characters of their stories. By the mid-1930s the newsstands were deluged with monthly, bi-monthly and even weekly mystery-detective magazines, and it was getting hard to tell the hard-boiled detectives apart. In the hope of engaging reader interest, many writers began endowing their series detectives with personality quirks that made them stand out from the crowd.

One of the more original was Hugh B. Cave's 80-proof detective, Peter Kane. A former cop, Kane epitomized the detective who was not immune to the snares of his vice-ridden environment, drinking his way through nine adventures written between 1934 and 1942. "The Brand of Kane" (1935) displays him at his wisecracking best, acting with more shrewdness and perspicacity while under the influence than any of his sober suspects.

Like Cave, many other *Dime Detective* writers found a way to leaven their hard-boiled tales with humor. Fred MacIsaac's bookish Addison "The Rambler" Murphy, hero of "Blond Cargo" (1936), was one of several reporters-cum-detective in the hard-boiled pulps, but probably the only one temperamentally incapable of handling advances from grateful female clients. Norbert Davis's William "Bail Bond" Dodd, hero of eight stories between 1940 and 1943, was a hard-boiled detective by default—a bail bondsman whose familiarity with a wacky assortment of petty felons and criminals plunked him down in the middle of such screwball capers as "Murder in the Red" (1940). Merle Constiner's detective buddy stories of erudite Wardlow "The Dean" Rock and his street-smart assistant Ben Matthews appeared in nineteen issues of the magazine between 1940 and 1945 and were renowned for making mysteries out of even more outlandish clues than the love potion, fake emeralds, boxing pictures, and wax dummy's arm found in "The Arm of Mother Manzoli" (1944).

Dime Detective dominated the pulp detective market not only through its own considerable strengths, but through Popular Publications buying up the magazine's competitors. Indeed, it even bought *Black Mask* in 1940. Three years later, it added another jewel to its crown, *Detective Fiction Weekly* (1924–1951), which it would ultimately absorb into *Dime Detective*. *Detective Fiction Weekly* had been created by the Frank A. Munsey Company, inventors of the pulp magazine, to cash in on the burgeoning mystery pulp market. Even after *Black Mask's* success, it refrained from turning completely into a hard-boiled magazine, as can be seen from Erle Stanley Gardner's "The Kid Clips a Coupon" (1934), one of several adventures of The Patent Leather Kid. Gardner, who would later achieve fame as the creator of Perry Mason, conceived his stories of gentleman detective Dan Seller and protégé Bill Brakey as tough variations on the Robin Hood theme. In doing so, he helped create the prototype for pop culture heroes such as Batman and the Green Hornet.

At the magazine's other extreme, though, was Satan Hall, the hero of Carroll John Daly's "Mr. Sinister" (1944) and arguably the toughest of all hard-boiled detectives. A literal avenging angel, the misanthropic Hall was always the last resort of his police force. He had a reputation as the only detective whom criminals actually feared, and only his police badge justified the number of kills he racked up in twenty-two adventures between 1931 and 1954. Readers familiar with Mickey Spillane's shoot-first-ask-questions-later detective Mike Hammer know that Spillane cited Daly as a major influence on his writing.

One of the more interesting sources for pulp mystery and detective fiction was Popular Publications' *Dime Mystery Magazine* (1932–1950), which began as a straight mystery magazine before turning into a "shudder pulp" in less than a year. The shudder pulps were a handful of magazines published in the mid-1930s to early 1940s that specialized in tales of weird menaces with seemingly supernatural origins, but that turn out to have perfectly logical (if contrived) explanations. Women were almost invariably victims in the weird menace stories, and their husbands and boyfriends virtually useless, which is one reason why Ray Cummings's "The Case of the Frozen Corpses" (1939), featuring the husband-and-wife detective team of George and Dot Stevens, was so unusual.

Popular Publications' success with its line of shudder pulps inspired several other publishers to try their hand at it. Better Publications' *Thrilling Mystery* (1935–1943) was one of the more memorable, in large part because it sought out the work of weird fiction writers in addition to mystery writers. Fritz Leiber's "Power of the Puppets" (1941), for example, is clearly a tale in the hard-boiled tradition, but it's also something of a rewrite of his 1943 *Weird Tales* shocker, "In the X-Ray." In "Death is a Vampire" (1944) Robert Bloch, author of many vampire stories for *Weird Tales* and other magazines, imagined (with tongue firmly in cheek) the sort of caper that might happen if one of horror's most famous monsters were to encounter a hard-boiled reporter.

Notwithstanding its similar title, *Thrilling Detective* (1931–1953), a sister magazine to *Thrilling Mystery*, was more firmly entrenched in the hard-boiled tradition. Frank Gruber's Oliver "The Human Encyclopedia" Quade was one of the more eccentric hard-boiled dicks, an encyclopedia salesman with a photographic memory who drew on his vast resources of knowledge to solve violent crimes. (Rumor has it that Gruber, a prolific writer, came up with the idea for Quade after searching an encyclopedia for story ideas.) "Death at the Main" (1936) was the second of fifteen Human Encyclopedia stories published between 1936 and 1940 in *Thrilling Detective* and *Black Mask*.

The extent to which the hard-boiled influence penetrated in the pulp magazines can be found in "Names in the Black Book" (1934) by Robert E. Howard, who is better remembered today as the creator of Conan the

Barbarian. The second of two stories featuring waterfront detective Steve Harrison and occasional friend Joan La Tour, Howard's tale, published in the short-lived *Super Detective Stories* (1934), is essentially an exotic adventure story turned crime thriller through the appearance of arch-villain Erlik Khan, an obvious homage to Sax Rohmer's criminal mastermind Fu Manchu.

With Robert Leslie Bellem's Dan Turner, the roscoe-toting hero of "Homicide Hunch" and over a hundred other stories published between 1934 and 1950, the hard-boiled detective tale comes full-circle. Turner's beat was Hollywood, meaning there were always racy scandals and supple starlets clamoring for his—and the reader's—attention. But one turned to the Dan Turner stories for their prose as much as their mystery. Turner was the rare hard-boiled detective who actually spoke the lingo of the streets, with all of its insensitive slang, bad grammar, and Runyonesque hyperbole. He first began appearing in *Spicy Mystery* but became popular enough in 1942 to sustain his own publication, *Dan Turner, Hollywood Detective* (1942–1950), the only hard-boiled detective so honored.

By the mid to late 1940s, the pulp series detective was on the wane and the crime *noir* story on the rise. Leigh Brackett, who was better known as a writer of science fiction and fantasy (and perhaps less well known as the screenwriter for film adaptations of Chandler's *The Big Sleep* and *The Long Goodbye*), wrote "I Feel Bad Killing You" (1944) for Popular Publications' *New Detective* (1941–1953), and gave almost as much emphasis to the dark landscape of her story as to Paul Channing, significantly an *ex*-detective back for one last chance to right a wrong. By the time John D. MacDonald wrote "The Lady is a Corpse" (1950) for Popular's *Detective Tales* (1935–1953), the detective had all but disappeared into a dog-eat-dog backdrop of a world of unseeming criminals and relatively anonymous crime solvers.

The hard-boiled spirit can be found in the work of many contemporary detective writers, but the roughness, tenacity, and sincerity of the hard-boiled pulp detective remains unique. They don't write stories like these any more—but that's because they don't make tough guys and dangerous dames like these any more.

Stefan Dziemianowicz
New York, 1993

Sail

Lester Dent

The fish shook its tail as the knife cut off its head. Red ran out of the two parts and the fluid spread enough to cover the wet red marks where two human hands had failed to hold to the dock edge.

Oscar Sail wet the palm of his own left hand in the puddle.

The small policeman kept coming out on the dock, tramping in the rear edge of glare from his flashlight.

Sail split the fish belly, shook it over the edge of the yacht dock and there were some splashes below in the water. The stuff from the fish made the red stain in the water a little larger.

When the small policeman reached Sail, he stopped and gave his cap a cock. He looked down at Sail's feet and up at Sail's head.

The cop said, "Damned if you ain't a long drink of water."

Sail said nothing.

The cop asked, "That you give that yell a minute ago?"

Sail showed plenty of teeth so that his grin would be seen in the moonlight. He picked up the fishhook and held it close to his red-wetted left palm.

"Little accident," he said.

When the cop put light on the hand, Sail tightened the thumb down and made a wrinkle in the palm. Red was squeezed out of the wrinkle and two or three drops fell on the dock. It was enough like seepage from a cut the fishhook might have torn that Sail went on breathing.

"Hook, eh?" the cop said vaguely.

He put the toe of his right shoe into the fish head's open mouthful of snake-fang teeth.

"Barracuda," he added, not sounding as if that was on his mind. "They don't eat 'em in Miami. Not when you catch the damn things in the harbor, anyhow."

Sail's laugh did not go off so well and he turned it into a throat clearing.

He said, "People get hot ideas."

The policeman did not say anything and began spearing around with his flashlight beam. He poked it over the edge of the dock at one of the fish organs floating on the stained water. He held it there for what seemed a year.

After he finally began pointing the beam at other places, the light located the bugeye. The bugeye was tied at the end of the dock with springlines. Sloping masts were shiny and black and black canvas covers were on the sails. The hull looked black, neat, new.

The cop dabbed his light up and down each of the two bugeye masts and asked, "Yours?"

Sail said, "Yep."

"What you call that kind of a boat?"

Sail began talking heartily about the boat.

He said, "Chesapeake Bay five-log bugeye. She is thirty-four feet long at the waterline and forty-five overall. Her bottom is made out of five logs drifted together with Swedish iron rods. She has twelve foot beam and only draws a little over two feet of water with the centerboard up. A bugeye has sloping masts. You tell 'em by that, and the clipper bow they always put on them. They're made—"

"Yeah," the cop said. "Uh-huh."

He splashed light on Sail.

Sail would have been all right if he had been a foot or two shorter. His face would never wear a serious look successfully. Too much mouth. Sun and salt water was on its way to ruining his hair. Some of the black had been scrubbed out of his black polo shirt and black dungarees. Bare feet had long toes. Weather had gotten to all of the man a lot.

The policeman switched off his light.

"That was a hell of a funny yell," he said. "And damned if you aren't the tallest thing I ever saw."

He stamped his feet as he walked away.

Sail shut and opened his eyes slowly and by the time he got rid of the effects of the flashlight, the officer was out of sight on shore.

Sail held both hands out about a foot from his eyes. There was enough moonlight for him to see them. A slight breeze made coolness against one side of his face. Loud music came from the Take-a-Sail-in-the-Moonlight-for-a-Dollar-a-Couple boat at the far end of the City Yacht Basin, but a barker spoiled the effect of the music. Two slot machines chugged alongside the lunch stand at Pier Six.

After he had watched his hands tremble for a while, Sail picked up hook, line, fish, knife, and got aboard the bugeye.

Sail, name of the bugeye, was in white letters on the black life preservers tied to the main stays.

Sail grasped a line, took half hitches off a cleat, and pulled a live-box made of laths partly out of the water. Some crawfish, crabs and two more live barracuda were in the live box. He cut the line close to the live-box and let the weighted box sink.

The tiny cabin of the bugeye had headroom below for a man of ordinary height. Sail had to stoop. The usual gear was neatly, in places cleverly, stowed in the cabin.

Sail popped the fish into a kettle in the galley, hurrying.

With the point of the fishhook, he gouged a small place in his left palm, making faces over the job.

He straightened out the stuff in the tackle locker enough to get rid of signs that a hook and line had been grabbed out in haste.

After he had washed and held the mouth of a mercurochrome bottle against the gouge, he looked out of the hatch.

The young policeman was back where the fish had bled and was using his flashlight. He squatted and picked up the fish head. He squeezed it and got fresh blood out of it. After a while, he stood up and approached the dock end. When his flashlight brightened the bugeye's dark sloping masts and black sail covers, Sail was at the galley, making enough noise cutting up the fish to let the cop know where he was and what he was doing.

Sail let four or five minutes pass before he put his head out of the hatch and looked. Perspiration had made the back of his polo shirt moist by then.

The cop had gone somewhere else.

Sail was still looking and listening for the policeman when he heard a man yell and a woman curse.

The woman said, "Dam' stinker!" and more that was worse.

The man's yell was just a yell.

The sounds came out of Bayfront Park, which lay between the yacht basin and Biscayne Boulevard.

Sail got out on deck and stretched his neck around. He saw a man run among the palms in the park. The man was alone.

Then the small policeman and his flashlight appeared among the palms. During the next five minutes, the policeman and his flashlight were not motionless long enough for him to have found anything.

Sail dropped into the bugeye cabin and stripped naked, working fast. His body looked better without clothes. The hair on it was golden and long, but not thick. He put on black jersey swim trunks.

Standing in the companion and looking around, his right hand absently scratched his chest. No one was in sight.

He got over the side without being conspicuous.

The water had odor and its normal quota of floating things. The tide was high slack, almost, but still coming in a little. Sail swam under the dock.

The dock had been built strongly because of the hurricanes. There was a net of cross timbers underneath, and anything falling off the south side of the dock would be carried against them by the tide.

Sail counted pilings until he knew he was under the place on the dock where he had used the fish. He began diving and groping around underwater. He was quiet about that.

He found what he was seeking on the sixth or seventh dive. He kept in the dark places as he swam away with it.

One of the little islands in the harbor seemed to be the only place that offered privacy. He made for it.

The island—an artificial half acre put there when they dredged the City Yacht Basin—was a heap of dark silence when Sail swam tiredly to it. Pine trees on the island had been bent by the hurricanes, some uprooted. The weeds did not seem to have been affected.

Sail tried not to splash coming out of the shallows onto the sand beach. He towed the Greek under water as long as possible.

Two stubborn crabs and some seaweed hung to the Greek when Sail carried him into the pines and weeds. The knife sticking in the Greek, and what it had done, did not help. Weeds mashed under the body when Sail laid it down.

Pulpy skins in the Greek's billfold were probably greenbacks, and stiffer, smaller rectangles, business cards. Silver coins, a pocket knife, two clips for an automatic. The gun was in a clip holster under the left armpit of the corpse.

Inside the Greek's coat lining was a panel, four inches wide, five times as long, a quarter of an inch thick, hard and rigid.

The Greek's wristwatch ticked.

Sail put the business cards and the panel from the coat lining inside his swim trunks, and was down on his knees cleaning his hands with sand when the situation got the best of his stomach. By the time he finished with that, he had sweated profusely and had a headache over the eyes.

He left the Greek on the island.

The water felt cold as he swam back towards the bugeye, keeping in what dark places he could find. The water chill helped the headache.

Having reached the bugeye with the stuff still in his swim trunks, he clung to the bobstay, the chain brace which ran from the bow waterline to the end of the long bowsprit. He blew the brackish bay water off his lips quietly and listened.

There was no sign anywhere that he had been seen or heard.

He made himself sink and began feeling over the parts of the dock which would still be under water at low tide. Everything under water was inches thick with barnacles and oysters.

He found a niche that would do, took the stuff out of his trunks and wedged it there tightly enough so that there was not much danger of it working out.

Sail clung to the bugeye's bobstay until all the water ran off him that wanted to run, then scrambled aboard and ducked into the cabin.

He had started to shed the bathing suit when the woman said, "Puh-lease!"

Sail came up straight and his head thumped a ceiling carling.

She swung her legs off the forward bunk. Even then, light from the kerosene gimbal lamp did not reach more than her legs. The feet were small in dark blue sandals which showed red-enameled toenails. Her legs had not been shaved recently, and were nice.

Sail chewed an imaginary something between two eye-teeth while he squinted at the girl. He felt of his head where it had hit the ceiling. Two or three times, he seemed about to say something, but didn't and went forward into one of the pair of small single staterooms. The shadow-embedded rest of her did not look bad as he passed.

He shut the stateroom door and got out of the swim trunks. He tied a three-pound fish sinker to the trunks and dropped them through a porthole into the bay, which was dredged three fathoms deep there. He put on his scrubbed dark polo and dungarees.

The girl had moved into the light when he opened the door and entered the cabin. The rest of her was interesting. Twenty something, he judged.

She smiled and said, "You don't act as if you remember me, Wesley."

Sail batted his eyes at her.

"Gosh," she said, "but you're tall!"

Sail scratched behind his right ear, changed his eyebrows around at her, gave the top of his head three hard rubs, then leaned back against the galley sink. This upset a round bottle. He caught it, looked at it, and seemed to get an idea.

He asked, "Drink?"

She had crossed her legs. Her skirt was split. "That would be nice," she smiled.

Sail, his back to her, made more noise than necessary in rattling bottles and glasses and pinking an opener into a can of condensed milk. He mixed two parts of gin, one of creme de cocoa, one of condensed milk. He put four drops from a small green bottle in one drink and gave that one to the girl, holding it out a full arm length, as if bashful.

They sipped.

"It's not bad without ice, Wesley," she murmured.

Sail said, "Thanks, lady," politely.

Her blue handbag started to slip out of the hollow of her crossed legs and she caught it quickly.

"For a husband, you're a darn polite cuss," she said.

Sail swallowed with a distinctly pigeon noise. "Eh?"

"My Gawd, don't you *remember?*"

"What?"

"If this isn't something! Two weeks ago Tuesday. Four o'clock in the morning. We were pretty tight, but we found a justice of the peace in Cocoanut Grove. You had to hock the engagement ring with the jeep for his fee and twenty dollars, and we all went out and had some drinks, and I kind of lost track of things, including you."

"I'll be—" Sail said vaguely.

The girl put her head back and laughed. The mirth did not sound just right.

"I didn't know what to do," she said. "I remembered you said you were a jewelry drummer out of Cincinnati. I sat around the hotel. Then I began to get a mad up."

An unnaturalness was growing in her voice. She pinched her eyes shut and shook her head. Her blue purse slid to the floor.

"I'm here to tell you I had a time locating you," she said. "I might have known you would be a sailor. Gawd, imagine! Anyway, Mama is right on deck now, Mister and I want something done about it. If you think you're not the man, you're going to have to prove it in a big way."

"You want me to prove my name, business and recent whereabouts? Is that it?"

"You bet."

Sail said, "That's what I figured."

She peered at him, winking both eyes. Then fright grabbed her face.

"You ain't so damn' smart!" she said through her teeth.

She started to get up, but something was wrong with her knee joints by now, and she slid off the bench and sat hard on the black battleship linoleum.

Sail moved fast and got his long fingers on the blue purse as she clawed it open. A small bright revolver fell out of the purse as they had a tug-o'-war over it.

"Blick!" the girl gasped.

Blick and a revolver came out of the oilskin locker. The gun was a small bright twin to the girl's. Blick's Panama fell off slick mahogany hair, and disarranged oilskins fell down in the locker behind him. Blick had his lips rolled in until he seemed to have no lips. He looked about old enough to have fought in the last war.

"Want it shot off?" he gritted.

Sail jerked his hand away from the girl's purse as if a bullet were already heading for it. He put his hands up as high as the cabin carlings and ceiling would allow. The upper part of his stomach jumped slightly with each beat of his heart, moving the polo shirt fabric.

The girl started to get up, couldn't. She said, "Blick!" weakly.

Blick, watching Sail, threw at her, "You hadda be a sucker and try that married-when-you-were-tight gag to find out who he is!"

The girl's lips worked with some words before they got out as sounds. ". . . was—I—know he—doped drink."

Blick gritted at Sail, "Bud, she's my sis, and if she don't come out of that, I wouldn't wanta be you!"

Sail watched the bright gun. Sweat had come out on his forehead enough to start running.

"She'll be all right," he said.

"What'd you give her?"

"Truth serum."

"You louse! Fat lot of good it'll do you."

Sail said nothing.

Blick ran his eyes up and down Sail, then said, "They sure left the faucet on too long when they poured you, didn't they, bud?"

Sail got his grin to operate. He said, "Let's see if some words will clear this any."

Blick said, "That's an idea, bud. I think I got you figured. You're some guy Andopolis rung in. It was like Andopolis to get himself some help."

"Andopolis was the one who got knifed?" Sail asked.

"You ain't that dumb."

"Was he?"

"Naw. That was Sam, my pal."

Sail rubbed the top of his head. "I'm sort of confused."

"You and us both," Blick said. "We're confused by you. We ain't seen you around before today. But me and Nola and Sam are watching Andopolis, and he starts out on this dock. You're the only boat out here, so it's a cinch he wanted to see you."

"He only made it about half way out the dock," Sail said dryly.

"Sure. Sam headed him off. Sam wanted to talk to Andopolis was all—"

"It wasn't all," Sail drawled. "What Sam really wanted was to make Andopolis tell him something. Andopolis had some information. Sam wanted it. Sam told Andopolis that if he didn't cough up on the spot he would get his entrails shot out, or words to such effect. Sam reached for his gun. But he had made the mistake of not unbuttoning his coat before he started the argument. Andopolis knew exactly where to put a knife. Sam went off the dock after he gave just one yell."

"And that brought the cop."

Sail squinted one eye. Perspiration was stinging it. He echoed, "And that brought the cop."

Blick was holding the gun steady. He said, "Andopolis ran before the cop got here. He hid in the park and Nola and I tried to get him later, but he broke away and ran."

"Then you came here."

Blick grinned thinly. "Let's get back to the time between the knifing of Sam and the arrival of the cop. You, bud, done some fast work. You were sweet, what I mean. You got a hook and line, grabbed a live fish out of your live-box, jumped on the dock and butchered the fish to hide the marks where Sam got it. You even got the insides of the fish into the water to hide any bloodstains where Sam sank. Then you fed the cop a line when he got there."

"You sure had your eyes open," Sail said.

"Did the cop go for your story?"

"I'm still wondering," Sail said thoughtfully.

Blick watched Sail. "How much do you know?"

Sail got rid of his made grin. "I'll bite. How much?"

"So you're going to start that," Blick said.

Nola was breathing noisily. Blick pointed at her, said, "Help me get her going!"

Sail grasped the girl and lifted her.

"Stay that way," Blick ordered, then searched Sail, found no weapon, and said, "Out."

Sail walked the girl up the companionway and on to the dock, then started to let go the girl and get back aboard.

"Along with us," Blick ordered. "It'd be swell if Andopolis has told you what we're trying to find out, wouldn't it?"

Sail said nothing. His breathing was as audible as the girl's. Blick got on the other side of the girl and helped hold her up. "We're tight," Blick said. "Stagger."

They staggered along the dock to the sidewalk, and along that.

Yacht sailors stood in a knot at the end of the Pier Six lunch stand, and out of the knot came the chug of the slot machines. Blick put his hand and small revolver into a coat pocket. They turned to the right, away from the lunch stand.

Sail said, "You might have the wrong idea about me."

"We'll go into that, bud," Blick said. "We'll go into that in a nice place I know about."

They scuffed over the sidewalk and Blick, walking as if he did not feel as if he weighed more than a ton, seemed to think of a possibility which pleased him.

"Hell, Nola! This guy covered up that knifing for Andopolis, so he's got to be with Andopolis all the way."

Nola did not answer. She was almost sound asleep. Blick pinched her, slapped her, and that awakened her somewhat.

A police radio car was parked at the corner of Biscayne Boulevard and the street they were traveling. Blick did not see it in time. When he did discover it, he took his breath in with a sharp noise.

"We're drunk," Blick warned. "Taking each other home."

Sail shoved a little to steer the girl to the side of the walk farthest from the prowl car. Blick shoved back to straighten them up. He also got mad.

Blick's gun was in his coat pocket, and if shooting started, it was no time for a gun to be in a pocket. Blick started to take it out, probably intending to hold it at his side where it could not be seen from the police car.

Sail watched the gun start out of the pocket. It had a high front sight and there was an even chance of it hanging on the pocket lining. It did.

Sail shoved Blick and Nola as hard as he could. Force of the effort bounced him towards the police car. He grabbed the spare tire at the back of the machine and used it to help himself around.

A policeman in the car yelled, "What the hell's this?" He wasn't excited.

Blick did not shoot. He got Nola over a shoulder and ran. A taxicab was on its stand at the corner. Blick made it.

Sail shouted, "Kidnapers!"

One of the cops leaned out, looked at him, said, "Huh?"

Blick leaped into the taxi with his sister. An instant later, the hack driver fell out of his own machine, holding his head. The taxi took off.

"They stole my heap!" the taxi-driver shrieked.

The police car starter began whining. It whined and whined and nothing happened. One cop wailed, "It never done this before!"

"Try turning on the switch!" Sail yelled.

The motor started.

An officer stuck his head out of the car, said, "You stick around here, wise guy!" and the machine left in pursuit of the cab.

Sail, who had the legs for it, ran away from there very fast.

Sail, when he reached the Pier Six lunch stand, planted his hip against the counter, and caught up with his breathing. A young man who looked as youths in lunch stands somehow always look came over, swiped at the counter with his towel, got a look at Sail, blinked and wanted to know, "How's the weather up there?"

"Dry," Sail said. "What you got in cans?"

Sail drank the first and second cans of beer in gulps, but did some pondering over the third. When it was down, he absent-mindedly put three dimes on the counter.

"Forty-five," the youth corrected. "Cans is fifteen."

Sail substituted a half dollar and put the nickel change in one of the slot machines, still involved with his thoughts. The one-armed bandit gave him a lemon and two bars, another bar just showing.

"Almost a jackpot," someone said.

"History," Sail said, "repeating itself."

A telephone booth was housed at the end of Pier Six. Sail dialed the O and asked for Police Headquarters.

The slot machines chugged at the lunch stand while he waited. A card on the phone box told how to report a fire, get the police or call an ambulance. He read part of it, and Headquarters answered.

Sail said, "I want to report an attempted robbery. This is Captain Oscar Sail of the yacht *Sail*. A few minutes ago, a man and a woman boarded my boat and marched me away at the point of a gun. I do not know why. I feel they intended to kill me. There was a police car parked at the corner of Biscayne, and I broke away. The man and woman fled in a taxi. The officers chased them. I do not know whether the officers have reported yet."

"They have."

"Did they catch the pair?"

"No."

Sail almost said that was what he had called to find out, but caught himself in time.

"It might help if you described the pair," the police voice said.

Sail described an imaginary couple that were not like Blick and Nola in any particular except that they were man and woman.

"Thanks," said the voice at Headquarters. "When you get aboard your boat, tell Patrolman Joey Cripp to give us a ring. I'm Captain Rader. You'll probably find Patrolman Cripp on your boat."

Sail was wearing a startled look as he hung up and felt for a nickel in the coin return cup of the telephone.

Three men were waiting in the cabin of *Sail* when Sail got there. Two wore police uniforms, the other had civilian clothes.

One policeman was using his tongue to lather a new cigar with saliva. The tongue was coated. His neck had some loose red skin on it. He was shaking, not very much, but shaking.

The second officer was the young small patrolman. He still had his flashlight.

The man in civilian clothes was putting bottles and test tubes in a scuffed leather bag which held more of the same stuff and a microscope off which much of the enamel had been worn. His suit was fuzzy gray, rimless spectacles were pinched tight on his nose, and he had chewed half of the cigar in his mouth without lighting it. The cigar was the same kind the policeman with the shakes was licking.

Sail said, "Captain Rader wants Patrolman Joey Cripp to call him."

"That's me," the young patrolman said, and started for the companionway.

"Wait a minute," Sail said. "You didn't happen to get a look at a man and a woman who left here with me a while ago?"

"I sure did. I was behind a bush in the park." The young officer went out.

The shaking policeman got up slowly, holding his damp cigar and looking miserable. He took a full breath and started words coming.

"Gracious but you're a tall man," he said. "I'm Captain Cripp and Joey is my son. This is Mister Waterman. You have a wonderful boat here. Some day I am going to get me a boat like this and go to the South Seas. I want to thank you for reporting your trouble to Captain Rader, which I presume you have just done. And I want to congratulate you on your narrow escape from those two. But next time, don't take such chances. Never fool with a man with a gun. We'll let you know as soon as we hear anything of your attacker and his companion. They got away from the radio car. I hope you have a good time in Miami, and no more trouble. We have a wonderful city, a wonderful climate." He shook with his chill.

Captain Cripp pulled out another cigar and a shiny cylindrical metal lighter. He took another breath.

"Smoke? Of course you do. Better light it yourself. I shake like a leaf. I've got the damned malaria, and every other day, I shake. That's an excellent cigar, if I do say so myself. One of our native products. Made right here in Miami, and as mild as an old maid's kiss. There! Didn't I tell you it was a good cigar?"

He took back his lighter. He did not touch the bright metal where Sail had held it and made fingerprints.

"Isn't admission charged to this?"

"Eh? Oh, yes, you are naturally puzzled by our presence here. Forget it. It means nothing at all. It's just an idea Captain Rader got after talking to Joey about a yell and a fish."

Patrolman Joey Cripp jumped aboard and came below.

"Captain Rader offers his apologies for sending us aboard your boat in your absence," Joey said. "And he wonders if you have anything you would like to say to us."

Sail, his scowl getting blacker and blacker, gritted, "I'm making an effort not to say it!"

Joey said, "Well, Mister Sail, if you will excuse me, we will be going."

The rabbity man, Waterman, finished putting things in his bag and picked up a camera with a photoflash attachment, pointed the camera at Sail. The outfit clicked and flashed.

"Thank you," he said, not very politely.

They left.

Sail threw the cigar overboard, then examined the cabin. Almost everything had been put back in place carefully. But in one spot, he found fingerprint powder enough to show they had printed the place.

Sail tried to sleep the rest of the night. He did get a little. The rest of the time he spent at the companion with a mirror which he had rigged on the tip joint of a fishing rod so as to look around without showing himself.

Boats at a slip do not usually have an anchor watch. But on a big Matthews at the opposite slip, somebody seemed to be standing at anchor. The watcher did not smoke, did not otherwise allow any light to get to his features. He might have been tall or short, wide or narrow. The small things he did were what any man would do during a long tiresome job.

There was one exception. The watcher frequently put a finger deep in his mouth and felt around.

Sail took a shower with the dock hose. It gave him a chance to get a better look at the Matthews. The watcher of the night was not in evidence.

The *Sail's* dinghy rode in stern davits, bugeye fashion, at enough of a tilt not to hold spray. Sail lowered it. He got a brush and the dock hose and washed down the black topsides, taking off dried salt which sea water had deposited. He dropped his brush in the water at different times. In each case, it sank, and he had to reach under for it.

The fourth time he reached under for the brush, he retrieved the stuff which he had taken off the Greek. The articles had not worked out of the niche between the dock cross braces under water, where he had jammed them.

Sail finished washing down, hauled the dink up on the davits, and during the business of coiling the dock hose around its faucet, looked around. Any of a dozen persons in sight might have been the watcher off the Matthews. The others would be tourists down for a gawk at the yachts.

He spirited the Greek's stuff below with the scrub brush.

One of the cards said Captain Santorin Gura Andopolis of the yacht *Athens Girl* chartered for Gulf Stream fishing, nobody catching more fish. The address was Pier Five.

The other twenty-six cards said Captain Sam Dokomos owned the Lignum Vitae Towing Company. An address and a telephone number for day calls only.

There was also a piece of board four by twenty inches, a quarter of an inch thick, mahogany, with screw holes in four corners. The varnish was peeled, rather than worn, as was some of the gold leaf. The gold leaf formed a letter, four figures.

K 9420

Sail burned everything in the galley Shipmate.

There was no one in the telephone booth at the end of the pier. He looked up the number of Pier Five, which was no more than two hundred feet distant, and dialed it.

"Captain Andopolis," he requested.

Through the window, he could see them go looking for Captain Andopolis. It took them almost five minutes to decide they couldn't find him.

"Maybe he went to the dentist, somebody thought," the one who had hunted suggested.

"Yeah?"

"Yeah. He's been having a toothache, somebody said."

Sail went back to the bugeye and put on a dark suit, tropical weight, a black polo shirt and black shoes. His shore cruising rig.

The cafeteria was overdone in chromium. The waiters who carried the trays were dressed in the same red that was on the walls. There were a score of customers and a boy who wandered among the tables selling newspapers and racing dope sheets. He sold more dope sheets than papers.

One man eating near the door did not put syrup on his pancakes or sugar in his coffee. When he finished, he put a finger in the back of his mouth to feel.

Sail finished his beer and doughnuts and strolled around the corner to a U-Drive-It.

The only car on which they did not want a deposit was a little six-cylinder sedan, not new. Sail drove it around, sticking his head out frequently to look for a tall building. He found it and parked in front of it.

He made a false start into the building, then came back to take another look at an upright dingus. Then he went inside.

He told the elevator operator loudly, "Five!" before they started up.

The fifth floor corridor was empty.

When the man who had felt of his tooth in the cafeteria came sneaking up the stairs, Sail was set. He had his belt strapped tight around his fist. The man got down on all fours to mew his pain. Sail hit again, then unwrapped the belt, blew on his fist, worked the fingers.

He had the senseless man in his arms when the elevator answered his signal.

"Quick! I gotta rush my friend to a place for a treatment!" he explained.

He drove five or six miles on a side road off the Tamiami Trail before he found a lonesome spot and got out. He hauled the man out.

The man began big at the top and tapered. His small hands were calloused, dirt was ground into the callouses, the nails broken. His face was darker than his hair.

A leather envelope purse held three hundred in old and new bills. There was a dollar sixty-one in change and the cashier's slip for his cafeteria breakfast in his trousers.

A knife was in a holster against the small of his back. It was flat and supported by a high belt. Sail threw it in the canal at the roadside. It was not the one with which he had knifed Sam. He had left that one in his victim.

Handfuls of water from the canal did not speed his revival much. When he finally came around, he groaned, squirmed, and started feeling of his bad tooth.

Sail stood back and showed him a fat blue revolver. "Just try to be nonchalant, Andopolis," he advised.

Andopolis immediately stood up.

"Sit down!" Sail directed sharply.

Andopolis walked towards him.

Sail shoved the gun out, gritting desperately, "This thing is loaded, you fool!"

Andopolis leaped. Sail dodged, but hardly enough. Andopolis hit him with a shoulder. The impact spun him. Since he didn't want to shoot, the gun was a handicap. It tied up his fists. Andopolis hit him on the belt buckle. Numbness grabbed the whole front of his body. Something suddenly against his back was the ground.

"Yah!" Andopolis screeched. "Yah!"

He jumped, feet together, at Sail's middle. Sail was too numb to move clear. The feet hit his chest, everything seemed to break, and red-hot pain knocked the numbness out. Sail got Andopolis' legs, jerked. Andopolis windmilled his arms, but fell.

Sail clamped on to one of the man's feet and began doing things to it and the leg. Andopolis, turning over and over, raised a dust cloud. He moaned and bellowed and made dog noises. When he judged Andopolis was dizzy enough, Sail pounced on the dust cloud. He hit, variously, an arm, the ground, a hip, and other places which he could not identify.

Andopolis, bewildered and with dirt in his eyes, failed to get his jaw out of the way.

Sail straightened, put back his head and started to take a full breath. He began coughing. Hacking, gagging, holding his chest, he sat down in the road. He began to sweat profusely. After a while, he unbuttoned his pants and pulled up his shirt. There was one purple print of the entire bottom of both of Andopolis' feet, and the chest was skinned, the loose skin mixed with the long golden hair. There was not much blood.

Andopolis got his eyes open and snarled, "Yah! I stomp you good if you don't lay off me!"

Sail coughed and got up. He kept his feet far apart, but did not teeter much.

He said thickly, "My Macedonian friend, you stood anchor watch on me all night and you were still trailing me this morning. Where do you get that lay off stuff?"

"Before that, I'm talk about," Andopolis growled.

"Eh?"

Andopolis took a breath and blew words out. "For two week now, you been follow me like dog. I go to Bimini two day, and you and that black bugeye in Bimini before long. I make the run from Bimini here yesterday. You make him too. Vat you take me for? One blind owl, huh?"

Sail asked, "Do you think you're bulletproof, too?"

Andopolis snorted. "Me, I don't theenk you shoot."

"What gave you that idea?"

"Go jump in hell," Andopolis said.

Sail coughed some, deep and low, trying to keep it from moving his ribs.

He said, "All right, now that we're being honest with each other, I'll tell you a true story about a yacht named *Lady Luck*. That's just so there won't be any misunderstanding about who knows what."

Andopolis crowded his lips into a bunch and pushed the bunch out as far as he could, but didn't say anything.

Sail began:

"The *Lady Luck*, Department of Commerce registration number K 9420, was as neat a little yacht as ever kedged off Featherbed Bank. She belonged to Bill Lord of Tulsa. Oil. Out in Tulsa, they call Bill the Osage Ogre, on account of he's got what it seems to take to find oil. Missus Bill likes jewelry, and Bill likes her, so he buys her plenty. Because Missus Bill really likes her rocks, she carries them around with her. You following me?"

Andopolis was. He still had his lips pursed.

"Bill Lord had his *Lady Luck* anchored off the vet camp on Lower Matecumbe last November," Sail continued. "Bill and the Missus were ashore, looking over the camp. Bill was in the trenches himself, back when, and is some kind of a shot in the American Legion or the democrats, so he was interested in the camp. The Missus left her pretties on the yacht. Remember that. Everybody has read about the hurricane that hit that afternoon, and maybe some noticed that Bill and his Missus were among those who hung on behind that tank car. But the *Lady Luck* wasn't so lucky, and she dragged her picks off somewhere and sank. For a while, nobody knew where."

Sail stopped to cough. He had to lay down on his back before he could stop, and he was very careful about getting erect again. Perspiration had wet most of him.

He said, "A couple of weeks ago, a guy asked the Department of Commerce lads to check and give him the name of the boat, and the name of the owner, that carried the number K 9420. That was the mistake."

"Pooey," Andopolis said, "on your story."

"The word got to me," Sail continued. "Never mind how. And it was easy to find you were the lad asking for the dope on K 9420. Inquiry brought out that you had had a fishing party down around Matecumbe and Long Key a few days before you suddenly got curious about K 9420. It was a little harder to locate the parties who had your boat hired at the time. Two Pan-American pilots. They said you anchored off Lower Matecumbe to bottom fish, and your anchor fouled something, and you had a time, and finally, when you got the anchor up, you brought aboard some bow planking off a sunken boat. From the strain as it was torn loose, it was apparent the anchor had pulled the planking off the rest of the boat, which was still down there. You checked up as a matter of course to learn what boat you had found."

Andopolis looked as if something besides his tooth hurt him.

"Tough you didn't get in touch with the insurance people instead of contacting Captain Sam Dokomas, a countryman of yours who had a towing and salvage outfit, and a bad reputation."

Andopolis growled, "Damn! You said somethin' then!"

Sail kept his voice lower to decrease the motion of his ribs in expelling air for words. "You needed help to get the *Lady Luck*. But Captain Sam Dokomas tried to make you cough up the exact location. Then you smelled a double-cross, got scared and lit for Bimini.

"I had been hanging around all this time, and not doing a good job of it, so you got wise to me. That scared you back to Miami. You had decided on a showdown, and were headed for my boat when Captain Sam collared you on the dock. You took care of part of your troubles with a knife right there. But that left Captain Sam's girl friend and her brother, Nola and Blick, or whatever their names are. They were in the know. They tried to grab you in the park after you fixed Sam up, but you outran them.

"Now, that's a very complete story, don't you think? Oh, yes. You got reckless and jumped me a minute ago because you figured I wouldn't shoot you because nobody but you knows the exact location of the *Lady Luck*. The two Pan-American boys fishing down there with you when you found the ship forgot to take bearings and didn't have a smell of an idea where they were at the time."

Andopolis was a man who did his thinking with the help of his face, and there was more disgust than anything else on his features.

"You trying to cut in?" he snarled finally.

"Not trying. Have."

Andopolis thought that over. The sun was comfortable, but mosquitoes were coming out of the swamp around the road to investigate, hungrier than land sharks.

"Yeah," Andopolis muttered finally. "I guess you have, at that."

"Let's get this straight, Andy. You and I, and nobody else."

Andopolis nodded. "Okey."

"Now just who is this Blick?"

"Nola's brother."

"Now, hell, Andy—"

"And Nola was married to that double-crosser, Sam."

Sail made a whistling mouth. "So it was Nola's husband you dirked. She'll like you for that."

"So what? She didn't go for him much."

"No?"

"Naw. That dame—"

"Skip it," Sail said suddenly. He put his shirt on, favoring his chest. "Dang, feller, you sure busted up my ribs. We've got to watch the insurance company. They paid off on Missus Bill's stuff. Over a hundred thousand. They'll have wires out."

Andopolis nodded. "What about stuff for diving?"

"There's sponger equipment aboard my bugeye," Sail said. "I tried that racket over in Tarpon Springs, but you can't compete with those Greeks over there."

"Let's go," Andopolis said.

He was feeling of his tooth when he got in the car. Sail drove slowly. The road, nothing more than a high dike built up with material scooped out to make the drainage canal, was rough. It hurt his ribs.

Sail had driven no more than half a mile when both front tires let go their air. Maybe the car would still have remained on the road. But bullets also knocked holes in the windshield. The car was in the canal before anything could be done about it.

The car broke most of its windows going down the canal bank. The canal must have been six feet deep. Its tea-colored water filled the machine at once. Sail's middle hurt, and he had lost his air, and had to breathe in, and there was nothing but water.

After the water had filled the car, it seemed to rush around inside. Sail tried the doors, but they wouldn't open. He did not touch Andopolis in his struggles. Andopolis did not seem to be in the car. Sail couldn't remember him having been thrown out.

The first window Sail found was too small. He pummeled the car roof, but hardly had strength enough to knock himself away from what he was hitting. Then he was suddenly out of the car. He didn't know just how he had managed it. He reached the top, but sank twice before he clutched a weed on shore, after which an attack of the spasms kept him at first from hearing the shots.

Yells were mixed in the shot noise. Sail squeezed water off his eyeballs with the lids, looked, and saw Andopolis on the canal bank. Andopolis was some distance away and running madly.

Blick and his sister Nola were running after Andopolis. They were shooting at Andopolis' legs, it seemed.

They all three ran out of sight, but the sounds told Sail they had winged Andopolis and grabbed him.

Sail had wrenched some of the water out of his lungs by now. He swam to a bush which hung down into the water and got under it. He managed to get his coughing stopped.

Andopolis was sobbing at the top of his voice when Blick and Nola dragged him up.

"Shoot his other leg off if he acts up, Nola," Blick said. "I'll get our tall bud."

Sail began to want to cough. He desired the cough until it was almost worth getting shot for.

"He must be a submarine," Blick said. He got a stick and poked around. "Hell, Nola, this water is eight feet deep here anyhow."

Andopolis bubbled something in Greek.

"Shut up," Blick said, "or we'll put bullets into you like we put 'em into the tires of your car."

Andopolis went on bubbling.

"His leg is bleeding bad, Blick," Nola said.

"Hell I care! He knifed your husband, didn't he?"

Air kept coming up in big bubbles from the submerged car. Sail tried to keep his mind off the cough. Blick stood for a century on the bank with his bright little pistol.

"He musta drowned," Blick said.

Andopolis moaned.

"Didn't you know we had been shaggin' you all night and mornin'?" Blick asked him. "Hell, if you hadn't been so occupied with that long lean punk, you'd have got wise, maybe."

Nola said, "We better get his leg fixed."

"If he ain't free with his information, he won't need his leg any more," Blick said. "Let's get the hell away from here."

Andopolis whimpered as they hazed him away. They apparently had a car in the bushes beside the canal some distance down the road. Its noise went away. Sail crawled out and had a good cough.

Captain Cripp looked wide-eyed and hearty and without a sign of a chill as he exclaimed, "Well, well, good morning, good morning. You know, we began to think something had happened to you."

Sail looked at him with eyes that appeared to be drained of everything but the will to carry on, then stumbled down the remaining three steps into the main cabin of Sail. He let himself down on the starboard seat. Pads of cotton under gauze thickened his neck and wrists. He had discovered the car windows had cut him. Iodine had run from under one of the pads and dried. He had just come from the hospital.

Young bony Patrolman Joey Cripp looked at Sail. His grin took the looseness out of the corner of his mouth.

"Tsk, tsk," he said. "Now that's terrible. You look a sight. By God, it's a wonder you're alive. I hope that didn't happen in Miami."

Sail gave them a look of bile. "This is a private boat, in case you forgot."

"Now, now, I hope we can keep things on an amiable footing," Captain Cripp murmured.

Sail said, "Drag it!" His face was more cream than any other color. He reached behind himself in the tackle locker and got a gaff hook. A four-foot shaft of varnished oak with a tempered bright steel hook of needle point. He showed them the hook and his front teeth. "I've got a six-aspirin headache, and things to go with it! You two polite public servants get out of here before I go fishing for kidneys!"

Patrolman Joey Cripp stood up. "I didn't think we'd have any trouble with you, Mister Sail. I hoped we wouldn't, on account of you acted like a gentleman last night."

"Sit the hell down, Joey," Captain Cripp put in. "Mister Sail, you're under arrest, I'm sorry to say."

Sail said, "Arrest?" He scowled. "Is this on the level?"

"It sure is."

"Pop said it," agreed young Joey.

Captain Cripp shook a finger at Sail. He said:

"Listen. Waterman found human blood in that fish mess on the dock last night. The harbor squad's diver went down this morning. He found a bathing suit with a sinker tied to it. He also found a live box with some live barracuda in it. It was a barracuda you butchered on the dock. Your fishline you had in your hand when Joey got there was wet, but it don't take a minute to wet a line. You described a man and a woman that looked a lot different from the pair Joey saw you with. We been doing some arithmetic, and we figure you were covering up."

"Now," Sail said, "I guess I'm supposed to get scared?"

"I don't know," Captain Cripp said, "but a dead Greek was found over on the island this morning. And in your bathing suit which the diver got was some island sand, and some stickers off the pine trees like grows on the island."

"I guess," Joey said, "it does look kinda funny."

"I regret that it does," Captain Cripp agreed. "After all, evidence is evidence, and while Miami has a wonderful hospitality, we do draw lines, and when our visitors go so far as to use knives on—"

"Let's get this straight!" Sail put in. "Pine tree stickers and sand are just about alike here and in Key West, and points between."

"You may be assured—"

Sail sprang up, gripping the hook. He began to yell.

"What's the idea of this clowning? I know two lug cops when I see 'em. If you got something to say, get it off your chests."

Joey sighed. "I guess courtesy is somethin' you can't acquire. Watcha say, Pop? Hell with the chief's courtesy campaign, huh?"

"Now that you mention it, Joey, okey." Captain Cripp pulled manacles out of his hip pocket. "We're gonna fan you into the can, and we're gonna work you over until we get the straight of this."

Sail slammed the gaff into a corner.

"That's more like. If you hadn't tried to fancy pants around last night, I'd have showed you something then."

Sail shuffled into the galley and got the rearmost can of beer out of the icebox. It gurgled when he shook it, but that was because of the small sealed jar of water which fitted inside it. Stuffed around the jar were some sheets of paper. He held the documents out to the two policemen.

Joey raked his eyes over the print and penned signatures, then spelled them out, lips moving.

"Aw, this don't make no difference," he said. "Or does it?"

Captain Cripp complained, "My glasses fell off yesterday when I was having one of my infernal chills. What does it say, Joey?"

"He's a private dick commissioned to locate some stuff that sank on a yacht called the *Lady Luck*. The insurance people hired him."

Captain Cripp buttoned his coat, squared it over his hips, set his cap with a pat on the top. "Who signed the papers, Joey?"

Joey said, "They're all right, Pop. From what it says, I guess this private op is the head of something called Marine Investigations. Reckon that's an agency, huh?"

Captain Cripp sighed and ambled over to the companionway. "Beauty before age, Joey."

Joey bristled. "Shamus or no shamus, I say it don't make no difference!"

"Let the next guy have the honor, Joey."

"Look, Pop, damn it—"

"The last private op I worked over got me two years in the sticks. He said something about me chiseling in on the reward, and the skipper believed him. It was a damned lie, except—well—out, Joey."

"But Pop, this stinker—"

"Out!" Captain Cripp barked. "You're as big a fool as your maw!"

Joey licked his lips, raking Sail with malevolent eyes. Then he turned and climbed the companion steps.

Captain Cripp looked at Sail. He felt for the bottom step with one foot without looking down. As if he didn't expect it to do any good, he asked, "You wouldn't want to cooperate?"

"I wouldn't."

"Why not?"

"I've done it before."

Captain Cripp grinned slightly. "Just as you say. But if you get yourself in a sling, it'd be better if you had a reason for refusing to help the police."

"All I get out of this is ten per cent for recovering the stuff. I can't see a split. I need the dough."

"And you with a boat like this."

"Maybe I like boats and maybe it keeps me broke."

"The only reason you're not in the can right now is that any shyster could make this circumstantial evidence look funny as hell. Forget the split."

"Thanks," Sail said. "Now I'm going to sound off. It just might be that you lads think you can let me finish it out, then step in, and maybe find the location of that boat for yourselves. Then, while I was in your bastile, trying to explain things you could think to ask me, the stuff might disappear off the boat."

"That's kind of plain talk."

"I feel kind of plain right now."

Captain Cripp's ears moved up a little with the tightening of his jaw muscles. He took his foot off the companion step. He gave his cap an angry adjustment. Then he put the foot back again.

"This malaria is sure something. I feel like a lark today, only I keep thinking about the chills tomorrow."

"Try whiskey and quinine," Sail said.

"I think the whiskey part gave it to me."

The two cops went away with Joey kicking his feet down hard at the dock planks.

Sail took rye and aspirin for what ailed him, changed clothes, took a taxi uptown and entered what looked like the largest hardware store. He asked where they kept their marine charts.

*   *   *

The nervous old salesman in the chart department had a rip in his canvas apron. He mixed his talk in with waving gestures of a pipe off which most of the stem had been chewed.

"Mister, you must have some funny things happen to you, you being so tall," he said. "Right now, you look as if you had had an accident."

Sail steadied himself by holding to the counter edge. "Who sells government charts here, Dad?"

"Well, there's one other store besides us. Hopkins Carter. But if you're going down in the Keys, we got everything you need here. If you go inside, you'll want charts thirty-two-sixty and sixty-one. They're the strip charts. But if you take Hawk Channel, you'll need harbor chart five-eighty-three, and charts twelve-forty-nine, fifty and fifty-one. Here, I'll show—"

Sail squinted his eyes, swallowed, and said, "I don't want to buy a chart. I want you to slip out and telephone me if either of a certain two persons comes in here and asks for chart twelve-fifty, the one which covers Lower Matecumbe."

"Huh?"

Sail said patiently, "It's easy, Dad. You just tell the party you got to get the chart, and go telephone me. Then stall around three or four minutes as if you were getting the chart out of the stock room. That will give me time to get over here and pick up their trail."

The nervous old man put his pipe in his mouth and immediately took it out again. "What kind of shenanygin is this?"

Sail showed him a license to operate in Florida.

"One of them fellers, huh?" The old man did not seem impressed.

Sail put a five-dollar bill on the counter. "That one's got a twin. How about it?"

The old man picked up the bill, squinted at it. "You mean this is a counterfeit or something. What—"

"No, no, control your imagination, Dad. The five is good, and it's yours, and another one like it, if you help me."

"You mean I keep this whether they show up or not?"

"That's the idea."

"Go ahead, Mister, and describe them people."

Sail made a word picture of Blick and Nola. Not trusting Dad's memory, he put the salient points down on a piece of paper. He added a telephone number. "That phone is a booth in a cigar store on the next corner. How far is this Hopkins Carter store?"

" 'Bout two blocks, reckon."

"I'll be there for the next ten minutes. Then I'll be in the cigar store. Ask for Chief Steward Johnson, when you call."

"That you?"

"Uh-huh."

Sail, walking off, was not as pale as he had been on the boat. He had put on a serge suit with more black than blue and a new black polo. When he was standing in front of the elevator, taking a pull at a flat amber bottle which had a crown and a figure on the label, the old man yelled, "Mister!"

Sail lowered the bottle, started coughing.

"Lemme look at this again and see if you said anything about the way he talked," the old man said.

Sail moved back to where he could see the old fellow peering at the paper which held the descriptions. The old man took his pipe out of his teeth. "Mister, what does that feller talk like?"

"Well, about like the rest of these crackers. No, wait. He'll call you bud two or three times."

The old man waved his pipe. "I already sold that man a twelve-fifty."

"The hell!"

"Around half an hour ago, I reckon."

"That's swell!" Sail pumped air out of his lungs in a short laugh which had no sound except such noise as the air made going past his teeth and out of his nostrils. "There was this one chance. They would probably want a late chart for their X-marks-the-spot. And now they've got it, so they'll be off to the wars." He kissed a palm sneeringly. "That for the whole works!"

He weaved around, a lot more unsteady than he had been a minute before. He put the flat flask between his teeth and looked at the spinning ceiling fan. By the time the bottle was empty, his head and eyes were screwing around in time with the fan blades. He got his feet tracking in the general direction of the door.

The old man said, "That there chart was delivered."

Sail maneuvered a turn and halt. "Eh?"

"He ordered it over the telephone, and we delivered. I got the address somewhere." The old man thumbed his order book, stopping to point at each name with his pipe stem.

"*Whileaway*," he said finally. "A houseboat on the Miami river below the Twelfth Street Causeway."

Sail cocked the empty bottle in a wastebasket, put five dollars in front of the old man and headed for the elevator. He was a lot steadier.

The houseboat *Whileaway* was built for rivers, and not very wide ones. Sixty feet or thereabouts waterline, she had three decks that put her up like a skyscraper. She was white, or had been. A man who loved boats would have said she should never have been built.

Scattered on shore near was a gravel pile, two trucks with nobody near them, a shed, junk from the hurricane, a trailer with both tires flat and windows broken, and two rowboats in as bad shape as the trailer.

Sail was behind most of the junk at one time or another on his way to the river bank. The river ran between wooden bulkheads at this point. Between Sail and *Whileaway*, two tugs, a yawl, a cruiser and another houseboat were tied to dolphins along the bulkhead. Nobody seemed to be on any of the boats.

Sail stripped to dark blue silk underwear shorts. He hid everything else under the junk. The water had a little more smell and floating things than in the harbor. After he had eased down into it, he kept behind the moored boats, next to the bulkhead. The tide carried him. He was just coming under the bow of *Whileaway* when one of the square window ports of the houseboat opened.

Sail sank suddenly. He thought somebody was going to shoot, or use a harpoon.

Something heavy—evidently it fell out of the porthole—hit the water. It sank quickly. Touching Sail, it pushed him aside. It went on sinking. Sail got the idea that a navy anchor was at the lowermost part of the sinking object.

He swam down after it. The river had only two fathoms here. He did not have much trouble finding it. When he clung to the object, the tide stretched his legs out behind.

Whoever had tied the knots was a sailor. Sailor knots, while they hold, are made to be easily untied. Sail got them loose. He began to think he wouldn't make the top with his burden. He was out of air.

His head came out of the water with eyes open, fixed in the direction of the square port. Nobody's head was there. No weapon appeared.

Sail looked around, then threw an arm up. He missed the first springline which held the houseboat to the bulkhead. He grasped the next one. He held Nola's head out.

Water leaked from Nola's nose and mouth.

Some of the rope which had tied her to the heavy navy anchor was still wrapped around her. Sail used it to tie her to the springline, so that her head was out of the water.

Then he had to try twice before he could get up the springline to the houseboat deck. Nola began gagging and coughing. It made a racket.

Sail stumbled through the handiest door. Waves of pain jumped from his ribs to his toes, from ribs to hair. The bandages had turned red, and it was not from mercurochrome.

*   *   *

The houseboat furnishings must have been something fifteen years ago. Most of the varnish had alligatored. Sail got into the galley by accident. Rust, dirt, smell. He grabbed the only things in sight, a quart brass fire extinguisher and a rusted ice pick.

He found a dining salon beyond the galley. He was half across it when Andopolis came in the opposite door.

Andopolis had a rusty butcher knife in one hand. He was using the other hand to handle a chair for a crutch, riding it with the knee of the leg which Blick and Nola had put a bullet through.

Clustered around Andopolis' eyes—more on the lids than elsewhere— were puffy gray blisters. They were about the size burning cigarettes would make. Two fingernails were off one of his hands, the one which held the butcher knife. Red ran from the mutilated fingertips down over the rusty knife.

Sail threw the fire extinguisher. He was weaker even than he had thought. The best he could do was bounce the extinguisher off the bulkhead behind Andopolis.

Andopolis said thickly, "I feex you up this time, fran!" and reversed the knife for throwing.

Sail threw his ice pick. It was a good shot. The pick stuck into Andopolis' chest over his heart. But it did not go in deep enough to trouble Andopolis. He never bothered to jerk it out. He already had enough pain elsewhere not to know it was there.

Feet banged through the boat behind Sail. They approached.

Andopolis threw. Sail dropped. His weakness seemed to help. The knife went over his head.

A uniformed cop had appeared in the door. Bad luck put him in the path of the knife. He made a bleating sound, took spraddling steps and leaned against a bulkhead, his hands trying to cover the handle of the butcher knife and his left shoulder. He made a poor job of it.

Sail got up and lurched around Andopolis. The chair crutch made Andopolis clumsy.

Once through the door behind Andopolis, Sail found himself in what had once been the main cabin, and pretended to be, still.

Blick sat on the cabin floor, his face a mess. His visage was smeared with blue ink. The ink bottle was upside down under a table on which a new marine chart was spread open. A common writing pen lay on the chart.

Andopolis came in after Sail, banging on the chair crutch. The ice pick still stuck in his chest by its point. He came at Sail, hopped on one leg, and swung his chair with the other.

Sail, coughing, hurting all over, tried to dodge. He made it, but fell down.

Andopolis swung the chair. Sail rolled, and the chair went to pieces on the floor.

Nola was still screaming. Men were swearing outside. More men were running around on the houseboat, trying to find the way below. A police siren was whining.

Andopolis held a leg of his chair still. It was heavy enough to knock the brains out of an ox. He hopped for Sail.

Sail, looking about wildly, saw the fire extinguisher on the floor. It must have bounced in here. Maybe somebody had kicked it in accidentally. He rolled to it.

Andopolis lifted the chair leg.

The extinguisher made sickly noises as Sail pumped it. No tetrachloride came out. Nothing happened to indicate it ever would. Then a first squirt ran out about a foot. The second was longer. The third wet Andopolis' chest. Sail aimed and pumped. The tetrachloride got into Andopolis' eyes.

Andopolis made snarling sounds and couldn't see any more.

Sail got up and weaved to the table.

The chart on the table had two inked lines forming a V with arms that ran to landmarks on Lower Matecumbe island in the Florida Keys. Compass bearings were printed beside each arm, and the point where the lines came together was ringed.

Several times, Sail's lips moved, repeating the bearings, the landmarks.

Then Sail picked up the pen. He made a NE into a NNE and a SSE out of an E.

His letters looked enough like the others that nobody would guess the difference. And the lines of the V were wavy. They had not been laid out with a protractor from the compass roses. Therefore, they did not indicate an exact spot. Probably they varied as much as a mile, for the *Lady Luck* seemed to lie well off Matecumbe. Nobody would locate any sunken boat from that chart now.

Sail was repeating the true bearings to fix them in his memory when Andopolis came hopping in. Andopolis was still blind, still had his chair leg.

Blick, on the floor, called, "Nola—kid—what's wrong?" He didn't seem to know where he was or what was happening.

Andopolis weaved for Blick's mumbling voice.

"Blick!" Sail yelled thickly. "Jump!"

Blick said foolishly, "Was that—you—Nola?"

Sail was stumbling towards him, fully aware he would not make it in time. He didn't. He woke up nights for quite a while hearing the sound Andopolis' chair leg and Blick's head made.

Andopolis hopped around, still quite blind, and made for Sail. He had his chair leg raised. Hair, blood and brains stuck to the hickory chair leg. Sail got out of the way.

Andopolis stopped, stood perfectly still, and listened. Sail did not move. He was pale, swaying. He squatted, got his hands on the floor, sure he was going to fall if he didn't. He tried not to breathe loudly enough for Andopolis to hear.

Captain Cripp, Patrolman Joey Cripp and the old man from the hardware store came in together looking around.

The old man pointed at Sail and began, "There's the man who asked about the feller that got the chart. I told you I told him the chart was delivered here, and he probably had come right—"

Andopolis rushed the voice, holding his chair leg up.

"Look out!" Sail croaked.

Andopolis instantly veered for where he thought Sail's voice had come from. He was a little wrong. It was hard for him to maintain a direction hopping on one leg. He hopped against a wall. Hard.

Andopolis sighed, leaned over backward and hit the floor. He had a fit. A brief fit, ending by Andopolis straightening out and relaxing. Hitting the wall had driven the ice pick the rest of the way into his chest.

Sail remained on all fours on the floor. He felt, except for the pain, as if he were very drunk on bad liquor. He must have remained on his hands and knees a long time, for he was vaguely aware that Captain Cripp and Joey had walked around and around him, but without speaking. Then they went over to the table and found the chart.

They divided their looking between the chart and each other.

"It's it," Joey said.

"Yeah." Captain Cripp sounded thoughtful. "What about it, Joey?"

"You're the boss, Pop."

Captain Cripp turned the corners of his mouth down. He folded the chart, stuck it inside his clothing, under his belt. Then he straightened his uniform.

A doctor came in at last. He seemed to be a very silent doctor. He picked up Andopolis' wrist, held it a while, then put it back on the floor carefully. The wrist and arm were more flexible than that much rubber would have been. The doctor did not speak.

Sail was still on all fours. The doctor upset him gently. Sail had his tongue between his teeth. The doctor explored with his hands; when he came to Sail's chest, a small amount of sound escaped between Sail's tongue and teeth.

"My God!" the doctor said.

Four men helped with the stretcher as far as the ambulance, but only two when it came to getting the stretcher into the ambulance. Two could manage it better, using a system which they had. The ambulance motor started.

Captain Cripp got into the ambulance with Sail. He was holding his right hand to his nose.

"About Joey," he said. "I been wondering if Joey believed in something on the side, when he could get it. You know, kinda the modern idea."

He took his hand from his nose and quickly put a handkerchief in its place. The handkerchief got red at once.

Then he put the folded marine chart under Sail's head.

"Joey," he chuckled, "is as old-fashioned as angels, only he about busted my beak before I could explain."

The Magician Murder

Raoul Whitfield

rom the spot in which Jo Gar was seated the two fighting cocks were whirling, feathered forms bouncing from the dark earth of the pit. Filipinos, Japanese, Chinese, Malays and Portuguese filled the rising tiers of wooden benches; their shouts were shrill and fierce. The betting was good; already there had been several fights. The event now under way was the last fight of the evening; one of the cocks, a small bird named *Riazo*, was the champion of a distant Philippine province. *Riazo* seemed to be winning and the majority of the crowd liked it.

The Island detective rolled the brown-paper cigarette between two short brown fingers of his right hand. His face was expressionless; it was as though he were unconscious of the excitement around him. At intervals he raised his right hand so that it was before his brown face. The fingers of the hand were spread carelessly; his blue-gray eyes looked between them.

Cardoro sat on his right, some twenty feet away, in the small box reserved for persons of importance. Cardoro was a magician—Cardoro the Great. He was Spanish, but spoke several languages. Only five days ago he had reached Manila from Australia, and already he was the talk of the city. Crowds stormed the box office of the theatre at which he executed his magic. His name was on the lips of the mixed breeds of the Islands. He was a savage magician, working with knives and poisons. He made incisions on people and there was blood in evidence. Yet it was only a trick. The audience saw incisions that did not exist, and blood that was only colored water. But they liked it, and Cardoro was great. Therefore he occupied the box of honor.

The shrill shouts now became a scream. Jo Gar smiled slightly as the favorite sank on the dark ground. It rose and launched itself into another attack. The larger bird met the attack with a more vicious one. The silver spurs glittered in the light shooting down on them. *Riazo* was battered back, fell on its side. The larger bird was on top of it now, spurs working. *Riazo's* movements were convulsive. Suddenly there were no more movements. The shrill of the crowd hushed. Filipinos were in the pit—bending over the birds.

Jo Gar said very softly: "Another champion is dead."

He raised his right hand again, spreading the fingers. Cardoro was on his feet in the box. He was staring towards the ground of the pit. He had large black eyes and a face that seemed very pale among the brown ones about him. His body was straight; he was a big man. His face seemed strained.

A Filipino standing in the pit raised a short arm and said into the silence: "*Riazo* is dead!"

He spoke in Spanish, and before he could repeat the announcement in another language Cardoro had cried out. His voice carried over the close-packed circular arena.

"No!" he cried in Spanish. "It cannot be!"

Heads were jerked in his direction. A jeering voice from somewhere below reached Jo Gar's ears.

"It *is* so—*Riazo* is even too dead for *your* magic, Señor Cardoro!"

Jo Gar narrowed his blue-gray eyes very little. There was the edge of a smile on his tight-pressed lips. He looked down at the one who had jeered up at the magician. It was Markden, an American who handled many bets. Many bets that were large. Markden was a gambler; it was rumored that he made good sums on the fighting cocks. It was also rumored that some of his bets were placed after he had advance knowledge of certain facts. The Chinese did not trust him, and the Chinese were known as the wisest of the gamblers.

Cardoro's big body was swaying a little from side to side. His arms were drawn upward, the elbows extended, and his fists were clenched. There were white gloves on his hands; he wore them to protect his fingers, which were long and extremely sensitive. He called above the murmur of the crowd:

"I will not—"

His voice ceased abruptly. Jo Gar watched him turn from the box, saw a rather pretty girl lift a hand as though to stop him. But the magician paid no attention to her. The Island detective watched Cardoro move down wooden steps to a narrow exit. When he looked at Markden again the gambler was facing the direction in which the magician had gone. He was a small, slight man—slighter even than Jo. There was a set expression on his face. His body was tense under the glare of the lights, but as Jo's eyes watched he saw the man relax. He shrugged his narrow shoulders, looked down at the form of the dead bird.

The Filipino official who had announced the defeat of the champion now lifted the live winner in his hands. He turned slowly with the fighting cock above his head.

"The new champion!" he called. "*Garcia the First!*"

There was shrill sound in the arena. A group of Portuguese sailors started down towards the pit. There was the odor of varied tobaccos and of heat of people. Betel-nut chewers passed Jo, and there were red stains on the planks. It was very hot.

The Island detective went slowly towards an exit from the cock fight arena. The crowd milled around the dry ground beyond the entrance, chattering excitedly. *Calesos* and noisy, battered cars were making sound. Cardoro was not in sight, but there was talk of him. A well-dressed Chinese near Jo stated to his companion that the great one had lost much money. He had backed *Riazo* to the limit. Such a bet had not been made in many Sundays.

Jo Gar moved slowly to his *caleso*, nodded to the driver, who drowsed on the seat. Señor Ronisa passed close to the *caleso*, spoke cheerfully to Jo.

"I was lucky," the fat one stated. "I have won many *pesos*. But most have lost."

Jo Gar's eyes were very small. He placed a Panama carefully over his gray hair.

"It is not good—when most lose," he said quietly.

The fat one shrugged. "It is good for the few who win," he replied. "The winning is greater."

Jo Gar smiled a little, climbed into the *caleso*. The driver lifted the reins and spoke shrilly to the ancient horse. Jo said in a toneless voice:

"And the hating of the losers is greater."

He closed his eyes and relaxed in the seat. The *caleso* jerked forward and the light wind fanned greater heat against his face. When he opened his blue-gray eyes they were smiling. But the smile was a hard one, and very thoughtful.

*   *   *

Sadi Ratan frowned across the few feet of Jo Gar's office that separated the two. He looked cool despite the heat; his khaki uniform was spotless, well pressed. He said with a slight accent, speaking in English:

"You have perhaps seen that the magician, Cardoro, is dead, murdered?"

Jo Gar leaned back in the wicker chair. He nodded very slowly.

"Yes," he replied.

The Manila police lieutenant's frown deepened. There was a short silence broken by the whistle of small craft on the Pasig.

"The crime was committed by the American, Markden," Sadi Ratan announced. "The gambler, Markden. He has been in difficulty before this. He has vanished. The Constabulary has been notified."

Jo Gar smiled pleasantly. "Is that so?" he said thoughtfully. "So it was Markden who knifed Señor Cardoro?"

Lieutenant Ratan nodded again. He stood erect, but did not smile.

"That is the way it was," he stated. "He had been betting against Markden three nights since he has arrived here. Large sums. He had lost each time. Last evening he made a big bet. It was Sunday and he had little money. He agreed to cable his bank in Australia this morning, if he lost. He lost and he refused to pay. At dusk tonight he was knifed to death by Markden in his room at the Manila Hotel. Markden escaped, but he will be caught."

The Island detective continued to smile. "Of course," he said simply.

There was another silence, and during it Sadi Ratan watched Jo closely.

"The knife we have not found. Perhaps it was not a knife. Beside the body was a blood-stained spur such as the cocks fight with. A knife spur. The wounds were on the back of the neck—many of them. The spinal column was struck. Markden was seen drinking very much at six o'clock. He talked of what he would do to Cardoro if he failed to pay. Perhaps it was that he fastened the silver spur to wood, and used it that way. He entered the room while Cardoro was sleeping. There was no struggle. Cardoro was stunned with the first blow and before he staggered from the bed to die on the floor. Markden had struck many others. Then he fled."

Jo Gar lighted a brown-paper cigarette. "Why did Señor Cardoro refuse to pay his bet?" he asked, after a short time.

Lieutenant Ratan smiled a little. "He had been told, before the cock fights, that the champion bird, *Riazo*, had been drugged. The fight was not fair. Markden had bribed the Filipino who cared for *Riazo*."

Jo Gar smiled with his eyes almost closed. "Why did he not cancel his bet?" he asked.

Sadi Ratan shrugged. "Perhaps he was not sure. Perhaps Markden would not allow it. The fight was not a good one. *Riazo* did not attack. Cardoro refused to pay. Markden drank *sake* and thought about it. He murdered the magician."

Jo Gar looked at the ceiling fan that whirled at slow speed, spreading tepid air around the small office.

"A foolish man," he observed. "He knew that murdering Cardoro would not get him the money he had won. He knew that leaving the knife spur behind would betray him. He knew that running away would make matters worse. Yet he did all three of these things."

Sadi Ratan smiled narrowly. "He hated," he said simply. "It is a hot country. He drank and he brooded. Perhaps he did not *intend* to leave the spur behind. He fled when he discovered it was lost, or when he sobered. He knew the police would think of him."

"And they *did* think of him," Jo said pleasantly.

Lieutenant Ratan frowned again. "I attended the cock fights and was near Cardoro. I saw Markden mock him, jeer at him. And I heard the magician call out: 'I will not—' I knew that he meant he would not pay his bet."

The Island detective nodded. "It was fortunate you were so near," he observed. "After the murder you thought instantly of Markden. You questioned the bird handlers and learned that *Riazo* had perhaps been drugged and was unfit to fight, and that Cardoro had been warned of this fact. You have had the red on the spur knife analyzed and you know that it is human blood. It is common knowledge that Cardoro was betting heavily. Markden has vanished. Thus, he is the murderer."

Sadi Ratan's dark eyes had widened. They narrowed now. He spoke in a tone of triumph.

"That is so."

Jo Gar inhaled deeply on his cigarette. He regarded the police lieutenant with faint interest, reached for the palm leaf fan that was on the desk near his chair.

"And it being so, why do you visit me?" he asked softly.

The police lieutenant smiled, his white teeth showing.

"The Señor Markden was seen with you, not long before the hour of the first cock fight," he said slowly and clearly. "You were walking along the bank of the Pasig, talking seriously. You were seen by the police."

Jo Gar chuckled. "One never knows who watches," he said half to himself. His blue-gray eyes narrowed on the dark ones of the younger man. "It is true. We walked and talked together."

Sadi Ratan smiled coldly. "I think I should know what you talked about," he said.

The Island detective said thoughtfully: "I think you should. Señor

Markden wished me to learn if the cock fight—the final one—was to be honest. He stated that he had a large sum of money involved."

He paused and after a few seconds Sadi Ratan said impatiently:

"Well—did you accept the commission?"

Jo Gar nodded. "I made inquiries. I did my best. And I reported to him during the cock fights."

Sadi Ratan said: "You learned that the bird Cardoro was betting on was unfit to fight?"

The Island detective shook his head. "I reported to Markden that I felt the birds were evenly matched physically. It would be a matter of skill."

Sadi Ratan's brown face showed red color. He swore in Filipino. He said thickly:

"I do not think—"

He checked himself. Jo Gar smiled. "That I tell you the truth?" he asked quietly.

The police lieutenant's body was tense. "You are protecting an American. You have always protected them. You like them. He was your client."

Jo shrugged his narrow shoulders. "I was not paid that well," he said with irony. "I doubt that I could ever be paid that well. *Riazo* was not drugged. You have no proof of it."

Sadi Ratan said hotly: "I stood over Juan Derigo when he told me—"

Jo chuckled again. "A Filipino does not like to be beaten," he said. "He preferred to let you think as you wished."

The police lieutenant said: "It will not be good for you to protect Markden, Señor Gar. When we have caught him—"

The Island detective fanned himself. His smile was gone and he said slowly:

"The birds were in condition. Each of them. *Riazo* was defeated. That is all."

Sadi Ratan said excitedly: "It is not all. Markden was betting against Cardoro. Cardoro stood up and shouted that he would not pay. I saw Markden's face—there was hate in his eyes. And Cardoro was murdered. A spur knife was used. Markden has vanished. We have searched the city for him. He is the killer of the magician!"

Jo Gar sighed. "Then it is all very simple," he said quietly. "You will find him, and that will be the end."

His calmness infuriated the police lieutenant. He said fiercely:

"And you will be brought to trial for lying to me, a police officer!"

Jo Gar placed the palm leaf fan on the desk. It was almost midnight. He said thoughtfully:

"He was murdered at dusk—that would be about eight-thirty. You have been searching for the American for three hours. That would give the *real* murderer sufficient time to travel far."

Sadi Ratan swore again. He pointed a brown finger at Jo.

"We will not accept the alibi that you establish for the American," he said. "Remember that."

Jo Gar smiled pleasantly. "That is unfortunate," he said.

The police lieutenant went to the office door, turned and faced the Island detective.

"Markden was seen on the grounds of the Manila Hotel, at eight-fifteen," he stated grimly. "The sun was very low over the Bay. He was seen by several servants. And then he was not seen again. At the time he was seen the magician was in his room, sleeping. There is a porch through which one may enter."

Jo smiled cheerfully. "In a hot country the screened porch is desirable," he said softly.

Sadi Ratan pointed a finger at him again. His voice was rising as he spoke.

"It will be bad for you," he warned. "A murderer is a murderer."

Jo Gar leaned back in the wicker chair and closed his almond-shaped eyes.

"It is so," he agreed almost tonelessly. "And I think it would be wise for you to find this one."

Sam Markden sat slumped on the bench that faced the door of the dully lighted hut. A faint, hot breeze rustled the thatch roof. Markden seemed smaller than ever; his eyes moved at every sound. He was perspiring heavily. He spoke in a thick voice, softly and unsteadily.

"I tell you—they'll get me. They hate me in Manila. The fight was on the level. Maybe some haven't been in the past. This one was. They'll get me and frame me. You've got to do something, Señor Gar."

Jo Gar shook his head. "I have not *got* to do something," he corrected. "But your position is unfortunate. The police will not even believe me when I tell them you wished me to learn if the cock fight was to be fair. They will laugh at that. If I told them Cardoro had asked me that—they would have believed. But *you*—"

He checked himself. Somewhere beyond the hut on the edge of Manila, a dog howled. Markden shivered. Jo Gar said slowly and firmly:

"You have sent for me—you trust me. Do not trick me. Did you murder Cardoro?"

Markden sat up straight and struck clenched hands together.

"No—no!" he said desperately. "I threatened him, yes. That was in the afternoon. But I didn't kill him. I went to the hotel grounds, to talk to him again, just before dusk. But I was afraid to trust myself. I didn't see him. I went away. Then word reached me of what had happened. I hid out here—and sent for you."

Jo nodded. "It was difficult for me to reach you without being followed," he said. "The police are watching me carefully."

The American groaned. "They'll get me," he breathed. "I'd won from Cardoro. So much that I wanted this last fight to be absolutely fair. It had to be, or I knew he'd squeal. That's why I went to you."

Jo frowned. "It's a bad alibi, in any case. In this case—it's impossible."

Markden covered his soaked face with both palms and rocked on the bench. The dog howled again. Jo Gar said:

"You do not know of any enemies Cardoro might have had?"

Markden removed his hands, shook his head. "I didn't know him well. He was just a man with money, who wanted to bet."

The Island detective frowned. "You drank—and talked. Made threats before others?"

Markden's eyes were staring beyond Jo. "I drank *saké*. But I didn't make any threats. Only to Cardoro, and we were alone. I was careful not to make threats."

Jo sighed. "It is difficult," he said. "It was a good thing for someone who hated him enough to kill—this hatred of yours. But if we do not know the one who could have made use of it—"

He broke off. Markden muttered: "Billibid—I'll hang for it! They won't believe me."

Jo Gar half closed his eyes. He said in a calm voice:

"If *you* hang for it—*I* will be forced to leave the Islands. I think you are telling the truth. I do not wish to leave Manila. You do not wish to hang. You will stay here and I will do what I can."

Markden stared at him with bloodshot eyes.

"But what can you do?" he muttered. "All the evidence is against me. All that they have."

Jo Gar rubbed moist fingers together and smiled grimly down at the gambler.

"Perhaps there will be some evidence they do *not* have," he said softly. "There is a chance."

The American said bitterly: "It's a hell—of a chance!"

Jo Gar drew a deep breath, shrugged. "Even a *hell* of a chance is worth while," he observed steadily and softly, and went cautiously from the thatch-roofed hut.

* * *

The girl said: "It seems to me it's pretty late for me to have to talk about—this terrible thing."

Jo Gar stepped inside the large, high-ceilinged room, smiled apologetically.

"It is so, Miss Rayne," he said. "It is almost one o'clock. I am sorry."

The girl stood aside as he moved to the center of the room. There was moonlight beyond the Manila Hotel, on the water of the Bay. The girl was pretty, but her mouth and eyes were hard. She said huskily:

"I've been questioned—by the police."

The Island detective nodded. "Yes," he replied. "I suppose so. I am not of the police."

She watched him very closely. "I know. You're Señor Gar, a private detective."

Jo bowed slightly. The girl said: "Markden did this terrible thing. I was to have—married—Dario—next week—"

The Island detective said gently, looking at the older woman seated in the room.

"You think Markden killed Dario Cardoro?"

The girl said: "Yes—yes, I do! I'm sure of it. I was with Dario at the cock fights. He was sure he had been tricked. He said he would never pay. *Riazo* had no life, no fight. Dario left me in the box, hurried away. He was terribly upset."

Jo gestured towards a chair. "Please sit down," he said.

The girl went slowly to the chair, sat down. She looked at the older woman, said:

"This is my companion—Señora Riggia."

The Spanish woman bowed, her eyes on Jo's. She was short and thick-set. Her body relaxed in the chair.

"It is terrible," she said with an accent.

Jo Gar nodded. "It is bad for Señor Markden, the American," he stated. "He was owed money by the dead man. It was refused him. He threatened the dead man. He was on the hotel grounds not long before the murder was committed. He has vanished."

The girl said: "They will find him—the police."

The Island detective nodded. "I think so," he agreed. "But he is not the murderer of the magician, Cardoro."

The girl's brown eyes widened. She said in a half whisper:

"Not the—murderer—"

Jo smiled gently. His eyes were on the older woman. Her hands were gripping the sides of the wicker chair. Far out in the Bay a big boat whistled. Jo spoke slowly.

"Markden has been in trouble with the police before. He has shot a man. He possesses a gun. He did not use it on Cardoro."

The older woman said sharply: "That was because he did not wish to give himself away. He wished the police to think it was some other person—not an American. Americans do not use knives."

Jo Gar said: "That is good reasoning, Señora. Almost *too* good. He looked at the girl again. There was a short silence. Then Jo said pleasantly:

"I have been looking at the body. Cardoro was killed by a strong person."

The girl said: "A strong person? That is not so. The doctors have said that the spur blade did not penetrate more than an inch. A blow to the base of the brain—"

The Island detective interrupted, but his tone was cold and his words unhurried.

"And Markden is not a strong person?" he suggested.

The girl said with scorn: "Of course not. He is smaller even than you."

Jo bowed slightly. "That is so," he agreed. "I felt that you were aware of the fact that Markden is not strong."

There was a knock at the door of the room. The girl rose. Before she reached the door it was opened. Sadi Ratan entered. He said quickly, looking at the Spanish woman:

"I felt that you should know, Señora—"

He stared at Jo, broke off. The Island detective smiled at him.

"I came to talk with Miss Rayne, Lieutenant," he said.

Sadi Ratan frowned. Then his eyes narrowed until they were slits in his brown face.

"We have captured the American, Markden," he said grimly. "He has admitted that Señor Gar visited him tonight. That is bad for you, Señor Gar. You were protecting a murderer, one wanted by the police."

Jo Gar said quietly: "One wanted by the police, but not a murderer."

The police lieutenant said in a hard tone: "He will confess very soon. And even if he does not—"

The Island detective smiled with his lips. "You will try to hang him, anyway," he finished.

Sadi Ratan let his right hand go back towards a hip pocket. He said in a hard tone:

"It will be necessary for me to place you under arrest, Señor Gar, for interfering with the police and for aiding a murderer."

Jo shook his head. "Señor Markden is not yet a murderer," he reminded. "He has not been found guilty."

The girl said with scorn: "His record is not good. He has shot a man. He is a gambler and he has been caught cheating, before this happened. He killed Dario—because Dario refused to pay him."

Jo shook his head. His eyes were very small.

"You know much about the American," he said calmly. "Almost *too* much."

Sadi Ratan was watching him closely. Jo looked at the girl, addressed the police lieutenant.

"The Great Cardoro has done his tricks here often—for a period of years. He is Spanish—there is a bond between him and the Spanish here. There is a Spanish paper in Manila. News of Spaniards all over the world reaches it and is printed or filed away in the paper morgue. I have been looking through the morgue files. I find that Cardoro was worth twice as much two years ago than he was six months ago. His losses were due to gambling. I found a later item stating that Cardoro the Great had become engaged to an American girl of the theatre, Miss Jessie Rayne. And I found one more item of three months ago. In Melbourne a gambling place was raided. One of the heaviest losers had been Cardoro. He had stated then that he was willing his money to Miss Rayne, his fiancée, and that on the day of their marriage he would never gamble again."

The girl was watching him narrowly—her breathing was heavy. The older woman was tense in her chair. Jo said, smiling a little:

"So there you are."

Sadi Ratan said sharply: "There you are—where? What of it?"

Jo Gar shrugged. "But Cardoro has continued gambling. Continued losing. His fortune is willed to Miss Rayne. But will there *be* any fortune— would there *have been* any fortune—if Cardoro had not been—"

The girl shrilled at him: "You are telling me that *I* killed—Dario! You dare—"

Jo Gar shook his head. "I am not," he said quietly. "You did not love him, but you did not kill him. You do not know so much about knives, and you are not strong enough."

The girl's eyes were wide; her face was pale. Sadi breathed something that the Island detective did not catch. He said softly:

"But you realized, Miss Rayne, that the money you had married Cardoro for would not be for you, unless something was done. And you decided that something should be—death."

The girl cried: "No—"

Jo Gar said steadily: "Yes. You waited for the opportunity. The American, Markden, offered it. He had reason to hate Cardoro. He had a record and you knew about it. He was a gambler on cock fights, and that was why the blood-stained knife spur was found beside the dead man. But you went too far. Markden is an American, and he would not kill and then boast about it as a Filipino or a Spaniard might do. He would not hate that much."

He paused and said very slowly: "Cardoro was killed with a knife—not a cock fight spur. He was killed by a strong man or woman, who knew how to handle a knife. He was killed by—"

He turned and looked at the girl's companion. He said quietly:

"*You* murdered Dario Cardoro. You did not throw the knife far enough into the Bay, in your hurry. And you were seen throwing it. I have the knife."

The woman sprang from the chair. She screamed in Spanish, terribly. From the folds of her dress steel color caught the light of the room. Her right arm was lifted.

Jo Gar said: "Stop—"

The woman's right hand went down into the folds of the black dress she wore. She said in a hysterical tone:

"You lie—"

Jo Gar's right hand made swift movement; his Colt was low at his right side.

"No," he said steadily. "I do not lie. You murdered Cardoro. Drop the knife you were about to throw—on the floor."

The woman was breathing heavily; her eyes held a wild expression. But her hand remained in the folds of her black dress.

Jo said: "Quickly—drop it!" He raised the gun slightly.

The knife made clattering sound as it struck the wood of the floor. The woman in black slipped downward, slowly, in a faint. Jo said:

"Well, I have the knife *now*, anyway." He went over and picked it up. "She did not throw it into the Bay—and she was not seen throwing it. But I was coming close—and her nerves—"

The Rayne girl was on the divan, rocking back and forth. Her eyes stared somewhere beyond the figure of Jo Gar. She spoke in a monotone.

"She made me—tell her when Dario slept. She used the knife and left the knife spur, touching it in his blood. She hated him. He loved her once, but he sent her away. He was losing, gambling away all the money he had willed to me. She made me help her—she was to have some of—the money. I didn't want—to do it."

Jo Gar looked at Sadi Ratan. "I thought at first that he had been murdered outside, carried in. That was wrong. And I thought that the knife had been thrown away. That was wrong, too. But when I saw the woman's eyes, saw her watching me—"

He shrugged. The woman on the floor stirred and moaned. The Rayne girl said:

"He was brutal—it was self-defense. He was brutal to both of us—"

Jo Gar smiled slightly. "Your defense is your own affair," he said gently. "I am very little interested."

Lieutenant Ratan frowned and swore. Jo Gar said:

"You were so sure of the American. So sure he was guilty. Now you must free him."

Sadi Ratan muttered: "All the evidence we had—pointed to him."

Jo Gar sighed. "That is so," he agreed softly. And that was why I had to go to a newspaper and seek the evidence—you *did not* have."

BLACK

Paul Cain

The man said: "McCary."

"No." I shook my head and started to push past him, and he said: "McCary," again thickly, and then he crumpled into a heap on the wet sidewalk.

It was dark there, there wasn't anyone on the street—I could have walked away. I started to walk away and then the sucker instinct got the best of me and I went back and bent over him.

I shook him and said: "Come on, chump—get up out of the puddle."

A cab came around the corner and its headlights shone on me—and there I was, stooping over a drunk whom I'd never seen before, who thought my name was McCary. Any big-town driver would have pegged it for a stick-up, would have shoved off or sat still. That wasn't a big town—the cab slid alongside the curb and a fresh-faced kid stuck his face into the light from the meter and said: "Where to?"

I said: "No place." I ducked my head at the man on the sidewalk. "Maybe this one'll ride—he's paralyzed."

The kid clucked: "Tch, tch."

He opened the door and I stooped over and took hold of the drunk under his armpits and jerked him up and across the sidewalk and into the cab. He was heavy in a funny limp way. There was a hard bulge on his left side, under the arm.

I had an idea. I asked the kid: "Who's McCary?"

He looked self-consciously blank for a minute and then he said: "There's two—Luke and Ben. Luke's the old man—owns a lot of real estate. Ben runs a pool-hall."

"Let's go see Ben," I said. I got into the cab.

We went several blocks down the dark street and then I tapped on the glass and motioned to the kid to pull over to the curb. He stopped and slid the glass and I said: "Who's McCary?"

"I told you."

I said: "What about him?"

The kid made the kind of movement with his shoulders that would pass for a shrug in the sticks. "I told you—he runs a pool-hall."

I said: "Listen. This guy came up to me a few minutes ago and said 'McCary'—this guy is very dead."

The kid looked like he was going to jump out of the cab. His eyes were hanging out.

I waited.

The kid swallowed. He said: "Let's dump him."

I shook my head slightly and waited.

"Ben and the old man don't get along—they've been raising hell the last couple of weeks. This is the fourth," he jerked his head towards the corpse beside me.

"Know him?"

He shook his head and then—to be sure—took a flashlight out of the side-pocket and stuck it back through the opening and looked at the man's dead face. He shook his head again.

I said: "Let's go see Ben."

"You're crazy, Mister. If this is one of Ben's boys he'll tie you up to it, and if it ain't . . ."

"Let's go see Ben."

Ben McCary was a blond fat man, about forty—he smiled a great deal.

We sat in a little office above his pool-hall and he smiled heartily across all his face and said: "Well, sir—what can I do for you?"

"My name is Black. I came over from St. Paul—got in about a half hour ago."

He nodded, still with the wide hearty smile; stared at me cordially out of his wide-set blue eyes.

I went on: "I heard there was a lot of noise over here and I thought I might make a connection—pick up some change."

McCary juggled his big facial muscles into something resembling innocence.

"I don't know just what you mean, Buddy," he said. "What's your best game?"

"What's yours?"

He grinned again. "Well," he said, "you can get plenty of action up in the front room."

I said: "Don't kid me, Mister McCary. I didn't come over here to play marbles."

He looked pleasantly blank.

"I used to work for Dickie Johnson down in K C," I went on.

"Who sent you to me?"

"Man named Lowry—that's the name on the label of his coat. He's dead."

McCary moved a little in his chair but didn't change his expression.

"I came in on the nine-fifty train," I went on, "and started walking uptown to a hotel. Lowry came up to me over on Dell Street and said 'McCary,' and fell down. He's outside in a cab—stiff."

McCary looked up at the ceiling and then down at the desk. He said: "Well, well"—and took a skinny little cigar out of a box in one of the desk-drawers and lighted it. He finally got around to looking at me again and said: "Well, well," again.

I didn't say anything.

After he'd got the cigar going, he turned another of his big smiles on and said: "How am I supposed to know you're on the level?"

I said: "I'll bite. What do *you* think?"

He laughed. "I like you," he said. "By——! I like you."

I said I thought that was fine and, "now let's try to do some business."

"Listen," he said. "Luke McCary has run this town for thirty years. He ain't my old man—he married my mother and insisted on my taking his name."

He puffed slowly at his cigar. "I guess I was a pretty ornery kid"—he smiled boyishly—"when I came home from school I got into a jam—you know—kid stuff. The old man kicked me out."

I lighted a cigarette and leaned back.

"I went down to South America for about ten years, and then I went to Europe. I came back here two years ago and everything was all right for a while and then the old man and I got to scrapping again."

I nodded.

"He'd had everything his own way too long. I opened this place about three months ago and took a lot of his gambling business away—a lot of the shipyard men and miners. . . ."

McCary paused, sucked noisily at his cigar.

"Luke went clean off his nut," he went on. "He thought I was going to take it all away from him. . . ." McCary brought his big fist down hard on the desk. "And by the——! I *am*. Lowry's the third man of mine in two weeks. It's plenty in the open now."

I said: "How about Luke's side?"

"We got one of the——" he said. "A runner."

"It isn't entirely over the gambling concession?"

"Hell, no. That's all it was at first. All I wanted was to make a living. Now I've got two notch-joints at the other end of town. I've got a swell protection in with the law and I'm building up a liquor business that would knock your eye out."

I asked: "Is Luke in it by himself?"

McCary shook his head slowly. "He don't show anywhere. There's a fellah named Stokes runs the works for him—a young fellah. They been partners nearly eight years. It's all in Stokes' name. . . ."

"What does Stokes look like?"

"Tall—about your build. Shiny black hair, and a couple of big gold teeth" —McCary tapped his upper front teeth with a fat finger—"here."

I said: "How much is he worth to you?"

McCary stood up. He leaned across the desk and grinned down at me and said: "Not a nickel." His eyes were wide and clear like a baby's. He said slowly: "The old man is worth twenty-five hundred smackers to *you*."

I didn't say anything and McCary sat down and opened another drawer and took out a bottle of whiskey. He poured a couple of drinks.

"I think the best angle for you," he said, "is to go to Stokes and give him the same proposition you gave me. Nobody saw you come in here. It's the only way you can get near the old man."

I nodded. We drank.

"By——! I like your style," he said. "I've been trying to get along with an outfit of yokels."

We smiled at one another. I was glad he said he liked me because I knew he didn't like me at all. I was one up on him, I didn't like him very well either.

Stokes sat on a corner of the big library-table, his long legs dangling.

He said: "You're airing Ben—how do we know you'll play ball with us?" His eyes were stony.

I looked at the old man. I said: "I don't like that fat—son of yours—and I never double-cross the best offer."

Luke McCary was a thin little man with a pinched red face, bushy white hair. He sat in a big armchair on the other side of the table, his head and neck and wild white hair sticking up out of the folds of a heavy blue bathrobe.

He looked at me sharply. He said: "I don't want any part of it."

"Then I'll have to act on the best offer."

Stokes grinned.

The old man stood up. He said: "Why—damn you and your guts. . . ." He opened a humidor on the table and took out a small automatic. "I can shoot the buttons off your vest, young fella . . . I can shoot you for a yegg right now, and no one'll ever know the difference. . . ."

I said: "*You'll* know the difference—for not having taken advantage of talent, when you had the chance."

He put the automatic back in the box and sat down and smiled gently at Stokes.

Stokes was looking at the floor. He said: "Five grand if you wipe out the whole outfit. Run 'em out of town, stick 'em in jail, poison 'em . . . Anything."

"Wouldn't you like a new railroad station too?"

They didn't say anything for a minute. They looked at me.

I went on: "No sale. I'll take care of Ben for that—but busting up the organization would mean sending for a few friends—would cost a hell of a lot more than five. . . ."

The old man looked the least bit scared for a second—then he said: "Ben'll do."

"How about laying something on the line?"

Stokes said: "Don't be silly."

The old man cackled. "Well I never saw such guts," he said.

I said: "All right, gentlemen. Maybe I'll call you later."

Stokes went downstairs with me. He smiled in a strange way. "I never knew the old man to go for anything that looks as tricky as this. I guess it looks good because Ben thinks you're working for him."

I nodded. I said: "Uh huh—Ben's a swell guy. He'll probably blast me on sight."

"I don't think you'll find him at his joint."

I waited and Stokes leaned against the door, said: "There's a big outfit downstate that's been running twelve trucks a week through here from the Border. They've paid off for this division of the highway for years—to the old man. The last two convoys have been hi-jacked at Four-mile Creek, north of town—a couple drivers were killed. . . ."

He paused, looked wise a minute, went on: "That was Ben. There was a convoy due through last night—they run in bunches of four, or six—it didn't show up. It's a cinch for tonight—and that's where Ben'll be."

I said: "That's fine. How do I get there?"

Stokes told me to follow the main highway north, and where to take the cutoff that crossed Four-mile. I thanked him and went out.

I walked down to a drugstore on the corner and called a cab. When it came, I got in and had the driver jockey around until he was parked in a spot where I could watch the front door of the McCary house.

After a while, Stokes came out and got into a roadster and snorted up past us and turned down the side street. I told the driver to follow him. I don't think the driver knew who it was. It didn't matter a hell of a lot anyway.

I got out and told the driver to wait and walked on down Dell Street, keeping close to the fence. It was raining pretty hard again. I passed the place where Lowry had come up to me, and I went on to the corner; and then went back the same way until I came to the narrow gate I had missed in the darkness.

It was more a door than a gate, set flush with the high fence. I finagled with the latch for a while and then pushed the gate open slowly and went into a yard. It was a big yard, full of old lumber and old box-car trucks—stuff like that. There was a long shed along one side, and a small two-story building on the far side.

I stumbled along as quietly as I could towards the building and then I went around the corner of a big pile of ties, and Stokes' roadster was sitting there very dark and quiet in the rain. I went past it and up to the building and along the wall until I saw the lighted window.

I had to rustle around quietly and find a box and stand on it to see through the little square window. The panes were dirty; the inside looked like a time-office. Stokes and Ben McCary and another man were there. They were arguing about something. McCary was walking around waving his arms; Stokes and the other man were sitting down. I couldn't hear a word they said. The rain was roaring on the tin-roof of the shed and all I could hear was a buzz of voices.

I didn't stay there very long. It didn't mean anything. I got down and put the box back and wandered around until I found McCary's car. Anyway, I guessed it was his car. It was a big touring-car and it was parked near the gate on the opposite side of the block from Dell Street, where Stokes had come in.

I got in and sat in the back seat. The side-curtains were drawn and it was nice to get out of the rain for a while.

In about ten minutes, the light went out and I could hear voices coming towards the car. I sat down on the floor. The three of them stood outside for a minute talking about "a call from Harry"—then Stokes and the other man went off towards Stokes' car, and McCary squeezed into the front seat and stepped on the starter.

I waited till we had burned through the gate and were halfway up the block, and then I put a gun against the back of McCary's neck. He straightened out in the seat and eased the brake on. I told him to go on to the old man's house.

We sat in the big room upstairs. The old man sat in the big armchair by the table, and Ben sat across from him. I was half lying down in another chair out of the circle of light and I had the gun on my lap.

The old man was fit to be tied. He was green with hate and he kept glaring at Ben out of his little red-rimmed eyes.

I said: "Well, gran'pa——if you'll make out that check now, we'll finish this business."

The old man swallowed.

"You can give me *your* twenty-five hundred in cash," I went on to Ben. "Then I'll put the chill on both of you—and everybody'll be happy."

They must have thought I meant it. Ben got rigid, and the old man cleared his throat and made a slow pass at the humidor.

I fiddled with the gun. I threw a pack of cigarettes on the table and said: "Smoke?"

The old man looked at the cigarettes and at the gun in my hand, and relaxed.

I said: "Still and all—it don't quite square with my weakness for efficiency, yet. Maybe you boys'll get together and make me an offer for Stokes. He's the star—he's been framing both of you."

I don't think Ben was very surprised—but the old man looked like he'd swallowed a mouse.

"He's been in with Ben on the truck heistings," I went on. "He's been waiting for a good spot to dump you—working on your connections."

The old man said: "That's a—damned lie."

"Suit yourself."

I went on to Ben: "He made the five-grand offer for your hide, in Luke's name, tonight—and he gave me the Four-mile steer. . . ." I hesitated a moment. "Only you wouldn't try three in the same spot, would you?"

Ben finally got his smile working. He started to say something but I interrupted him:

"Stokes told me you rubbed the two boys on the trucks, too."

Ben's smile went out like a light. He said: "Stokes shot both those men himself—and there wasn't any need for it. They were lined up alongside the road. . . ."

Something in the soft way he said it made it sound good.

I said: "He'll be around your place—no?"

"He went home."

Ben gave me the number and I called up, but there wasn't any answer.

We sat there without saying anything for several minutes, and then the door downstairs opened and closed and somebody came up.

I said to Ben: "What'll you bet?"

The door opened and Stokes came in. He had a long gray raincoat on and it made him look even taller and thinner than he was. He stood in the doorway looking mostly at the old man; then he came in and sat down on a corner of the table.

I said: "Now that the class is all here, you can start bidding."

The old man laughed deep in his throat. Stokes was watching me expressionlessly, and Ben sat smiling stupidly at his hands.

"I'm auctioning off the best little town in the state, gentlemen," I went on. "Best schools, sewage system, post-office. . . . Best street-lighting, water supply. . . ."

I was having a swell time.

The old man was staring malevolently at Stokes. "I'll give you twenty-five thousand dollars," he said to me, "to give me that pistol and get out of here."

If I'd thought there was any chance of collecting, I might have talked to him. Things happen that way sometimes.

I looked at my watch and put the gun down on the arm of the chair where it looked best and picked up the phone.

I asked Ben: "Where's the business going to be pulled off tonight?"

Ben wanted to be nice. He said: "A coffee joint about six miles north of town." He glanced at Stokes. "This—tried to swing it back to Four-mile when he thought you'd be there sniping for me."

"The boys are there now?"

He nodded. "The trucks have been stopping there to eat lately."

I asked the operator for long-distance, and asked for the Bristol Hotel in Talley, the first town north. The connection went right through. I asked for Mister Cobb.

When he answered, I told him about the coffee place, and that I wasn't sure about it; and told him he'd find the stuff that had been heisted in the sheds of the yard on Dell Street. I wasn't sure of that either, but I watched Ben and Stokes when I said it and it looked all right. Cobb told me that he'd gotten into Talley with the convoy about midnight and had been waiting for my call since then.

I hung up. "There'll be some swell fireworks out there," I said. "There's a sub-machine-gun on every truck—double crews. And it don't matter much," I went on to Ben, "how good your steer is. They'll be watching out all the way."

Stokes stood up.

I picked up the gun. "Don't move so far, Skinny," I said. "It makes me nervous."

He stood there staring at the gun. The water was running off his raincoat and it had formed into a little dark pool at his feet.

He said: "What the hell do you want?"

"I wanted you to know that one of the kids you shot up last week at Fourmile was my boss' brother. He went along for the ride."

I don't think Stokes could move. I think he tried to move sidewise or get his hand into his pocket, or something, but all he could do was take a deep breath. Then I shot him in the middle of the body where he shot the kid, and he sank down on the floor with his legs crossed under him, like a tailor.

The old man didn't get up. He sat a little deeper in his chair and stared at Stokes.

Ben moved very fast for a fat man. He was up and out the door like a bat out of hell. That was OK with me—he couldn't get to the coffee place before the trucks got there. I had the keys to his car, and it was too far anyway.

I got up and put the rod away and went over to the table and picked up my cigarettes. I looked down at the old man, said: "Things'll be a little quieter now, maybe. You'll get the dough for haulage through your territory, as usual. See that it gets through."

He didn't answer.

I started for the door and then there was a shot out in front of the house. I ran on down to the front door. It was open and Ben was flat on the threshold —had fallen smack on his face, half through the door.

I ducked back through the hall and tried a couple locked doors. When I came up through the hall again, the old man was on his knees beside Ben, and was rocking back and forth, moaning a little.

I went through another room and into the kitchen and on through, out the back door. I crossed the backyard and jumped a low fence and walked through another yard to a gate that led into an alley. I sloshed along through the mud until I came to a cross-street, and went on down to the corner that was diagonally across the block from the McCary house.

A cab came down the street and I waited until it was almost to the corner, stepped out in front of it. The driver swerved and stepped on the gas, but he had slowed enough to give me time to jump on the running-board.

I stuck my head in to the light from the meter. That turned out to be my best hunch of the evening because in another second, the driver would have opened up my chest with one of the dirtiest looking .45's I ever saw, at about two feet. It was the kid who had picked Lowry and me up. He hesitated just long enough when he saw who I was.

We nearly ran into a tree and I had time to reach in and knock that cannon out of his hand. He stepped on the brake, and reached for the gun, but I beat him to it by a hair and stuck it in my overcoat pocket and got in beside him.

I said: "Shame on you—almost crashing an old pal like me."

He sat tight in the seat and got a weak grin working and said: "Where to?"

"Just away."

We went on through the mud and rain, and turned into a slightly better lighted street.

I said: "How did you know Ben shot Lowry?"

The kid kept his head down, his eyes ahead. "Lowry and me have lived together for two years," he said. "He used to be in the hack racket too, till he got mixed up with McCary. . . ."

"Lowry won a lot of jack in one of Ben's crap games a couple days ago, and Ben wanted him to kick back with it—said everybody that worked for him was automatically a shill, and couldn't play for keeps. But Lowry's been dropping every nickel he made in the same game, for months. That was okay with Ben. It was all right to lose, but you mustn't win."

I nodded, lighted a cigarette.

"Ben shot Lowry tonight at the joint on Dell Street. I know it was him because Lowry's been afraid of it—and that's why he said 'McCary.' "

"Did you know it was Lowry when you picked us up?"

"Not until I used the light. Then, when we got to Ben's I saw him get out of his car and go in just ahead of you—then I was sure. I took Lowry up to his pa's after you went in."

The kid drove me to the next town south. I forget the name. I got a break on a train—I only had to wait about ten minutes.

The King in Yellow

Raymond Chandler

I

George Millar, night auditor at the Carlton Hotel, was a dapper wiry little man, with a soft deep voice like a torch singer's. He kept it low, but his eyes were sharp and angry, as he said into the PBX mouthpiece: "I'm very sorry. It won't happen again. I'll send up at once."

He tore off the headpiece, dropped it on the keys of the switchboard and marched swiftly from behind the pebbled screen and out into the entrance lobby. It was past one and the Carlton was two thirds residential. In the main lobby, down three shallow steps, lamps were dimmed and the night porter had finished tidying up. The place was deserted—a wide space of dim furniture, rich carpet. Faintly in the distance a radio sounded. Millar went down the steps and walked quickly towards the sound, turned through an archway and looked at a man stretched out on a pale green davenport and what looked like all the loose cushions in the hotel. He lay on his side dreamy-eyed and listened to the radio two yards away from him.

Millar barked: "Hey, you! Are you the house dick here or the house cat?"

Steve Grayce turned his head slowly and looked at Millar. He was a long black-haired man, about twenty-eight with deep-set silent eyes and a rather gentle mouth. He jerked a thumb at the radio and smiled. "King Leopardi, George. Hear that trumpet tone. Smooth as an angel's wing, boy."

"Swell! Go on back upstairs and get him out of the corridor!"

Steve Grayce looked shocked. "What—again? I thought I had those birds put to bed long ago." He swung his feet to the floor and stood up. He was at least a foot taller than Millar.

"Well, Eight-sixteen says no. Eight-sixteen says he's out in the hall with two of his stooges. He's dressed in yellow satin shorts and a trombone and he and his pals are putting on a jam session. And one of those hustlers Quillan registered in Eight-eleven is out there truckin' for them. Now get on to it, Steve—and this time make it stick."

Steve Grayce smiled wryly. He said: "Leopardi doesn't belong here anyway. Can I use chloroform or just my blackjack?"

He stepped long legs over the pale-green carpet, through the arch and across the main lobby to the single elevator that was open and lighted. He slid the doors shut and ran it up to Eight, stopped it roughly and stepped out into the corridor.

The noise hit him like a sudden wind. The walls echoed with it. Half a dozen doors were open and angry guests in night robes stood in them peering.

"It's O.K. folks," Steve Grayce said rapidly. "This is absolutely the last act. Just relax."

He rounded a corner and the hot music almost took him off his feet. Three men were lined up against the wall, near an open door from which light streamed. The middle one, the one with the trombone, was six feet tall, powerful and graceful, with a hairline mustache. His face was flushed and his eyes had an alcoholic glitter. He wore yellow satin shorts with large initials embroidered in black on the left leg—nothing more. His torso was tanned and naked.

The two with him were in pajamas, the usual halfway-good-looking band boys, both drunk, but not staggering drunk. One jittered madly on a clarinet and the other on a tenor saxophone.

Back and forth in front of them, strutting, trucking, preening herself like a magpie, arching her arms and her eyebrows, bending her fingers back until the carmine nails almost touched her arms, a metallic blonde swayed and went to town on the music. Her voice was a throaty screech, without melody, as false as her eyebrows and as sharp as her nails. She wore high-heeled slippers and black pajamas with a long purple sash.

Steve Grayce stopped dead and made a sharp downward motion with his hand. "Wrap it up!" he snapped. "Can it. Put it on ice. Take it away and bury it. The show's out. Scram, now—scram!"

King Leopardi took the trombone from his lips and bellowed: "Fanfare to a house dick!"

The three drunks blew a stuttering note that shook the walls. The girl laughed foolishly and kicked out. Her slipper caught Steve Grayce in the chest. He picked it out of the air, jumped towards the girl and took hold of her wrist.

"Tough, eh?" he grinned. "I'll take you first."

"Get him!" Leopardi yelled. "Sock him low! Dance the gum-heel on his neck!"

Steve swept the girl off her feet, tucked her under his arm and ran. He carried her as easily as a parcel. She tried to kick his legs. He laughed and shot a glance through a lighted doorway. A man's brown brogues lay under a bureau. He went on past that to a second lighted doorway, slammed through and kicked the door shut, turned far enough to twist the tabbed key in the lock. Almost at once a fist hit the door. He paid no attention to it.

He pushed the girl along the short passage past the bathroom, and let her go. She reeled away from him and put her back to the bureau, panting, her eyes furious. A lock of damp gold-dipped hair swung down over one eye. She shook her head violently and bared her teeth.

"How would you like to get vagged, sister?"

"Go to hell!" she spit out. "The King's a friend of mine, see? You better keep your paws off me, copper."

"You run the circuit with the boys?"

She spat at him again.

"How'd you know they'd be here?"

Another girl was sprawled across the bed, her head to the wall, tousled black hair over a white face. There was a tear in the leg of her pajamas. She lay limp and groaned.

Steve said harshly: "Oh, oh, the torn-pajama act. It flops here, sister, it flops hard. Now listen, you kids. You can go to bed and stay till morning or you can take the bounce. Make up your minds."

The black-haired girl groaned. The blonde said: "You get out of my room, you damned gum-heel!"

She reached behind her and threw a hand mirror. Steve ducked. The mirror slammed against the wall and fell without breaking. The black-haired girl rolled over on the bed and said wearily: "Oh lay off. I'm sick."

She lay with her eyes closed, the lids fluttering.

The blonde swiveled her hips across the room to a desk by the window, poured herself a full half-glass of Scotch in a water glass and gurgled it down before Steve could get to her. She choked violently, dropped the glass and went down on her hands and knees.

Steve said grimly: "That's the one that kicks you in the face, sister."

The girl crouched, shaking her head. She gagged once, lifted the carmine nails to paw at her mouth. She tried to get up, and her foot skidded out from under her and she fell down on her side and went fast asleep.

Steve sighed, went over and shut the window and fastened it. He rolled the black-haired girl over and straightened her on the bed and got the bedclothes from under her, tucked a pillow under her head. He picked the blonde bodily off the floor and dumped her on the bed and covered both girls to the chin. He opened the transom, switched off the ceiling light and unlocked the door. He relocked it from the outside, with a master key on a chain.

"Hotel business," he said under his breath. "Phooey."

The corridor was empty now. One lighted door still stood open. Its number was 815, two doors from the room the girls were in. Trombone music came from it softly—but not softly enough for 1:25 A.M.

Steve Grayce turned into the room, crowded the door shut with his shoulder and went along past the bathroom. King Leopardi was alone in the room.

The bandleader was sprawled out in an easy chair, with a tall misted glass at his elbow. He swung the trombone in a tight circle as he played it and the lights danced in the horn.

Steve lit a cigarette, blew a plume of smoke and stared through it at Leopardi with a queer, half-admiring, half-contemptuous expression.

He said softly: "Lights out, yellow-pants. You play a sweet trumpet and your trombone don't hurt either. But we can't use it here. I already told you that once. Lay off. Put that thing away."

Leopardi smiled nastily and blew a stuttering raspberry that sounded like a devil laughing.

"Says you," he sneered. "Leopardi does what he likes, where he likes, when he likes. Nobody's stopped him yet, gum-shoe. Take the air."

Steve hunched his shoulders and went close to the tall dark man. He said patiently: "Put that bazooka down, big-stuff. People are trying to sleep. They're funny that way. You're a great guy on a band shell. Everywhere else you're just a guy with a lot of jack and a personal reputation that stinks from here to Miami and back. I've got a job to do and I'm doing it. Blow that thing again and I'll wrap it around your neck."

Leopardi lowered the trombone and took a long drink from the glass at his elbow. His eyes glinted nastily. He lifted the trombone to his lips again, filled his lungs with air and blew a blast that rocked the walls. Then he stood up very suddenly and smoothly and smashed the instrument down on Steve's head.

"I never did like house peepers," he sneered. "They smell like public toilets."

Steve took a short step back and shook his head. He leered, slid forward on one foot and smacked Leopardi open-handed. The blow looked light, but Leopardi reeled all the way across the room and sprawled at the foot of the bed, sitting on the floor, his right arm draped in an open suitcase.

For a moment neither man moved. Then Steve kicked the trombone away from him and squashed his cigarette in a glass tray. His black eyes were empty but his mouth grinned whitely.

"If you want trouble," he said, "I come from where they make it."

Leopardi smiled, thinly, tautly, and his right hand came up out of the suitcase with a gun in it. His thumb snicked the safety catch. He held the gun steady, pointing.

"Make some with this," he said, and fired.

The bitter roar of the gun seemed a tremendous sound in the closed room. The bureau mirror splintered and glass flew. A sliver cut Steve's cheek like a razor blade. Blood oozed in a small narrow line on his skin.

He left his feet in a dive. His right shoulder crushed against Leopardi's bare chest and his left hand brushed the gun away from him, under the bed. He rolled swiftly to his right and came up on his knees spinning.

He said thickly, harshly: "You picked the wrong gee, brother."

He swarmed on Leopardi and dragged him to his feet by his hair, by main strength. Leopardi yelled and hit him twice on the jaw and Steve grinned and kept his left hand twisted in the bandleader's long sleek black hair. He turned his hand and the head twisted with it and Leopardi's third punch landed on Steve's shoulder. Steve took hold of the wrist behind the punch and twisted that and the bandleader went down on his knees yowling. Steve lifted him by the hair again, let go of his wrist and punched him three times in the stomach, short terrific jabs. He let go of the hair then as he sank the fourth punch almost to his wrist.

Leopardi sagged blindly to his knees and vomited.

Steve stepped away from him and went into the bathroom and got a towel off the rack. He threw it at Leopardi, jerked the open suitcase onto the bed and started throwing things into it.

Leopardi wiped his face and got to his feet still gagging. He swayed, braced himself on the end of the bureau. He was white as a sheet.

Steve Grayce said: "Get dressed, Leopardi. Or go out the way you are. It's all one to me."

Leopardi stumbled into the bathroom, pawing the wall like a blind man.

II

Millar stood very still behind the desk as the elevator opened. His face was white and scared and his cropped black mustache was a smudge across his upper lip. Leopardi came out of the elevator first, a muffler around his neck, a lightweight coat tossed over his arm, a hat tilted on his head. He walked stiffly, bent forward a little, his eyes vacant. His face had a greenish pallor.

Steve Grayce stepped out behind him carrying a suitcase, and Carl, the night porter, came last with two more suitcases and two instrument cases in black leather. Steve marched over to the desk and said harshly: "Mr. Leopardi's bill—if any. He's checking out."

Millar goggled at him across the marble desk. "I—I don't think, Steve—"

"O.K. I thought not."

Leopardi smiled very thinly and unpleasantly and walked out through the brass-edged swing doors the porter held open for him. There were two nighthawk cabs in the line. One of them came to life and pulled up to the canopy and the porter loaded Leopardi's stuff into it. Leopardi got into the cab and leaned forward to put his head to the open window. He said slowly and thickly: "I'm sorry for you, gum-heel, I mean sorry."

Steve Grayce stepped back and looked at him woodenly. The cab moved off down the street, rounded a corner and was gone. Steve turned on his heel, took a quarter from his pocket and tossed it up in the air. He slapped it into the night porter's hand.

"From the King," he said. "Keep it to show your grandchildren."

He went back into the hotel, got into the elevator without looking at Millar, shot it up to Eight again and went along the corridor, master-keyed his way into Leopardi's room. He relocked it from the inside, pulled the bed out from the wall and went in behind it. He got a .32 automatic off the carpet, put it in his pocket and prowled the floor with his eyes looking for the ejected shell. He found it against the wastebasket, reached to pick it up, and stayed bent over, staring into the basket. His mouth tightened. He picked up the shell and dropped it absently into his pocket, then reached a questing finger into the basket and lifted out a torn scrap of paper on which a piece of newsprint had been pasted. Then he picked up the basket, pushed the bed back against the wall and dumped the contents of the basket out on it.

From the trash of torn papers and matches he separated a number of pieces with newsprint pasted to them. He went over to the desk with them and sat down. A few minutes later he had the torn scraps put together like a jigsaw puzzle and could read the message that had been made by cutting words and letters from magazines and pasting them on a sheet.

TEN GRand BY TH U RS DAY NI GHT,
LEO PAR DI. DAY AFTER *YOU* OPEN AT
T HE CL U B SHAL OTTE. OR EL SE—CUR-
TAINS. FROM HER BROTHER.

Steve Grayce said: "Huh." He scooped the torn pieces into a hotel envelope, put that in his inside breast pocket and lit a cigarette. "The guy had guts," he said. "I'll grant him that—and his trumpet."

He locked the room, listened a moment in the now silent corridor, then went along to the room occupied by the two girls. He knocked softly and put his ear to the panel. A chair squeaked and feet came towards the door.

"What is it?" The girl's voice was cool, wide awake. It was not the blonde's voice.

"The house man. Can I speak to you a minute?"

"You're speaking to me."

"Without the door between, lady."

"You've got the passkey. Help yourself." The steps went away. He unlocked the door with his master key, stepped quietly inside, and shut it. There was a dim light in a lamp with a shirred shade on the desk. On the bed the blonde snored heavily, one hand clutched in her brilliant metallic hair. The black-haired girl sat in the chair by the window, her legs crossed at right angles like a man's and stared at Steve emptily.

He went close to her and pointed to the long tear in her pajama leg. He said softly: "You're not sick. You were not drunk. That tear was done a long time ago. What's the racket? A shakedown on the King?"

The girl stared at him coolly, puffed at a cigarette and said nothing.

"He checked out," Steve said. "Nothing doing in that direction now, sister." He watched her like a hawk, his black eyes hard and steady on her face.

"Aw, you house dicks make me sick!" the girl said with sudden anger. She surged to her feet and went past him into the bathroom, shut and locked the door.

Steve shrugged and felt the pulse of the girl asleep in the bed—a thumpy, draggy pulse, a liquor pulse.

"Poor damn hustlers," he said under his breath.

He looked at a large purple bag that lay on the bureau, lifted it idly and let it fall. His face stiffened again. The bag made a heavy sound on the glass top, as if there were a lump of lead inside it. He snapped it open quickly and plunged a hand in. His fingers touched the cold metal of a gun. He opened the bag wide and stared down into it at a small .25 automatic. A scrap of white paper caught his eye. He fished it out and held it to the light—a rent receipt with a name and address. He stuffed it into his pocket, closed the bag and was standing by the window when the girl came out of the bathroom.

"Hell, are you still haunting me?" she snapped. "You know what happens to hotel dicks that master-key their way into ladies' bedrooms at night?"

Steve said loosely: "Yeah. They get in trouble. They might even get shot at."

The girl's face became set, but her eyes crawled sideways and looked at the purple bag. Steve looked at her. "Know Leopardi in Frisco?" he asked. "He hasn't played here in two years. Then he was just a trumpet player in Vane Utigore's band—a cheap outfit."

The girl curled her lip, went past him and sat down by the window again. Her face was white, stiff. She said dully: "Blossom did. That's Blossom on the bed."

"Know he was coming to this hotel tonight?"

"What makes it your business?"

"I can't figure him coming here at all," Steve said. "This is a quiet place. So I can't figure anybody coming here to put the bite on him."

"Go somewhere else and figure. I need sleep."

Steve said: "Good night, sweetheart—and keep your door locked."

A thin man with thin blond hair and thin face was standing by the desk, tapping on the marble with thin fingers. Millar was still behind the desk and he still looked white and scared. The thin man wore a dark gray suit with a scarf inside the collar of the coat. He had a look of having just got up. He turned sea-green eyes slowly on Steve as he got out of the elevator, waited for him to come up to the desk and throw a tabbed key on it.

Steve said: "Leopardi's key, George. There's a busted mirror in his room and the carpet has his dinner on it—mostly Scotch." He turned to the thin man.

"You want to see me, Mr. Peters?"

"What happened, Grayce?" The thin man had a tight voice that expected to be lied to.

"Leopardi and two of his boys were on Eight, the rest of the gang on Five. The bunch on Five went to bed. A couple of obvious hustlers managed to get themselves registered just two rooms from Leopardi. They managed to contact him and everybody was having a lot of nice noisy fun out in the hall. I could only stop it by getting a little tough."

"There's blood on your cheek," Peters said coldly. "Wipe it off."

Steve scratched at his cheek with a handkerchief. The thin thread of blood had dried. "I got the girls tucked away in their room," he said. "The two stooges took the hint and holed up, but Leopardi still thought the guests wanted to hear trombone music. I threatened to wrap it around his neck and he beaned me with it. I slapped him open-handed and he pulled a gun and took a shot at me. Here's the gun."

He took the .32 automatic out of his pocket and laid it on the desk. He put the used shell beside it. "So I beat some sense into him and threw him out," he added.

Peters tapped on the marble. "Your usual tact seems to have been well in evidence."

Steve stared at him. "He shot at me," he repeated quietly. "With a gun. This gun. I'm tender to bullets. He missed, but suppose he hadn't? I like my stomach the way it is, with just one way in and one way out."

Peters narrowed his tawny eyebrows. He said very politely: "We have you down on the payroll here as a night clerk, because we don't like the name house detective. But neither night clerks nor house detectives put guests out of the hotel without consulting me. Not ever, Mr. Grayce."

Steve said: "The guy shot at me, pal. With a gun. Catch on? I don't have to take that without a kickback, do I?" His face was a little white.

Peters said: "Another point for your consideration. The controlling interest in this hotel is owned by Mr. Halsey G. Walters. Mr. Walters also owns the Club Shalotte, where King Leopardi is opening on Wednesday night. And that, Mr. Grayce, is why Leopardi was good enough to give us his business. Can you think of anything else I should like to say to you?"

"Yeah. I'm canned," Steve said mirthlessly.

"Very correct, Mr. Grayce. Good-night, Mr. Grayce."

The thin blond man moved to the elevator and the night porter took him up.

Steve looked at Millar.

"Jumbo Walters, huh?" he said softly. "A tough, smart guy. Much too smart to think this dump and the Club Shalotte belong to the same sort of customers. Did Peters write Leopardi to come here?"

"I guess he did, Steve." Millar's voice was low and gloomy.

"Then why wasn't he put in a tower suite with a private balcony to dance on, at twenty-eight bucks a day? Why was he put on a medium-priced transient floor? And why did Quillan let those girls get so close to him?"

Millar pulled at his black mustache. "Tight with money—as well as with Scotch, I suppose. As to the girls, I don't know."

Steve slapped the counter open-handed. "Well, I'm canned, for not letting a drunken heel make a parlor house and a shooting gallery out of the eighth floor. Nuts! Well, I'll miss the joint at that."

"I'll miss you too, Steve," Millar said gently. "But not for a week. I take a week off starting tomorrow. My brother has a cabin at Crestline."

"Didn't know you had a brother," Steve said absently. He opened and closed his fist on the marble desk top.

"He doesn't come into town much. A big guy. Used to be a fighter."

Steve nodded and straightened from the counter. "Well, I might as well finish out the night," he said. "On my back. Put this gun away somewhere, George."

He grinned coldly and walked away, down the steps into the dim main lobby and across to the room where the radio was. He punched the pillows into shape on the pale green davenport, then suddenly reached into his pocket and took out the scrap of white paper he had lifted from the black-haired girl's purple handbag. It was a receipt for a week's rent, to a Miss Marilyn Delorme, Apt. 211, Ridgeland Apartments, 118 Court Street.

He tucked it into his wallet and stood staring at the silent radio. "Steve, I think you got another job," he said under his breath. "Something about this set-up smells."

He slipped into a closetlike phone both in the corner of the room, dropped a nickel and dialed an all-night radio station. He had to dial four times before he got a clear line to the Owl Program announcer.

"How's to play King Leopardi's record of 'Solitude' again?" he asked him.

"Got a lot of requests piled up. Played it twice already. Who's calling?"

"Steve Grayce, night man at the Carlton Hotel."

"Oh, a sober guy on his job. For you, pal, anything."

Steve went back to the davenport, snapped the radio on and lay down on his back, with his hands clasped behind his head.

Ten minutes later the high, piercingly sweet trumpet notes of King Leopardi came softly from the radio, muted almost to a whisper, and sustaining E above high C for an almost incredible period of time.

"Shucks," Steve grumbled, when the record ended. "A guy that can play like that—maybe I was too tough with him."

III

Court Street was old town, wop town, crook town, arty town. It lay across the top of Bunker Hill and you could find anything there from down-at-heels ex-Greenwich-villagers to crooks on the lam, from ladies of anybody's evening to County Relief clients brawling with haggard landladies in grand old houses with scrolled porches, parquetry floors, and immense sweeping banisters of white oak, mahogany and Circassian walnut.

It had been a nice place once, had Bunker Hill, and from the days of its niceness there still remained the funny little funicular railway, called the Angel's Flight, which crawled up and down a yellow clay bank from Hill Street. It was afternoon when Steve Grayce got off the car at the top, its only passenger. He walked along in the sun, a tall, wide-shouldered, rangy-looking man in a well-cut blue suit.

He turned west at Court and began to read the numbers. The one he wanted was two from the corner, across the street from a red brick funeral parlor with a sign in gold over it: Paolo Perrugini Funeral Home. A swarthy iron-gray Italian in a cut-away coat stood in front of the curtained door of the red brick building, smoking a cigar and waiting for somebody to die.

One-eighteen was a three-storied frame apartment house. It had a glass door, well masked by a dirty net curtain, a hall runner eighteen inches wide, dim doors with numbers painted on them with dim-paint, a staircase half-way back. Brass stair rods glittered in the dimness of the hallway.

Steve Grayce went up the stairs and prowled back to the front. Apartment 211, Miss Marilyn Delorme, was on the right, a front apartment. He tapped lightly on the wood, waited, tapped again. Nothing moved beyond the silent door, or in the hallway. Behind another door across the hall somebody coughed and kept on coughing.

Standing there in the half-light Steve Grayce wondered why he had come. Miss Delorme had carried a gun. Leopardi had received some kind of a threat letter and torn it up and thrown it away. Miss Delorme had checked out of the Carlton about an hour after Steve told her Leopardi was gone. Even at that—

He took out a leather keyholder and studied the lock of the door. It looked as if it would listen to reason. He tried a pick on it, snicked the bolt back and stepped softly into the room. He shut the door, but the pick wouldn't lock it.

The room was dim with drawn shades across two front windows. The air smelled of face powder. There was light-painted furniture, a pull-down double bed which was pulled down but had been made up. There was a magazine on it, a glass tray full of cigarette butts, a pint bottle half full of whiskey, and a glass on a chair beside the bed. Two pillows had been used for a back rest and were still crushed in the middle.

On the dresser there was a composition toilet set, neither cheap nor expensive, a comb with black hair in it, a tray of manicuring stuff, plenty of spilled powder—in the bathroom, nothing. In a closet behind the bed a lot of clothes and two suitcases. The shoes were all one size.

Steve stood beside the bed and pinched his chin. "Blossom, the spitting blonde, doesn't live here," he said under his breath. "Just Marilyn the torn-pants brunette."

He went back to the dresser and pulled drawers out. In the bottom drawer, under the piece of wall paper that lined it, he found a box of .25 copper-nickel automatic shells. He poked at the butts in the ash tray. All had lipstick on them. He pinched his chin again, then feathered the air with the palm of his hand, like an oarsman with a scull.

"Bunk," he said softly. "Wasting your time, Stevie."

He walked over to the door and reached for the knob, then turned back to the bed and lifted it by the footrail.

Miss Marilyn Delorme was in.

She lay on her side on the floor under the bed, long legs scissored out as if in running. One mule was on, one off. Garters and skin showed at the tops of her stockings, and a blue rose on something pink. She wore a square-necked, short-sleeved dress that was not too clean. Her neck above the dress was blotched with purple bruises.

Her face was a dark plum color, her eyes had the faint stale glitter of death, and her mouth was open so far that it fore-shortened her face. She was colder than ice, and still quite limp. She had been dead two or three hours at least, six hours at most.

The purple bag was beside her, gaping like her mouth. Steve didn't touch any of the stuff that had been emptied out on the floor. There was no gun and there were no papers.

He let the bed down over her again, then made the rounds of the apartment, wiping everything he had touched and a lot of things he couldn't remember whether he had touched or not.

He listened at the door and stepped out. The hall was still empty. The man behind the opposite door still coughed. Steve went down the stairs, looked at the mailboxes and went back along the lower hall to a door.

Behind this door a chair creaked monotonously. He knocked and a woman's sharp voice called out. Steve opened the door with his handkerchief and stepped in.

In the middle of the room a woman rocked in an old Boston rocker, her body in the slack boneless attitude of exhaustion. She had a mud-colored face, stringy hair, gray cotton stockings—everything a Bunker Hill landlady should have. She looked at Steve with the interested eye of a dead goldfish.

"Are you the manager?"

The woman stopped rocking, screamed, "Hi, Jake! Company!" at the top of her voice, and started rocking again.

An icebox door thudded shut behind a partly open inner door and a very big man came into the room carrying a can of beer. He had a doughy mooncalf face, a tuft of fuzz on top of an otherwise bald head, a thick brutal neck and chin, and brown pig eyes about as expressionless as the woman's. He needed a shave—had needed one the day before—and his collarless shirt gaped over a big hard hairy chest. He wore scarlet suspenders with large gilt buckles on them.

He held the can of beer out to the woman. She clawed it out of his hand and said bitterly: "I'm so tired I ain't got no sense."

The man said: "Yah. You ain't done the halls so good at that."

The woman snarled: "I done 'em as good as I aim to." She sucked the beer thirstily.

Steve looked at the man and said: "Manager?"

"Yah. 'S me. Jake Stoyanoff. Two hun'erd eighty-six stripped, and still plenty tough."

Steve said: "Who lives in Two-eleven?"

The big man leaned forward a little from the waist and snapped his suspenders. Nothing changed in his eyes. The skin along his big jaw may have tightened a little. "A dame," he said.

"Alone?"

"Go on—ask me," the big man said. He stuck his hand out and lifted a cigar off the edge of a stained-wood table. The cigar was burning unevenly and it smelled as if somebody had set fire to the doormat. He pushed it into his mouth with a hard, thrusting motion, as if he expected his mouth wouldn't want it to go in.

"I'm asking you," Steve said.

"Ask me out in the kitchen," the big man drawled.

He turned and held the door open. Steve went past him.

The big man kicked the door shut against the squeak of the rocking chair, opened up the icebox and got out two cans of beer. He opened them and handed one to Steve.

"Dick?"

Steve drank some of the beer, put the can down on the sink, got a brand-new card out of his wallet—a business card printed that morning. He handed it to the man.

The man read it, put it down on the sink, picked it up and read it again. "One of them guys," he growled over his beer. "What's she pulled this time?"

Steve shrugged and said: "I guess it's the usual. The torn-pajama act. Only there's a kickback this time."

"How come? You handling it, huh? Must be a nice cozy one."

Steve nodded. The big man blew smoke from his mouth. "Go ahead and handle it," he said.

"You don't mind a pinch here?"

The big man laughed heartily. "Nuts to you, brother," he said pleasantly enough. "You're a private dick. So it's a hush. O.K. Go out and hush it. And if it *was* a pinch—that bothers me like a quart of milk. Go into your act. Take all the room you want. Cops don't bother Jake Stoyanoff."

Steve stared at the man. He didn't say anything. The big man talked it up some more, seemed to get more interested. "Besides," he went on, making motions with the cigar, "I'm softhearted. I never turn up a dame. I never put a frill in the middle." He finished his beer and threw the can in a basket under the sink, and pushed his hand out in front of him, revolving the large thumb slowly against the next two fingers. "Unless there's some of that," he added.

Steve said softly: "You've got big hands. You could have done it."

"Huh?" His small brown leathery eyes got silent and stared.

Steve said: "Yeah. You might be clean. But with those hands the cops'd go round and round with you just the same."

The big man moved a little to his left, away from the sink. He let his right hand hang down at his side, loosely. His mouth got so tight that the cigar almost touched his nose.

"What's the beef, huh?" he barked. "What you shovin' at me, guy? What—"

"Cut it," Steve drawled. "She's been croaked. Strangled. Upstairs, on the floor under her bed. About midmorning, I'd say. Big hands did it—hands like yours."

The big man did a nice job of getting the gun off his hip. It arrived so suddenly that it seemed to have grown in his hand and been there all the time.

Steve frowned at the gun and didn't move. The big man looked him over. "You're tough," he said. "I been in the ring long enough to size up a guy's meat. You're plenty hard, boy. But you ain't as hard as lead. Talk it up fast."

"I knocked at her door. No answer. The lock was a pushover. I went in. I almost missed her because the bed was pulled down and she had been sitting on it, reading a magazine. There was no sign of struggle. I lifted the bed just before I left—and there she was. Very dead, Mr. Stoyanoff. Put the gat away. Cops don't bother you, you said a minute ago."

The big man whispered: "Yes and no. They don't make me happy neither. I get a bump once'n a while. Mostly a Dutch. You said something about my hands, mister."

Steve shook his head. "That was a gag," he said. "Her neck has nail marks. You bite your nails down close. You're clean."

The big man didn't look at his fingers. He was very pale. There was sweat on his lower lips, in the black stubble of his beard. He was still leaning forward, still motionless, when there was a knocking beyond the kitchen door, the door from the living room to the hallway. The creaking chair stopped and the woman's sharp voice screamed: "Hi, Jake! Company!"

The big man cocked his head. "That old slut wouldn't climb off'n her fanny if the house caught fire," he said thickly.

He stepped to the door and slipped through it, locking it behind him.

Steve ranged the kitchen swiftly with his eyes. There was a small high window beyond the sink, a trap low down for a garbage pail and parcels, but no other door. He reached for his card Stoyanoff had left lying on the drainboard and slipped it back into his pocket. Then he took a short-barreled Detective Special out of his left breast pocket where he wore it nose down, as in a holster.

He had got that far when the shots roared beyond the wall—muffled a little, but still loud—four of them blended in a blast of sound.

Steve stepped back and hit the kitchen door with his leg out straight. It held and jarred him to the top of his head and in his hip joint. He swore, took the whole width of the kitchen and slammed into it with his left shoulder. It gave this time. He pitched into the living room. The mud-faced woman sat leaning forward in her rocker, her head to one side and a lock of mousy hair smeared down over her bony forehead.

"Backfire, huh?" she said stupidly. "Sounded kinda close. Musta been in the alley."

Steve jumped across the room, yanked the outer door open and plunged out into the hall.

The big man was still on his feet, a dozen feet down the hallway, in the direction of a screen door that opened flush on an alley. He was clawing at the wall. His gun lay at his feet. His left knee buckled and he went down on it.

A door was flung open and a hard-looking woman peered out, and instantly slammed her door shut again. A radio suddenly gained in volume beyond her door.

The big man got up off his left knee and the leg shook violently inside his trousers. He went down on both knees and got the gun into his hand and began to crawl towards the screen door. Then, suddenly he went down flat on his face and tried to crawl that way, grinding his face into the narrow hall runner.

Then he stopped crawling and stopped moving altogether. His body went limp and the hand holding the gun opened and the gun rolled out of it.

Steve hit the screen door and was out in the alley. A gray sedan was speeding towards the far end of it. He stopped, steadied himself and brought his gun up level, and the sedan whisked out of sight around the corner.

A man boiled out of another apartment house across the alley. Steve ran on, gesticulating back at him and pointing ahead. As he ran he slipped the gun back into his pocket. When he reached the end of the alley, the gray sedan was out of sight. Steve skidded around the wall onto the sidewalk, slowed to a walk and then stopped.

Half a block down a man finished parking a car, got out and went across the sidewalk to a lunchroom. Steve watched him go in, then straightened his hat and walked along the wall to the lunchroom.

He went in, sat at the counter and ordered coffee. In a little while there were sirens.

Steve drank his coffee, asked for another cup and drank that. He lit a cigarette and walked down the long hill to Fifth, across to Hill, back to the foot of the Angel's Flight, and got his convertible out of a parking lot.

He drove out west, beyond Vermont, to the small hotel where he had taken a room that morning.

I V

Bill Dockery, floor manager of the Club Shalotte, teetered on his heels and yawned in the unlighted entrance to the dining room. It was a dead hour for business, late cocktail time, too early for dinner, and much too early for the real business of the club, which was high-class gambling.

Dockery was a handsome mug in a midnight-blue dinner jacket and a maroon carnation. He had a two-inch forehead under black lacquer hair, good features a little on the heavy side, alert brown eyes and very long curly eyelashes which he liked to let down over his eyes, to fool troublesome drunks into taking a swing at him.

The entrance door of the foyer was opened by the uniformed doorman and Steve Grayce came in.

Dockery said, "Ho, hum," tapped his teeth and leaned his weight forward. He walked across the lobby slowly to meet the guest. Steve stood just inside the doors and ranged his eyes over the high foyer walled with milky glass, lighted softly from behind. Molded in the glass were etchings of sailing ships, beasts of the jungle, Siamese pagodas, temples of Yucatan. The doors were square frames of chromium, like photo frames. The Club Shalotte had all the class there was, and the mutter of voices from the bar lounge on the left was not noisy. The faint Spanish music behind the voices was delicate as a carved fan.

Dockery came up and leaned his sleek head forward an inch. "May I help you?"

"King Leopardi around?"

Dockery leaned back again. He looked less interested. "The bandleader? He opens tomorrow night."

"I thought he might be around—rehearsing or something."

"Friend of his?"

"I know him. I'm not job-hunting, and I'm not a song plugger if that's what you mean."

Dockery teetered on his heels. He was tone-deaf and Leopardi meant no more to him than a bag of peanuts. He half smiled. "He was in the bar lounge a while ago." He pointed with his square rock-like chin. Steve Grayce went into the bar lounge.

It was about a third full, warm and comfortable and not too dark nor too light. The little Spanish orchestra was in an archway, playing with muted strings small seductive melodies that were more like memories than sounds. There was no dance floor. There was a long bar with comfortable seats, and there were small round composition-top tables, not too close together. A wall seat ran around three sides of the room. Waiters flitted among the tables like moths.

Steve Grayce saw Leopardi in the far corner, with a girl. There was an empty table on each side of him. The girl was a knockout.

She looked tall and her hair was the color of a brush fire seen through a dust cloud. On it, at the ultimate rakish angle, she wore a black velvet double-pointed beret with two artificial butterflies made of polka-dotted feathers and fastened on with tall silver pins. Her dress was burgundy-red wool and the blue fox draped over one shoulder was at least two feet wide. Her eyes were large, smoke-blue, and looked bored. She slowly turned a small glass on the table top with a gloved left hand.

Leopardi faced her, leaning forward, talking. His shoulders looked very big in a shaggy, cream-colored sports coat. Above the neck of it his hair made a point on his brown neck. He laughed across the table as Steve came up and his laugh had a confident, sneering sound.

Steve stopped, then moved behind the next table. The movement caught Leopardi's eye. His head turned, he looked annoyed, and then his eyes got very wide and brilliant and his whole body turned slowly, like a mechanical toy.

Leopardi put both his rather small well-shaped hands down on the table, on either side of a highball glass. He smiled. Then he pushed his chair back and stood up. He put one finger up and touched his hairline mustache, with theatrical delicacy. Then he said drawlingly, but distinctly: "You son of a bitch!"

A man at a nearby table turned his head and scowled. A waiter who had started to come over stopped in his tracks, then faded back among the tables. The girl looked at Steve Grayce and then leaned back against the cushions of the wall seat and moistened the end of one bare finger on her right hand and smoothed a chestnut eyebrow.

Steve stood quite still. There was a sudden high flush on his cheekbones. He said softly: "You left something at the hotel last night. I think you ought to do something about it. Here."

He reached a folded paper out of his pocket and held it out. Leopardi took it, still smiling, opened it and read it. It was a sheet of yellow paper with torn pieces of white paper pasted on it. Leopardi crumpled the sheet and let it drop at his feet.

He took a smooth step towards Steve and repeated more loudly: "You son of a bitch!"

The man who had first looked around stood up sharply and turned. He said clearly: "I don't like that sort of language in front of my wife."

Without even looking at the man Leopardi said: "To hell with you and your wife."

The man's face got a dusky red. The woman with him stood up and grabbed a bag and a coat and walked away. After a moment's indecision the man followed her. Everybody in the place was staring now. The waiter who had faded back among the tables went through the doorway into the entrance foyer, walking very quickly.

Leopardi took another, longer step and slammed Steve Grayce on the jaw. Steve rolled with the punch and stepped back and put his hand down on another table and upset a glass. He turned to apologize to the couple at the table. Leopardi jumped forward very fast and hit him behind the ear.

Dockery came through the doorway, split two waiters like a banana skin and started down the room showing all his teeth.

Steve gagged a little and ducked away. He turned and said thickly: "Wait a minute, you fool—that isn't all of it—there's——"

Leopardi closed in fast and smashed him full on the mouth. Blood oozed from Steve's lip and crawled down the line at the corner of his mouth and glistened on his chin. The girl with the red hair reached for her bag, white-faced with anger, and started to get up from behind her table.

Leopardi turned abruptly on his heel and walked away. Dockery put out a hand to stop him. Leopardi brushed it aside and went on, went out of the lounge.

The tall red-haired girl put her bag down on the table again and dropped her handkerchief on the floor. She looked at Steve quietly, spoke quietly. "Wipe the blood off your chin before it drips on your shirt." She had a soft, husky voice with a trill in it.

Dockery came up harsh-faced, took Steve by the arm and put weight on the arm. "All right, you! Let's go!"

Steve stood quite still, his feet planted, staring at the girl. He dabbed at his mouth with a handkerchief. He half smiled. Dockery couldn't move him an inch. Dockery dropped his hand, signaled two waiters and they jumped behind Steve, but didn't touch him.

Steve felt his lip carefully and looked at the blood on his handkerchief.

He turned to the people at the table behind him and said: "I'm terribly sorry. I lost my balance."

The girl whose drink he had spilled was mopping her dress with a small fringed napkin. She smiled up at him and said: "It wasn't your fault."

The two waiters suddenly grabbed Steve's arms from behind. Dockery shook his head and they let go again. Dockery said tightly: "You hit him?"

"No."

"You say anything to make him hit you?"

"No."

The girl at the corner table bent down to get her fallen handkerchief. It took her quite a time. She finally got it and slid into the corner behind the table again. She spoke coldly.

"Quite right, Bill. It was just some more of the King's sweet way with his public."

Dockery said "Huh?" and swiveled his head on his thick hard neck. Then he grinned and looked back at Steve.

Steve said grimly: "He gave me three good punches, one from behind, without a return. You look pretty hard. See can you do it."

Dockery measured him with his eyes. He said evenly: "You win. I couldn't . . . Beat it!" he added sharply to the waiters. They went away. Dockery sniffed his carnation, and said quietly: "We don't go for brawls in here." He smiled at the girl again and went away, saying a word here and there at the tables. He went out through the foyer doors.

Steve tapped his lip, put his handkerchief in his pocket and stood searching the floor with his eyes.

The red-haired girl said calmly: "I think I have what you want—in my handkerchief. Won't you sit down?"

Her voice had a remembered quality, as if he had heard it before.

He sat down opposite her, in the chair where Leopardi had been sitting.

The red-haired girl said: "The drink's on me. I was with him."

Steve said, "Coke with a dash of bitters," to the waiter.

The waiter said: "Madame?"

"Brandy and soda. Light on the brandy, please." The waiter bowed and drifted away. The girl said amusedly: "Coke with a dash of bitters. That's what I love about Hollywood. You meet so many neurotics."

Steve stared into her eyes and said softly: "I'm an occasional drinker, the kind of guy who goes out for a beer and wakes up in Singapore with a full beard."

"I don't believe a word of it. Have you known the King long?"

"I met him last night. I didn't get along with him."

"I sort of noticed that." She laughed. She had a rich low laugh, too.

"Give me that paper, lady."

"Oh, one of these impatient men. Plenty of time." The handkerchief with the crumpled yellow sheet inside it was clasped tightly in her gloved hand. Her middle right finger played with an eyebrow. "You're not in pictures, are you?"

"Hell, no."

"Same here. Me, I'm too tall. The beautiful men have to wear stilts in order to clasp me to their bosoms."

The waiter set the drinks down in front of them, made a grace note in the air with his napkin and went away.

Steve said quietly, stubbornly: "Give me that paper, lady."

"I don't like that 'lady' stuff. It sounds like cop to me."

"I don't know your name."

"I don't know yours. Where did you meet Leopardi?"

Steve sighed. The music from the little Spanish orchestra had a melancholy minor sound now and the muffled clicking of gourds dominated it.

Steve listened to it with his head on one side. He said: "The E string is a half-tone flat. Rather cute effect."

The girl stared at him with new interest. "I'd never have noticed that," she said. "And I'm supposed to be a pretty good singer. But you haven't answered my question."

He said slowly: "Last night I was house dick at the Carlton Hotel. They called me night clerk, but house dick was what I was. Leopardi stayed there and cut up too rough. I threw him out and got canned."

The girl said: "Ah. I begin to get the idea. He was being the King and you were being—if I might guess—a pretty tough order of house detective."

"Something like that. Now will you please—"

"You still haven't told me your name."

He reached for his wallet, took one of the brand-new cards out of it and passed it across the table. He sipped his drink while she read it.

"A nice name," she said slowly. "But not a very good address. And *Private investigator* is bad. It should have been *Investigations*, very small, in the lower left-hand corner."

"They'll be small enough," Steve grinned. "Now will you please—"

She reached suddenly across the table and dropped the crumpled ball of paper in his hand.

"Of course I haven't read it—and of course I'd like to. You do give me that much credit, I hope"—she looked at the card again, and added—"Steve. Yes, and your office should be in a Georgian or very modernistic building in the Sunset Eighties. Suite Something-or-other. And your clothes should be very jazzy. Very jazzy indeed, Steve. To be inconspicuous in this town is to be a busted flush."

He grinned at her. His deep-set black eyes had lights in them. She put the card away in her bag, gave her fur piece a yank, and drank about half of her drink. "I have to go." She signaled the waiter and paid the check. The waiter went away and she stood up.

Steve said sharply: "Sit down."

She stared at him wonderingly. Then she sat down again and leaned against the wall, still staring at him. Steve leaned across the table, asked "How well do *you* know Leopardi?"

"Off and on for years. If it's any of your business. Don't go masterful on me, for God's sake. I loathe masterful men. I once sang for him, but not for long. You can't just sing for Leopardi—if you get what I mean."

"You were having a drink with him."

She nodded slightly and shrugged. "He opens here tomorrow night. He was trying to talk me into singing for him again. I said no, but I may have to, for a week or two anyway. The man who owns the Club Shalotte also owns my contract—and the radio station where I work a good deal."

"Jumbo Walters," Steve said. "They say he's tough but square. I never met him, but I'd like to. After all I've got a living to get. Here."

He reached back across the table and dropped the crumpled paper. "The name was—"

"Dolores Chiozza."

Steve repeated it lingeringly. "I like it. I like your singing too. I've heard a lot of it. You don't oversell a song, like most of these high-money torchers." His eyes glistened.

The girl spread the paper on the table and read it slowly, without expression. Then she said quietly: "Who tore it up?"

"Leopardi, I guess. The pieces were in his wastebasket last night. I put them together, after he was gone. The guy has guts—or else he gets these things so often they don't register any more."

"Or else he thought it was a gag." She looked across the table levelly, then folded the paper and handed it back.

"Maybe. But if he's the kind of guy I hear he is—one of them is going to be on the level and the guy behind it is going to do more than just shake him down."

Dolores Chiozza said: "He's the kind of guy you hear he is."

"It wouldn't be hard for a woman to get to him then—would it—a woman with a gun?"

She went on staring at him. "No. And everybody would give her a big hand, if you ask me. If I were you, I'd just forget the whole thing. If he wants protection—Walters can throw more around him than the police. If he doesn't—who cares? I don't. I'm damn sure I don't."

"You're kind of tough yourself, Miss Chiozza—over some things."

She said nothing. Her face was a little white and more than a little hard.

Steve finished his drink, pushed his chair back and reached for his hat. He stood up. "Thank you very much for the drink, Miss Chiozza. Now that I've met you I'll look forward all the more to hearing you sing again."

"You're damn formal all of a sudden," she said.

He grinned. "So long, Dolores."

"So long, Steve. Good luck—in the sleuth racket. If I hear of anything—"

He turned and walked among the tables out of the bar lounge.

V

In the crisp fall evening the lights of Hollywood and Los Angeles winked at him. Searchlight beams probed the cloudless sky as if searching for bombing-planes.

Steve got his convertible out of the parking lot and drove it east along Sunset. At Sunset and Fairfax he bought an evening paper and pulled over to the curb to look through it. There was nothing in the paper about 118 Court Street.

He drove on and ate dinner at the little coffee shop beside his hotel and went to a movie. When he came out he bought a Home Edition of the *Tribune*, a morning sheet. They were in that—both of them.

Police thought Jake Stoyanoff might have strangled the girl, but she had not been attacked. She was described as a stenographer, unemployed at the moment. There was no picture of her. There was a picture of Stoyanoff that looked like a touched-up police photo. Police were looking for a man who had been talking to Stoyanoff just before he was shot. Several people said he was a tall man in a dark suit. That was all the description the police got—or gave out.

Steve grinned sourly, stopped at the coffee shop for a good-night cup of coffee and then went up to his room. It was a few minutes to eleven o'clock. As he unlocked his door the telephone started to ring.

He shut the door and stood in the darkness remembering where the phone was. Then he walked straight to it, catlike in the dark room, sat in an easy chair and reached the phone up from the lower shelf of a small table. He held the one-piece to his ear and said: "Hello."

"Is this Steve?" It was a rich, husky voice, low, vibrant. It held a note of strain.

"Yeah, this is Steve. I can hear you. I know who you are."

There was a faint dry laugh. "You'll make a detective after all. And it seems I'm to give you your first case. Will you come over to my place at once? Twenty-four-twelve Renfrew—North, there isn't any South—just half a block below Fountain. It's a sort of bungalow court. My house is the last in line, at the back."

Steve said: "Yes. Sure. What's the matter?"

There was a pause. A horn blared in the street outside the hotel. A wave of white light went across the ceiling from some car rounding the corner uphill. The low voice said very slowly: "Leopardi. I can't get rid of him. He's —he's passed out in my bedroom." Then a tinny laugh that didn't go with the voice at all.

Steve held the phone so tight his hand ached. His teeth clicked in the darkness. He said flatly, in a dull, brittle voice: "Yeah. It'll cost you twenty bucks."

"Of course. Hurry, please."

He hung up, sat there in the dark room breathing hard. He pushed his hat back on his head, then yanked it forward again with a vicious jerk and laughed out loud. "Hell," he said, "*That* kind of a dame."

Twenty-four-twelve Renfrew was not strictly a bungalow court. It was a staggered row of six bungalows, all facing the same way, but so-arranged that no two of their front entrances overlooked each other. There was a brick wall at the back and beyond the brick wall a church. There was a long smooth lawn, moon-silvered.

The door was up two steps, with lanterns on each side and an iron-work grill over the peep hole. This opened to his knock and a girl's face looked out, a small oval face with a Cupid's-bow mouth, arched and plucked eyebrows, wavy brown hair. The eyes were like two fresh and shiny chestnuts.

Steve dropped a cigarette and put his foot on it. "Miss Chiozza. She's expecting me. Steve Grayce."

"Miss Chiozza has retired, sir," the girl said with a half-insolent twist to her lips.

"Break it up, kid. You heard me, I'm expected."

The wicket slammed shut. He waited, scowling back along the narrow moonlit lawn towards the street. O.K. So it was like that—well, twenty bucks was worth a ride in the moonlight anyway.

The lock clicked and the door opened wide. Steve went past the maid into a warm cheerful room, old-fashioned with chintz. The lamps were neither old nor new and there were enough of them—in the right places. There was a hearth behind a paneled copper screen, a davenport close to it, a bar-top radio in the corner.

The maid said stiffly: "I'm sorry, sir. Miss Chiozza forgot to tell me. Please have a chair." The voice was soft, and it might be cagey. The girl went off down the room—short skirts, sheer silk stockings, and four-inch spike heels.

Steve sat down and held his hat on his knee and scowled at the wall. A swing door creaked shut. He got a cigarette out and rolled it between his fingers and then deliberately squeezed it to a shapeless flatness of white paper and ragged tobacco. He threw it away from him, at the fire screen.

Dolores Chiozza came towards him. She wore green velvet lounging pajamas with a long gold-fringed sash. She spun the end of the sash as if she might be going to throw a loop with it. She smiled a slight artificial smile. Her face had a clean scrubbed look and her eyelids were bluish and they twitched.

Steve stood up and watched the green morocco slippers peep out under the pajamas as she walked. When she was close to him he lifted his eyes to her face and said dully: "Hello."

She looked at him very steadily, then spoke in a high, carrying voice. "I know it's late, but I knew you were used to being up all night. So I thought what we had to talk over—Won't you sit down?"

She turned her head very slightly, seemed to be listening for something. Steve said: "I never go to bed before two. Quite all right."

She went over and pushed a bell beside the hearth. After a moment the maid came through the arch.

"Bring some ice cubes, Agatha. Then go along home. It's getting pretty late."

"Yes'm." The girl disappeared.

There was a silence then that almost howled till the tall girl took a cigarette absently out of a box, put it between her lips and Steve struck a match clumsily on his shoe. She pushed the end of the cigarette into the flame and her smoke-blue eyes were very steady on his black ones. She shook her head very slightly.

The maid came back with a copper ice bucket. She pulled a low Indian-brass tray-table between them before the davenport, put the ice bucket on it, then a siphon, glasses and spoons, and a triangular bottle that looked like good Scotch had come in it except that it was covered with silver filigree work and fitted with a stopper.

Dolores Chiozza said, "Will you mix a drink?" in a formal voice.

He mixed two drinks, stirred them, handed her one. She sipped it, shook her head. "Too light," she said. He put more whiskey in it and handed it back. She said, "Better," and leaned back against the corner of the daven-port.

The maid came into the room again. She had a small rakish red hat on her wavy brown hair and was wearing a gray coat trimmed with nice fur. She carried a black brocade bag that could have cleaned out a fair-sized icebox. She said: "Good night, Miss Dolores."

"Good night, Agatha."

The girl went out the front door, closed it softly. Her heels clicked down the walk. A car door opened and shut distantly and a motor started. Its sound soon dwindled away. It was a very quiet neighborhood.

Steve put his drink down on the brass tray and looked levelly at the tall girl, said harshly: "That means she's out of the way?"

"Yes. She goes home in her own car. She drives me home from the studio in mine—when I go to the studio, which I did tonight. I don't like to drive a car myself."

"Well, what are you waiting for?"

The red-haired girl looked steadily at the paneled fire screen and the unlit log fire behind it. A muscle twitched in her cheek.

After a moment she said: "Funny that I called you instead of Walters. He'd have protected me better than you can. Only he wouldn't have believed me. I thought perhaps you would. I didn't invite Leopardi here. So far as I know —we two are the only people in the world who know he's here."

Something in her voice jerked Steve upright.

She took a small crisp handkerchief from the breast pocket of the green velvet pajama-suit, dropped it on the floor, picked it up swiftly and pressed it against her mouth. Suddenly, without making a sound, she began to shake like a leaf.

Steve said swiftly: "What the hell—I can handle that heel in my hip pocket. I did last night—and last night he had a gun and took a shot at me."

Her head turned. Her eyes were very wide and staring. "But it couldn't have been my gun," she said in a dead voice.

"Huh? Of course not—what—?"

"It's my gun tonight," she said and stared at him. "You said a woman could get to him with a gun very easily."

He just stared at her. His face was white now and he made a vague sound in his throat.

"He's not drunk, Steve," she said gently. "He's dead. In yellow pajamas— in my bed. With my gun in his hand. You didn't think he was just drunk— did you, Steve?"

He stood up in a swift lunge, then became absolutely motionless, staring down at her. He moved his tongue on his lips and after a long time he formed words with it. "Let's go look at him," he said in a hushed voice.

VI

The room was at the back of the house to the left. The girl took a key out of her pocket and unlocked the door. There was a low light on a table, and the venetian blinds were drawn. Steve went in past her silently, on cat feet.

Leopardi lay squarely in the middle of the bed, a large smooth silent man, waxy and artificial in death. Even his mustache looked phony. His half-open eyes, sightless as marbles, looked as if they had never seen. He lay on his back, on the sheet, and the bedclothes were thrown over the foot of the bed.

The King wore yellow silk pajamas, the slip-on kind, with a turned collar. They were loose and thin. Over his breast they were dark with blood that had seeped into the silk as if into blotting-paper. There was a little blood on his bare brown neck.

Steve stared at him and said tonelessly: "The King in Yellow. I read a book with that title once. He liked yellow, I guess. I packed some of his stuff last night. And he wasn't yellow either. Guys like him usually are—or are they?"

The girl went over to the corner and sat down in a slipper chair and looked at the floor. It was a nice room, as modernistic as the living room was casual. It had a chenille rug, café-au-lait color, severely angled furniture in inlaid wood, and a trick dresser with a mirror for a top, a kneehole and drawers like a desk. It had a box mirror above and a semi-cylindrical frosted wall light set above the mirror. In the corner there was a glass table with a crystal greyhound on top of it, and a lamp with the deepest drum shade Steve had ever seen.

He stopped looking at all this and looked at Leopardi again. He pulled the King's pajamas up gently and examined the wound. It was directly over the heart and the skin was scorched and mottled there. There was not so very much blood. He had died in a fraction of a second.

A small Mauser automatic lay cuddled in his right hand, on top of the bed's second pillow.

"That's artistic," Steve said and pointed. "Yeah, that's a nice touch. Typical contact wound, I guess. He even pulled his pajama shirt up. I've heard they do that. A Mauser seven-six-three about. Sure it's your gun?"

"Yes." She kept on looking at the floor. "It was in a desk in the living room —not loaded. But there were shells. I don't know why. Somebody gave it to me once. I didn't even know how to load it."

Steve smiled. Her eyes lifted suddenly and she saw his smile and shuddered. "I don't expect anybody to believe that," she said. "We may as well call the police, I suppose."

Steve nodded absently, put a cigarette in his mouth and flipped it up and down with his lips that were still puffy from Leopardi's punch. He lit a match on his thumbnail, puffed a small plume of smoke and said quietly: "No cops. Not yet. Just tell it."

The red-haired girl said: "I sing at KFQC, you know. Three nights a week— on a quarter-hour automobile program. This was one of the nights. Agatha and I got home—oh, close to half-past ten. At the door I remembered there was no fizzwater in the house, so I sent her back to the liquor store three blocks away, and came in alone. There was a queer smell in the house. I don't know what it was. As if several men had been in here, somehow. When I came in the bedroom—he was exactly as he is now. I saw the gun and I went and looked and then I knew I was sunk. I didn't know what to do. Even if the police cleared me, everywhere I went from now on—"

Steve said sharply: "He got in here—how?"

"I don't know."

"Go on," he said.

"I locked the door. Then I undressed—with that on my bed. I went into the bathroom to shower and collect my brains, if any. I locked the door when I left the room and took the key. Agatha was back then, but I don't think she saw me. Well, I took the shower and it braced me up a bit. Then I had a drink and then I came in here and called you."

She stopped and moistened the end of a finger and smoothed the end of her left eyebrow with it. "That's all, Steve—absolutely all."

"Domestic help can be pretty nosy. This Agatha's nosier than most—or I miss my guess." He walked over to the door and looked at the lock. "I bet there are three or four keys in the house that knock this over." He went to the windows and felt the catches, looked down at the screens through the glass. He said over his shoulder, casually: "Was the King in love with you?"

Her voice was sharp, almost angry. "He never was in love with any woman. A couple of years back in San Francisco, when I was with his band for a while, there was some slap-silly publicity about us. Nothing to it. It's been revived here in the hand-outs to the press, to build up his opening. I was telling him this afternoon I wouldn't stand for it, that I wouldn't be linked with him in anybody's mind. His private life was filthy. It reeked. Everybody in the business knows that. And it's not a business where daisies grow very often."

Steve said: "Yours was the only bedroom he couldn't make?"

The girl flushed to the roots of her dusky red hair.

"That sounds lousy," he said. "But I have to figure the angles. That's about true, isn't it?"

"Yes—I suppose so. I wouldn't say the only one."

"Go on out in the other room and buy yourself a drink."

She stood up and looked at him squarely across the bed. "I didn't kill him, Steve. I didn't let him into this house tonight. I didn't know he was coming here, or had any reason to come here. Believe that or not. But something about this is wrong. Leopardi was the last man in the world to take his lovely life himself."

Steve said: "He didn't, angel. Go buy that drink. He was murdered. The whole thing is a frame—to get a cover-up from Jumbo Walters. Go on out."

He stood silent, motionless, until sounds he heard from the living room told him she was out there. Then he took out his handkerchief and loosened the gun from Leopardi's right hand and wiped it over carefully on the outside, broke out the magazine and wiped that off, spilled out all the shells and wiped every one, ejected the one in the breech and wiped that. He reloaded the gun and put it back in Leopardi's dead hand and closed his fingers around it and pushed his index finger against the trigger. Then he let the hand fall naturally back on the bed.

He pawed through the bedclothes and found an ejected shell and wiped that off, put it back where he had found it. He put the handkerchief to his nose, sniffed it wryly, went around the bed to a clothes closet and opened the door.

"Careless of your clothes, boy," he said softly.

The rough cream-colored coat hung in there, on a hook, over dark gray slacks with a lizard-skin belt. A yellow satin shirt and a wine-colored tie dangled alongside. A handkerchief to match the tie flowed loosely four inches from the breast pocket of the coat. On the floor lay a pair of gazelle-leather nutmeg-brown sports shoes, and socks without garters. And there were yellow satin shorts with heavy black initials on them lying close by.

Steve felt carefully in the gray slacks and got out a leather keyholder. He left the room, went along the cross-hall and into the kitchen. It had a solid door, a good spring lock with a key stuck in it. He took it out and tried keys from the bunch in the keyholder, found none that fitted, put the other key back and went into the living room. He opened the front door, went outside and shut it again without looking at the girl huddled in a corner of the davenport. He tried keys in the lock, finally found the right one. He let himself back into the house, returned to the bedroom and put the keyholder back in the pocket of the gray slacks again. Then he went to the living room.

The girl was still huddled motionless, staring at him.

He put his back to the mantel and puffed a cigarette. "Agatha with you all the time at the studio?"

She nodded. "I suppose so. So he had a key. That was what you were doing, wasn't it?"

"Yes. Had Agatha long?"

"About a year."

"She steal from you? Small stuff, I mean?"

Dolores Chiozza shrugged wearily. "What does it matter? Most of them do. A little face cream or powder, a handkerchief, a pair of stockings once in a while. Yes, I think she stole from me. They look on that sort of thing as more or less legitimate."

"Not the nice ones, angel."

"Well—the hours were a little trying. I work at night, often get home very late. She's a dresser as well as a maid."

"Anything else about her? She use cocaine or weed? Hit the bottle? Ever have laughing fits?"

"I don't think so. What has she got to do with it, Steve?"

"Lady, she sold somebody a key to your apartment. That's obvious. You didn't give him one, the landlord wouldn't give him one, but Agatha had one. Check?"

Her eyes had a stricken look. Her mouth trembled a little, not much. A drink was untasted at her elbow. Steve bent over and drank some of it.

She said slowly: "We're wasting time, Steve. We have to call the police. There's nothing anybody can do. I'm done for as a nice person, even if not as a lady at large. They'll think it was a lovers' quarrel and I shot him and that's that. If I could convince them I didn't, then he shot himself in my bed, and I'm still ruined. So I might as well make up my mind to face the music."

Steve said softly: "Watch this. My mother used to do it."

He put a finger to his mouth, bent down and touched her lips at the same spot with the same finger. He smiled, said: "We'll go to Walters—or you will. He'll pick his cops and the ones he picks won't go screaming through the night with reporters sitting in their laps. They'll sneak in quiet, like process servers. Walters can handle this. That was what was counted on. Me, I'm going to collect Agatha. Because I want a description of the guy she sold that key to—and I want it fast. And by the way, you owe me twenty bucks for coming over here. Don't let that slip your memory."

The tall girl stood up, smiling. "You're a kick, you are," she said. "What makes you so sure he was murdered?"

"He's not wearing his own pajamas. His have his initials on them. I packed his stuff last night—before I threw him out of the Carlton. Get dressed, angel—and get me Agatha's address."

He went into the bedroom and pulled a sheet over Leopardi's body, held it a moment above the still, waxen face before letting it fall.

"So long, guy," he said gently. "You were a louse—but you sure had music in you."

It was a small frame house on Brighton Avenue near Jefferson, in a block of small frame houses, all old-fashioned, with front porches. This one had a narrow concrete walk which the moon made whiter than it was.

Steve mounted the steps and looked at the light-edged shade of the wide front window. He knocked. There were shuffling steps and a woman opened the door and looked at him through the hooked screen—a dumpy elderly woman with frizzled gray hair. Her body was shapeless in a wrapper and her feet slithered in loose slippers. A man with a polished bald head and milky eyes sat in a wicker chair beside a table. He held his hands in his lap and twisted the knuckles aimlessly. He didn't look towards the door.

Steve said: "I'm from Miss Chiozza. Are you Agatha's mother?"

The woman said dully: "I reckon. But she ain't home, mister." The man in the chair got a handkerchief from somewhere and blew his nose. He snickered darkly.

Steve said: "Miss Chiozza's not feeling so well tonight. She was hoping Agatha would come back and stay the night with her."

The milky-eyed man snickered again, sharply. The woman said: "We dunno where she is. She don't come home. Pa'n me waits up for her to come home. She stays out till we're sick."

The old man snapped in a reedy voice: "She'll stay out till the cops get her one of these times."

"Pa's half blind," the woman said. "Makes him kinda mean. Won't you step in?"

Steve shook his head and turned his hat around in his hands like a bashful cowpuncher in a horse opera. "I've got to find her," he said. "Where would she go?"

"Out drinkin' liquor with cheap spenders," Pa cackled. "Pantywaists with silk handkerchiefs 'stead of neckties. If I had eyes, I'd strap her till she dropped." He grabbed the arms of his chair and the muscles knotted on the backs of his hands. Then he began to cry. Tears welled from his milky eyes and started through the white stubble on his cheeks. The woman went across and took the handkerchief out of his fist and wiped his face with it. Then she blew her nose on it and came back to the door.

"Might be anywhere," she said to Steve. "This is a big town, mister. I dunno where at to say."

Steve said dully: "I'll call back. If she comes in, will you hang onto her? What's your phone number?"

"What's the phone number, Pa?" the woman called back over her shoulder.

"I ain't sayin'," Pa snorted.

The woman said: "I remember now. South Two-four-five-four. Call any time. Pa'n me ain't got nothing to do."

Steve thanked her and went back down the white walk to the street and along the walk half a block to where he had left his car. He glanced idly across the way and started to get into his car, then stopped moving suddenly with his hand gripping the car door. He let go of that, took three steps sideways and stood looking across the street tight-mouthed.

All the houses in the block were much the same, but the one opposite had a FOR RENT placard stuck in the front window and a real-estate sign spiked into the small patch of front lawn. The house itself looked neglected, utterly empty, but in its little driveway stood a small neat black coupe.

Steve said under his breath: "Hunch. Play it up, Steve."

He walked almost delicately across the wide dusty street, his hand touching the hard metal of the gun in his pocket, and came up behind the little car, stood and listened. He moved silently along its left side, glanced back across the street, then looked in the car's open left-front window.

The girl sat almost as if driving, except that her head was tipped a little too much into the corner. The little red hat was still on her head, the gray coat, trimmed with fur, still around her body. In the reflected moonlight her mouth was strained open. Her tongue stuck out. And her chestnut eyes stared at the roof of the car.

Steve didn't touch her. He didn't have to touch her to look any closer to know there would be heavy bruises on her neck.

"Tough on women, these guys," he muttered.

The girl's big black brocade bag lay on the seat beside her, gaping open like her mouth—like Miss Marilyn Delorme's mouth, and Miss Marilyn Delorme's purple bag.

"Yeah—tough on women."

He backed away till he stood under a small palm tree by the entrance to the driveway. The street was as empty and deserted as a closed theater. He crossed silently to his car, got into it and drove away.

Nothing to it. A girl coming home alone late at night, stuck up and strangled a few doors from her own home by some tough guy. Very simple. The first prowl car that cruised that block—if the boys were half awake—would take a look the minute they spotted the FOR RENT sign. Steve tramped hard on the throttle and went away from there.

At Washington and Figueroa he went into an all-night drugstore and pulled shut the door of the phone booth at the back. He dropped his nickel and dialed the number of police headquarters.

He asked for the desk and said: "Write this down, will you, sergeant?

Brighton Avenue, thirty-two-hundred block, west side, in driveway of empty house. Got that much?"

"Yeah. So what?"

"Car with dead woman in it," Steve said, and hung up.

VII

Quillan, head day clerk and assistant manager of the Carlton Hotel, was on night duty, because Millar, the night auditor, was off for a week. It was half-past one and things were dead and Quillan was bored. He had done everything there was to do long ago, because he had been a hotel man for twenty years and there was nothing to it.

The night porter had finished cleaning up and was in his room beside the elevator bank. One elevator was lighted and open, as usual. The main lobby had been tidied up and the lights had been properly dimmed. Everything was exactly as usual.

Quillan was a rather short, rather thick-set man with clear bright toadlike eyes that seemed to hold a friendly expression without really having any expression at all. He had pale sandy hair and not much of it. His pale hands were clasped in front of him on the marble top of the desk. He was just the right height to put his weight on the desk without looking as if he were sprawling. He was looking at the wall across the entrance lobby, but he wasn't seeing it. He was half asleep, even though his eyes were wide open, and if the night porter struck a match behind his door, Quillan would know it and bang on his bell.

The brass-trimmed swing doors at the street entrance pushed open and Steve Grayce came in, a summer-weight coat turned up around his neck, his hat yanked low and a cigarette wisping smoke at the corner of his mouth. He looked very casual, very alert, and very much at ease. He strolled over to the desk and rapped on it.

"Wake up!" he snorted.

Quillan moved his eyes an inch and said: "All outside rooms with bath. But positively no parties on the eighth floor. Hiyah, Steve. So you finally got the axe. And for the wrong thing. That's life."

Steve said: "O.K. Have you got a new night man here?"

"Don't need one, Steve. Never did, in my opinion."

"You'll need one as long as old hotel men like you register floozies on the same corridor with people like Leopardi."

Quillan half closed his eyes and then opened them to where they had been before. He said indifferently: "Not me, pal. But anybody can make a mistake. Millar's really an accountant—not a desk man."

Steve leaned back and his face became very still. The smoke almost hung at the tip of his cigarette. His eyes were like black glass now. He smiled a little dishonestly.

"And why was Leopardi put in an eight-dollar room on Eight instead of in a tower suite at twenty-eight per?"

Quillan smiled back at him. "I didn't register Leopardi, old sock. There were reservations in. I supposed they were what he wanted. Some guys don't spend. Any other questions, Mr. Grayce?"

"Yeah. Was Eight-fourteen empty last night?"

"It was on change, so it was empty. Something about the plumbing. Proceed."

"Who marked it on change?"

Quillan's bright fathomless eyes turned and became curiously fixed. He didn't answer.

Steve said: "Here's why. Leopardi was in Eight-fifteen and the two girls in Eight-eleven. Just Eight-thirteen between. A lad with a passkey could have gone into Eight-thirteen and turned both the bolt locks on the communicating doors. Then, if the folks in the two other rooms had done the same thing on their side, they'd have a suite set up."

"So what?" Quillan asked. "We got chiseled out of eight bucks, eh? Well, it happens, in better hotels than this." His eyes looked sleepy now.

Steve said: "Millar could have done that. But hell, it doesn't make sense. Millar's not that kind of a guy. Risk a job for a buck tip—phooey. Millar's no dollar pimp."

Quillan said: "All right, policeman. Tell me what's really on your mind."

"One of the girls in Eight-eleven had a gun. Leopardi got a threat letter yesterday—I don't know where or how. It didn't faze him, though. He tore it up. That's how I know. I collected the pieces from his basket. I suppose Leopardi's boys all checked out of here."

"Of course. They went to the Normandy."

"Call the Normandy, and ask to speak to Leopardi. If he's there, he'll still be at the bottle. Probably with a gang."

"Why?" Quillan asked gently.

"Because you're a nice guy. If Leopardi answers—just hang up." Steve paused and pinched his chin hard. "If he went out, try to find out where."

Quillan straightened, gave Steve another long quiet look and went behind the pebbled-glass screen. Steve stood very still, listening, one hand clenched at his side, the other tapping noiselessly on the marble desk.

In about three minutes Quillan came back and leaned on the desk again and said: "Not there. Party going on in his suite—they sold him a big one—and sounds loud. I talked to a guy who was fairly sober. He said Leopardi got a call around ten—some girl. He went out preening himself, as the fellow says. Hinting about a very juicy date. The guy was just lit enough to hand me all this."

Steve said: "You're a real pal. I hate not to tell you the rest. Well, I liked working here. Not much work at that."

He started towards the entrance doors again. Quillan let him get his hand on the brass handle before he called out. Steve turned and came back slowly.

Quillan said: "I heard Leopardi took a shot at you. I don't think it was noticed. It wasn't reported down here. And I don't think Peters fully realized that until he saw the mirror in Eight-fifteen. If you care to come back, Steve—"

Steve shook his head. "Thanks for the thought."

"And hearing about that shot," Quillan added, "made me remember something. Two years ago a girl shot herself in Eight-fifteen."

Steve straightened his back so sharply that he almost jumped. "What girl?"

Quillan looked surprised. "I don't know. I don't remember her real name. Some girl who had been kicked around all she could stand and wanted to die in a clean bed—alone."

Steve reached across and took hold of Quillan's arm. "The hotel files," he rasped. "The clippings, whatever there was in the papers will be in them. I want to see those clippings."

Quillan stared at him for a long moment. Then he said: "Whatever game you're playing, kid—you're playing it damn close to your vest. I will say that for you. And me bored stiff with a night to kill."

He reached along the desk and thumped the call bell. The door of the night porter's room opened and the porter came across the entrance lobby. He nodded and smiled at Steve.

Quillan said: "Take the board, Carl. I'll be in Mr. Peters' office for a little while."

He went to the safe and got keys out of it.

VIII

The cabin was high up on the side of the mountain, against a thick growth of digger pine, oak and incense cedar. It was solidly built, with a stone chimney, shingled all over and heavily braced against the slope of the hill. By daylight the roof was green and the sides dark reddish brown and the window frames and draw curtains red. In the uncanny brightness of an all-night mid-October moon in the mountains, it stood out sharply in every detail, except color.

It was at the end of a road, a quarter of a mile from any other cabin. Steve rounded the bend towards it without lights, at five in the morning. He stopped his car at once, when he was sure it was the right cabin, got out and walked soundlessly along the side of the gravel road, on a carpet of wild iris.

On the road level there was a rough pine board garage, and from this a path went up to the cabin porch. The garage was unlocked. Steve swung the door open carefully, groped in past the dark bulk of a car and felt the top of the radiator. It was still warmish. He got a small flash out of his pocket and played it over the car. A gray sedan, dusty, the gas gauge low. He snapped the flash off, shut the garage door carefully and slipped into place the piece of wood that served for a hasp. Then he climbed the path to the house.

There was light behind the drawn red curtains. The porch was high and juniper logs were piled on it, with the bark still on them. The front door had a thumb latch and a rustic door handle above.

He went up, neither too softly nor too noisily, lifted his hand, sighed deep in his throat, and knocked. His hand touched the butt of the gun in the inside pocket of his coat, once, then came away empty.

A chair creaked and steps padded across the floor and a voice called out softly: "What is it?" Millar's voice.

Steve put his lips close to the wood and said: "This is Steve, George. You up already?"

The key turned, and the door opened. George Millar, the dapper night auditor of the Carlton House, didn't look dapper now. He was dressed in old trousers and a thick blue sweater with a roll collar. His feet were in ribbed wool socks and fleece-lined slippers. His clipped black mustache was a curved smudge across his pale face. Two electric bulbs burned in their sockets in a low beam across the room, below the slope of the high roof. A table lamp was lit and its shade was tilted to throw light on a big Morris chair with a leather seat and back-cushion. A fire burned lazily in a heap of soft ash on the big open hearth.

Millar said in his low, husky voice: "Hell's sake, Steve. Glad to see you. How'd you find us anyway? Come on in, guy."

Steve stepped through the door and Millar locked it. "City habit," he said grinning. "Nobody locks anything in the mountains. Have a chair. Warm your toes. Cold out at this time of night."

Steve said: "Yeah. Plenty cold."

He sat down in the Morris chair and put his hat and coat on the end of the solid wood table behind it. He leaned forward and held his hands out to the fire.

Millar said: "How the hell did you find us, Steve?"

Steve didn't look at him. He said quietly: "Not so easy at that. You told me last night your brother had a cabin up here—remember? So I had nothing to do, so I thought I'd drive up and bum some breakfast. The guy in the inn at Crestline didn't know who had cabins where. His trade is with people passing through. I rang up a garage man and he didn't know any Millar cabin. Then I saw a light come on down the street in a coal-and-wood yard and a little guy who is forest ranger and deputy sheriff and wood-and-gas dealer and half a dozen other things was getting his car out to go down to San Bernardino for some tank gas. A very smart little guy. The minute I said your brother had been a fighter he wised up. So here I am."

Millar pawed at his mustache. Bedsprings creaked at the back of the cabin somewhere. "Sure, he still goes under his fighting name—Gaff Talley. I'll get him up and we'll have some coffee. I guess you and me are both in the same boat. Used to working at night and can't sleep. I haven't been to bed at all."

Steve looked at him slowly and looked away. A burly voice behind them said: "Gaff is up. Who's your pal, George?"

Steve stood up casually and turned. He looked at the man's hands first. He couldn't help himself. They were large hands, well kept as to cleanliness, but coarse and ugly. One knuckle had been broken badly. He was a big man with reddish hair. He wore a sloppy bathrobe over outing-flannel pajamas. He had a leathery expressionless face, scarred over the cheekbones. There were fine white scars over his eyebrows and at the corners of his mouth. His nose was spread and thick. His whole face looked as if it had caught a lot of gloves. His eyes alone looked vaguely like Millar's eyes.

Millar said: "Steve Grayce. Night man at the hotel—until last night." His grin was a little vague.

Gaff Talley came over and shook hands. "Glad to meet you," he said. "I'll get some duds on and we'll scrape a breakfast off the shelves. I slept enough. George ain't slept any, the poor sap."

He went back across the room towards the door through which he'd come. He stopped there and leaned on an old phonograph, put his big hand down behind a pile of records in paper envelopes. He stayed just like that, without moving.

Millar said: "Any luck on a job, Steve? Or did you try yet?"

"Yeah. In a way. I guess I'm a sap, but I'm going to have a shot at the private-agency racket. Not much in it unless I can land some publicity." He shrugged. Then he said very quietly: "King Leopardi's been bumped off."

Millar's mouth snapped wide open. He stayed like that for almost a minute—perfectly still, with his mouth open. Gaff Talley leaned against the wall and stared without showing anything in his face. Millar finally said: "Bumped off? Where? Don't tell me—"

"Not in the hotel, George. Too bad, wasn't it? In a girl's apartment. Nice girl too. She didn't entice him there. The old suicide gag—only it won't work. And the girl is my client."

Millar didn't move. Neither did the big man. Steve leaned his shoulders against the stone mantel. He said softly: "I went out to the Club Shalotte this afternoon to apologize to Leopardi. Silly idea, because I didn't owe him an apology. There was a girl there in the bar lounge with him. He took three socks at me and left. The girl didn't like that. We got rather clubby. Had a drink together. Then late tonight—last night—she called me up and said Leopardi was over at her place and—he was drunk and she couldn't get rid of him. I went there. Only he wasn't drunk. He was dead, in her bed, in yellow pajamas."

The big man lifted his left hand and roughed back his hair. Millar leaned slowly against the edge of the table, as if he were afraid the edge might be sharp enough to cut him. His mouth twitched under the clipped black mustache.

He said huskily: "That's lousy."

The big man said: "Well, for cryin' into a milk bottle."

Steve said: "Only they weren't Leopardi's pajamas. His had initials on them—big black initials. And his were satin, not silk. And although he had a gun in his hand—this girl's gun by the way—*he* didn't shoot himself in the heart. The cops will determine that. Maybe you birds never heard of the Lund test, with paraffin wax, to find out who did or didn't fire a gun recently. The kill ought to have been pulled in the hotel last night, in Room Eight-fifteen. I spoiled that by heaving him out on his neck before that black-haired girl in Eight-eleven could get to him. Didn't I, George?"

Millar said: "I guess you did—if I know what you're talking about."

Steve said slowly: "I think you know what I'm talking about, George. It would have been a kind of poetic justice if King Leopardi had been knocked off in Room Eight-fifteen. Because that was the room where a girl shot herself two years ago. A girl who registered as Mary Smith—but whose usual name was Eve Talley. And whose real name was Eve Millar."

The big man leaned heavily on the victrola and said thickly: "Maybe I ain't woke up yet. That sounds like it might grow up to be a dirty crack. We had a sister named Eve that shot herself in the Carlton. So what?"

Steve smiled a little crookedly. He said: "Listen, George. You told me Quillan registered those girls in Eight-eleven. *You* did. You told me Leopardi registered on Eight, instead of in a good suite, because he was tight. He wasn't tight. He just didn't care where he was put, as long as female company was handy. And you saw to that. You planned the whole thing, George. You even got Peters to write Leopardi at the Raleigh in Frisco and ask him to use the Carlton when he came down—because the same man owned it who owned the Club Shalotte. As if a guy like Jumbo Walters would care where a bandleader registered."

Millar's face was dead white, expressionless. His voice cracked. "Steve—for God's sake, Steve, what are you talking about? How the hell could I—"

"Sorry, kid. I liked working with you. I liked you a lot. I guess I still like you. But I don't like people who strangle women—or people who smear women in order to cover up a revenge murder."

His hand shot up—and stopped. The big man said: "Take it easy—and look at this one."

Gaff's hand had come up from behind the pile of records. A Colt .45 was in it. He said between his teeth: "I always thought house dicks were just a bunch of cheap grafters. I guess I missed out on you. You got a few brains. Hell, I bet you even run out to One-eighteen Court Street. Right?"

Steve let his hand fall empty and looked straight at the big Colt. "Right. I saw the girl—dead—with your fingers marked into her neck. They can measure those, fella. Killing Dolores Chiozza's maid the same way was a mistake. They'll match up the two sets of marks, find out that your black-haired gun girl was at the Carlton last night, and piece the whole story together. With the information they get at the hotel they can't miss. I give you two weeks, if you beat it quick. And I mean quick."

Millar licked his dry lips and said softly: "There's no hurry, Steve. No hurry at all. Our job is done. Maybe not the best way, maybe not the nicest way, but it wasn't a nice job. And Leopardi was the worst kind of a louse. We loved our sister, and he made a tramp out of her. She was a wide-eyed kid that fell for a flashy greaseball, and the greaseball went up in the world and threw her out on her ear for a red-headed torcher who was more his kind. He threw her out and broke her heart and she killed herself."

Steve said harshly: "Yeah—and what were you doing all that time—manicuring your nails?"

"We weren't around when it happened. It took us a little time to find out the why of it."

Steve said: "So that was worth killing four people for, was it? And as for Dolores Chiozza, she wouldn't have wiped her feet on Leopardi—then, or any time since. But you had to put her in the middle too, with your rotten little revenge murder. You make me sick, George. Tell your big tough brother to get on with his murder party."

The big man grinned and said: "Nuff talk, George. See has he a gat—and don't get behind him or in front of him. This bean-shooter goes on through."

Steve stared at the big man's .45. His face was hard as white bone. There was a thin cold sneer on his lips and his eyes were cold and dark.

Millar moved softly in his fleece-lined slippers. He came around the end of the table and went close to Steve's side and reached out a hand to tap his pockets. He stepped back and pointed: "In there."

Steve said softly: "I must be nuts. I could have taken you then, George."

Gaff Talley barked: "Stand away from him."

He walked solidly across the room and put the big Colt against Steve's stomach hard. He reached up with his left hand and worked the Detective Special from the inside breast pocket. His eyes were sharp on Steve's eyes. He held Steve's gun out behind him. "Take this, George."

Millar took the gun and went over beyond the big table again and stood at the far corner of it. Gaff Talley backed away from Steve.

"You're through, wise guy," he said. "You got to know that. There's only two ways outa these mountains and we gotta have time. And maybe you didn't tell nobody. See?"

Steve stood like a rock, his face white, a twisted half-smile working at the corners of his lips. He stared hard at the big man's gun and his stare was faintly puzzled.

Millar said: "Does it have to be that way, Gaff?" His voice was a croak now, without tone, without its usual pleasant huskiness.

Steve turned his head a little and looked at Millar. "Sure it has, George. You're just a couple of cheap hoodlums after all. A couple of nasty-minded sadists playing at being revengers of wronged girlhood. Hillbilly stuff. And right this minute you're practically cold meat—cold, rotten meat."

Gaff Talley laughed and cocked the big revolver with his thumb. "Say your prayers, guy," he jeered.

Steve said grimly: "What makes you think you're going to bump me off with that thing? No shells in it, strangler. Better try to take me the way you handle women—with your hands."

The big man's eyes flicked down, clouded. Then he roared with laughter. "Geez, the dust on that one must be a foot thick," he chuckled. "Watch."

He pointed the big gun at the floor and squeezed the trigger. The firing pin clicked dryly—on an empty chamber. The big man's face convulsed.

For a short moment nobody moved. Then Gaff turned slowly on the balls of his feet and looked at his brother. He said almost gently: "You, George?"

Millar licked his lips and gulped. He had to move his mouth in and out before he could speak.

"Me, Gaff. I was standing by the window when Steve got out of his car down the road, I saw him go into the garage. I knew the car would still be warm. There's been enough killing, Gaff. Too much. So I took the shells out of your gun."

Millar's thumb moved back the hammer on the Detective Special. Gaff's eyes bulged. He stared fascinated at the snub-nosed gun. Then he lunged violently towards it, flailing with the empty Colt. Millar braced himself and stood very still and said dimly, like an old man: "Goodbye, Gaff."

The gun jumped three times in his small neat hand. Smoke curled lazily from its muzzle. A piece of burned log fell over in the fireplace.

Gaff Talley smiled queerly and stooped and stood perfectly still. The gun dropped at his feet. He put his big heavy hands against his stomach, said slowly, thickly: "'S all right, kid. 'S all right, I guess . . . I guess I . . ."

His voice trailed off and his legs began to twist under him. Steve took three long quick silent steps, and slammed Millar hard on the angle of the jaw. The big man was still falling—as slowly as a tree falls.

Millar spun across the room and crashed against the end wall and a blue-and-white plate fell off the plate-molding and broke. The gun sailed from his fingers. Steve dived for it and came up with it. Millar crouched and watched his brother.

Gaff Talley bent his head to the floor and braced his hands and then lay down quietly, on his stomach, like a man who was very tired. He made no sound of any kind.

Daylight showed at the windows, around the red glass-curtains. The piece of broken log smoked against the side of the hearth and the rest of the fire was a heap of soft gray ash with a glow at its heart.

Steve said dully: "You saved my life, George—or at least you saved a lot of shooting. I took the chance because what I wanted was evidence. Step over there to the desk and write it all out and sign it."

Millar said: "Is he dead?"

"He's dead, George. You killed him. Write that too."

Millar said quietly: "It's funny. I wanted to finish Leopardi myself, with my own hands, when he was at the top, when he had the farthest to fall. Just finish him and then take what came. But Gaff was the guy who wanted it done cute. Gaff, the tough mug who never had any education and never dodged a punch in his life, wanted to do it smart and figure angles. Well, maybe that's why he owned property, like that apartment house on Court Street that Jake Stoyanoff managed for him. I don't know how he got to Dolores Chiozza's maid. It doesn't matter much, does it?"

Steve said: "Go and write it. You were the one called Leopardi up and pretended to be the girl, huh?"

Millar said: "Yes. I'll write it all down, Steve. I'll sign it and then you'll let me go—just for an hour. Won't you, Steve? Just an hour's start. That's not much to ask of an old friend, is it, Steve?"

Millar smiled. It was a small, frail, ghostly smile. Steve bent beside the big sprawled man and felt his neck artery. He looked up, said: "Quite dead . . . Yes, you get an hour's start, George—if you write it all out."

Millar walked softly over to a tall oak highboy desk, studded with tarnished brass nails. He opened the flap and sat down and reached for a pen. He unscrewed the top from a bottle of ink and began to write in his neat, clear accountant's handwriting.

Steve Grayce sat down in front of the fire and lit a cigarette and stared at the ashes. He held the gun with his left hand on his knee. Outside the cabin, birds began to sing. Inside there was no sound but the scratching pen.

IX

The sun was well up when Steve left the cabin, locked it up, walked down the steep path and along the narrow gravel road to his car. The garage was empty now. The gray sedan was gone. Smoke from another cabin floated lazily above the pines and oaks half a mile away. He started his car, drove it around a bend, past two old boxcars that had been converted into cabins, then on to a main road with a stripe down the middle and so up the hill to Crestline.

He parked on the main street before the Rim-of-the-World Inn, had a cup of coffee at the counter, then shut himself in a phone booth at the back of the empty lounge. He had the long-distance operator get Jumbo Walters' number in Los Angeles, then called the owner of the Club Shalotte.

A voice said silkily: "This is Mr. Walters' residence."

"Steve Grayce. Put him on, if you please."

"One moment, please." A click, another voice, not so smooth and much harder. "Yeah?"

"Steve Grayce. I want to speak to Mr. Walters."

"Sorry. I don't seem to know you. It's a little early, amigo. What's your business?"

"Did he go to Miss Chiozza's place?"

"Oh." A pause. "The shamus. I get it. Hold the line, pal."

Another voice now—lazy, with the faintest color of Irish in it. "You can talk, son. This is Walters."

"I'm Steve Grayce. I'm the man—"

"I know all about that, son. The lady is O.K., by the way. I think she's asleep upstairs. Go on."

"I'm at Crestline—top of the Arrowhead grade. Two men murdered Leopardi. One was George Millar, night auditor at the Carlton Hotel. The other his brother, an ex-fighter named Gaff Talley. Talley's dead—shot by his brother. Millar got away—but he left me a full confession signed, detailed, complete."

Walters said slowly: "You're a fast worker, son—unless you're just plain crazy. Better come in here fast. Why did they do it?"

"They had a sister."

Walters repeated quietly: "They had a sister . . . What about this fellow that got away? We don't want some hick sheriff or publicity-hungry county attorney to get ideas—"

Steve broke in quietly: "I don't think you'll have to worry about that, Mr. Walters. I think I know where he's gone."

He ate breakfast at the inn, not because he was hungry, but because he was weak. He got into his car again and started down the long smooth grade from Crestline to San Bernardino, a broad paved boulevard skirting the edge of a sheer drop into the deep valley. There were places where the road went close to the edge, white guard-fences alongside.

Two miles below Crestline was the place. The road made a sharp turn around a shoulder of the mountain. Cars were parked on the gravel off the pavement—several private cars, an official car, and a wrecking car. The white fence was broken through and men stood around the broken place looking down.

Eight hundred feet below, what was left of a gray sedan lay silent and crumpled in the morning sunshine.

CHAINS OF DARKNESS

Frederick Nebel

I

Death for Two

The loose, flat jangle of the telephone bell sounded in the darkened room. Eastward, over the rooftops, a post-midnight elevated train slammed south. The bell stopped ringing. Wind from the East River bellied white curtains inward, rattled the wooden rod of a half-drawn shade. The bell rang again.

Cardigan moved in the bed, raised himself to his elbows, yawned boisterously, cocked a sleepy eye at the illuminated dial of the clock on the bed table. He muttered, cursed, reached out. A glass and bottle went down from the table with a crash. The clock followed. And then Cardigan got his hand on the telephone, yanked it savagely across to the bed.

He barked: "Hello . . . Yes; hello, Mike . . . Who said so? . . . Did, did he? And so I suppose just because my name is alphabetically first, you wake me up out of a sound sleep! . . . Listen Mike; this is the second time in a week that tramp Murfree pulled this stunt! . . . I know, I know," he grumbled; then he snapped: "O.K. I'll go up."

He pronged the receiver, found the bed light and snapped it on. Getting out of bed, he took most of the covers with him. Two buttons were off his pajama coat and one leg of his pajama pants was hitched up past the knee. His hair, at no time a barber's delight, was now a tousled shambles. He went growling and grumbling into the bathroom, gargled loud enough to be heard several apartments away. He dressed, slapped on his lop-eared hat, got the collar of his shaggy ulster inside instead of out, but went plodding down the corridor unaware. He was still only half awake by the time he reached the lobby.

The cold winter night helped to rouse him, but in the Napoli, in Fortieth Street, he drank a double Scotch that went much farther toward removing the cobwebs from his eyes. Then he took a cab, lounged back with a cigarette, and was whooped up and over the Park Avenue ramp. Five blocks farther north, in a side street off Park, the cab came to a halt. Cardigan flipped the driver a half dollar, swung his long legs across the sidewalk and punched in the heavy brass-and-mahogany swing door of the Hotel Gascogne. He was quite awake by this time, but he still wore the somewhat sour expression of a man who has been roused from a sound sleep.

He made his way long-legged across the vast, opulent lobby, and reached the black marble and chrome desk where a dapper young man stood pensively pruning his fingernails.

Cardigan said: "He get back?"

"I beg pardon."

"Murfree—did he get back? I'm Cardigan, from the Agency."

"Oh, I see," the man said; and then his face tightened irritably and he snapped: "This is the second time."

"I know. What time did he go out?"

"At ten. And he said he would be right back—at least in time to make the midnight rounds. It seems to me—"

"O.K., I'll make 'em."

Cardigan went down a corridor back of the desk, entered a small office and hung up his hat and overcoat. The Agency had been supplying the Gascogne with a house detective for the past two months, and Murfree had been on the job nights for the past two weeks. Murfree, Cardigan knew, was a souse and something of a ladies' man, and once before he'd gone out for a drink and not shown up until three hours later. Cardigan had wanted to fire him then, but his senior partner, George Hammerhorn, was by nature soft-hearted.

It was ten past one when Cardigan started on his rounds. He took an elevator to the top—the twenty-second—floor, got off and walked the corridors trying doors. Every door was supposed to be locked after midnight, and if it wasn't, it was the house officer's duty to knock and tell the occupant to lock his door. Cardigan worked his way down, poking into linen rooms, trying door after door. He found two unlocked by the time he reached the eighteenth floor. He toned down a drunken party on the seventeenth. On the fifteenth he helped a drunk find his room. On the thirteenth he found a husband who had been locked out by his wife.

The tenth was all right until he came to one of the wings. The door of 1024 gave under his hand. He closed it again, then knocked. He received no response and he knocked again. He waited another minute, then palmed the knob, turned it and opened the door. Lights were glowing in a large apartment living room. He opened the door far enough to step into a small foyer, and then his bushy black eyebrows snapped downward. He reached behind him and pulled the door shut.

There was a man lying face-down in the center of the living room, one arm beneath his body, the other stretched out ahead. He had an overcoat on, but no hat; the hat was lying several feet beyond. Cardigan started toward the body, then stopped as he saw, lying in front of a broad divan at the opposite side of the room, a woman in a négligé. There came to his ears a faint sound like the far-away humming of a dynamo. His eyes cruised the room, stopped on a radio. It was evidently tuned in on a station that had gone off the air.

His eyes dropped back to the man. He moved swiftly now, bent down. A grunt chopped out between his teeth. The man on the floor was Murfree—pale and handsome even in death. Cardigan gripped his body, lifted it, and saw that the hand beneath held a revolver; and he saw a large red blotch on Murfree's chest, and on the carpet. He eased the body back to the floor.

Cardigan stood up, his jaw hardening, a black shimmer coming into his eyes. The thick carpet muffled his footfalls as he crossed rapidly to the woman. She was young, slender, with a fine head of jet-black hair, and she must have been very beautiful, alive. She was very dead now, a caked smear across her breast. Her négligé was torn in many places.

Rising, his eyes took on a glassy, introspective stare. On a small table at one side of the divan, the side nearest the wall, he saw a shattered bowl. He leaned over, and saw on the floor a square, leather-backed clock. He reached down and picked it up and found the lower part of it pierced. The hands had stopped at three minutes to eleven. He set the clock down on the table.

He crossed to the radio, made a mental note of the station at which it was tuned but did not touch the dials, nor did he turn off the switch. He found no other gun in the room. Crossing to the telephone, he picked it up and called the desk.

"Who's registered in Ten Twenty-four? . . . I see. You'd better call the police . . . Dead . . . Yeah—dead . . . Murder, I guess." He hung up quietly.

Molly Shane had lived a lifetime in twenty-two years. From the age of fifteen onward she had kicked, pirouetted and cartwheeled her way across more stages than most people see in a normal lifetime. At various times she had been the darling of Paris, London, Rio and New York—a score of other cities. She had completed a circle. She had begun in New York and ended in New York. A bullet put an end to Molly Shane.

Doake, the plainclothes sergeant, said: "It went right through her." He juggled the twisted lead slug he had picked up from the floor beneath the end table by the divan. He nodded. "Went through her and busted that bowl and busted that clock. Stopped that clock at"—he nodded again—"three of eleven. It smacked her high between the breasts; she could have been sitting or standing—sitting on the divan, I mean." He tossed the slug, caught it. "It's a thirty-eight," he said dully. He was a dour, disillusioned-looking man, with a hard medium-sized body, a hard white nape.

The man from the medical examiner's said "Ah, so" while bending over the body of Murfree.

Dirigo, holding Murfree's gun by the end of the barrel, said: "Murder and suicide," and threw a sly, droll look toward Cardigan.

Cardigan snorted and walked away into the bedroom, came back into the living room again, a mutinous dark look in his eyes.

The medical examiner's man said cheerfully: "You can see this fellow's coat is powder-burned."

"Two shells in this gun exploded," Dirigo drawled. "One in the jane. One in Murfree."

"It looks like suicide," the medical examiner's man sighed.

Doake said to Cardigan: "Did Murfree know her?"

"I don't know."

"Sure he did," a voice rose from the depths of an armchair. It was Barney Evans' voice; he represented The Daily Call. His hand floated a cigarette around languidly. "Saw him. Mean, saw him with her."

"Where?" Doake growled.

"Here and there. The Falstaff, for instance. She was dancing at the Falstaff, you know. Saw her at his table. He always got himself nice janes."

Cardigan snapped: "He made forty bucks a week. How the hell could he travel in this company?"

"He had looks," Dirigo said. "And bedroom eyes."

The medical examiner's man stood up. "The bullet's in him, of course. Ballistics will have to check up when we get it out of him.

"How long's he been dead?" Cardigan asked.

"Let's see. It's one-thirty now. Oh, for the past two or three hours. We'll check up better, later."

Dirigo was smiling. "Sure." He turned the radio on. "These rooms are supposed to be pretty soundproof, and the radio helped. A jazzband was on that station at that time. Not so swell for the dear old Cosmos Agency, huh, Cardigan?"

"Why don't you bust out laughing and be done with it?"

"Trouble with you, Irish, you can't take it."

"I'd call you a lousy Dago if I was sure that's the only kind of blood in you."

Dirigo's eyes snapped, his nostrils quivered.

Doake chopped in: "Both you guys lay off!"

The medical examiner's man pointed downward at the body. "He was wearing a wrist watch on his left wrist. When he fell, I guess he smashed it."

Cardigan took three long strides, knelt down. The glass face was gone; so were the hands. He found splinters of glass in the carpet where he had first seen Murfree's outstretched left hand lying. Later he found the hands—broken, twisted. The watch on Murfree's wrist was also shattered, soundless —a corner of it had dug into his wrist.

The medical examiner's man was saying: "Of course, he had been drinking."

"Sure," Dirigo snarled, still bristling under Cardigan's last taunt. "He got tight and tried to make her and when he couldn't he let her have a slug. And then he saw what he did and he put one into himself. I'm not surprised. The Cosmos Agency seems to pick its men up out of the gutters anyhow."

Cardigan stood up, red color flooding his face. "You keep your dirty mouth shut!"

"You don't like that, do you? Swell!"

"Keep your mouth shut till you know more about this! And lay off the Agency! We have to live on our salaries and we don't ride around in swell cars that are bought with shake-down money."

"Watch your lip, Irish."

"I'll watch it when you watch yours. You ought to go back to South Brooklyn where you made your first dough shaking down the burlesque houses."

"Shut up!" Doake barked.

Cardigan spun on him. "Then tell this white trash to lay off me! I'll kick his face in if he opens it again!"

Dirigo was licking his lips. "You'll—"

"Damn it, you shut up too!" Doake hammered out.

Cardigan said crisply: "I'm staying here till you get a fingerprint man up. When Murfree's taken to the morgue, I want his clothes and effects."

"Yes," sighed the medical examiner's man, "I'd say it's murder and suicide. There's powder burns on Murfree's coat—and the way he fell, the way he was lying here, with his gun hand doubled beneath him—" He shrugged, sighed again. "Of course, we have yet to see if the bullet inside him was fired from this gun. If it was, then of course that will—practically, so to speak—convince me that it was murder and suicide."

"Of course!" Dirigo snapped. "This guy was hot after the dames, he was tight when he came in here—"

"I'll tell you something," Cardigan cut in savagely. "I'll tell you this: even if you find that the bullet in his body was fired from his own gun, and the bullet that killed her was fired from the same gun—I tell you that even then I won't believe it's murder and suicide!"

"And why?" sneered Dirigo.

"Because—simply because Murfree *was* a ladies' man. Because he had too many dames on the string to lose his head over one."

"Nuts! That logic's nuts!"

Cardigan said: "Sure it is—to you. You can't see beyond your nose, Dirigo —and you've got a damned small nose at that."

II

Cardigan Discovers Poetry

George Hammerhorn, the broad, blond and bland head of the Cosmos Agency, was a man who affected gray tweeds and a stick. His cheeks were fleshy without being fat, and they were pink, and he had a kindly blue eye, a sound and genuine air about him. He came into the inner sanctum of the agency next morning more rapidly than was his custom.

Patricia Seaward was at his desk sorting his mail, separating the chaff, the crank letters, from the important matter of the day.

"Ah, Pat," he sighed gravely, hanging up stick, hat and overcoat, "that was a tough one."

Pat was grave too. "Murfree you mean?"

He nodded, sighed again, ran broad palms back over the speckled gray above his ears. He tossed a newspaper on the desk. "See that song-and-dance?"

"I read it over the tomato juice. That's dirty."

He ground the heel of one hand into the palm of the other, stared hard at the desk. "I don't like the implications. Certain parties in this city have been trying for a long time to paint this agency as a collection of crooks. And it looks," he added, dropping his voice, "that this time they get a break."

"Dirigo, huh?"

He nodded.

She said: "I was speaking with Cardigan on the phone about an hour ago."

"What'd he say?"

"First, of course, he told me of a number of things he'd like to do to Detective Dirigo—"

"Dirigo's had it in for him—for us—for a long time. What else did he say?"

"That this would be a swell opportunity for someone to get an injunction against us, close us up, take away your license to operate. But wait. He said to hold everything. Give no newspaper interviews. He said he was sure we'd get clear. He's over at headquarters now, I guess."

Hammerhorn sat down, sighed. "Maybe I should have fired Murfree when Cardigan wanted me to. It would have avoided this, and I suppose Murfree would still be alive. I wonder if he really did lose his head and do it."

Pat said: "Of course, Murfree couldn't let a skirt go by. I wouldn't be surprised. Still—" She broke off, shrugged, then said: "I'm darned if I know."

"If he did it—if he did it"—Hammerhorn held up his hands—"we're through as an agency. This new Civic Rights Commission will nail us."

It was eleven A.M. when the outer door banged open, heavy feet hit the floor, and Cardigan came plowing into the inner sanctum. His face was wind-reddened, his lop-eared hat rode crazily over one ear, and he was eating an apple.

Hammerhorn laid down a pen, leaned back, folded his hands on his stomach and said nothing.

"The news," said Cardigan in a heavy, jocular tone, "is not the kind you'll be crazy about."

"Autopsy—"

"Yeah." Cardigan bit into the word with a grim smile. "It was Murfree's gun did both jobs. The revelation threw that nice-faced bum Dirigo into a spring dance and gave me a bellyache. But wait," he said roughly, as Hammerhorn wagged his head, "I got over the bellyache right away."

"How about the time of death?"

"They say both at approximately the same time; at eleven."

Hammerhorn's voice tightened. "That's bad—bad!"

"On the face, George, it's lousy."

"We're in for it, Jack!"

Cardigan chuckled. "Sure we're in for it."

"It's no laughing matter."

"Listen, George. I haven't begun to sink my teeth into this thing yet. What the hell—give Dirigo rope. He's wanted to hang me for a long time and just now he's foaming at the mouth for pure delight. O.K., let him; let the South Brooklyn punk go ga-ga. I've been around, George—and I pinched a pass key to the late Molly Shane's apartment. I like to let the cops fan a place first. I can always depend on it they take the worthless and overlook the worthwhile."

"How about fingerprints?"

Cardigan, sitting down, shook his head. "They didn't find any but her's, Murfree's, and the maid's."

"Ouch!"

"Buck up." Cardigan drew a paper packet from his overcoat pocket, unsnapped a rubber band. "Molly was a poet in her spare time—a pretty awful poet, but still a poet. I snagged her scrapbook. It's interesting. After each little poem she put a date. Here's one written two weeks ago."

> *"You're my light and you're my darkness,*
> *Chains of love and chains of darkness;*
> *The stars, the moon, the restless sea—*
> *But you, you will be the death of me."*

"It rhymes," Hammerhorn said.

"It's punk. Get this."

> *"You came out of the night, dark-eyed;*
> *And though I tried and tried and tried*
> *To ward you off, you followed me*
> *Till I was lost, no longer free."*

Hammerhorn said: "But what does it mean?"

"She loved him. Swallow this one."

> *"Your clothes, the boutonnière you wear,*
> *The sheen of your dark midnight hair,*
> *The pirate's life you lead, the ice*
> *And blood of you; and mine the price."*

"That girl had things on her mind, Jack."

"You're telling me? And just two more lines. Listen—"

> *"The blood you've taken, here and there,*
> *Is like the ruby that you wear."*

Cardigan slapped the scrap-book shut.

Hammerhorn said: "Did the cops see that?"

"Dirigo thumbed it and chucked it down. Now wait. The dress she wore last night when she came in was lying across a chair in her bedroom. In the bodice of it I found a few bits of confetti. On the flesh just below her elbow —the part she'd lean on at a table—I saw an imprint—the letters I A M. Ink —the ink of some lettering—as though some card or paper was wet when she leaned on it and the print came off on her arm. This ought to prove that she hadn't washed yet when she was killed. She probably came home, got undressed—or almost—her underclothes were still on—and then put on a négligé to admit whoever came in. I saw these letters on her arm before the medical man came. In handling her, he must have rubbed them off."

"How about the elevator boys at the hotel?"

"There was a dance in the hotel at the time and a lot of people were going up and down in the elevators. She wasn't noticed. My contention is that she came home early from wherever she was. In a tantrum maybe. And that whoever she was with, he followed later."

"But where does Murfree fit in? The hotel desk said she didn't call for help. Murfree wouldn't have been in the halls at the time unless he'd been called. How do you figure him in it?"

"I can't yet. If I could, the case might be a snap."

The afternoon papers cut loose with a flock of pictures of Molly Shane, ran stick on stick of highly spiced high-points in the life of the late dancer. There'd been a lot of men in her life, but scandal had not touched her. Dig as the scandal mongers did, they found nothing in her career worth pitching at an I-told-you-so public. The conservative sheets remained conservative; the yellows gagged themselves on adjectives and superlatives, were strong for the murder-and-suicide theory—because it was colorful. One writer hashed up an imaginary playlet of how the crime had happened. News trickled in, and kept trickling, to add to the stated fact that Chris Murfree knew Molly Shane well. The whys and wherefores were traced back five years, at a time when Murfree, working for another agency, had been engaged to guard Molly Shane against the advances of a psychopathic young man who was later jugged on a Westchester attack charge, and was still in the jug. More recently, Murfree had been seen with Molly Shane in the Falstaff and in a number of small, out-of-the-way eating places.

With no evidence to the contrary, a verdict was handed down that Murfree, in a drunken rage, had tried to attack Molly Shane and being repulsed had shot her to death and then committed suicide. To the rank and file, it was open and shut. This line was particularly significant: "Christopher Murfree, who at the time of his death was a private detective in the employ of the Cosmos Agency—" The Hotel Gascogne, bristling, intended to begin suit for damages against the Cosmos Agency.

"We're sunk," George Hammerhorn said. "You see now the beginning of the end of the Cosmos Agency."

"My eye!" said Cardigan.

At this moment William H. K. Plankett, attorney for the agency, came in with his spats and his walking stick and blew his nose zestfully. He was a one-hundred-and-ten-pound fashion plate, aged fifty, with more brain matter than any one man deserved.

"Good news," he said. "The attorney for the Civic Rights Commission apprised me of the fact that your dear old agency is to be ransacked."

"Clear that up," Hammerhorn said.

"They're applying for a court order to investigate your files and to cross-examine every man and woman in your employ. Also, of course, they'll want an injunction to prohibit further operations on your part."

"So what?"

"Send your employes to Capri for the winter and burn the old office down."

"Seriously, I mean."

"Oh, don't worry about it. I'll just get an injunction against their injunction and I'll try to make them show reason why, because one of your employes committed a crime in no way connected with the agency—why, in consequence thereof, the agency should be submitted to the humiliation of an inquest, and so on, so forth. But don't go in a funk. Remember, prosperity is just around the corner." He leaned over, whispered: "And if there happens to be anything in your files, you understand, that might cause a furrowed brow—well, expunge, take out, delete."

"There's nothing in our files I'm afraid of."

"Good." Plankett twirled his stick. "Well, so long, toodle-oo, *auf Wiedersehen!*" Swishing out, he bumped into Pat Seaward. "Ah, Patricia! How about supper some night?"

"Make it lunch and I'll know you're on the level."

"But, Patricia, I am!"

She smiled good-humoredly. "I know—like an escalator."

III

Rigatti

Cardigan, stretching his legs up the dark street, hugged the buildings. For the rain was hard, a steady downpour, threshing on the sidewalk, making silver needles around the street lights. Ahead, he saw a white blob of light suspended above a door. Reaching it, he turned and ducked down three stone steps. The door opened as he reached for it. A small man barged out, and Cardigan, stopping short, dipped his head as the small man, also stopping short, looked upward. A half-pint of water was jerked from the hollow in the crown of Cardigan's hat and flung neatly into the small man's face.

"I beg your pardon," said Cardigan.

The man spluttered and cursed and bounded up the steps, hailed a cab.

Inside, a swart fat girl reached for Cardigan's hat, but he shook his head, went through the anteroom and passed into a bright, prosperous-looking bar. The Rome was supposed to be one of the flashier speaks in the Sheridan Square neighborhood. Three bartenders were on duty, and between twenty and thirty men stood at the bar. Nearby was an elaborate free-lunch counter, and facing the bar was a broad frescoed archway that opened onto a large dining room that tried to look like an Italian Garden, with its fountains, its synthetic trees and vines, and its mandolin-playing troubadour, who from time to time sang from a vine-clad balcony. There was no dancing. Here came the local politicians, the men in the money, some celebrities from Broadway and the Forties. The prices were high, the main reason why Cardigan knew next to nothing about it or its personnel.

He ordered a rye highball and drank it down before saying to the bartender: "Who's the manager here?"

"You wanna see him?"

"That's right."

The bartender craned his neck. "See that fountain in there? He's standing in front of it."

"What's his name?"

"Rigatti."

Among the slick and well-groomed men, Cardigan stuck out like a sore thumb. His hat, more lop-eared than ever because of the rain, was a disgrace. His ulster looked soggy and it had that pungent smell which genuine wool takes on when wet; and the damp made his thick hair bunch and curl eloquently about his ears and on his nape.

"Rigatti? My name's Cardigan and I want to talk to you."

Rigatti had a face like a hard-boiled egg that has been shelled; it shone, but not with delight.

"About what?"

"Your office'll do, or the washroom."

"What's the matter with right here?"

"Nothing—except that I want to talk to you alone."

"I don't get you."

"Ever hear of the Cosmos Agency?"

"Yeah."

"I'm half of it."

Rigatti jerked his chin and Cardigan followed him along the wall, through a doorway into a small, cluttered office. Rigatti closed the door, looked at his fingernails, said without looking up: "What's on your mind?"

"On the night of January Twenty-second, Rigatti, what kind of a party was thrown here?"

"Here?"

"Yeah."

"Nothing."

"Your memory's lousy. You ordered a batch of paper hats, those paper ribbons you toss, some noise-makers, and confetti. You ordered 'em from the Star-Comic Novelty Company for the Twenty-second. They hadn't arrived by noon, and you or somebody else here telephoned and said you had to have 'em for that night."

"Oh, that! Yes, I remember."

"So what?"

"Hell, is this the only place had stuff sent that day?"

"No. There were twenty-one others, and I've been around to seventeen. I just asked you a question."

"What was the question? I told you yes and—"

"I mean, Rigatti, who threw the party?"

"It was just a kind of celebration on our part."

"Public?"

"Yeah."

"Out in your dining room, huh?"

"Sure."

Cardigan laughed. "Come on, Rigatti—lay off that."

"Lay off what."

"A girl I know was down here on the night of the Twenty-second and there was no public party."

Rigatti stood back on his heels, his eyes became dull as they settled on Cardigan's face. "You know a lot, don't you?"

"Not half as much as I'd like to know. Who threw the party?"

"I don't know."

"It was thrown upstairs, wasn't it, in a private banquet room?"

"Maybe it was." Rigatti's face was cold. He turned. "I got a job to take care of."

Cardigan stepped in his way. "So have I."

Rigatti's thick upper lip quivered, tried to curl like a wolf's, didn't quite succeed. He said: "You heard me." He picked up a menu card from the desk, started for the door again.

Cardigan ripped the card from his hand. "Listen to me, Wop—"

The door opened and two bull-necked waiters stood there.

Rigatti said: "Toss him out."

"Quit it!" Cardigan snapped. He added: "I'll walk."

"You're wise," Rigatti said.

Cardigan flung him a dark look, shouldered between the two waiters and made his way to the bar. He did not stop. He went through the anteroom, opened the door, climbed the steps and lunged through the rain into a taxicab parked at the curb.

"Drive east," he said.

He sat back, wiped the rain from his face, and then suddenly found that he still had the menu card he had ripped from Rigatti's hands. Switching on the cab's dome light, he squinted at the card, at the printing at the top.

Beniamino's
THE ROME

He squinted hard, and a dark, intense light came into his eyes. He thought back. Molly Shane's arm just below the elbow. He looked down again at the card—Ben*IAM*ino's . . .

Cardigan got out of the cab in Grove Street, where street lights are few and far between, ducked across the sidewalk, down six stone steps into a black well of an areaway. The iron gate was ajar, and he pushed open the heavy wooden door beyond, tramped down a wide, uncarpeted corridor and took a swing door into a high-ceilinged, old-fashioned bar.

"Rye highball, Chip," he said.

"Swell weather out, huh?"

"For ducks."

"Paper says fair tomorrow and I see a guy of yours up and pulled himself off a crime of passion."

"You don't want to believe everything you hear in the papers, Chip."

"Me-ow!" sighed a voice nearby.

Cardigan turned and saw Barney Evans, of The Daily Call, with his face in a glass of beer.

Cardigan smiled grimly, dagger-eyed. "There's a howling example of what I mean."

"Anyhow," belched Evans, "I'm good to my mother. And I lead blind old men across crowded streets. I also sing hymns. Want me to sing a hymn?"

"Listen, lug," Cardigan said, grabbing his arm. "Come over here a minute."

He piloted the rubber-kneed reporter to a booth at the far end of the bar and shoved him down onto one of the benches. He took the bench opposite, and the table was between them. Evans promptly got the hiccups. Cardigan went to the bar and came back with a glass of water. He made Evans stand up, told him to bend way over and drink from the opposite side of the glass. Evans did this and his hiccups vanished.

He sat down, grimacing. "Water's bad for the system."

"Now, listen, Barney. You're a lousy souse-pot, but I like you, and there's a break that maybe we can split two ways."

"I don't bet on the horses anymore. The horses I follow always follow other horses."

"Shut up and give your ears a chance. Listen. You know the Rome, don't you?"

"Oughta. Wasn't I tossed out once for singing hymns?"

"And you know Rigatti?"

"Yes. A nice guy. Nice, I mean—like a snake in the grass. He doesn't like hymns."

"Listen, Barney. Listen, now. On the night of the Twenty-second—"

"Where was I? Why, playing checkers with my mother."

Cardigan groaned. He drummed on the table, bent a dark exasperated stare on Evans, and finally snapped: "Will you listen!"

"Pro-proceed."

Cardigan leaned way over the table. "On the night of the Twenty-second there was a hi-de-ho party thrown at Beniamino's Rome. Upstairs. Private. You hear?"

"Party . . . Twenty-second . . . Rome."

"Good! Now . . . do you know who threw it?"

"Lemme see. M'm. Um. No. Nope, I don't."

"Any way you can find out?"

"Ha! Trying to put me on my mettle, eh? Ha!"

"Talk sense! Can you find out?"

"I can check up. Uh—listen, write it down, will you? Here, write it on this hunk of paper. Write, 'Who threw party at Rome night of Twenty-second?' That's so I won't forget, in case I get drunk."

"In case you get drunk! You're plastered now!"

"Phooey! That's just an optical illusion of yours."

Cardigan wrote as Evans directed, and when he looked up the reporter was sound asleep. Cardigan did not rouse him. He slipped the note in Barney's vest pocket—the pocket containing his watch, so that it would not be overlooked.

He walked back to the bar and set down his glass as Dirigo came in. Dirigo's face warped in a sly, amused smile, and he came the last few steps lightly on the balls of his feet, put his tongue archly in his cheek.

"Got a new job in mind, Cardigan?"

"You'll be out of a job before I will, Dirigo."

"Quoth he!" He drawled to the bartender: "Scotch, Chip. Give Cardigan one, too. I want to drink his health."

Cardigan said: "Pass it up, Chip."

"Tender, eh?" Dirigo drawled. "Don't like to drink with your betters, eh?"

"Betters?"

Dirigo smiled, his eyes drooping.

Cardigan tilted his jaw, said: "I hear you lay down in a gutter once and a rat got up and walked away."

"Yeah?"

"Yeah. Another rat came along and lay down beside you, and the first rat saw him and went off and told all the other rats. And the other rats got together and said, 'We must cast our brother from us. He lay in a gutter with one named Dirigo.' "

Dirigo colored, and his collar suddenly seemed too tight for him. A muddy look came into his eyes, and his nostrils quivered.

"And if you don't like that," Cardigan said, "say so and ask me to take it back and see if I'll take it back."

"Some day, Irish," Dirigo grated, "you'll go too far."

"When I do, Wop, it'll take a couple of good surgeons to fix up that Dago pan of yours." He looked Dirigo up and down, laughed scornfully, pivoted and went swinging his long legs out of the bar.

IV
Murder by the Clock

At nine next morning Cardigan walked into the Fifth Avenue jewel firm of Abbott & Mars. An elegant young man met him at the door, and Cardigan caught a whiff of chypre and said: "Mr. Abbott in?"

"Who shall I say is calling?"

"Cardigan of the Cosmos Agency."

"A little moment, please—just a little moment."

Cardigan grinned to himself, wandered around the shop. In a minute the elegant young man reappeared, beckoned. Cardigan walked to the rear of the store, climbed a short circular staircase to a mezzanine and entered a large, luxurious office.

"Hello there, Cardigan," old Abbott said. "I see your agency is being taken for a ride."

"So I suppose we'll lose your account."

"Not until you fold up. That what you came about?"

"No. I finally managed to get Murfree's effects from the cops, and I'd like you to help me—and keep it secret." He drew a small wad of tissue paper from his pocket, opened it and laid Murfree's shattered wrist watch on the desk. "That broke when Murfree fell on the floor. The glass was shattered and the hands fell off. The hands broke too. What I want is this—I want to see if you can tell just when this watch stopped. Can you?"

"I guess so. We can replace the hands. You see, the hour hand would go on first, and then the minute hand. The hole of the hour hand is a little large, and is not really a hole but a small oblong that will fit only two ways. I mean, if I just put the hand on haphazardly, fitting it over the small bar, it might be twelve. I could lift it off, turn it around, put it on again, and it would be six. But nothing else. It would have to be exactly opposite. The same with the minute hand. It could be placed in only two positions; if placed at a quarter to twelve, or a quarter to any hour, the opposite could be only a quarter after any hour. You see?"

"I catch on."

"I'll take it down the lab and see if I can fit a couple of hands. I'll do it personally."

"Swell."

"You'll wait?"

"Yeah, I'll wait."

*   *   *

It was twenty minutes later when Cardigan left the shop. He stood for a moment on the curb outside, the wind clapping the skirt of his ulster and humming past his hat. He turned at last and headed south, swung west at Thirty-third and wound up at Herald Square. He spent a minute or two cogitating, then went on west past Macy's, reached Seventh Avenue and entered Penn Station. He made a couple of telephone calls from a booth—one to the office and one to Barney Evans.

"Beniamino threw the party, Cardigan. And listen, I'll tell you how I found out. Max Schmeil runs a photographer's shop on Sixth north of Waverly, and I knew he did all the photography for those joints around there. Listen, Cardigan . . ."

Cardigan listened, made a few notes on the margin of a page of the telephone directory; hung up, tore out the page and whistled his way blithely out of the booth. He went downstairs in the terminal, caught a West Side subway train south and got off at the station marked Christopher Street & Sheridan Square. He crossed the Square, went up Grove Street, turned right into Waverly Place, followed it to Sixth Avenue and turned north beneath the elevated structure.

Max Schmeil's was a hole in the wall. Out front was a glass box containing pictures of the local swains and belles and of chubby little bambinos, immense Italian housewives, a locally prominent plumber and a late alderman.

"On the night of the Twenty-second," Cardigan said, "you went over to Beniamino's Rome."

Max was a young, knotty-haired Jew who wore large, dark-rimmed spectacles. "Sure. I went over and took a flashlight picture."

"Of a private party Beniamino was throwing."

"Yeah."

"How many were there?"

"I don't remember. But I got a picture here."

Cardigan nodded, smiling. "Yeah; that's what I want to see."

Max disappeared into a rear room, came back in a couple of minutes saying: "Yeah, I got several here." He placed three large glossy prints on the counter. "I took 'em from different angles."

Cardigan switched on a light above his head, lifted the photographs. Carefully, shutter-eyed, he scrutinized each picture. He used an index finger to count the number of persons seated at the long banquet table. He tapped the picture he now held and said: "I notice two chairs here, side by side, are empty."

"I guess maybe them two didn't come."

"What time did you take these pictures?"

"Oh, about ten. I know I left here at nine-thirty."

"Got a magnifying glass?"

"Yeah."

Cardigan screwed the glass into his eye, peered. "H'm," he said.

"What?"

Cardigan said: "Mind if I borrow one of these?"

"Sure, go ahead."

"Remember, keep this under your hat."

"That's what Barney Evans said. Sure. Barney gives me lots of breaks—tips me off about hot subjects—accidents or something—and I run off and take the pictures and clean up sometimes selling 'em to the papers hot."

Cardigan went out and in a drugstore used a booth phone to call Barney Evans. He said: "Can you get a big sedan? . . . O.K., get it—now—and meet me in half an hour at Sixth and Waverly . . . I'll tell you when you get here . . . Are you drunk? . . . You would be!"

He hung up, bought a nickel cigar and strolled down Sixth. He stopped at the corner of Waverly, stood looking down at the photograph of Beniamino's party. He recognized several faces: a local two-fisted politician; Beniamino grinning; Rigatti in the background; an ex-judge, now considered a potent political gun without portfolio. But mainly Cardigan's gaze dwelt on the two empty chairs; on the table in front of these chairs two persons had eaten. He saw two wine glasses, half empty; two rumpled napkins; bits of food on two plates.

Pat Seaward was drawing a tumbler of water from the iced cooler in the inner sanctum, and George Hammerhorn was figuring up his bank balance, when a rattle and clatter sounded in the outer office. Miss Myrtle O'Hara, the stenographer, opened the glass-paneled connecting door and then jumped out of the way and Cardigan came in carrying an armchair. Behind him with another came Barney Evans, puffing and groaning. The chairs were heavy, seated and backed with dark red leather.

Barney planked his down and staggered toward the cooler. "Water! Water!" he cried. He stopped short, staggered around, shook his head. "No! No! . . . Spirits! Spirits!"

George Hammerhorn gave him a drink of Scotch, said: "What the hell kind of a picnic is this?"

Cardigan said: "Is Engle in?"

"Back in the lab."

"Good."

Hammerhorn said: "But what are you doing with those chairs?"

Barney Evans burst into a fit of laughter and walked round and round the office holding his stomach.

Cardigan was deadly serious. "We got them upstairs in the Rome—that place Beniamino runs. Nobody there at this hour. I got Barney to drive around with a sedan and then we broke in the joint, got up to this banquet room and snitched these chairs."

Barney fell into a chair, still laughing.

"But why," George Hammerhorn said, "why the chairs?"

Cardigan pointed. "Fingerprints. I want to see if Engle can get off some fingerprints. I've got it in my nut that Molly Shane and a guy were at Beniamino's party. I want to see if Molly's prints are on one of these chairs. I want," he added, "to see whose prints are on the other."

"How do you know these are the chairs?"

"I'm guessing. They were the only two unoccupied chairs when the picture was taken. A Jew photographer took a flashlight. This," he said, tossing the photograph to the desk. "The leather back of each chair is tooled differently. You can see the variations in the photograph with a magnifying glass."

Cardigan called in Engle and said: "Take these two chairs, Pete, and see what kind of prints you get off. Look particularly on the arms, where a person would naturally grab to shift the chair back when getting up. But look all over."

Hammerhorn had begun to sweat. "Do you realize this is—is burglary?"

Cardigan was offhand. "Sure. And don't you realize that if we twiddle our thumbs the grand old Cosmos Agency is going up the flue?"

"Faint maid," Barney said dramatically, "never won fair heart, to quote the Scriptures. I got a swell new hymn—"

"Please, Barney," said Pat, "no hymns." She sighed, looked at Cardigan. "Anyhow, it's a relief it wasn't a bar you wanted."

At three that afternoon Pat was holding down the inner sanctum when she heard voices in the outer office. She looked up as Miss Myrtle O'Hara opened the connecting door and began to stutter: "Ah—huh—S-s-s—"

"That's O.K., miss," plainclothes Sergeant Doake said, coming in. Dirigo sauntered after him, and Doake said bluntly: "Where's your boss, Miss Seaward?"

"I'm on deck, sergeant."

"Well, there was a place busted into down near Sheridan Square this morning and a couple of chairs stolen."

Dirigo, rocking on his heels, slurred: "Yeah, and we're looking for that big Turk Cardigan."

"I'm sorry," said Pat sweetly; "he's not in." She added: "Would you like to leave a message?"

Doake was blunt. "No. We came here looking for the chairs."

"How ridiculous!"

"Can that," Dirigo said.

"But why," Pat said, "would Cardigan steal a couple of chairs?"

Doake said: "Rigatti, the guy manages the place, seems to think it was Cardigan, and anyhow we're looking for them here."

"So sorry," Pat sing-songed. "Were they expensive?"

"This jane's horsing us," Dirigo snapped. "Come on; let's fan the joint."

"Wait," Doake said, holding out his arm; and to Pat: "Suppose you show us around, Miss Seaward."

"I tell you it's absurd, sergeant! Please believe me—"

Dirigo snarled: "She's horsing us! Come on!"

Pat jumped up, her eyes flashing. "You get out of here! There are no chairs here, I told you, and if you want to search this place you know where to get a warrant!"

Dirigo laughed: "She learned those cracks from Cardigan! Come on, Doake—what the hell!" He started for the other door.

Pat jumped in his way, and Dirigo, vicious-eyed, struck her down. Doake looked disapprovingly at him but said nothing. Pat jumped up, and as Dirigo swung the door open Pat picked up a glass paper weight and bounced it off his head. Dirigo swung and came at her, but Doake, cool and hard-faced, stopped him.

Doake muttered: "Cut it, Dirigo!" and shoved him on into the laboratory.

Engle said: "What's the row?"

Doake and Dirigo went through the laboratory, looked in closets, in the photographic dark room. Dirigo swiveled and snapped at Engle: "Where the hell's those chairs?"

Engle was innocent-faced. "Chairs?"

"You heard me! Chairs!"

Doake said: "Come on, Dirigo. They're not here . . . Come on, I tell you!"

Dirigo went hotly back into the office, and Pat said: "If I wanted to be real mean, Dirigo, I could tell Cardigan about that pass you made at me—and then inform a hospital of an impending disaster."

Doake hustled Dirigo out.

Pat turned to Engle. "What happened—"

"I heard them," Engle said. He turned and pointed to a groundglass window. "I tied the chairs to a rope, hung 'em in the shaftway."

Pat fanned herself. "Whew! Did you use your head!"

V
Roman Holiday

Cardigan came out of the subway kiosk at Christopher Street & Sheridan Square. The wind lifted a sheet of newsprint from the sidewalk and plastered it against his face. He yanked it off, and the wind caught it, kited it away. He cut across the Square, went up Grove Street to West Tenth. He walked on, stretching his long legs, his hands jammed into the pockets of his shaggy ulster, a butt jutting from one side of his mouth and his lop-eared hat crammed low down on his forehead, with brim up like a cowboy's riding into the wind.

He saw, ahead, the yellow blob of light that marked the Rome. He reached the door, pinched his butt between thumb and forefinger and snapped it out into the middle of the street. He dropped down the steps, palmed the door open and towered into the anteroom. The fat girl reached for his hat and coat.

He shook his head, said, "Uh-uh," and passed on into the bar. It was a little past six and a cocktail crowd was in the bar. The shakers were going fast, and the troubadour was singing *Valencia* to a handful of persons in the dining room.

Cardigan dropped his elbows on the bar. "Side-car," he told the bartender. He downed the side-car at three gulps, cleared his throat and felt better. He paid for the drink, saw Rigatti standing in the dining-room entry and went toward him.

"In your office, Rigatti—come on."

"So you're here again."

"And you're going to see a lot of me. Come on. I've got the words and I've got the music."

"Take it outside."

Cardigan got close to him, looked darkly down into Rigatti's muddy eyes. "Dago, I'm here on business. Get in your office."

Rigatti shrugged and led the way into the little office, and Cardigan kicked the door shut, unbuttoned his overcoat and dug his hands into his pants pockets.

He said with deadly calm: "I want to see Beniamino."

"You could have asked me that out there."

"I want," said Cardigan, "to see Beniamino in here. Go get him."

The door opened and Dirigo came in, closed the door, leaned back against it, said: "I saw that little play."

Cardigan jerked a thumb. "You're not wanted."

A waiter opened the door, beckoned to Rigatti: "Just a minute, boss."

"I'll be back," Rigatti said, and followed the waiter out.

Cardigan sat on the edge of the desk, dangled a leg. "Dirigo," he said, "you're going to get your nose dirtied if you hang around."

"I'd like to know who piled in here this morning and h'isted two of the Rome's Spanish chairs. Burglary, you know."

"Is that right? . . . Well, why don't you find out?"

"I'm trying now."

Cardigan stood up, took his hands out of his pockets and went over to face Dirigo. "Copper, when I see you I see red. You're in my way tonight. I'm a wild Mick on the loose and I'm warning you—take the air before I step on you. You're breaking your neck to bust me and bust up George's agency. You're dirty about it, but that doesn't surprise me, because you're dirty anyhow. You hear me—stay the hell out of my way!"

Dirigo's eyes were dark, his nostrils twitched. "I'll break you and the Agency. How do you like that?"

"I hate it."

"Swell!"

Cardigan hit him. All the accrued hatred and bile came out in the form of a big fist driven, chopped upward. Dirigo said, "O-o-o-o" quietly, and his knees buckled, his eyes rolled and showed the whites as he slumped downward.

Cardigan picked him up, shook him. Dirigo's eyes rolled and he cursed, staggered back and forth on his feet. Cardigan held his arm firmly, steadied him. He opened the door. By main strength he guided Dirigo to the bar, piloted him through it to the anteroom, got him out into the street. He opened the door of a waiting taxicab and hoisted Dirigo in. Dirigo slumped back into the seat.

Cardigan slipped the driver a bill. "Take my friend to Grand Central. He's plastered and has to make a train."

"O.K., chief!" The cab drove off.

Cardigan stood on the curb, brushed his hands together, whistled a few bars and went back into the Rome. He didn't see Rigatti in the bar or in the dining room. He walked through the dining room, pulled black curtains aside and found himself in a corridor. There was a broad staircase which he mounted, a few steps at a time, listening. He reached the corridor above. Moving from door to door, he listened at each.

He was halfway down the corridor when he heard a door open and saw Rigatti appear farther down the hallway. Rigatti closed a door and took half a dozen steps before he saw Cardigan. Then he stopped short, his features tightening, freezing. He came on swiftly, his fists clenched, his brows bent in a sudden, furious scowl.

"Who the hell told you to come up here?" he snarled.

"Don't show your teeth at me, Rigatti. Where's Beniamino?"

"You get downstairs!"

"Why should I? And come up again?"

"This is private up here!" Rigatti rasped, his eyes blazing. "Get down!"

Cardigan grinned. "Now listen, Rigatti—"

Rigatti shot a hand toward his hip. Cardigan grabbed, caught Rigatti's wrist; he shifted his feet quickly, tightened his loins; his bent arm hardened, lifted while it corkscrewed upward. Rigatti rose from the floor, gritting his teeth, his body supported by his bent arm. Suddenly Cardigan relaxed. Rigatti's body dropped a couple of inches; and then Cardigan's arm did a whipsnap and instantly Rigatti was flat on his face. He pawed for his gun; his hand didn't seem to work properly.

Cardigan said: "I sprained your wrist, Rigatti. You're wasting time trying to get that gun."

He reached down, took the gun from Rigatti's pocket, thrust it into his own. He left Rigatti panting and aching for breath, and still on the floor. Below, the troubadour was singing *Marcheta*. Cardigan came up to the door through which he had seen Rigatti emerge. He grasped the knob with his left hand, turned it; he opened the door, and walked into a large, old room furnished with large, modern pieces at odds with the Georgian fireplace.

"Take your time, Beniamino," he clipped.

A lucious little red-head, all hosiery and white shoulders, was sitting in fat, swart Beniamino's lap. Beniamino had a fat wife and ten bambinos up-town. The red-head, taking one look at Cardigan, grabbed fat Beniamino around the neck and cried: "Oh, Popsy-wopsy!"

Cardigan let a low, brittle chuckle escape. "Popsy-wopsy!"

Beniamino ordinarily had the face of a fat angel, but now it showed a mixture of anger, fear and embarrassment.

Cardigan's smile vanished, his face grew cold. "Chase the dame, Beniamino," he said.

"I—I'd say you're Cardigan."

"That's right. Now chase her."

Beniamino, his fat eyes fixed on Cardigan, patted the red-head's shoulder, urged her away with a movement of his body. Goggle-eyed, she fled across the room, while Cardigan looked her over from head to foot and said, as the girl went out and closed the door: "You pick 'em, you old playboy, you!"

Beniamino looked breathless, mournful. "What do you want?"

"I want . . ." He paused, came a few steps closer, showed his teeth in a hard, brazen smile.

Beniamino gulped: "Yes?"

"Can't guess, huh?"

"N-no."

"Joe Polarmo."

Beniamino's fat swart face seemed to jounce once, and was then motionless and mournful, saggy-eyed. "Joe Polarmo," he said in a far-away whisper.

"Joe Polarmo," Cardigan said, matter-of-factly now.

Beniamino giggled, made a silly gesture. "Oh, yes. Yes. Oh, you mean Joe Polarmo! Joe Polarmo, you mean."

"Yeah."

"Yeah," Beniamino giggled. "Uh—have a drink?"

"I'll have Joe Polarmo instead."

Beniamino groped to his feet, coughed, blew through his teeth, made silly gestures, said: "I—I—yes—I'll have a d-drink."

Cardigan stepped between him and the table. "I'm in a hurry, Beniamino. Where's Polarmo?"

"Well—heh-heh!—you see, I don't—that is—I don't j-just know where Joe is."

Cardigan's voice hardened. "Beniamino, I want Polarmo! He was here at a banquet on the night of the Twenty-second!"

"Yes. Sure he was here. He was here all right."

"What time did he leave?"

"Oh, about two A.M."

"What time did he come here?"

"Eight-thirty."

Cardigan grinned ironically. "Got his alibi all fixed, huh?"

"Look now, Cardigan—"

"You're lying like hell! Because Polarmo left during the banquet, you dumb potato!"

Beniamino said dramatically: "There's twenty men and women know he didn't."

"They're liars too!" He stopped short, remained silent for a moment and then his voice rushed out violently. "Me and the agency I work for are headed for the rocks! I'm not crazy about my job but I have to eat and I'm damned if I'm going to lose it. And I want, you fat Italian sugar-daddy, I want Polarmo! I don't want any arguments and I don't care how many people say he didn't leave your banquet. I know he did. I want him, you hear!" He whipped out the gun he had taken from Rigatti and jammed it hard against Beniamino's middle. His voice chopped: "Get him. Phone him. Get him here."

"N-no!"

Cardigan rushed him halfway across the room. Beniamino landed in an armchair so hard that he almost bounced out again. His jowls jounced.

"Mother o' God, Cardigan—"

"I want him!" Cardigan snarled. "Get up!" He yanked Beniamino out of the chair, turned him, pressed the gun against the back of Beniamino's neck. "I want him, Beniamino!" he snarled.

It was this simulated madness that frightened, horrified the Italian. He stumbled to the telephone, dialed a number. The instrument shook in his hands.

"Joe—Joe. This is Beniamino. I got to see you—quick!"

He hung up, groaned. He gulped: "Let me get outta here."

"Wait."

The door whipped open and Dirigo stood there with his gun drawn. "Drop it, Irish!"

Cardigan looked over his shoulder.

Dirigo rasped: "Drop it! Or move—move an inch, baby, and I'll let you have it—and like it!"

Cardigan let the gun drop to the floor.

Dirigo was breathless. "Send me on a buggy-ride to Grand Central, will you? O.K., smart guy. This is a pinch."

Cardigan had turned. "For socking an officer of the law?"

"Yeah—for socking an officer of the law. I'll see you spend six months in the can for this!"

Cardigan raised his palms, went toward Dirigo. "Now wait a minute. I can't be pinched right now. I'm on a job—"

Dirigo was simmering, his eyes were blazing, and his voice shook with suppressed passion. "You heard me, Cardigan! I've stood enough from you—enough! You're going over to headquarters and you're going to spend the night there." He snapped up his chin, steadied his gun. "Get out in the hall."

"Dirigo, listen—"

"Get out!" rasped Dirigo. "Shut your mouth! I don't want to hear a word out of you!"

Beniamino, at first shocked, now breathed in deeply and looked like a man who had been told his world would end and then found that it would not. But he said nothing. His jowls quivered with excitement.

Cardigan walked into the hall, passing Dirigo and looking down at him with dark, malignant intensity. He began: "I just—"

"Shut up!"

* * *

Cardigan inhaled deeply, held his breath, then let it out slowly, sighing hopelessly. His face became red with chagrin, his eyes sultry and mutinous. Dirigo, he knew, was mad to the core, bitter and resentful and determined to make him, Cardigan, pay in full for past victories and abuses. Dirigo was on top, riding the crest. Cardigan thought, "I'm a fool—a sap. I should never have pasted that guy." He reached the head of the staircase, saw a group of waiters waiting expectantly below. The troubadour was singing *The Peanut Vender.* "Pe-e-e-e-e-nuts . . ."

"Dirigo, for crying out loud—"

Dirigo struck Cardigan a blow on the head and Cardigan involuntarily took three steps down. His face grew darker, redder, and he licked his lips, felt himself beginning to sweat as he walked down the stairway. He reached the bottom, looked straight ahead as he walked past the waiters. He heard a few snickers and one Bronx cheer. His face was taking on a very dark red color and his eyes seemed to become bloodshot.

Rigatti hissed: "I'll send you some ice cream, Cardigan—and put arsenic in it!"

Cardigan did not move his head. He walked through the dining room, passed into the bar. Dirigo was behind him, a step behind him. He turned and faced Dirigo and his big face was warped.

"I tell you, Dirigo, I came here to make a—"

"Mug, get on!" rasped Dirigo.

Cardigan turned and headed for the anteroom, but the man coming into the bar made Cardigan stop. He felt Dirigo's gun prod him in the back, but he did not budge. The man was young, dark-clothed, darkly handsome. He held a cigarette in his mouth, and a large ruby shone redly on his small finger; a flower was in his lapel.

"Polarmo!" Cardigan muttered.

The man had not noticed him; he was making his way swiftly toward the dining room.

"Get!" snapped Dirigo.

But Cardigan raised his jaw. "Polarmo!" he barked.

The sleek young man spun.

Cardigan turned on Dirigo. "There's your man, Dirigo! Nab him! There's Joe Polarmo!"

Polarmo was unaware of the situation that existed between Dirigo and Cardigan. He did not know Cardigan, but he must have known that Dirigo was a detective. And he saw the gun in Dirigo's hand—he saw the savage, bitter, murderous look on Dirigo's face, but he did not know that it was meant for Cardigan and not for him.

Joe Polarmo made one sleek dive, twisted as he ran toward the door through which he had just come. He must have had things on his mind. Metal flashed in his hand and his gun boomed. Women screamed. Dirigo looked silly, made a wry face, shook himself, took one step forward, one backward, then turned around like a dog sitting down—and sat down.

Cardigan's hand sliced beneath the left lapel of his coat. He started off, drawing his gun from its shoulder holster. He heard the front door bang. Going through the anteroom, he saw the fat checkroom girl holding her ears. He leaped over a man lying on the floor. He reached the door, yanked it open and dived out on hands and knees.

He heard running feet. Rising out of the small well, he climbed the stone steps, saw a dark figure fleeing west. He waited until he saw the figure speed beneath a street light. Then he raised his gun, fired. The bullet hit an ashcan and scared away a couple of cats. It made Joe Polarmo run faster.

But Polarmo spent a second at the next corner to spin. He used the corner of the building as a shield—and he fired, but he fired as Cardigan flopped behind the ashcan; and the bullet whanged into galvanized iron. Cardigan got a mouthful of cinders. Spitting them out, he rose and raced on; skidded up to the corner, bent way down and looked around the corner with his chin almost touching the sidewalk.

Polarmo fired and bits of brick dribbled down onto Cardigan's hat. Cardigan, kneeling, fired twice in succession. He saw Polarmo stagger. He saw a truckdriver jump from a truck and race out of sight. Jumping up, Cardigan broke into a run; saw the flash of Polarmo's gun, heard a window two feet from his head fly to pieces. The crash of the glass commingled with the crash of his own gun. The echoes banged in the narrow dark street.

Going on, he saw Polarmo walking around in a circle. It was curious, he thought, the way Polarmo kept walking faster and faster, in the same circle, round and round. And then Polarmo suddenly stopped walking and fell to his knees. He remained on his knees for a moment and then fell over backward.

Doake sat on a straight-backed chair in his office, his feet far apart but planted solidly on the floor.

"Yeah," nodded Cardigan. "Yeah. I shot Polarmo up because he shot Dirigo. It makes good reading matter—so what the hell. I could have given Dirigo a pinch there. But no. He was so lousy mad at me that he was blind —he couldn't even get it through his nut that Polarmo was drawing on him. I could have saved him these three weeks in the hospital he's going to spend, but I'm no dummy. I knew damned well that if I so much as started toward my lapel Dirigo would have blown my heart out. So I let him take that slug. I had to. And then I went after Polarmo."

"How the hell did you tie down on Polarmo?"

Cardigan shrugged. "First off, you guys and a lot of other guys were bent on running the Agency out of business. Then I didn't believe Murfree did it, and I told you why. The confetti in Molly Shane's dress gave me an idea. It meant a party. I walked my feet off finding where parties had been held on the night of the Twenty-second. I knew that Murfree didn't do the shooting because I found out that Murfree was down by the time Molly was shot."

"How'd you know?"

"His watch. His wrist watch. The bullet that killed Molly stopped the clock on the table behind her at three to eleven. When Murfree was shot, he fell—he fell and smacked his watch on the floor. I took it to a jeweler, who put new hands on it, and I found then that his watch had stopped at twenty past ten—thirty-seven minutes before Molly was shot. Pictures had been taken of Beniamino's party. I saw the pictures. Two chairs, side by side, were empty. I swiped the chairs. Off one I got Molly's prints; off the other I got some prints I brought down here and looked up: they were Polarmo's. I went out to find Polarmo. Molly wrote poetry. When I met him in the Rome, I knew him right away from the pictures I'd seen here—but I would have known him from her bum poetry too."

Doake sighed, shook his head.

Cardigan said: "You know, of course, what Polarmo did. He told you in the hospital. He wanted Molly to help him dispose of Murfree's body. Murfree knew Polarmo. He saw Polarmo go into the Hotel Gascogne, and Murfree, on the job, wanted to find out what Polarmo was doing there. He found out. Polarmo was drunk and attacking Molly. And afterward Polarmo wanted her to swear she wouldn't tell who killed Murfree—and she wouldn't swear—and Polarmo shot her. Murfree was a sap. He walked into that apartment with his gun in his pocket. Polarmo took it away from him and Murfree was sap enough to try hand-to-hand. Murfree should have walked in with his gun drawn."

Doake shoved his hands into his pockets, frowned, bit his lip. He said dully: "When Dirigo comes out of the hospital, he goes back to harness."

"You're getting wise to him, huh?"

"I been wise a long time—but I never acted." He kept staring hard at the floor, thrust out his hand.

Cardigan reached out, shook it.

The Arm of Mother Manzoli

Merle Constiner

I

The Lovesick Professor

Nine out of every ten amateur murderers look upon themselves secretly as hotshot geniuses. It's the other lad, the tenth, that's really bad medicine. He doesn't think he's any smarter than his fellow man. He just works his way through the night school of homicide the hard way, plugging along, planning ahead, taking care of details. He's original, cagy—and can do a lot of killing before he's scotched.

This was the sort of baby behind the University Court slayings—as crafty and vicious a murder-sequence as we ever tackled.

We'd just finished lunch and were in the office-bedroom. I stood at the window in my stocking feet, deftly balancing a saucer of peanuts and a glass of tepid ale. The Dean was fiddling at his workbench beneath his green student's lamp.

I recognized the signs and they worried me. He was sulking. There was no telling why. Maybe it was something that had happened at breakfast, maybe it was some minor irritation he'd been subjected to last week and just got around to brooding over. I asked: "What's your favorite song, chief?"

He looked startled. "Song? I can't say offhand. Why?"

"You're griping about something you can't even remember. As long as you stay this way we'll starve. I thought perhaps you'd like to join me in a little two-man community sing. Psychologists say it's elevating to the spirit."

He parted his angry lips to loose a withering retort when there was a noise out front. We heard the door open and the sound of footsteps in the reception room. I cut my eye at the chief. He said mulishly: "Tell them to get out. No clients today, please."

I said: "What's the matter with me? I'll take over." I put on my house slippers and left the room.

There was a brace of them, assorted—one male and one female—sitting side by side on the Dean's *ante bellum* loveseat.

The little brunette was just a kid, in her late teens or early twenties, and plenty attractive. She had sulky lavender eyes with long lashes and a boyish little figure, but there was an air of helpless feminine humility about her that rang about as true as a lead quarter.

The lad with her was right out of the sporting ads. Obviously wealthy— and super-obnoxious. He was middle-aged, powerfully built, and dressed in as gaudy a swatch of hound's-tooth check yardgoods as I've seen outside a tailor's window. He had a big red face with silky silver eyebrows and tiny, porcelain-cold eyeballs that lurked back in their fleshy caves, frosty and suspicious.

I tried to mimic the Dean. "Well, who was here first? Raise your hands, please."

He blinked, took a short, gasping breath. He'd had a speech all ready to reel off and I'd mixed him up. He drew himself up, said crossly: "I'm sure your insolent tone is accidental, sir. I am J. Bogardus Keane." He paused. I looked blank. He added petulantly: "You know, Keane, the—ahem—retired woolen goods magnate. This is Miss Marcia Cowen. We're not competing, as you rather crassly imply. We came in together and wish to consult you jointly. You're Wardlow Rock, I presume."

"Monkey food! I'm Ben Matthews. Mr. Rock is engaged. What do you want?"

They exchanged questioning glances, decided that while I was just riffraff, I was better than nothing. Miss Cowen straightened her short dress modestly, said: "I wish to retain you. Mr. Keane is sort of sponsoring me, so to speak. We'd like your help on two points. The first is the love-potion. I understand Mr. Rock is a student of medieval alchemy. I want him to stew up some kind of an antidote. That's the main thing. Then there's Mr. Saxby, my fiancé, who's beginning to show signs of being mentally upset. We want you to find out what it is that's injuring his reason and remove it."

Already I was in over my head. I tried to get organized. "Let's get this clear. Then J. Bogardus, here, isn't your betrothed?" They both looked horrified. I asked: "Who are you people? And who is this Saxby, and if he's your fiancé why does he have to hop himself up with a love-potion?"

Miss Cowen waved me down with a gesture of her limp hand. "It's not that way at all. We all live out in the University Court neighborhood. That's why we're all friends. Steve Saxby and Beanie, here"—the sporty man smirked—"and myself. Well, up on the corner in an old run-down house, lives Professor Eggleston. He has some kind of tenuous affiliation with the college but he's getting rather ancient now and spends most of his time at home. He's quite a character."

I listened patiently. "No doubt, no doubt."

The kid continued: "University Court isn't snooty—it's just that we all have kind hearts. Of late, Professor Eggleston has been walking the streets in a rather shabby condition."

Miss Cowen went on: "It is just heartbreak to watch the poor old fellow. Bogardus suggested the professor needed a feminine hand to guide him. I volunteered. Every morning I drop in for an hour and fix him up—mend and darn and see that he has clean linen."

I said gustily: "I bet the old professor likes that!"

"He didn't know how to refuse at first, so he tolerated me." The gal frowned. "I sure wish those days were back! In the meantime, he's mixed up this love-potion for himself, and now he just sits and drools while I sew. He keeps this drug in a bottle, says it's cough syrup. I've brought it along without his knowledge—" She produced a small parcel twisted in brown paper, laid it on the table. "I want Mr. Rock to analyze it and prescribe an antidote. It's a pathetic thing to see a dignified old man in the throes of puppy love."

J. Bogardus looked indescribably sad. "Marcia's right. It fairly wrings your—"

"I know." I cut him off. "What's this about Mr. Saxby?"

"I'm worried about him." Miss Cowen smiled somberly. "We're practically engaged and he's beginning to do such erratic things. Last month he decided to be a treasure-hunter and went out and made maps of the neighborhood. He's given that up, thank goodness. The other day he suddenly went in for prizefighting. I don't mean he fights; he's making a study of all the pioneer pugilists. He has pictures of these coarse persons all over his house! Something is making him do these strange things. We want to know what."

"You and Beanie?" I grinned. "You folks are certainly hounds for charity work. O.K., you've hired a detective." I ushered them to the door. At the threshold, the big man hesitated. He fumbled in his pocket, came out with a glossy, pigskin wallet. "Here, sir, is fifty dollars—your retainer fee."

Mr. Keane closed the door behind them. Abruptly, he re-opened it, called through the slot: "You are now in my employ. Remember, no man can serve two masters! Tally-ho!" Before I could retort, the door slammed.

University Court! I knew I had something hot. I ambled into the office-bedroom with the banknote and the package.

The Dean was lolling in his broken-down Morris chair, his eyes closed, the black snip of a Cuban cigar screwed into the corner of his mouth, when I drifted in. I gave him a detailed review of my seance with our new clients. When I'd finished he tried to belittle me, but his heart wasn't in it. "What fol-de-rol! Treasure-hunters, prizefighters—and love-potions!" He reached forward. "So this is Professor Eggleston's cough syrup?"

He unwrapped the stiff brown paper. It was an ordinary four-ounce medicine bottle—empty. He glanced at the label and almost dropped the vial in his astonishment. "Good Lord, Ben! Take a look at this."

I peered over his shoulder. The sticker was a messy job, pasted over the regulation drugstore label. It had been typed on an old-fashioned typewriter and said:

> 1,000   parts strass
> 8   parts oxide of copper
> 0.2 parts oxide of chromium

"What is it?" I asked. "Some slow-acting poison?"

"Benton, my boy, this is big—and there's going to be big money in it for us. It hurts me to reprimand you but I must take this occasion to inform you that I am the proper person to interview prospective clients, and that by exceeding your authority we are indeed fortunate that you have not jeopardized . . ."

The same old merry-go-round! I swear, I wonder a dozen times a day how I ever manage to hang on. The Dean likes to pose as an amiable crackpot, and as long as I've known him, sometimes even I can't figure him.

I used to be a troubleshooter for a small safe company. He picked me up when I was down and out and gave me a job. I'm no big-brain. All I know is guns and locks.

I said bitterly: "Clients come. You turn deaf. I take them on. And now you're graveling because—"

"But University Court, Ben. That was the tip-off. You should have run screaming for me when you heard University—"

*　*　*

Actually, I didn't kid myself—I knew he was right. It was a strange mix-up. The case had broken about four months ago. The papers were full of it. Nobody could make heads or tails of it. An old lady named Taggart lived alone in a ramshackle mansion out in the University Court section. One night she had two lodgers and about ten the next morning, when they didn't answer her knock for breakfast, she entered their room and found them dead in bed. A man and his wife. They'd been shot at close range and a rusty old Iver Johnson lay on the coverlet.

Miss Taggart told the law that she didn't have the slightest idea who they might be. Around six, the night before, they'd come up on her porch and said they'd like a room for the night. They'd seen the "Tourists Accommodated" sign in her parlor window, they said. They were fortyish and seedy looking, but shabby through neglect, she judged, rather than through poverty. The man was bald-headed and his wife wore a pair of those nose glasses with a black ribbon. They looked somber but respectable. She took them in, and during the night they killed each other.

The tragedy must have occurred about eleven because that was the time she always took Ophelia, the cat, out for her walk. There were no shots after Miss Taggart returned—on that point she was definite.

The law had put it down as a suicide pact. There had been a mild flurry of mystery to it at first—the mystery of the third andiron. It seemed as though the couple had been extremely cautious about destroying all marks of identity. They'd cut out the window screen, laid it on the andirons in the fireplace, like a grate, and had burned the woman's pocketbook, the man's wallet, and an assortment of private papers. That part was natural enough, but the andirons themselves presented a riddle. The two regular ones had cats on them, and in between the cats was a third—an andiron with an owl on it. Miss Taggart said she kept this set in a storeroom at the end of the hall. She had no further explanation.

So it was a suicide pact, and the newspapers gave it a heart-throb banner. But the next day it almost jelled into murder. Almost but not quite.

An anonymous telephone call informed the police that Miss Taggart wasn't in the habit of taking in tourists. The speaker, a man, said that he was a neighbor of the old lady's, that he'd passed the house many times and seen no sign in the parlor window. He suggested flatly that Miss Taggart had placed the placard in the window the morning of the deaths, that she'd found the bodies, grabbed a pen and ink, and dashed off a "boarders-taken-in" card—after the murders.

Miss Taggart, confronted with this new evidence, admitted exactly that. She said never before had she taken roomers. However, the man and his wife introduced themselves as friends of Professor Eggleston's, in town for the night. The next morning, when she'd discovered the corpses, she phoned the professor. To her astonishment, he violently disclaimed any knowledge or relationship with her guests whatever. It was then that Miss Taggart, panicky, drew up the fake sign.

A month later, Miss Taggart, alone in her big house, died from an overdose of sleeping powders and gimmicked the whole affair tighter than a drum. The mysterious guests were never identified.

"And now the guy pops up again!" I exclaimed. "Eggleston, and this time he's lovesick. In my opinion, he's—"

"Let's not rush to any shaky conclusions, Ben. Maybe we'd better have a brief chat with this scholarly gentleman." Out front the reception room door opened. The boss frowned. "More visitors. And I think I recognize those stalwart hoofbeats."

II

Homemade Emeralds

This time it was the law. Lieutenant Bill Malloy and Captain Kunkle. The captain was holding a cheap straw suitcase clamped beneath his arm.

The Dean bowed stiffly, said: "Greetings, sires." He pointed a peremptory index finger at the suitcase under Kunkle's arm. "May I inquire, Captain, as to what you're mothering so tenderly? I seem to sense that this is somehow the object of your visit."

Captain Kunkle took three short steps forward, placed his polished shoes at careful right angles. "First, I wish to state that our call here is unofficial, you might even say social. The lieutenant and I were having a bit of an argument and, as we happened to be passing, we thought we'd drop in and get you to settle it. Ahem. Now here is our puzzler—you know those wax figures of famous criminals that you see in penny arcades and carnival concessions. Here's what we want to know. What do they look like underneath their clothes? The limbs, for instance. Are they crudely shaped or are they carefully sculptured like the hands and faces?"

"And the color," added Malloy. "Underneath the clothes are those wax people all grayish and drab?"

The Dean was gitting nettled. "What is this? Stop beating about the bush!"

Kunkle laid his straw suitcase on the table beneath the lamp, opened the lid. We stared. The captain said hoarsely: "Isn't it grisly? Isn't it horrendous?"

* * *

Inside, on a nest of shredded newspapers, was an arm. It looked exactly like a human arm, except it was a faded sort of gray. It was a large arm, bent slightly at the elbow, and heavily muscled. I could hardly believe it was artificial. You even could see the texture of the skin and the fingernails looked almost alive. The upper end had been modeled in a gruesome way, as if the arm had been lopped off by a surgical instrument. You could make out veins and arteries and stuff.

The Dean was speechless with admiration. Finally, he spoke. "Gad! This is a pleasure I never expected. I can hardly believe it! It's a gem, isn't it? What a beauty!"

Captain Kunkle looked nauseated. "To me it's highly revolting. What makes it so gray?"

"Because it's so very old. No, this is no makeshift from a carnival concession." The chief closed the suitcase affectionately. "Treat it with great care. It's very valuable. By the way, where did you get it?"

Malloy shifted his feet. He said gruffly: "Thanks, Rock. For what, I don't know. We'll be getting along, eh, Captain?"

"I'll make a deal," the Dean said hastily. "I admit I've been holding back on you. You tell me how it came into your possession and I'll tell you what you've got. That's one of the arms of Mother Manzoli. The Manzoli family were skilled craftsmen in wax figures. They lived in the middle of the eighteenth century in Bologna and specialized in anatomical models. Their works are museum pieces. How came you by this treasure?"

The officers paused on the threshold. Captain Kunkle showed beads of sweat across his brow. "It's all so confusing. This suitcase with its contents was found on the doorstep of the Elite Diner this morning when the proprietor opened up."

The Dean pursed his lips. "The Elite? I don't believe I—"

"A greasy-spoon lunchwagon out by the college. In the University Court neighborhood."

"I see," the Dean answered vaguely. "I see. Well, good afternoon, gentlemen."

After they were gone, the chief said briskly: "Just as I suspected—the Taggart-Eggleston affair is a long way from being closed in the official books. Well, let's be on the move. We've a mighty busy evening ahead of us."

I'm tenderloin born and raised. I didn't go for it. I said: "Boss, this job's too spooky for me. A treasure-hunter wacky over old-time prizefighters. A wax arm. And a college professor doping himself on love-potions!"

"Love-potions?" The Dean looked bewildered. "Oh, you mean the bottle. That wasn't a love-potion. That romantic touch was the product of Miss

Marcia Cowen's neurotic imagination." He chuckled. "Strass and oxide of copper and oxide of chromium! That's not out of *Materia Medica!* Strass is a kind of clear glass. The prescription on the bottle is not a prescription at all, but a formula the professor hoped to conceal from prying eyes. It's the traditional formula, tried and true, *for imitation emeralds!* Yes, the venerable scholar, for some reason or other, intends to turn out a batch of homemade gems!"

To my surprise, I learned that the Dean was perfectly at home in the University Court neighborhood. It developed, too, that he had made a purely academic study of the district months ago, at the time of the tragedies, and wasn't entirely unfamiliar with the names and addresses of our clients. He was one man you simply couldn't calculate.

The Court was a dreary little community a few blocks from the college campus. A bizarre mixture of the old and the new, of ancient rotting mansions in their groves of gnarled and blighted oaks interlaced with patches of tiny, modern bungalows, trim and spanking in new paint. The sodden afternoon sky was breaking into layered clouds, lipped with dull silver, and the desolate yards of pavements were illumined by a watery, sepulchral light. The Dean slowed up, said: "Well, here we are."

My first look at Professor Eggleston's home clashed with my mental image of it. The gal had referred to it as "an old house on the corner" and I'd conjured up a picture of a stark, ominous place with broken window panes and a front lawn overgrown with weeds. The neat story-and-a-half structure was set up on a terraced, close-clipped plot of grass. It was of white brick and almost clinical in its severity. A small one-room annex was built out at one side, like a garage, but there was no drive leading from it. "The professor's workshop," the Dean explained. "See. There's a light showing. He's tinkering around at something."

We ascended the tired steps, took a narrow cement walk around the side of the building, and knocked. Leisurely footsteps sounded from within, the door opened.

I goggled at the little man in the doorway. It was difficult to believe that this was the fellow whose name had been jumping into the case so frequently and so unexpectedly at every crook and turn. He was a twisted, dwarfish chap, turnip-shaped, with big shoulders and a chest that dwindled away to scrawny thighs and tiny midget feet. His baggy black suit was rusty with age. A small, round baby head emerged from his tieless collar. He nodded and beamed and waggled his chin in an ecstasy of pleasure at seeing us. "Visitors!" he rhapsodized. "Visitors. Well, I do declare! Come in, gentlemen, come in. Old Eggleston gets so lonely!"

We walked into the workshop.

"Professor Eggleston," the Dean said politely, "I am Wardlow Rock, and this is Benton Matthews, my firebrand assistant. We're detectives. We've come for a bit of information. I understand that since you've retired from teaching you accepted the responsibility of the curatorship of the college museum."

Eggleston seemed pleased. "That's right. So you've heard of me? I'm curator. We're building up quite a valuable accumulation. It's slow work, but we're building it up. . . ."

The Dean sympathized. "Through bequests, eh?"

"That's right. Rich collectors die and leave us their collections."

We took in our surroundings. The workshop was bare, with a bench along one wall, a rack of nondescript tools. On a table in the corner was a screw press with an iron wheel. The Dean strolled over, said with interest: "Binding a book, I observe. You're quite a talented craftsman, sir."

"Rebinding a book, Mr. Rock." Professor Eggleston looked annoyed. "I'm bothered with deathwatches!"

The boss clucked his tongue, suddenly grinned at me. "Don't look so impressed, Ben. Deathwatch sounds macabre but it's simply the proper term for bookworm. When the beetles and their larvae get into a library, they can certainly devastate it. What is this book, sir? And may I ask how long you've had it?"

Eggleston was enjoying the sociability. "It's a rare and valuable volume from my personal library. I've had it for many years. It's a medieval lapidary."

"A lapidary?" The Dean was intent. "Tell me about it."

A great emotion suddenly filled the little professor. He tried unsuccessfully to conceal his excitement. "To you and your friend, jewels are baubles, ornate toys to embellish your garb. The ancients knew differently. Gems, gentlemen, are more than mere stones. They have power, power for good and evil. The wise ones, the scientists of ancient times, understood the ruby and the diamond and the emerald. However, they erred in attributing this inner power of gems to latent demoniacal influence. The scientist of the future will understand the true nature of the energy of gems! Take the mineral radium, sirs. Can anyone deny its brutal force?" He controlled himself. "To answer your question, a lapidary is a treatise on jewels and their peculiar influences on the human body."

The Dean bowed courteously. "A very enlightening discourse, Professor. Er—you say you've had the volume for quite some time?"

"Goodness gracious, yes. For twenty years at least. Everyone seems to ask the same question. Bogardus Keane and Miss Cowen were quite persistent on the point. Even Steve Saxby registered curiosity." Professor Eggleston's baby face broke into a rollicking, cherubic smile. "By the way, you said you are detectives. May I inquire why you honor me with your presence?"

"It's about Anna Morandi Manzoli, the Italian wax sculptress of the eighteenth century." The Dean chose his words carefully. "I've been informed that the college museum has an arm done by that eminent *artiste*. I thought perhaps, as curator, you might remember seeing this piece—"

Professor Eggleston rubbed his stumpy fingers. "You're on the right road, but you've the cart before the horse. You're no doubt referring to the Simpson collection. Mr. Simpson, an extremely wealthy manufacturer, and one of our most respected alumnae, passed away not long ago and left us his private collection. It's rumored that Simpson, among his other treasures, possessed a Manzoli arm."

"What do you mean, it's rumored? Haven't—"

"No, we haven't received the stuff yet. It should be along any day now." The Dean looked puzzled. "Most private collections have a catalog."

"That's true. Indeed they do. But Mr. Simpson considered catalogs barbaric and impersonal. He loved his art objects as though they were—"

The Dean spoke casually. "Generally, after a death come the appraisers. I wonder how Mr. Simpson's collection avoided such an invoice?"

Eggleston said helpfully: "It appears that Mr. Simpson was intending to erect a tiny museum on his estate. He had the stuff crated up, ready to move. Nobody bothered to unpack it. They're shipping it along to the college in the original crates."

We picked up our hats, prepared to leave. The Dean paused in the doorway. "I want to thank you for an edifying visit, sir. Believe me, I don't intend to run a subject into the ground, but this Simpson collection—did it contain any rare volumes, such as, say, lapidaries?"

The dwarfish little man contorted his neck affably. "I wouldn't know."

"Did it contain any priceless gems, such as rare historical emeralds?"

"Quite possibly." Professor Eggleston glowed happily. "We'll find out when the crates get here, won't we? Good day, gentlemen, good day."

Outside, on the sidewalk, I got my brain to working. We walked along a bit in silence. Finally, I said: "This job's shaping up fast, isn't it? Like you always claim, if you get enough facts the picture materializes all by itself. You know who I've been thinking about, chief? Sam the Switchman. I bet you ten to one he's got a finger in this somewhere. What say we drop in on him?"

"And just who is Samuel the Switchman?" The Dean laughed, added seriously: "No, Benton, this is no time to be introducing new personalities. Let's not fly off at tangents. Saxby, Eggleston, Keane and Cowen—three merry gentlemen and a lonesome maiden. Somewhere within this charming little group of cozy humans lurks the lethiferous motive which—" He cut his eye at me, remarked queerly: "Is it possible that you've reached some sort of conclusion so soon, that you've already solved the case?"

I looked innocent, said: "To quote lovable old Professor Eggleston, I wouldn't know. I'll give you a hint, though. How are you making out on that imitation emeralds formula? Break that down and you've got the motive."

"I've been trying to," the Dean said, nettled. "There's something devilishly elusive about it. I think I've got it and then it evades me. Frankly, I fear we'll have to garner a bit more information before it makes sense." We turned from the pavement, through a pair of low pink boulder gateposts, found ourselves on a broad, landscaped lawn. "The domicile of Mr. Stephen Saxby," the Dean announced gustily. "We shall now see what we shall see!"

It was a big, lumpish house of gray fieldstone and red Spanish tiles, set in a scraggly clump of silver poplars. It looked like money. The Dean took a dirty envelope and a pencil stub from his breast pocket, made a quick, swashbuckling crisscross of lines. "This is University Court, Ben. These are the residences of Keane and Miss Cowen. This is Saxby's. Here, where I make the X, is the late Miss Taggart's. On this corner, back here, is Eggleston's. Do you observe that our principals reside in a rough circle about the Taggart place? Let's always keep this diagram in mind." Before I could retort he was off up the drive.

I followed him onto the impressive flagstone porch. He dropped the knocker on its escutcheon, said from the corner of his mouth: "Hold on to your hat. Here we go again!"

III

S. Saxby's Secret Sorrow

The fellow that answered our knock was lanky, slight-framed, with the gaunt hatchet face of an incurable busybody. He had a lock of tousled hair over his bony forehead, an oversized aristocratic, chisel-bladed nose that flared into two hairy nostrils over a fussy, V-shaped mustache, and a team of hungry little brown eyes that skipped ceaselessly over you, here and there, never meeting yours, always checking and analyzing and estimating. I wouldn't have trusted him to run up to the drugstore and bring back the deposit on a pop bottle. He was wearing a showy, quilted dressing-robe and had a stag-and-hound meerschaum drooping from his clenched jaw. He waited hostilely for us to explain ourselves.

The Dean said pleasantly: "It's a beautiful afternoon, isn't it, Mr. Saxby? May we step in a moment? We've come to certify you."

Saxby's malevolent little brown eyes bugged out. "Certify me? Who the hell are you, anyway? You mean you think I'm balmy?"

"Ah-ah-ah!" The boss shook a reproving finger. "We didn't say that—yet. There have been reports, you know, and—ahem—complaints. We're employed by Mr. J. Bogardus Keane. He asked us to sort of—er—examine you. The procedure is perfectly painless. It's rather like a guessing game. May we . . ."

Saxby's rodent lips writhed in fury. When he spoke, his voice was icy calm. He said: "So Keane's behind this? Just come inside, please. I'd like to do a little examining on my own."

We entered a small ante chamber. Inside, the house didn't seem so grand —it was jerry-built, flashy but cheap. The rug on the floor was imitation Oriental. To our left, the staircase ascended upward to the second floor. The massive newelpost with its ram's-horn was imitation mahogany, and so was the banister. It was here in the hallway, alongside a cheap reproduction of an antique grandfather's clock, that we saw our first prizefighter. This was something different—a genuine collector's item. The Dean strolled forward and examined it with interest. Matted in the center of a rather large gilded frame, it hung exhibition-height, about on the level with your eyes. It was the picture of a barrel-chested boxer, an old-timer, with handle-bar mustaches. He was dressed in tight pants, naked above the waist, and held his fists raised stiffly in a boxer's guard.

"Figg!" The Dean exclaimed. "The king of the bare-knucklers! That's a nice print, sir. Gracious, I'd like to own it!"

Saxby said: "This way, please."

We turned right, through an archway, and followed our host into a great parlor. Same old tawdry imitation of wealth—huge imitation marble fireplace, more imitation Oriental rugs. In this room, there were more prizefighter pictures, one on each of the four walls. We passed through the parlor, through an open door at the rear, and found ourselves in Mr. Saxby's cut-rate den.

The cubbyhole was offensively swanky. Goat hides on the floor, a bookcase loaded with gaudy bindings, mail order mooseheads and Indian blankets. Suddenly, I realized that Saxby had run out of prizefighters. There were no boxing pictures in the den.

Our hatchet-faced host gestured us rudely to chairs, sat down confronting us. "So you're hirelings of Beanie Keane's, eh? So now he's trying to sock me in the nut foundry! First he steals my gal and now he's trying to—"

The Dean cleared his throat insinuatingly. "We're men of justice and honor. And ethics. We desire to represent only the most worthy of clients." He rolled his eyes, added slyly: "For a minor increase in honorarium we can be persuaded to, well, shift our allegiance."

Saxby shook his head. "No soap. You don't scare me. There's no reason for me to deal with you at all. Here's the set-up, as I get it. Keane and Marcia came to you, asked you to fiddle around and frighten me off. To tell the truth, I don't give a hoot or the kid any more, but I don't like being pushed around. We're engaged, I've got letters to prove it, and I'm damned if I'm going to release her under pressure. Men can sue for breach of promise, too, you know!"

The Dean assumed a wheedling attitude. "Why not forget the girl entirely? Why not sign a paper I've got here in my pocket, rejecting all claims on her? Be a good sport. Don't force us to publicize your—er—eccentricities."

Saxby purpled. "Eccentricities! So that's the frame-up. I'm as sane as you are."

"Miss Marcia doesn't say you're completely gone. She feels, however, that it's sneaking up on you. She seems to feel that Professor Eggleston is somehow upsetting you. A healthy young man like you under the spell of an old crackpot like—"

"I'm not under anyone's spell, and Marcia damn well knows it!" Saxby's jaw pivoted from side to side in suppressed rage. "Such nonsense! How can she say such things! She associates with the professor as much as I do, and lately, more. As a matter of fact, it was at one of the professor's Hello-Neighbor parties that she met that fat slob, Beanie Keane!"

"Just a second," the Dean put in. "I don't quite follow you. What's this about Hello-Neighbor parties?"

"It's a goofy name, isn't it? Just the kind of idea an academic recluse would dig up. Some weeks ago a handful of us University Court residents received notes from Eggleston. He said that he was getting lonesome in his old age and was ashamed of not knowing any of his neighbors any better. He suggested that we gather at his house once a week for old-fashioned corn-popping and horse-and-buggy sociability. Well, we felt sorry for the old boy and accepted his invitation. We've been meeting ever since. Had a meeting last night, as a matter of fact. Pretty boring, but it seems to cheer him up."

"Last night?" The Dean arched his eyebrows. "Then he showed you the book he was binding?"

"He didn't show it to me—I happened to notice it. Funny thing about that book. He says the bugs are getting in his library and that he's rebinding it to protect it. Well, for one thing, he's got at least a thousand volumes. One at a time like that is ridiculous. Secondly, you don't strip the back off a rare book, as you would a banana peel, to 'protect' it. That's sacrilege and would completely devaluate it. However, if you had a stolen book, say with a name or other identifying marks on the end-papers, you might find it advisable to do just that—rebind it."

The Dean wasn't listening. He asked casually: "About this Hello-Neighbor Club, it actually fascinates me. By any chance did the late Miss Taggart belong to your little group?"

"Yes." Saxby nodded. "She did. Eggleston organized it just after she'd had all those unfortunate doings at her home. At the time, we all suspected that he was really thinking of her, that he was attempting to cheer her up through her period of adversity. When she died from too many sleeping powders, we all chipped in and bought her a big wreath. Now, we don't much miss her."

"Nor she, you." The Dean grinned. "Well, Saxby, though I wouldn't want to be quoted, you seem perfectly sane to me. My personal advice is that you release the girl to Bogardus if you really want to get even with her. But you seem to have contrary opinions on the subject. By the way, off the record, you know she can make out a pretty good case of lunacy against you. She claims you're entertaining delusions that you're a treasure-hunter, that you've been out mapping the surrounding community."

"That's true. I like charts. They're my hobby."

"Phooey, sir!"

Saxby smiled wryly. "Take it or leave it."

"We'll leave it for the time being. Now, Miss Marcia Cowen is most concerned over these prizefighter pictures which embellish your halls and chambers. She declares that she's quizzed you on this point and you respond that you've suddenly taken an interest in old-time bare-knuckle boxing. "Now why did you hang these boxers? There must be a reason. What is it?"

Saxby looked embarrassed. He said quietly: "I'm going to do a strange thing, I'm going to tell the truth. I've got a quirk in my brain, had it ever since I was a kid. I've got to be a bigshot, put on the dog. I have a small income and I spend it all on front. I picked up this house for a song. It's a rat-trap, an orange crate. It looks good on the outside but in here it's cheap as hell! Floors sag, baseboards don't meet, and so on. I try to cover everything up but it seems as though every few days something else goes bad on me. I had those old prints up in a trunk. They're mementos of better days. I was forced to get them out and put them to work. Take a look at this."

We followed him into the parlor. He swung a picture out on its wire, gave us a glimpse behind it. The plaster had crumbled from the laths in a patch as large as your hand. He replaced the frame. "If I have it replastered I'll have to have the entire room repapered, and the same out in the hall. And I don't have the kale. It would be torture for me to stare at those tenement house blemishes!"

The Dean asked: "How long has it been since these walls got this way? You imply that it happened rather abruptly."

He took us to the front door. "Abruptly, hell. The Saxby mansion has been slowly disintegrating ever since I moved in. To answer your question, I should say those walls went bad on me about a month or so ago. I remember it was while I was attending one of Professor Eggleston's parties. Keane and Miss Cowen walked as far as the gate with me. I asked them in for cake and coffee but they declined. When I got inside, I was glad they didn't come. I would have died of mortification if they'd witnessed my actual poverty."

The Dean said gently: "My friends somehow enjoy looking at cracked walls and patched wallpaper. I guess they just don't know any better. Good afternoon, sir."

All the way back to town, the chief seemed smugly self-satisfied. I grabbed the old pump handle and got to work on him but the more I questioned him, the tighter he clammed up. Finally, I said: "Boss, I've changed my mind. Eggleston's out and Saxby's in. Yep, Saxby's our baby. You know that patch of bare lath behind the picture he showed us. Let me tell you something. That plaster didn't fall off—it was chiseled off. Saxby removed it himself!"

"It's a man-made job, all right," the Dean agreed. "But it brings up a delicate problem which we'd better not go into just at this moment." He came to a stop at the curb, said: "You go back to the apartment. I'm half expecting our clients to make a return visit. Not in pairs, this time, but in singles. I have a feeling that they were—er—inhibited this afternoon by each other's presence. Take them as they come, find out what they have to add to their original story, and give them the bum's rush. I'd rather they'd not meet." He paused. "And keep an eye peeled. It might interest you to learn that we're in deadly peril. I'll be along shortly. Just a little stroll to settle my nerves—and I'll join you."

Nerves. He had no more nerves than that wax arm in Captain Kunkle's straw suitcase. Always, when a case really got rolling and the pressure began to gather, he'd amble off and leave me hanging on to the safety valve. He had friends in all walks of life, folks I'd never seen—bartenders, elevator operators, newsboys. When he needed some particular tidbit of information, he'd fluff me off and do his circuit alone. He usually came back with the dope, too. I never asked him where he'd been. Confidential information was just that to the Dean, and wild horses couldn't force him to betray a friend.

All at once, I had an idea. I put on an act. "I'm just a bond-boy," I griped. "Just a peon. Go back to the apartment, he says loftily, and I needs must fly. I'm nothing but a robot, and he's the master carrying my brain around in his watch-case." I groveled, asked servilely: "And which route must I select on my return, sire? Shall I go by Cherry Street or shall I go by Fourth?"

He said frostily: "Quit clowning. Go any way you like. This is no time for amateur theatricals, this is murder!"

So I returned home via Dorrigan's Alley.

Of course it was ten blocks or so out of the way, but Sam the Switchman kept shop in Dorrigan's Alley.

The neighborhood was bleak and grim, squalid with run-down eateries and cut-throat hockshops. Tenderloin—and lowgrade tenderloin at that. The setting sun struck through the cloud splits in the sodden sky, painted the shabby storefronts in lavender-and-rose in the exact irridescent tint of putrifying meat. The sidewalks were deserted. Here, the denizens didn't leave their holes until nightfall. I only hoped I came out of this all right. The Dean had one strict rule—no free-lancing on my part—and I knew he'd really melt my ears down if I bungled it. I turned at a dingy second-hand clothing emporium, and entered the brick-paved channelmouth of the alley. I'd peddled papers as a kid and since then, in one way or another, I'd knocked about our fair city until I knew it pretty well. This was one section I kept away from.

Dorrigan's Alley was plenty mean.

Just a half-block long, and dead end, it was a warren of filthy flats, dead-falls and hideouts. A sullen double row of blank, blistered doors set in the windowless brick facing. I picked my way through the littered trash, the foul ashcans and the stinking refuse, and began counting doors. The Switchman's, I'd heard, was on the ground floor of Number Seven—down toward the end of the line.

The guy's real name was Sam Franzell and he was one of the town's leading fences. The story, as I'd gotten it, was that he was strictly upper bracket, that if there was any big stuff floating around you could bet that the Switchman had taken a peep at it. He was reputed to be as cagy as a vixen—and dangerous.

I twisted the nicked china doorknob, stepped into a dank hall lit by a feeble, fly-specked bulb. If Mr. Saxby was allergic to cracked plaster and stained wallpaper, he should have seen this place. I walked the length of the vile corridor, knocked at the door at the end of the hall. A cheery, melodic voice sung out an invitation to enter.

* * *

The Switchman's office was rigged up like a flophouse bedroom. The warped floorboards were bare of rugs, there was an iron-pipe bed, a dresser with peeled veneer, a kitchen table—and a safe. Like I said, safes used to be my profession. This box stood in the corner and was of the vintage of the Spanish-American War. Beside the safe was a closet door.

Franzell was seated at the table. He was a sloppy-looking fat man, unshaven, with a wet, pendulous under-lip and smoky green eyes. His fawn shirt was wrinkled and dirty and he was dressed in a shoddy gray suit, like a respectable tradesman in hard luck. He had a deck of cards in his hand and was dealing out a little Canfield. There was a score-pad by his elbow. He dropped the cards on the tabletop, wheeled around on his chair seat and asked: "You the rent collector?" His rich baritone was jovial, ingratiating.

I laughed. "Hardly. I got hot news for you. My brother-in-law sent me."

"Who," the Switchman asked blandly, "is this brother-in-law?"

"An old reliable customer of yours, Mr. Franzell. A guy that's got your best interests at heart. We'll let it stand at that. He's been here to see you many a time."

Franzell waited, deadpan.

For no reason at all, I kept worrying about that old-time safe. A big dealer like the Switchman would have a better box than that. I glanced about the walls. They were bare, no tell-tale pictures. Then I doped it. He had a floor-safe. He had a floor-safe—in the closet. I'd installed many a similar job myself in the past. I said: "This is for free, just to be sure we're being honest with each other, Mr. Franzell. A college professor named Eggleston is all set to make up a batch of phony emeralds. Does that make sense to you?"

Did it? He batted his eyes like a frog snapping at a horsefly. "No, friend, it makes no sense whatever. I never heard of anyone named Eggleston, and I'm not interested in emeralds, genuine or fake. However, as a token of mutual trust I give you Doctor Mary and Doctor John. How are we doing?"

I frowned. "Not so good. I don't get it."

The Switchman fingered his juicy hanging lip in reverie. "Let's go back to the beginning. I'd dearly love to hear a bit more about this brother-in-law. Just who did you say he was?"

"Sorry. No can do. He's just a gink that trades with you. Once you did him a favor—now he wants to even things up." I lowered my voice, spoke urgently: "The cops are wise. They know you've been tampering with the Simpson collection. They don't know how you did it, but they know you've managed somehow to get to it! If you've still got the stuff in your possession you'd better put it back where it came from, and quick. The law's about ready to crack down!"

Franzell shook his flabby jowls sorrowfully. "I swear on my dear mother's grave that I've never heard of the Simpson collection. Frankly, I consider it a figment of your enterprising imagination. I believe I finally make you. You almost fooled me for a moment. You're just another live-wire sharpshooter trying to move in on me! It's an old story to me, son. And, as usual, I've got a good answer. I'm going to hate to do this, but a man in my position, you know—I've got a reputation to keep up . . ."

While he was rambling on, I happened to take a gander at the pad on the table by the deck of cards. He hadn't been totaling his Canfield wins—it was a pinochle score, for two players! One column was headed *Me,* that was Franzell, and the other said *Virgil.* I'd busted into a sociable little game. And where was Virgil?

I thought I knew, and I didn't enjoy the thought. Virgil was behind me, in the clothes-closet, no doubt holding a bead between my shoulderblades. I decided to scram. I said carelessly: "You got me wrong, Mr. Franzell. I'm trying to be a pal. If you feel that way about it, I'll be going. So-long. I've said my piece. You don't seem to relish my presence—"

"But I do!" The fat man smiled nastily. "I do relish your presence. In fact, I'm going to request that you remain." He raised his voice, called softly: "Oh, Virgil. I seem to be needing you."

There was the sound of footsteps behind me. I half turned my head, got a glimpse of the open closet filled with coat-hangers and dirty linen, saw Virgil ambling toward me.

I know a gunman when I see one. This specimen was crying for trouble. He was the smart-aleck type, and that's the worst, resplendent in flashy tweeds and with a fancy marcelled hair-do that had everything but ribbons and perfume. He held a big-caliber automatic in his bony, effeminate hand. He ignored me, asked: "What's on your mind, Mr. Franzell?"

"Take him out to the quarry."

Just like that. No arguments, no long sermons. I began to sweat. I said calmly: "O.K., let's go, Virgil. I want to talk to you."

The dapper gunman smirked. "What you want to tell me?"

"I want to talk to you about my brother-in-law. He's got quite a noodle on his shoulders. Ben, he says to me, the Switchman's a funny one. Take a big-shot fence like Franzell—imagine all the dough he has to keep on hand! Yet he's only got a tin-can safe that you could open with a tackhammer. It isn't logical, he says."

Virgil was entranced. He nudged me with his gun muzzle. "I ain't interested. Let's get going." His tone was nervous, excited.

I went on. "My brother-in-law is a good friend of Mr. Franzell's, but he's quite a curious fellow. Every time he's been here, he sort of cases the place. The safe there in the corner, he thinks, is a blind. The money's hidden somewhere else. Where? Well, my brother-in-law favors the clothes-closet. He says—"

Virgil cut me off. "On your way, bud. Let's get going." He spoke in a monotone but he couldn't conceal a note of eagerness.

Franzell made up his mind. His big, mobile face had been twisting itself in indecision. "Put the gun away, Virgil," he ordered. "We'll give him another chance. I just wanted to show him I mean business." He addressed me: "You —get the hell out of here! Keep out of my affairs! And tell that brother-in-law of yours to button up his big mouth before he catches himself some misery."

The Switchman's roly-poly face wasn't so merry now. His smoky green eyes bored into mine in cloudy hate. I said: "Methinks I will now promenade. Good day all."

When I hit the street, my armpits were wringing wet. It was a mighty close call in anybody's book, and I knew it.

IV

Highbrow Pocket Pool

Dusk had fallen by the time I returned to our apartment. From the light in the reception room window, I saw we had a guest.

J. Bogardus Keane, the retired self-styled tycoon, this time alone, was giving the poor folks an encore of his exalted personality. Obnoxious in his hound's-tooth plaids, he was posed on the loveseat as though it were a throne—elegant wrist poised on meaty thigh, his big red chin ensconced impressively in the cupped palm of his other hand. No telling how long he'd been holding the position. He looked as if some serf had swiped his crown and scepter and someone was going to get scolded. His head reared back as I entered, his tiny porcelain eyeballs popped open in their little sacs of withered skin. He said angrily: "You've kept me waiting twenty-four minutes and thirty-one seconds!"

I used one of the Dean's favorite tricks. When clients got high-horse with him, he put them in the old mortar and ground them down to a fine powder. I said absently: "Oh, hi there, whatchumacallit! Come back tomorrow. This is our busy day."

That rocked him. He changed his manner to a wheedle, said: "I'm Mr. Keane, remember? I paid you a fifty-dollar retainer this noon. You're work-ing for me, don't you recall? Miss Cowen and I—"

"The lady, I remember—you, I forget. What's on your mind?"

"Ah, yes. Sweet Marcia!" He tried unsuccessfully to appear boyishly bashful. "What a lucky chap I am to be favored by her tender affection! Which happens to bring me to the point of my visit. On our earlier call, under the stress of emotion, Miss Cowen got her story a bit jangled. Now if you're going to help us, and her in particular, I felt that I'd better drop by and straighten things out—just for the record. You see—"

"Make it snappy. This is after closing hours. I'm getting ready to lock up." Closing hours, I thought. What a blissful pipedream!

He could talk fast and sensibly when he had to. "It's this. I believe Miss Cowen stated that these little visits she's been paying to Eggleston's—you know, the button-sewing and patching and so forth—were our idea, her's and mine. It's an act of sacrificing charity on her part and I only wish I could share in the glory. However, the actual facts are a bit different. I have the definite impression that these calls were started at the professor's instigation, not Miss Cowen's. Maybe a phone call, maybe a note. The professor's a great note writer—"

"What about the old man's puppy love?"

"That part's true enough. He begins throwing calf eyes every time she heaves into sight. Another thing—he has his own goofy pet name for her. She says whenever they're alone he always calls her Doctor Mary. It's so strange it scares her. He just ogles her and it's Doctor Mary this and Doctor Mary that!"

"No kiddin'? Does he, by any chance, refer to you as Doctor John?"

Keane looked irritated. "Never. I'm a man, sir. Men don't call each other by pet names. I'll be extremely relieved when you people get this all cleared up. I didn't say so this noon, but I feel sinister forces at work. There's much more here than shows on the surface. I'm getting the gradual impression that the goings-on out at University Court, the Hello-Neighbor Club and all that, are somehow linked with that Taggart tragedy! I feel that perhaps there's more to come!"

"And what," I asked sternly, in the Dean's best manner, "and what brings you to that morbid conclusion?"

"There's a man in our neighborhood who has been spying on us all. This person has been sneaking around, prying. He's been in my backyard, and in Marcia's, and no doubt Professor Eggleston has seen him prowling about on his premises, too. When he's confronted and questioned as to his disgusting behavior, he laughs brazenly and spouts nonsense about searching for treasure. Please don't ask me to name him. He's an old beau of Marcia's and I feel it would be more proper to keep him anonymous."

"You mean Saxby?" I yawned. "You told me all about him before."

"Gracious! Did I? Did his name slip through my lips?" Keane got to his feet. "I'll be getting along. Er—I never hired detectives before. What's the customary time, I mean how long before I can expect results?"

I ushered him to the door, said as he departed: "An inferior agency can usually crack a simple case like this in about three months. We're twice as good as most agencies so we should be able to do it in twice the time. Give us six months and I guarantee—"

He stamped down the hall, puffing and snorting.

It was the Dean's habit, when a tough case really began to barrel, to forego all thought of food. The Lord only knows how many meals I've skipped since I've been with him. Bearing this in mind, I took advantage of the lull which followed the exit of J. Bogardus. I retired to the kitchen, tossed up a stack of sandwiches and brewed a pot of coffee. I'd just placed the grub on the table when the chief came in through the back door. Without a word of greeting, he pulled up a chair, sat down, and cleaned the platter before I realized what was happening. By sheer luck, I salvaged a child's portion for myself. I wrestled him for the coffee pot, said angrily: "Hey!"

"I need sustenance, Benton," he explained amiably. "I've been out on the campus, poking around in cellars and so on. I found it. It was back in a sort of sub-basement under the old abandoned Library Building. Gad, it was a sight to behold! I phoned Malloy, disguised my voice, and reported it. Has Bogardus Keane been in?"

I nodded.

"The girl?"

"Nuh-huh. Not yet."

He yanked out his huge antique silver watch. "We'll give her a quarter of an hour. And then we must be off. Things are crystallizing. It's about all over now. It's a peculiar affair. I know who, but I don't know why!"

I saw he was trying to suck me in but I couldn't help it. I asked: "What did you find in the basement of the College Library? Another corpse?"

"You need a bromide," he declared solicitously. "You're developing acute necrophilia." We heard the *clickety-clack* of spike heels in the corridor. "There's Miss Marcia Cowen. And she sounds like she's loaded for bear!"

We reached the reception room just as she came steaming through the door. That fake attitude of helpless feminine humility had completely disappeared. Her boyish little figure was tense. She asked curtly: "Has Mr. Keane been here?"

"Beanie?" The Dean knotted his brows. "I haven't seen him. If he came, I was out. Why?"

She looked relieved. "I'm glad I got here first. If you should see him and he has anything to say, don't believe it. I swear, I have the worst luck with my men. Steve Saxby goes lunatic on me and I shift to Beanie. Beanie welcomes me with open arms, so to speak, and at first we get along O.K. The last few days it's been different. I've had the queer sensation that he's using me somehow, that I'm a kind of a tool. Golly, I think I'll go hogwild and marry Old Eggleston!"

The Dean appeared mildly amused. "You feel Mr. Keane is using you? In what way?"

"It's hard to explain. Take Steve Saxby. Beanie rants and raves over him and asks me dozens of questions about him. At first I put it down to jealousy but he's so persistent that sometimes I get the idea he's not really envious at all, that he's just pretending, using that as an excuse to quiz me about my ex-fiancé. I even get the impression that he doesn't care for me at all and that his only interest in me is my previous relationship with Steve. Now Professor Eggleston comes in for abuse. It's the same thing all over again, like with Steve. What did the professor say to me, how did he act, did he give me any presents?" Her delicate jaw went hard.

"I'm not particularly adept in the field of domestic relations," the Dean said timidly, "but I can't help wondering why, if Beanie's so nauseating, you don't boot him out of your pretty little life?"

"And go back to Steve Saxby? Hardly!" She looked suddenly frightened. "Steve's essentially a dangerous man. He's vindictive and he holds a grudge. Like I keep telling you, he's stark, raving mad! What do you think of this?" She opened her pocketbook, handed the chief a sheet of note-paper. He laid it on the table, studied it. I joined him.

It was a diagram made in heavy pencil. There was a longish rectangle and on the inside of the rectangle, diagonal lines cut crisscross from one side to another. At the corners of the rectangle, and halfway down each side, were small circles. Down at the bottom of the paper was written: *Mercator's Projection, 19 feet above sea level. Scale one quarter inch to one foot. S. Saxby, cartographer.*

"What in the heck is it?" I asked.

The Dean was befuddled. "Believe it or not, it's a map of a pool table! This heavy rectangle is the table, these little circles are the pockets, these lines must represent banks or caroms. I can't seem to figure it. This Mercator's Projection, sea level, and so forth, is all malarkey, of course, to confuse the issue." Suddenly he grinned. "Gad! I've got it. Think of that!" He turned to the girl. "How did this come into your hands?"

"One night, some weeks ago, while I was still going with Steve, I dropped in to visit him. He had a cold and was back in his study amusing himself by working on this. When I left, I hooked it. I don't know why, except I guess even then I realized his mind was buckling."

"Does Steve have a pool table?"

She shook her head.

"Do you?"

"Heavens, no." She considered. "Beanie Keane has one, up in his attic. It's past the state of being usable. The cushions are no good, the felt is all torn. Why?"

The Dean was brusque. "I must ask you to leave now. Here are my final instructions. Be at Steve Saxby's tonight at nine. And bring Mr. J. Bogardus Keane."

She faltered. "Beanie won't come. He loathes—"

"I don't mean for you to put a halter on him and drive him there. Just phone him that you're spending the evening with your ex-fiancé. He'll come galloping up, tossing his mane, flinging his fetlocks. And don't tell anyone you've been here."

After she had gone, I began to gripe. "Now it's a map of a pool table! Before it was a wax arm, imitation emeralds, and the mystery of a third andiron!"

He looked disgusted. "Are you still harping on that third andiron? Andirons come in sets of two. It's never been the mystery of the third—it's actually the mystery of the fourth! Where is the extra one?"

I was just about to tell him about Keane's visit and my adventure with Sam the Switchman when Lieutenant Bill Malloy walked in on us.

Malloy had an ominous cat-and-the-canary gleam in his eye, as though he finally had the Dean just where he wanted him. He said softly: "I'm glad I caught you in, Rock. Remember that Manzoli arm the skipper had, the one that was found on the doorstep of the lunchwagon out at University Court? Well, there have been developments along that line. Would you be interested?"

The Dean nodded eagerly. "Indeed I would. What—"

"After we left you this noon, the skipper checked on your story. He found out that the arm was really a museum piece, like you said, and that it came from the collection of a man up-state, a rich hombre, recently deceased, named Simpson. This Simpson, it appears, left his art treasures to the local college. We got in touch with the university museum and they informed us that the stuff was no doubt in transit, was expected daily."

"Gad. Think of that!"

"Yep. Well, tonight comes the payoff. The janitor of the college phones us that he's discovered some big boxes in the basement of the Library Building. We go out and find this Simpson collection. The crates had been ripped open, the stuff laying around on the floor. We haven't been able to learn as yet if anything's missing—other than the arm, of course. How does it sound?"

"Very intriguing, I must admit." The Dean seemed entranced.

"You haven't heard it all, at that." Malloy grinned. "The college janitor told us he hadn't phoned."

"Maybe," the Dean suggested suavely, "it was the assistant janitor, Lieutenant."

"Maybe it was. I'd like to have a talk with him. He used such fancy language—all loaded with expressions like Jove! and Gad!"

"Jove, sir!" the Dean exclaimed. "I can hardly believe it."

"Rock," Malloy said quietly, "how did you find that cache? The express company says it was delivered last week and signed for by a Dr. Douglass. There's no Douglass on the faculty. What does it all mean?"

"It's the sequel to those deaths two months ago, out at Miss Taggart's. It means murder!"

Malloy flinched. "The Taggart case again, eh? I hoped that mess was settled with the old lady's suicide."

The Dean scoffed. "Suicide. Phooey! You're just taking the easiest solution. Listen, according to you, either the two victims committed suicide or they were slain by their hostess. Who, in that case, committed—oh, baloney. It was murder, three times. Miss Taggart was a victim—not a killer."

"And the slayer's still at large?" Malloy was hesitant. "I can't say that I agree. The old lady must have done it. Here's why. Recall the old lady took her cat, Ophelia, out for a stroll every evening about eleven? The conclusion was that the shots let loose while she was gone. Perhaps. But—we asked a few questions around the neighborhood. This so-called walk Miss Taggart always took wasn't a real walk at all, just a turn up to the corner and back. Grant that the pistol went off while she was out of hearing. Even then she must have returned right on the heels of the detonations. According to you, the killer must have been in the house at that moment. And he must have stayed. Remember he rifled the bodies and burned wallets and such—that takes time."

"Could be, Lieutenant."

"Unlikely. Here's the reason. The old lady always locked all the doors from the inside with turned keys. The keys were untouched the next morning. The windows have old-fashioned clamps that hold them half open. No chance of a prowler escaping there. And furthermore, the old lady was a light sleeper. Her room was on the ground floor at the foot of the stairs. She was hopped up over having strangers with her and swore she didn't sleep a wink, said that the upstairs hall and the staircase squeak at the slightest provocation. She heard absolutely nothing."

"Maybe," the Dean said, leering horribly, "maybe he's still there! Living in the cabinet under the kitchen sink. A loathesome creature, ragged, bearded, creeping out at night, stalking through the old mansion to stretch his legs. Half-man, half-ape, living on rats and moths and bats!"

Malloy looked shocked. "That's no way to talk!" He picked up his hat, arose.

The Dean said: "Don't go away mad. Actually, Lieutenant, it's about finished. Meet me tonight at nine, at Steve Saxby's out in University Court. Bring Professor Eggleston. We shall see what we shall see."

V

Doctor Mary and Doctor John

The instant Malloy left us, and we were alone again, I got it off my chest. I gave the boss a detailed report of my experiences in the interim, while we had been separated. I started off with Keane and then, because I couldn't see any way out of it, I made a clean breast of the matter and related my adventure at the Switchman's. I expected him to fly off the handle in a tantrum of violent sarcasm—he was mighty temperamental about me free-lancing—but, to my astonishment, he patted me on the back as if I were a water-spaniel and said: "Good boy, good boy!"

All at once his eyes went blank. He looked as though he'd been socked on the skull with a maul. He said: "Do my ears deceive me? Did you say Doctor Mary and Doctor John? Did Malloy say Douglass?" He rubbed his jaw in trancelike concentration. "It's the master-key, Ben!" he exclaimed jubilantly. "Just a minute, please, while I make sure."

He hurried into the office, came back with a thick paper-bound volume. I got an upside-down look at the title while he thumbed the pages. *Catalog Historical Gems, Private Collections, Foundations, Etc. 1933–1943.* He found his place, read eagerly: "Doctors Mary and John Douglass. Private Traveling Collection. Lectures by Owners. Exhibits, preferably academic, can be arranged by contacting owners, Two Stag Ranch, R.F.D. 2, Meadville, Colorado." He closed the book, laid it on the mantelpiece. "That does it. Now we know the motive. That explains Professor Eggleston and his formula for imitation emeralds! And Steve Saxby's prizefighters! Let's go!"

Darkness had settled down over the desolate landscape by the time we paid our second visit to University Court. If the neighborhood had been dreary in daylight, it was downright sepulchral in the shifting moonglow.

We passed by Saxby's, and the sidestreet where Keane and Miss Cowen lived. I figured we were heading for Old Eggleston's, but we passed the professor's white brick cottage, too.

A block beyond Eggleston's, we turned left and, after three more squares, left once more. Abruptly, the chief stopped. "The Taggart house," he said quietly. "Keep your wits about you. Anything can happen from here on in!"

All afternoon we'd been skirting around it—finally, we'd come to case it. Two months had elapsed since the deaths. I couldn't believe it might hold any importance at this late date.

I didn't like its looks. A cumbersome old frame mansion, it sat back in a weedy lawn, waiting for the gentle hand of time to shove in its sagging roof. It must have been a knockout in its day but now its gingerbread scrollwork had rotted from the cornices, its clapboards were warped and cupped from the siding. I followed the boss across the unkempt yard to the rear. We stood a moment in the shadow of a grape arbor while he scrutinized the back of the building. He did it leisurely, studying the dilapidated facing from eaves to foundations.

Directly opposite us was a one-story summer kitchen built flush to the side. The kitchen roof sloped up twelve feet or so to a row of three second-story windows. Three black windows, like three missing teeth. I said: "We don't need to go in, do we? We can solve it by just peeping, can't we? Maybe we should have brought camp stools."

The Dean was unruffled. "Peeping, like everything else, has its place, my boy." He stepped into the moonlight and approached the summer kitchen. I tailed along.

The summer kitchen had no basement and there was a kind of lattice grille between the floor joists and the ground. The Dean reached down, removed a section of this latticework. He bent forward, threw the beam of his flashlight under the porch. "Ah," he said. "This is more like it." I stooped over, took a look.

There, on the ancient, spongy earth, lay the fourth andiron. An owl andiron—and beside it was a neat coil of hair-thin wire. "Well, well," I murmured. "Now we got it, what do we do with it?" The Dean straightened up. "We leave it where it is. Let's get inside. I want to see the murder room."

The lock on the back door was an old-time mortise job. I opened it with a dime-store skeleton key. Old houses have a queer, stale human smell. We went through a high-ceilinged kitchen, into the front hall. There, as Malloy had said, next to the parlor and at the foot of the stairs, was Miss Taggart's bedroom. We ascended to the second floor.

* * *

The murder room was at the end of the corridor and hadn't been touched since the slayings. It was a melancholy tomb—eighteen-ninety flowered wallpaper, a red rug, dusty knick-knacks and faded crayon portraits. The three andirons were still in the fireplace, and so was the patch of window screen. The bloody bedclothes were gone, of course, and the mattress had been turned over to hide the blemish. The Dean made straight for the window. I heard him chuckle. "Observe," he whispered. "Observe and ponder."

A small awning hook had been screwed in the center of the trim above the window. Smugly, he showed me the hole in the top of the upper sash. It was a tiny auger hole and if he hadn't pointed it out, I would have missed it. "From a legal point of view," he declared, "this is a momentous discovery. It proves that the murder was done by an outsider who, as a consequence, is still at large."

"How—how . . ."

"Miss Taggart came home and went to bed while the slayer was still in the house. The slayer anticipated this and had made plans for it. The shots were fired while she was away, the escape was made after she had retired. Now observe this window. It presents quite a problem for an escapee. It's old-fashioned and has no sash-weights. Little spring clamps in the sides of the sash can be adjusted to hold the window half open, not clear open—and half open isn't enough to permit the convenient exit of a fugitive."

"How did he do it?" It had me stumped.

"Quite simply. He used the andiron as a counterweight. He opened the window, fed his wire over the awning hook and through the auger hole, tied the andiron on it and lowered it to the ground. He'd doubled the wire so that later, when he was out, he could reeve it back to him. The loop-end he slipped on the finger lift at the bottom of the sash. The lower sash was thus held open for him. The screen, I might add, was pure genius. He was confronted with a screen, so he cut it out of its frame, laid it across the andirons in the fireplace and pretended to use it as a grate. Once outside, after he'd climbed down the kitchen roof to the ground, he pulled his wire back to him, the window lowered itself, and the spring clamps caught it, held it half open!" He smiled happily. "Wait till Bill Malloy hears of this!"

We descended to the ground floor. We'd started again for the kitchen when we noticed the portieres. Heavy mildewed velvet curtains, on a pole and rings, about a third of the way down the hall. Curiously, the Dean thrust forward an index finger like a rapier, parted them, and swung his flash beam into the opening. "Jove!" he exclaimed. "This is a treat! I didn't imagine any of these things had survived." He stepped inside. I strolled in after him.

We were in a small, musty room and such a room I'd never conjured up—

even in my wildest dreams. There was a Hindu *punkah* on the ceiling, a big Oriental divan in the corner piled with silken pillows. The walls were draped in rotting, purple brocade and everywhere were incense burners and *hookahs* and Asiatic brass lamps. I couldn't grasp it. I asked: "What is this? An opium layout? Did the old lady hit the pipe?"

"Nothing of the kind," the Dean retorted crossly. "This is a Turkish Corner. They were very much the vogue in faddish homes about the turn of the century. To us now it seems foolish and silly but the maidens of yesterday considered them very exotic and romantic. Miss Taggart's Turkish Corner, however, is getting a little on the putrid side."

I said: "It's very adorable and all that, but who does that foot belong to? That foot sticking out from those comfy pillows on the divan?"

We shoved the cushions aside, and uncovered the portly body of J. Bogardus Keane, deader than a nickel's worth of stew-meat. His forehead had been bashed in and I'm here to tell you he made a mighty repulsive corpse. He lay there spread-eagled, his tiny bird-eyes glazed, his sporty checked suit bagged and lumpy about his elbows and knees. I said moodily: "He knew this was coming—he just the same as told me so!"

The Dean showed no sympathy. "He brought it on himself! When you go messing around in murder, you can expect disaster to—"

"Ain't that the truth!" A cruel, husky voice spoke up from behind us. "Turn around—and slow!"

The Switchman and his dapper bodyguard, Virgil. And they weren't fooling. They were a couple of earnest tradesmen working on a project, and they were all set to do a professional job. They carried big-bore guns close to their hips in the best hoodlum style. Franzell brought his huge body to an easy stop, asked: "Why'd you knock off the stiff on the couch, there?"

The elegant Virgil, his hat back on his head so you could see his beautiful marcel, echoed his boss: "Yeah, why?"

The Dean said archly: "I'm a detective. If you wish to ask me questions I must ask you to deposit a retaining fee with Mr. Matthews, my assistant. If you're just a couple of gawking sightseers, fan out of here! We're busy."

In his own mind, the Switchman considered himself a big-shot. It was like slapping him in the face. He flushed. The Dean turned to Virgil, the dapper underling, said: "Evidently you are here for a purpose. As you, sir, are the best dressed, I presume you are the head-man and this ragamuffin is your servant. What brings you to this house?"

Virgil looked pleased and flattered. He patted his fancy hair-do, said: "I ain't exactly head-man. We're sorta partners. You see—"

Franzell cut him off viciously. "I'm the number-one man in this little party, my friend. And I'll ask the questions." He lashed out verbally at the Dean. *"Where's the rest of the Douglass collection?"*

"Oh-oh!" The Dean exclaimed. "I place you now. You're Franzell, the fence. Gah! You're a filthy looking specimen, I must say. I know all about you. I've been anxious to meet you."

The Switchman's jowls quivered in insensate rage. "You know all about me?"

"I do indeed. Two months ago a man and woman came to this old house and asked Miss Taggart, the owner, for a night's lodgings. These people were Doctor Mary and Doctor John Douglass. I, like yourself, am interested in gems, but from a slightly more honest angle. I've known about the Douglasses for years. They possessed a most valuable collection of historical jewels. They took this collection on tours, in person, and gave lectures to academic groups. How they happened to be here in town is another story."

Franzell sneered. The Dean continued: "About eleven o'clock on the night of their arrival, they were murdered in their beds. The slayer stole the gems and escaped through the window."

"Are you saying that I murdered these—"

"No. Not actually—but later you became involved. The killer, an amateur, wasn't certain just how to market his plunder. He selected a few less valuable items and contacted you. You beat him down so mercilessly on his blood money that he decided to hold back the rest until a better market came along. You wormed out of him where he had acquired them, but you didn't suspect that the batch you bought wasn't the sum total. Didn't suspect it, that is, until Mr. Matthews, here, visited you this afternoon and set you back on the trail. You came here thinking the slayer might have secreted them here in some hiding place—"

Franzell said: "Nuts! If these Douglasses were so important, why aren't they missed?"

"They are missed—out in Meadville, Colorado, at Two Stag Ranch. Their visit to town was obviously a side trip and went unreported." He paused, added: "Any way you twist it, you see, it's murder and you're an accessory after the fact. Now, I guess we'd all better be getting down to police head-quarters, eh?"

That did it. He was deliberately goading them. Virgil was nervous, unde-cided. Franzell was trembling, loose-lipped in fury. The big man broke first. He swung his gun muzzle and I went for the bulldog in my belt. It was like living in two worlds, a world of sound and a world of movement. The Dean's hand bent suddenly at the wrist and his big, blue Magnum came out from its shoulder-clip, firing as the gunsight cleared leather. Virgil got in two rounds and then the deep-throated .357 of the chief smacked my ear drums, three times, hand-running. Franzell's enormous body buckled and collapsed. A little purple blossom appeared on Virgil's cheek. He splayed his fingers, dropped to the floor as if he'd been blackjacked.

One second the racket was stunning, the next the room was dead still. The Dean said: "Ben?"

"Yes, chief."

He pointed to my short-gun, limp in my grasp, half out of my belt. "Touch that thing off. Fire a charge in the ceiling, son."

"In the ceiling? Why?"

"It's repressed. Relax it. It got to the party late—all dressed up and no place to go!"

I tried to take it but it was wormwood and gall to me. Sometimes I get to thinking I'm a little better than I am with a hand-gun and when I fall down he always rubs a pinch of salt into my wounded vanity. He does it for my own good, and I know it, but it's mighty hard to swallow. I said: "Let's get out of here."

Saxby met us at his front door as if we were a couple of typhoid carriers. His anemic, hatchet face twisted itself into an expression of extreme distaste. We edged by him into the hall, sauntered into the living room. Bill Malloy and the professor had not yet arrived. Marcia Cowen was perched daintily on the edge of the sofa, her handkerchief balled in her lap, her pretty eyes red-rimmed. It was obvious that our genial host had been working on her, trying to talk her into returning to him. A strange picture it was, the barnlike room with its cheap rugs and borax furniture, the domineering, pigeon-chested little man—and the weeping gal. I sat down on a pseudo-Duncan Phyfe chair, hooked my hat on my knee.

No one said anything. The Dean remained standing. He kept yanking out his watch, studying it. That didn't settle our nerves any. When the doorbell cut loose, we all jumped. Saxby left the group, returned with the lieutenant and Old Man Eggleston. Malloy was poker-faced, lowering. His dwarfish, bespectacled companion gazed about in dreamy confusion. The Dean said heartily: "Welcome, Professor. You're just in time. I'm about to explain the bizarre enigma of the arm of Mother Manzoli!" He addressed Miss Cowen: "Did you contact Mr. Keane?"

"I phoned," the kid said, "but I couldn't get an answer."

"Well, we won't wait. We might as well begin. It won't take long." The Dean began to lecture. "Two months ago, a Doctor Mary and Doctor John Douglass, possessors of a valuable gem collection, stopped in at the home of your neighbor, Miss Taggart, to spend the night. They were murdered in their beds, the killer escaped with the jewels. Later, as a safeguard, he killed the old lady, too. Somehow their identity got out to a closed group here in University Court. Maybe Miss Taggart remembered things about her guests and relayed them to her neighbors. Anyway, a pack of jackals got on the trail of the stones. Everyone spying on everyone else!"

Saxby listened gravely. Professor Eggleston said: "Tsk! Tsk!"

"It was you, Professor," the Dean continued, "who had the cleverest scheme, and if I hadn't come in when I did, doubtless it would have worked. It was this elaborate stratagem of yours, by the way, that revealed the whole unholy mess to me. We'll never know what your intentions were—I'm inclined to give you the benefit of the doubt and say that you were working for law and order in your own devious way. You knew that the gems had been stolen, for it was you, I imagine, who invited the Douglasses to town and sent them to Miss Taggart's for lodging. After the theft you set about after the recovery of the stones and the exposure of the criminal."

Eggleston looked bewildered.

"Don't deny it," the Dean said. "First you formed your Hello-Neighbor Club to get everyone together. You invited the girl into your home as a helpmeet—to pump her. This was all preliminary to your big plan. You knew the Simpson collection, a collection of some fame, was due to arrive in your custody. You put out the word to your friends. You carefully implanted in their minds the impression that you were about to loot it. Take the rebound book, for instance—even Saxby thought it was illegally acquired."

Malloy frowned. The girl started to speak, stopped. The Dean went on: "The Simpson collection arrived. You tore open the crates, took out the arm of Mother Manzoli, left it on the lunchwagon steps for the police to find and investigate. You wanted publicity. When the time was ripe, you would anneal a nice big imitation emerald and flash it surreptitiously to your Hello-Neighbor Club. That was the bait to bring the killer again to action. The thief's natural deduction would be that you had pilfered a priceless stone from the Simpson collection."

Professor Eggleston gave us all a toothy smile. "So I'm a murderer?"

"Of course not. You're evidently misunderstanding me. You're not even guilty of petty larceny. The wax arm is back where it belongs, the book you were rebinding is one of your own." He turned to Lieutenant Malloy. "Saxby's your man, Lieutenant. Watch him—he's a four-time killer!"

Saxby smirked. "Don't be silly! Where's your proof?"

"You prowled the neighborhood pretending to make treasure-hunting maps, spying on your friends. Keane suspected you, so finally you were forced to eliminate him."

"Proof," Malloy insisted. "You've not offered one single grain of evidence!"

The Dean herded them all into the den at the rear. "Wait here." He disappeared toward the front of the house, was gone a moment, showed himself again in the living room. "Keep your eyes on me," he called.

He walked to the picture on the wall, the picture of Dutch Sam, the prizefighter. Deftly, he lifted the print from the frame. Behind the mat was a mirror.

We stared at him as he worked. Abruptly, a startling thing happened. No sooner had he revealed the mirror than three other mirrors sprang up in its reflection. We found ourselves looking around three walls, through two rooms, into the front hall, at the staircase.

"There were no glasses over Mr. Saxby's boxing prints," the Dean remarked. "There couldn't be, because they had to be removable. He had it arranged so he could sit back there in the study and watch. It was a problem in angles of reflection and incidence—the same proposition afforded by a pool table. As a matter of fact, he used a diagram of a pool table to help him calculate."

Saxby said viciously: "So what? I can sit back here and watch my front door. Does that make me a killer and a robber? There've been so many murders going on, I'm scared of my life!"

"But you're not watching the front door," the Dean corrected. "You're watching—"

"The stairs, eh?" Malloy shook his head. "It's suspicious, all right, Rock. But it's no case!"

The Dean began to gripe. "Won't anyone let me talk? I've got important things to say. He's not watching the stairs, or the front door, either. *He's watching the newelpost!* He's got the loot hidden in the hollow of the newelpost!"

Saxby scrambled to his feet. Quick as a flash, Malloy had the cuffs on him.

The Dean picked up his hat. "Good night, Miss Cowen. May the Fates be more solicitous of your love-life in the future, And good night to you, gentlemen. I will now go home, bite my fingernails, and wait for the insurance company to mail me its customary percentage-reward."

Murder in the Red

Norbert Davis

I

The Tart from Kester Street

It was still raining when Dodd's taxi slid to the curb in front of the court-house. He pulled the collar of his coat up around his throat and sloshed quickly across the sidewalk, went three at a time up the long, broad flight of granite steps. He pushed through one of the revolving doors, went into the hall, puffing a little.

Meekins, Dodd's runner, was leaning against the wall under a square gold-lettered sign that said—*Room 101, Night Court.* Meekins was small and mild and nondescript, and the only cue to his age was the fact that he was bald and sensitive about it. He always kept his hat on whenever it was possible, and he had it on now, pulled down low over his weary eyes.

"You ain't any too soon," he said. "He's up now, and he's soundin' off again."

"What judge?" Dodd asked.

"Crane. He's new."

"Oh, hell," said Dodd.

"I don't know why you think you got to front for that screw-ball, anyway," Meekins said. "It ain't as if there was any dough—"

"Later, later," said Dodd, opening the door to 101.

It was a long, high-ceilinged room, brightly lighted with the spectator's seats in long, curving rows in front of the railing that separated them from the court proper. There were a few bedraggled people, sitting in the seats, and sure enough Riganov was up and sounding off again.

Dodd was a big man, tall and loose-jointed, with deceptively wide shoulders, and his feet made thudding echoes as he hurried down the aisle. He wore a pair of horn-rimmed glasses patched over the nose-piece with a strip of white adhesive tape, and his eyes were blue and blandly good-humored behind their rain-misted lenses. He had to fumble with the catch on the gate in the railing.

Riganov went right on talking, loudly. "I got a right! I got a right in the Constitution! It says so. It says free speech in the Constitution, and I'm a citizen and I got a right!"

Judge Crane was a thin little man, looking shrunken and pale in his black robes, and he was regarding Riganov with an air of mildly absentminded interest.

"Quite so," he said. "Quite so, Mr.—ah—Riganov. I flatter myself that I am as familiar with your constitutional rights as you are. However, the state —in this case, the municipality—has a right, also. It is known, generally, as its police power. Under that right, it has the power to forbid acts that endanger the safety of its citizens. No one objects to your holding meetings, but you can't do it on street corners where you block traffic and menace the safety of passers-by."

"It's a plot!" Riganov yelled. "You're just a fascist tool of the special interests—"

Dodd got through the gate and reached him. He caught one of Riganov's bent, thin shoulders, whirled him around, and slammed him down in a chair.

"Shut up!" he whispered fiercely. He straightened up then, smiling, apologetically, and said: "Your honor, I'm sorry to interrupt the court in this abrupt manner, but may I be allowed to speak for the defendant?"

"Who are you?" Crane asked mildly.

"My name is William Dodd, sir."

"Are you an attorney, Mr. Dodd?"

"No, sir. I'm a bondsman—the defendant's bondsman."

"That's interesting," said Crane, "but hardly relevant at this stage of the proceedings. You may well be the defendant's bondsman, but that doesn't give you any status in this court."

Dodd nodded. "I know that. I'm not acting in my professional capacity, your honor. I've furnished bond for the defendant several times, but I've never received any money for it. He's just a friend of mine."

"A philanthropic bondsman!" Crane said. "That's astonishing, Mr. Dodd. In fact, almost unbelievable. You've succeeded in arousing my curiosity. Go ahead."

Riganov popped out of his chair. "It's a plot! It's a filthy fascist plot to silence—"

Riganov had a shock of bushy black hair, and Dodd put his hand on top of it and pushed hard. Riganov sat down.

"Your honor," said Dodd in his most persuasive manner, "this man is the janitor in the building where I have my offices. He's slightly cracked on the subject of fascist plots, but other than that he's perfectly harmless."

"He's charged with holding an unauthorized meeting on a street corner, blocking traffic and disturbing the peace. I understand he has been arrested repeatedly for the same or similar offenses."

"That's correct," Dodd agreed. "But he's still perfectly harmless. He only does things like that because his wife beats him."

"Ah?" said Crane in amazement.

Dodd nodded earnestly. "She beats him. He has to express his defiance and independence and general manhood in some way, so he gets on a soap-box and yells at people."

Riganov didn't get up this time. Instead he wriggled forward in his chair and twisted his thin, brown face into a horrible grimace. "Any day, now," he said, "we blow up all courthouses!"

"All of them, Mr. Riganov?" Crane inquired, interested.

"Yes!" Riganov snarled dramatically. "All! This one here, I attend to myself personally. I put ten tons of dynamite in the cellar and then *whoom!* Nothing but a hole in the ground!"

Crane looked at Dodd. "That's a rather dangerous program for him to advocate."

"It doesn't mean a thing," Dodd insisted, glowering at Riganov. "He'd run like a rabbit if he saw a stick of dynamite."

"And jails!" said Riganov. "We let everybody out of jail and arrest all policemen and judges and put them in!"

"Your honor," Dodd said desperately. "I've known Riganov for a long time, and he never does anything but talk. He has a good job, and if he's put in jail he'll lose it."

"He doesn't sound very safe to me," said Crane.

Dodd said: "He's trying to get you to put him in jail, your honor."

"He has a good chance of succeeding," said Crane. "But just why does he want me to put him in jail?"

"His wife is here waiting for him."

Crane looked up at the audience. "If Mrs. Riganov is in the court, will she stand up, please?"

A woman sitting in the front row of spectators' seats stood up slowly. She was six feet tall, but she was so enormously broad she looked much shorter. She had a round, impassively smooth olive-skinned face and dark, narrowed eyes that had dangerous greenish flecks of light in them. She was hatless, and she wore an old man's overcoat fastened with a safety pin in front.

"Yes," said Crane thoughtfully. "I can understand that Mr. Riganov might have reason to be apprehensive if his wife disapproved of his actions."

"She outweighs him by a hundred pounds," Dodd said. "And she gets mad when he talks on street corners."

Crane stroked his chin. "Well, I'll tell you, Mr. Dodd. I appreciate your motives, and after seeing Mrs. Riganov, I'll discount a lot Mr. Riganov has said, because I can understand that he'd probably prefer the safety and quiet of a jail to having an interview with his wife in the privacy of their home. But nevertheless, in view of the defendant's record, I can't just simply dismiss his case. I'll put him under a hundred-dollar peace bond, Mr. Dodd."

"A hundred dollars?" Dodd said, swallowing.

"Yes. You may furnish it if you wish. Arrange it with the clerk."

"Thank you, sir," Dodd said glumly.

He arranged for the bond with the clerk. Riganov was still sitting in his chair with a look of dazed despair on his face, and Dodd hauled him up with a grip on one thin arm and steered him through the gate in the railing and on up the aisle. Mrs. Riganov padded quietly and sinisterly along behind them.

Safely out in the hall, Dodd let go of Riganov and said: "Now, listen, you. I—"

Riganov suddenly thrust against him, pushing him back into Mrs. Riganov, and darted frantically for the front door. Mrs. Riganov got Dodd out of her way by the simple method of cuffing him one alongside the head and knocking him into the wall. She went after Riganov in a deadly swift, ponderous rush and caught him just at the door.

Riganov squealed once. His wife took a good grip on the back of his collar and dragged him back to Dodd. Dodd was feeling gingerly of the ear that had stopped her slap.

"What?" Mrs. Riganov asked gutturally. "What happens in there?"

"He's loose—for the time being," Dodd explained. "I put up a peace bond for him."

"Peace bond? What is that? Money?"

Dodd nodded sadly. "And how. A hundred dollars. If he gets arrested again, I lose it."

"He makes speeches—you lose money?"

"That's it."

"He don't make speeches," said Mrs. Riganov. "He—don't—make—speeches." She emphasized her words by hitting Riganov four times—twice

on one side of the head and twice on the other. Riganov's head bobbed like
a punching bag.

Meekins came down the hall, making a cautious detour around Mrs. Riganov, and spoke to Dodd. "There's some more comin' in now. Women. We
ain't got any in this batch, so can I go out and have me a beer?"

"I guess so," said Dodd.

The prisoners came in through the passageway that led across to the jail.
There were six of them in charge of two matrons who looked enough alike
to be twins, and were almost as big as Mrs. Riganov. The prisoners filed
along toward the rear door of the night court with an air of dispirited
defiance—bedraggled drabs seined up out of the city's slums—all except the
last one.

Dodd stared at her unbelievingly.

She was swaggering along with her head up in the air and her hands in the
pockets of a fur jacket that had cost plenty of money. She was slim and very
young, and she had bronze-red hair and a pert, tip-tilted nose. She looked
like she knew just what she was doing and was very proud of herself for
doing it.

"That last one?" Dodd asked Meekins, watching her disappear through the
door.

"I thought so, too," said Meekins. "The coat is worth six months of what
you laughingly call my salary, but she wouldn't put it up for security, and
she hasn't got a dime cash on her, and besides she told me to scram."

"What's her name?"

"Tessie Smaltz—she says."

"What's the charge?"

"Soliciting. She must be dumber than hell. She talked back to a plainclothesman down on Kester Street, so of course he run her in."

Riganov coughed. "She stops me too."

Mrs. Riganov shook him viciously. "What? What?"

"Wait," Dodd said. "Wait, now. What's this, Riganov? That girl—Tessie
Smaltz—stopped you?"

"Yes. I am hurrying to make my speech, and she stops me and says, 'Wait a
minute,' and I say, 'I got no time, please,' and start to walk away fast, and she
stops me again and puts her fingers in my pocket to hold me, like this . . .'"

Riganov poked two fingers in the breast pocket of his coat to illustrate,
and his voice trailed off into a mumble. He opened his mouth and shut it
again, carefully.

Mrs. Riganov grabbed his wrist and hauled his hand out of his pocket.

Expertly she opened his clenched fingers. A flat red stone gleamed with incredible fiery brilliance against the grime on his palm.

"*Whooie!*" Meekins said in a reverent whisper.

Mrs. Riganov slapped her husband and then slapped him again, harder. "So! Taking jewelry from no-goods!"

"No!" Riganov wailed. "No, no! I didn't! I didn't know it was even there!"

"Let me see it," said Dodd.

"Give," said Mrs. Riganov.

Riganov handed the stone over. "But I didn't know! She puts it there when I don't know! I didn't—"

"Liar," said Mrs. Riganov, slapping him.

"Wait, now," said Dodd quickly. "What happened after she put her hand in your pocket?"

"I knock it away," said Riganov plaintively. "I am in a big hurry to make my speech. I don't say nothing else to her at all, and I don't even see her again until now. Honest!"

"Is it real?" Meekins asked in the same reverent whisper.

Dodd nodded. "Yeah. Get in there and pay her fine. Quick."

Meekins darted through the front door of the courtroom.

Mrs. Riganov pointed a finger. "You keep."

"Keep—this?" Dodd asked, holding up the stone.

"Is no good. Is no good to take jewelry from bum girls."

"Mama!" Riganov protested. "Mama, but—"

She slapped him. "Shut up. You come home. I fix you."

She dragged him down the hall. Riganov tried to hold back, wailing tearfully, but to no avail. Mrs. Riganov hauled him through the door and out into the night.

II

Vanishing Redhead

Meekins came out of the courtroom so fast his hat-brim was blowing up in front. He stopped beside Dodd, skidding his heels on the damp tile.

"Listen, boss! Sam Rudolph is in there. He got the clerk to call her case first, plead her guilty, and paid her fine without batting an eye. They're coming now."

"Rudolph," Dodd repeated thoughtfully. "What's he doing in a night police court?"

Meekins had no time to answer because Sam Rudolph and the girl with the bronze hair came out of the night-court entrance and started down the hall.

"Hi, Sam," said Dodd, getting in their way.

Sam Rudolph was a thin little man with a pouter-pigeon chest. He wore specially built-up shoes, but even they weren't enough to bring the crown of his carefully creased hat higher than the top button on Dodd's vest. He had a dark, sharply sallow face and a voice so gratingly unpleasant that it was rumored judges gave him his many successful decisions just to keep from having to listen to him any longer. He was a crack criminal attorney, with all that implied. The Bar Association had been following him around for years, but had never been able to catch up with him.

He tilted his head back and scowled up at Dodd. "Uh? Oh, hello, Dodd. Busy, now. Some other day."

"Wait a minute," said Dodd easily. "You've got enough time for me to say a word or two to Tessie, here, haven't you?"

"No!" said Rudolph, trying to get around him.

But the girl with the bronze hair pulled back on his arm, anchoring him. She looked even better at close range. She had a clear tanned skin and nice blue eyes that she had opened very wide now in a burlesque imitation of a baby stare.

"Oh, let's talk to the nice man. You *are* a nice man, aren't you?"

"Positively," said Dodd.

"Are you a reporter, too?"

"No!" said Rudolph sharply. "He's a bail bondsman. Come along."

The girl still dragged back. "But I want to see a reporter! I thought there were always reporters in courtrooms to take your pictures and things."

"This is night court, Tessie," Dodd said. "But you can talk to me. I talk to easily, even if I don't carry a camera."

Rudolph put his hand against Dodd's chest and shoved. "Now, listen here, Dodd! You stop annoying my client! I'm in a hurry—"

Outside, in the street, there was a sharp, cracking report that multiplied itself in fluttering echoes. Instantly after it there was another.

"Shots," Meekins exclaimed.

He darted for the front door with Dodd pounding heavily right behind him. They stopped for a second on the wet granite steps, staring both ways through the mist.

"There!" Meekins said, pointing to the left.

A tavern occupied the corner a half-block away, light showing orange and dim through its painted windows. Its front door was open now, swung wide, and a man lay flat on the sidewalk in the column of light that splashed through it.

"Hey!" said Meekins. "That—that looks like—"

"It's Riganov!" Dodd said.

He went down the steps in long, awkward leaps, skidded dangerously on the smeared sidewalk, and then hunched his broad shoulders forward and ran for the corner. Several of the saloon's customers had their heads poked cautiously out the door now, looking at the sprawled body on the sidewalk with stupid curiosity.

Riganov lay half twisted on his side, as though he had started to turn and got his legs tangled in the process. One arm was out limp beside him and the other was across his eyes, hiding his face.

Dodd knelt down beside him, swearing in a whisper. Gently he moved the arm that covered Riganov's face. All the animation seemed to have fled from it, and it was stiff as wax. There was a deep, slashed cut over the eyes, and the nose was flattened and slewed sideways. Blood mixed with rain ran messily down both Riganov's sallow cheeks.

Mrs. Riganov appeared silently and ponderously out of the wet darkness. She shoved at the tavern customers that had ventured outside to form a ring around Dodd and Riganov, knocking several of them aside.

"Get out! You get out!" She knelt beside Dodd and put one square, muscle-padded hand softly on her husband's shoulder. "He is dead?"

"No," said Dodd. "He's been knocked around plenty, but I can't find where any shots—"

"They don't shoot at him, they shoot at me."

Around the corner a siren sounded in a long dismal wail. Dodd stared at Mrs. Riganov. Her smooth face was as impassive as ever, but her eyes were all green now, as round and luminous as a cat's.

"You?" said Dodd.

"Yes. I leave him here while I go inside to get a beer. He cannot have a beer because he makes speeches after I tell him no. Two men come and hit him on the head and knock him down. I run out and chase them. They shoot at me." She touched a long rip in her overcoat, waist-high on the left side, and shrugged indifferently.

"They don't shoot so good, but they run good."

The ambulance on call at the police station whipped around the corner, skittering wildly on the wet asphalt, and bore down on them with the siren still wide open.

Meekins was standing on the runningboard, holding on to the door-post with one hand and the brim of his hat with the other. He hopped off when the ambulance pulled in to the curb.

"Is the little screw-ball dead?" he asked anxiously.

"No," said Dodd. "A couple of birds hammered him around with brass knucks. Got a concussion, I think."

The ambulance attendants were handling Riganov's limp body with expert precision. They lifted him quickly and gently on a rolling stretcher.

Mrs. Riganov stood silent and impassive, watching them.

Dodd pulled at her sleeve. "Did you recognize the birds that hit him?"

"No. I not see good. I find, though."

"What?" said Dodd.

"I find," said Mrs. Riganov. "Nobody hits my husband but me. Nobody. I find." She nodded her head once at Dodd and climbed into the back of the ambulance with her husband.

Dodd leaned in and called to the attendant. "Doc! Give him a private room and the trimmings. It's on me."

"O.K., Dodd. Roll her, Casey."

The back doors slammed shut, and the ambulance bored away into the night with another rising howl from the siren.

Dodd suddenly remembered Sam Rudolph and the girl with the bronze-red hair. He turned hurriedly to go back to the courthouse and nearly fell over Meekins.

"They beat it," Meekins said, divining the cause of Dodd's sudden move. "Rudolph had that green locomotive of his parked in front of the courthouse. She got in it with him, and they went off in a cloud of smoke."

Dodd squinted thoughtfully through the moisture that smeared the lenses of his patched glasses.

"You think them two birds were after that red rock Riganov had?" Meekins murmured.

"Maybe," Dodd said.

"You sure it's real? I didn't get a good squint at it."

"It's real. I can't tell whether it's flawed or not, without a glass, but it's a swell job of cutting."

"Ruby?"

"Yeah."

"Boy, oh, boy!" said Meekins. "Oh, boy! Do you suppose the dame really slipped it to Riganov like he said?"

Dodd nodded. "Yes. He wouldn't have tried to sell his wife such a goofy story if it hadn't been true. Anyway, you could tell from his face that he didn't know it was in his pocket until he reached in there."

"Do you suppose," said Meekins, "that the dame has any more like that? Do you suppose she'd maybe hand us over a half-dozen or so if we asked her pretty?"

"I'd like to know," said Dodd.

"And me," said Meekins. "And how! Hey, look. When I ducked through the station on the way to get that ambulance, I spotted a dame that might give us some business. Want to see her?"

"Yes. I'd like to find Rudolph and Tessie Smaltz, but there isn't much chance of that if he wants to keep her under cover. He's got too many hide-outs."

They walked across the street and diagonally across the small park south of the courthouse. Behind them, a radio car rolled up in front of the tavern.

"Remind me I got to make a report on that as an eye-witness," Meekins said. "I told the boys I would when I flagged the ambulance through. You better, too. I didn't want Riganov lyin' there on the sidewalk until them dopey cops got through with their pinochle game and got around to an-swerin' the call."

"All right," said Dodd absently.

Meekins jerked at his soaked hat-brim. "Gee, you finally did cash in on that little screw-ball, didn't you? I couldn't figure why you was always front-ing for him for no dough."

"I wasn't trying to cash in on him," Dodd said shortly. "I like him. He's a harmless little devil, goodhearted as the day is long, even if he does have nitwitted ideas. I didn't want to see him get thrown in jail and lose his job."

"All right, all right," Meekins said soothingly. "But I'd sure hate to be the birds that pasted him. I wouldn't want that wife of his on my tail. Them eyes of hers give me the assorted shivers."

They went around the back of the courthouse and along a dimly lighted alley and across the paved court toward the green light that marked the side entrance of the police station.

"In here," said Meekins.

Dodd preceded him through the door and down the grimy, stale-smelling hall past the deserted pressroom. The sergeant in charge was the only officer present in the booking-room. He had his elbows on his desk and was looking wearily at the girl who stood on the other side of the wooden railing in front of it.

"Well, really," she was saying in a clear, arrogant voice, "it doesn't seem to me that you can be very intelligent."

"Oh, I'm hellishly intelligent," the sergeant said. "All us cops are."

The girl was slim and tall and young. She wore a close-fitting blue tailored coat with a high fur collar. Her hair was blue-black, cut in a long page-boy bob, glistening sleekly with moisture now, and her eye lashes were long and langorous, over sleepily dark eyes. She was staring at the sergeant as though he were some form of lower animal life.

"It's a plain question," she said. "Surely you can answer it if you want to try."

The sergeant shook his head sadly. "Look, lady. I sit here eight hours a day, doin' nothin' but bookin' people in. How can I remember what one particular dame looks like?"

"You could remember this one. She looks very refined, and she has red hair."

"Red hair," the sergeant said slowly. "Refined. Sorry, lady. It don't mean a thing. Hello, Dodd."

Dodd nodded to the girl and said: "Perhaps I can help you. You were looking for a girl with red hair?"

She tilted her head back to stare up at him. "And just who are you, may I ask?"

"I forgot," said the sergeant. "Pardon me. She don't speak to strange men without a proper introduction. If you'll allow me, lady, I'll present you to Mr. William Dodd."

"Are you a reporter?" she asked Dodd flatly.

"No, lady," the sergeant answered for him. "He's a bail bondsman. That's a brand of vermin that infests police stations. We can't get rid of 'em. We tried fly spray and rat poison and what-not, but they're a hardy breed."

Dodd smiled at her. "You were looking for a girl with red hair? Was she wearing a short mink jacket?"

She was suddenly eager. "Did you see her?"

Dodd shrugged. "Maybe. What's her name?"

"That's none of your business!"

"Oh," said Dodd. "Well, I guess I haven't seen her, then."

"You have! You're lying!"

"You're probably right, lady," said the sergeant. "Do you want to bet on it, Meekins?"

"The hell with you," said Meekins. "You've won enough of my dough."

The sergeant rubbed his hands. "That reminds me, Meekins, my friend. There was a little matter of two dollars on that fight last night."

"Collect from Dodd," Meekins said glumly. "He owes me last week's salary."

The dark-haired girl stamped one small, high-heeled pump. "You! All of you! Answer my questions!"

"Well, now," said Dodd blandly, "if you'd only tell me your friend's name, perhaps I could tell you if I'd seen her."

"I won't! It's none—"

Running feet thumped along the hall, and a man came through the door and jerked to a breathless halt when he saw the girl.

"Donna!" he exclaimed, staring in bewilderment from Dodd to the sergeant to Meekins. "I got here as soon as I could. What—what is it?"

He was a young man with a finely drawn, pale face. He was wearing a long blue overcoat with velvet lapels over a dinner jacket. He took off his black felt hat now and brushed absently at the moisture on the brim, watching with worried eyes.

The girl took him by the arm, pulled him into the far corner of the room and whispered urgently in his ear. Dodd and Meekins and the sergeant watched curiously.

The young man had white, thinly nervous hands, and he kept jerking them in subdued gestures of protest as the girl whispered to him. Finally she finished and gave him a little push in the direction of the railing.

"But, Donna!" he protested. "I can't—"

The girl nodded her sleek, dark head determinedly. "You do it."

He shrugged and came up to the railing and spoke to the sergeant. "I'd like to inquire whether or not a girl has been booked here tonight?"

"Name?" the sergeant asked, interested now.

The man made a helpless gesture. "I don't know her name. I can give you a description—"

"If it's the same one she gave me," the sergeant said, jerking his head to indicate the dark-haired girl, "I already told her at least a hundred times I don't know who you mean."

The young man drew in his breath. "I'm an attorney, sergeant, and the girl in question is my client. I have a right to know whether or not she's being held here and the charge."

"Attorney?" said the sergeant. "What's your name?"

"Howard Linden."

Dodd looked at Meekins and nodded. Meekins went quietly back along the hall to the pressroom, and Dodd could hear him dialing on one of the telephones there.

"Look, Mr. Linden," said the sergeant. "I'm not trying to put anything over on anybody. I don't remember anybody like the lady describes, but that don't mean she ain't been here. If you give me her name, I could look it up, but if you don't, I can't. There's been about a hundred prisoners in here tonight. Some of 'em are still here and some of 'em went through night court already and some are goin' through now. If you wanta, you can inquire over there."

Linden nodded. "Thanks." He turned to the girl. "That's the best thing to do, Donna. It's no good staying here."

The girl pointed at Dodd. "He knows."

"Do you?" Linden asked.

Dodd shrugged and smiled blandly.

"Offer him money, you fool," the girl said.

Dodd smiled more broadly. "No. You tell me the girl's name, and I'll tell you whether I've seen her or not."

Linden turned to the dark-haired girl. "Donna, can't I—"

"No!"

"Then, no sale," said Dodd.

Linden looked around helplessly and then said: "Come on, Donna. Perhaps at the night court . . ."

She let him lead her out, turning for one last arrogantly angry stare at Dodd.

Meekins came in and said to Dodd: "Linden is connected with McKay, Dunlop and Riley, and they're hot-shot legal guys that handle corporate and financial stuff only. No court work. Linden ain't a partner or anything. Just sort of a glorified office boy."

"Nothing much there," said Dodd. "He and the brunette are evidently friends of the redhead. See if you can find out the brunette's last name. The first is Donna."

"I'll find out," said Meekins. Dodd knew he would, too. Meekins had weird and wonderful sources of information.

"What's all the gagging?" the sergeant asked.

"We're trying to find out," Dodd answered. "Look up Tessie Smaltz and see what address she gave when she was booked."

"Oh, is that who they were after?" the sergeant said, pawing through an index. "Why the hell didn't you tell 'em?"

"I didn't want to," Dodd said. "I've got a reason."

"Here," said the sergeant. "She gave her address as Thirty-seven-sixteen West Forty-fifth."

"Dummy," said Meekins. "There ain't no such number. Forty-fifth ends in the thirty-four-hundred block."

"Oh, hell!" the sergeant exclaimed. "That's right."

Dodd shrugged. "Well, that's that. Let's go over to night court, Meekins. They might dig something out of the clerk over there, and maybe we can tag along."

Meekins nodded at the sergeant. "Tell the boys in car twelve I'll make out an eye-witness statement before I leave tonight."

"You'd damned well better, smarty," the sergeant told him, "or you won't leave for very long. And don't forget that two dollars."

III
Gus Gillen—Gambler

Meekins and Dodd came in through the back door of the courthouse and walked around the turn in the corridor in time to see Howard Linden and the girl called Donna coming out of the entrance of the night court. She was talking to him with a sort of angry disgust, and her voice carried plainly.

"Well, you did it, and you should have had better sense. The idea of telling a person a thing like that!"

"But, Donna!" Linden protested. "I didn't know. I didn't think. I supposed of course she knew."

"You're a fool, Howard," Donna said shortly. "Now who is this man Rudolph the clerk told you about?"

"He's a criminal attorney. He has a very shady reputation."

"How would he know her? Why should he pay her fine?"

"Donna, I don't know! I haven't the faintest idea!"

"Then we'll have to find him and ask. Come on."

Without even looking in the direction of Dodd and Meekins, they went along the hall and out through the front entrance. They met a man at the wide doors, and he stepped aside quietly to let them pass. They didn't notice him.

Meekins nudged Dodd. "They're going to have one hell of a time finding Rudolph if he don't want them to. Rudolph is—" He let his voice trail off, staring.

"What?" Dodd asked.

Meekins moistened his lips. "That guy, there. That's Gus Gillen!"

The man Donna and Linden had passed in the doorway was coming down the hall now. He was short and pudgy, and he had a round face that was pink as a baby's. He wore a shiny blue suit that didn't fit him very well and was spotted on the shoulders with rain drops. He wore thick, rimless spectacles, and he had an amiable, shy smile.

"Who?" Dodd asked out of the corner of his mouth.

"Gus Gillen," Meekins whispered. "Big shot from the West. Hangs out in Reno."

Gillen came right on toward Dodd and Meekins and stopped in front of them. He lowered his head a little to peer over the tops of the thick glasses.

"You recognized me?" he asked in an embarrassed tone.

"Yes," Dodd admitted. "If you're Gus Gillen."

"That is my name. And yours?"

"Dodd. I'm a bail bondsman. This is Meekins. He works for me."

"Dodd," Gillen repeated gently. "Dodd. I'll remember. I came in tonight on a hurry-up trip. It is private business, purely. I would rather it were not known I was here."

"Oh," said Dodd noncommittally.

"You were watching the young couple who just went out. You are interested in them?"

"After a fashion," said Dodd.

"A bail bondsman wouldn't be interested in them."

"No?" said Dodd.

"Maybe I should say a bail bondsman *shouldn't* be interested in them," Gillen said, correcting himself. He was still smiling.

"We ain't interested in them," Meekins said quickly. "Not any more, Mr. Gillen. Not a bit!"

Dodd looked at him indignantly and was about to say something to Gillen, when a man came around the curve in the corridor behind them and said: "Hi, Dodd. Hi, Meekins. Say listen, either of you two know anything ripe about a gal with red hair and some rubies?"

His words echoed a little in the emptiness of the corridor, and after that the silence seemed to grow so heavy it was like a thick weight pressing down. Gillen was wearing yellow shoes with upturned toes, and he rocked forward and back on them, making them squeak gently.

"Well," said the other man. "Do you?"

He was taller even than Dodd, and much thinner, and he had a harassed air, as though he had a lot of things to do and not enough time to do them. He was wearing a ragged raincoat hung around his shoulders like a cape, and he held a blackened, stubby pipe in one corner of his mouth.

"Is it a riddle?" Dodd asked smoothly.

"Huh? No. Somebody called up and rooted me out of my evening's siesta and told me to come down to the courthouse if I wanted something hot. I said I'd heard that one before, and they said to look for the redheaded girl with the rubies. I thought it was a rib at first, and then I got to thinking about it, so I trailed down here."

"It must have been a rib," said Dodd.

"Undoubtedly," said Meekins.

The tall man was looking at Gus Gillen with a calculating squint in his eye. "Seems like I've seen you before somewhere, mister. Not in person, but your picture."

"Perhaps you have," said Gus Gillen gently.

"This is Mr. McCray," Dodd said to the tall man, indicating Gillen with a wave of his hand. "Mr. McCray is a—a real-estate broker from—out of town. Mr. McCray, this is Donald Craig. He's a reporter on the *Times*."

"It's a pleasure to meet you," Gillen said politely.

"McCray," said Craig. "Real estate. That doesn't sound familiar. Must be you look like someone else. Dodd, are you sure you haven't seen any red-headed gals or rubies around here?"

"Oh, no," said Dodd.

"Absolutely not," Meekins seconded.

"Was it a man or woman who called you?" Dodd asked.

"Woman," Craig answered. "Sounded young, if that means anything. That's why I thought it was a gag. Thought it was some chorus biddie looking for publicity."

"Is that all she said?" Dodd inquired.

"Yeah. But somebody called right afterwards and said, 'Who's this?' and I said, 'It's the *Times*, if it's all the same to you,' and they hung up on me without another peep. The funny thing was though, that on both calls there was music playing in the background, and it was the same piece. Damn funny music, too. It sounded like somebody playing swing on a fire-siren."

Meekins made a strangling noise in his throat and Dodd said hastily: "It certainly is wonderful the things people will do for a gag these days."

"Yeah," Craig said sourly. "Very wonderful, indeed. If I catch pneumonia, I'll laugh myself to death. Well, I'll dodge into night court and see what gives. So long."

He went through the back door of the night court and left Dodd and Meekins looking at Gillen.

"Thank you very much, Mr. Dodd," Gillen said shyly, "for not revealing my identity. If you'll excuse me now, I will go into the court, too. I find night sessions very instructive and stimulating."

"Oh, very," Dodd agreed vaguely.

He watched Gillen until he had disappeared through the front entrance of the court and then turned on Meekins.

"Well—why the funny noises?"

Meekins looked like he had been holding his breath. "What Craig said—that the music sounded like swing played on a fire-siren! A couple of weeks ago we pulled a guy named Windy Moore out of the pokey when he was in for getting on a marihuana jag. This Moore's an entertainer. He plays pieces by blowing up an inner tube and letting the air come out through a rubber squee-jee on the valve. I heard him. It sounds like a fire-siren. He's playin' now at Shine Brevani's clip-joint on Clark just off Kester."

"Well," said Dodd thoughtfully. "On Clark off Kester, huh? And the red-headed doll was picked up on Kester."

"Listen, boss," said Meekins earnestly, "I think we better take that red rock and get ourselves under cover somewhere. Real far under cover."

"How so?" Dodd asked, annoyed.

"Look," said Meekins. "Riganov got batted around with brass knucks on account of that ruby, and that's all right. I'll fight with them knucks for a purse like that any day. But I don't want any part of Gillen or Shine Brevani."

"I'm curious," Dodd told him. "Here's a nice-looking girl hanging out on Kester Street giving strange guys rubies and getting hauled up for soliciting and getting Sam Rudolph to front for her. I want to know why."

"I don't," said Meekins. "Don't let that mild air of Gillen's fool you. He's big-time in the gambling racket in Nevada, and he's got his fist in lots of other things, I hear tell. And not only that but he knows a hundred guys who'd just as leave rub you out as spit. And Shine Brevani is just naturally bad from way back. I positively don't want to get in between him and Gillen."

"I think I'll look around," Dodd decided, ignoring him.

"Where?"

"On Kester Street. What plainclothesman picked the redhead up?"

"Harris. You can catch him in the back room of Casey's Haven. He ducks in for a drink every hour or so. But listen, boss, if I were you—"

"You aren't, so don't let it worry you. You get to work and find out what Donna's last name is and anything else you can pick up in a hurry. Call me at Casey's Haven."

"I'll call you," Meekins agreed gloomily, "but I don't know as you'll hear me."

IV
Old Smoke

Dodd came in through the swinging green doors of Casey's Haven and breasted a solid wave of noise that beat up unavailingly against the low ceiling. The longshoremen and dock-workers—heavily muscled men with big voices and bigger thirsts—were crowded three deep along the bar, and clouds of rank tobacco smoke swooped and swirled crazily over their heads. Dodd stepped over a redfaced man who was squatting on the floor pounding on the bottom of a brass spittoon with an empty beer bottle and howling some queerly rhythmic dirge. He worked his way through the press to the hinged gate at the end of the bar.

Casey, himself, was there, sitting on a spindle-legged stool and looking wearily philosophical about it all.

"How's it going, Casey?" Dodd asked.

"You can look around this mad-house and ask that?" Casey said.

"How many fights tonight?"

"Six—not counting a political argument."

"I'm looking for Harris. Have you seen him?"

Casey stared up at the cracked dial of the clock over the back-bar. "He'll be here any minute. Your man, Meekins, wants you to call him at the police station."

"Thanks. Fix me a rye highball."

Dodd pushed through to the phone booth in the corner, got the police operator, the booking-sergeant, and finally Meekins.

"Well, what?" he asked.

"Hot stuff," Meekins said. "Sam Rudolph had an argument about the right-of-way with a lamp post over on Center Street. They had to scrape his car off the pavement."

"How about the redhead?" Dodd demanded.

"She wasn't with him. Sam's got two cracked ribs and a couple of black eyes, and he isn't talking very much. He said he skidded, but that's hard to figure because it happened in the middle of a block, and there wasn't any traffic. I think the dame decided not to go any further with him and just gave the wheel a jerk and steered him into the lamp post and then beat it."

"Probably," Dodd agreed. "Anything else?"

"I always save the best for the last. Donna's last name is Barstow, and her old man is E. P. Barstow, and he's a heavy market-operator in mining stock. I found that out from Craig. So then I called up the Barstow joint and gave somebody a little song-and-dance about being a society reporter, and this somebody tells me that Miss Donna Barstow is home on vacation from Miss Wiggenbottom's Seminary for Girls and get this.

She has as her guest, during the vacation, another student from the same school, her room-mate, by the name of Patricia Gilwyne! And this Patricia Gilwyne has very beautiful auburn hair!"

"Ah!" said Dodd triumphantly. "Good work!"

"I always deliver," Meekins said modestly.

"Call me back if you get anything more."

Dodd went back to the end of the bar.

Casey had set out two drinks. He pointed to one and said: "This is yours. Harris is in the back room now. You can take the other one to him."

Dodd paid for the two drinks and took them with him through the rear door of the saloon and down a narrow, dark hall to another door that was marked—*Private—No Admittance—This Means You* in large red letters. He opened the door, maneuvered himself and the drinks through, and kicked it shut behind him.

"Hello, Harris," he said. "Have a drink with me?"

"That I will," said Harris heartily.

He was a tall, enormously broad man with a red, square face and blue eyes that had little white laughter creases at the corners. He took the drink from Dodd, threw it down with one big gulp, and waited for it to hit bottom.

"Ah!" he said in a satisfied tone, when it did. "There's nothing like good Irish whisky. Damn all water, I say, and especially when it's rain. How are you, Dodd?"

"Good enough," said Dodd. "And expecting to be better shortly. I hope. I want to ask you a question. Do you remember a redheaded girl who gave her name as Tessie Smaltz? You picked her up tonight earlier."

"Ha!" Harris grunted. "Do I remember her! Ha! Are you going to use that drink of yours, or are you just going to sit and hold it?"

"Take it," Dodd invited. "It's rye."

"Better than nothing," Harris said, pouring it after the first one. "Tessie Smaltz, eh? Sure I remember her. I spotted her over near Clark, and I thought she'd be one to watch on account of the coat she was wearing. You see, I used to work on the Loft Squad, and I know mink when I see it, and there's others around here who do, too, but not for the same reason. So I thought she'd wind up in an alley with a sore head and no coat to cover her if I didn't keep an eye open. And then what do I find but that the little tart is going along hitting guys up on Kester."

"And then?" Dodd urged.

"So I stop her, and I say, 'Listen, cutie, run yourself home to your mama before I sick the truant officer on you.' Ha! And what did she say? She said, 'Listen, apeface, I'll do what I damn please and walk where I damn please.' So I say, 'No, you won't, my dear. You'll ride to the station.' I was just bluffing, hoping it would scare her, but she laughed in my face, so I had to send her along. She was a crazy one, but then the young ones are all crazy now. She had no eye for prospects, I'll say that. She hit up two of the worst you could find if you sifted this town like sand."

"Only two?" Dodd asked casually.

"Yup. One was Riganov, that screeching little crack-pot who has a wife that would cut his ears off if he looked at another woman, and the other was Old Smoke."

"Old Smoke?" Dodd repeated.

Harris laughed. "That old stew-bum! He'd rather look into a glass of whisky than into the eyes of any woman that ever lived!"

"Where could I find him?" Dodd asked.

"Old Smoke? He lives in a shack on Butcher Flats, on a little spit that sticks out just south of Crane's Packing House. He'll be drunk by this time—stiffer than a log."

Dodd stood up. "I'll take a look."

Harris pointed a thick forefinger. "Watch your step, my boy, down that way. It's one of our most exclusive neighborhoods. Exclusively bad."

The taxi bounced over a culvert with a sideways twist that made the springs groan protestingly and pulled up to a stop under the feeble yellow glow of a streetlight.

"We're at the end of the line, doc," the driver said. "This here is a taxi, not an ocean liner."

Dodd got out and paid him. "I won't be long. Will you wait for me?"

"Doc," the driver told him, "in this neighborhood at this time of night, I wouldn't wait five minutes for the King of England. There's guys around here that would cut your throat for a dime, and I mean ten cents."

"All right," Dodd said.

He started down the slanting, slick cobblestones. Behind him the taxi's motor made a fluttering blast as it backed and turned hurriedly. It banged back over the culvert, and then the sound of its motor faded smoothly into the distance.

It had stopped raining, but there was a yellow, moving mist in the air that felt slickly smooth against Dodd's face. There were warehouses all around him, great blocks of them hunched in squat darkness. Somewhere close ahead water slapped monotonously against a piling, and the sour salt smell of the bay floated heavily in the mist.

Dodd came to a corner, under the feeble yellow eye of another street-light. He turned around very quickly there and ducked down a little, staring up the slant of the street. He caught the dim sway of a figure outlined for a second against the first streetlight. It was gone instantly, and it didn't appear again. Dodd swore to himself in a whisper.

The sound of the slapping water was closer, and he walked in front of a warehouse on planks that were ground to rough splinters by the constant wear of the iron wheels of hand-trucks. A red light on a buoy dipped and swayed tipsily making ruddy, gleaming streaks on the greasy surface of the bay.

Dodd went on past the warehouse and ducked into a velvet-black niche between it and the next one. He stood flat against the wall there, waiting. A boat whistle sounded low and dull, off somewhere in the night.

Footsteps touched the splintered planks and came along in a quick, stealthy shuffle. Dodd could hear the man breathing before he saw him, and then he was just a dark, bent outline. Waiting until he was even with the niche, Dodd stepped out behind and slid his right arm across in front of the man's throat.

"Hah!" the man said in a sudden shrill gasp that ended when Dodd tightened his arm and bent slightly sideways, pulling the man against him and bending him backward across Dodd's out-thrust hip.

The man fought, clutching desperately with both hands, trying to kick back at Dodd's shins.

"Quit it," Dodd said, "or I'll crack your neck."

The man relaxed instantly, with a choked gurgling noise. Dodd relaxed his strangle-hold slightly, and the man sucked in air with a wheezy sob.

"Let go! Let go me! I didn't—I wasn't—"

"Oh, hell!" said Dodd in a disgusted tone. He released the man and gave him a shove. "So it's you, is it?" He found a match in his pocket, snapped it on his thumbnail, and held it in front of his own face.

"Hah! Dodd!"

"Yeah. I didn't think I'd see you again, Maxie, since you owe me ten bucks. Haven't got it on you, have you?"

The man's voice dropped into an accustomed whine. "I'm just dead broke, Dodd. Honest. I ain't got enough to eat, even."

"That certainly isn't food I smell on your breath," Dodd agreed. "So you've taken to rolling lushes now, have you, Maxie? Better watch your step. One more trip-up and they throw the book at you."

"I got to have something to eat—"

"Ever think of working?"

"I can't get no job, Dodd. Them cops keep after me all the time—persecutin' me and houndin' me. I ain't got a place I can turn, and I ain't got a friend—"

"Too bad, too bad," said Dodd unfeelingly. "You should write a letter to the governor about it, only don't forget to tell him you had three jobs since you got paroled the last time, and lost them all because you couldn't keep your mitts out of the cash register. But never mind that. Where does Old Smoke live from here?"

"Down the next block and through that alley toward the bay. What's everybody want that old stew-bum for?"

"What do you mean—everybody?"

"There was a guy after him earlier."

"How do you know? Try to stick him up?"

"No! I never did! I just asked him for a match, and he stuck a gun right in me. He was a reporter, he says. Name of Craig. And he wanted to interview Old Smoke. I say it's a hell of a fine note for a reporter to stick guns in people!"

"If it was Craig, it was probably just a pipe."

"A pipe! No, it wasn't no pipe! I know a gun when I see it, and that's what this was he stuck in me. He ain't got no right to stick a gun in a person just because a person asks him polite for a match."

"You don't seem to be having very good luck tonight. Don't follow me around any longer, because I might get mad."

"Sure not, Dodd. Say, could you maybe spare four bits for an old pal that ain't had a bite to eat for three days? Just four bits, huh, Dodd? I'll pay you back next week."

Dodd gave him a coin. "All right, all right. But when you get picked up drunk tonight, don't holler for me to go your bail, because I'm not going to."

"Thanks. Thanks, pal. I ain't drinkin' no more. No, sir. I turned over a new leaf, Dodd. Thanks."

"Scram."

"Sure, Dodd. Sure. Thanks. I'll pay you back next week. Honest. So long."

Dodd stood and watched the bent shuffling figure until it went under the yellow circle of the streetlight and turned up the block.

He shrugged then and turned around and went past the next warehouse and across another of the narrow, cobblestoned alleyways. The shoreline turned a little here, and there were warehouses on both sides of Dodd again. He went along in between them accompanied by the hollow, empty sound of his footsteps, until he saw a blackened notch in the solid walls.

Dodd turned into it, slowing up. The ground softened, and his feet crunched on soggy refuse. He went on, feeling his way with one hand against the rough stone of a wall, and suddenly the alley opened out and he almost fell into a pond of scummed, stagnant water.

He stopped, squinting ahead through the mist, and made out the shadowy blur of a shack straight ahead. Ten feet to his right there was a long board stretched across the pond. Dodd tested the board with his foot, gingerly, and then walked quickly across it, balancing himself with his arms extended wide. The board slapped the water under him, groaning with his weight.

He jumped the last five feet and landed in mud that sucked hungrily when he pulled his feet free. The shack was directly ahead of him, a sagging patternless pile of battered odds and ends of lumber that had been salvaged from the bay. One window in the wall on Dodd's side stared like a bleary blinded eye.

"Smoke!" Dodd called. "Old Smoke!"

His voice bounced off the warehouse walls and echoed flat and empty across the water. There was no answer.

Dodd walked around the shack, his feet slopping wetly in the mud, and found what served as a door. He pounded on it and shouted again.

"Hey, Smoke!"

There was no stir and Dodd muttered disgustedly to himself: "Must be drunker than an owl." He put his weight against the door and pushed. The hinges groaned dolorously, and the bottom scraped against rough board.

Putting his head inside, Dodd breathed in stale air loaded with the odors of sweat and burned grease and alcohol.

Dodd struck a match on the wall, and the flame sputtered up yellow and wavering and showed a blurred, impressionistic picture of the cave-like interior of the shack.

It was like a medieval horror painting, with the wasted form of Old Smoke lying on the soiled mattress in the corner, spread-eagled there with his arms flung wide and his eyes staring glassily at the ceiling. There was a round black hole punched in the skinny muscle of his neck, just under the angle of his stubbled jaw, and the blood had seeped down and soaked into the blanket that was twisted under him.

Dodd stood there, frozen, until the match burned his fingers. He dropped it then, and lighted another, breathing heavily. The blood had turned the blanket into a purple, clotted mass. Dodd stepped closer, forcing himself to hold the match steady, and saw that every one of Old Smoke's pockets had been turned inside out.

The match went out and he dropped it and found another, fumbling in his haste. He held this one high over his head, staring around the shack. The place was filthy as a pig-sty, but it gave no evidence of having been searched.

"He found it," Dodd said in a whisper.

He felt the cold moisture of perspiration on his face, and it was hard for him to breathe.

Dodd stepped outside the shack, slamming the door shut behind him. He wiped the back of his hand across his forehead, staring blankly at the greasy water of the bay.

"Craig," he said slowly. "Craig, hell!"

He jerked himself into motion then, and dodged around the corner of the shack and trotted back to the board that bridged the stagnant pool. He wasn't so careful this time. He went across the board, taking long, hurried steps, and when he was in the middle of it, it cracked gently under him, slipped sideways and then turned.

Dodd went up in the air and came down again, churning his arms and legs frantically. He hit the water with a hollow, dull splash and turned it into dirty froth.

It was only knee deep, but there was a foot of soft mud under it. Dodd staggered to his feet, cursing and spluttering. He fought his way through the mud to the edge of the pond.

He was soaked through, and the mud was thick and slimy on his face and hands. He fumbled with stiff fingers, still cursing monotonously, until he found his handkerchief. He made a damp, wadded ball out of it and swabbed the mud out of his eyes. His patched glasses were floating placidly on the roiled water, and he leaned over and groped until he got hold of them.

He began to trot back through the alley, his trousers slapping wetly and uncomfortably against his legs. He turned out into the narrow street and back past the warehouse where he had tackled Maxie. He turned again under the streetlight and labored up the slant of the street to the intersection where he had left the taxi.

His breath was beginning to burn in his throat now, and his heart made pounding thunder. He kept at it, trotting steadily along with the water squishing in his shoes, heading back toward the blurred color-smear of lights that marked the downtown section of the city.

It was fifteen minutes later, and he was staggering on numb sticks of legs that had no feeling and no give at the knees when he came out on a wider street and saw the red and green lights of a cruising taxi a half-block away. Dodd had just enough breath left to whistle. He put his fingers in his mouth and did the best he could.

The taxi kept on going, floating tantalizingly away from him, and Dodd collapsed on the curb. He was all through. He didn't even have energy enough to swear, but he began to think dizzily of the things he was going to say when he did.

Then the taxi slid up and stopped beside him, and the driver said, without much hope: "Taxi, mister?"

Dodd got up and grabbed the door handle before he could get away again. "Aragon Apartments," he managed to gasp.

"Hey, listen!" the driver protested. "You're all fulla mud. You're gonna get my cushions all smeared—"

"All right, all right," Dodd panted. "I'll sit on the floor and pay double the meter. Just get going. I want a bath and I want one right now!"

V

Rubies and a Redhead

The Aragon Apartments had a small, austerely correct lobby, but there was no desk in it, and it was late enough now so that all the tenants had retired to their respective apartments, if not to bed.

Dodd was glad enough to have no audience. He went across the lobby in a hurry, still trailing dribbles of muddy water behind him, and took the self-operated elevator to the third floor. He went down the long hall, still hurrying, fumbling with wet, muddy fingers for his key ring.

He fitted the key in the lock of the door of his own apartment, but it wouldn't turn. His fingers slipped off it once and then again. He swore in an undertone and wiped his hand on his coat, smearing his fingers more than before. He tackled the key again, and this time the door opened of its own accord, and left him standing there, staring incredulously.

Craig, the reporter, was sitting in the big chair under the crook-necked bridge lamp. He was sitting there very still, looking awkward and gaunt and uncomfortable, and he was watching Dodd with eyes that were wide open and that didn't blink.

Dodd said: "Well—" and then didn't finish the sentence.

Craig's stubby pipe had fallen from his mouth. It was lying in his lap, and the ashes in it had spilled a gray streak across one trouser-leg. There was a hole like an oversize black period in the center of Craig's forehead. Not very much blood had come out of it.

Dodd released his breath in a long sigh. He stepped into the apartment and closed the door quietly and firmly behind him. He stood there for a moment, still staring incredulously, and then stepped closer.

"Yeah," a voice told him. "He's still here."

Dodd spun on his heel. There was a man standing in the open doorway of the bedroom. He was a small man with a face as pale and shiny as old parchment and his eyes were flat and deadly close on either side of the swollen, formless bulge of his nose. He was wearing a pearl-gray derby, the crown spattered with rain drops, and a greenish pin-stripe suit. He was holding a .45 automatic that looked grotesquely huge and deadly clasped in his thin hand.

He nodded gravely and said: "Hi, Dodd."

Dodd moistened his lips. "Hello, Luke. I didn't know you were back. I thought this town was too hot for you."

"Not any more," said Luke. "Shine Brevani is taking care of me now. He wants to see you."

"Does he?" Dodd asked absently.

The front door of the apartment opened, and another man slipped inside. He was squat and bow-legged, with long muscular arms out of all proportion to the rest of him. His eyes were shifting, colorless little pin-points under glove-scarred brows, and his left ear was bent over and thickened.

"Well," said Dodd. "Shine sent a regular greeting committee, didn't he? Hello, Mushy."

Mushy lifted his rubbery, thickened upper lip in a leering half-smile. "Yah," he said in a whispering croak.

"Go over him," Luke ordered.

Mushy slid around behind Dodd and slapped his pockets with quick deft hands. "No gun, Luke."

"That's why he went out," Luke said. "He was ditching it, but what I want to know is where? Where, Dodd?"

"Where, what?" Dodd asked.

"The gun. Where'd you put it?"

"What gun?"

Luke jerked his head toward Craig.

Dodd grinned wryly. "Hell, you're not trying to talk me into thinking I killed Craig, are you? That's the kind of stuff you go in for, Luke. I had you tagged for the job."

"I was afraid maybe you had," Luke said softly. "Take another look at his pockets. Mushy. Careful this time."

Mushy went through Dodd's clothes with the expert precision of a pickpocket and found the ruby in Dodd's lower vest pocket.

"Yah!" he said triumphantly, showing it to Luke.

Luke watched Dodd silently for a moment and then said: "We'll go see Brevani. We got a car downstairs. You want to walk to it, or do you want to be carried?"

"You'll frighten me if you don't watch out," Dodd answered, "but I'll walk. I'm hardly wearing the proper dress, though, to appear in such a tony dive as Shine runs these days."

"You might look worse—later," Luke told him.

It was a small, black sedan, a new one and indistinguishable from thousands of others that had come off the assembly line before and after it. Mushy was driving, and Dodd was sitting in the back seat with Luke. Luke wasn't holding the .45 on Dodd. He had it deposited casually in his lap, and apparently he wasn't even looking at Dodd, but Dodd knew that he was watching out of the corners of his eyes, waiting for Dodd to make a move. Luke was an old hand at this, and Dodd sat carefully still.

Mushy turned the sedan off Clark into a narrow alley and coasted along it slowly until he came to a board fence that barred the end. He stopped there, and Luke picked up the automatic and said: "Out, Dodd. And don't try to be funny."

"I'm fresh out of jokes," Dodd said.

He opened the door and stepped down on the rough paving. Luke slid out behind him. Mushy used a key to open a padlock on a gate in the board fence. He preceded Dodd and Luke through the gate, closed it behind them, and then led the way around the corner of a building and across a small back yard to a door in the rear of another building.

"Servants' entrance?" Dodd asked.

Luke said: "Just keep the trap shut."

Mushy opened the door, and the three of them went into a long, dimly lighted hall. When Mushy closed the door, Dodd could hear the faint clatter of plates and tinkle of silverware. At the back of the hall, a narrow carpeted stairway led up to the second story, and Dodd climbed the steps with Mushy ahead of him and Luke close behind.

There was another closed door at the top of the stairs, and Mushy scraped lightly on its panel with his thumbnail and then turned the knob.

"In," said Luke, pushing Dodd with the automatic.

Dodd stepped into Shine Brevani's private office. It was a small, square room, its one window masked with heavy black drapes. The big, flat desk in the center filled up most of the floor space, and Shine Brevani was sitting on a corner of it, casually swinging one leg back and forth.

Shine Brevani took his name from his hair. It was so black it looked purple in streaks along the top where the light caught it, and it was so heavy with grease that it didn't look like hair at all, but a flat, viscous mat curved sleekly over the bony outline of his skull. He had a long, sallow face and a mouth that was a pursed, colorless line. He was dressed very dapperly in a navy blue tuxedo, and he wore patent-leather shoes and gray spats.

He looked at Dodd and waved one hand languidly.

"Over there."

Mushy put his hand in the center of Dodd's chest and shoved him hard. Dodd stumbled backwards, and his knees hit the edge of a chair. He sat down in it with a thump.

Shine Brevani turned his head back again and continued to stare thoughtfully at the girl with the red-bronze hair. She was sitting in a chair beside the desk, and she didn't look proud or confident any more. She looked scared, but still defiant, and she was holding her hands clasped tightly together in her lap.

Luke still had the big .45 clasped casually in his right hand, and he stepped into the center of the room where he could watch Dodd without turning his head.

"Where'd you get her?" he asked Brevani.

"She just walked in," Brevani explained. "Right after you left. So I brought her up here to have a chat. So far we haven't been getting on too well. All right, cutie. Once again. What's the big idea?"

The girl's lips were pressed into a determined line, and she shook her head stubbornly.

Brevani leaned forward and slapped her in the face, hard. Her head jerked sideways with the impact, and her blue eyes widened with a sort of unbelieving terror.

"Speak up, cutie," Brevani said.

"Slap her again, and you'll have a one-man riot around here," Dodd said flatly.

Mushy was standing beside his chair. He brought his fist out of the sagging pocket of his coat now. He was wearing a set of brass knuckles, and he slashed downward at Dodd's face with them. Dodd jerked his head aside, and the brass knuckles struck his shoulder with a force that numbed his whole side.

Luke raised the .45 automatic and leveled the heavy barrel at Dodd's chest.

"Never hit a man with glasses on, Mushy," Brevani advised gently. "You know that's against the law."

Mushy grinned and flicked out the stiffened fingers of his left hand, knocking Dodd's patched glasses on the floor. He raised his right fist in a glinting arc, aiming more carefully this time.

"Oh, don't!" the girl gasped in a sickened whisper.

Dodd stared at Brevani, blinking a little. "What I said still goes. I can take it. I hope you can when it gets around to your turn."

"He means it," Luke said. "He don't scare very easy, or maybe he's only nuts."

"Cut it, Mushy," Brevani said. "So you think we're going to get a turn, hey, Dodd?"

"You'll want bail some time."

Brevani laughed contemptuously. "You think we'd ask a two-bit operator like you for it?"

"No matter who you ask you won't get it if I put the finger on you. Bail bondsmen stick together."

Brevani's face grew tight and still. "Maybe you won't put the finger on anybody but a couple of fish at the bottom of the bay. Let's hear you do some talking. Ever see this before?"

*   *   *

Brevani picked up a round blue circle from the desk and flipped it at Dodd. Dodd batted at it nearsightedly, knocked it to the floor by his glasses. He leaned over and picked it up, his glasses too. It was a poker chip, and he turned it over in his fingers and saw the name *Brevani* printed in small golden letters on its back. He looked up.

"You still running games here?"

"Two roulette tables and craps and a black-jack layout," Brevani said. "But I asked you a question, Dodd."

"No. I've never seen this chip before—nor any other one like it. I didn't even know you were running tables here now."

"He had one of the red rocks on him," Luke said. "Give it to Shine, Mushy."

Mushy handed Brevani the ruby he had taken from Dodd. Brevani turned it over in his fingers absently and then showed it to the girl.

"Yours, cutie?"

She nodded her head once, still holding her lips pressed tightly together.

"Where'd you get it?" Brevani asked Dodd.

"From Riganov. She gave it to him. He gave it to me before Mushy clipped him. You might as well break down and tell me what this is all about, Shine."

"That's what I want to know," said Brevani. "This doll comes in early this evening. She wants to see me, and when I let her, she asks me what I know about Gus Gillen. I know plenty about that baby-faced, double-crossing rat, and I told her some of it. So she just sits and takes it without a peep, and then says 'Thanks' and goes over and sits by herself in a corner of the bar. I noticed when she talked to me that she's wearing this ruby and another one like it in a big dinner ring. I tell Mushy to keep an eye on her. So she borrows an ice-pick from the bartender and starts taking these two rocks out of their setting."

"It's my ring," said the girl. "It's my business what I did with it."

"Shut up," Brevani ordered. "So Mushy can't figure that one out, and he's too dumb to come and tell me. So the doll makes a phone call. Mushy does spot the number and calls it back and finds out she talked to the *Times*. She beats it then, and Mushy comes and tells me, so I send him and Luke out to see what she's up to. She stops that little screw-ball, Riganov, and Old Smoke, and then she runs up against Harris who pinches her."

"I knew that," Dodd said.

"Never mind what you knew. So Luke sees Old Smoke lean over to pick up a snipe, and one of these rubies pops out of his pocket. Old Smoke grabs it and rushes into a bar. Luke and Mushy can't get at him in there, so they come back. I called up Sam Rudolph and told him to get the doll out and find out what the hell eats her, and send Luke and Mushy down to back his play. They see Riganov and figure he's got the other rock and make a play for him and botch it. The doll gets loose from Sam. So Mushy and Luke went down to Old Smoke's joint, and they find the old stew-bum with a bullet in his gizzard, and they find that blue chip from my joint lyin' on the floor beside him."

"So?" said Dodd.

"So, I'm in the middle here, and I don't like it. Suppose the cops find Old Smoke croaked and that chip on the floor with my name on it? They come right back here, and they find out about this redheaded doll and her rubies startin' out from here. Then where do we go?"

"For a ride in the paddy wagon," said Dodd. He looked speculatively at Luke. "So maybe you didn't knock Craig over?"

"What?" Brevani demanded sharply.

"Craig," said Luke. "Reporter from the *Times*. We found him in Dodd's apartment—deader than a kippered herring."

"Yeah," said Dodd. "And Craig was writing a series of articles on vice and gambling in the city, wasn't he?"

Brevani came up off the desk as though something had stung him. He stood rigid for a second, staring hard at Dodd, and then sat down slowly again. He swore in a low, bitter monotone.

"That Gus Gillen. That damned backstabbing Gus Gillen." He glared at the redheaded girl. "Listen, cutie, I got no more time to stall around with you. What's your name?"

"Patricia Gilwyne," Dodd said.

The girl jerked her head around to look at him. Surprise wiped away the lines of sullen defiance in her face, and it looked round and soft and childish.

"You—!" Dodd blurted in amazement. "Gilwyne—Gillen! You're some relation to Gus Gillen! You look like him!"

She drew a long, tremulous breath. "I'm his daughter."

There was a dead, tense silence and then Brevani said very softly: "So? Gus Gillen's daughter. His daughter, hey?" He slid off the desk. "Then we'll just forget about the rubies. Yeah. They don't matter much. I've been lookin' for a chance like this. I owe Gus Gillen a thing or two." He stepped slowly closer to the girl, and he was grinning with a sort of savage vindictive glee.

"Here!" said Dodd sharply. "What—"

Brevani didn't even turn his head. "Take him, Mushy."

"Yah!" said Mushy thickly. He raised his brass-knuckled fist.

Dodd ducked sideways, swinging both stiffened legs sideways, and

knocked Mushy's feet out from under him, and in that same instant the
door-latch made a soft click and one of the hinges creaked a little.

Dodd lunged forward, ignoring the menace of Luke's gun, and landed
with both knees in the middle of Mushy's stomach. Mushy grunted in
agony. He heaved up in an arc and threw Dodd off him, and as Dodd rolled
away from him, he caught a hazily blurred picture of the rest of the room.

Mrs. Riganov was standing in the doorway.

"I find," said Mrs. Riganov.

Luke was spinning around, and as he turned he fired with the big automatic. The blasting roar of the report filled the room, and Dodd saw the .45
buck up in Luke's hand and saw the bullet rake a long, splintered gash in the
door-post.

Mrs. Riganov didn't seem to move fast. She raised her right hand. She was
holding a flat-iron in it. It was not an electric iron. It was an old-fashioned
flat-iron—an ugly wedge-shaped piece of solid metal—and Mrs. Riganov
threw it at Luke.

Luke tried to dodge but he was too close. The flat-iron hit him in the face
with a sound like a board slapping water and carried him clear across the
room and smashed him into the wall. He dropped to the floor and didn't
move.

Mushy was up on his knees. He struck viciously at Dodd now with his
brass knuckles. Dodd ducked the blow by falling flat on his face, and then
Mrs. Riganov leaned over and clipped Mushy neatly across the back of the
neck with the hard edge of her palm. Mushy's head jerked, and he seemed
to come all unstrung. He flopped limply over on top of Dodd.

Brevani had lunged clear over his desk and was frantically jerking at a
drawer on the other side, trying to get it open. Mrs. Riganov got her hands
around his thin neck, picked him up off the desk and slammed him head-
first into the wall. Brevani screamed shrilly. Mrs. Riganov drew him back
and slammed his head into the wall again, harder.

Dodd was trying frantically to scramble out from under Mushy. "Wait!" he
yelled. "Don't!"

Brevani screamed, and Mrs. Riganov slammed him into the wall again
with methodical precision.

Brevani quit screaming with horrible abruptness.

Dodd kicked Mushy off him and got to his feet. He grabbed Mrs. Riganov by one massive arm. "Wait! You'll kill him!"

"Sure," said Mrs. Riganov.

"Wait," Dodd groped for an inspiration. "Listen! If you kill him I'll lose
that money I put up for a peace bond for your husband!"

"Oh," said Mrs. Riganov. "All right. I don't kill him—now." She dropped

Brevani in a limp sprawl on the floor and eyed Patricia, who was still sitting stiffly terrorized in her chair. "She's the one that starts this?"

"No, no," said Dodd quickly. "Oh, no! She didn't have anything to do with these others. She's a friend of mine."

"*Ummm,*" said Mrs. Riganov doubtfully.

"Positively," Dodd hastened to assure her. "How did you find these boys, anyway?"

"I ask. I ask every woman on this street. One sees them following this girl and knows they are Brevani men. I guess they don't beat my husband up no more."

"I'll bet they don't either," Dodd agreed emphatically.

VI

The Blue Chip

The taxi made a U-turn in the middle of the wide, tree-lined street and rolled to a stop in front of an apartment house that was a massive, dark peak of granite with high, needled spires on its four corners. Dodd got out and held the door open for Patricia Gilwyne. She was still remembering the scene in Shine Brevani's office, and her face had a drawn frightened look.

"Would—would you come up with me?" she asked. "I'd like awfully to explain—"

"Sure," said Dodd. The mud on his clothes had dried and stiffened now, and he crackled every time he moved. His shoulder ached, and his glasses were twisted at the patch so that one lens sat high and the other low, but he was feeling very pleased with himself in spite of all that.

He paid the driver, and he and Patricia were going up the steps of the apartment building, when there was a long, high squeal of skidding tires behind them, and Donna Barstow's voice called: "Pat! Patricia!"

She was driving a long maroon roadster, and Howard Linden was riding with her. They both got out of the car and hurried across the walk.

"Patricia!" Donna said. "We've been looking everywhere for you! I got the note you left for me saying you were going out to get yourself arrested, and I simply couldn't understand—" She recognized Dodd under the mud and said, instantly arrogant: "And just what are *you* doing here?"

Patricia held out her hand pleadingly. "Donna, please. He's my friend. He—he's been so decent and so kind—"

Donna accepted Dodd on that recommendation without the slightest hesitation.

"Oh, I didn't know. I'm sorry. Now, Patricia, what in the world does all this mean?"

Patricia nodded toward Linden, who was fidgeting uneasily in the background. "Didn't he tell you about—about my father?"

"He did," said Donna. "And I told him what I thought about him for telling you."

Linden protested: "But I didn't realize you didn't know, Pat. I'm sorry. I—"

"You're a fool," said Donna. "Really, Howard, you are, and I'm getting very annoyed with you. Now what's all this got to do with your father, Pat?"

"He's a crook and a gambler and a m-murderer. He's so crooked that even other crooks don't trust him!"

"Pooh!" said Donna, dismissing it with a wave of her hand. "That doesn't matter a bit!"

"It does, Donna! He never told me anything about his business—just that he was a banker. And—and I was so proud of him! And I've been going to Miss Wiggenbottom's school and being entertained at all the best homes—like yours—and all the time my father is a notorious criminal!"

"Oh, pooh!" said Donna. "That's not your fault. What do I care what your father is? Now you come up to the apartment and forget all this foolishness."

"But your father—He's so—well-bred."

"Bah! Come along. And you, too, Mr. What's-Your-Name. And I guess you can come, Howard, although I'm pretty well disgusted with you for telling Patricia about her father."

Linden appealed to Dodd. "It wasn't my fault. I was looking over some old newspapers, looking up publication on a divorce hearing, and I saw Gus Gillen's picture. I thought he looked like Patricia, and the name was similar, and so I just saved it and showed it to her as a joke. I never thought of it being her father. I had never seen—"

"Oh, be quiet," said Donna. "Come on."

They went through the severely modernistic lobby and up to the tenth floor in a self-operated elevator. The Barstows' apartment evidently took up the entire floor. There was only one door off the small entry-hall. Donna opened that with her key, and they went through into a long, low living-room.

A spindle-legged ornamental desk that evidently belonged discreetly in one corner of the room had been hauled out in the middle of the floor, and a man who could have been no one but E. P. Barstow was sitting on a chair in front of it. He was a short, bald-headed man with a fiery red face. There were papers scattered on the desk and in a loose circle on the rug around it. Barstow was chewing on the end of a pencil and staring in grim determination at the papers. As they came in, he spat out part of the pencil's eraser, picked up a bottle of beer from under the table and took a big swallow.

"Dad!" said Patricia in a choked voice.

Gus Gillen was sitting quietly on the couch in the corner. He smiled and nodded shyly.

"Uh?" said E. P. Barstow. "Oh, hello, Donna. This is Gus Gillen, Patricia's father. You've never met him, have you? Gus, this is Donna, and that one is Howard Linden. I don't know your other friend, Donna."

"The name is Dodd," Dodd told him.

"I have met Mr. Dodd," Gus Gillen said, smiling.

"All right," Barstow said, beginning to chew the pencil again. "If you want to make noise, go somewhere else. I've made a mistake here and I can't find it."

"Dad!" said Patricia in an agony of embarrassment. "What—what are you doing here?"

E. P. Barstow looked up. "What? What do you mean, what is he doing here? Can't I even entertain my partner in my own house any more?"

Patricia stared. "You said—partner?"

"Yes, yes!" E. P. Barstow barked. "Partner! He furnishes the money and the brains, and I do the work."

Donna said: "Dad, you never told me—"

E. P. Barstow glared. "Do I have to tell all my business to everyone? Gus is my silent partner. Now, go away, all of you. I'm trying to add these figures."

"No," said Patricia. "No, wait. I want to know—to understand—" She was looking at Gus Gillen. "I saw—an old paper today. There was a picture of you in it. It said that you were a notorious g-gambler and had been arrested in connection with a murder."

"Murder!" E. P. Barstow exploded with laughter. "Gus? What a joke!"

Gus Gillen blinked apologetically. "My dear, that was just the work of a young district attorney who was making publicity for himself. I had met the murdered man only once. He was killed in New York, and I was in San Francisco at the time and easily proved it. I wasn't even held for questioning."

"But Shine Brevani said you—you—"

Gus Gillen sighed. "I own stock in three race tracks, Patricia. Brevani tried to fix a race at one of them, and I caught him and had him ruled off every track in the country for life. He's tried to get even with me several times since."

"But you told me you were a banker!"

"Well, I own a bank."

"Three," E. P. Barstow corrected. "And not one worth a damn if you ask me. Gus bought them up to keep them from going under during the depression."

Patricia still looked dazed. "The paper said—gambling—"

"Sure," said E. P. Barstow. "Gus owns three clubs that run gambling in Reno and Las Vegas. That's his end of our partnership, along with the race tracks."

Dodd cleared his throat. "It's legal to gamble in Nevada, Patricia."

"Well, sure it is," said E. P. Barstow. "What do you think we are—crooks or something?"

Patricia seemed to crumple a little. "Dad! why didn't you *tell* me?"

Gus Gillen looked worried in a bewildered way. "Well, dear, you see your mother used to worry terribly about these speculative businesses of mine. She was afraid I'd lose all my money—and I did, too, several times—and I didn't want you to worry at all. I wanted you to feel secure and—and happy—"

Patricia straightened up. "Oh, I've been a fool!" She stared at the others blindly. "You see, when Howard showed me that old paper with Dad's picture in it, I—I just couldn't believe, couldn't think straight. I thought I had been going under false pretenses and that my father was a c-crook. I'd heard Shine Brevani was a gambler, and I went to ask him, and he told me those lies about Dad. So—so I decided that no matter what my Dad was, he was my Dad, and I was proud of him. I decided I wouldn't pretend any more to be what I wasn't. I was going to get arrested and get my picture in the paper.

"I gave those rubies to those funny men because I wanted to make a good story out of it. I was going to say I was d-drunk, and everyone would be trying to find the rubies, and the story would go all over the country, and all my friends would see it, and that would show them I didn't care what my father was, and that I was just as bad as he was, and that if they didn't like him, they didn't have to like me any more, either. Oh, I've been such a fool!"

"You don't seem to have very good sense," E. P. Barstow agreed. "But then maybe you'll grow up after awhile. Now, will you please kindly get out of here so I can add these figures?"

"Wait a minute," said Dodd. "Speaking of those rubies. There's a couple of things I don't understand, Linden. Mud and your shoes."

"Mud?" Linden said blankly. "My shoes? There's no mud on my shoes."

"No," said Dodd. "That's what I can't understand."

Donna said: "Well, Howard, you know very well your shoes were covered with filthy mud, and that I took you home to change them—"

"Yes," said Dodd. "I thought so. I used to have a customer by the name of

Grouchy Smith. He was an expert pickpocket. He taught me some of his tricks. Look." He held out his right hand and opened his fingers. A flat ruby glowed red on his palm. "I got this out of your pocket on the way up in the elevator, Linden."

Linden slapped his hand against his lower vest pocket. "You lie! You couldn't possibly—" He stopped short, his thin face suddenly sickly white.

"Yes," Dodd agreed amiably. "I lie. The twin of this ruby—the one you took from Old Smoke when you shot him—is still safe in your pocket."

"You—you're crazy," Linden whispered.

"No. You showed that picture to Patricia on purpose. You were sure it was her father, and that she didn't know he was a gambler. You told her about Shine Brevani and followed her to his place because you knew Brevani hated Gus Gillen. He's always popping off about it, and you gamble there a good deal. You figured Patricia would be sick with the shock, and that then you could move in and offer her the sanctity and purity of your honored name, and that she'd jump at it like a shot rather than be known as the daughter of such a notorious character as the newspaper and Shine Brevani painted Gus Gillen as being, and that you would then be in line to get some of Gus Gillen's dough. You weren't making any progress in your attempt to marry Donna for her money, so you thought you'd try someone else."

Linden backed against the wall. "That's a lie!"

"I don't think so. You were desperate for money, and when you saw Patricia give those rubies away, you went after them. You tackled Old Smoke first. He was drunk on the credit he got on the strength of the ruby, but not drunk enough not to know that it was worth a lot more cash than you were offering. He wouldn't deal with you, and you shot him. You thought probably you had been seen and noticed in that district, so you tried to poke the thing off on Craig.

"You knew Craig and knew he was a newspaperman because it was from the *Times* you had gotten the old newspaper you showed to Patricia, and the interview gag was the best reason you could think of at the moment for anyone prowling around and looking for Old Smoke in the middle of the night. But, unfortunately for him, Craig also knew you. My man, Meekins, questioned Craig about Donna and you, and Craig began to connect things up. He didn't know about Old Smoke but he knew about you and the old newspapers, and he found out from the court clerk about Patricia and Sam Rudolph, and he must have remembered who Gus Gillen was. He had seen Gus Gillen at the night court. Why were you there, Mr. Gillen?"

Gillen shrugged, still looking anxiously worried. "I always go to night court when I can. I was just passing the time away, waiting for Ed."

Barstow was staring grimly at Linden. "Gus pays fines for bums in night courts. That's his private charity."

Dodd said: "Craig went to my place to wait for me. He wanted some more information. He was an expert at picking locks, and he let himself into my place and made himself comfortable. While he was waiting, he called you up, and he said too much. You knew he could and would connect you with Old Smoke's murder as soon as he got the lowdown on Patricia and the rubies. You went to my apartment and shot him."

Donna said in a sick voice: "Howard, that was—was the phone call you got at your apartment when you were changing you shoes, and that—that was where I drove you afterwards—"

Dodd went on in the same casual tone: "Also you dropped a poker chip in Old Smoke's shack. That tripped you up badly, because Shine Brevani thought someone was trying to frame him."

Linden stood stiff and white and still against the wall. "You couldn't prove it," he whispered. "You couldn't—" He made a stiffly awkward gesture with his right arm, and then he was holding a small nickel-plated automatic. "Stand still! All of you, stand—"

All in one motion, E. P. Barstow leaned over and picked up the beer bottle and threw it with an expert backward flip of his wrist. The heavy end of the bottle took Linden squarely between the eyes. His head banged into the wall back of him, and then he dropped loosely to his knees and slid forward on his face.

"Hah!" said E. P. Barstow. "See that, Gus? And I haven't heaved a beer bottle since I used to tend bar."

"Dad!" Donna shrieked. "You—a bartender?"

"Sure," said E. P. Barstow. "That's how I met Gus. I was tending bar at the *Golden Lady* at Frying Pan Creek when Gus was running the faro game there. I was a damn good bartender, too, I'll have you know, young lady. I'll prove it. Dodd, you sit down here, and I'll fix you a drink. We might as well be comfortable while we wait for the police, and I want to talk to you about writing some fidelity bonds for some of my employees, and then, damn it, I want you all to get out of here, while I add these figures. Gus is going to think I'm holding out on him if I don't get the right answer soon."

Brand of Kane

Hugh B. Cave

I

Water-Logged Corpse

Mr. Michael Aloysious Kelly, night watchman on board the steamship *Concord*, took a corncob pipe out of his face and stretched himself. Being alone on board the half-submerged hulk of a wrecked steamship did not annoy him so much as did the endless yammering of rain around and about him. Rain-mutter had been disturbing the Kelly eardrums for hours.

He peered around the ship's dining room, spat smoke from his wrinkled lips and slouched erect. It was not easy to walk without staggering. For one thing, though the *Concord* had been aground since yesterday noon, the distance between ship and shore was alarmingly great, and the moiled waters in which the *Concord* now rolled were apparently suffering a severe hangover from the storm which had aroused them.

The *Concord*, after crashing head-on into the side of a Tampico-bound freighter, had shivered herself loose, wallowed helplessly through more than a mile of mountainous seas, and finally bogged down in shallow water offshore. And though the ship still lay in a reasonably upright position, the carpet beneath Mr. Kelly's feet was damp, and the floor pitched and swayed disturbingly as he made his way into the ship's salon. From adjoining staterooms came sounds of sea-water sloshing sluggishly against walls and bunks.

Mr. Kelly swayed to a slow stop, stood listening, and puffed his red face into a scowl. He was hearing things. The sound that disturbed him was a dull thumping noise that accompanied the gurgling of sea-water in a nearby stateroom.

He opened the stateroom door and thumbed a lightswitch. When the switch failed to function, he unhooked an enormous searchlight from his belt and used that. The glare of the searchlight showed him an inundated oblong of floor, a stool, a washbasin, and a double bunk.

Mr. Kelly stared at the floor. He took a step backward and opened his eyes to white-rimmed bigness. Breath rattled in his throat. The hand that gripped the flashlight began to tremble.

The thing on the floor was not pretty to look at. Its feet were somehow wedged beneath the bunk, and from the looks of things the rest of it had been wedged there also, until dislodged by the ship's continued lurching.

It had been dead a long while. Its face was white and bloated, its mouth hung open, and its wide eyes peered glassily into Mr. Kelly's own. With every sluggish roll of the ship, the body lurched as though alive, its pajama-clad torso wallowing in dirty water, its head thumping the base of the washstand in rhythm.

Mr. Kelly backed away from it and quickly pushed the door shut. His heart was pounding furiously. His legs were limp with terror as he hastened back to the dining room.

On a sideboard in the dining room, the police had installed a telephone. Michael Aloysious Kelly seized the instrument in trembling fingers and called police headquarters.

Peter Kane, ace shamus of the Beacon Agency, sat in a backroom booth at Limpy's on Stuart Street and stared moodily at a dark, square bottle of Scotch on the table before him. The bottle was half empty. An hour ago it had been full.

Life, Kane reflected, was very good. With a bottle of Scotch on hand and nothing to disturb a man's drinking time, life could be very pleasant indeed.

Limpy, proprietor of the establishment, waddled into the back room and tapped Kane's shoulder. "Listen, Kane," Limpy said, "Joe Henderson is out front lookin' for you. Will I tell him where you are?"

Joe Henderson was a fellow slave on the Beacon payroll. His presence was ominous. Kane sighed, tamped out a half-smoked cigarette, and realized that life was no longer pleasant.

Henderson peered searchingly into the Kane countenance. He sat down, pushed the square bottle out of the way. "You're assigned to the *Concord* job, Kane," he grinned.

"The police," Kane said, "are already—"

"This is private. The steamship company just called up the office and hired Peter Kane. It seems a dead guy was found on board the wreck last night, after they thought all the bodies had been removed. It also seems the dead guy is a company official. So you're hired to look into things. It must be they think you're good."

Henderson helped himself to a drink. "Me, personally, I think you're a hollow-legged souse, with a taste for a lousy brand of likker," he grinned. "Have a good time, pal. They tell me Moroni is doing the snooping for the police. I feel for you, Kane, I feel for you!"

Life, for Kane, had suddenly become very lousy. He groaned. It was not enough that the peaceful routine of his drunken existence was about to be disturbed. On top of that, the job was one that would necessitate close contact with a lot of bilious-looking green ocean.

"Sure as hell," Kane mumbled, "I'll get seasick. I feel sick already."

He was more than sick when he climbed out of his own coupé a couple of hours later and hiked across a broken-down wharf that fronted on a bulging, heaving expanse of that same despised ocean. The *Concord* had gone aground off Sanders Cove, and Sanders Cove had apparently been used from time immemorial as a dumping ground for clam shells, deceased fish, and sea-spawned refuse that stunk to high heaven.

The odors assailed Kane's innards as he paraded forward. His face had taken on a hue that matched the pale, muddy green of his battered hat. The mingled stenches of things dead and decaying did not harmonize with the quantities of liquor already reposing in the Kane stomach.

"I'm gonna hate this job," Kane groaned.

He went toward an end of the wharf where a large individual in hip boots and dirty clothes was messing about on board a fishing boat. The fellow looked up and blinked watery eyes.

"Take you out around the wreck for a dollar, mister," the fellow said.

Kane stepped aboard. "Take me to it, not around it," Kane groaned. "And for God's sake avoid the bumps. Water—especially a whole lot of it like this —always does things to me."

He had a ghastly upside-down feeling in the pit of his stomach when the fishing boat finally chugged alongside the *Concord*.

Resolutely he climbed the ladder that hung over the steamer's side. The broad grin on the fisherman's leathery face did not bother him. He was beyond being bothered by trivialities.

Kane said, "Stick around, guy," and steered a crooked course along the *Concord's* deck. Opening a door, he marched through a narrow passageway and went down a flight of stairs into the salon.

Moroni and another dick from headquarters were talking near the news-stand and turned to eye Kane as he approached. A scowl hooked Moroni's large face and the scowl became a broad grin. "Well, look what's here," he beamed. "The great Peter Kane himself, in person. You don't look so good this morning, Kane. You sick?"

Kane stared at the bulge of Moroni's big stomach. He thought dully that if Mr. Moroni's large belly were as full of sickness as Peter Kane's little one was, Mr. Moroni would be a very sick man indeed—and that would be swell.

Lowering himself onto a divan, he pulled a pint bottle of whiskey from his pocket and had a long drink. On a job like this, with Large Mouth Moroni and a lot of heaving green ocean all over the place, the only thing to do was get thoroughly plastered and remain that way.

Moroni said: "Sorry, Kane, but you got to clear out. We're under orders from the steamship company to bar anyone who don't have official business or a permit."

"The trouble is," Kane groaned, "the steamship company hired me, so I got to stay." Wearily he helped himself to a long look around the salon.

The place had several occupants. On the other side of the room sat a dumpy, red-faced man who had a corncob pipe stuck in his face and was slouched down in a big leather chair, intently watching everyone else, but saying nothing.

Most likely the fellow was Mr. Michael Aloysious Kelly, who according to the papers, had discovered the body last night.

Mr. Kelly seemed particularly interested in a woman who, at the moment of Kane's arrival, had been opening and closing stateroom doors but who was now standing very still and straight at the foot of the staircase. She was a small woman with dirty-gray hair and a woodenish body that had no curves. Her face was gray and one side of it kept twitching. She had small dark eyes that drilled holes in Kane's soul and made him feel itchy all over.

From the looks of things the woman was either going to throw a fit or fall into a nervous collapse.

Upstairs a couple of men who looked like insurance dicks were nosing around and yelling back and forth to each other.

"Whereabouts," Kane demanded, "is the body?"

The body was on a bunk in the stateroom where Michael Kelly had reputedly discovered it. Kane prowled forward, pushed open the stateroom door. With Moroni trailing him, he entered and took a long look around, bent over the body and stared down into a white, unlovely face that was very dead.

"The dame out there," Moroni said, "is this guy's wife. Says she's positive he was a passenger on the boat and was traveling under an assumed name because he had some other dame in tow. The way she prowls around here, snooping into this and that, would give anybody the living creeps."

Kane said: "Who is this guy?"

"The name is Mr. Clarence Waite—with an 'e'. He's a big shot with the steamship company."

Kane braced himself against the hulk and made a careful inspection, had to forcibly hold down the contents of the Kane stomach while he turned the body over and examined it. It was bad enough to be drunk and seasick both, without having to mess around with a pajama-clad body which was bloated with sea-water and had already begun to decompose.

"You won't find anything," Moroni shrugged. "The guy was drowned. Chances are he tried to get out of bed when the crash came and got himself jammed under the bunk. That's why the body wasn't discovered until later when the roll of the ship dislodged it."

Kane felt the need of another long drink from the bottle in his pocket. He had one. "This guy's name on the passenger list?" he demanded.

"I guess you don't read the papers," Moroni said. "They didn't have no passenger list. The purser's office downstairs was wiped out in the crash, and, thanks to a lot of official dumbness, there wasn't a duplicate list on shore."

Kane made a rumbling noise in his throat. On his way out of the state-room he again peered at the woman who stood near the staircase. If she was the wife of Mr. Clarence Waite, she probably knew things that might be of importance.

He started toward her, changed his mind and stopped. Someone else, coming down the stairs, was apparently bent on engaging the woman in conversation.

Kane put a cigarette in his mouth, walked unobtrusively to a divan and sat down. A scowl twisted the corner of his mouth that was not filled with cigarette. He wondered what Dr. Nicolas Ackerman was doing on board the *Concord*. Ackerman, tagged with a shady reputation which extended far back into the past, was supposedly the head of a private hospital in Plymouth. The man towered above Mrs. Clarence Waite, had a hand on the woman's elbow as he talked to her in low tones that failed to reach Kane's ears.

He had a string-bean body and stooped shoulders, an angular dark-skinned face that would have harmonized nicely—and probably did—with operating rooms and the midnight moans of patients. When he was through talking he gently patted the woman's arm, shook his head to toss a mop of black hair away from his high forehead, and walked away. Kane watched him.

The man nodded to Moroni, peered darkly in Kane's direction and strode along the passageway that led to the dining room.

Kane stood up, blew cigarette smoke through quivering nostrils. He had met Dr. Nicolas Ackerman before; had, in fact, been assigned to investigate certain shady dealings in which Ackerman had been involved. The presence of Ackerman aboard the *Concord* was something to think about.

Moroni had evidently thought about it. "That guy," Moroni said, "gives me the creeps, Kane. How he got a permit to snoop around here, I wouldn't know. He says one of the crash victims was a staff member at his hospital, but if that's any excuse for him to go prowling around like a walking corpse—"

Kane had the neck of a pint bottle in his throat and was gurgling noisily. He gagged, spat a spray of whiskey at the floor, muttered darkly: "With guys like him hanging around, and a water-logged corpse to mess over, and a floor that won't keep still under a man's feet, this is one lousy job."

He paced forward, pawed the wall in an effort to keep the Kane torso on an even keel. Then, because someone called him by name, he dragged his unsteady feet to a stop and turned.

The young man who came toward him had, for the past half hour, been sitting at the desk in the salon, methodically filling pages of paper with what was probably an official report. He was slender, good-looking, and had a lick of black hair curling gracefully over one temple.

He said: "You're Detective Kane, aren't you?"

"I was," Kane growled, "before I came aboard this damn barge."

The young man did not smile. His gray eyes scrutinized Kane from head to foot. "I'm Frank Deasy," he said. "The company sent me down to make an estimate of the financial loss. If there's anything I can do—"

"You work for Coastal Steamship?"

The young man nodded. "Mr. Waite," he said, with a movement of his head toward the door of the stateroom where Clarence Waite lay sprawled on the deathbunk, "was my superior."

Kane exhaled slowly, put a hand on the young man's arm and steered him to a divan. If the corpse cargo of this wrecked barge had formerly been Mr. Deasy's superior, it was just probable that Mr. Deasy might be able to furnish pertinent information.

Mr. Deasy could and did. "It's probably true," he said, sitting with his knees apart and his gaze focused on the floor, "that Mr. Waite was on the passenger list under an assumed name." He glanced at Kane quickly and put a hand out to touch Kane's arm. "Understand, I have no proof. I only know that Waite took frequent trips to New York whenever home conditions got too stiff for him. Usually he took along a companion."

Kane nodded, glanced across the room to where Clarence Waite's wife had been standing at the foot of the staircase. The woman was no longer there. Evidently she had quietly gone upstairs.

"So you think Waite was a passenger?" Kane murmured.

"Yes, I do." Frank Deasy blew ashes from the glowing tip of a cigarette and screwed his good-looking face into a scowl. "In the first place, he'd been working hard at the office, preparing the semiannual financial report for the auditors. It was at times like that that he usually helped himself to impromptu vacations and slipped away without saying a word to any of us." Deasy stood up. "If I can help you in any way, let me know. Right now I've got to get back to the office."

Kane sat for ten minutes with his legs stuck out in front of him and his gaze focused on his shoes. The Kane brain was at last beginning to function, probably because of the increased amount of liquor in the Kane stomach.

In the beginning, this thing had looked like a case for an undertaker, not for a private shamus who disliked messing about in surroundings where people got seasick. Yet the Coastal Steamship Company had hired Peter Kane to investigate the discovery of Clarence Waite's body.

That meant that the officials of Coastal Steamship were inclined to disagree with the theory that Clarence Waite had been a passenger.

Perhaps, after all, Mr. Clarence Waite had not been a passenger.

Kane pushed himself erect and found Moroni. He said: "Has the medical examiner seen Waite yet?"

The Moroni countenance wig-wagged sideways. "Not yet. We're taking the remains with us when we get through here."

In the chair beside Moroni sat the chalk-faced form of Mr. Michael Aloysious Kelly. Mr. Kelly was obviously frightened. From the looks of things, Moroni had been doing a great deal of involved thinking and had arrived at the conclusion that Mr. Kelly would bear questioning. Having decided upon that, Moroni had apparently, in the usual Moroni manner, taken Michael Aloysious Kelly apart to see what made him tick. Mr. Kelly looked very ill.

Kane glanced into Kelly's gray face, sighed, and took himself away from there. The pint bottle in his pocket was empty, and the sickness in his own stomach was insidiously creeping higher.

He took himself out on deck. A grunt of relief gurgled in his throat when he saw the guardian of the fishing boat had obeyed orders and hung around.

II

A Shadowy Assassin

It was two P.M. when the Kane chariot groaned to a stop on Atlantic Avenue in Boston, in front of the building occupied by Coastal Steamship Lines, Inc. Kane had used up the best part of two hours in driving back from Sanders Cove; had stopped twice en route, parked himself in drinking establishments, and consumed large quantities of liquor in a vain attempt to rid his mind of the ghastly, unshakable vision of green ocean that clung there.

Nothing but a prolonged diet of good Scotch whiskey would ever budge that ghastly vision and return the Kane innards to normal.

He got out of the car and steered a crooked course up the steps of the building before him. Instinct warned him to avoid such stomach-lifting vehicles as elevators, so he used the stairs.

For half an hour he sat in conference with the officials of Coastal Steamship and acquired information concerning the past history and habits of Mr. Clarence Waite.

The information checked quite nicely with that which had already been volunteered by Mr. Waite's underling, the athletic young man whose name was Frank Deasy.

Waite had made frequent trips to New York on the quiet. Undoubtedly his very angry and very nagging wife had known a great deal about it.

And it was unfortunate that Waite had seen fit to return from his last New York visit as an incognito passenger on board the ill-fated *Concord*. Most unfortunate. It meant that the company's financial report would now be unavoidably held up, and would have to be completed by Waite's understudy.

"How come you're so positive," Kane demanded, "that Waite traveled under an assumed name? I thought the passenger list was lost."

"Yes, yes, the passenger list *had* been lost. But the purser, whose duty it was to see that all passengers were duly listed, was a man who had a good memory. He was positive that no such name as Clarence Waite had appeared on the list.

"So you see, Mr. Kane," murmured one smirking gentleman who apparently did the most of Coastal's hiring and firing, "we were really on the wrong track when we requested your services. There is nothing now to investigate. We really won't need you after all. I'm sorry."

A sigh of relief whispered on Kane's whiskey-sweet breath. "That," he murmured, "is a break. You don't have any idea."

He felt so good that he took the elevator on the way down. That was a mistake. The sudden drop of the elevator car pushed the contents of the Kane stomach into the Kane throat and brought a weird whiteness to his face.

When he got into his car he sat very still for ten long minutes, while the heaving sensation in his mid-section subsided to normal. Then he drove to Limpy's on Stuart Street.

It was six P.M. when Joe Henderson, fellow slave on the Beacon Agency payroll, again found him in Limpy's back room. The quart bottle on Kane's table was two-thirds empty. Kane was plastered.

A grin was on Henderson's large face. He sat down, murmured gently: "I hear you got relieved of that steamship job. That made you mad, huh?"

Kane had a silver cigarette case in one hand and a pony of Scotch in the other.

"About fifteen minutes ago," Henderson went on, "the Coastal Steamship outfit called the office and re-engaged the services of a guy by the name of Peter Kane. It seems the medical examiner found some interesting stuff in the stomach of Mr. Clarence Waite. Poison, in fact. And so the whole thing looks very dark and dirty all of a sudden, and your vacation is over."

Kane stared, made rumbling noises in his throat. A look of pain came into his countenance. "I'sh a cruel world," he said solemnly.

"The boss," said Henderson, "told me to tell you to hie yourself down there to the wreck and get on the job before you get plastered or something. He figures you'll stay sober down there."

Darkness had blurred the greenish-gray hue of the Atlantic when Kane got out of his car in Sanders Cove and paced sluggishly across the wharf. A light glowed in the window of the wharf shanty. At Kane's drunken "hallo," the guardian of the fishing boat emerged from the shack's doorway.

"There ain't a livin' soul on board except Kelly, the watchman," the fellow informed Kane while guiding his chug-chug boat through restless waters that disturbed the Kane intestines. "Mr. Moroni, he told me not to take no one out there tonight unless they got a written permit, but I guess you're all right, seein' as how you're a detective."

Kane was silent. His mouth was clamped shut and he kept it that way for reasons best known to Peter Kane. When he had climbed the ladder and gained the *Concord's* deck, he closed his eyes and hung onto the rail.

The chug-chug man called up to him: "You want me to wait?"

Kane shook his head, opened his mouth, said, "Come back in a couple of hours," very quickly, and closed his mouth again. Then he pawed his way along the deck and descended into the steamer's bowels.

A ship's lantern was burning in the salon, and Kelly, the night watchman, came scuffing from the dining room, staring with big eyes and gripping an enormous searchlight in one outthrust fist.

"Oh, it's you," Kelly mumbled. "I was wonderin' who in the name of Gawd at this time of night—" He shuddered, peered fearfully around. "This job is enough to give a man the holy shakes, Mr. Kane."

Kane said: "You all alone?"

"I—I think so. But sometimes I ain't so sure. I'll be sittin' here, readin' out of a magazine or somethin', and I'll hear the strangest noises."

Kane walked crookedly to a chair and sat down. He had come here to do things, to look around and make his own kind of investigation without the interference of Moroni and others who might veto the Kane method of research.

The lantern swung slowly back and forth. Malshaped shadows, created by its yellow glare, did the same thing. Kane's innards followed suit.

A groan of misery spilled from Kane's lips. Then, very suddenly, he stared straight ahead.

His hands tightened on the arms of the chair he was sitting in and his big body stiffened. His eyes widened, refused to blink.

At the head of the stairs, some twenty paces distant, stood a dark, ill-defined shape that did not belong there.

The shape was grotesquely tall in actuality and looked gigantic because of the shadows that enveloped it. It had two glowing eyes that returned Kane's stare. For twenty seconds Kane's blood ran cold with creeping dread of things sinister and supernatural. Then the menacing monster moved.

It descended the stairs slowly and paced forward into the glow of the lantern. Kane relaxed, dragged breath into his numbed lungs and pushed himself erect, scowling. His left hand slid into a pocket of his coat.

"Good evening, Mr. Kane," the shape said.

Kane growled, "Is it?" and stood wide-legged, glaring. If the presence of Dr. Nicolas Ackerman on board the *Concord* had been ominous before, during daylight hours, it was doubly so now. The man's thin-lipped smile was ominous, too, and in the ochre glow of the lantern his shadowed face possessed a corpse pallor.

The man had stopped within five feet of Kane and was standing motionless, smiling as though fully aware of Kane's uneasiness. He stiffened slightly as Kane jerked toward him.

Kane said grimly: "All right, Ackerman. What's the big idea?"

The man's eyebrows and shoulders went up in unison. "I do not understand what you mean."

"You're here, aren't you? What for?"

"I have a permit—"

"Your permit's no good at night and you know it! How'd you get aboard?"

Again that ominous half-smile curled Ackerman's mouth. "It is really quite simple, Mr. Kane. I hired a man to bring me here in a rowboat."

"Where is he now?"

Ackerman calmly raised one arm and peered at his strapwatch. "By now he should have returned. I told him to come back in an hour. Really, Mr. Kane, my motive for coming here tonight was quite reasonable. I'm neither a vampire, as you seem to think, nor a thief in the dark. I came here to take pictures."

"To what?"

"To take pictures." Quietly, Ackerman displayed a small but expensive camera, rolls of films, flash-sheet equipment. "This morning, while I was here to check on the unfortunate death of one of my assistants who was a passenger, I was deeply impressed by the macabre atmosphere of the ship. Photography is my hobby, Mr. Kane—especially the photographing of things weird and unusual. So I took the liberty of returning here tonight—"

Kane's eyes narrowed, clouded with suspicion, but the vague smile did not fade from Ackerman's thin lips. With a shrug the doctor stepped backward. "Now, if you are quite reassured, Mr. Kane, I had perhaps better be leaving."

Kane watched him go, felt damp and clammy all over. He returned slowly to his chair and helped himself to a long stiff drink from the quart container he had brought with him. He needed it. The evil stare of Ackerman's eyes had eaten right through to the Kane arteries and soured the blood that coursed there.

His gaze focused again on the ship's lantern. The lantern was still swaying horribly to and fro, and the floor of the salon was doing the same thing. Kane groaned, closed his eyes and gulped hard. But closing his eyes did not help.

Peter Kane, ace dick of the Beacon Agency, was a sick shamus. Nothing less than a team of mules could have dragged him out of the chair he was sitting in. He wanted very much to die and get it over with.

Instead, he spent the next half hour guzzling from the quart bottle. And for the first time in his eventful life he passed out before the supply of liquor was finished.

The strapwatch on his wrist said four twenty A.M. when he came to, but he did not know it. His gluey eyes jerked open, focused groggily on the swaying lantern. His mouth was full of a whiskey-thick tongue and his big body was piled like a deflated blimp in the chair.

He groaned, hauled himself to a more upright position. And the sound which had aroused him from his drunken stupor came again, whispering its way into his consciousness.

He hunched forward, stared. From a passageway upstairs, in gloom beyond the head of the staircase, came a sound of slow footsteps.

Frowning, Kane pushed himself to his feet and swayed forward.

He was seasick and suffering from a monstrous hangover but he managed somehow to keep on an even keel as he swayed across the salon floor. Sometimes, despite its usual load of Limpy's bad liquor—or perhaps because of that—the Kane brain functioned clearly when other brains might be expected to wallow in darkness. Right now the Kane brain was full of a disturbing intuition that something was very wrong.

The gloom around him was alive with strange noises that might be considered normal on board a wrecked hulk which lay at the mercy of heaving seas. But that other sound—that sluggish whisper of footsteps in the passage above—was somehow ominous.

Kane pawed the bannister, ascended slowly. Hangover-hammers pounded a dull dirge inside his skull and his throat was gummy with the fusel oil in Limpy's liquor. When he reached the head of the stairs he stopped, dragged breath into his lungs and gathered himself together.

The sound of footsteps had ceased.

Kane moved slowly into gloom, tip-toed along a corridor where stateroom doors frowned darkly on both sides. Ahead of him a sliver of light crept from beneath a closed portal and yellowed the floor.

In a dozen slow strides Kane reached the door, thrust a hand toward the knob. From inside came sounds of a bunk creaking. The light was suddenly extinguished.

The stateroom door swung open in Peter Kane's face.

The liquor in Kane's big body went to his legs as he lunged sideways to avoid the pile-driver fist that lashed out at him. His shoulder crashed the side of the doorframe; the impact spun him off balance, left him wide open. The fist raked one side of his face.

It was a hard fist full of knuckles. The blow jarred Kane's head on his shoulders and drew blood. It would have knocked a sober man out. Instead of doing that to Kane, it shook some of the whiskey-mist from his eyes and brought a savage snarl from his bleeding lips.

He staggered forward, cursed the darkness that blinded him to the flailing arms that sought to drive him back. One thing he was sure of—he was fighting a man who knew how to fight. An upthrust knee ground into the pit of his stomach. When he stumbled back, gasping, his assailant rushed him with lowered head, both fists working like pistons.

One of those fists held something big, solid—probably the searchlight whose glow had lured Kane along the corridor. The weapon crashed down on Kane's head, crashed again and again as he got his arms around the killer's body and tried to drag the man down.

It found a vital spot. Blood trickled from Kane's gasping mouth. He stumbled, clawed the wall as he collapsed.

The killer lurched away from him, turned, wrenched open a shuttered window that gave access to the cat-walk outside. For an instant Kane's eyes, blurred by the blood, focused on a contorted shadow shape that clambered through the aperture.

The shape thudded loudly on the deck outside, made more noise as it clambered onto the ship's rail. Through the shuttered window Kane caught a dim vision of something big and dark leaping out into space. A muffled splash echoed up from the sea below.

Kane didn't hear the splash. It was smothered by the groans that issued from his own battered mouth as he crawled on hands and knees into the corridor.

He clung hard to consciousness, refusing to pass out. At the end of the passage he clutched the bannister at the stairhead and hauled himself erect.

"Kelly," he croaked hoarsely. "Kelly!"

Then he collapsed in a gurgling contortion and slid grotesquely down the carpeted stairs, to land in a sprawled heap on the floor below.

III

Call for Kane

A sidewalk clock on Huntington Avenue said four thirty P.M. when Kane hiked out of the Peter Bent Brigham and thumbed a passing cab. Getting out of the hospital had not been as easy as getting into it. He had known nothing whatever about getting in. Michael Aloysious Kelly and a Sanders Cove doctor had driven him to the city in his own car, after Kelly and the pilot of the fishing boat had lugged him ashore. When consciousness had finally filtered through the blood-mist in Kane's brain, his blurred gaze had focused in bewilderment on the hovering face of a hospital doctor and the white walls of an accident ward.

Getting out of the place had necessitated a lot of loud talk, threats, and the signing of certain papers which relieved the hospital of all responsibility for what might happen after the exodus.

Kane said grimly to the cab driver: "I got a car parked in the Huntington Garage, or so they tell me. Drive over there."

It was after six when he reached Sanders Cove. The ocean was a monstrous caterpillar that crawled away into gathering gloom. The owner of the fishing boat, lured from his wharf shanty by the sounds of the car's approach, stopped abruptly in the lighted doorway and gaped as if seeing a ghost.

Kane said huskily: "I hope to God you got a drink around somewhere. I need one. My brand is Scotch, but anything you got will do."

When he climbed the *Concord's* ladder and descended into the ship's salon some ten minutes later, he felt better. The owner of the boat had possessed a pint of amber-hued liquid that smelled like the concentrated juice of crushed bedbugs and tasted worse than it smelled. Even that, however, felt better than the ether fumes which had worried the Kane stomach for the past many hours.

He walked crookedly across the salon and was oblivious to the amazed stares of Moroni, of Mr. Michael Aloysious Kelly, and of others who were assembled there. He looked worse than he felt. One side of his face was swathed in bandages and his greenish hat was cocked at a grotesque angle because of the strips of adhesive that humped his forehead.

Moroni, recovering from the shock, gasped out: "Where the hell did you come from?"

Kane made a face and sat down. "I guess you heard what happened."

"Yeah, sure. Some guy beat you up with a flashlight. We got the light right here. Found it in the stateroom. But how—"

Kane stood up stiffly and walked to the news counter, peered down at the searchlight. "Any fingerprints on this?" he demanded.

"The guy must've worn gloves," Moroni said.

Kane stared around him, encountered the gaping stare of Kelly's big eyes and saw a thin, hawk-faced woman talking to one of Moroni's men on the other side of the room. The woman was Mrs. Clarence Waite. Kane hooked his mouth into a puzzled frown and took a long look before turning his attention elsewhere.

He wondered how it was that some women, after nagging their husbands all through life, suddenly took a large interest in them after death.

He poked a cigarette into his mouth and sat down. To Moroni he said, suddenly: "Has Ackerman been around?"

"Thank God, no. He gave me enough creeps yesterday." The Moroni jaw-muscles tightened ominously. "Whatever Ackerman does from now on, I'll know about it. I put a man to keep tabs on him."

"When?"

"Last night."

"Last night," Kane said, "the good Doctor Ackerman was—" He stopped talking, peered across the room at the approaching figure of Frank Deasy. Deasy had come from the dining room, was staring at Kane in open-mouthed astonishment as he paced forward.

"Last night Ackerman was what?" Moroni demanded.

"Skip it," Kane said. "I want a look at that stateroom upstairs." He put his feet under him, stood up.

Frank Deasy, gaping at him, exclaimed loudly: "Good Lord, Mr. Kane, what are *you* doing here? Kelly told me you were at the Peter Bent Brigham!"

"They serve lousy liquor in hospitals," Kane said, "and they're stingy as hell with it. I didn't like the joint."

He strode across the salon and went upstairs, felt wobbly in his legs as he prowled along the upstairs passageway and pushed open the same door that had opened in his face the night before.

Before entering the stateroom he shot a quick glance both ways along the corridor. Inside, he closed the door behind him, pulled a flashlight from his pocket and looked around.

The room contained nothing worth looking at.

He strode to the shuttered window and peered out. A moment later he was on the cat-walk outside, leaning over the ship's rail. The sea was an undulating carpet far below. The light in the wharf shanty, on shore, was a long way off.

Scowling, Kane went back downstairs, knew before he reached the foot of the big staircase that something had happened during his absence. Moroni was hiking the floor, chewing savagely on a sodden stump of black cigar.

He looked up and glared as Kane approached. "I just had a phone call," he said thickly, "from Moe Finch at headquarters. It seems Finch had a hurry call from some girl who works for Coastal Steamship. The girl was one of Clarence Waite's secretaries."

"This has possibilities," Kane murmured.

Moroni evidently thought so. "This girl's been out of town on vacation, see? Just this afternoon she got back to the city and heard about Waite's death. So she calls up police headquarters and says she knows where there's some very important information to be had."

Moroni spat cigar smoke out of a twisted mouth. "So Moe Finch, being too busy betting on the ponies or something, tells her to come down and tell me all about it. Then he calls me up and tells me to hang around till she gets here."

Obviously Moroni did not relish the idea of hanging around. Neither did Peter Kane. Kane murmured softly: "So she works in Waite's office and she knows something, does she?" Rocking around, he hiked toward the stairs.

Moroni said: "Hey, what's the idea? Where you goin'?"

"Only a dumb dick like you," Kane grunted, "would even think of hanging around after getting a phone call like that."

It was after eight o'clock when he got to Boston and later than that when he parked his car on Atlantic Avenue in front of the Coastal Steamship Building. He used up half an hour in rounding up a sleepy-eyed night janitor and convincing the man that Peter Kane, being currently in the employ of Coastal, had a right to be let into the Coastal offices.

The janitor, after much deliberation, turned on some lights, reluctantly manned an elevator, and ushered Kane into the very dark and very gloomy rooms on the building's fourth floor.

Kane went straight to the private office of Mr. Clarence Waite but he had a feeling he would be too late getting there.

He was.

With a hand on the light switch inside the door, he gaped at the scene of upheaval before him. The carpeted floor was strewn with papers; the contents of desk drawers and filing cabinets had been dumped out, pawed through and flung aside. Wax records of a dictating machine had been spilled from their containers and smashed into chunks of black, gleaming stuff that crunched under Kane's feet as he advanced.

He turned a slow circle, stared around him. Half an hour later, when he paced wearily out of the office, the hangdog look on his face would have soured milk. He had listlessly waded through all the stuff that the intruder before him had condescended to leave behind. He had methodically explored Clarence Waite's domain from end to end.

The sullen curve of his mouth was proof enough that he had wasted half an hour of good drinking time.

When he left the building he drove uptown to Limpy's and from there drove to the Back Bay apartment house where Peter Kane's name adorned a brass mailbox. The ache in his battered head had grown to alarming proportions. Letting himself into his three-room apartment on the third floor, he savagely kicked the door shut and paraded into the living room.

At four thirty A.M. the next morning, when the phone rang, Peter Kane was sitting deep in a big easy chair with his stockinged feet propped on an endtable and a large bottle of Limpy's very bad Scotch squatting on the floor beside him.

The voice on the phone was vaguely familiar.

"Mr. Kane!" the voice wailed. "This is Frank Deasy. You've got to come down here!"

"Down where?" Kane mumbled.

"Here—to the *Concord!* Something frightful has happened! You've got to come, Mr. Kane. Our company hired you—"

Kane made loud grumbling noises and asked questions, hung up when he realized that Frank Deasy was too excited to supply coherent answers. Something undoubtedly had happened. It was essential that Mr. Kane rush at once to the scene of the happening.

"If ever there's a lousy job around," Kane groaned, "I'm elected."

It occurred to him later, as he sat behind the wheel of the car, that after all he might as well be glad of a chance to get the job over with. During the past few hours the Kane thinking apparatus had spawned several loose ends of ideas that were beginning to blend together.

He had to get the owner of the fishing boat out of bed, had to bang on the shanty door and bellow loudly before a light went on in the shack and the fellow appeared. Out on the steamer's hulk other lights were visible, and between steamer and wharf lay an expanse of bulging ocean that looked dark and mean.

"You wouldn't have any more of that brimstone-branded brew of yours around, would you?" Kane said. "Sure as hell I'll be sick as a goat without some little thing to bolster me up."

The fellow had some. But despite the liquor's potency, it was sea-sickness, not the pale contents of the bottle, that caused Kane to stagger drunkenly when he entered the ship's salon some ten minutes later.

The salon was empty.

From the direction of the dining room came a murmur of voices that dragged Kane to a halt, made him stop and peer around. He went slowly past the foot of the staircase, paced along the passageway. The voices emanated from a stateroom set back in a small side-passage off the end of the dining hall.

Moroni was doing most of the talking.

Kane pushed over the threshold, stood staring. It was a big stateroom and had a pair of iron beds instead of a bunk. Moroni, in the middle of the floor between the beds, had his hands hipped and his legs spread wide and was glaring into the dark, unlovely face of Dr. Nicolas Ackerman.

Michael Aloysious Kelly stood with his back against a wall, his big eyes bulging, his face, for once, empty of the corncob pipe.

Frank Deasy was methodically rummaging through a small overnight case that lay opened on a chair.

"Well, for goo'nesh sakes," Kane croaked.

The occupants of the room turned toward him, and Moroni grunted disdainfully: "Oh, it's you." Frank Deasy had a sheepish look on his face as he straightened above the overnight case and came forward.

"I guess I should have waited a while before I called you, Mr. Kane," he said. "There really was no need for you to come down here."

"Thanks," Kane said. Slowly he paced toward the cot on the far side of the room, stood there and peered down.

IV

Death in a Dumb-Waiter

The girl who lay there had a crumpled blue dress on, and the dress was soiled and wet looking. The girl was young. She lay with one leg bent at the knee and the fingers of one hand pressed rigidly into her stomach. Her face was gray and dirty and her hair was a stringy mop that bulged out over the pillow.

From the looks of things, she had been dead some time.

"Where," Kane demanded in a low voice, "did *this* come from?"

No one was in a hurry to answer him. Michael Kelly was gawking. Moroni had jerked his large head in Kane's direction but was still standing over the stiff, chalk-faced form of Nicolas Ackerman, who sat like a propped-up wax figure on the other cot.

Frank Deasy said, slowly: "Kelly was the one who found her. He was making his rounds, and when he entered this room he heard a kind of creaking noise that seemed to come from over there." He aimed an unsteady hand at the corner of the room, where a door hung open. "The noise came from behind that door, but he couldn't get the door open, so he went and got help."

Kane said softly: "The door was locked?"

"No, it wasn't. It was stuck. Mr. Moroni and I got it open and found— her."

Kane strode forward and would have hiked over the threshold. He stopped just in time, used a searchlight from his pocket and screwed his face into a puzzled frown. It was a queer layout. The enclosure beyond the threshold was a small-sized closet of some kind, but the closet had no floor.

"When the company bought this ship," Deasy said, "the dining hall was half again as big as it is now, and these staterooms didn't exist. Apparently this was a dumb-waiter leading down to the kitchen. When the staterooms were built, the dumb-waiter was blocked up with a false door."

Kane leaned forward, peered down into the depths and heard a gurgle of water down below. "You found the girl in here?"

"Yes. She was wedged in the shaft. The creaking noise Kelly heard was caused by the pressure of her body against the walls, every time the ship rolled."

Moroni said grimly, from the other side of the room: "The idea is, the girl was a passenger on the night of the crash. She got panicky and made a dive for the door. The door was supposed to be locked but it wasn't—or else the lock was so damn ancient that she had strength enough to get it open. She thought she was getting out into a corridor or something, and instead of that she took a nose-dive down the dumb-waiter and got jammed tight. And she's been there ever since. That," said Moroni, "is what Deasy thinks, anyway."

Kane peered at the overnight bag.

"Where did that come from?"

"We found that down in the shaft with her," Moroni shrugged. "Deasy thinks she snatched it up when she made the break. Maybe Deasy is right about the whole business. Me, I think different."

"And just why do you think different?"

Moroni scowled, jerked his head toward the girl's body. "It so happens, Kane, that this girl's name is Helen Tilson. It also happens that she's the dame who was supposed to come to me a long time ago with some important information. About two minutes after you barged out of here, the gal called up and said she'd be late. Said she was going to the steamship office first, to get the papers that contained that important information. Well— here she is."

Moroni had his theories but was not sure of them. He went into doubtful detail. "Maybe," he said, "the phone calls to Moe Finch and me were just gags. Maybe the gal who did the phoning had a good reason for using this gal's name. It's possible, all right, that this dame was a passenger the night of the crash. Sure as hell, this corpse could have been jammed down that dumb-waiter for a couple of centuries without ever being discovered except by accident."

Moroni screwed his face around to glare into the gray features of Dr. Nicolas Ackerman, "But it also happens that I found *this* mug snoopin' around here about an hour ago, and so help me, he says he was takin' pictures!"

Moroni had evidently worked long and hard on the good doctor. Ackerman showed pathetic signs of having been subjected to the usual Moroni method of third-degree. "I—I *was* taking pictures," he insisted.

Kane took a long drink from the pint bottle of vile-smelling liquor he had acquired from the owner of the fishing boat. He felt wobbly from being so long in a stuffy stateroom. "If it's all the same to you people," he mumbled, "I'll go take a walk."

He closed the stateroom door behind him and was scowling as he paraded across the dining hall and went out on deck. The Kane brain had begun to do a great amount of deep thinking.

Half an hour or so later, when Moroni and the others appeared, Peter Kane was apparently plastered and his eyes had taken on a sickly green hue from peering so long at so much ocean. Moroni had a look of triumph on his face and a firm grip on the arm of Dr. Nicolas Ackerman.

The expression on the face of Mr. Michael Kelly, who shuffled along in the rear of the procession, was strangely enigmatic. The Kelly mouth seemed to bear a slight suggestion of triumph, too.

Moroni said: "That's where you're goin', Ackerman. Right straight to headquarters until you come clean. I got this thing all figured out, and it ain't often I figure things out wrong." He shoved Ackerman to the rail and yelled down to the admiral of the fishing boat. To Kane he said: "Hang onto this mug a minute."

"Poshitively," Kane gurgled.

Kane was plastered, and when he released his grip on the rail and turned around, his feet crossed and he went off balance. The deck was slippery with spray. Less than three paces distant, the railing had a break in it where the ladder hung over the ship's side.

Kane pawed empty air and let out a yell. His big body teetered, went out on one foot and hung over vacant space. Moroni stabbed a hand at Kane's legs, missed. Frank Deasy yelled incoherent words. Kane went overboard.

He struck with a huge splash, went down a long way into undulating wet darkness and made blubbering sounds when he broke surface. A searchlight gleamed yellow on deck and the beam picked him out, clung to him as he dogpaddled wildly in a frantic effort to stay afloat.

From the looks of things he either couldn't swim or was too drunk to remember how. He was blubbering under a second time when a hurtling shape shot head foremost from the steamer's deck and sliced the water beside him.

The hurtling shape was Frank Deasy.

Deasy could swim. With a minimum of effort he dragged Kane up from under, lugged him to the ladder. Moroni and Michael Kelly hauled Kane to the deck. Moroni growled: "Well, of all the drunken souse-brained idiots, you're it."

Frank Deasy came up the ladder hand over hand and spat out a mouthful of sea-water.

Kane stood up. "Thanks, Deasy," he said. Oddly enough he did not look half as plastered as before. His eyes were narrowed and there was nothing fuzzy about the metallic rasp of his voice. "Thanks, Deasy. That's all I needed to know."

Moroni gaped at him. Deasy took a step backward, staring, and said: "What?"

"It was either you or Ackerman," Kane murmured. He took a police thirty-eight from a pocket of his drenched coat and toyed with it. The gun dripped water, but the chances were ten to one it would work if called upon. Deasy made large eyes at it and stood stiff as wood.

"At first," Kane said, "I figured it was Ackerman. I figured he and Mrs. Clarence Waite were in cahoots and engineered Waite's murder between them. That was before the girl called Moe Finch and said she worked for Waite and knew where to put her hands on some important information."

Kane was drunk enough to be enjoying himself. The scared look on Deasy's face amused him, brought a twisted grin to his lips. "I guess you got into a jam with the finances or something, huh?" he gurgled. "Why not come clean?"

Moroni said, frowning: "For God's sake, Kane, what's eating you? Do you go nuts like this all the time?"

"This mug murdered Waite because Waite knew things," Kane shrugged. "He'll tell us all about it in a minute. Just stick around. He murdered Waite, and figured to do it in a way that would leave him a loophole in case things got hot. You can't burn a man for murder unless you first prove the victim was murdered. The poison in Waite's stomach didn't mean a thing. The guy might've been drinking poisoned liquor the night this barge cracked up.

"The fireworks began when this Helen Tilson girl, or whatever her name is, came back to town and called Moe Finch. Maybe you don't remember it, but Deasy here was in the salon when you were blabbing to me about getting the call from Moe—and you weren't talking in a whisper. I guess Deasy was still there when the girl called you and said she was going to the steamship office. The chances are, you even told him all about it."

"Sure I did," Moroni growled. "Why wouldn't I?"

"Sure you did. So Deasy faded out of here and got to the steamship office ahead of me, and got his paws on the girl, and went through the joint with a cootie comb. I bet you never even knew he left the ship."

Moroni put thick fingers into his hair and scratched. He seemed to be remembering things that heretofore had seemed unimportant.

Kane said: "Until I took a look around Waite's private office, I was on the wrong track. I figured on Ackerman and Waite's wife being in on some dirty scheme that spelled murder. But there were some funny things done in that office. For one thing, a whole bunch of dictating-machine records were smashed."

The Kane orbs drilled holes in Deasy's white face. "Only a guy who worked pretty close to Waite," he said, "would even figure to suspect that Waite might have put that important information on the dictating machine. I guess you better come clean."

Frank Deasy's nerves were in good shape. Despite the lack of blood in his stiff face, he forced a sickly grin to his mouth. "You're altogether wrong, Mr. Kane," he said. "I assure you—"

"There was another thing had to be figured out," Kane mused. "The mug who murdered Waite and Miss Tilson had to be a good swimmer. He couldn't have lugged those bodies aboard by boat, because the risk was too big. So he had to be a guy with enough swimming ability to tote them through the water. I figured on finding out if you could swim well enough to tote a dead man through the ocean, Deasy."

Moroni jerked a step forward, stood glaring. He was no longer interested in Dr. Nicolas Ackerman. "So you weren't plastered when you went overboard? You can swim?"

"I can—" Kane caught his answer, changed it quickly. "I can swim like a hunk of lead pipe, mister. It was a chance I had to take." The gun in his fist drooped a little as he swung again on Deasy. "How about coming clean, mug?"

Deasy went limp, had a look of resignation in his face. He had an eye on the opening in the rail where the ship's ladder hung over the side. He shrugged his shoulders.

"Did you get the important information or is it still in the steamship offices somewhere?" Kane demanded.

"It—it's still there," Deasy mumbled. A glint of black hate gleamed in his eyes. "I couldn't find it. Only for that, I'd have a chance to get out of this, damn you!"

"Tell us about it."

"You know about it already." Deasy's voice dropped low, became a mumble. "I was in deep. I—well, I'd stolen enough to send me to prison for—a long time. I'd been playing the horses." He put a trembling hand to his face and wiped away beads of perspiration. "Waite was preparing a report for the auditors," he groaned, "and he found out what I'd done. I—well, I had to shut him up. I despised him anyway."

"And being a bright young man," Kane grunted, "you figured to plant the body on board ship where it would look like Waite had been a passenger the night of the crash. What's the rest of it?"

"You know the rest," Deasy mumbled. "When Helen Tilson called up, I realized that Waite must have made out some kind of a report before I killed him. I had to get to the office before she did. I—I guess I should have hidden there and waited for her to find the papers, but I was nervous. When she showed up, I—"

He shuddered, stared helplessly at Kane. "Then I got her into my car and drove down here and dumped the body into the dumb-waiter shaft. The overnight case didn't belong to Helen. It was something I found in one of the other staterooms the day after the crash."

"You're not so dumb," Kane muttered.

"I didn't think the body would be discovered so soon," Deasy moaned. "When Kelly stumbled on it, I had to think fast. That's why I called you. I— well, I thought it would clear me of suspicion, and you'd be so drunk you wouldn't guess the truth anyway, and—"

Deasy's voice ended in a sucking intake of breath as he lunged forward. The distance to the rail was about eight feet. He took it in a headlong rush, cleared the opening with inches to spare and streaked down into darkness. The guttural drone of his voice was still alive on deck when the heaving black waters of the Atlantic sucked him under.

Moroni and Ackerman and Michael Kelly stood gaping. Peter Kane ploughed forward, stood in the open space above the ship's ladder and peered down at the widening rings of black water below.

The sight of so much water brought a pained look to Kane's face. He pulled a pint bottle from his pocket, dropped it and growled to Moroni: "Take care of that. I'll need it!" His big body shot out and down, sliced the water and reappeared almost instantly. A stream of gurgling white foam trailed out behind him as he surged away from the ship.

Moroni, gasping, said in a hoarse voice: "For God's sake!"

Frank Deasy could swim, but the torpedo-like shape behind him caught up with him. Deasy twisted around, put both hands out of the water and raked savagely at Kane's face, battered wildly as Kane closed in. Terror made a contorted mask of his face and sucked a lurid shriek from his lips.

Kane growled, savagely, "I owe you this one, mug!" and drove a sledge-hammer fist into the killer's screaming mouth.

The fist crunched home, brought a sobbing sound from Deasy's throat. Thrashing wildly, he flung himself back, spun in the water and again headed for the distant light in the wharf shanty on shore.

He turned when Kane's big body again bore down on him. The surface in front of Kane was suddenly a boiling upheaval. Deasy shot down, vanished. Savage hands clawed at Kane's legs, dragged him under. Water rushed into Kane's breath-sucking mouth.

Twisting at the hips, Kane hooked himself double and got both hands on the shape beneath him. He was sore, and the sea-water in the pit of his stomach was making him sick. The fingers of his left hand tore into a mass of wet hair. His right hand, balled into a fist, struck three times with trip-hammer precision under water. Bubbles of blood gurgled to the surface.

After that, Peter Kane hooked one arm in a strangle-hold around the limp neck of his assailant and swam wearily back to the steamer. Moroni and Michael Kelly helped him haul Deasy's unconscious form up the ladder.

"He figured," Kane mumbled, "I couldn't swim. *Tsk.* I was a Boy Scout once."

Moroni and Michael Kelly gaped at him. Walking crookedly around Deasy's crumpled body, Kane gathered up the pint bottle and stood swaying. His face in the broad beam of Moroni's searchlight was the color of seaweed.

"About one half the Atlantic Ocean," he groaned, "is inside my stomach. In a couple of minutes I'm gonna be sick. Awful sick."

He glared at Moroni, pulled the cork from the bottle and gurgled until the container was empty.

"When I come to," he said thickly, "the first guy that hands me a drink of water—any kind of water—will get—" His legs buckled under him, let him down. A groan of torment mumbled up with the heaving contents of Kane's stomach. "Will get—hell," Kane finished. "It ain't my brand."

Two Biers for Buster
William Campbell Gault

I t isn't only that you're a detective," she said, "but you knew him in training camp. You were a friend of his, weren't you?"

"I knew him," I said. *He hadn't had many friends,* I thought, but didn't say. Not after the time he'd been caught with phony dice.

"He died at Tarawa," she said. "He was buried there. That's why none of it makes sense."

Tarawa was three years back—November of '43. I studied her, and wondered how a lug like Buster Cowan had ever made this league. A honey blonde, small and trim, dressed in beautiful taste, all woman, all lovely.

I said: "Some angle shooter, some racketeer." I made some marks on my scratch pad. "I'd ignore it. It's a bad neighborhood." I looked up to meet her gaze fully. "Mrs. Cowan, your husband never made any secret of the fact that he was well-to-do. One of his former buddies is probably in trouble, and is working this angle. If you want, I'll go over and see this fellow. But I'd recommend the police."

She looked down at her hands, folded in her lap. She looked up. "I'm not sure I want the police in this," she said.

I could understand that. Buster had left a lot of money, but none of it was clean. She dressed like a woman who needed a lot of money.

"O.K.," I told her. "I'll run over there this afternoon and find out what he wants. I'll phone you."

She nodded and rose. "Will there be a retainer, or do you prefer to bill me later?"

I told her I'd bill her later, and she left.

I sat there, thinking back four years. Most of our cycle in training camp had gone east, to Europe, through Fort Dix. But Buster and one other had gone west, through Fort Ord. Who had that other one been? The name eluded me, but I remembered him, a big boy, from out on the coast somewhere.

Outside, the wind was working itself into a gale. It was November, and anything can happen in November in this town. I went out, locking the door behind me, and down the steps to the street.

There were a few broken branches in the road and dead leaves lining the gutters. There was a black Lincoln Continental convertible parked directly behind my coupe. Somebody was slumming—my neighborhood doesn't support Lincolns.

I climbed into the coupe, and headed it toward the Hotel Metropole.

The coupe fought the wind all the way. On Eighth, I had to detour, because of a huge branch which had crashed. Then I was driving along Front Street, which follows the river.

It's a neighborhood of cheap rooming houses and crummy hotels, of sailor's taverns and missions and small garment shops. One of the crummiest hotels was the Metropole.

It was an ancient wooden structure, with a cupola, weather-beaten, beginning to tilt on its foundation. A faded sign proclaimed *Rooms By The Day Or Week.* Only two gilt letters remained of the *Hotel Metropole* on the grimy front lobby window.

I parked the coupe close to the entrance. The water of the river was choppy, the odor from the river was strong and unpleasant. I lit a cigarette and stepped out into the wind. The odor was stronger, and I was glad for the cigarette.

There was no one behind the desk in the lobby, but there was a bell, and a sign. The sign said: *Ring for service,* which I did.

A fat man in a pair of shiny pants and a blue work shirt came through the door behind the desk and looked at me blankly.

"I'm here to see a Mr. Sam Nelson," I explained.

"He expecting you?" The eyes still blank.

I lied with a nod.

His head inclined toward the stairs. "Second floor, back—Room 218." He turned, and went through the door again.

The stairs were covered with the shreds of carpeting. I followed them up into the musty dimness of the second floor hall. Down the hall to 218, where I knocked.

The door opened almost immediately, and a big man stood framed there. A big man with small eyes, wearing a dirty white shirt and a two-day growth of beard and a scowl.

Surprise, swiftly guarded in the small eyes. "Red Barry, you old—" He tried to smile, but it was work.

I knew him. It was the man who'd gone to Ord with Buster. I couldn't remember the name, but I knew it wasn't Sam Nelson.

I groped for it while he said: "What brought you here? How'd you know I was here?"

"I didn't," I said. "Mrs. Cowan sent me, I'm working for her."

There was no sound but the wind. He stared at me, then stepped aside. "Come in," he said, and I went in.

A chipped enameled bed. A leaning wash stand, with a bowl on it, a bathing girl calendar on the wall, a rug that seemed to be growing on the floor, like moss. An acrid odor. Two kitchen chairs, formerly white.

He indicated one of the chairs, and I took it. He shook his head, staring at me. Then: "You pitching in that league? You making time with that broad?"

I shook my head. "I'm a private detective. I'm working for her."

He swore. He said, "A private eye," and swore again. "No," he said, "mmm-mmm. I'm not working through no copper."

I shrugged. "That's what she wants. What have you got that's worth money to her? Buster's dead. She's got his money. If it's a piece of his character you're trying to peddle her, you won't get far. What's a dead man's character?"

He didn't answer that. He said: "I want to talk to her. You tell her that. If she don't want to come here, I'll go and see her. But I'm not working through no copper."

"You went to Ord with Buster, didn't you?" I probed. "Did you ship out from there with him, too?"

He didn't answer. He stared at me stubbornly. He reached over for a pack of cigarettes on the bed, and brought one up to his mouth. He was staring at me, again, and then his eyes went past me, toward the door, and grew wide and filled with horror . . .

Sound exploded from behind me, and I hit the floor, rolling for the bed, for coverage. There were three shots, all together . . .

The smell of powder still lingered in the room, overpowering the other odors. Mike Markatti, alias Sam Nelson, still lay on the floor, two holes in his face and one in his neck.

Lieutenant of Detectives Jeremiah Kost was a thin man of medium height and a little better than medium mentality. He took me out into the hall, away from the others.

He asked: "You were on a job?"

I admitted it.

"Tell me how it was."

I told him how it was. "After I felt safe," I finished, "I went to the window, in the hall, there. I saw this black Lincoln convertible going up the block like a bat out of hell."

"You get the number?"

I hadn't, I told him.

He studied the threadbare green carpet on the floor. "Who's your client?"

I hesitated—and told him.

"Cowan's widow, huh?"

"That's right."

"Stay here," he said, and went back into the room. A moment later, he reappeared. "C'mon, we'll take a run out and see her."

Outside, the wind was steadier, less gusty. Kost said: "If it's all right with you, we'll take your car. I'll leave the department car here."

I said it was all right with me.

We followed Front Street to the Avenue and the Avenue down to the Drive. We followed the Drive all the way out to Shore Hills.

An upper middle class suburb, this Shore Hills, with a small shopping district and a scattered residential district. The Cowan home was Georgian, red brick, white trim, set well back from the street, a little more pretentious than its neighbors.

Kost said, "I'll do the talking," and led the way to the front door. Dead leaves swished dryly as they swept across the gray grass.

A girl in a fawn-colored uniform answered Kost's ring. She said gravely: "Mrs. Cowan is resting right now. She isn't feeling very well."

Kost displayed his badge.

The girl nodded, without perceptible interest or emotion, and held the door wide.

We went into a small entrance hall, and through that to the living room. It was a long, wide room, furnished in an early American motif, cheerful but not comfortable. Kost and I sat on a maple, bright-cushioned davenport, while the maid went to get Mrs. Cowan.

Kost lighted a panatela and blew smoke at the ceiling, saying nothing, looking thoughtful, ignoring me.

She came in presently, wearing a blue robe and mules, her honeyed hair up. A contrast, I thought, with this homy, neat house. Because she had poise, but she also had fire. Maybe she had the poise because she was afraid of the fire. I speculated on that.

Kost and I rose, and Kost said: "Just a few questions, Mrs. Cowan." His voice wasn't so matter of fact now.

She said: "Is it about—about that man who phoned, that Nelson?"

Kost nodded. "I'd like to have your story on that."

She took a chair near the fireplace, and we sat down again on the spring-gless davenport.

She looked at her hands, in her lap, and said: "He phoned me yesterday morning. He said he had some information that would be valuable to me."

"Did he say what it was about?"

The blond head rose slowly, and she looked directly at Kost. "He—said it was about my husband. He said I was in danger."

Kost said nothing.

"He said I should come down there and see him, that it wasn't safe for him to come up here. I didn't know what to do." She looked down at her hands again. "I remembered that Mr. Barry had been a friend of Buster's, and I went to see him. I thought he was a *private* detective."

"He was, and is," Kost said, "only there's been a murder, Mrs. Cowan. There's nothing private about a murder."

Silence in the room. The sound of the dying wind, outside. Her head came up slowly, and the blue eyes were wide and dark. "Murder," she whispered.

Kost nodded. "This Nelson's real name was Markatti. He's a hoodlum, an ex-pug. He was killed about an hour ago, while Red—Mr. Barry—was talk-ing to him."

She looked at me, and away. Her hands were no longer in her lap, but clenching the arms of the chair. The poise was gone, but the fire was there. "Murder," she repeated, and put her face into her hands.

Kost said: "If there's anything else you know, now would be the time to tell it."

"There's nothing," she said, her face still hidden. "I guessed that my hus-band's business wasn't always—legal, but there's nothing I know about it. And *now*—why should they bother me *now?*"

"That's what we mean to find out," Kost said. "That's why I want *all* the information you have."

A few drops of rain spattered on the windows. The wind had brought it in. Some of Mrs. Cowan's poise had returned, and she faced Kost reason-ably. "One man I know my husband feared. A Jess Revolt, a gambler. But my husband is dead. He died in the service of his country."

Kost's dead cigar rolled in his mouth. "Jess Revolt," he said, and seemed to be trying to place the name. "He live in this town?"

"I believe so. He did when my husband was alive."

Kost rose, and I rose with him. Kost said: "We'll do all we can on this, Mrs. Cowan. There might be some more questions later."

She nodded, and accompanied us to the door. She said to me: "Call me later, won't you? I'm afraid I'll still need you."

I promised her I would.

Kost and I hurried down through the rain to my car. He said: "Take me to the station. They must be all through at the Metropole by now."

We drove for a while in silence. Then I asked: "How'd you know this Markatti? He's no local mug, is he?"

"He was for a long time. Then he went out to the Coast. He and his brother ran a policy game here."

I said: "He was drafted from the Coast. He was in our training cycle at Camp Wolters."

"That's an angle," he said. "I think I'll send a wire or two to the War Department." No change in his casual voice. "Why do you suppose she still wants you on the job?"

"I don't know. I'll let you know as soon as I do."

He nodded. There was no further conversation until I pulled up in front of the station.

Then, getting out, he said: "Some babe, huh Red?"

"First-rate," I admitted.

He turned to face me, and said, "Watch your step there, Red," and was hurrying up the walk to the wide door.

Me and my reputation.

I drove back through the rain to the office. From there, I phoned Mrs. Cowan. I said: "I don't quite understand just why you'd need me further, Mrs. Cowan."

A silence. Then: "I've a feeling it isn't finished. I'm frightened, Mr. Barry."

"O.K.," I said. "I'll dig at it. This Markatti may have some friends." I asked: "You don't, by any chance, know anyone who drives a black Lincoln convertible, do you?"

A longer silence, this time. A hell of a long silence. I don't know why, but I knew she was lying when she finally said: "No, I don't."

Outside, the rain came down. In my office, the radiator began to hiss. I went over to the wash bowl in the corner to wash my hands. I had my back to the door while I was doing this.

When I turned to reach for a towel, I saw the man near the doorway. Thin and fairly short, dark and oily. Looking as though he had come for trouble. I stood there, staring, saying nothing.

"Who killed him?" he said. His hands were at his sides, and empty, but the threat of a gun was somehow implied. "Who killed Mike?"

I shook my head. "I don't know. I'm being paid to find out. Who are you?"

"His brother," he said. "Who's paying you, copper?"

I said nothing. I started to walk toward my desk.

His hand went to a coat pocket, and I continued to walk, as calmly as I could. I sat down in my chair behind the desk.

He said: "I followed you out to that place in Shore Hills. She lives there, doesn't she—Cowan's widow? This is all a part of that Cowan business."

"What Cowan business?" I asked him. "If you know something about him, I'll be glad to pay for it."

"Never mind what I know. What do you know, copper?"

"I know it's raining," I said. "I know you'd be a damned fool if you pulled that gun out of your pocket. Maybe what we've got together makes a story. Way it looks to me, we should work together."

"With a cop?" He sneered. "Me work with the law?"

"I'm not the law," I said. "I'm a private operative."

"You smell like the law to me," he said. "What'd the babe have to say?"

"She doesn't know anything," I told him calmly. "She doesn't know as much as you do. Weren't you working with your brother?"

"I didn't even know he was in town." His eyes moved around the room, and came back to my face. "How about Jess Revolt?"

"Never heard of him," I lied. "If you didn't know your brother was in town, how could you have followed me out to Shore Hills? You must have been in the neighborhood of the Metropole."

"I got the word," he said, "in time to get over there."

"Did you get over there in a black Lincoln convertible?" I asked.

"No." He looked puzzled. "How does that figure?"

"I don't know," I said. "I was just making sound."

He walked over close to the desk. His eyes were bright, and he was trembling. "Start making some sense, monkey. I don't like your lip."

I tried not to look as nervous as I felt. I tried to keep my voice level. The drawer of my desk was open now, and my hand was in the drawer. I brought out my .38. "Maybe *this* makes sense to you," I said.

His hand was still in his pocket, and he didn't move a muscle.

I said: "I've a license for mine. I can use it in self-defense. Take your hand out of your pocket. Take it out empty."

His hand came out slowly, and dropped at his side. "All right," I said. "What did you mean by the 'Cowan business'?"

He was still trembling, and his eyes had lost none of their luster. He said: "Cowan and my brother were in some pitch together. They took Revolt for fifty grand. That was before the war. Revolt's been on the trail ever since."

I studied him, trying to determine if he was lying.

He asked again: "How does the Lincoln figure?"

It was none of his business, I knew. But I thought if I told him he'd be more with me than against me. In my business, I don't spurn allies. I told him how the Lincoln figured.

He looked at the top of my desk, and at me. He was nervously chewing his lips, and some of the brightness was gone from his eyes.

"Revolt drives a Lincoln," he said.

The rain had stopped. A low sun glinted off the wet window panes. I said: "I'll give that to the law. Stay away from Revolt. The police will take care of him."

He didn't answer by so much as a nod. He turned his back on the gun I held, and quietly walked from the room. I heard him go down the stairs, and I went to the front window.

He was driving a convertible, himself, I saw, but it wasn't a Lincoln.

I called the Department, and got Mike Kost. I told him about the Revolt angle. I should have saved my breath.

"We've got the call out for him now," he said. "He looks like the man I want. I think we can wrap this one up."

I thought so, too. I went out to supper.

After supper, I called Mrs. Cowan from the restaurant, and told her all the angles. "The police will handle it from here in," I explained. "I'll send you a bill for the one day's work."

"No," she said. "I'm not satisfied with that. Will you come out, tonight, and see me?"

I said I could be there in a half hour, if it was all right with her. That was all right with her.

She was wearing a black wool, soft wool, dress when I got there. She was wearing a rather disturbing perfume, not quite strong enough to hide the odor of whiskey on her breath. She looked frightened.

The shades were down in the living room. We sat in there. She lit a cigarette from a nearly empty pack, and offered me one, which I refused.

She didn't look at me but at the cigarette, as she said: "I knew Mr. Revolt drove a Lincoln convertible. He came here to see me once."

I said nothing.

She looked at me. "He said that Buster owed him forty thousand dollars. He thought I should pay it."

"I heard it as fifty thousand," I said.

She nodded. "That's what it was, originally. But he said that Buster had sent him ten thousand from the Coast before he shipped out. He wanted the rest from me." She took a puff of the cigarette, a deep puff. "I wouldn't have paid it if I had it. And I didn't have it."

"Fair enough," I said. "But what's that got to do with *now*? Everything's washed up. If Mike Markatti knew something about Buster, he's not able to tell it. It wouldn't be wise for you to get mixed up with any of Buster's playmates. No percentage in it."

"How about Mike's brother? Maybe he knows something."

"Knows what? Nothing that will help you, nothing with which you should be concerned."

"I don't know," she said quietly. She rubbed her forehead with the back of one hand. "I don't know—" She bit her lower lip. "I never heard from Buster, not a line, after he left California."

"That could be explained."

"Yes—of course. But you know—he was listed as missing first. It was an ammunition dump that blew up. They never made positive identification. There were no fingerprints—available. I wondered if—perhaps—"

She must have loved him, I thought. *She must still be carrying the torch.* I said gently: "Even if he wasn't killed at Tarawa, he'd never be able to leave there on anything but government transportation. He'd never make it. Were you thinking he might have deserted?"

Again, she rubbed her forehead. "I don't know what I was thinking. I was feeling, more than thinking. What else could Mike Markatti have told me?"

"Maybe," I said, "he knew where Buster had some cash hidden out. Maybe he knew something that would be worth money to you—and to him."

While I was talking, some part of my brain must have been elsewhere. Because it came up with this idea. Just a crazy, half-idea at first, and then it began to grow. It was fantastic, and my mind wanted to reject it. But it persisted.

She said: "There's more in this thing than we know. Much more. I'm frightened. I don't know why. Call it intuition." Her voice rose. "Call it insanity if you want. But I think Buster is alive."

She'd been drinking. She was worked up to a nervous pitch. Her words could be discounted, should be discounted. There was no reason for me to feel that they might be true.

"It's highly improbable," I told her. I was telling myself at the same time. "It's impossible."

The cigarette was out now, and she put it in a well-filled ashtray. She covered her eyes with one hand.

I said: "It's something you've wanted to believe so badly that you've worked yourself into a mental state."

She looked up. Her smile was bitter. "Mental state? You mean insanity?"

"Not insanity," I said evenly. "You're nervous, upset. You need a rest, to get away from this town. You need a trip."

She nodded slowly. Her eyes were directed downward. She said: "I'm afraid, in this house. I want to leave." She looked at me defiantly. "But I won't leave. I want to be here, if Buster comes back."

I felt a chill, and tried to ignore it. I said: "If Buster came back, it would mean he was a deserter."

"I don't care about that," she said. "It wouldn't matter." Her voice thickened. "Maybe he won't come back—alive."

The words seemed to stay in the room with us. I looked at the drawn shades, at the filled ashtray. I smelled the whiskey in the air. This luscious, lovely blonde and that—that *jerk*. What did he have, what had he had? Women, I will never understand.

She said: "I want you to talk to Mike Markatti's brother. I'll pay whatever he wants if he can tell me what Mike Markatti was going to tell me."

"All right," I said, and rose. This idea grew bigger and bigger in my mind, and all the day's business seemed to support it. I picked up my hat. "I'll try to find Markatti," I promised. "I'll do all I can."

"Thank you," she said softly. "I knew you were a friend of Buster's."

I remained outwardly composed. Inside, I winced.

She walked with me to the door. She locked it securely after me.

It was dark out. No moon, no stars, the light from the street lamp distant and hazy. A gentle wind stirred the leaves littering the walk, making a dry, grating sound.

I thought: *We all had a delay en route. Buster had one, too. Eighteen days from the finish of the training cycle to the day we hit the P. O. E. But who'd be sucker enough . . . Although, for enough money . . .*

I went down the walk to the curb. I walked around to the driver's side of the coupe and opened the door.

There was a shadow in the coupe. A crouching shadow, below the window level. Light glinted faintly off a gun barrel. The shadow said: "Get in and drive. Drive up to the corner and turn right. Stop a half a block down, on Parkway."

I didn't argue. It wasn't the kind of voice that one argued with. I drove up to the corner and turned right. A half block down I stopped and cut the motor. There was a long black sedan parked here, the motor running.

The shadow said: "Get out, on my side." He opened the door and stepped out backward, keeping the gun trained on me. I climbed out. I could see the shadow more distinctly now. I thought I could recognize him, Jed Abel, a grifter and gunman.

The man who held open the door of the big sedan I didn't recognize. He was blond and broad and tall. He had a face that seemed entirely devoid of emotion, a stone face.

Jed said: "Get in the back." I started to climb in.

That was when Stone-face sapped me. That's when the skyrockets went off in my mind . . .

I was playing ball—I was pitching. The ball seemed to be made of velvet or velour, fuzzy to the touch, but hard underneath. I threw my clincher, my fast one right down the groove, and this giant at the plate smashed it right back at me. I tried to duck. I tried to protect myself, and I turned, but it caught me in the temple, and I went down. Then it was raining—my face was wet. The manager was sopping my face with a cold, wet towel . . .

It was Jed Abel, all right. He had a wet cloth in his hand, and he was stroking my forehead, my temples. He looked back over his shoulder to say: "He's coming around, boss."

My hands were flat, palms downward on the floor, and it was a fine rug, under their touch. Jed said: "The rug's getting wet, boss."

A chuckle. A hearty voice. "A little water won't hurt a Royal Kashan, Jed. You can quit now."

Jed stepped out of my line of vision.

The light was dim, from two floor lamps. Stone-face sat on a long low davenport. The boss sat next to him. He was a big man, this one who'd chuckled, looking well-fed, well-clothed and content. He had light eyes in a dark, tanned face, and a mouth like a woman's, well shaped and soft.

He was smiling down at me as he asked: "Think you could get up, now? I'm sure my friend here underestimated his strength."

Stone-face permitted himself a smile, a stony smile. He was smoking, watching the end of his cigarette carefully.

I tried to get up, and the fireworks sputtered in my brain again. I put one hand to the floor and pushed. Then Jed came over to help me to a chair. I sat down, and closed my eyes.

When I opened them again, Jed was near the door. The other two sat quietly on the davenport, waiting. I rubbed the back of my neck.

The boss said: "You seem determined to pin a murder charge on me, Mr. Barry. I had you brought here so I could find out why."

"I don't even know you," I said.

The womanish lips pursed. "You identified my car. A gun registered in my name was found in the hall of the Hotel Metropole. It was the gun used to kill Mike Markatti."

I hadn't known about the gun. I said: "You're Jeff Revolt."

He nodded. Stone-face put his cigarette out carefully. Revolt, watching him, said: "You smoke too much, Danny. It's bad for you." Then he turned to me. "We'll have your story now, Mr. Barry."

Despite his manners, he was no one to defy. I gave him the story straight. When I'd finished, he looked thoughtful. He said: "You weren't carrying a gun."

"I rarely do."

He nodded thoughtfully. "You weren't expecting trouble, then?"

"I thought it was all washed up. Mrs. Cowan believes that Buster is still alive, and it might be, but the odds are against it."

"Alive?" The soft mouth was slack in disbelief. "How could that possibly be?"

"Buster," I said, "went to Fort Ord practically alone from our class at Camp Wolters. He had a delay en route. He had enough time to find a stooge to take his place. The stooge would need to be a man with some military experience to get by, and enough need for the money to take a chance. He'd report in at Fort Ord as Buster Cowan. He'd die at Tarawa as Buster Cowan."

Revolt looked at Danny. Danny lit another cigarette and Revolt looked at me. "You said 'practically alone,' Mr. Barry. Who else went to Fort Ord with Buster?"

"Mike Markatti," I said.

The pale blue eyes were darker now. They were on Stone-face. "What do you think of that story, Danny?"

Danny shrugged. Danny looked tight and nervous.

Revolt chuckled again. "Quite a story. This Markatti would be the only one who knew, wouldn't he?"

"Mike and his brother," I said. "His brother came to see me this afternoon."

Near the door, Jed Abel moved quietly. There was a gun in his hand, and he was alert. My headache throbbed rhythmically.

Revolt's smile was a strange, cold contortion. "Would you like to hear another story, Mr. Barry?"

I shrugged. "Why not? I'm not going anyplace."

He said: "Danny, here, brought me ten thousand dollars from Buster Cowan, as a partial payment on a debt. Danny also brought me a message. The message was that Buster would be back, after the war, to clear the rest of the debt up." He looked at Stone-face. "Am I right?"

Stone-face nodded, his eyes straight ahead.

Revolt looked at me. "I gave Danny a job with me. He's a remarkable young man. He's risen very rapidly in my organization." He shook his head. "I wonder what happened to Buster?"

"I don't know," I said. "But if he were smart, he'd have gone to a first-rate plastic surgeon and have his face made over. He might even come back to his own home town and get a job with his old rival. *He might even frame his old rival—and take over the business.*"

On the davenport, Danny stirred. Near the door, Jed Abel was taut and braced.

Revolt was musing aloud. "He might, at that. He'd have the keys to my car, and access to my guns. He'd hear, through my organization, that Mike Markatti was in town. It wouldn't be difficult, for a man in a trusted position."

Silence, a heavy silence.

I broke the silence. I said: "I remember Buster's voice. Don't you remember Buster's voice, Mr. Revolt?"

He sighed. "I don't. I'm not as observant as a man in my position should be." He turned. "Do you remember Buster's voice, Danny?"

Danny shook his head nervously.

"Answer politely, Danny. Don't just shake your head. Do you remember Buster's voice?"

Silence. I waited, Revolt waited, and at the door, gun raised, Jed Abel waited . . .

The rest is still confused to me. I heard the explosion, and saw Jed Abel go slamming back into the wall near the door. I saw him fold. I heard Revolt's "Damn it," almost petulant, and I saw Danny moving for the door, his back to it, his heavy automatic trained on Revolt.

Revolt didn't move. Danny reached around behind him, and opened the door.

Again I heard explosions, three of them, and caught a momentary glimpse of the dark, oily face of Mike Markatti's brother. He must have followed me, or perhaps he'd been out there before we came. I saw Danny collapse . . .

They picked up Nick Markatti in St. Louis, but they electrocuted him here. The fingerprints of Buster Cowan, in Washington, checked with the fingerprints of Danny, and they found the scars on Danny's face, near the hairline. His widow gave him a fine funeral, nevertheless. I heard, later, that she married some old gent with millions, and it might be true, but I didn't want to believe it. Jeff Revolt offered me a job, and it paid a lot more than my business, but I turned him down. Ethics, I guess.

I keep wondering who that guy was who died at Tarawa . . .

Blond Cargo

Fred MacIsaac

I

Panama Puzzle

His name on the first-cabin passenger list was Addison Francis Murphy, and that was all anybody knew about him, except that he spent most of his time in a deck-chair on the promenade deck with a volume of the *Encyclopedia Britannica* open on his lap.

He was not a good-looking man; neither was he bad-looking, and he was fairly young. The situation upon the *Delphian*, bound from Los Angeles to New York via Panama was, as usual, an abundance of pretty girls, quantities of doddering grayheads, and a few youths who hadn't been using a razor long enough to become expert in its management.

During the first couple of days nobody noticed Mr. Murphy, but after that he was remarked upon because he made no acquaintances, apparently did not wish to make any.

Anyone who knew Addison Francis Murphy knew that he was not unsocial, so there must have been good reason for his making a man of mystery of himself. It was really quite simple. Murphy, after purchasing a first-class ticket and laying aside the necessary sum needed for shipboard tipping, was practically without funds. Acquaintances beget expense. Enough said.

When the ship arrived in New York, Murphy would walk ashore more or less penniless, but that did not bother him a jot or tittle, whatever they are. For Murphy was reasonably certain that wherever newspapers were published he could manage to land a job.

The ship's purser, whose name was Fitzgibbon, was a fellow with an insatiable curiosity. On the third day he dropped into the deck-chair beside the student and said: "Look here, Murphy, what's eating you? Look at all the pretty girls. They want dancing partners and swimming partners and people to flirt with. You're a young fellow. Close that damn book and do your duty."

Murphy returned his Irish grin with another equally broad. He said: "Wherever you go you'll find girls but this is the first time I ever had thirty-six volumes of the *Britannica* and eighteen days to read them. It is full of the most interesting information. Try it sometime."

The purser rose. "You're a nut," he said disgustedly. "I'm going to believe what I believe and not be looking through fine print."

"Who is that man going by with the pretty blonde?" asked Murphy.

"Name of Beckett. John C. Beckett. Owns a string of horses. He's bought more champagne than anybody on the ship."

"I still don't like him."

"Cut him out with the blonde. Name's Vivian Darcey. Her old man owns all the copper in Montana. What do you do for a living?"

"Newspaper reporter. Not working."

"Well, I'll be seeing you," said the purser. "I'll introduce you to Miss Darcey if you like. Matter of fact, she told me to bring you round."

"I have twenty-eight volumes to read yet. No time."

"Bah," said the disgusted purser.

It became very warm on the third day out. The sea was like a sheet of shimmering blue glass, the sky like a cerulean dome unflecked by a single cloud. Porpoises put in an appearance, and so did purple blazers and flannel pants and light dresses. Owning only the blue serge suit which he wore, and the plain black shoes on his feet, Addison Francis Murphy did not make any change in his costume. He stopped wearing his old gray felt hat, and his stiff reddish hair was revealed to be much in need of tonsorial attention. The sun burned his face to the color of rare old brick. He was putting on weight. His body was becoming—as it usually suggested when well fed—a slab.

In his quiet way he was enjoying himself and was already up to K in the *Encyclopedia*. It was six bells of the afternoon watch when the next deck-chair was suddenly occupied by a beautiful young blonde with dancing blue eyes and a divine smile. She wore a sea-green sweater, a white linen skirt and snub-nosed sports shoes that still couldn't make her feet look big.

"What's the matter with you, Mr. Murphy?" she asked impudently. She was impudent because she had never met the gentleman.

Murphy glanced up and smiled at her, and for the first time she had a chance to see that he had fine white teeth.

"Why, I'm fine," he said pleasantly. "You're Miss Darcey, aren't you?"

"Fancy your knowing my name!" she exclaimed.

"I've heard people addressing you as 'Miss Darcey'."

"Well, why have you been avoiding me?" she demanded with a saucy smile. "You are the only man on board who hasn't danced with me."

"I've got a sore foot," he said untruthfully.

"No, you just don't like me," she stated dolefully.

"I think you're swell. I'm reading a very interesting article on Kalamazoo. Do you know anything about Kalamazoo?"

"No, thank heaven," she said tartly. "If you think I came here to flirt with you, it shows how conceited men are. I want you to give me five dollars. I'm collecting a fund for prizes for the masquerade."

"I'm sorry," he said with some embarrassment. "I don't like masquerades, and I don't think the right people ever get the prizes, and I can't afford to contribute five dollars."

"You're just being mean," she said with a pout.

"Economical. I'm on a budget. There's nothing in it regarding masquerade contributions."

She rose. "Well, Mr. Murphy," she said acidly, "in my opinion you're a complete wash-out. Good-afternoon." She departed gracefully though in dudgeon. Murphy gazed after her with regret.

The following morning the ship arrived at Matzalan down in the southwest corner of Mexico, and the passengers piled into the tender and went ashore for a gay day. Murphy leaned on the rail and watched them depart. He would have liked to go ashore but a day in Matzalan was not included in his budget.

The purser stepped up beside him. "Read the bulletin about the new treaty between the United States and Panama?"

"Yep. What of it?"

"We've relinquished our right to dictate the foreign policy of the Republic. We've paid them off and told them to roll their own hoop."

"I got that. What of it?"

"It means that that there will be trouble down there—revolutions, plots, and such. They'll get cocky, knowing that the Marines won't use their clubs in the shadow of the capital, and our passengers will have to behave as if they really were in a foreign country."

"Can't get drunk and beat up the natives with their former impunity?"

"Right. Why don't you get ashore here like everybody else?"

"I figure on going through the J's in the *Encyclopedia*."

"You're a queer egg," said the purser with a laugh, and strolled away.

A moment later a page boy touched his arm. "Telegram just came aboard for you Mr. Murphy. At the purser's office."

Murphy strolled to the main companion, descended to the deck and collected a telegram. He controlled his surprise, although he expected no messages.

"Greetings, Rambler," the telegram began. "Wire if you'll open office for Round-World Press Association, Panama. Seventy-five a week. New set-up down there. Learned from Los Angeles correspondent you sailed on *Delphian*." It was signed Wallace, New York.

His impulse was to wire a refusal and go back to the thirty-six volumes. What influenced him to do otherwise was vanity. If he took this job, the fifteen dollars he had allotted for expenses between Panama and New York would be velvet. He could tell the Darcey girl he had been joshing about the masquerade contribution and that his sore foot had got well. He'd stick around Panama for a couple of months, resign and continue on to New York.

And he might as well, under the changed circumstances, go ashore in Matzalan.

He went down to his cabin, secured his hat and asked the steward where he took the tender. "Go all the way aft along this alley," said the steward. "Go down two flights to D Deck at the companionway you come to, turn left and you'll see the open port where the gangway is."

He followed directions as well as he could, not being very familiar with the interior of big passenger ships, but turned right at the foot of the stairs on the D Deck, instead of left, followed a corridor with an open door leading out on deck and emerged upon a part of the ship he hadn't even known existed. It was a covered promenade-deck that ran to the stern. There were no deck-chairs but many benches and upon the benches sat girls, some of them pretty, and all of them blondes. He whistled softly. He became aware of a number of pairs of bright eyes inspecting him curiously and he spoke to a steward who happened along.

"What's this? Tourist accommodations?"

"No, sir. Steerage. The tourists have much better quarters than these. You see we don't often have many steerage passengers on these ships and then mostly darkies and spigs. We put the darkies and spigs up in quarters near the bow on this voyage on account of having all these actresses."

"Actresses!" he exclaimed.

"Sure. They're going to work in an American show in Panama City."

The steward passed on. Murphy met the clear-blue eyes of a girl in a yellow wash-dress sitting on a bench a dozen feet away. She smiled at him.

"Hello, Redney," she said huskily. "Got a cigarette?"

* * *

He grinned and produced a package of cigarettes. He sat down on the bench beside her the better to light the weed. He inspected her sharply. She wore no stockings and her black slippers were shabby and run down at the heels. The dress she had on could be bought on Geary Street, San Francisco, for forty-nine cents, he thought. His fingers touched the palm of her hand which was rough and calloused.

Her face, however, was round, soft and pretty. Her hair was thick and naturally yellow.

"How do you like the sea voyage?" he asked.

"The sea is oke," she told him, "but the chuck is vile and the rooms are down in the bottom of the boat. Some of us have been sleeping on deck. Come down and see us sometime."

"Are you a member of this troupe?"

"Me? Oh, yeah."

"They don't look like actresses very much—except you, of course."

"Actresses, huh! A lot of clucks. I'm the only one with stage experience. And I ain't had a job for four years. I've been walloping pots in a snide hotel in Frisco. Any kind of a ride looked good to me. Say what's it like up on them top decks?"

"A bit more luxurious. If these girls haven't any stage experience, how do they expect to appear in a musical show in Panama?"

She laughed loudly. "Well, now, Clarence, mamma isn't worrying about that. They get us cheap because they got to train us. The manager says them South Americans are crazy about blondes, and so we don't have to be performers. All we have to be is blondes."

"How many of you are there?"

"Thirty-two."

"A big troupe."

"Yeah, that's why we have to travel tourist instead of first class."

"Do you think you're traveling tourist?" he asked, surprised.

"Certainly. Ain't we?"

He shook his head. "Steerage."

"Ain't that the same thing?"

"Well, not quite."

"Put something over on us, did they?" she said vindictively. "Say, can you spare that pack of smokes? I ain't got a dime to buy any."

"You mean you didn't get an advance?"

"They bought our tickets and they pay the tips. Our dough doesn't start to come in till we get to Panama."

He handed her the cigarettes. "What kind of work have these girls been doing?" he asked.

"Chambermaids, hash-slingers, manicures, and a lot of them come out of canning factories." Murphy was inspecting those within range of his eyes. Few of them were really pretty. Most of them were girls with heavy features, thick ankles and large feet. They would satisfy Panama audiences, perhaps, but they couldn't get by in the United States.

"What's your name?" she demanded.

"Murphy. What's yours?"

She giggled. "O'Brien. Same breed of goats, eh?"

He grinned; then eyes narrowed as a man came out of a companion entrance and moved in the Rambler's direction. His appearance caused a commotion amongst the girls. They surrounded him. They demanded cigarettes and beer. Why couldn't they go ashore like the other passengers?

He pushed them aside and bore down upon the couple on the bench.

"Who's this guy, eh?" he demanded truculently of Miss O'Brien.

Miss O'Brien tossed her head impudently. "Friend o' mine. Do you mind?"

He looked Murphy over. "Scram, guy," he said roughly. "You don't belong down here." He was a tall thin man with broad shoulders and a wasp waist. He wore an expensive, light-blue suit with a belt, Panama hat and corrugated-leather sports shoes.

"Neither do you, Slocum," said Murphy quietly.

The fellow's black brows bent. A look of wonder and then anger spread over his rather good-looking countenance. Recognition now was mutual.

"Scram, O'Brien. I want to talk to this bozo," he growled.

"Her master's voice," said Miss O'Brien satirically. "Come and see us again, Handsome." This to Murphy. She retreated in good order.

He sat down on the bench. "You been on this ship from Frisco?"

Murphy shook his head. "San Diego. I've seen you topside. So you're in show business, now, Slocum?"

"That's right. What of it?"

"Nothing. You've a pretty seedy-looking troupe."

"Well, we're cheaping it, and that's a fact," admitted Mr. Slocum.

"When did you get out of jail, Slocum?" asked Murphy quietly.

The man's face twisted with anger but when he replied it was without heat. "A couple of years ago. I don't bear no hard feeling. You was working for your newspaper and I got caught in the clean-up in Baltimore. Who you working for now?"

"I'm taking over the Panama office of the Round-World Press," Murphy grinned. "I suppose I'll get press-seats for your opening night?"

"Oh, sure," declared Slocum.

"Beckett your money-man?"

"What makes you think that?" asked Slocum sharply.

"I've seen you talking to him. Any of the girls in the first cabin, that you've been dancing with, know about your harem down here?"

"Are you going round shooting off your mouth about this?" demanded Slocum truculently.

"I kind of like that O'Brien kid. I may sneak down here. O.K.?"

Slocum laughed relievedly. "Why sure," he said heartily. "Play the whole field. I ain't wasting my time on these floozies with the fillies there are in first cabin."

Murphy rose. "I'll be going. Oh, by the way, tell Beckett to keep away from Miss Vivian Darcey. That's important."

Slocum jumped up. He clenched his fists. "Who the hell do you think you are?" he shouted.

"Never mind. I'll tell him myself."

"Look here, Murph, Beckett has nothing to do with this enterprise and if he had, it's legitimate. He's a millionaire, he is. Made his dough in oil. Got a string of race-horses."

"Don't let me see him in the vicinity of Miss Darcey, Slocum. That's all."

II

Thirty-two Blondes

The Rambler went through the opening into the alley which had led him inadvertently to the steerage promenade-deck. Slocum stood looking after him breathing heavily, fists clenched and muttering aloud.

"The sneaking, nosy mugg," he muttered. "He had to be on this boat. And he's going to stay in Panama. And Beckett has to keep away from that dame. Well, Mr. Rambler Murphy, maybe you ain't going to get to Panama, and what do you think of that?"

But Rambler Murphy was not unaware that he had left behind him a man breathing threats. There had been a time in Baltimore when this same Jack Slocum had engineered a ride for Addison Francis Murphy. He had returned from the ride and sent Slocum up for five years. Slocum must have got a couple of years off for good behavior.

He located the elevator, rode up to the top deck and entered the radio room. He wrote a radiogram addressed to Joe Wallace, his new employer in New York, which was as follows—

> Get me a complete line of activities of John C. Beckett, sportsman of San Francisco. Cable care U.S. Consul at Panama.
>
> Murphy.

Murphy had no further interest in going ashore. He secured a volume of the *Encyclopedia* and resumed his intensive study of the world's history and geography. He was thus engaged when the tenders brought back the passengers, full of Mexican liquors and laden with Mexican trinkets.

After dinner there was a dance on deck, and for the first time Addison Francis Murphy appeared in the gay throng. He was watching for Miss Darcey and she appeared, for a wonder, alone, from the smoke-room entrance.

Murphy confronted her.

"Oh, Miss Darcey," he said. "I wanted to give you the five dollars for the masquerade."

She lifted her pretty chin, narrowing her pretty eyes.

"The books are closed and the names of the contributors sent to the printer," she stated.

"I was kidding, yesterday," he said with an embarrassed grin.

"Indeed. It was the only opportunity you will ever have to kid me, Mr. Murphy," she said. "Kindly let me pass."

There was nothing for him to do but to step back, and the girl walked straight into the arms of John C. Beckett who whirled her out upon the dance-floor—which caused Rambler Murphy's Irish blood to boil. A moment later he spied Slocum fox-trotting with a pretty child of seventeen. He had to walk all the way to the rear end of the first-class promenade to cool his wrath about that.

It was dark down there and cooler than up forward where the windows of the promenade-deck were closed to protect the young women in their scanty ballroom raiment. Murphy leaned on the rail and looked down at the black water with its fringe of white foam where the ship's side cut through it like a knife.

Someone touched his arm. He looked up. Had Miss Darcey sought him out to apologize for her rudeness? To his astonishment, the O'Brien girl stood beside him. She wore a bright-red evening-dress, cut daringly low. Her yellow hair was braided tightly around her small head, and she looked beautiful in the semi-darkness.

"How on earth did you get up here?" he demanded.

She laughed softly. "I figured if you got down to our awful place, I could get up the same way. I put on my evening-dress—only got one—and I sailed through that door into the main-deck house. A steward stopped me, and I gave him the Ritz. 'How dare you?' I said like Lady Vere de Vere. 'I beg your pardon, mum,' he said, and let me pass. I reckon he thought I was a swell doll who had been slumming. I kept climbing stairs and finally got up here. It's swell, ain't it?"

"Not bad."

"Say, Slocum knows you, don't he?"

Murphy nodded.

"Well, the real reason I wanted to get up here was to give you a tip. I heard him talking about you to a guy named Ferguson that's giving us dancing-lessons every day. He said he hated your guts and this ship wasn't big enough to hold you and him. What did he mean by that?"

"What he said, I suppose. I've run up against him before, Miss O'Brien, and know all about him."

"Aw, call me 'Kate'."

"Well, Kate, he's a bad egg. Look out for him."

She nodded. Her face wore an expression of anxiety. "You look out for him. Listen, Mr. Murphy, what are us girls up against?"

"I don't know. What do you think you're up against?"

"Well, I know this show won't ever open. Most of these dames are so dumb they can't be taught anything. Say, a chorus number by them would make even the spigs die laughing. I'm worried. They must be crazy, thinking they can do anything with a flock of clucks like them."

Murphy drew forth a pencil and an old envelope. "I'm a newspaper man from away back," he said. "I'm opening an office in Panama for the Round-World Press Association. I don't know where I'll locate. But, if you get in trouble, go to the American consul and ask him my address. Here's my full name and the name of the Association. You may get in trouble for coming up here. Better go down right away."

As he spoke the band struck up. Looking along the deck they could see the space reserved for dancing. A multitude of Chinese lanterns made the scene gay, and the bright dresses of the young women made it brilliant. The band was playing *The Music Goes Round and Round*.

"Gee," she said wistfully. "That's my favorite tune. I wish I could only get one dance." He saw tears in the girl's eyes.

"Well, why not?" he asked recklessly.

"You mean it?"

The Rambler laughed, took her arm and led her to the dance-floor.

"Won't we get in trouble?"

"No, you're as well dressed and better looking than most of them."

In another moment they were whirling round in time to the music. The dancing-space was crowded but Murphy, though an infrequent dancer, was a good one and Miss O'Brien was light as a feather. They wove their way in and out, and the rapture of the girl communicated itself to her partner.

"I beg your pardon," said a man who had backed into Miss O'Brien.

"Keep the change," she said happily.

Murphy looked around. It was Beckett, dancing with Vivian Darcey. An expression of astonishment and then wrath spread on his countenance. Murphy encountered the cold-blue eyes of Miss Darcey who looked right through him.

"See that guy?" Kate said. "He's the boss. He was the one that hired us in Frisco."

"Name of Beckett?"

"That's him. He can travel up here but he sticks us down with the freight. Gee, look at the grub, will you?"

"Come and have some," suggested the Rambler, glad to end the dance.

There was an elaborate buffet spread on snowy tables on the far side of the dance-floor. There were turkeys, chickens, glazed hams, salads and ices shaped like fruits and birds and beasts. Kate O'Brien ate like a horse. Murphy, who'd eaten a very hearty dinner, sipped coffee and enjoyed watching the kid eat. Apparently, the girl had been half starved during the voyage.

With a deep sigh she finally ended her amazing consumption of victuals.

"Jiminy cricket," she said, "I never had such a good time in my life!"

"That's swell," he said. "Now, I'll take you back to the steerage. Come along."

"Things like this is what makes Bolsheviks," she stated. "Well, I got mine for once. I'm ready to quit."

He conducted her along devious passages and left her at the door which gave out upon the steerage promenade-deck.

She put out her hand. "Gee, you're a swell egg," she said. "If I can ever do anything for you—"

"Good-night," he said. "Remember—the American consul will have my address."

He went back to the dance, hovered on the outskirts. It was there the purser found him. Fitzgibbons beckoned him out of hearing of those who ringed the dance-floor.

"Who was this dame you were dancing with a little while ago?" he asked gravely.

"I don't know. Why?"

"Did you know she was a steerage passenger?"

"What of it?" asked Murphy, laughing. "You and I are a couple of Democrats."

"I advise you to say you didn't know it," said the purser solemnly. "Then she gets all the blame."

"Well I knew it and I'm damn glad I gave the child a good time for a little while."

"That's too bad, Mr. Murphy. You're under arrest."

Murphy stared at him blankly. "Are you serious?"

"Yes, damn it. You brought up a cheap cabaret-singer from the steerage and flaunted her in front of the young ladies in the first cabin. What's her name?"

"Go to the devil and find out," growled the Rambler.

"Trouble is that this fellow Beckett complained to the skipper. The skipper told me to learn if you knew that she had no right up here. You admit you knew what she was. You will be confined to your cabin until we get to Panama. Captain's orders."

"I won't stand for it."

"You chump, the captain of a ship can hang you if he wants to. It won't be so bad. We'll be there in a few days. You'll have all your meals served in your room. About all you do is read books, and I'll send 'em down to you."

"Let me see the captain."

"Take my advice and don't. He's an old so and so, and you're Irish. Talk up to him and you'll wind up in the brig in irons."

"Any way to fix this?"

"It's Beckett. He's a big shot, and the captain has orders to be nice to him. He don't give a damn about you, so you are the goat. Are you coming to your cabin, or have I got to send for the master-at-arms?"

"I'll go. I'll sue the company."

Fitzgibbon laughed. "You haven't a leg to stand on. We have a right to confine any passenger who makes himself objectionable in any way. In bringing that moll up here you technically insulted everybody in the first cabin."

"Well, I'm glad I did. Let's go."

Three days later, in the afternoon, the big ship steamed into the harbor of Balboa. Addison Francis Murphy had a partial view of the beautiful tropical harbor and entrance to the Panama Canal, through his porthole. He heard the band playing up on the promenade-deck. He glimpsed navy planes flying low, circling the steamer like giant seagulls. He heard the shouts of passengers to friends on the government pier, cries of those below who had come to meet the ship. For three days the Rambler had been in a humor of a kind which boded ill for John C. Beckett and his lieutenant, Jack Slocum.

The ship was fast to the dock, gangplank in position. Passengers were going ashore. Murphy tried his cabin door. It was locked. He rang for the steward but nobody came—all the stewards were busy carrying hand-luggage ashore. Time passed. He saw the passengers on the pier, he saw them meeting their friends. Unable to see the steerage gangway, he obtained no sight of Miss O'Brien and her fellow actresses. But he did observe Miss Darcey welcomed by an old gentleman in the uniform of a general in the United States Army.

She introduced John C. Beckett to the general, then shook hands with Beckett and went off on the arm of the soldier. Beckett moved out of view. The throng on the pier lessened. Motor-cars and horse-vehicles were departing with the passengers. Murphy kept ringing his bell but continued to get no reply. Finally the pier was deserted.

At the end of two hours the steward unlocked his door. Purser Fitzgibbons was at his elbow, grinning like a Cheshire cat.

"I bet you're sore," he remarked.

"I certainly am. Why, wasn't I turned loose when we docked? What right have you to keep me imprisoned?"

The purser dismissed the steward and sat down on Murphy's bed.

"What's this Beckett got against you?" he asked curiously.

Murphy hesitated. "Why?" he inquired.

"It was all right to report you for bringing one of those tough babies from the steerage to the first-cabin dance—you should have been reported—but he asked the old man, as a favor to him, to hold you on board for a couple of hours after docking. How could that be a favor to him?"

"I'll have to find out."

"You're a funny egg," remarked Fitzgibbon. "You don't give the gals in first cabin a tumble—you bury your nose in the *Encyclopedia*. Next thing we know you're pals with one of the dese-dem-and-dose dames from the hold. You got low tastes? That it?"

"Listen, you thick Mick, I'm a newspaper man. I'm on the trail of a big story. I'm the correspondent of an important news-service in Panama. You tell the captain that I wouldn't want to promise him, but I may be able to have him put on the beach for being an accessory in a major crime."

"What you need is a drink," declared the purser with a horse-laugh. "It's on me."

"O.K. I'll have one."

"Has that job lot of actresses from the steerage gone ashore?" Murphy asked.

"Yep. A special bus took 'em away. Slocum went with them. He didn't tell anybody in first cabin he was a theatrical manager but I knew it, of course."

"You'll be surprised to know that Beckett is the boss of that troupe."

"Aw, say, he wouldn't bother with a piking proposition like that. He's got a lot of dough. I know that."

"Well, I'm leaving this ship here. I don't know Panama. Where do we meet for dinner? I'm buying."

"Hotel Central. At seven o'clock. Ship sails at five A.M. so I'll have to leave you early, about four."

Murphy picked up his suit-case, refused to give it to the steward who had been his jailer, forgot completely the small matter of tips, and went ashore.

Beckett, Slocum and the thirty-two blondes were mixed up in something —that would bear investigating.

A taxi rushed him through the American town of Ancon into the old city of Panama and drew up before the entrance to the U.S. Consulate. But all doors were closed—it was six P.M. Dismissing the cab, he went into a saloon and made some inquiries.

Yes, there was an American newspaper, the Panama *Herald*. He secured the address, took another cab and arrived at the office of the paper, located in a tumbled-down building near the sea wall. A man in white linen sat tapping leisurely upon a typewriter, only occupant of the cityroom. He leaned back, when the Rambler entered, a thin man with a large brown mustache turned up at the ends.

"How are you?" he asked genially. "Got a piece for the paper?"

"Name of Murphy. Opening an office for the Round-World Press. Came in on the *Delphian*."

"That's an item. I'm the city editor and head reporter. I've just had an interview with Miss Vivian Darcey. Guest of General Shusther in the Zone. Meet her on the trip?"

"I exchanged a few words with her," said the Rambler with a wry grin. "There was a big theatrical troupe on board. Thirty-two girls. What theater are they going to play in?"

"You mean a chorus of thirty-two girls? Man alive, the only real theater here is the opera house, and it's closed. No honky-tonk can employ as many girls as that. A dozen is the limit."

"This is a big musical enterprise, I understand. Who's promoting it?"

"Whoever is—is keeping it dark. There are only half a dozen men in Panama City who promote shows, and they're all pikers."

"Ever hear of John C. Beckett?"

"Nope."

"Jack Slocum?"

"Unknown to me."

"They brought the girls down. They came over from Balboa in a special bus."

The city editor grinned. "Good looking?"

"Anyway they're all blondes," said Murphy with an answering grin.

"Central Americans like blondes but thirty-two— We'll spend money for a group picture of 'em. That's news in this man's town. I'll telephone around. Make yourself at home. My name's Barnett. Used to work in Hartford, came down here twenty years ago and went to hell. Got so I like the Tropics."

He went into a phone-booth and was busy for ten minutes. He came back looking perplexed.

"No showman knows anything about this troupe," he said, "and they are not at any of the hotels or boarding-houses. The Vanishing Blondes, eh?"

"Just what would these two fellows be able to do with all those women?"

Barnett laughed. "Marry them to our leading citizens if they are blond enough. There's a good story in this. I know the town like a book and I'll go out on it after dinner. Perhaps somebody plans to open up the opera house, at that. Drop back here about eleven o'clock. I'll probably have some information for you."

They shook hands, and Murphy took a cab to the Central Hotel where he was dining with Purser Fitzgibbons. It was a large, typically Spanish structure set on the edge of a spacious plaza, thickly populated with blacks and tans. He saw a number of persons whom he knew had been among the *Delphian's* passengers but no sign of Beckett and Slocum.

There was a story, here; a crime of some sort was being committed and it looked like he would make good with the Round-World Press from the start.

The musical enterprise had seemed fishy from the first. Beckett had caused him to be confined to his cabin to keep him from getting a line on his game, and had had him detained on board long enough to get clear away with his strange cargo. Murphy grinned. He wouldn't be able to hide away thirty-two blondes very long in a country where blondes were as scarce as snake's teeth.

"Paging Mr. Murphy," called a yellow bell-boy.

Murphy snapped his fingers, and the boy approached. "I'm Murphy."

"A letter, señor."

III
Invitation to Sudden Death

The letter was on the stationery of the steamship company, and the Rambler sensed the contents before he tore it open. Fitzgibbons was unable to leave the ship and sent his regrets. As he folded the letter and put it in his pocket, a hand touched his shoulder. He looked up to observe a derisive smile upon the countenance of Mr. Jack Slocum.

"Wise guy, eh? Had a taste of jail yourself, eh?"

"Short sentence, though," replied Murphy blandly. "No hard feelings, as you told me. Say, I'd like to see more of that O'Brien girl. Where is your troupe stopping?"

"Buy you a drink?" suggested Slocum.

"Why not?"

"Planters' punch is a specialty. Let's get a table."

The two mortal enemies sat down together, and Slocum ordered the drinks.

"Beckett is a bad boy to monkey with," remarked Slocum. "I had to tell him what you said. Did he work fast? I ask you?"

Murphy chuckled. "He worked fast. When does your show open and where?"

"We'll put on operettas in the opera house. Beckett is going to get a subsidy from the government. That's under your hat."

"Can any of them sing?" inquired Murphy.

Slocum laughed. "The principals can sing. They haven't arrived yet. Coming down from New York. We're up against a delay so we took the molls out to a cheap joint on the way to Old Panama. Road-house. A dollar a day per dame, board and lodgings. Drop out. Kate O'Brien is the best of the bunch, at that." He drew a scrap of paper from his pocket and scribbled an address. "Cost you a couple of bucks to get out there, so maybe it ain't worth it?"

"It was just an idea I had."

Slocum downed his drink. "Got a date with a dame from the first cabin for dinner," he said. "No hard feelings, Murph, eh?"

"None whatsoever," the Rambler assured him blandly.

He watched his retreating back sardonically. It was very probable that this address was a trap. If Beckett and Slocum had no objections to him knowing where the girls were lodged, why have him held on board ship until they were safely away?

On the other hand he knew that the troupe had not been quartered in the city, thanks to the Panama *Herald* man's inquiries. And he had read, somewhere, that these South American republics actually paid subsidies to theatrical companies. Not to an outfit like this, though. Was the game to display these blondes, collect a subsidy and disappear leaving the girls stranded? Not enough money in it for Beckett.

It was quite likely that the company had been taken out of town and lodged in some cheap road-house, but it was not likely to be the place to which Slocum had kindly directed him.

Just the same Murphy knew he was going out there to have a look, and was perfectly well aware that he would be taking his life in his hands. Slocum would murder him with great satisfaction if he thought there would be no come-back.

Not being a one-hundred-per-cent idiot, he decided to have a talk with City Editor Barnett before embarking upon this wild enterprise.

After sampling chicken with Spanish rice, Murphy put in the time rambling through the streets of the town. There was a moon shining down, band playing in the plaza, crowds in the parks and on the main streets. Quickly leaving the business streets, he drifted down one narrow side street, up another. The buildings were mostly one story in height and the inhabitants overflowed into the thoroughfares. Many homes had no windows, only a door like a barn door which was wide open, and families went through the business of living in full view of passersby.

At eleven he reported at the newspaper office to be informed by a young Spaniard, in charge at the time, that Barnett had phoned in he had no information for Mr. Murphy and would not return to the office. Murphy showed the address Slocum had given him to this youth, who said: "I don't know the place but there are quite a few joints out that way. Bad liquor and poisonous food. Stick to the town bars."

Five minutes later the Rambler was in a motor-car headed for Casa Casaba, Bellavista, Panama.

In five more minutes the car crossed the railroad tracks and was running through a large, fairly modern suburb which seemed to be sound asleep.

Shortly after, they were out of the region of street lights. The car was running over smooth macadam. If there were houses, they were invisible in the darkness. Unseen vegetation perfumed the warm air. The stars overhead glittered brightly but shed no light on the landscape. Murphy tried to pick out the Southern Cross but gave it up. He had tried to locate it on the ship and hadn't succeeded.

He had no plan. It was possible that Slocum had sent him on a wild-goose chase, perhaps to get him out of the way while something was pulled off in Panama. It was possible he was rushing into a trap. It was not possible that

Slocum sympathized with his feigned interest in the O'Brien girl. It was curious that Barnett had lost interest in the Vanishing Blondes. He had been keen about them when Murphy had left him at the newspaper office. Well, Barnett was a run-to-seed reporter. Perhaps he had been bribed.

Half an hour passed, and the car turned into a dirt road.

"How much farther?" he demanded.

"Two, three miles, señor."

The Casa Casaba was a brick-and-plaster building, built on three sides of a courtyard. It was two stories high with a flat roof. Its age must have been a couple of centuries for originally it had been a *hacienda*. It had been abandoned a quarter of a century before by a half-Spanish, half-Indian named Juan Morales, an innkeeper who had secured the place, fixed it up and opened it as a road-house. He had a notion that Panama would be filled with tourists because the Panama Canal had just been opened and also because it lay between the city and the ruins of old Panama destroyed by Morgan, the buccaneer, three centuries earlier.

His enterprise failed but he hung on there because he had no other place to go, and his son, Juan, took it over when he died, running a truck-farm. He married a woman out of a dive, in what they call the "Cocoanut Grove" in Panama City, who had other ideas for the place. It became a hide-out for Panama lovers. That phase passed and now it had degenerated into a cheap *cantina* with few customers. There were, however, a dozen rooms with beds in them on the second floor, a large bar equipped with a nickel-in-the-slot piano, a bad-smelling restaurant and an assortment of the cheapest sort of liquors. Juan finally gave up the ghost, closed the place and moved into the city.

On this night, however, it looked as if the dream of the old man had come true. The bar was brightly lighted. Female voices were lifted in song, not Spanish songs but such ditties as *Moon Over Miami*.

The old piano occasionally played a discordant American tune of ten years' vintage, and the girls sang to its accompaniment. Two waiters were serving beer to a strictly female patronage. In the courtyard was a large, ancient motor-bus with its side curtains down. The bar was on the left-hand wing of the Casa Casaba. The other wing was dark, but there was a light in a window on the ground floor of the center wing.

A motor-car blew its horn three times and then rolled into the courtyard. A door in the center wing opened, and a man peered out.

"It's Beckett," he called. "We're in here, John."

John C. Beckett, wearing black evening-clothes with a Panama hat, got out of the car and approached the door. Slocum stepped back and ushered him into the lighted room.

"Good-evening, Frank," said Beckett cheerily. "Hello, Ramon."

Frank was a huge man, wearing dirty white trousers, a dirty white shirt, open at the neck and which revealed a thick growth of black hair on his chest. He had black hair but light-blue eyes, somehow out of place in a face tanned the color of sole leather. Ramon was a tall lean Latin, good looking save for a hard mouth, and dressed in clean whites.

"Where in hell have you been?" demanded Frank. "Rushing the dames off the boat at the Union Club?"

Beckett poured himself a drink from the bottle of Scotch on the table. "Just that," he said pleasantly. "Why not?"

"We got important business," growled Frank.

"Shut up," snapped Beckett. Few people would have suspected Beckett of being other than he appeared—a typical business man with sporting inclinations. Athletic in build, he looked younger than his forty-five years, his smile frank, open over his teeth, white and regular.

"Murphy shown up?" he asked of Slocum.

"Nope."

"Think he'll come?"

"Yes," said Slocum firmly. "That guy ain't afraid of man or devil. I told you what he did in Baltimore. He'll show up."

"He smells a rat," said Frank. "He'd better come, or we'll go after him."

"And when he comes," said the Spaniard softly, "a knife right at this spot"—he indicated his heart—"and we'll bury him in the old cemetery back there, in the same tomb with old Juan Morales."

"Which sounds to me like a very good idea," said Slocum, with relish.

Beckett smiled. "I have a better one," he said. "But first catch your rabbit. This fellow doesn't believe you gave him the location of this place out of friendship?"

"Naw. He knows it's a trap but he's the kind of guy that walks into traps—and usually gets out."

"What precautions have you taken?"

"Two men, watching the road. They'll close in on him from behind."

Beckett poured himself another drink. "There is no way he could have learned about our plans, but that kind of fellow can make a guess fairly near the mark. Valdez says he told a reporter on a Panama paper named Barnett that you and I, Jack, aren't going to use these girls in show business."

"Say," exclaimed Frank. "If he's talked to this reporter there will be questions asked when he don't show up tomorrow."

"Diego Valdez has that reporter under his thumb," said Beckett. "However, that isn't important, as it happens. I've something on that's terrific, Jack. I'll tell you about it."

Slocum's eyes sparkled. "Oh, yeah?"

"It makes this deal a side-show—"

"Look here," shouted Frank. "This ain't no side-show. I'm up to my neck in it. Don't you try any funny business, Beckett."

"You're in on it, Frank Hogan, so shut up. You, too, Ramon. What do you muggs say to half a million dollars?"

"Nuts," growled Hogan. "We got fifty thousand cinched—I'm no hog."

"It fits in neatly with my plans. Ramon, go out and tell your men not to let Murphy see them, not to interfere with him. I want him to walk into the bar and make himself at home. That is, if he's fool enough to come."

"Say," protested Slocum. "You can't fool with Rambler Murphy. He's dynamite. Ramon's right. A knife between the ribs and a quick burial."

Beckett laughed contemptuously. "You've a grudge against him. I'm going to make him useful. I need him in this new business."

Frank, the hairy man, got up and thumped the table. "Nothing doing, you damned dude," he bellowed. "What? Oh, all right."

For an automatic had appeared magically in Beckett's white hand and was pointed at the middle of the big man's chest. "This is my show," he said through clenched teeth. "And you play my way."

"Give us an idea what it is, boss," pleaded Slocum. "Put up that rod. You can't blame Frank. You know what'll happen to him down there if his deal flops."

"I'll tell you in good time. There is no risk—"

Ramon entered hastily. "A man's walking up the road alone," he said. "Has a gray suit on."

"That's him," exclaimed Slocum excitedly. "If we let him get away—"

Beckett's laugh was harsh. "He won't get away," he said confidently.

IV

The Dead Lie Long

The chauffeur pointed to lights in the distance. "There is the Casa, señor, I thought, maybe it was closed." Murphy laughed at the naive remark. The chauffeur had unscrupulously taken him for this long drive under the impression they would have to turn round and go back again.

"Joke's on you," he said.

"Señor, I do not understand."

"You don't have to. When you get within half a mile, stop the car."

"Si, señor. Why not drive you to the entrance?"

"Stop here," he commanded, a few minutes later. "Here's your five dollars."

"I shall wait to take the señor back to Panama."

"No. Perhaps, I won't go back." Under his breath he added: "And there may be more truth than poetry in that."

The driver, still protesting, took his fare and turned his car around.

Murphy stepped off the road and waited several minutes, listening intently. Finally he continued on toward the road-house. Presently, two shadows came out of the fields and followed him at a distance of a hundred yards. He was unaware of their presence but he moved with extreme caution. When within a short distance of the house, he listened incredulously. Female voices were raised in song. A violent chorus was singing *Be Still My Heart*.

Being almost certain that wherever the human sheep had been hidden, it would not be here, their presence was astonishing. A grin spread over his countenance. "Why, the girls are whooping it up!" Unconsciously he quickened his steps; he was almost off guard.

Lights were blazing from a row of windows in the left wing of the old building, throwing radiance upon the driveway. He swung off to the left, approaching the outside of the left wing. Four windows on this side were lighted. The singing continued, some very dreadful voices in this chorus. It meant that Slocum and Beckett hadn't even bothered to try the voices of their chorus girls.

Convinced that he was not observed, he crept up to the side of the building, stood on tiptoe beneath an uncurtained window, peered in.

Then he laughed aloud. There was nobody inside save the girls, two waiters and a bartender. Half a dozen pairs of the ex-steerage passengers were dancing while the rest sat at tables, thumped beer-mugs on the table-tops and sang the waltz at the top of their lungs. Flushed with beer and excitement, the young women looked better than when sprawled around on the steerage-benches. Suddenly, he spied Kate O'Brien. She was sitting with a dark girl, legs crossed, hands folded across her knees, a somber expression on her pretty face.

It decided Murphy. Slocum had told him the absolute truth. Kate O'Brien was where he had said she would be. Slocum had invited him to call. Slocum, a murderous crook, hated him but, if it were true that the ladies were waiting here until called for rehearsal at the Opera House, it was unlikely that he would want trouble with a newspaper reporter whom he knew had a job in Panama. If it were not true, something would drop on Mr. Murphy. Yet, it was worth the risk of finding out.

He boldly walked round the wing of the building, located the entrance on the courtyard side, opened the door and stepped into the bar. The singing died instantly. The dancers stopped dancing. Thirty-two pairs of eyes were fixed on him in astonishment.

"My Gawd, a man!"

"It's the man that was on the ship."

"You got a noïve, mister!"

All of a sudden Kate O'Brien was clinging to his arm. Tears were streaming down her cheeks. "You came," she breathed. "Say, am I glad to see you!"

"Hello Kate," he said, smiling.

There was a burst of shrill laughter; they crowded round in a circle. The Rambler, whom women easily embarrassed, was the color of a ripe tomato.

"You can't have him, Kate," said a buxom blonde stridently. "We'll take turns dancing with him."

"Make him buy whisky. All they'll give us is beer," proposed another.

"You dames scram," screamed Kate. "Mr. Murphy came to see me. I invited him. He's a particular friend of mine."

"That right, feller?" asked a new voice.

"You bet," declared the Rambler.

"Well, let them alone."

"You bet you'll let us alone," said Kate fiercely. It was evident she dominated the others, probably by superior moral force, for they drifted away although continuing to stare at him from all parts of the bar. A waiter appeared, asked his order. Murphy produced a five-dollar bill. His money was evaporating rapidly.

"Beer all around," he commanded. He led Kate to a table in a corner. "Everything all right?"

"I guess so. We have to sleep three in a bed, the beds are awful, the grub is worse than on the boat and has too much garlic in it, but they give us all the beer we want and told us to have a good time."

"Slocum here?"

"He looked in a couple of hours ago. I suppose he's around."

"Where is your show going to play?"

"We got to stay here for a week or so, and then the principals arrive and we move into Panama. This is an awful dump."

"When I couldn't locate you in the city I was a bit worried."

"Oh, I guess nothing worse can happen to us than getting hit with bum eggs when we open the show," she said with a slightly hysterical laugh. "Gee, I'm glad to see you, Mr. Murphy. You certainly treated me swell that night on the boat. I was kind of disappointed that I didn't see you anymore."

"They made a fuss about my taking you to the dance."

"I'm awful sorry. I was afraid they would. Darn it, here's Slocum!"

Slocum appeared at the door, observed Murphy and came over, a broad smile on his face. "No matter how dumb they are, they can still catch fish," he observed. "Eh, Kate?"

"No dirty cracks. I'm not afraid of you," she said fiercely.

He sat down uninvited. "You must be stuck on the dame," he said to the Rambler.

"If he is, is it any of your business?" she demanded. "Did I ask you over here?"

"I told him where you were staying," he said cheerfully. "Now, I get bawled out."

She was full of contrition. "Oh, I didn't know that."

"The drinks are on me," said the man who had no hard feelings against the person who had sent him to jail for several years. "I'll chase these floozies off to bed, first. No more beer!" he shouted. "You girls hit the hay. You know your rooms. Go there."

"How about lights?" demanded somebody. "There ain't any lamps in my room."

"You use candles. The waiters will light you up with lamps. That goes for you, Kate."

"But he's only just come."

"Can't help it. Boss's orders."

The girls were reluctantly filing out. Half a dozen bracket kerosene-lamps lighted the bar. The waiters took two of them and led the way. Miss O'Brien lingered.

"Am I going to see you tomorrow?" she asked anxiously.

"Two Scotch and sodas," called Slocum to the bartender. "None for you, Kate. Scram." She rose reluctantly. The bartender was preparing the drinks. "Good-night," she said softly.

Murphy felt a qualm. "If the poor kid is falling in love with me," he thought, "why that's terrible!"

She walked slowly toward the exit beyond the bar into the corridor. Murphy watched her sadly. Slocum had his back turned. At the door she swung about. She pointed to the bartender—made a gesture of lifting a drink in her hand, then shook her head violently.

"I get you. Good-night!" called the Rambler.

"Get what?" asked Slocum, whirling round.

Murphy smiled. "She threw me a kiss."

"Oh, well she ain't so bad. Not my style."

"Every man to his taste," Murphy remarked sententiously. The bartender placed a drink in front of each man. Murphy reached over, took Slocum's drink and placed his in front of Slocum.

"What's the idea?" inquired Jack.

"Good luck, that's all," said Murphy.

"Good luck, yourself," replied Slocum with an equally bland smile and switched the drinks again.

The Rambler sprang up. His right fist shot out. It struck the jail-bird between the eyes, and its force was great enough to knock him and his chair over on the floor. Murphy made a swift rush for the door but as he approached it, it flew open and three men blocked the exit. One was John C. Beckett. The second was a huge, heavily tanned, blue-eyed man, and the third was a Spaniard.

Murphy charged them savagely. He shouldered Beckett out of the way, dropped Ramon with a right swing and hit Frank in the stomach without the slightest effect upon the giant. Frank opened his arms and embraced the Rambler. His hug was like a grizzly's. He raised Murphy off his feet, lifted him high in the air and hurled him upon the floor. The Rambler came up, but very groggy. Slocum was coming from the rear, a gun in his hand. Ramon was up, brandishing a knife with an eight-inch blade. The huge right fist of Frank collided with the jaw of the dauntless but shaken reporter, and Murphy hit the floor again, lay still.

Ramon lifted his knife, bent over. Beckett grasped his wrist. "None of that," he snarled. "I need this guy. Carry him out."

The four men lifted the unconscious interloper and carried him into the courtyard.

"I tell you he's dynamite," exclaimed Slocum. "For God's sake, boss, lemme finish him off. I owe him plenty."

Beckett drew him to one side. "I need him for the go-between," he whispered.

"Go-between for what? Are you crazy? We don't need a go-between."

"Oh, yes we do. We're taking him with us, and we're sending him back."

"I suppose you know what you're talking about," muttered Slocum.

"We got him. What'll we do with him?" demanded Frank.

Murphy, who was lying on the stone flagging, suddenly sat up.

"Hit him again and harder," commanded Beckett. Frank closed his big right fist, drew it back and let it go. It crashed against the right temple of the Rambler, and he lay back on the flagging, out for a long period.

"Ramon, you said something about a tomb," said Beckett smiling. "Let's have a look at it."

The Spaniard looked startled, then sighed. "You mean put him in the tomb of Juan Morales?"

"If it will hold him. He'll be safely out of the way until tomorrow night."

"Bury him alive," exclaimed Slocum. "What? I'm for that!"

"How far is this cemetery?" demanded John C. Beckett."

" 'Bout a couple of hundred yards."

"Pick him up and let's look it over."

Three dark-skinned fellows had arrived on the scene. Ramon gave an order in Spanish and they lifted Murphy upon their shoulders. He was heavy for the little men, so Frank lent a hand. The singular procession filed out of the courtyard and moved around the right wing of the Casa Casaba.

They moved across a field of scrubgrass through a broken place in a stone wall, and then the bearers began to mutter protests. An oath from Ramon silenced them. They had entered a private cemetery. It had been the burial-place of the original owners of the *hacienda*. Not more than forty persons were buried here, but there were half a dozen large tombs. Ramon stopped before the tomb of the late Juan Morales, and the bearers let the still unconscious Murphy drop upon the ground.

Beckett went forward and lighted a match. It was a brick-and-plaster tomb, but much of the plaster coating had fallen off. There was a big iron door. The structure was about five feet high by eight feet square. A rusty padlock was on the door.

"It ought to hold him," remarked Beckett. "Break this padlock. I'll leave somebody to stand on watch, of course." More protests came from the peons, who crossed themselves. Violation of a tomb! Slocum examined the padlock, produced a revolver, inserted the barrel in the hasp, used leverage and it opened easily. The iron door swung back with a clang and whining of rusty hinges. There were moans of terror from the peons, but no ghosts emerged.

"Toss him in," commanded Beckett. "Wait!"

He lighted a match, stepped inside the door of the tomb and looked around. Three stone coffins were piled one upon another at one side of the interior. The other side was empty. "All right," he reported, "it ought to hold the lug."

Frank and Slocum carried Murphy in and laid him on the stone floor. The Spaniards would not have entered even if threatened with death. They emerged, the door was closed and the broken hasp of the padlock passed through the staple.

"No chance of his getting out," stated Beckett, "but put two of those spigs on guard here, Ramon. I know they don't like cemeteries. See if this will cheer them up." He produced two ten-dollar bills and the objections of the natives were stilled.

"Another drink, and we'll all turn in," said Beckett cheerfully. "And I'll tell you fellows what it's all about."

"And I certainly want to know," declared Frank.

They returned to the room and Slocum filled the glasses. "We have a perfect set-up for a snatch," declared Beckett, "and the easiest snatch on record." He seemed very confident about it, too.

"What do you mean?" demanded Frank.

"At nine tomorrow night the *Guadalupe* leaves Panama harbor and she'll be off Starrat at ten, looking for the lights from our launch."

"I made the arrangements," declared Frank. "I ought to know."

"Tomorrow afternoon, Vivien Darcey, daughter of William Darcey, the Copper King, goes out to see the ruins of Old Panama with General Shusther and his daughter and yours truly. I'll arrange things so we won't get there until dusk. I'll get her away from the old folks—she rather likes me. Jack will be waiting with a car. You know the jungle grows right up and almost over the ruins—you can get fifty feet away from people and lose them. I'll give her the needle, get her into Jack's car, and we take thirty-three girls south instead of thirty-two."

"And then what?" demanded Frank. "There's radio, airplanes—there will be hell to pay!"

"The general will hunt for us. He won't leave for a couple of hours. It will be ten o'clock before he gets to Panama. He'll send searching-parties back and accompany them. There are old wells, trapdoors, secret passages in the old castles—we might have fallen through into a pit. They'll search all night. The *Guadalupe* has sailed before the loss of Miss Darcey and myself was reported. Nobody on the ship will know that she isn't one of the girls— the sick one. It's a cinch. And her old man will pay half a million for her."

Frank drew a long breath. "It's a great idea," he said. "I suppose we can get away with it."

"You'll be suspected, John," warned Slocum. "If they look you up, your record ain't so sweet. You can never go back to the U.S.A."

Beckett laughed. "I can't, anyway. I haven't told you, but the federals are after me for an affair in Kansas City."

"How do you expect to use that guy in the tomb?" demanded Frank.

"We take him with us. We send him back by plane. Land him in Panama. He goes to General Shusther, tells him that the ransom money is to be sent in English pounds to Pedro Dominguez in Cacacoa, Colombia, with author- ity to deliver it to the people who bring Miss Darcey to his office. If the directions are given out, if there is anything phony, they will never see the girl again. This isn't like an American snatch. They can't do business with the authorities down there. Frank's the authorities, ain't you Frank?"

"I can make 'em jump through," said Frank complacently.

Slocum scowled. "It lets Murphy out, though. I don't like that."

"You damn fool, they'll jug him. We won't make any restrictions regarding Murphy. When they pay the money and get the girl back, they'll give him twenty years for kidnaping."

Slocum smiled with satisfaction. "That's right. Never thought of that. Let's have a drink to Murphy, doing a twenty-year stretch."

Beckett rose. He crossed the room on tiptoe while the others gazed at him in surprise. There was a door which gave directly upon the patio and one which opened into the corridor that ran around the house. Beckett suddenly flung the inner door open. A girl stood there. The bright light dazzled her, fright petrified her. She stood, eyes wide, her right fist pressed against her mouth.

"Why you—you—" he sputtered and drove his right fist viciously against the little chin of Kate O'Brien. The girl crumpled up and fell in a still heap upon the floor of the corridor.

"Listening!" snarled Slocum. "Well, let's break her bloody neck."

"Yeah?" shouted Frank. "I suppose you'd tear up a couple of thousand-dollar bills?"

Jack, whose right foot had been drawn back to kick the unconscious young woman, hesitated. "That's right," he said. "But this is Murphy's gal, boss, and she probably got it all. She tipped him to the Mickey Finn I was preparing to feed him. That's why he slugged me and tried to lam it."

"Why isn't she in her room?" demanded Beckett sharply.

"We pulled all the boys to go to Murphy's funeral," said Jack. "Nobody was watching the second floor."

Beckett shrugged his shoulders. "We need her in our business," he said. "Tie her up and stick her in a closet until we're ready to pull out tomorrow night. When we're aboard the *Guadalupe,* she can talk her head off if she likes. Not a bad-looking filly." He gazed down upon her dispassionately.

"The best of the lot, says I," declared Frank. "She'll be the belle of the oilfields. You hadn't ought to have hit her so hard, Beckett."

"Bah, she had it coming. You and Ramon rope and gag her and stick her in someplace you can lock up."

V

Man into Mole

Rambler Murphy was coming to slowly. He had taken fearful punishment, was weak, groggy—but he didn't have any broken bones. He lay on the stone floor. He sat up, felt in his pockets, found they hadn't frisked him. He had his wallet, watch, paper of matches and small penknife. He got shakily on his feet, then bumped his head against the low stone roof. He scratched a match. It flared. Then, as he saw where he was, he dropped the match in consternation.

He was in a tomb—buried alive! Coffins were piled up there. This was a very old tomb, some cemetery in the vicinity of the Casa Casaba. He couldn't have been unconscious long, so this place couldn't be very far from the house. He was not afraid of the ancient dead in those stone coffins, but he did not relish the idea of being locked up with them. His hair was standing on end, his body was covered with goose-pimples.

He quickly got over that, faced the real horror. A tomb in an old cemetery, in a remote spot like that where the Casa Casaba was located, would be an ideal place in which to dispose of a person. Nobody was going to open an old tomb. Unless released or able to break out, he might remain here forever.

This could not be an underground vault—there was plenty of fresh air. He lighted another match, located the iron door, drew back and hurled himself against it. A dull metallic *clank* resounded, but the door held solidly. He ran his fingers around the door's edges. There was perhaps a quarter of an inch space through which the air gained entrance. He might starve to death but wouldn't die of suffocation.

The clang of the tomb door reverberated upon the night air, reaching the ears of the two peons guarding the living dead. They listened, looked at each other—and with one accord took to their heels. Probably this was the man they had thrust into the tomb, but he might have died and his ghost was stirring. A ghost could get out of a tomb. They didn't care to meet it.

The tomb was no longer guarded but this did the Rambler no good, inasmuch as he was alive and could not pass through solid substances. He lighted another match, studying the situation.

The tomb had been built of brick and was covered with plaster. Patches of the plaster had fallen away, revealing the bricks. Since he couldn't budge the door, he must see what he could do about the wall. The cement between the bricks was hard in some places, powder-like in others. He opened his pen-knife, attacking the cement. It was tough going but at the end of several hours he had three bricks out. It revealed another layer of brick, however, and the cement on these, having been protected from the action of air over a couple of centuries, was solid as rock.

In the end, the Rambler lay down on the stone floor and, being exhausted, was able to fall immediately asleep.

The clanging of the door awakened him. Sunlight was pouring in and Slocum, backed by two other men, was peering in at him.

"Hello, Murph, how's tricks?" demanded Slocum. He had an automatic in his right hand which prevented the Rambler from plunging at him.

Murphy growled: "Going to let me starve to death in here?"

"Sure, why not?" replied Slocum. "Say, I had to half beat the life out of your girl friend. She was listening at doors. Know where she's going? Down to the new oil region on the west coast of Colombia. Thousands of men down there, and no women except Indians. You can imagine how those boys will go for blondes."

Murphy, who was crouching, sprang at him despite the menace of the gun. But Slocum stepped back, slammed the iron door and Murphy crashed against it. He heard the fellow's laugh.

"Just looked in to see if you were O.K.," he called. "This is worse than any jail, eh Murph?"

Then Slocum departed.

Murphy sat on his haunches and gazed stolidly at the three stone boxes in which bodies had been placed long, long ago. There was no charnel odor in this tomb—flesh had long since departed from the bones in the coffins. A dim light in the tomb came from narrow spaces above, below and at the sides of the door. They intended to bury him here permanently, since they hadn't troubled to give him food and drink. Nobody in Panama knew him; nobody would come to look for him.

He examined the walls again. They were a foot and a half thick, judging from an inspection of the door-frame. And the door, though rusty, was solid. He hurled himself against it to try the hinges but they didn't give in the slightest degree.

He came as near despair as a man of his type was apt to come. He gazed stolidly at the floor. It wasn't stone, but Spanish tiles. Tiles might be broken. He looked round for a weapon, but there was none. He rose, inspecting the top coffin. It was a stone slab and laid on, not fastened, with hinges. With a shudder he lifted it. It weighed fifty pounds. He was unable to refrain from gazing within. A skull grinned up at him.

He took the heavy slab, up-ended it and dropped it upon a tile. It did not break the tile. The slab was almost as tall as the tomb, and he could not wield it effectively. He let it fall flat on the floor and it broke neatly in the middle. Now, he had something. He moved toward the back of the tomb and, with his three-foot weapon, attacked another tile. At the third blow, the tile cracked. In ten minutes he had it broken in a dozen places. Dropping the slab, he squatted and endeavored to lift out the broken tile with his fingers. It was slow, discouraging work but he finally pried loose a piece three inches in diameter, about an inch thick. Beneath was earth—hard-packed, sandy, soil. Murphy was getting excited.

In fifteen minutes he had removed the entire tile. Scooping out earth with his hands, he burrowed under the neighboring tile, succeeded in inserting the edge of the stone slab and easily lifted out the tile. He laughed aloud. If they didn't catch him at it, he was going to get out.

At the end of two hours he had removed a floor space three feet square, and now attacked the hardest part of the job. With nothing but hands and penknife, he had to dig a tunnel under the rear wall up to open air.

It was slow but painful labor. It became horribly hot in the tomb as the terrible sun of early afternoon in Panama got on the job. Murphy was perspiring from every pore, but making progress. When he had dug a hole a foot and a half deep he had an incredible piece of luck. He came upon a buried conch-shell. Now, he had a fair substitute for a scoop; he could lift a pound of earth at a time with it and the sharp edge of the shell cut into the ground like the blade of a shovel.

It was dark when he reached the bottom of the wall which had been sunk two feet deep into the ground. But that was so much the better, as he could get away under cover of night. Hours passed but the time came when the human mole came up out a hole and stood upon the surface. His clothing was torn, he was exhausted but—triumphant.

Now, how far was he from the Casa Casaba? He couldn't locate it. He had no notion in which direction to proceed to get anywhere. However, the farther he got from his tomb the better. He started to walk. He was ravenously hungry. And suddenly a dark building loomed up ahead of him.

He approached it cautiously, identifying it. It was the Casa Casaba. But it was dark. Not a light anywhere. He crept along the wall of the house, peered into the courtyard. The moon came from behind a cloud and he saw that the big bus and the motor-car, which had been there the night before, were gone.

So they had moved after burying him alive. He swore softly but savagely.

With extreme care he ventured into the courtyard. He crossed to the bar, peered in a window. Empty and abandoned. He became aware that he was ravenously hungry and would take any risk for food. The door was open, he entered, felt his way to the bar. Lighting a match, he hunted on the shelves beneath the bar and found crackers, stale bread and cheese. There was beer in bottles. Murphy feasted.

When the inner man was satisfied he was able to consider the situation. Why had the place been abandoned? Not on his account. They considered him safe where they had put him. What did it mean? Moving a multitude of women around was a big job and probably a costly one. Exactly what was their game?

The quicker he got back to Panama the better. He had money enough, thanks to their consideration in not robbing him—no doubt they had intended to do that at their leisure—to hire an automobile at some village to take him into the city.

He rose. He didn't feel tired, now, despite his super-human exertions during the day and early evening. He left the Casa Casaba and started briskly down the driveway. He reached the road by which he had come, started along it. There wasn't a pin-point of light visible to indicate a habitation, but the moon was shining and showed him his way. After he had walked a mile he saw, some distance ahead, a female form in the road. Somebody from whom he could ask directions. He hastened his pace, gained on her rapidly. Fifty feet behind, he shouted: "Hello there!"

To his astonishment, the woman broke into a run. He had to talk to her—he ran after her. She rushed off the roadway and plunged into thick bush. He heard her crashing through shrubbery.

"I won't hurt you!" he shouted. "I just want to ask how to get to Panama!"

He heard a scream. The bushes parted, and the girl rushed toward him.

"Oh, Mr. Murphy," she cried. "Oh, I'm so glad!" Then she fell sobbing into his arms."

"Well I'm damned!" he exclaimed. "Where did you come from? What's happened? Where's everybody?"

But Kate O'Brien was sobbing hysterically and it took several minutes to soothe her. "They were going to take you with them. They were going to put you in jail for twenty years," she moaned. "Oh, I'm so glad!"

"Come on, kid, everything's all right. Where are they?"

"They've gone," she said with a sigh. "Excuse me for being such a fool, but you ain't got no idea what I've been through."

"Where have they gone?"

"They are going on a ship. I don't know where. They were going to take you with them. They kidnaped a girl they're going to get half a million for, and you were going to be the go-between and go to jail for twenty years."

He patted her shoulder. "Calm down, kid. What you say doesn't add up right. I'm here, aren't I? And you're here. How long ago did the outfit pull out?"

"About three quarters of an hour," she said, rubbing her eyes with her fists.

"How does it happen you didn't go with them?"

"Because I listened last night and heard them talking. You see, I knew you had a fight with them, and I was afraid they'd hurt you. When they came back I hadn't gone to my room. I saw a light on the ground floor and listened at the door of the room to find out what happened to you."

"Why, you brave kid!"

"And that's how I learned they were taking us on a ship to a place called Colombia."

"It's a country."

"It's south, anyway, on a ship called the 'Gaddalop,' or something like that, and they had you a prisoner and were going to send you back when they got the Darcey girl down there—and—"

"Miss Darcey!" he exclaimed. "They've kidnaped her? Are you sure?"

"Sure? I *saw* her. They brought her to that house up there. They took her off in the bus with the other girls."

His mind was turning somersaults. Of course—Vivian Darcey, the Copper King's daughter. What a prize! And they were going to the west coast of Colombia, a vast region so far from Bogota, the capital, that it was almost without law and authority. And Slocum, who expected the Rambler to die in that tomb, told him what would happen down there to Kate O'Brien. White slavery it was, working out of Panama, no longer strictly supervised by Uncle Sam, to the new oil regions of western Colombia.

"How did you get away?" he asked gently. So she told him what had happened. They had left her in that closet and released her only an hour before departure. Frank, the big man, had taken her into the bar where the other girls were already assembled, told her to keep her mouth shut or she'd get her head beaten off, and left her. A few minutes later, a car had driven into the courtyard and Kate, through a window, saw Beckett and Slocum lifting out a young woman who seemed unconscious. They carried her to the bus, placed her in it. Slocum had gotten in with her.

Beckett had then appeared, and made an announcement. He told the girls that they were going to be lodged in a good hotel in Panama City and were leaving at once. Their scanty luggage was already being placed on top of the bus. Kate had no friends in the crowd, and the rest were all delighted at the transfer. Only Kate knew where they were really going. They moved in a mob into the courtyard, were lined up alongside the bus and counted by one of the Spaniards with a flashlight. Kate was in a state of mortal terror. Everything was over for her, if she got into that bus. In the confusion and darkness, she stooped, slipped underneath the bus, came out on the other side and sped across the courtyard.

Her escape was not noticed. She reached the corner of the building without being observed by the gang herding the girls into the bus. She got a safe distance from the place and lay flat on the ground. Shortly afterward the bus departed and was followed by the car which had been used to kidnap Miss Darcey, and another car. The place had been abandoned.

"So I started to walk to Panama or somewhere," she finished.

"A ship called the *Guadalupe*," he said thoughtfully. "Maybe we can have her held at Panama. What time does she sail?"

"I think they said at nine o'clock."

"If we could get to a place with a telephone— What time is it now?"

"I don't know."

"My watch is stopped. I forgot to wind it this morning. I had other things on my mind," he said grimly.

"But they ain't going on board at Panama. It stops for them at a place called 'Stare-it' or something like that and they go out in a launch. That's at ten o'clock."

"And it must be eight—we're miles and miles from anywhere. Come on. Let's walk."

VI
Slugs for Snatchers

He set off, half dragging her, at a stiff pace. He wasn't even sure he was going in the direction of Panama but, in a crisis like this, he couldn't stand still. Familiar as he was with criminal ingenuity, this set-up was one to awaken his admiration. First, get this herd of ignorant girls out of the United States and land them in a foreign country under false pretenses, then rush them under cover of darkness on board some tramp which would transport them to a place where the law wouldn't be interested in their fate. It was a crime with no possibility of a kickback—white slavery made easy.

But endeavoring to get Miss Darcey down there with them was not so easy. Her kidnaping would make a rumpus. The radio would broadcast the alarm, warships from the Canal Zone would search all ships, if it were known that she had been kidnaped. But let a day or two elapse before her disappearance was discovered, and the *Guadalupe* would land her and the other human freight at some point in Colombia before a warship could overtake and search that ship. The only person who might betray the plan was Kate, and they assumed that she was on the bus and would later be safely on the *Guadalupe*. Beckett had rightly assumed that if he got Miss Darcey into the interior of Colombia, her father would have to pay to get her back. It was a country where G-men would not be welcome.

Lights ahead.

"My feet hurt," protested Kate. "You walk too fast."

"Can't help it," he said grimly. "I'll go on ahead, if you like."

"No, don't leave me."

He took her arm again and half carried her along. In ten minutes they entered a small town—six or eight houses sprawled by the roadside and a gas station. There was a native boy sitting on the ground outside the station shack, and Murphy addressed him.

"Telephone in this town?" he asked.

"No, sah. No telephone."

"Do you know a place called 'Stare-it'?"

"No sah. No, I don't." He hesitated. "You mean Starrat, maybe."

"That's it. Where is it?"

He made gesture with his arm. " 'Bout five or six miles on the coast."

"Any cars to rent?"

"No, sah. No cars."

"What's that one there?" He pointed to an open Ford, parked back of the shack.

"That am the boss's car."

"What time is it?"

"You certainly ask lots of questions, boss," said the boy, displaying two rows of enormous white teeth.

Murphy drew forth one of his two remaining bills, a five-dollar bill.

"You can take me there and back in an hour, can't you? Five dollars?"

"I reckon I could shut up for that five dollars," said the Negro. He leaped to his feet and glanced into the shack. "Five minutes past nine," he said. "Come on, white folks."

Kate and the Rambler piled into the car, and Murphy realized that he was very tired. Kate almost collapsed on the seat.

"Is Starrat a big place?" he asked the driver as the car started.

"No, sah. Just a little place."

"Any telephones there?"

"I reckon there is, sah."

The car left the boulevard and started over a road across country. It creaked, groaned and didn't do better than fifteen miles an hour. There was very little time. But the road grew better, the car traveled faster and in about sixteen or eighteen minutes the lights of Starrat appeared.

"Is there a police-station at Starrat?" he demanded.

"No, sah. They don't need no policeman."

"What are you going to do?" she demanded.

"Stop them from getting on the ship."

"How?"

"Somehow. Be still. I want to think."

They came abruptly upon the waterfront. Starrat consisted of a row of one-story buildings along the beach. There was a small pier, a few bath-houses, and that was all. "Stop. Here's your money," said Murphy and leaped out. "It must be close to nine thirty."

They had arrived at the upper end of the beach. The street was deserted but there were bright lights in half a dozen places.

"You stay here," he said curtly to Kate. "I'm going to be busy."

She grasped his arm. "You can't stop them. They'll kill you," she protested.

"I'll take no risks," he lied. "You do as I say."

"All right," she meekly agreed.

He left her and walked in the direction of the pier. There was a street leading inland from the pier, and as he looked into it he saw the dim outline of a bus parked a hundred yards up. He looked at the pier and saw a large launch tied up there. There were no other craft visible. He crossed the street and came to a *cantina* into which he glanced cautiously. There were two or three natives inside, but none of Beckett's gang. They would be guarding the bus.

"Have you a telephone?" he hopelessly asked the bartender. To his surprise the man pointed to an inner room. Joyfully, he went in, closed the door and called the operator. "Connect me with U. S. Army headquarters at Ancon." He dropped twenty-five cents into the machine.

In a minute he had the connection. "This is Murphy of the Round-World Press in Panama," he said. "Do you know that Miss Vivian Darcey has been kidnaped?"

"What? Just a minute. Hold the line." Somebody else came on the line.

"Captain Pope speaking. You are a newspaper man named Murphy? Well, Miss Darcey hasn't been kidnaped. She is lost somewhere in the ruins of Old Panama. Searching-parties are looking for her now."

"Listen, Captain Pope. At ten o'clock Miss Darcey will be taken on board a ship bound for Colombia with thirty-two other girls brought down yesterday from San Francisco on the *Delphian*. White slavery. They intend to get half a million ransom for Miss Darcey when they have her in Colombia—"

"Wait a minute—"

"No time. The girls are here in a big motor-bus, guarded by the slavers. A place called Starrat. They will take them out to the *Guadalupe* in a launch at ten o'clock."

"My God, man, it's nine thirty now!"

"How soon can you get here?"

"It's ten miles out. Half an hour. I'll send a bunch of army officers immediately, but they'll be aboard before we get there."

"I'll try to detain them. Good-by."

Help was coming but it might arrive too late. Murphy went out upon the street. He was unarmed. If he approached the bus he knew what would happen. What in the devil was he to do? His eye rested on the launch. Too dark to see who was in it, but undoubtedly somebody was on board.

He walked a hundred yards along the beach, stripped to his shirt and shorts, kicked off his shoes and stockings and went into the water. He swam out beyond the pier. The moon was shining but the launch was in the shadows, which was good.

He swam swiftly but noiselessly. Keeping out of sight of the launch, he approached the pier, swam beneath it, close to the side of the motor-craft. Its gunwale was too high to reach—a disappointment. A roller threw him against a barnacle-covered pile and he struck a spike. There were spikes sticking out of the pile, one of the supports of the pier. He got his feet on one, found another higher up and laid hands on the gunwale of the launch. Looking seaward, he spied the lights of a ship standing in. Looking shoreward the outline of a man smoking a pipe up near the bow was visible. His back was turned.

In a moment, Murphy was on board the launch. A monkey-wrench lay beside the engine in the center of the craft. He picked it up. The boatman heard a noise, turned and saw the intruder. He shouted something in Spanish, and the Rambler plunged at him. The man thrust his hand in his pocket and pulled out a revolver. He fired one shot, and the bullet whined its way past Murphy's right ear. Immediately after that the monkey-wrench collided with the top of the man's head, and he went down. The Rambler picked up the revolver, fished the fellow's pockets for cartridges. He found a box containing fifty. He broke the gun, ejecting and replacing the spent cartridge.

The bus rolled down to the beach, followed by two motor-cars. A man jumped out, came running to the pier. "What's the matter there?" he shouted.

Murphy was trying to cast off the line, but the knot was a Spanish knot which resisted his inexperienced fingers. The fellow was so big he must be the one who had felled him in the bar.

"José, what's the matter?" he bellowed. Murphy took careful aim and shot him in the right leg. He went to the ground, his weapon flying from his hand and falling into the water.

Murphy was working at the knot again—if he only had a knife! He stooped over the man he had knocked out but he didn't have a knife.

Three or four men were approaching. "Look out," bellowed the wounded Frank. "Somebody fired on me."

Those approaching, spread out and bent over but continued to advance. Murphy recognized both Beckett and Jack Slocum. If he could cut the rope, the boat would drift out into the harbor and everything would take care of itself.

Slocum fired and immediately dropped flat. The bullet hit the bow of the launch. Somebody far over at the right fired, and the bullet came within an inch of ending the career of Rambler Murphy. He had been standing upright to watch the pier, the floor of which was on the level with his chin, and he had to drop down behind the bulwark of the launch.

He heard the tramp of feet on the pier. He straightened up, fired and hit a man in the chest—a Spaniard by the look of him. A second man, Slocum, dropped flat.

A bullet from the fellow at the right. Murphy could not stoop for shelter now. If they got over him on the pier it was the end. He kept a watchful eye on the pier but did not forget the man at the right on the shore who was about fifty yards distant. The fellow made the mistake of getting up and Murphy winged him in the right shoulder. He fired a shot at Slocum, who was crawling along the pier, missed, but stopped his progress. And then there was a shout from Beckett who was well up the beach.

"Quit firing!" he cried. "You, in the boat—who are you? What do you want?"

"A voice from the tomb," called Murphy loudly. "I don't want a damn thing. Keep back. You can't have this launch."

"Murphy," called Beckett, "you can't hold us off! You'll get your brains blown out. Come out of there, and we'll let you go free."

Wha-ack!

Murphy had fired at the head of Slocum who had reached the edge of the wharf and dared to thrust head and right arm over. He was only thirty feet away and his bullet left his gun almost simultaneously with that of Murphy's. But Murphy's bullet hit him in the side of the head; he was finished.

There had been seven in all, not counting the boatman. The Rambler had wounded three and killed one. He reloaded his revolver. He became aware of loud screams from the bus; and the population of the village was awake. Up the beach and down, at a safe distance, crowds were assembling.

"How would you like to make five grand?" cried Beckett. He was out of the range of Murphy's vision.

"Go to the devil!" Murphy bellowed back.

And then something very heavy descended upon him from the pier and bore him to the bottom of the boat.

Ramon had followed Murphy's method. He had gone into the water on the far side of the pier, swum to the end, climbed upon the pier and crept down in the rear of the fighting Irishman. Crouching on the platform, he had seized the moment when Beckett was trying to parley to jump upon the head of the man blocking the expedition.

It would have been the end of Rambler Murphy save for a fortunate accident. As the pair went down, Ramon's forehead came into violent contact with one of the handles of the steering-wheel, and the knife in his hand clattered to the deck. Murphy found an unconscious enemy on top of him, threw him off and was up in time to deter Beckett who had rushed down the pier, firing wildly.

Beckett dropped flat and Murphy, grasping the knife, cut the rope he had been unable to unfasten. The bow of the launch swung wide but there was a line at the stern. He plunged in that direction and drew two or three shots, which missed. The second line was cut, and the tide was dragging the launch out into the bay. Murphy lay flat and contented in the bottom, and the cries of rage from the survivers ashore was music to his ears.

The original boatman was conscious and sitting up now, but the Rambler's revolver kept him quiet. Ramon was still out.

A steamer was drifting along a couple of miles out, her signals like twinkling stars. Her captain wanted his passengers to hurry.

Then came honking of horns and headlights were visible on the street leading from the pier. In a few seconds six motor-cars reached the beach, and men were springing out of them. There were men in uniform and men in evening dress, and they surrounded the bus puzzled as to what to do. Then a young woman appeared among them and told them.

"Let's go," said Murphy to the boatman. "Start the engine. Back to the pier."

As Murphy came ashore, an American army captain grasped both his hands. "I'm Pope," he said. "You were all there, sir. General, this is Mr. Murphy. General Shusther is Miss Darcey's uncle."

The gray-haired general didn't shake hands; he embraced the Rambler. And when he released him a very beautiful but rather pale young woman stood in front of him.

"Will you shake hands?" she asked. "I was hateful to you on the ship, but that awful Mr. Beckett had told me dreadful things about you. I can't express myself. I know what you've done for me—for no reason. You didn't even like me."

"I thought you were swell," said Rambler Murphy.

"We had no notion it was a kidnaping," the general told him. "We thought Vivian and Mr. Beckett had fallen into a pit in the castle at Old Panama. We were searching there when your message was relayed to me. I assure you her father will know how to thank you, sir."

"Miss O'Brien," called the Rambler. Kate came forward timidly.

"I want to introduce you all to Miss O'Brien," he said. "Miss Darcey, Miss O'Brien, is one of the girls brought down from San Francisco to appear in Panama in a musical comedy. Actually, it was a plot to take the young women down to Colombia on that steamer waiting there. Miss O'Brien became suspicious and overheard Beckett, Slocum and others planning to kidnap you and take you along for ransom. She escaped from the place. I encountered her walking back to Panama. I knew nothing whatever about the plot against you. You owe your gratitude to Miss O'Brien."

Miss Darcey threw her arms around Kate and kissed her. "I thank you so much," she said and burst into tears.

Captain Pope laughed. "You didn't do a damn thing Murphy, did you?"

An hour later the Rambler was banging a typewriter in the cable office, shooting to the Round-World Press Association, in New York, an exclusive story of the advantage taken of the new set-up in Panama, by American white slavers. Accompanying the story was a request for five hundred dollars for the expenses of opening the new office. Before he had finished the last take, the first part of the story had reached New York and a highly congratu-latory message had come in from his boss, Mr. J. Wallace. Even more welcome was an order for the cash. The Rambler was in funds again.

The smooth crook, John C. Beckett, and his surviving accomplices were speedily tried in the Panama courts and sentenced to life-imprisonment.

A few days after the trial had concluded Murphy, Miss Darcey, General Shusther and a group of army officers put Miss O'Brien aboard the steamer for San Francisco. Kate was dressed as became a young lady who had now found grateful friends.

"Will you kiss me good-by?" she asked Murphy.

He kissed her, shamefaced, because the others were watching them. Kate burst into tears.

Miss Darcey went down the gangplank, her arm inside that of Murphy's. "Are you in love with her?" she asked. "You kissed her."

"That was good-by," he said, much embarrassed. "Why, I'll kiss you good-by when you sail for New York day after tomorrow—if you'll let me."

"I'll let you. Didn't you save my life?" she exclaimed. "But I'm not going to New York day after tomorrow."

"You're not?"

"I've decided to remain in the Zone for a month or two," she said. "Aren't you glad?"

Murphy looked troubled. "Why, sure."

"And we'll see a lot of each other?"

"Why, sure," he said, more troubled. "You bet."

"Come Vivien," called the general. The Rambler put her in the general's car and waved good-by as it rolled away. Kate was a fine girl, and Vivien was a very fine girl. She had practically told him she was remaining on his account. She was rich as mud, and whoever married her would not have to worry about the future.

He drove into the city, went into his office, sat down and stared at the wall. He reached for a cablegram blank. He chewed the end of a pencil and wrote a message to the Round-World Press.

> Send down a new boy. Sailing for New York tomorrow night. No action down here.
> Murphy.

That made him feel better. "She certainly is a grand girl," he muttered. "So it's time for me to ramble."

Mʀ. Sɪɴɪsтᴇʀ
Carroll John Daly

I

Death Gives an Order

If you have a little better food, a little better cooked and for a little better price, more people will wear a path to your door than any "better mouse trap" racket, despite the old adage. And that was the way of things at Mike the Greek's place. It was a small restaurant down three steps on a dark side street.

It was almost seven-thirty and despite the lateness, for the patrons of the Greek's did not observe the formal dining hour, the single room was more than comfortably filled.

There was little to notice about the people who ate at Mike the Greek's. You could drag a net down most any New York City street and catch yourself a hundred or so just like them. Still, one little old lady had an eye for detail and a good memory.

She spotted the man alone at the table for two and noted that he faced the back of the room rather than the street. She always faced the street herself when possible for she liked to watch the crowds filing in and out. This man was the only one who sat alone at a table, for Mike didn't bow to the niceties of seclusion while dining—and why should he at sixty-five cents including two cups of coffee? So she wondered why the man was alone. Several people had approached the vacant chair at his table. One or two actually sat down. But both had arisen before they gave their orders.

Old Mrs. Tremont was sure that the man at that table had not spoken. He had simply raised his head and looked at them. Long? Certainly. Steadily? She thought so. But she could not see the man's face. A waiter approached the table and said something to him in a low voice. The man got up and walked down the aisle toward the kitchen and lifted up the receiver of the pay phone that was fastened on the wall. There was no booth—no box-like stand, even—no privacy of any kind to this phone planted black and naked against the white wall—or fairly white wall.

She could not hear the man's voice. She didn't even know if he said anything, for she was not in a position to see his lips move. But she did see him return to his table and did see him sit down in the opposite chair, this time facing the entrance to the restaurant. She doubted, too, that anyone else would have noticed he had changed his seat. He did it so naturally.

Then with a single movement of both hands he leaned across the table and dragged the pie plate, the coffee, the few utensils and even the water glass and napkin toward him. Just a single gathering movement, and for a moment she even wondered if he hadn't been sitting in the same seat before.

It was a few minutes after that she saw his face. For a second as it turned toward her. It startled her, for she couldn't exactly describe it. It hadn't stood out in detail. Simply one quick impression. Disgusting was not the word. Revolting wouldn't fit it either. And certainly ugly was out of the question. She knew it was sharp and finally, being a stickler for the right word, she laid one on it. Sinister. That was it. Nothing else would fit that face. She nodded her head. She was pleased with herself.

She watched him light a cigarette and place it between thin lips beneath a hooked—well, she at least thought it was a sharp nose. She saw his left hand fooling with the spoon in the coffee cup, his right hand toying with his napkin. She was wondering if she knew any gentleman who permitted a cigarette to dangle in his mouth. Offhand she could think of no one who smoked that way. Besides—

Mrs. Tremont turned her head as the sinister man raised his head and looked toward the door. Then she stopped thinking. At least she was unable to put coherent thoughts together. But she did take in the entire picture.

Three men had thrown open the restaurant door, and they strode determinedly into the room. One was in the lead. Two others flanked him. They didn't wear masks and they didn't wear caps. But the dark fedoras they wore hid their faces sufficiently.

She could not see at first what the man in front carried in his hand as he walked quickly to within almost twenty feet of the sinister man at the table. Then she saw it. She had seen too many movies not to recognize its black, horrifying significance. She thought she shrieked out "Tommy gun," but she heard no words. Yet it was a machine gun and it was pointing directly at the body of the sinister man.

Then the man with the gun spoke. His words were loud and commanding and triumphant.

"Okay, feller," he said, "you asked for it. Now you can take—"

Mrs. Tremont's eyes nearly popped out of her head. She had expected a fusillade of shots, but there had been only one single report. She didn't see any smoke or any flame come from that Tommy gun. She simply saw the cold, cruel living eyes of its possessor turn to glassy, expressionless dead ones. She heard the machine gun fall to the floor, saw the man who held it clutch at his left side as he sank slowly to his knees. Then he toppled forward on his face.

Things happened quickly after that, almost too quickly for even Mrs. Tremont to follow. She knew that one of the men behind the dead machine gunner raised his hand and that there was a snub-nosed pistol in it. She knew that the third man ran toward the door. She knew too that the man with the gun suddenly cried out in terror and started toward the door after his companion. She heard the words plainly before the sinister man arose from his seat.

"No—" he whimpered in terror. "For God's sake—"

That was all he did say. The sinister man had shot him down and was stepping over the body and running into the street. Before that door fully closed she heard the single roar of a gun—the racing of a powerful motor. Then pandemonium broke loose in the restaurant.

She didn't know if the sinister man came back, but someone had stood in that doorway and forced the people back into the dining room. She didn't know what he said for she had remained seated at her table. Her Uncle George, when she was a very little girl, had told her always to do that, in a panic. After that a uniformed policeman was there. The proprietor, Mike, was speaking, and even before other policemen came the waiters had restored some semblance of order.

She was proud of her city and her police force. In no time the place seemed full of men in uniform and others who weren't. But she wasn't going to be fooled by the big, brusque man who kept his hat on when he questioned her. She didn't like his manner. It wasn't the roughness of it she disliked, but rather the indifference. He was ready, she thought, to pass her up as another frightened female. She got to her feet, pulling up her huge bulk haughtily, and crossed over to the table where the sinister man had sat.

"Yes, lady," said the detective from homicide. "Fifty people have told us the man sat there. We want only a simple statement of what happened."

"Simple." She shook her head. "Well, what I have to say can be said only to the commissioner of police himself. I knew him when I was a little girl."

Which was not true, for when she was a little girl the commissioner had not yet been born, and besides she knew him only from his pictures in the paper. Which last fact the detective found out to his sorrow.

The commissioner of police was a big man who sat far back in his chair and let his fingers drum together when he talked. He had not come up the hard way from the force. His life had been a busy one and successful. His appointment had been entirely a matter of ability, of having ideas of his own on running a great police system, and of a long standing friendship with the mayor, despite his lack of interest in politics. The boys in the know had looked at him as an experiment. They still did, for that matter, but they had discovered that the experiment was to be theirs.

Everyone knew the commissioner was too big a man, too wealthy and too important to be shoved around. It was only later they found out that he was also too big a man to be soft-soaped, cajoled or misled into any action of political expedience.

Now the commissioner was not sitting in that chair. He was walking up and down the room. Occasionally he looked out the window at the scurrying little people far below. He felt a great responsibility to those people. He turned again and regarded the man who sat so quietly in the chair by his desk.

That man had the body of a god and the face of a devil. His whole head was shaped almost like the letter V. Even his green eyes planted and his ears tapered and there was again the peculiar V-shaped growth of his jet-black hair. The commissioner didn't know when the name was first attached to this detective who was the terror of criminals, big and little throughout the city. Officials didn't like him. Newspaper editorials had appeared against him. And the first time the commissioner had seen him was when he talked to him before he dismissed him from the force. That was some time back and Detective—er—the commissioner couldn't remember his real first name now—well, Detective Satan Hall had been with him ever since. Working direct, for him.

"Well—" The commissioner spoke after a while. "Haven't you got anything to say?"

Satan's wide shoulders moved slightly.

"It was messy, I suppose," he said, without apparent feeling. "They dragged the third man into the car. We'll soon be finding out who he was."

"His friends in the car may take care of him."

"They wouldn't have much use for a dead body."

"You know he's dead?"

"I shot to kill. You're not going to threaten to fire me again, are you?"

"It wouldn't do you any harm." The commissioner smiled. "Chicago called me up today. They'd like to offer you a good job out their way. The man you killed was—the first one—Lawson King, a real killer and a dead shot."

"Maybe." Thin red lips parted and white teeth showed. "But he talked too much. He talked himself to death. Now what's the beef?"

"There is no beef," said the commissioner. "All three were notorious Chicago hoodlums. It's your flair for the dramatic, Satan. A respectable residential street—a crowded restaurant."

"I didn't pick the time nor the place."

"Didn't you?" The commissioner leaned forward. "Don't tell me you didn't know it was coming."

"Never had any idea before I dropped in to eat," Satan answered innocently.

The commissioner said with meaning, "There was a machine gun covering you—and you drew and fired. Is that it?"

"He wanted to talk," said Satan.

"Where's the napkin?" And when Satan looked at him blankly, "The napkin you jammed into your pocket when you went after man number two!" And when Satan still stared, "The napkin you held your gun under and shot through."

"Oh, that," said Satan. "I'm keeping it as a souvenir. It's not a bad idea."

"Are you in the habit of eating dinner with a gun clutched in your right hand and that right hand and what it contains hidden by a napkin? I want the truth, Satan. There was a Mrs. Tremont in that restaurant with a nose for crime and an eye for detail. She was watching you. She watched you go to the telephone. Watched you return and reverse your position so you sat facing the door. No—she didn't see you slip your gun under the napkin but she saw you slip that napkin in your pocket when you ran from the place."

"She knows me?"

"No," said the commissioner. Then with a grin, "She described you as the Sinister Man. Don't scowl. It is not a bad description. So you see you could have avoided the dramatic. Someone telephoned you that the death trap was set for you. You could have left, couldn't you?"

"Yes," said Satan.

"Why didn't you?"

"Because," said Satan, "no criminal, no hoodlum, no slimy murderer is going to drive me from my dinner."

"As simple as that, eh?" the commissioner said, but there was no irony in his voice. He hadn't expected such an answer, yet it didn't surprise him, coming from Satan. What's more he knew it was true.

Another look out the window and the commissioner said, "Of course, I am not going to ask you who telephoned you. Do you know?"

Satan hesitated a long moment. Then he said, "I think I know."

"Was it a woman?"

Satan only grinned and the commissioner tried again.

"Lawson King must have had a reason for coming on from Chicago. You didn't know him before?" And when Satan shook his head the commissioner went on. "It would take a big man to bring him on—big money, too, for a man to attempt your life. I know many who would want to see you dead—but do you suspect anyone of hiring Lawson King?"

"Yes." Satan's lips snapped closed.

"Who?"

"You won't like it."

"You have told me enough things I don't like, Satan, but when they were true I took them—and liked it."

"It was Tony Paro," Satan said. And after a pause, "Do you want to know why?"

"I can tell you what you'll tell me," the commissioner said. "Paro runs the biggest gambling establishment in the city of New York above his night club. Paro has protection. You are not in tune with my views that for the present at least we should tolerate certain things that are crimes on our statute books. I don't believe, Satan, that you can legislate morals. I know we should enforce the laws but I would rather keep an eye on our vices than drive those vices up back alleys."

"Yes." Satan nodded. "Paro runs his night club downstairs as a blind for his gambling upstairs—but what you won't believe is that Paro runs his gambling rooms to hide other crimes."

"You mean what I haven't proof of, Satan." And suddenly swinging around and staring long at him, he said, "Go after the man. Bring me that proof."

For the first time Satan showed emotion—at least physical movement. He said, "The politicians won't like it." And when the commissioner still stared at him, he added, "You have guessed the truth, perhaps. Paro is big. He is getting bigger. I doubt if there is a thousand dollars worth of marijuana sold in the city today from which Paro does not get a rake-off. Opium is coming in again. He will control that. I don't believe there is even a small-time crook in the entire city who gets murdered that within twenty-four hours Paro doesn't know who killed him and why." Satan shrugged his shoulders. "He will, if not stopped, rise to a great power—a power for evil in the nation."

"He must have a great deal of money."

"No," said Satan, "he hasn't. As a matter of fact he's in debt. Not that he doesn't make plenty—tax free money. He counts his small change in thousand-dollar bills, I imagine. But he's an opportunist. His rise to success must be quick, spectacular and sensational. He's throwing back every cent he can get his hands on into his business—the business of power."

"He doesn't consort with criminals."

"Not publicly. But remember, Commissioner, that a president of a great bank can be as much a thief as the ragged burglar who climbs the fire-escape of a tenement house. And the dishonest stock-broker takes more money from widows and orphans in one day than the subway purse-snatcher takes in his entire lifetime. Paro is beginning to get into exclusive clubs. Partly through his influence in politics—partly through the social contacts he has made. Partly because he'll take a second mortgage on a socialite's property. It won't be long before he is accepted by the best people. It won't be long before he has a grip on the party in power—or puts in his own party. He has killed or had killed well over a hundred men."

"You exaggerate there, Satan."

"No, I don't exaggerate. I underestimate, if anything. For the last time— and that's not a threat, Commissioner—I'm telling you, because it won't be much longer before Paro is too big to handle."

"You could handle him now?"

Satan's lips clicked in pleased determination. "I might goad him into drawing a gun on me."

"No," said the commissioner very seriously. "He wouldn't draw a gun on you. It couldn't be that easy."

"You'd like to see him dead?"

"Yes," the commissioner said, "I'd like to see him dead."

"You'd like to see me kill him?" Satan leaned forward now.

"No." The commissioner shook his head. "If I believed in murder, Satan, I wouldn't ask another man to do the killing for me. But I do believe in justice. I want that proof against Paro. I'm out to get him now."

"You have sent that word down the line?" There was disbelief in Satan's voice.

"No, I haven't." And then he said suddenly, "I haven't been a good commissioner, Satan. I'm afraid it's personal with me now, this Paro business. He's been seeing a lot of Elsa Drake. I spoke to her about it. She said she was going to marry him."

"Who," asked Satan, "is Elsa Drake?"

The commissioner smiled.

"Evidently not a criminal, or you wouldn't forget. Her father was a bank president—a good and dear friend of mine who, since his wife's death, gave more time to his business and less to Elsa. She got to running around night clubs. She was seventeen then, so the law was with us. You pushed around the hoodlum she admired and dragged her out of the place. Her reaction was peculiar, Satan. She transferred her affections to you. Came to see me about working with you against crime. Told her father she was going to marry you, wrote you some letters, then went away to school."

Satan leaned back and laughed.

"Sure, sure," he said, "I remember her. A painted child of wealth. I think I told her exactly what I thought of her, and cured her."

"You told her, but evidently you didn't cure her," the commissioner said grimly.

"I'll drag her out of this for you," Satan said. "If that's all that is worrying you and her father. Nice old duck, her father. Full of high-sounding words and a little flowery when he made his speech of appreciation on my saving his daughter." He smiled. "Also a hint that he wouldn't be the least bit sore about it if I didn't see her again. Offered me money, too. Can't he handle her now?"

"He's dead—two years nearly. Her uncle, Leslie Drake, is her guardian. She comes into a great deal of money shortly. You can't bully her around, Satan. She's too old and she winds her uncle around her finger. We've got to get Paro before he gets her."

"Like that. This Paro takes a grip on eight million people in the city of New York and you do nothing. Then he puts a finger on one single girl and you holler to high heaven." Satan opened his mouth as if to laugh but no laugh came. He closed it again. Came to his feet. "Commissioner," he said, "you are quite a friend. I don't know what I can do but I'll worry hell out of Paro."

Just before Satan opened the door the commissioner said, "Don't you want to know what she said to me, when I spoke to her? She said, 'If I can't run with the hounds, why, I'll run with the hares.' "

"Love of adventure, eh? Wants excitement. I'll try to furnish her with plenty of both. Paro has hard work clearing up his past. He had a lot of women friends." Satan shook his head. "When they become troublesome he sends them to South America, and they never return. He's got one now who will take trouble getting rid of. She helped build his 'career.' She won't stand for another girl." He turned back and gripped the commissioner's arm. "This Mrs. Tremont. She won't talk?"

"So that was the girl who called you up!" The commissioner's voice grew excited. "That may be it, Satan. Paro's girl friend can talk."

It was then that the telephone rang. The commissioner picked up the phone. He didn't say anything for a long time. Then he said simply, "All right," and put the phone back in its cradle.

It was a full moment before he spoke to Satan. Then he asked, "Was her name—Paro's girl friend's name—Betty Barber?"

"Yes," said Satan. "So Mrs. Tremont talked."

"I don't think so," said the commissioner solemnly. And then he added in a very tired voice, "We won't get anything from Betty, Satan. She won't talk. She can't talk." And after a pause, "The medical examiner said her tongue was cut out, before she died." And after a moment's pause, "They're looking for Razor Jenkins. He threatened to cut out her tongue, I'm told."

II

The Gunmaster

The Club Elite did not cater to the ordinary run of café society. Tony Paro was making it live up to that name. It provided only the best entertainment and never leaned toward the vulgar. Paro liked to look on it as like the Sherry's or Delmonico's of bygone days. There were drunks, of course, but they leaned heavily toward the middle-aged or elderly side. Young bloods didn't turn the place into a brawl even on Saturday nights.

Society people of another era were already beginning to venture out again for dinner or supper at the Club Elite. Their ears were not offended by boisterous talk nor their eyes by shameful misbehavior. The prices bumped even the hardiest, but at that Paro was losing money on the place.

Upstairs things were slightly different. One drank a bit more—one laughed a bit more—and one talked a bit louder—but just a bit. These gambling rooms above, Paro fancied, were run on the style of the former famous Bradley's at Palm Beach. The entrance was directly beyond the bar and up a flight of stairs where an attendant welcomed you or rejected you through a steel-barred little square in a heavy door.

Paro was in his office back of these rooms when Lieutenant Harrison of the police, natty and smart in a dark blue suit, breezed in.

"Thought I'd drop in and see you, Mr. Paro," he said. "Wanted to thank you for the donations to the Widows and Orphans Fund. Besides, I felt kind of lucky. Thought maybe I'd take a one shot at the wheel."

Paro liked Lieutenant Harrison. He was a man who was going places. He was a man who knew his way around. He had a nice way, too, of offhandedly dropping police department gossip that helped Paro a lot. And he was a man who knew the value of information. But he never broke the bounds of propriety by suggesting anything so low as a bribe.

"What's new?" Paro asked, indifferently, dipping his hand into a box of chocolates.

"Nothing. Detective Satan Hall has been acting up a bit after his shooting at Mike the Greek's. I don't think he likes you, Mr. Paro." Then, with a laugh, "Which wouldn't bother a man like you much. He might pay you a visit—some excuse about gambling. Maybe he'd like to make trouble. Well," as he backed toward the door, "I feel sort of lucky. What do you think?"

"How lucky do you feel?" Paro's eyes were friendly enough, nice blue that set off the wavy brown of his hair. He was a big man and handsome, and he carried himself well. He didn't drink, seldom smoked, but almost continually ate chocolate creams from a specially constructed humidor. A small candy manufacturer in Detroit made them exclusively for Paro—always vanilla— and always two dollars and fifty cents a pound.

Harrison said, "Oh—I thought I might win three or four hundred dollars."

"Five hundred," said Paro, with a smile. "That's what I'd go out to win if I were you." He pressed a button on his desk and a tall, slim, stooped man all dressed in black appeared at the door. "Lieutenant Harrison feels lucky, Parson," Paro said to him. And as Harrison turned toward the door, Paro raised five fingers in the air.

Parson nodded but did not speak.

Ten minutes later Parson came back into the room.

Lieutenant Harrison went whistling down the stairs, out the iron-windowed door, swung right instead of passing the bar, and still whistling, stepped through the little door that led into the alley. He turned toward the street. Lieutenant Harrison was a wise guy who recognized the fact that a too honest cop simply remained a too honest cop. Not that he had ever done anything exactly dishonest. There'd been a few little things like tipping off Paro. But then the big boys in the city took care of Paro too. If he wanted to make a bet occasionally, didn't he have the same right as the ordinary citizen? If he won? Well, some guys were lucky.

About Satan Hall. Word had sort of slipped out to Harrison that Satan Hall had learned that the commissioner wouldn't cry over any trouble he caused Paro. If Paro had suggested it, Harrison would have stayed around and handled Satan for him if Satan went stalking through the club making trouble. Sure, Lieutenant Harrison knew of men even on the force who feared Satan Hall—but then that must have been because he was "the commissioner's pet." Harrison would like to see the guy who would intimidate him by making faces. He had never met up with Satan and probably never would. He had seen him of course—and Harrison turned out of the alley and bumped into a man.

Harrison was a little surprised at that bump. He was a big man and when he collided with anyone it was generally the other fellow who gave ground. Now he was not only rocked back on his heels but sent staggering along the sidewalk almost into the arms of a uniformed cop. It was the officer in harness who caused Harrison to act the way he did. Ordinarily he was an easy going man who left well enough alone. Not now. His dignity was hurt. He ran several steps forward and grabbed the man who had turned into the alley, and swung him around.

"You big lug," Harrison boomed, for the benefit of the officer who was sauntering up. "I have a good mind to punch you smack in the nose."

The man raised his eyes and set them long and steadily on the bellowing Harrison. He didn't speak. He suddenly jerked the lieutenant toward him, and like a member of the force of many years standing, actually frisked Harrison.

Lieutenant Harrison was stunned. It was so quick and so unexpected. Then the officer was beside him and Harrison was free. He raised his hand to strike. The officer cried out:

"Hall—by God, it's Hall. Detective Satan Hall."

Lieutenant Harrison didn't know then and never did know what stayed his hand. Certainly he was not a coward. But something did stay his hand. But nothing stayed his mouth. He wished later something had. He wished it then. For the words he spoke were certainly not the words he wanted to speak. He said:

"Detective Hall, eh? I'm Lieutenant Harrison. You're drunk. You are relieved from duty and ordered to report to your nearest—"

Harrison stopped, then. Satan's lips had parted and his teeth showed. He thought the man was smiling but when he looked at those green eyes he wasn't sure. Then Satan spoke. Harrison was startled. He had never heard so much of bitterness in a man's voice before. Satan said:

"I hate crooks, but I hate above anything else a crooked cop. This is yours, I believe." Satan Hall raised his hand and slapped something into Harrison's face. Then he turned and went down the alley.

The cop watched Lieutenant Harrison pick up the bits of paper which had struck him in the face. He counted them. There were ten of them. And each piece of paper was a fifty-dollar bill.

Harrison came erect—shoved one of the bills into the officer's hand.

"Something for the missus," he said. "Forget the incident. I'll attend to that lad later."

"No, thank you, sir." Officer Riordan refused to take the money. "I'll forget the incident, sir, and you'd be well advised to forget it too. He was in an unpleasant mood, sir, and he's going in to see Mr. Paro."

"And what would a punk like Satan Hall do to a big shot like Mr. Paro?" Harrison sneered.

"Well," said Officer Riordan, who was a realist, "he could shoot him to death, for one thing."

What the other thing might be Lieutenant Harrison didn't inquire.

Detective Satan Hall had no trouble in dodging garbage cans and turning in the rear door of the Club Elite. The kitchen help used that door continuously and certainly Paro gave the impression that he had nothing to hide. He reached the hall that led from the rear to the bar and went quickly up the stairs to the little dark landing where the barred square identified the privileged who wished to enter the gaming rooms. Satan kept his felt hat on and his head slightly down when he tapped on that door.

Wood slid back and the heavy bars appeared. The attendant, a shrewd, highly paid man, could not recognize Satan. His voice was soft.

"We don't admit anyone to this section of the club," he said. "It's reserved for private parties."

"I am a new member." Satan spoke just as softly. "I have a card here. If you will take it to Mr. Paro he will admit me. Indeed, he would be rather disturbed if he did not see me."

"I see," said the attendant, in a voice that was supposed to convey that he was greatly impressed. "May I have the card?"

"Certainly." Satan held a card up close to the window. Fingers raised to grasp it reached between the bars. It might be an honored guest of course. It might be the same old attempt to get inside. Nothing ever bothered the suave attendant and nothing surprised him.

That is, nothing until that precise second.

He did not see the hand move that clutched his fingers, dragging his arm its full length through those bars and forcing his face close against the uprights of steel. And forcing his face against something else too, against the black snub nose of a heavy automatic. He saw also green evil eyes, a thin red gash that was a mouth and he heard the voice that spoke. It said:

"Don't press an alarm button. Unlock the door and let me in, or I'll blow your face out of its frame."

And then quite unnecessarily, "The name is Satan Hall."

The attendant was not a man who was easily bluffed. At the same time he was not a man to have his face shot apart, either. He didn't know if he believed Satan's threat. But he knew of other men who had not believed it— and were dead. He wasn't panic-stricken. He was quite calm. He knew it would be nice to say, "Sure, I showed Satan up for the bluff that he is." But it was nicer still to be alive.

So he simply snapped free the lock, felt the unpleasant sensation of being torn apart by an opening door that he hung on. Then his arm fell back through the opening and Satan Hall was in the little vestibule beside him.

"I will have to report your forced entrance, and your threat." The attendant had recovered now, and his voice was still soft.

"Sure." Satan nodded. "I was kidding, of course. I wanted to see if you could be intimidated."

Satan swung up the remaining steps, shook his head at the pretty little page girl who wanted his hat and was in the main foyer of the gambling rooms. Eddie Fallow, the manager, spotted Satan almost at once and was in front of Satan as he started toward the private office of Tony Paro.

Satan Hall did not find the door locked. Indeed, he almost bumped into the creeping, black-clad Parson as he swung down the final few feet. Parson wasn't quite sure what happened. He knew that he had been thrust aside. He knew that the door he was closing had been jerked violently open and as violently closed, and a tall man with broad shoulders had disappeared inside. He also heard the key turn in the lock.

Paro looked up from the telephone. If anything showed in his face it was simply a slight start. Paro said into the phone:

"Yes, you're quite right. He's a fast worker. He's here now. Thank you." Then he dropped the phone, put a chocolate carefully into his mouth, and looked up at Satan.

"It was Harrison, wasn't it?" Satan asked, but he didn't wait for an answer. He knew he wouldn't get it. "I told him to tell you I was coming."

It was some time before Paro spoke again. Satan waited. He was going to let Paro worry about his sudden appearance and the locking of the door. The two men studied each other. There was character in Paro's face, strong character, but then Satan knew that character was both good and bad.

The mild blue eyes were searching, but not visibly hostile, though apparently annoyed. The lips were thick and sensuous and Paro held them closely together, the upper one drawn tightly down. It was hardly noticeable any more, but Paro was still conscious of the fact that his upper lip protruded, puckered slightly.

That here was a third person in that room Satan knew. But he didn't turn his head and it was quite possible from his position that he might not have seen that person. It was Paro who finally spoke.

"You are Detective Hall, of course. I presume that you have something of great importance."

"Skip it," Satan said suddenly. "Your girl friend, Betty Barber, was murdered tonight."

"My girl friend!" Paro straightened in his chair. "What a vulgar way of expressing it."

"How would you put it? You went around with her, didn't you? You tired of her, didn't you? She talked, didn't she? Well, her tongue was cut out before she died. But she rang me up at Mike the Greek's the other—"

"Stop!" Paro was jarred out of his boasted calm. "There is a lady present."

Satan turned slightly and looked at Elsa Drake. She had changed a great deal since he had last seen her, but he knew her. She was just as pretty, maybe beautiful now in a sophisticated sort of way. She was dressed entirely in black, bare shoulders, no adornment of any kind but a single small white flower in her hair. Her smile seemed very pleasant. She said, in a low voice:

"Satan Hall. You don't remember me, but I remember you. No one would forget such a—such—should I say such a compelling face."

Satan said, "I remember you. You are Elsa Drake. I got you out of a particularly nasty situation with another gangster a few years back."

Paro was on his feet now. His upper lip protruded. The years swept back. For a moment he wondered if he could reach into the open drawer of his desk, grip the gun that was there and shoot Satan dead before he turned from the girl. He wondered, too, what the girl would say in court, if it ever reached court. But he didn't reach into the desk.

Satan said, "There's a key in the door that the young woman can turn and walk out. If you prefer, we'll talk alone."

For the first time in his life Paro knew real fear. For a moment he felt the beads of perspiration coming out on his forehead. He had almost waved a hand for Elsa to go, then he remembered all he had heard about the man Satan Hall. He wondered what would happen in that room with the two of them alone. It would be his word only if he killed Satan. And that was where the beads grew on his forehead.

It would be Satan's word only if Satan killed him. That would be murder. And Satan never went to murder. Or did he? And that was a point in question that the great Paro didn't want to prove—or at least disprove—at that time. He said, and his voice, though controlled and quite natural, sounded husky and uncertain to him, "No. Miss Drake and I are engaged to be married. There is nothing I would not wish her to hear." And feeling on thicker ice now, he added, "We might dispense with the details."

"The same honest old Tony." Elsa Drake crossed to the desk and ran a hand through that wavy brown hair. "I'll go downstairs and have a sandwich. I'm starved." And when she reached the door and spun the key in the lock, "I'll see you before you leave, Mr. Satan Hall, and you can renew an unpleasant acquaintance."

She was gone and Paro had not spoken. He had half raised his hand, but the gesture was never completed. He sat down at the desk and let his hand creep close to the open drawer. Satan was leaning over now, both hands on the desk. A half minute, a few seconds only, to draw and shoot—and Satan's hands both on the desk. Yes, he was sorely tempted, as many a killer had been before him. Then a voice behind Satan, a warning voice, said simply:

"Don't do it, boss. Don't do it."

The blood rushed back into Paro's face as he saw Parson standing there behind Satan. He had slipped in the door and closed it softly. And he saw, too, the expression on Parson's face, the lowering of his eyes and the movement of his right hand in his jacket pocket. He saw Satan's green eyes steadily on him, but he saw with more satisfaction those hands with the long, strong fingers spread flat on the desk—empty. Satan didn't even turn when Parson spoke.

Paro was his old self now. His lips grew firm. He said to Satan, "Do you know how long it would take me to get you dismissed from the force? Just as long as it would take me to lift this telephone here."

Satan said easily, "There's a little matter of news interest, about the dead girl calling me on the phone and warning me there would be an attempt on my life."

Relief appeared on Paro's face. Satan wondered. Was it possible that Paro didn't know who made the call? Was it possible that that call had not been the immediate cause of Betty Barber's death?

"Why are you here?" Paro asked.

"Simply to ask you where you were last night. Many others are going to ask you. You are going to answer them. An alibi might help you—with me —now."

"It's not your business. It's not your line. You are here for personal reasons."

"And what personal reason?"

"To—well, to do everything possible to break up my contemplated marriage with Miss Drake."

Satan's laugh was a grating hollow sound. He said, "I'd break up your marriage with any decent girl if I could. But I'm not here because of that girl. I'm here because of another girl."

"Another girl?" Paro's eyes opened wide. But there was no disbelief in them. Somehow Satan's voice was full of sincerity, his eyes too.

"Yes. Betty Barber. I won't say that she saved my life. But she may have. That was what I started to tell you. She called me at the Greek's the night— the night three men died. I owe her something. I owe myself something. I am going to get the man who killed her. I am going to get the man who ordered her killed. Don't you get the point, Paro? It's common gossip along the Avenue. You tossed her out, but she swore vengeance. She swore she'd talk. She talked to me and she died."

Paro smiled.

"I can clear that point up for you, Satan. I swear I never knew that Betty called you."

"You knew," said Satan slowly, "that I have tried to interest the authorities in you for a long time. You knew, too, that my efforts were bearing fruit." And, raising his voice slightly, "I know what you are thinking, Paro."

"You are thinking how easy it will be to hire men to do the job you are afraid to do yourself. Well, you have one more chance—and one chance only. See that the man you hire doesn't fail. For if he does I'll come blasting into this office again, and that time I will be on the kill."

"That," said Tony Paro easily, "will be murder."

"If you can get any satisfaction out of that thought—why, call it murder." And straightening from the desk, "I'll be leaving now, Tony Paro. If that man behind me has his hand on a gun when I pass him, I'll shoot him to death."

Satan spun suddenly on his heels and Parson's hand jerked from his pocket, empty. A moment later the door closed and Tony Paro faced Parson. He said:

"Louie Spatz lied about Betty. He said he was with her all that evening and she never went near a phone."

Parson nodded. "She was a nice armful, Mr. Paro. I guess Louie got to like her pretty much."

Tony Paro got up and paced the room. He dipped his hand into the candy box; finally said, "Do you know, Parson, I could bear up if I never saw Louie Spatz again."

"Right," said Parson, as he reached for the phone.

There was not a great deal of interest next day when Louie Spatz's body was picked out of the East River.

III

"I Like to Make Trouble!"

Ilsa Drake leaned out of the darkness at the end of the stairs and gripped Satan's arm.

"You're not even surprised," she told him. "I thought you'd pull a gun or blackjack me, or something."

"I saw you," Satan said simply. "And I knew you'd be here."

"How marvelous is our detective. Not only sees in the dark but reads the mind, and my mind above all others. And why am I here?" There was light banter in her voice.

"To try to justify yourself. To hear yourself talk. To make yourself believe that you are doing the right and noble thing. To tell me that you have refused to stay in the rut that society cut out for you, which inheritance and environment demanded. That you are above the petty things of life. That here is a man who has fought his way up alone, the world against him and—"

Her laugh stopped him, then. It seemed so natural and pleasant.

"How flattering," she said. "It is almost word for word what I told you when I was a child, isn't it? And you remember it. I said that I loved you, too —that I'd never marry any other man. You spurned me."

Satan looked at her a moment, then started by her toward the rear.

"Wait," she said. "I have reserved a little booth back beyond the bar. It's cozy and quiet and has a little shaded light. Just the place for us, Satan, while you point out the error of my ways."

"I am not interested in you. At all."

"But the commissioner is. He threatened me with you, I think—or maybe I suggested it. For friendship's sake, for the commissioner's sake, aren't you going to tell me what a big, bad man Tony is? The commissioner is very fond of both of us, you know. Are you afraid to tell me about Tony? Afraid I'll tell him? Afraid of what he may do about it? Or haven't you anything to tell?"

"Are you going to marry Tony Paro?"

"Do you mean are we engaged?"

"Isn't that the same thing?"

"No," she shook her head. "We are not engaged. I know he told you that upstairs. That's what I like about him. He's so possessive. Yet there are times when he—when I think he is a little afraid of me."

"He kills what he fears," Satan said, abruptly and brutally.

Elsa Drake shivered visibly. "How thrilling," she said. "Do tell me about it."

Satan followed her to the little table three booths down from the end of the bar. After all, he might learn something. Again, he might leave the girl with an impression that might make her hesitate about marrying Tony Paro. He noticed the thick vase and the yellow flowers it held upon the table. He noticed, too, that the other little booths didn't have flowers. The girl said:

"You see my little arrangements. We can put our heads close to the flowers and talk. No one can overhear us then. She straightened the vase slightly and some leaves on the side fell off. Even in the semidarkness Satan could not help seeing the network on the side of the vase. He leaned over and tried to lift it from the table, but it gave very little. Satan smiled grimly and jerked the vase free. A wire snapped beneath it, broke. Satan tossed the vase and the flowers into the empty booth across from them. He didn't say anything when the girl quickly laid her purse down on the exposed wiring where the vase had been. A dictograph. Satan screwed up his mouth, but when the waiter came running he said simply:

"I don't like flowers. See what the young lady wants. I'll take a bottle of coke. And open it at the table."

"It's all right about the flowers, Johnson," the girl said to the waiter. "We were fooling. I'll have a Martini—a double one."

"But Mr. Paro said—" The waiter started and stopped as Elsa Drake interrupted him.

"We won't bother with what Mr. Paro said tonight, Johnson."

"We won't be overheard now," Satan said pointedly, when the waiter had left, but he didn't directly mention the wired vase. The girl ignored it too. She said:

"Tell me about Betty Barber—the details Tony didn't want me to hear. He's always taking such care of me. He's so considerate."

"She was tortured to death," said Satan. "Nicked with razor blades—face and upper part of her body. Her tongue was cut off before she died. So she couldn't talk and—What's the matter, Miss Drake?" The girl had turned a sudden white. A finger moved up to her throat as if to pull down something tight that wasn't there. After a moment she said:

"Or maybe because she wouldn't talk?"

"What made you think of that?"

"I—I—there was Razor Jenkins, you know. He threatened to kill her. He was very fond of Betty Barber once, and she was close to Tony later. Jenkins might have wanted to know things. He—" The waiter came then and she leaned out and grabbed the Martini from the tray and drank it down at once. "Another one, Johnson," she said. "Don't stand there staring at me. Bring another one."

The waiter hesitated, opened his mouth, said nothing. Then he walked away.

Elsa Drake asked, "Razor Jenkins has been arrested, hasn't he?"

"Don't you know?"

"No," she said. "No. How should I know? I guess the details are a little gruesome. Can't we talk about something else?"

"Well," said Satan, "Razor Jenkins has been pulled in by this time, I guess. He always was a big mouth. It was common gossip that he told Betty Barber that he'd cut her tongue out if she talked about him. John Smith knew it.

John Brown knew it. Joe Doe knew it." And, after a pause, he said, "Tony Paro knew it."

"So that's it," she said. "You are trying to lay the crime on Tony Paro. Because you are out to get Paro. The commissioner wants him—because of me."

"The commissioner didn't know the girl was dead when he spoke to me about you. Tony Paro, Miss Drake, is a very smooth and a very dangerous killer. I have traced back his life and he was once tried for for murder. He was twenty-one then and he was acquitted. I think he was guilty. Since then —well—" Satan leaned forward. "Haven't you ever heard him express the wish not to see such a person again, and haven't you thought it quite a coincident that the person died after that?"

"No man could hire another for such a brutal, beastly murder," she said, after the second drink had been brought.

"No. Even if a man could, I don't think he'd let himself out on the limb that far. It's a murder that a man would have to commit himself."

"And do you think Tony Paro would hack a woman to death, himself? It wouldn't be true to character."

"No," said Satan again. "With all I know about the man, it wouldn't be true to his character."

"There, you see?" Elsa Drake said triumphantly.

"But," said Satan, "if Razor Jenkins didn't commit the murder, the one who did was not committing it in his own character, but in the character of Razor Jenkins. He would be playing a part, and would have to play it true to character. True to Razor Jenkins' threat to cut Betty Barber's tongue out."

"You tell me this, knowing I am so close to Tony. You think I won't tell him?"

Satan shrugged his shoulders.

"What does your uncle think of this—contemplated marriage?" he asked abruptly. "What would your father have thought?"

"Father would not have liked it. He was of the old school. My Uncle Leslie doesn't approve or disapprove of the things I do. He is a banker and simply the guardian of my money. But he approves of Mr. Paro personally. He invites him to our house. To his club. He is an esteemed depositor at my uncle's bank."

"Your uncle," said Satan coldly, "is not the man your father was. He holds a very small position at the bank. Makes an insignificant salary, lives well and—visits the rooms above the club. No doubt"—and Satan went on watching her closely—"he is a man who plays only when he feels lucky?"

The girl waited some time before she spoke. Then she said, "My uncle owes Tony nothing."

Satan looked her over slowly.

"Let's us hope, Miss Drake, that we roast Paro for murder before that marriage takes place."

"He has an alibi," she said. "Before, after, and at the time of the murder. He was with my uncle."

"The uncle of the luck in the gaming rooms? Leslie Drake?"

The girl reddened slightly.

"Yes," she said. "I suppose you would have the same sneer in your voice if I told you that I was present too?"

"Really," said Satan, "it grows very interesting, doesn't it? But you didn't tell me you were there." And without raising his eyes from hers he said, "Here comes Paro. I am surprised he didn't interrupt our little talk sooner."

"He doesn't tell me what to do," said Elsa.

But Paro did tell her what to do. Told her brusquely, too.

"Give me that cocktail, Elsa," he said. "Now." He gripped her wrist.

She held onto the glass tightly and looked up at him, surprise more than anger in her eyes.

"Take your hand off my wrist, Tony," she said. "It hurts."

"It's meant to," he said, his voice very low. "Give me that cocktail."

"You heard the lady," said Satan. "She said take your hand off her wrist—it hurts her." And when Paro just glared at him, "If you don't, I will remove it in a way that will positively amaze you."

Paro dropped the wrist as if it had been a hot coal. His action was almost involuntary. So was his action to grab it again, but he controlled it in time. He turned without a word and left the table.

Elsa Drake said, "You had better go now—or rather, I will." She came to her feet and slid gracefully from the booth. "You are a very foolish man, Mr. Satan Hall." And just before she left she turned back again and whispered softly, "And a very courageous one."

Then she was gone. Satan sat in silence a few minutes, sipping the remains of his coke. Then he smiled. She was a clever girl. And, he thought, a dangerous one. The commissioner mightn't do better than let her marry Paro.

IV
Satan Takes Over

Razor Jenkins didn't take his beating too long. And Satan had little trouble in getting in to see him. Indeed, there was great rejoicing among the boys. The stenographer was even then typing out the full statement of Jenkins' confession. Satan asked a swarthy sergeant:

"So you got another confession. Won't you ever learn?"

The big sergeant beamed on him.

"You've gotten confessions that way yourself, Satan. Real ones. This time it will stick, for we've got enough on Jenkins without it. But it makes for good newspaper reading, keeps the D.A. happy, and leaves the grand jury nothing to do but turn in an indictment. After that the fun begins."

"What fun? Razor has no friends."

"He's got money, then. He's got a right smart lawyer. Sam Renwick."

Satan whistled. Renwick was big money. Not the best criminal lawyer in the city, perhaps, but one who'd go further than any other with perjured witnesses, fixed jurors and all the trimmings. He was a man, too, who used money freely in a case. So somewhere behind the show was big cash. He turned now and saw Renwick with Captain Sheridan. Sheridan was saying:

"Cut and dried, Mr. Renwick. Confession signed and no one laid a hand on him."

"How droll," said Renwick. "How very quaint. Poor Jenkins—such mastery by the police. I have always said we had the greatest police force in the world. Don't tell me you promised to give Jenkins back his lollypop?" And poking the captain in the stomach and chuckling at his own joke, "Well, do I see him, or do I have to tell the newspapers how you kept me from him"— and significantly—"for a little while?"

"Give me a break, Sergeant," Satan said. "Hold off the legal talent for fifteen minutes—ten, even. Renwick will probably offer Captain Sheridan a ten-cent cigar with a hundred-dollar bill for a wrapper."

"If he hands me any such cigar," the sergeant said with a grin, "you won't have your ten minutes. But shoot through and I'll see what I can do."

Razor Jenkins was sitting on the end of his iron bed when Satan was let into his cell. There was a little blood on Jenkins' lips but otherwise he wasn't marked. He was a skinny little man with shifty, mud-colored eyes, sparse hair, and he held a cigarette between yellow-stained fingers. He looked up at Satan and said:

"Hell, you! Aren't they satisfied with the confession? What else do they want?"

"We haven't much time." Satan sat down close to Jenkins on the iron bunk. "You know I don't work along with homicide. I work alone. They are going to fry you, Jenkins. It's a frame."

"A frame," Jenkins' shifty eyes became steady. "The cops, you mean?"

"No. Cops don't frame guys, Jenkins. They do the best they can with the evidence they have, and they have plenty. Someone else is framing you. I don't believe you did it. I want to help you."

"You help a guy—a crook? That's a laugh."

"I want to get the man who killed her, Razor. I think I know who he is. He put the finger on you."

"Paro?" said Jenkins.

"Paro."

"I thought on that," said Jenkins. "I thought on that the minute I saw her body. But he's too big. Besides, he don't do his own killing any more. And if he did, not like that. A bullet through her head, or if that was too noisy, a pillow over her head. Or a knife across her throat. I often—"

"Often thought on it." Satan finished the sentence for him. "Don't look so startled. Often talked about it, too. They'd bring that up in court. They'd put guys on the stand who'd heard you."

"I got a lawyer—one who is tops. He'll fix me up. He said so."

"When did you see him?"

"See him?" Razor Jenkins hesitated and then said brightly, "I didn't see him. I gave him a buzz on the phone. I knew they'd be looking for me."

"Where did you get the money for Renwick? Don't lie, Razor. You've been broke a long time. Now listen. He called you, didn't he? He knew where you were hiding out. How did he know where? Because someone told him. Who? Someone who must have followed you from Betty Barber's apartment.

"You must have known something like that had happened when Renwick called you. He told you to wait there, didn't he? Told you he'd come and get you and turn you in and protect you. You got in a panic and left. The cops picked you up, and this lawyer is looking for you now. What friends have you got? Who'd lay five grand—maybe ten—on the line to get Renwick? Just one man. The man who framed you. Paro."

"Nuts," said Razor, "he framed me all right, but why try to protect me now? Why sic a high-priced, high-powered mouthpiece on me? It don't make sense."

"It does make sense," said Satan, "if something went wrong at the killing. That you discovered something, or saw something that Paro doesn't want you to beef about." And seeing the surprise in Jenkins' eyes, he went on, "So Renwick called you, and you told him just what had happened at Betty

Barber's apartment. And he said 'Don't talk—don't talk at all until I see you. And above all don't mention—' something. Something in particular. Right?"

"He told me not to talk." Jenkins' eyes were very wide now.

Satan gripped his arm. "Something went wrong, Jenkins, or Paro wouldn't have sent Renwick to you. And who else would? What friends have you got? Jenkins—you're going to cook. There is only one person besides the murderer in the city who believes you didn't do it. That's me. Tell me the things you aren't to mention. I give you my word never to use it against you.

"Look, Jenkins, it's your last chance. I won't be able to see you again. Renwick will see to that. Now's your last opportunity. You'll think of it again. You'll wish you had told me. You'll think of it when they strap you in the chair and the smell of burning flesh—your own flesh—is in your nostrils."

"There—there—" Jenkins began to shake. "There was another person there, outside the door. He's right, Satan. Renwick is right. We keep that person out of it. A mention in the newspaper and she'll—the person will disappear. This way, maybe the person won't know I saw—saw—"

"Her," said Satan.

"Yes—yes—and Renwick will trace her and put private dicks on her. And he'll find out the play and—bing! Just like that. I'm out and free."

"Did you recognize the girl?"

"No," said Razor Jenkins, "I never seen her before. It was like she come out of the apartment and—and—" He tossed his cigarette on the floor and stamped on it. "Not a word to Renwick, Satan—not a word. You swore you wouldn't."

"No," said Satan, "and not a word from you." And suddenly, as he heard a gate clank far down and heavy feet beat along the cold steel floor he jerked the newspaper from his pocket and held the picture of the girl close to Jenkins' face.

"Was that the girl?" he asked. "Was that—"

It was a long time before Jenkins spoke, and then shadows broken by black bars made pictures on the wall.

"Yes—no—I don't know," said Jenkins.

Satan had pushed the newspaper back into his pocket and had come to his feet when the guard let Renwick into the cell.

"Well, well," boomed Renwick, smiling at Satan. "So you got a confession of the crime too. Wasn't one enough? I know he confessed to you, Satan. Otherwise you would have shot him dead. None of this slow, lingering torture for you. You are a man of action. No hard feelings, Detective Hall, but this will be your last visit. After all, my client is not on public display, you know."

Satan went back to the commissioner's office and said, "You want me to go after Paro, Commissioner? To break up this marriage? That's certain, isn't it?"

"You can't very well shoot Paro to death. And you can't very well arrest him for murder."

"No," said Satan, "but I can arrest the girl. That's right, Commissioner. Elsa Drake."

"For murder?" The commissioner was amazed.

"She was in the room with the dead Betty Barber. Certainly she can be held as an accomplice before or after the fact."

"It's not a pretty prospect for a young girl—a highly strung young girl whom I—"

"Yes, yes," Satan cut in, "whom you dandled on your knee as a child. Well, a dead girl on the floor with her tongue cut out is not pretty either. I thought I'd tell you before I got the warrant."

"Satan," said the commissioner slowly, "you don't believe *she* committed such a crime?"

"If she didn't," Satan said, "she could say a lot of words that would probably straighten the crime out. I'm going to put the squeeze on her. She talks or I drag her in."

The commissioner got up and paced the room. He had handled men for a long time. He had even handled Satan Hall, which no one else in the department, great or small, ever claimed to have done. Finally he turned and faced Satan.

"Satan," he said, "I am not going to stand in the way of you and what you feel is justice. This young girl is in trouble. Her father was my best friend. I'm not saying she is doing anything to enhance an honored name. She's doing plenty to hurt it. I hoped to prevent her from hurting it, and herself, more. You know, of course, that to place her at the scene of the crime will smear her for life."

Satan smacked his lips. The sound was not a pleasant one.

"That," he said, "was the chance she took when she went there."

"Well," said the commissioner, "I think you are wrong. But you do what you think is right. I brought you into this thing because I thought you were the only man in the department who could handle it alone, without outside help. If you can't, get that help, of course."

Satan grinned.

"I could handle it alone," he said, "if not another cop in the city raised a hand to help me. If not—" And seeing the commissioner's smile, he said, "Okay, Commissioner. Maybe you are smarter than I am." He walked toward the door, put a hand on the knob and pulled it open. "I won't get any warrant, but I'll tear this case wide open. And if the cards fall that way, I'll blast it into the open if it lifts the roof right off the city hall. You won't interfere?"

The commissioner opened his mouth twice to speak, but it was the third time before the words came. Then he said simply:

"I won't interfere."

Satan didn't believe that Elsa Drake had committed that murder. He felt that something or someone had sent her to the scene of the crime.

He took a trip to see the medical examiner, and established the time of death of Betty Barber as between nine p.m. and eleven p.m. Old Doc Newberry wouldn't put it officially closer than that. He said to Satan:

"Death didn't take place before nine and certainly not after eleven o'clock. . . . I understand the case is closed. Razor Jenkins gets the chair."

"Takes the rap, you mean," Satan said.

Doc Newberry straightened.

"Like that, eh? You don't believe he did it? It's a rather ordinary murder, Satan." And after a moment's hesitation, for Dr. Newberry rather like Satan, "They say you'd like to pin it on—a certain man—a big man. Suppose he is too big to roast?"

"No man is too big to die." Satan wheeled then and strode out of the doctor's house, and the doctor went back to his beer and cheese on rye.

It was then close to nine o'clock in the evening and Satan, ignoring a cab, hopped a subway up to 72nd Street, walked up Broadway a few blocks and turned toward Central Park West. The stone steps of the brownstone front that echoed dully under his feet was the well-worn entrance of the Drake residence.

Mr. Leslie Drake felt that he was of some importance in the bank. And in a way he was. His brother had been president and Leslie had grown great in his shadow. Now, though somewhat diminished, he was thriving on his niece's shadow; at least, that part of the shadow cast by the money her father had left and of which Leslie was trustee.

He dressed the part of the man he thought he was and the way he thought such a man should be dressed. His clothes were always somber. His face was always somber and the black ribbon that ran from his pince-nez down into his waistcoat was just a bit thicker than even he thought his importance called for.

When the door bell rang he got up quickly from his chair and placed a detective thriller behind some books in the shelf, straightened his tie and took a squint at himself in the mirror. Even his niece had never seen him in what he liked to call his leisure moments. He didn't have to replace the detective book for another. One was already lying on the table before him, carefully turned over to be picked up at any moment.

The book before him was called *The Human Side of Banking.* It meant nothing to him, but a friend at the club had said that it meant a great deal to the customers—providing they read no further than the cover.

The hour was late for him, almost five minutes of ten. He wondered if it was his niece, Elsa, coming back for a forgotten key, as it never entered his head that she would be returning at such an early hour—for her.

He went to the door and pulled it open and was somewhat surprised at the man who pushed his way in, and, relieving him of the door, pushed it closed with—well, if not exactly a bang, certainly with considerable unnecessary force.

"Hall," said his visitor. "Detective Hall of the police."

Leslie Drake did not lose his dignity though it was slightly ruffled. He said, "Isn't the hour rather late?"

"It's about the same time that a girl was murdered. Murderers and cops don't work regular hours. Is that the library? I want to ask you a few questions."

"I don't think we shall talk at all." And when Satan blocked the hand that would have majestically thrown the front door open for his dismissal, Mr. Drake continued, "Do you know, Detective Hall, just how long it would take me to have you removed from the force?"

"Just as long as it would take you to lift the phone," Satan said. "I've heard that one before. I'm here on serious business, Mr. Drake, and you'll have to be on your own." And when the dignity still remained, "All right, you'll have to have it, then. Things have happened that connect you up rather closely with the death of Betty Barber."

If the man was acting, he certainly was a great actor, Satan thought. The look on his face was one of utter amazement. He turned, seemed to feel his way toward the open door of the library, though there was plenty of light in the hall. He was inside and sitting in his chair and not fully recovered when Satan, following him in, spoke again.

Standing before the great broad desk, Satan said, "Maybe I tossed it at you a little hard. But no matter how I put it, it's not going to be an easy dose to swallow. If you feel that you wish to have your attorney present or someone from the bank, all right. But what I say is going to involve the honor of your family." And, as the banker seemed to brighten a bit, he added, "Yourself as well as your niece."

"Now listen. You made a statement to the D.A. over the phone, but an inspector of police got a signed statement. I have read it. Was it all true?"

"To the best of my knowledge and belief."

"Your niece, Elsa, never left you between the hours of eight o'clock and midnight. You were playing Gin Rummy, isn't that it? You and Elsa and Paro —and Elsa never left."

"I couldn't say she never left the room. I didn't say that. There were light refreshments, I believe, and she was in and out."

"But never more than ten minutes. You were sure of that. You signed a statement to that effect."

"Er—fifteen, perhaps—She—"

"You signed ten." And leaning forward, "As a matter of fact, wasn't she gone for hours? Was she here at all?" And when Drake would have come in indignantly, "All right, Mr. Drake. Here it is. I have placed Elsa Drake directly at the scene of the murder, and I can produce people who saw her. Now, do you want to change that statement? Was your niece here at all that evening? Was Paro here?"

"Good gracious. Tony Paro was the one who said we must say she was with us. He—but what am I saying! What—Yes, I will see an attorney. I will say nothing more. Surely, you can't believe—"

"You can see your attorney down town," Satan cut in abruptly. "I know your rights and I know you know them. I have a warrant for your arrest here in my pocket. Get your hat and coat."

Satan heard the step and saw the figure as he heard all steps and saw all figures, before the girl spoke. She said:

"You have been very noble, Uncle. You won't have to explain." And turning to Satan, "Paro is out in the hall. He'd like to talk with you. If you want me then—well, you can have me. If you are set on making a mess out of it."

"Someone made a mess out of the Barber woman," Satan said calmly. "I'll talk to Paro." Satan was always willing to listen to anyone who wanted to talk. So many men had talked themselves to death. He couldn't put things quite together yet. But somehow he did feel that there was an attempt all around to protect the girl. Then when he saw Paro he didn't know. His mind was working like clockwork now. Paro's assured smile was not so assured. A quick blast hit Satan's mind. Was Paro with the banker when the girl was murdered? Couldn't Paro have plotted the whole thing? Arranged to have the girl go to—And Paro spoke.

"I'm not armed, Satan," he said, spreading his dinner jacket open. "My top coat is on the chair. You can frisk me if you wish."

And he was surprised as Lieutenant Harrison had been with the suddenness and thoroughness and quickness of that search.

"No," said Satan, "you're not armed. What do you want to say?"

"First off, that I know the truth—why you want to get me. You loved Elsa once, you love her still." And not liking the look on Satan's face, he went on hurriedly. "I don't blame you for that."

"Who told you that? The love interest—on my part. Her uncle?"

"No, Satan, no. And denials won't help you. Elsa told me herself."

Satan cut in, "That's not the talk I want to hear." And looking hard into Paro's eyes. "So you know why I'm here."

"Yes." Paro nodded. "Razor Jenkins told you he saw Elsa in Betty's apartment. That won't stand up in court—perhaps he may even deny it."

Satan's lips parted and his teeth showed. Though his eyes remained hard, Paro imagined that he smiled.

"It won't matter," Satan said. "I'll have prints made of the girl's picture. Someone will have seen her. More than one with an honest record. It was fairly early. When you have your subject it's not too hard to find witnesses. You know that."

Satan whirled. But it was only Elsa Drake coming down the stairs. She carried no bag. Her dress was sheer. Her hands were empty. "Well, Tony, will he come up in the sewing room and talk? Or is he afraid?"

"He's searched me," said Paro. "Anyway, he wouldn't be afraid."

"No," said Satan, "I wouldn't be afraid. Not if you had two guns on you, Paro. But I'm afraid you have nothing worth listening to."

"Will you have to tell him the truth?" the girl said, in a low voice.

"Yes." Paro nodded, very grimly. "I guess I'll have to tell him the truth. Satan Hall, come upstairs. I'll tell you who murdered Betty Barber. Then you can call the commissioner and see if he likes the way you broke the case."

"And it wasn't Razor Jenkins?" asked Satan.

"No," said Paro. "It's wasn't Razor Jenkins. I guess you've guessed it, Satan. You're smart. I knew Jenkins didn't do it, so I hired him a good lawyer."

"So he wouldn't say he saw Elsa Drake there?"

"Yes." Paro's grin was not pleasant. "That was a part of it, of course. Even the lawyer doesn't know where the money came from. But he had his instructions."

"Uncle will hear if we talk here," Elsa cautioned from the bottom of the steps.

"All right," said Satan, "I'll listen. It'd better be good. And I make no promise of it being off the record."

"We can't hide it now." Paro's arms came far apart. And then, frowning, he said, "You are a big man, Satan, and you dislike me. Will you leave your firearms below?"

Satan didn't even smile. He simply shook his head. He said, "It's a big house. Men have been known to hide in the dark and shoot from the dark. I never shot a man to death who wanted to say what I wanted to hear."

V

Scene Set for Murder

Paro and the girl preceded Satan up the stairs. Green eyes behind them peered into the darkness ahead of them. One white hand of Satan's slipped along the bannister, the other hung empty at his side.

Did he feel that Paro would not attempt to have him killed there in that house? No, he wasn't even sure of that. It would be a desperate move even if Paro felt any hope of carrying it off, and it would only be attempted at all if Paro himself had been guilty of the killing of Betty Barber. Not only guilty of the brutal murder but pretty sure of having the crime pinned on him. What would hit Paro the hardest—the breaking of his alibi, of course, and already Satan had broken one link in it. Certainly the girl was not with Paro when the murder took place.

Somehow, Satan felt that Paro was guilty. He didn't expect to believe the story he was going to be told, but he wanted to listen to Paro. Would Paro be like a lot of criminals before him—talk himself smack into the electric chair?

They were in the sewing room now and Satan had closed the door behind him and spun the key in the lock. At least, the girl had called it a sewing room, but she was talking now as Satan, with his eyes never off the pair, opened the one closet and looked in.

The girl was saying, "It used to be a sewing room. I sort of fixed it up as a study. And what do you think I'm studying, Satan? What do you think all those books along the wall are about? Crime. Remember—I told you once I wanted to work for the police. Work with you, wasn't it? And you laughed at me. But now, look at that collection."

She waved her hand around the room. It seemed unconsciously to hover for a moment over Paro. Satan said:

"Yes, quite a collection." He had covered the room with his keen eyes. The couch against the wall. No room to hide under it or behind it. Shades drawn at the window, curtain pulled back and not reaching to the floor. Not any place big enough to hide even a cat.

He looked at the open, two-pound box of candy on the table, saw that the top layer was pretty well gone, said, "Shall we sit here at the table? You there, across from me, Paro. You at the end, close to me, Miss Drake."

The girl reached over and lifted the candy box, offered one to Paro. Satan watched him pore over the candy and finally select one, saying:

"Chocolate creams—vanilla—my only real dissipation. Last one, I'm afraid."

The girl offered the box to Satan. He shook his head.

"Afraid of poison?" she asked.

"I am not," said Satan, very slowly, "afraid of anything. I am not afraid of guns in other men's hands. Yet, I don't look down the muzzles to see if they are loaded."

The girl said nothing. She took a piece of candy and laid it on the table. Her hands remained in her lap. Paro's hands were plainly on the table. Satan placed his hands on the table, looked at the girl. Her smile was not very pleasant, but she put her hands on the table.

Paro said, "I am not going to try to make a deal with you, Satan. I am not even going to ask you to promise that you will not divulge where your information came from, though I know the lowest criminal is entitled to that consideration. To begin with, a certain man fell deeply, or at least passionately, in love with Betty Barber. I am human. I loved, I do love Elsa very much. I encouraged this other attachment. This man—Do you want the details first or the name of the murderer and then the details?"

"The name of the murderer. Now. And the proof."

"The proof should be quite easy. I'm afraid he won't deny it. All right, it's going to make a smell. But it won't put the name of Miss Drake so far above mine. She'll be marrying a man who has tried to live down the past. I will be marrying a girl whose—well, her uncle killed Betty Barber."

Satan was surprised. If he could be shocked he was shocked. Green, suspicious slits of eyes opened wide.

"Leslie Drake killed her, like that?"

"Just like that," Paro nodded. "He knew his niece was there. He saw her, I think. He called me in to alibi her, and incidentally himself. Yes, I got it out of him. They can't hang me for that. After all, he was the uncle of the girl I love and intend to marry."

"And you weren't with Leslie Drake that night, at all?"

"No," said Paro. "Not at all. I won't have any trouble proving where I was that night, but I was experiencing a devil of a job proving that I was with Leslie Drake."

"What made him do it—a murder like that?"

Paro shrugged his shoulders.

"He says it was a blind rage of jealousy. You ask him. When I repudiate his alibi—why, he'll talk."

"But Razor Jenkins—and Miss Drake here."

There was a blank look on the girl's face as she lifted the candy box, and, taking a piece, put it into her mouth.

"I don't know," she said, in a far-away voice. "I don't know about Jenkins. I suppose it was like me. Betty Barber called me to come. At least it was a woman who said she was Betty Barber. She said not to tell a soul. She said it was something that affected my entire future, with Tony here." She looked toward Paro. "It wasn't suspicion and distrust, Tony. It was—I thought maybe I could help you. Here—" She held the box of candy toward him and when Paro shook his head, "The bottom row under the paper—creams, there—look." She lifted up the paper.

Satan knew and he didn't know. He knew that the girl suddenly dropped the box upon the table, jerked back and toward him and threw out her arms, crying in a high-pitched voice:

"No—no—Uncle Leslie. He couldn't have—"

Then her body had spun and she was behind Satan and both those waving arms were clasped tightly about his body, pinning his arms to his side. Satan knew, then. He saw the gun in Paro's hand, knew that it came from the candy box. He saw the gleam in Paro's eyes—recognized it as the lust to kill. And then his right arm had shot out, knocking the girl across the room, and his left hand had gone under his right arm and come out again before Paro pressed the trigger.

It was death, yes. Satan knew that. But he knew something else, and his lips set in a grim satisfaction. It would be death for Paro, too. His finger was closing on the trigger now and his head instinctively ducked to one side when the yellow blue flame belched from Paro's gun, almost blinding him.

There were hardly six feet between them, and Paro's fingers had closed on the trigger a good second before Satan had fired. Powder burned Satan's face but he knew that Paro had missed, and then the slug from his gun pounded into Paro's chest. It lifted him out of his chair and sent him crashing backward to the floor.

Paro moved a bit upon his shoulders, then lay still. Satan came slowly erect and looked at the girl, who was getting to her feet.

"It's too bad I had to kill him," Satan said, evenly and without viciousness in his voice. "You'd have made a good pair—a couple of rats. When the time came to shoot he turned yellow and missed—missed at that distance." And walking across the floor he looked down at Paro, kicked the gun out of his twitching fingers, said:

"It wasn't her fault, Paro. She did her part. You can take that thought to hell with you. When your big moment came, you failed. But it wouldn't have made any difference to you. We'd have died together, that's all."

"I'm going to die?" Paro gasped.

"What do you think?" There was a noise in Satan's throat that might have been a laugh. "There's a hole in your chest big enough to drive a truck through."

Paro said, "I know—What will you do for her—the girl—if I talk?"

Satan shrugged his shoulders.

"You'll be dead. I'll pin the murder on you. Or if I don't—I always know— and you'll be dead anyway. So you sent for Jenkins. You sent for the girl, Elsa Drake. You told her uncle you'd help him alibi her and so alibi yourself."

"She—she—I thought she was going cold on me. I'd risk anything for her. I had a dame telephone Elsa and say she was Betty Barber, that she'd tell her things about me. Then I did Betty in. That way—so it would look as if Jenkins did it. I—I didn't know Jenkins would see Elsa. I had Jenkins trailed."

"If you didn't know Jenkins would see her, why did you send her there?"

"I loved her," Paro gasped. "I wanted to have something on her so she'd marry me. I told her uncle—I told Elsa—that she was seen in the murdered girl's apartment. I could have told her that even if Jenkins hadn't seen her and so—so—"

"So force her into marriage if she hesitated." Satan bobbed his head up and down. "So that's the way love works? But, then, I wouldn't know. You threatened her, too, I guess, so she'd hide the gun in the candy box for you. To kill me—shoot the knowledge about her out of my head." And looking down at the dying man, as he thought of the torn body of the Barber woman, he said, "You'll never know, Paro, if Elsa Drake planted that revolver there because she loved you, or because she feared for her own self. You—"

Satan straightened. There would be no more words coming. He could accept what Paro said as a confession. Tony Paro was dead. Far too dead to talk. Satan swung on the girl, said:

"When did you know Paro killed her?" And when Elsa Drake stared at him, "All the time?"

"No—no." Elsa Drake shook her head. "I suspected when he grew jittery about Razor Jenkins telling you I was there. But I knew—yes, I knew when he asked me to plant the gun for him."

"To kill me?"

"To try and kill you," she corrected him. "He didn't, you know."

"I know," Satan told her, "but you planted the gun and held my arms at my side."

"He's dead now." Elsa Drake came close to Satan and placed two small white hands with delicate fingers upon his shoulders. "I never loved him, Satan. I haven't changed any from seventeen to twenty—not that way. You laughed at me then. That was a mistake."

Satan took both her hands from his shoulders, held them very tightly at her side.

"Yes, that was a mistake," he echoed her words. "I'm not laughing at you now."

Her wide eyes looked directly into his. She said, "What do you intend to —to do about me?"

"It was a good name—Drake," Satan said, thoughtfully. "The commissioner said so. Your father was a fine man. The commissioner said that too. Your uncle is—well, maybe a good man, but a fool for people like you. I hate criminals. All of them—men and women."

Thin lips grew even thinner, hard eyes grew even harder.

"What am I going to do with you? The commissioner dandled you on his knee. He is my only friend in life. I am going to do something I never thought I was even capable of doing. So—You never put that gun in the candy box. You never lifted the box for Paro to grab it. You never held my arms. In fact, you were never in this room when the shots were fired. Paro drew and he missed and I killed him. You rushed in and heard his confession. We may need that for the record." And as a loud knocking pounded on the door and the hysterical voice of Leslie Drake called out, Satan continued:

"We won't have to place you at the scene of the crime at all. Razor Jenkins won't talk, for I'll have him sprung under that condition."

"You might even," the girl said eagerly, "say I really assisted you in gathering evidence." And smiling at the utter disgust in his face, she finished off, "Because of your esteem for the commissioner."

"Get out!" was all Satan said.

He walked to the door, and unlocking it, threw it open. The white face of Leslie Drake stood out. He was talking but no coherent words came.

"Paro is dead," said Satan, thrusting the girl into the hall. "She ran in after I shot him. What's this hollering about the police?"

"Should I call them? You are a detective, I know." Words suddenly came pouring through Leslie Drake's dry lips.

"Wait in the hall," said Satan, and, closing the door, he went back to look the room over again. What a wild story Paro had concocted, he thought. No one would believe it after a little thought. But Paro's gun had come before the thought. The fear in Paro's face before he shot. But no—Satan remembered now that there was no fear in Paro's face. It was hard and cold and cruel and his eyes—yes, so sure.

Satan ran his hand across his chin. His eyes still burned from the powder. His hand came away from his face dark and smudged. "Powder," he said, half aloud, "gun powder." Yet the bullet had missed him and hit the wall. About here. He turned and faced the wall. And "about here" proved to be a picture that still hung on the wall. He looked for the bullet hole—couldn't find it; looked for the slug that might be upon the floor. But there was no slug.

Then he crossed the room quickly, knelt down by the dead body, lifted up the gun. He looked at the barrel. He broke the gun open. Blanks! The heavy thirty-eight that Paro used had been fully loaded—but there wasn't, hadn't been a live shell in it.

Satan sat down by the table. For the first time in his life he actually admitted surprise. The girl had left her uncle's study, below, and quite evidently had come up to the sewing room by the rear stairs. She had planted the gun in the candy box as planned by Paro. Clever, too, for Paro was always eating chocolates. But what hadn't been planned by Paro was the substitution of the live shells for blanks. That explained the lack of fear in Paro's face when he fired. And, Satan thought, that might explain, too, why he was still alive and Paro was dead.

But having the blanks handy showed more than just the will to save Satan's life. It showed premeditation. At least, it showed forethought. Satan put his chin in his hands and thought deeply. There at the Club Elite, how clumsy Elsa had been in knocking away the greens that disclosed the microphone. Or how clumsy he had thought she was.

He got up after a while and shook the cobwebs from his head. Then he jarred erect. Fool, he thought. Why hadn't he guessed it when he first knew that Betty Barber wasn't killed because she telephoned him at Mike the Greek's? And the answer was so simple. Paro didn't know Betty telephoned him at the Greek's because—well, because it wasn't Betty Barber who telephoned him. He recognized the voice now, or thought he did. It was Elsa Drake. All along she had been playing a part. A dangerous part. A desperate part. And she had been playing it for him.

He opened the door and strode out into the hall, started down the stairs. He met Leslie Drake at the bottom. Satan said:

"I must call the commissioner."

"There's a phone there, in my study." And as Satan walked toward the door, "My niece is in there now."

Satan hesitated, half turned, started to ask if there was another phone, then didn't. He had never shirked his duty before. He wouldn't shirk it now. He walked straight toward the door, flung it open. The girl stood in the center of the room. Satan closed the door slowly. She looked at him a long time, searching for the truth in his face. Then she came forward and put both her arms around his neck.

"Yes, Satan," she said, as if answering an unspoken question. "I was the one who telephoned you at Mike's, too."

She kissed him then. She was slightly surprised and a little pleased when he didn't knock her down.

THE KID CLIPS A COUPON

Erle Stanley Gardner

I

The Clue of the Jam

Dan Seller lounged in the big chair and listened as Police Inspector Phil Brame recounted the circumstances of the crime for the edification of the small group of cronies who frequented the choice corner of the club.

"Just a plain case of murder," Inspector Brame was saying, "and a bit of strawberry jam is going to send the guy to the chair."

"I don't think Dan Higgins intended to commit murder when he broke into the place. Mrs. Morelay, paralyzed from the hips down, was in the living room, seated in her wheel chair, going over a bunch of account books. Higgins broke in to get some food. Mrs. Morelay heard him moving around in the kitchen. There was a telephone attached to her wheel chair. She called police headquarters and reported someone in her kitchen, stealing food.

"Higgins heard her telephoning. It sent him into a furious rage. The man was hungry. He dashed into the room and split the woman's head open with a hatchet he had picked up in the kitchen. Then he helped himself to food. He spread some homemade strawberry jam on a slice of bread and ate it. He spilled some jam on his necktie without knowing it. He had gone less than a block from the place when the police radio car came along.

"Higgins looked like just the type who would be stealing food—a half-starved chap with clothes that were pretty much the worse for wear. Our men stopped and picked him up on suspicion and then went to the house and found that murder had been committed. Higgins denied he'd been near the house, and he'd evidently learned his lesson about fingerprints, because there were no fingerprints on any of the stuff in the kitchen. The police found a pair of dirty gloves in his pocket. Evidently he'd worn those while he was eating. But there was strawberry jam on his tie. The jam was analyzed. The amount of sugar it contained was carefully noted by the police chemists, and then an analysis was made of the strawberry jam in the jar in the sink. The jam on the tie Higgins was wearing at the time of his arrest came from that jar of homemade jam."

"Wasn't there some one who saw him leaving the house?" Renfroe, the banker, asked.

"Yes," Brame said. "Walter Stagg, the man who acts as manager for Mrs. Morelay, drove up to the house in his automobile. He arrived there almost at the same time that the police did. He was just coming up the cement walk when the police car rounded the corner. He said that he had seen Higgins coming around the back of the house, as though he had either slipped out of a window, or had been snooping around the house. Stagg said he intended to unlock the front door—which was always kept on a night latch—and see if anything was wrong. If anything was missing, he was determined to jump into his car and follow the man until he could notify a policeman. Stagg was unarmed so he didn't want to encounter an armed crook unless he had an officer handy."

Bill Pope, the explorer, stared steadily at the curling smoke of a cigarette.

"It seems strange," he said, "that a man would have gone ahead and eaten heartily after having committed a murder, particularly the murder of a helpless old woman who had done nothing to injure him."

"She telephoned for the police," Inspector Brame said. "Don't forget that."

"But," Dan Seller pointed out, "if that was the motive for the crime and the man knew she had telephoned for the police, he'd have been doubly foolish to have murdered her and then gone on eating, knowing that the police were on their way in a radio car."

Inspector Brame's face flushed.

"More of *your* amateur detective stuff," he said. "It's an easy thing for you wealthy young coupon-clippers to construct theories proving that the police are always wrong. Doubtless, an attorney for the defense will try to bamboozle a jury into believing the police got the wrong man. But he won't be able to—not with that strawberry jam on the man's necktie."

"Was there," asked Bill Pope, "robbery as well?"

"Apparently not. Higgins had nothing in his possession when he was arrested. He might have taken something from the body and buried it somewhere in the vicinity. She was supposed to have a large sum of cash money which she always kept on hand, but there wasn't any money found on her body.

"Higgins was wise. He didn't leave a single fingerprint. We fingerprinted everything about the body, and didn't find a thing. The books that were open in front of her didn't have a single fingerprint on the page other than the prints of Walter Stagg, the manager, who kept all the books and submitted them to Mrs. Morelay for examination."

"Perhaps a draft of wind might have blown one of the pages," Dan Seller said. "Did your men take prints on the other pages to see if that had happened?"

"As it happens, my bright young man," the inspector said, "we did that very thing, although we didn't need to, because when the woman's skull was split open, blood spattered upon the pages of the open account book, and we had no difficulty in telling what page was in front of her at the time."

"Very clever detective work, inspector," Renfroe, the banker, said. "Undoubtedly the man will go to the chair on the strength of that strawberry jam."

"Mrs. Morelay was wealthy?"

"Quite wealthy. She leaves no will. The property goes to a niece, Tess Copley. She's the only surviving relative."

"Live here in the city?" Renfroe asked.

"Yes."

"They found the weapon with which the crime was committed?" Bill Pope inquired.

"Oh, yes, of course. It was there in the room. There could be no question about it. A blood-stained hatchet that had been taken from the kitchen."

Bill Pope's clear eyes surveyed Inspector Brame.

"You should feel pretty happy, inspector," he said, "but you seem to be down in the dumps."

Inspector Brame sighed.

"It's that damned Patent Leather Kid," he said.

"What about him?" asked the explorer.

"He's been meddling again. The man is a crook, a gangster, a public enemy. And yet, he appeals to the public. He tries to pull some of this Robin Hood stuff, and the people fall for it. Slowly but surely he's becoming a public hero, and he's making the police appear ridiculous."

"Why don't you catch him," asked the banker, "and put him away?"

"Have you," asked Bill Pope, "got anything definite on him? His methods are irregular, perhaps illegal, but can you get him on any specific felony and make it stick?"

Inspector Brame's voice was ominous.

"Listen," he said, "when we get that guy, we'll make something stick. Don't worry about that. I wouldn't want to be quoted publicly on the thing, you understand, but that fellow has been a thorn in the side of the Police Department long enough. It wouldn't take very much framing to pin a good murder case on him."

"Don't you think framing him for murder is pretty steep?" the explorer asked.

"Well, perhaps not for murder," Inspector Brame said. "I was speaking impulsively. But I can promise you this, that if we ever get our fingers on The Patent Leather Kid, he'll go away for a long, long time."

Dan Seller arose, yawned, and took a cigarette from a hammered silver case.

"Referring to that murder case once more, inspector," he said, "didn't Walter Stagg agree to notify Tess Copley, and fail to do so?"

"Notify her of what?" the police inspector asked.

"Of her aunt's death."

"He promised to go and get her, but he had some trouble starting his car. His battery was weak, and in the end the police telephoned and had a messenger sent to her. Tess Copley was working in a place where the girls weren't allowed to receive telephone calls."

"Then," Dan Seller said, "her aunt didn't part with any money while she was alive."

"I'll say she didn't," Inspector Brame said. "She was as tight as the bark on a tree—one of those misers who salted money away in gold coin. She'd been collecting gold for some time."

"And hadn't turned it in?"

"No."

"What was the amount of the money?"

"I don't know exactly. No one does. She had been collecting it for years."

Dan Seller lit his cigarette, nodded casually to the small group. "Well," he said, "I'll be seeing you later."

Bill Pope, the explorer, followed Dan Seller with quizzical, speculative eyes, but said nothing.

II

Fingerprints and a Stalled Car

The process by which Dan Seller, the wealthy club man, became The Patent Leather Kid, spectacular figure of the city's underworld, was tedious and complicated. However, it left no back trail, and when The Patent

Leather Kid entered the apartment hotel where he maintained a penthouse, he might as well have appeared from thin air for all the trail he had left.

The manager greeted The Kid with deference.

Gertie, the telephone operator, flashed him a glance from eyes that were starry, as she reached for the switchboard to notify Bill Brakey that The Kid was on his way up.

The Kid's private elevator whisked him directly to the roof. Bill Brakey, ensconced behind bullet-proof doors, made certain that The Kid was alone, and that there was no trap laid by police or gangster enemies before he opened the door.

Bill Brakey's face never showed the slightest nervousness. Only his hands and his eyes betrayed the everlasting watchfulness, the readiness to explode into instant action.

"You made a short trip this time, Kid," he said.

"Yes," The Kid told him. "Let's go in where we can have a drink and talk. I've got something on my mind."

The Kid dropped into a chair, stretched out his feet and sighed.

"Seems good to be back, Bill," he said.

Bill Brakey brought out a bottle of Scotch, drew the cork and poured out whiskey and ginger ale.

"What's on your mind, Kid?"

Brakey's eyes were not fastened upon The Patent Leather Kid, but were slithering about in a nervous survey of the windows and doors. It made no difference that he knew no one could get through the roof without a warning coming over the telephone, without an automatic alarm shrilling a strident warning should the only elevator which communicated with the penthouse start on its way without The Kid's key having first unlocked an electrical contact.

Bill Brakey's watchfulness was purely mechanical, purely a matter of long habit.

"I'm interested," The Patent Leather Kid said, "in the murder of Mrs. Fannie Morelay."

"Inside stuff is," Brakey said, "that Higgins is going to the chair because he had some strawberry jam spilled on his necktie. He didn't leave any fingerprints, but it looks as though it was a dead open and shut case."

"Except for one thing," The Patent Leather Kid said, slowly.

"What's that?" asked the bodyguard.

"This fellow, Stagg."

"You mean the manager?"

"Yes."

"He's okay," Bill Brakey said. "The police looked him up just to make sure.

He's got the highest references. He's been with Mrs. Morelay for years. He handled all of her business affairs. You see, she couldn't get around at all by herself, and she had quite a bunch of business interests. She was worth over a million dollars. Nobody knows just how much more."

"Stagg was just coming up to the house when the police came. He'd just driven up in his car, and saw Dan Higgins moving about as though he'd been prowling around the house."

Bill Brakey flashed The Kid a sharp glance.

"Even if he was lying about *that*," he said, "the strawberry jam on Higgins' necktie is enough to send him to the chair. Higgins says he wasn't near the house. The chemists can absolutely identify that jam. No two batches of homemade jam are made according to the same actual recipe. There are minor variations of sugar content, and that sort of stuff, and—"

"That's all right," The Patent Leather Kid remarked, "but when Walter Stagg wanted to notify Tess Copley, the niece, of what had happened, his car didn't start; the battery was weak."

"Well," said Brakey, "what about that?"

"If he had just driven up to the house," The Kid said, "his car would have been warm. And, what's more, the battery would have been freshly generated from a run. It would have turned over a warm motor. The fact that it didn't turn over the motor indicates that the motor was cold. It's more probable that Stagg had left the house and was running toward the car, trying to make a getaway, when he heard the police car coming, and, knowing that he couldn't get away, turned and started back toward the house, pulling out his key to open the front door as he did so."

There was an interval of silence. The Kid sipped his highball thoughtfully.

"Of course," Brakey said, "that doesn't prove anything. It's a suspicious circumstance—that's all."

"That's why I didn't call it to the attention of the police," The Kid said. "It's something that we've got to run down."

Bill Brakey nodded.

"When do you want to start, Kid?" he asked.

"Sometime tonight," The Kid told him. Brakey's poker face did not change.

"There's a police guard at the place?"

"I presume so. I don't know. I can find out."

The Kid let smoke stream from his nostrils.

"Better slip out there this afternoon, Bill," he said. "Look the ground over and make a report. I'll get a little sleep and get caught up on some of my reading. As soon as you come back with the report, we'll have dinner and then proceed to look the premises over."

Bill Brakey nodded.

"I'll have all the low-down on it," he said.

"Another thing," The Patent Leather Kid muttered, hesitatingly, "that doesn't check, is the fingerprints on the book of accounts. They found the fingerprints of Walter Stagg on those books. No other print."

"Higgins was wearing gloves," Brakey said.

"I know," The Kid said, "but if this woman had been checking over the books of account, it's almost a cinch that *her* fingerprints would have been on the books somewhere."

"That's so," Brakey agreed.

"Apparently they weren't. Just Stagg's prints."

"What do you make of that, Kid?"

The Patent Leather Kid shrugged his shoulders so slightly that the action was all but imperceptible.

"That," he said, "is something which remains to be determined."

"They were the books she was working on, all right," Brakey said, "because there were blood stains on the leaves. They were the books she was working on when she was murdered, regardless of who did the murder."

"Then why weren't her fingerprints on the pages, Bill?" The Patent Leather Kid pointed out.

"Gosh, Kid, I don't know," Brakey confessed.

"That's something we're going to find out."

III

Inside the Murder House

The Patent Leather Kid adjusted the black patent leather mask which covered the upper half of his features. He worked his hands into soft, pliable leather gloves, nodded to Bill Brakey.

"Ready, Bill," he said.

Bill Brakey jimmied the window.

The Patent Leather Kid was the first one through. He paused for a tense moment while he listened; then muttered to Bill Brakey: "Okay, Bill, let's go."

Brakey slid noiselessly after him.

The place was musty, with a peculiar suggestion of death.

The Kid produced a flashlight.

"This the window he came through, Bill?" he asked.

"This is it."

"And the murder took place in this next room?"

"Yes. On the other side of that swinging door."

The men moved upon silent feet. The Kid pushed open the swinging door and gazed upon the room in which the crime had been committed.

Inasmuch as Tess Copley, the sole beneficiary of the estate, did not care to occupy the house, the police had left the room just as it had been found when the crime was discovered. All that had been removed was the corpse of the victim. For the rest the furniture remained undisturbed. The shades were drawn so as to shut out any light, and The Patent Leather Kid let his flashlight flicker around the room, taking in the various details.

"There's a guard in front, Bill?" he asked.

"Yes. A harness bull that was taken off his beat. He doesn't take it very seriously. He's probably dozing off right now. For some reason, the district attorney wants to keep the room just as it was so that he can show it to the jury. In order to do that, he'll have it appear that the place was guarded by an officer who will testify he was there to see nothing was disturbed."

The flashlight centered upon a lacquered box.

"What's the box, Bill?"

"That's a lock-box they found in the room. There was nothing in it. There was a file of papers by the side of it that probably were taken from the box."

The Kid knelt by the box. It was unlocked. He lifted back the lid and stared at the interior.

"Notice the way the enamel is chipped on the inside, Bill," he said. "That wouldn't have been done by papers."

He pulled the lid of the box back and looked at the metal handle.

"Notice the bulge in the top of the box," he said. "It looks as though it had been filled with something very heavy and lifted repeatedly."

"Gold?" asked Bill Brakey.

"Looks like it."

"Where was the manager's office, Bill?" asked The Kid. "Did he have one here in the building?"

"Yes, he had one way in the front."

"Let's take a look."

They traversed a corridor, went through a bedroom, and came to another room in the front of the house, which had evidently been designed as a bedroom, but which had been used as an office.

"Take it easy," whispered Bill Brakey. "The cops are right outside there on the walk."

"The curtains aren't down here," The Kid observed, in a whisper. "Why would they have the shades drawn in the rest of the house and not have them drawn here?"

"Looks as though the manager had been working here," Brakey said.

"You've got a plan of Stagg's house?"

"It ain't a house. It's a flat."

"Has he got the lower or upper flat?" The Kid asked.

"Upper. It's a three-story flat. He's on the top floor."

"An attic above him?"

"Probably. I haven't been in the place. I was waiting for you."

"Okay," The Kid said, "I've seen enough here. Let's go take a look at this man Stagg. I'd like to talk with him."

"You're the boss," Bill Brakey said.

The men left the place as silently as they had entered it. They slipped through the window, oozed through the darkness to the alley, followed the alley to a side street, and there picked up their car.

Bill Brakey drove to a district given over largely to small apartment houses and flats. He parked the car by the curb.

"That's the place over there," he said.

"Well," The Kid said, "there's a light on the upper floor. That means our friend will be up."

"Do we bust in on him?" asked Bill Brakey.

"I think," The Kid said, "we bust in on him, tie him up and make a search. Maybe we can throw a scare into him."

"Just what do you expect to find?" Brakey asked.

"I don't know," The Kid told him. "Maybe we'll let the police find it."

"How do you mean?"

"Go in and pull out a few drawers, mess things up a little bit, tie him up, and then notify the police. They'll start making a search to see what we took and to see whether we left any fingerprints."

"He's too clever for that," Brakey said. "If there's anything hidden there, it'll be hidden where the police wouldn't find it. The police may have made a search already. They're not so dumb."

"Inspector Brame is," The Kid said. "His whole idea of handling a case is to make a quick arrest and then make sure of getting a conviction. After a man is once arrested for a crime, Brame never bothers about any clues that don't point to the guilt of that man."

Bill Brakey opened the car door.

"Well," he said, "we might as well . . . That car, watch it."

A big sedan purred smoothly along the road and slid gently to the opposite curb. It was a car that had been designed with plenty of power under the hood. From it a big, well nourished man stepped to the sidewalk. For all of his size, he moved with the lithe grace of a panther.

" 'Pug' Morrison, the prizefighter who turned gangster," Bill Brakey said in an undertone. "What the hell is *he* doing here?"

"Perhaps," said The Kid, "he's looking around the same way we are."

"When that guy looks around," Bill Brakey said, "he's looking around on a hot scent."

"Uses his noodle, does he?" asked The Kid.

"He uses his muscle," Brakey said. "That bird is one of those cheerful guys that always wants to give the other fellow his cut provided his cut isn't more than one and a half per cent. Pug figures that around ninety-eight or ninety-nine per cent is his fair share of the take."

"Well," The Kid said, "he's going up."

"Hell," Brakey ejaculated, "going up! He's ringing the bell."

The door of the flat opened and the broad-shouldered form of Pug Morrison moved through the lighted oblong.

Bill Brakey slid out from behind the steering wheel. The Kid got to the ground on the other side. They had no need for words. They crossed the street with swift steps. Bill Brakey had his skeleton keys in his right hand while they were still six feet from the door. It took him less than ten seconds to find the right key and shoot back the spring latch. A long flight of stairs loomed before them—stairs which were broken by one landing.

Men's voices were audible when they were still a dozen steps from the top. The voices came from the left, and sounded only as an undertone of booming sound, interspersed at intervals by a voice that was higher in pitch, less in volume, and which spoke with nervous rapidity.

A dimly lighted reception hall was at the front of the stairs. A door opened from it to what was evidently a corridor. The door on the left was closed. From under it shone a ribbon of bright light. Evidently the conference was taking place in a front room on the left hand side.

Once more the men exchanged glances. The Patent Leather Kid adjusted the distinctive black mask of patent leather from which he had derived his name. His shoes were of patent leather. His gloves were also black.

Bill Brakey wore no gloves. At times such as these, he needed to have his swift hands, with their long, delicate fingers, where they could whip guns from the shoulder holsters without the faintest suggestion of a fumble. It was an unspoken law between them that The Kid touched those things upon which fingerprints might be left; that Bill Brakey's hands remained free to reach for and use weapons.

The Kid crossed the reception hall, twisted the knob on the door, disclosing the long corridor which stretched the length of the flat. He picked the first door on the left, twisted the knob, and entered a bedroom. He brought his flashlight into play, slid quietly across the bedroom to a bathroom which opened to his left, entered the bathroom, and crossed to a small dressing room. On the other side of this dressing room was a door through which came the mumble of voices.

The Kid worked with swift efficiency. He gripped the knob tightly with his gloved right hand, pulled the door as tightly against the jamb as he could force it, and then twisted the knob, moving it so slowly as to make the motion all but imperceptible. When the latch cleared its seat in the jamb, there was no faintest suggestion of a click. Slowly, The Kid pushed the door open—an inch, two inches.

IV

A Playmate for The Kid

They listened to the mumbling noise of the conversation, conversation which became audible as the door opened. At the slightest break in the rhythmic flow of that conversation, The Kid would have flung the door open and crouched. Bill Brakey, a gun in either hand, would have stood in the doorway, commanding the situation.

But there was no break. The door was in a dark corner of the room; the illumination came from floor lamps. The men who occupied the room were far too engrossed in what they were saying to pay attention to the shadows of the room.

". . . kidnaping is a serious business," said the deep, booming voice of Pug Morrison. "I don't go in for it."

"You go in for making money, don't you?" asked the higher-pitched, nervous voice of Walter Stagg.

"Sure I do, but I don't go in for death penalties and life sentences."

"Oh, bosh and nonsense," Stagg said. "You go in for murder."

"Who says so?" asked Morrison, with sudden menace in his voice.

"Don't take offense," Stagg said, "I'm telling you what everyone says. I'm not talking about any specific killing. I'm talking about the reputation you've got. Remember, I'm not trying to frame you with anything. I'm in this thing just as deep as you are."

Pug Morrison laughed.

"The idea," he said, "of a guy like you trying to frame me! I could tell you what's on *your* mind right now. You've been manager for Mrs. Morelay. She was murdered. It looks like a dead open and shut case against this guy Higgins, but I'm not so certain that you ain't mixed up in it now. You've been handling all the gravy for the old woman, and now that she's croaked, there's going to be an administrator appointed and you've got to make accounting. There's probably a will some place that you're holding out. It provides that the niece takes all the property, unless she should die first; and then it all goes to you. Something like that. Therefore, you want us to snatch the kid and bump her off. You'll come into the big coin."

"You'd better get your cards on the table, buddy. If you're playing around with the big coin, we want to know it. You can't hold out on us anyway. We'd keep coming back and shaking you down from time to time until we got a fair split, so you'd better give us a break."

Stagg's voice lost much of its assurance, but maintained its nervous, almost hysterical, rapidity of articulation.

"Now, look here," he said, "you know as well as I do, that if it's just a matter of getting somebody bumped off, I can find lots of people who are willing to do it for a thousand dollars."

Pug Morrison laughed, a laugh that contained no mirth, but plenty of scorn.

"Sucker," he said. "You'd pay a grand to have a bump-off and you'd get bled white for the rest of your life. You deal with me and you're going to pay and you're going to pay plenty. But if you're on the square, you're going to pay once and that's going to be all. You know that, and you know I can't afford to get mixed into this thing any more than you can, so you figure we're going to shoot square with each other. Now, go ahead and give me the lowdown."

"Well," Stagg said, "there was some cash in the estate. Not liquid cash, you understand, but cash in the bank. It's stuff that I can't touch without a court order, see?"

"No, I don't see," Pug told him. "Cash in the bank doesn't mean anything to me. It's cash in my right fist that talks music."

"That's just the point," Stagg went on hurriedly. "I've got that kind of cash, too."

"Oh, you have, have you?"

"That is, I know where I can put my hand on it."

"Go ahead," the gangster said, "and get to the point."

"I figured that you could snatch this girl and make a demand on the estate for seventy thousand dollars' ransom."

Morrison's tone showed sudden interest.

"Why seventy grand?" he asked.

"Because," Stagg told him, "that's the amount I *could* raise, and that's about the amount on deposit in the bank."

"Go ahead," Morrison said, with a voice that had lost much of its mocking scorn, and was almost respectful.

"The snatching job," Stagg said, "wouldn't look like it was done by any professional gang, but it would look like it was done by a bunch of amateurs. You'd make it look that way in your ransom notes."

"That's old stuff," Pug Morrison said. "That doesn't fool anybody. All regular snatchers try to make their stuff look like the work of cranks and amateurs."

"But, this would be different," Stagg went on. "You'd be snatching a woman that you couldn't get any money out of. In other words, you'd make a demand for seventy thousand dollars, the amount of money that Fannie Morelay left in the bank. Then, no matter how badly any executor of the estate wanted to pay it, he couldn't pay it under the law. The girl would have the money coming to her, but only after the estate had gone through probate. So you'd really have snatched a girl who didn't have any money or any opportunity of getting any immediate cash. There wouldn't be any relative who could pay. The newspapers would play it up big. It would be the work of blundering amateurs."

"Go ahead," Morrison said. "Maybe you've got something in your bean after all."

"Then, of course, having snatched the girl and not being able to get any money, you'd murder her. That would account for a motive. If I had the girl killed without having some other motive for the murder, someone might start suspecting me. It would look as though I might be in a position to profit by the killing."

"I see," Morrison said, musingly.

"Now, you get your letters ready. You take the girl. You get seventy thousand dollars, and you kill the girl."

"Listen," Morrison said, thoughtfully, "how do we know we ain't going to double-cross one another?"

"You can't double-cross me," Stagg said, "because I've thought it all out in advance. I'm not going to double-cross you, but I'm going to show you how you can keep me from giving you anything that looks like a double-cross."

"Go ahead," Morrison said, "show me. I'm listening."

"You take the girl," Stagg said. "And when you take the girl, you take seventy thousand dollars at the same time. And at the same time you take the money, you deliver the letters demanding payment of a ransom."

"You mean we get the cash at the same time we make the snatch?" asked the gangster.

"That's right."

"Well," Morrison said, slowly, "that's jake with me, but how about you? You said you'd done some figuring on your own account. Let's have it."

"I'm figuring this way," Stagg said. "It's got to be a genuine snatch. Therefore, as soon as you make the demand, you're in the kidnaping racket. You don't dare to turn the girl loose then because she could identify your men and you'd be on the dodge. You've got to kill her once she finds out what she's up against."

"How are we going to work this?" Morrison asked.

"I'm going to tell you where you can contact with the girl. She's going to hire a detective."

"The hell she is!" Morrison exclaimed.

"Yes, she's going to go to the Victoria Hotel and register as Ethel Mason. She has an appointment for a detective to meet her there at eleven thirty tonight."

"So what?" asked Morrison.

"So," Stagg said, "you go there about an hour earlier—about ten thirty. The girl will be there. You tell her that you're the detective, that you got rid of the case you were working on earlier than you had expected. And that you're there to talk with her. She's going to tell you some stuff about the killing of her aunt. She's a little bit suspicious about it. You tell her you want to see the premises. You get her in your car and drive her out to the Morelay house. But don't stop. Tell her you're going on past. There's a drug store about two blocks down the street. Tell her you've seen as much of the house as you want from the outside. Stop in front of the drug store and tell her that you want to see specimens of her aunt's signature; that it's important that you see them; that you would like to see some cancelled checks."

"Go on," Morrison said.

"The only way she can get those is by telephoning me," Stagg said. "She'll telephone me and ask me to send her some checks and documents that are specimens of her aunt's signature. She'll make some sort of an excuse. I'll put seventy thousand dollars in currency in a black bag and send it by a messenger the girl knows. I'll try and use a girl friend of hers. You take the bag, open it, look in it, find that there's seventy thousand bucks there, and then give the messenger a note to open after she's gone five blocks from the place. That note will be a demand for ransom.

"You get out of the car when you accept the bag, and you have a mask on your face. Do you get the sketch? If you aren't wearing the mask, you don't get the bag with the seventy grand. If you are wearing the mask and make the demand for ransom, you get the bag.

"The newspapers make a big hullabaloo about it, and then some wise guy finds out that the money couldn't be paid, no matter how badly Tess Copley might want it paid. The snatching is branded as the work of amateurs. The newspapers give you the horse-laugh. You retaliate by bumping the kid off and dumping the body by the side of the road somewhere. That's all there is to it."

There was a moment of silence.

Pug Morrison's voice was low and thoughtful.

"Buddy," he said, "you've got a brain on your shoulders. We need you in our gang. You've got something that we need."

"You can't get it," Stagg rasped. "I'm a business man. I've got affairs of my own to consider."

The gangster's voice was once more filled with respect.

"You made out a fake set of books," he said. "You'd been waiting for an opportunity to substitute them. You heard the old woman telephoning for the cops when the guy got in the kitchen. You recognized that as your opportunity. You waited until the bird sneaked out of the window, and then you stuck the fake books in front of the woman, slammed the hatchet in her head, ducked out, and tried to make a getaway. But the cops came around the corner just as you were getting to your machine. So you pretended you were getting *out* of your automobile instead of getting in, and started up to the house as though nothing had happened."

"Suppose I did," said Stagg, "what of it?"

"Nothing," said Morrison, "except that you used your noodle to make maybe a couple of million dollars for yourself, to say nothing of covering up any little shortages that might exist in your affairs."

"What makes you think there are shortages?" asked Stagg.

Pug Morrison's laugh was ironical.

"Seventy thousand bucks," he said, slowly, "seventy thousand bucks that you can 'put your hands on.' And don't bother about all that elaborate program, because you ain't going to cross me—not with a murder rap I can pin on you.

"You just send out the jane with the bag. Have seventy grand in the bag unless you want to go to the chair. We'll make the snatch. You kick through with your end."

The Patent Leather Kid turned to Bill Brakey, and nodded his head.

Brakey turned and tiptoed across the floor of the bathroom. The Patent Leather Kid was at his heels. As noiselessly as two shadows, they slipped to the back of the house, found a back door, opened it and flitted like silent shadows downstairs to a back yard which opened on an alley.

Pug Morrison was driving away as the pair reached the cross street.

"What a sweet little playmate *that* guy is!" Bill Brakey said.

"Playmate is right," The Patent Leather Kid told him, "because we're going to play with him."

V
According to Schedule

Pug Morrison was too smart to make the contact himself. The Patent Leather Kid, lounging in the lobby of the Victoria Hotel, had left word with the telephone operator that he was to be signalled when a call was put through to the room of "Ethel Mason." The flash of a detective's badge and a five-dollar tip had been all that was necessary to secure her cooperation.

When The Kid got the signal, he carefully studied the man who was at the telephone desk over which appeared the sign, "TELEPHONES TO GUESTS' ROOMS."

The man was very smooth-shaven. His hands were well manicured. His clothes bore the stamp of expensive workmanship. His shoes fitted like gloves. There was an assurance about the manner in which he held his head, a quick restlessness about his hands that was reminiscent of Bill Brakey's long, tapering hands.

The man hung up the telephone, moved with quick, nervous steps to the elevator, and was whisked up.

The Patent Leather Kid smoked in contemplative silence.

Twenty minutes elapsed before the man returned. This time there was a young woman at his side. She was wrapped in a heavy cloth coat with a wide fur collar. She wore a tight-fitting black hat trimmed with white. Her eyes were large and black. Her lips had been carefully applied so that they were quite crimson. The Kid could not see too much of her figure because of the heavy coat, but he gathered that she was slim-waisted, and she carried her head with a little tilt to one side which indicated something of the vibrant individuality which seemed to radiate from her.

The Kid got to his feet, stretched, yawned, tossed away the end of his cigarette and nodded to Bill Brakey, who was standing near the door.

The man and the young woman left the hotel, went directly to a shining closed car which was drawn up in front of the curb. Bill Brakey, getting The Kid's signal, had placed himself in a position of vantage, where he could see the interior of the car. The Kid, standing in the doorway of the hotel, stretched and yawned, as though debating just how to spend the evening.

There was a moment while introductions were performed, and The Kid knew from the introductions that there was only one other man in the car. That man, of course, would be Pug Morrison himself. Morrison wouldn't make a contact in a public hotel with a young woman who was subsequently to be murdered. On the other hand, he would not delegate the receipt of seventy thousand dollars in cash money to any of his subordinates.

The young woman entered the car. The door slammed. The car purred away, Tess Copley occupying the front seat with the driver, who, The Kid surmised, would be Pug Morrison. The contact man occupied the rear of the car.

The car purred into smooth motion and rounded the corner. The Patent Leather Kid nodded to Bill Brakey. Bill Brakey moved over to the place where The Kid's high-powered machine was parked against the curb. He slid in behind the wheel and had the motor started by the time The Kid jumped into the seat and said, "Step on it, Bill. I think they're going to the Morelay house, but there's no use taking chances. We'll keep them in sight until we make sure that's the way they're heading."

They swung around the corner. Bill Brakey snapped the car into high gear. They accelerated into swift speed, and within three blocks picked up the tail light of the big sedan.

"Okay," The Kid said. "Let's drop behind now."

They followed for four blocks, and then The Kid nodded.

"They're headed for the Morelay place. We can cut through on the side streets and get there a little before they do."

The Kid sat back against the cushions while Bill Brakey piloted the car with deft skill. They passed the location of the grim tragedy where Mrs. Morelay had been done to death, swung up a side street, and parked the car.

The Patent Leather Kid got out.

"Let's look it over, Bill," he said.

They moved as silently as shadows down the side street to the corner, waited until they heard the sound of a car, then peered out at the headlights that showed first as two gleaming eyes of white fire, then purred past, giving them a glimpse of the big sedan as it slid smoothly to a halt, exactly as Walter Stagg had planned.

The big sedan waited, the motor running. After a few minutes, the motor was shut off. A woman crossed to the drug store and returned.

The Kid nodded to Bill Brakey.

"Looks," he said, "as though it's going through according to schedule."

A man emerged from the car as automobile headlights came in sight down the street. The man paused to adjust a mask about the upper part of his face. From the interior of the big sedan came the sound of a woman's scream, a scream that was promptly suppressed.

The masked man moved to the rear of the car, flung a cloth over the rear license plate. The man in the driver's seat started the car. The purring sound of the running motor was audible to the waiting pair.

"Better start our car, Bill," The Patent Leather Kid said.

Bill Brakey started the powerful motor, settled down behind the steering wheel, opened the door opposite him so that The Kid could jump in without the loss of a moment.

The headlights of the other car showed more plainly, then a taxicab rattled past. A girl sat in the rear of the cab. The cab slid to a stop by the side of the big sedan. The cab driver picked up a small suitcase from the floorboards, started to step from the cab. The young woman was fumbling with the door catch.

The masked man stepped forward, so that the headlights of the taxicab showed not only his mask, but the blued-steel of the automatic which he held in his right hand. There was the sound of a scream from the girl. The taxicab driver slowly elevated his hands. The bag dropped to the street. The masked man shoved an envelope in through the partially opened window of the taxicab, motioned with his gun. The cab driver slid back to his place behind the wheel. The cab rattled into slow motion. The masked figure raised his gun and fired twice, deliberately shooting out both front and rear tire on the right hand side. Then he scooped up the bag, turned and ran to the sedan. The sedan almost instantly glided into swift motion.

The Patent Leather Kid raised his arm in a beckoning gesture and gave a shrill whistle. Instantly, Bill Brakey shot the powerful car into motion. It slid to a stop beside The Kid. The Kid climbed the running board on the side near the wheel.

"It's going to be a gun fight, Bill," he said. "I'll take the wheel."

Bill Brakey slid over to the other seat and snapped the door closed. The Patent Leather Kid adjusted himself behind the wheel. His patent leather shoe pressed down on the throttle. The car shot ahead.

As The Kid sent the car into a turn at the corner, he snapped the band of the black patent leather mask about his forehead, adjusted the mask so that his eyes fitted the eye-holes. The car was continually accelerating its speed.

They passed the crippled taxicab, and as they passed, The Kid snapped the gearshift into the over-drive. His car swept ahead with the grace of a seagull swooping down to skim the surface of ocean waves. The big sedan rounded a corner. The Kid swung wide, skidded his car into a turn, stepped on the strottle.

"They know we're on their tail, Bill," he said. "They're going to run for it."

The sedan swung wide, swayed far over on two wheels as it took a corner. The Kid, grinning, swung his car at the same corner, keeping all four screaming wheels on the pavement. Bill Brakey slipped a heavy caliber gun from its shoulder holster, nestled it in his right hand.

"Don't shoot until they do," The Kid told him, shifting gears as he spoke.

The cars roared down a paved side street devoid of traffic, traveling at a mad pace. The Kid's car gained.

The driver of the sedan tried one more turn, not realizing that The Kid's low-hung car was far less topheavy. The driver lost control of the sedan. It ran on two wheels, came back to four wheels with a terrific jolt which swayed the big body on its springs.

A hand knocked out the rear window. A gun spatted viciously. A bullet struck the side of the windshield support on The Kid's car and ricocheted off into the night.

"Try for the driver, Bill," said The Patent Leather Kid calmly, and swung his car wide so that Bill Brakey would have a clear shot around the side of the windshield.

Brakey's gun crashed twice. The dark hulk of the driver's body jerked and swayed. The big sedan screamed into a skid, whipped entirely around, crashed against a curb, hung balanced for a moment, and then toppled to its side with a roar of breaking glass and the sound of grinding steel.

Bill Brakey flung open the door of the car, jumped to the ground. The Patent Leather Kid was out from behind the wheel and on the ground ahead of him. Together, they raced toward the big sedan.

"Look out!" yelled The Kid suddenly. "They've got a cover-car!"

Headlights came into view as a car skidded around the corner.

"Quick!" shouted The Patent Leather Kid. "I'll get the girl and the bag. You hold the car."

Bill Brakey dropped behind a fire hydrant. His gun crashed once. The headlights of the approaching car wobbled. The car screamed as the driver applied brakes and skidded in close to the curb. Little flashes of gunfire spurted into the night. The Patent Leather Kid tugged at the jammed door of the sedan, finally wrenched it open.

A young woman stared at him from wide black eyes. As she caught sight of the black mask which covered the upper half of The Patent Leather Kid's face, she screamed.

"It's all right, Miss Copley," The Kid said. "I came to get you."

He leaned forward and pulled her through the doorway.

Pug Morrison was lying unconscious, his head badly gashed. The man who had been in the rear seat was making futile motions, clawing with his fingers at the upholstery on the back of the seat.

"Your friends will be here in a minute, buddy," The Kid said. "In the meantime, fork over that bag. Walter Stagg said we'd find seventy grand in it."

He caught sight of the bag, lurched toward it, and then grinned at the girl.

"We've got to make a run for it," he said. "There's a battle going on."

The street echoed and re-echoed to the sound of shots. Men had jumped out of the cover-car, taken refuge behind such protection as they could find, and were directing a cross-fire at Bill Brakey.

The Kid sprinted to the car. Someone shot at the pair, but the bullets were wide of the mark. The Kid flung the girl into the seat.

"Bend over low," he said.

He jumped in behind the wheel and tooted the horn, signal to Bill Brakey.

Bill Brakey suddenly stood erect. His guns roared in a pealing crescendo of rapid fire, a fire of such scathing accuracy that it drove his enemies to cover, and in the moment when they were ducking to cover, Bill Brakey sprinted for the car.

The Kid had it in second gear. The car gave a terrific lurch and then snarled into speed.

Behind them came a burst of fire. The bullet-proof body in the rear of the car deflected half a dozen bullets that thudded into the steel.

"They'll try the gasoline tank and the tires," Bill Brakey said, slipping a fresh clip of cartridges into his gun. "I'll give them something to keep their minds occupied."

He fired four or five well directed shots, then slid in beside the girl.

"Here they come," he said.

"We'll make a run for it," The Kid told him. The car by this time was in high gear. The Kid waited until it was going fifty-five miles an hour before he flung in the over-drive. The car swept into instant response, screaming down the pavement at better than sixty miles an hour, a sixty which soon became seventy, eighty-five. The speedometer needle quivered around ninety miles an hour.

A car came out of a side street.

There was a moment of tense silence, but The Kid swung his car in a deft skidding turn, so that he swept past the obstructing car, the driver of which had lost his head and left the car in such a position that it blocked the intersection.

The pursuing car tried a similar swerving turn. The driver was not skilled enough. The car went out of control, swung completely around in a circle, and then crashed into an ornamental lamp post.

"Okay, Kid," said Bill Brakey, "slow down and let's introduce ourselves to Miss Copley."

VI

A $70,000 Coupon

Walter Stagg was nervously pacing the floor, cracking the knuckles of his right hand against the extended palm of his left hand. From time to time he glanced nervously at the clock on the wall.

The doorbell rang. Stagg did not wait to work the electric buzzer, but dashed madly down the stairs to open the door.

A white-faced young woman staggered in through the opening and handed him an envelope.

"Tess!" she screamed. "She's been kidnaped!"

Walter Stagg ripped open the envelope with trembling fingers and stared at the demand for ransom.

"What happened?" he asked. "Tell me about it."

"I took the papers out in a cab," the young woman said. "A man was waiting. He had a mask. He threw a gun on us and took the papers. Then he gave us this demand and told us we'd never see Tess alive again unless we did just as we were instructed."

Walter Stagg heaved a great sigh of relief. "Take this to the police at once," he said.

"But they were going to kill her if we went to the police."

"Don't be a fool!" he said. "We've got no money. The money is all tied up in the estate. We couldn't pay any ransom. We've *got* to go to the police. Did you get a description of the man?"

"He was masked," she said. "He was a big man with a black suit—I saw that much."

"Take this letter," Walter Stagg said, "and go to the police."

She hesitated a moment, looking at him in white-faced anguish.

"Tess was with them," she said, "in the car—and—"

"Go to the police," Walter Stagg told her, "otherwise you'll be compounding a felony. It's up to the police to handle the case. We can give publicity to it. The newspaper can feature the fact that none of the money can be paid out except on an order of the court, and a court can't order moneys paid from an estate."

The girl took the envelope, turned and ran to a taxicab which was waiting with the motor running. Walter Stagg stood in the doorway for a moment, watching her, then slammed and bolted the door. He walked back up two flights of stairs, and a smile of serene satisfaction twisted his lips.

He entered the living room on the front of the flat, turned and locked the door behind him, then suddenly gave a convulsive start.

A man was stooping over the wall safe, and, as Stagg looked, the lock clicked and the man pulled the door of the safe open.

Walter Stagg's hand shot to his hip. The gun at which he tugged caught for a moment in the lining of his hip pocket. Then, as he freed it, he became conscious of another figure which was seated comfortably in one of the overstuffed chairs, holding a blued-steel gun levelled steadily at him.

"Better drop it," said the voice of Bill Brakey.

The Patent Leather Kid did not even look up as Walter Stagg's hands shot into the air and the gun slipped from his nerveless fingers and thudded to the floor.

The Patent Leather Kid pulled out some papers, looked through them and chuckled.

"Here's the will, Bill," he said. "Stagg was suppressing it."

"Who the devil are you?" screamed Stagg.

The Patent Leather Kid looked up. His enigmatical eyes glittered through the eye-holes in the patent leather mask.

"They sometimes call me," he said, "The Patent Leather Kid."

He turned back to the safe.

"Good heavens!" he said, "here are the original books! The damn fool hadn't destroyed them as yet."

Stagg took two quick steps forward, stopped only when he heard Bill Brakey's voice, low with ominous menace.

"One more step," said Brakey, "and I'll shoot your legs out from under you."

Stagg stopped, his face working with fury.

"Damn you!" he said. "You'll pay for this—both of you! The police will have you for this. The Patent Leather Kid, huh? Well, this is once they've got you where they want you."

"I neglected to tell you," said The Patent Leather Kid calmly, "that as soon as Pug Morrison had delivered the ransom note to the taxi driver, we rescued the girl and, incidentally, picked up the seventy thousand dollars. I inadvertently dropped a remark which makes him think we were working for you."

There was a moment of silence while the full force of The Kid's words struck home to Stagg.

"Think you're working for *me?*" he screamed.

"Yes," The Kid said, "he sort of thought you had double-crossed him. What makes it bad is that there was a cover-car following along behind. It had some of Morrison's men in it. He didn't trust you all the way. I'm afraid there'll be trouble."

Stagg's upstretched hands slowly drooped. There was not enough strength in his arms to hold them up.

"Good God!" he exclaimed. "You . . ."

Bill Brakey nodded toward the door.

"We got you into it," he said. "We'll give you a chance to get out. You can beat it if you want to."

"But it's a death sentence," Stagg said. "They'll gun me out. They'll . . ."

"Better get started," Bill Brakey told him.

Stagg turned, ran to the door, struggled with the lock with futile, nerveless fingers which simply wouldn't coordinate. Bill Brakey opened the door for him, saw him into the corridor, listened to the wild beat of his steps as Stagg dashed down the staircase and wrenched open the front door. A moment later he heard the *ker-flop, ker-flop, ker-flop, ker-flop* of his running steps on the cement sidewalk.

Bill Pope, the explorer, regarded Inspector Brame with twinkling eyes.

"At least, inspector," he said, "you've got to admit that The Patent Leather Kid did a good job this time."

Inspector Brame's face slowly flushed to a dark shade that was almost a purple.

"The damned outlaw!" he said. "He wounded one man and almost killed another in one car, and killed a gangster outright in another. He had bullets flying around the street like hail. It was the most lawless demonstration of gangster warfare that has ever been staged in the city."

Bill Pope chuckled.

"Nevertheless," he said, "the public has got a great kick out of it."

"It was murder, just the same," Inspector Brame said, "and when we get him, we'll—"

"Oh, no, it wasn't murder," Bill Pope said. "You forget that the girl testifies she was being kidnaped; that there's a letter to prove her claims. Also, a girl friend who is a witness. All The Patent Leather Kid did was to rescue the girl from the hands of her kidnapers."

"The police don't need to accept help at the hands of a crook," Inspector Brame said, with dignity.

"Where were the police at the time, inspector?"

"That's neither here nor there," Inspector Brame stormed.

"Neither were the police," chuckled the explorer.

Renfroe, the banker, clucked his tongue sympathetically against the roof of his mouth.

"I quite agree with you, inspector. It's a pretty pass when crooks have to come to the rescue of people who are being kidnaped. It's an insult to the police efficiency."

Dan Seller yawned, stifled the yawn with four polite forefingers and spoke suavely.

"Wasn't there another murder, inspector?" he asked. "Seems to me I heard something about it over the radio."

"Walter Stagg," said Inspector Brame grimly. "He was shot down by machine guns. Someone took him for a ride."

"Rather looks as though he'd been mixed up with the gangsters, doesn't it?" asked the explorer.

"Yes," Inspector Brame said, "we've got plenty on Walter Stagg. It's too bad they killed him. We could have sent him to the chair."

"What for?" asked Renfroe.

"For the murder of Mrs. Morelay."

"But I thought you said some tramp killed her."

"That," Inspector Brame said, "was merely a stall we were making in order to trap the real criminal. When we went to Walter Stagg's flat, we found unmistakable evidence that he had doctored certain books of account and had prepared a duplicate set ready to be substituted at the proper moment. He found his opportunity when Mrs. Morelay telephoned the police that a tramp was in her kitchen. He split her head open with a hatchet, substituted the duplicated book of account, and took the real one with him."

"You have evidence of that?" asked Dan Seller, almost moodily.

"I'll say we have. We searched his apartment and found the original books. They still had blood stains on them, and what's more, we found Mrs. Morelay's fingerprints all over them, showing that those were the books she had been examining at the time she was killed."

Dan Seller once more stifled a yawn.

"All this talk of shooting and violence," he said, "bores me dreadfully."

Inspector Brame snorted.

"That's the worst of you young coupon-clippers," he said, "you live a life of idle ease and luxury, and don't know anything at all about what goes on out on the firing line. You should have the job I have for a while—only you wouldn't last forty-eight hours. You wouldn't have the faintest idea about how to go after a crook."

Dan Seller nodded placid agreement.

"Doubtless you're right, old top," he said, "every man to his trade, you know."

Inspector Brame's grunted comment was inaudible, but Bill Pope, the explorer, surveyed Dan Seller with watchful, appraising eyes, in which there was just the suggestion of a twinkle.

"You look tired, Seller," he said, "as though you had been through something of a strain."

Dan Seller nodded.

"Yes," he said, "I clipped a coupon—a seventy-thousand-dollar coupon."

Renfroe, the banker, stared with wide eyes.

"What kind of a coupon would that be?" he asked.

"Oh, kind of a grab bag affair," said Dan Seller, casually.

Bill Pope, the explorer, was suddenly seized with a fit of coughing.

TARANTULA BAIT

Paul Chadwick

shriek, throaty and horrible, shattered the stillness of Hamilton Square. Night shadows lay like pools of ink on the serpentine asphalt walks. The dusty, heavy, midsummer foliage swayed lazily in the breeze, making faint, eerie whisperings.

Then the shriek came again, followed by another and another.

Heads appeared in windows of a half dozen nearby apartment houses. Radios were quickly snapped off. Men and women looked fearfully at each other, then gazed down into the square where the darkness made everything indistinct.

The cop on the beat running parallel with the square heard the shrieks, too. He whirled and dashed forward, vaulting over the low iron fence onto the grass, his nightstick clutched in his hand.

Swift footsteps sounded ahead of him. Then a figure burst from the end of one of the walks. It was a girl, running till her breath came in labored, sobbing gasps. Her face had the deathly whiteness of parchment. Her eyes were wide and staring. Strands of loosened hair whipped behind her and a gleaming white shoulder showed where one side of her dress had been torn away.

Her steps quickened when she saw the policeman. With a last burst of energy that made her high heels click over the asphalt, she ran toward him and collapsed at his feet, moaning hysterically. Then words came from her lips.

"I saw him," she gasped. "The Tarantula! He's back there—in the square. Don't let him get me—please!"

The cop bent down, but the girl had wilted suddenly, falling into a dead faint.

Figures began to slip out of doorways and move toward the spot. A small crowd was gathering. They pressed around the unconscious girl, turning to stare uneasily into the shadows of the square.

The cop growled at them: "Stand back—give her some air."

He stooped, gathered the girl in his arms and carried her into the lobby of the nearest apartment. Then he called headquarters, his voice hoarse and low.

Five minutes later the French type telephone in Wade Hammond's bachelor apartment jangled. Wade picked the instrument up. His gaunt, bronzed face with its pencil-thin moustache line tightened as he heard the excited voice of the desk sergeant at the other end.

"It's the Tarantula again, Hammond. The boys are on their way now. The square's only a few blocks from your place. Better run over and take a look. Something funny is up."

Wade replaced the instrument in its bed and slipped out of his tasseled lounging robe. Funny was no name for it. The first "Tarantula" scare had startled the city a few nights before. A man crossing Hamilton Square claimed that he'd seen a great, black, eight-legged creature moving over the grass, moving like the spirit of death itself. The thing, he said, was seven feet in diameter—and for want of a better name he called it a tarantula.

It was too fantastic to be believed. But it made good newspaper copy. The tabloids had played it up. Now the Tarantula had been seen by a girl.

Wade smiled grimly as he got into his coat. He was too hard-headed to take stock in such a thing. He wondered what new kind of a racket some one was trying to put over.

Men from the Tenth Precinct were beating through the shrubbery of the square when he arrived. Their flashlights gleamed everywhere.

They had almost finished their search and nothing had been found. A burly detective whom Wade knew approached and spoke:

"She musta been cookoo," he said. "There ain't nothing here, no tracks even. Better go in and talk to her, Hammond. The sergeant's there now."

Wade took the advice. He found the girl on a leather lounge in the apartment lobby. A negro janitress had put a screen in front of her so that curious people in the street couldn't stare in. A sergeant of detectives was bending over her, getting ready to shoot questions, and the girl was just coming to.

* * *

Wade moved close and nodded at the sergeant, whose name was Terrant. The girl's eyelashes were heavily mascaraed. Her lips were a vivid crimson against the white oval of her face; but when she opened her eyes there was something wistful and appealing about her.

She sat up and clutched at her torn dress.

"Don't mind us," said the sergeant. "Just tell us what you saw out there."

"The Tarantula," she whispered. "I saw its hairy legs and its horrible red eyes. It grabbed at me with its claw. It was the most terrible thing I've ever seen—like a nightmare."

The girl shivered and half closed her eyes as though to blot out the memory.

"It *must* have been a nightmare," said the sergeant pointedly. "What's your name, miss?"

"Faith Tashman. Please take me to the apartment next door—where my friends are."

The sergeant nodded. Cops held the curious crowd back while he and Wade escorted the girl along the sidewalk and into the next building.

As soon as they got inside Wade verified what he had already guessed. The girl was an actress. A couple of other young women crowded around her, asking questions and trying to comfort her. One was a platinum blonde; the other a red-head. Wade could tell by their speech and ultra-sophisticated dress that they were stage people.

"Faith and I were in the same troupe before the depression hit," said the platinum blonde.

Wade smiled. He wondered what Faith Tashman's real name was. The combination sounded too stagey to be genuine.

They ascended to the girls' rooms, and from glimpses he got through half-opened doors Wade judged that the place was a hangout for down-on-their-luck bohemians. The building was shabby and run-down, contrasting sharply with the expensive apartments on the south side of the square.

The platinum blonde spoke again.

"I'll make Faith lie down," she said. "The poor kid's got the jitters."

Wade watched Miss Tashman being led away. He saw her pale face and the look of terror that still lingered in her eyes. Whatever had caused it, her shock was real enough.

The sergeant began talking to the red-head.

"You people who live here must be hitting the booze to see things like that," he said. "It'll be snakes next."

He laughed, jollying the red-headed girl along till the platinum blonde made her appearance again. She came out, closed the door quietly behind her and put her fingers to her lips.

"I gave Faith a snifter," she said. "She's going to take a little nap. She was on her way to a party at Jack Winchel's across the square. But I don't believe she'll make it now."

"Well, we'll be going," said Terrant. "Don't let this Tarantula business frighten you kids. It's a lotta boloney. Some nut is—"

He suddenly stopped speaking and leaned forward. A sound echoed through the apartment. The faces of the two girls went white as death.

It was another shriek—a shriek of terror. It came from the door through which Faith Tashman had walked a few minutes before. From the room where she was supposedly lying, resting after her scare. The scream ended in a choking, inarticulate cry.

Wade Hammond leaped to the door and threw it wide. The chamber was brightly lighted. There was a small bed with rumpled coverings. The window was wide open—and Faith Tashman was gone!

The sergeant was close behind him as he thrust his head over the window sill.

"Look—there she is!"

Wade's eyes widened with horror as he glimpsed the crumpled form on the sidewalk three stories below. The girl lay there, pitifully sprawled out, and Wade knew that she must be dead.

"She jumped," said the sergeant hoarsely. "She got so scared she bumped herself off. She shouldn't have been left alone."

Wade turned away from the window.

"Where does that door lead?" he asked, pointing across the room.

Then, without waiting for an answer, he strode forward and flung the door open.

He found himself in the corridor again. Just as he stepped out another door down the hall opened. He looked into the eyes of a tall, somber-faced man; a man with thin lips, a hawkish nose and features that held a bizarre mixture of power and cruelty.

Wade had the feeling that the man had started to step back, then shown himself when he realized he'd been seen.

The two girls were coming out into the hall, too. The red-head was sobbing hysterically, but the platinum blonde was still calm.

"It's only Marko," she said, seeing the intent look on Wade's face as he stared at the man down the hall.

"Marko?" Wade's voice was questioning.

"Yes—Marko Dürer, the magician. A swell guy. I did a disappearing bathing beauty act with him at the New Century last winter."

Wade nodded and went on down the hall. His eyes rested on the tall man speculatively. The magician came forward as he reached the stairway.

"What's the trouble?" he asked softly.

"Miss Tashman saw the Tarantula," said Wade. "Now she's fallen out of her window and is down in the street—dead."

He looked sharply at Marko Dürer and saw the muscles in the man's leathery face go taut.

"Dead!" The word came like a gasp.

"She must be," Wade said. "It's three stories to the sidewalk."

He turned and ran down the stairs. Sergeant Terrant was beside him when he reached the huddled body on the pavement. A policeman, the same one who had helped her out of the square, was bending over her.

"She's finished this time," he said soberly. "The scare must have got her in the head—made her jump."

Wade bent down and stared at the face of the dead girl. He reached forward and brushed a strand of loose hair away from her neck, then he gave a stifled exclamation.

"My God—look!"

The others saw what he was staring at. Sergeant Terrant began cursing hoarsely.

On the girl's white neck, close to her throat, were two terrible wounds, crimson holes where gigantic fangs seemed to have penetrated.

"She would have died even if she hadn't fallen," said Wade. "This is murder, Terrant—the Tarantula has claimed his victim. Better question everybody in the house."

"But how did he get to her room? Some guy's doing this—but who? And why?"

"You've got me, Terrant. I feel as if I'd had a shot too many myself. Miss Tashman was three stories up. She was alone only two minutes or so—but there was that door leading into the corridor!"

Brakes shrilled as an expensive sport roadster roared around the side of the square and drew up at the curb. The door opened and an excited man stepped out.

"What's this I hear? What's happened to Faith?"

The man came forward, then recoiled in sudden horror as he saw the figure on the sidewalk. His finely chiseled but dissipated face went ashen.

Wade turned and stared at the newcomer.

"It's Jack Winchel, Jr," whispered the cop. "Lives across the square and spends his old man's dough on radio and high-stepping dames."

*　*　*

Wade remembered then. A few weeks back he had read about Winchel's amateur radio station on the roof of his apartment, the station where he experimented in a haphazard way. The slender antennae masts of his transmission set, duly licensed by the radio board, thrust steel fingers upward into the sky above Hamilton Square.

So this was Winchel, heir to the Winchel millions, dilettante, inventor and expert ladies' man! Wade looked at him closely. The thing was getting complicated. Marko, the magician—and Winchel. They both seemed strangely interested in the dead girl.

"What happened?" Winchel repeated, his voice shrill with fear.

"She saw the Tarantula," said Wade. "She's been murdered. Look at her throat."

Young Winchel did so, and the color left his face.

He said: "We were having a party at my place—most of the stage people who live here, and a lot of others. We were expecting Miss Tashman. I phoned, and the janitress told me there'd been an accident."

As though to prove his words, some of his guests who had hurried around the square after him came up. Wade recognized a few. There was Lucille Roberts, the blues singer, Bert Thelmo, vaudeville clown, Bowers and Bender, the trapeze team, and Manricki, the contortionist, who had played six years on the Keith Circuit.

They pressed in, staring curiously.

The strident clanging of an ambulance sounded, and the crowd parted to let the white-clad attendants reach the girl. But Wade wasn't interested. He knew without being told that Faith Tashman was dead, beyond human aid. He was looking at the faces around him, trying to read the subtle emotions hidden behind the masks of fear.

Bert Thelmo's expression was, as always, faintly idiotic; his lips twisted by years of professional grimacing. Manricki was a thin, emaciated man. The trapeze artists were contrasting types: Bowers powerful and stolid; Bender thin and weakly.

Then Wade raised his eyes and stared again into the face of Marko Dürer. The man had followed them down into the street.

He stood there, aloof, brooding, staring at the dead girl with an inscrutable look. But Wade sensed some deep emotion behind his unfathomable expression.

He was glad when he saw Sergeant Terrant questioning the man closely. Dürer would bear watching, though the police would be up against a blank wall when it came to connecting the Tarantula scare down in the square with the murder of Miss Tashman in her third-floor room.

Wade listened while the police inquiry went on. Then the ambulance bore its pitiful burden away, and the crowd began to thin.

Jack Winchel did not offer to take his guests back to his apartment. He drove off, looking drawn and shaken. The guests wandered away as though shunning the murder house.

Wade slipped into the square, feeling that in its eerie shadows lay the solution of the ghastly mystery. He found a bench partially hidden by shrubbery, yet giving him a view of the building where Miss Tashman had met her terrible end.

It was getting on toward eleven when he suddenly leaned forward, staring up at the roof of the building across the way. A faint flicker of light showed for a moment, then winked off. It came again as he stared. Someone was up there, but who?

He slipped out of the shadows of the square, crossed the street, and entered the building next to the one where Miss Tashman had been killed. He showed his special investigator's card bearing the signature of the police commissioner himself, then climbed to the top floor.

Cautiously he opened the door leading to the roof and stepped out. He crouched and crept forward. A low brick wall separated the roof of the building he was on from the next one.

He stared over it and saw the light again. Someone with a small flash in his hand was moving over the roofs along the edge of the square. Wade followed silently, then stopped as the flashlight ceased its flickering and a dim form loomed ahead.

He moved to the rear of the roof and crouched down, feeling a prickle of excitement along his spine. Then he drew in his breath sharply.

A figure came opposite and was silhouetted for an instant against the glow coming up from the street.

It was Marko Dürer, the magician, prowling along the dark roof, and his right hand was deep in his right coat pocket.

What was he up to? Did he suspect someone, or had he some more sinister reason for being there?

Wade remembered the door leading into the corridor from Miss Tashman's room, and the strange look on Marko Dürer's face as he had come out.

He saw Dürer quicken his pace then disappear through a skylight door in the building where he lived. Wade at once left the roof, went down into the street again, and strolled back into the square.

His eyes were alert now, his attitude tense. In a moment he saw Dürer come out. The man lighted a cigarette, tossed the match away, then crossed the street and entered the square also, following one of the asphalt paths.

Wade eased into the shadows near his bench till Dürer had passed. Then he came out and followed, sticking to the grass plot beside the path, moving silently as a shadow.

The magician walked with an air of determination, heading straight across the square toward the south side where the more expensive apartments were situated; where Winchel had his place.

He reached the exact center of the square and stepped into the little open space where a small fountain played. A thick-branched maple made mottled shadows close to the fountain.

For a moment Dürer's form blended with these, then he emerged again. But Wade bent forward, every muscle taut, hardly believing his eyes. The shadow behind Dürer seemed to spread; seemed to enlarge and creep forward.

Then there came a hideous, choking cry. Wade saw Dürer go down on his face, saw the thing that had seemed a shadow leap upon him, saw a horrible, black something lift up and reach down for Dürer's throat.

For a moment the body of the magician was blotted out by the darker thing crouching on his back.

Wade sprang forward, breath hissing through clenched teeth, his hand reaching for the gun in his armpit holster.

The shadow on Dürer's back twisted for an instant. Wade got a second's glimpse of two red eyes, baleful and devilish in their unhuman intensity. Then he saw the horrible black hairy legs, and he knew he was looking at the Tarantula; knew he had seen it strike another victim down.

He raised his automatic to fire; but the black, ghastly shadow was gone. It had disappeared as mysteriously as it had come, seeming to blend with and vanish into the larger shadows of the trees. All that was left to prove it had been there was Marko Dürer's sprawled form. Wade fired two shots as a signal to the detectives patrolling the edges of the square.

Then he went up to Dürer. The first glimmer of his flashlight showed the telltale throat wounds. A stream of crimson was running from them, glistening and spreading on the asphalt. The Tarantula had struck for Dürer's jugular veins.

Even in that moment of horror Wade's lips curled in a faint, grim smile. He was smiling at himself, at his own false hunch which had made him suspect Dürer as the murderer. Now the mystery of the Tarantula seemed more impenetrable than ever.

But suddenly he bent forward, eyes narrowing. On the asphalt beside

Dürer's head and shoulders was a faint streak of whitish powder. It was fresh, lying on the very surface of the walk.

Wade set his flashlight beside it. Then, with delicate care, scraped the powder onto a piece of paper which he took from his pocket. He had just finished the job when the first detective arrived.

He told his story then, told it briefly, and felt almost like a suspect himself, so fantastic were the details of the killing.

"Which way did the Tarantula go?" asked the detective.

Wade shrugged. "I couldn't tell. One moment I saw it against the asphalt. The next it was gone."

"It's a hell of a note," said the dick. "Two murders in one night on the same case. The inspector himself will want to look into this."

By daylight, with Inspector Thompson at his side, Wade went over the square again. The grizzled head of the city homicide bureau, who at first had taken the Tarantula case as a joke, was now deeply troubled.

"Any theories, Hammond?"

"Not yet, chief—none worth mentioning. Let's go call on Jack Winchel. His radio apparatus interests me."

"Are we studying radio or making a murder investigation?"

"Both." Wade spoke quietly. He didn't tell Thompson about the white powder. He wasn't sure how it fitted in himself, and it was his habit not to give voice to a theory till he had some facts to bolster it. The powder puzzled him. He had had it analyzed, established the fact that it was magnesia. But the idea that it suggested seemed too far-fetched to be real. He had nothing to back it up, no subsidiary theories to prop the main one. He stared up at the high, slender masts of Winchel's radio station as they crossed the square.

But Winchel was out, and the servant couldn't tell them when he would get back.

Thompson seemed dissatisfied; but there was a gleam in Wade Hammond's eyes.

That afternoon he rented a room on the south side of the square; in the only rooming house left in a row of high-class apartments. It overlooked the square, and from his windows he could see the shadows of the Winchel radio masts on the grassplots below.

The shadows lengthened as evening came, seeming to stretch over the square like long and sinister fingers. Then they dimmed as the sky darkened.

Wade went for a stroll in the square, every sense alert. He crossed it and met a party of stage people from the murder house on their way to dinner.

Manricki, Lucille Roberts, Thelmo, the clown, Bowers and Bender, and the two girls who had been near Miss Tashman's room were in the party. The platinum blonde greeted him.

"We're all going to move out at the end of the week," she said. "It gives me the heebee-jeebies to think of what happened to Marko and Faith. The rest feel the same way."

"And I've just taken a room across the square," said Wade. "The second floor front of the brown-stone house. I'll be near-by then if anything else breaks."

The blonde shuddered.

"Let's hope it doesn't. I didn't sleep a wink last night, and I won't tonight either."

Wade nodded. He didn't expect to get much sleep himself. But he had undertaken the job voluntarily. Crime riddles fascinated him, and he'd never run across one which seemed more mystifying than this on the surface.

It was another warm night. He left the window of his room wide open and turned the light out. He had a deeper reason than merely wanting to watch the square in taking a place so close to the scene of the murders. If certain theories of his were correct he knew he was playing a dangerous game.

The evening deepened and a deathly quiet settled over the square. People shunned it now. Everyone in the city had read the ghastly story. They even avoided its vicinity as much as possible.

Alert, Wade waited in his room, waited for something he was not sure about himself. The hours passed. Midnight came, and still the tomblike quiet of the square had not been broken.

He found himself getting drowsy. He, too, had been up a greater part of the night before.

He sat down in a chair for a few moments to rest his legs, facing the window, his gun near his hand. Another hour ticked by. It was wearying work, this waiting for something that might never come. Before he knew it his head had fallen forward and his eyelids closed.

Then a sound wakened him, a sound that seemed nothing more at first than a faint, mouselike scratching. But his eyelids opened, his head lifted up; and if he hadn't been a man with nerves and muscles under supreme control he would have cried out; shrieked aloud in the wave of stark horror that gripped him.

The square of the window, dimly illuminated by the street lights below, was now blotted out. In it was a huge, vague form; a black something with hairy legs entering the room.

He found himself staring at two red eyes set in a black, indistinct head. Then the thing came into the room and lunged toward him. A sense of

loathing mingled with the horror he felt, as though at a presence unspeak-
ably evil.

Against the window now he saw a black claw with gleaming points at the
end reach upward and outward toward him. He hurled himself sidewise in
the chair; dropped noiselessly to the floor and reached for his gun at the
same moment.

The thing seemed to hear him. Wade heard a scraping movement across
the floor, saw the black bulk leap backwards toward the window.

He fired just as the light was again blotted out as it went through. But the
indistinct bulk made a poor target.

Yet it seemed to him that his bullet must have struck home, that the killer
must have fallen. He leaped to the window half expecting to see it lying on
the street as he had seen the body of Faith Tashman.

But it was not there, and the night was empty, except for a strange
whisper of sound that seemed to fill the air, coming from everywhere at
once as the surface of the buildings reflected it. The uncanny whisper died
away as Wade listened. It died, and he heard only the running feet of the
detectives coming at the sound of his shot.

Wade ran to the door of his room. That strange whispering sound—the
powdered magnesia—the two things set his brain working, gave shape and
substance to the theory his mind had been evolving. His eyes were alight
now with the zest of the hunt.

He went out into the hallway, but instead of descending to the street to
meet the detectives and tell them what had happened he turned and ran up
the stairs to the roof. He opened the skylight and crept out into the night.

Like a wraith he stole across the roofs toward the higher bulk of the
building where Jack Winchel had his apartment. A fire-escape, not visible
from the street, snaked up the side of this. There was one landing at the rear
which could be reached from the roof Wade was on.

He climbed the iron ladders, passing window after window. There were
no lights in Winchel's apartment.

He was more cautious than ever as he went up the last slender ladder to
the roof. The masts and aerials of the experimental radio station showed.

Wade stopped and listened. A faint noise came, so faint that if his ears had
not been alert for it he would not have detected it. It was the scrape of metal
on metal, the soft clicking of well-oiled cogs. And high above him a shadow
was moving. Like the boom of a derrick, one of the steel radio masts was
lifting upward, lifting from an inclined position which had brought its top
over the center of the small square.

Wade stole forward toward its base. His gun was out now, his fingers clenched over the hard-rubber butt like the talons of a hawk.

He crouched, went forward on hands and knees, and suddenly leaped. A cry of terror broke the stillness of the night as he jabbed his gun forward, jabbed it against a man who was bending over the handle of a gear box from which cables led upward to the mast. Sweat streamed from the man's face.

"Drop it," said Wade tensely. "Drop it before I shoot."

The man's face went white.

"I had to do it—he made me—he would have murdered me."

Like a cringing cur the man groveled at Wade's feet.

"Get over there and stand still. Make any move and I'll kill you."

Wade pocketed his gun and took hold of the crank handle. The derrick-like boom of the mast, which had a ball and socket base, was almost vertical with the roof now. A few more turns of the crank and the steel cable leading through a pulley in the top of a still higher mast had drawn it up. It could be lowered and turned to alter the length and direction of the antennae.

Another cable led from the mast's end; a slender, almost invisible, wire. And from this something was dangling, swinging. The black shadow came in toward the end of the roof and landed as the slender wire unwound on a steel reel. A metal fastener was snapped open and the black shadow bounded toward Wade.

This time he fired coolly and accurately. Fired—and the thing collapsed into a shapeless heap. Wade's flashlight stabbed the darkness, played over the thing on the roof.

The shape of the Tarantula was visible then, legs sprawling. With a look of disgust he walked to it. From the heap of cleverly designed cloth and hair a harsh voice was swearing monotonously, swearing in pain.

Wade reached down, tore at the vicious head with its red reflecting lenses and disclosed a man's face—the face of Bowers, of the trapeze team of Bowers & Bender.

Bowers' left hand had a clawlike glove on it, set with two razor sharp blades on the end which could be pressed together with his thumb and forefinger. His right hand was uncovered and blackened, but the palm had whitish powder on it.

"You shouldn't have spilled that magnesia," grated Wade. "It started me thinking. I used magnesia myself in my own gym work—bought it at a drugstore to put on my hands and keep them from slipping. Then I heard the wire whisper when you swung away from the window after trying to kill me. Winchel will be surprised when he learns that you used his radio mast for a purpose he hadn't intended. Sneaked up the fire escape, didn't you? But what was your motive, Bowers?"

A stream of curses was his only answer.

But Bender, the Tarantula's white-faced partner, gave the details of the ghastly plot later.

"He made me help him," he repeated. "He was after Winchel's money. Faith Tashman was Bowers' wife, though she didn't live with him. He tried to play the badger game—compromise Winchel, and get a big cash settlement. But Faith got to like Jack and stalled along.

"Bowers read one of her letters—learned that she wasn't going through with it. That's why he swung up to her room and killed her after failing to get her in the square. Marko Dürer was sweet on Faith and suspicious of Bowers. Bowers guessed he might be wise and killed him for that reason, after seeing him prowling around the roofs. He liked the Tarantula stunt and was going to work it some. He had it all doped out and that's why he pulled the first scare in the square. He did a spider act at the Criterion two years ago. Climbed up a rope web and used the same costume."

Wade nodded. He had known all along that there was some simple and rational explanation. The deepest looking puzzles sometimes have the simplest solutions.

"He's got himself mixed up in another web now," he said quietly. "The web of the law—and he knows where it will land him!"

THE SINISTER SPHERE

Fred C. Davis

I

The Moon Man

It was robbery.

The French door inched open. A figure crept through, into the dark room. It paused.

It turned from side to side, as if looking around, a head that had no eyes, no nose, no mouth! From side to side it turned its head, a head that was a perfect sphere of silver! Mottled black markings covered the shining surface of the ball, reproducing the shaded areas of the full moon whose light streamed in through the windows.

If the silent figure had any face at all, it was the face of the man in the moon!

The silver, spherical head sat low on a pair of broad shoulders from which a long, black cape hung. A pair of black-gloved hands stole through slits in the sides of the cape.

The dark room was not silent. From below came the soft strains of dance music, mingled with laughter and the rhythmic moving of feet on polished floor. It was midnight; the party was at its height. The man whose head was a globe of silver nodded as though pleased.

He glided through the darkness across the room. At an inner door he drifted to a stop. He opened it carefully. The music became louder in the ears of him who had no ears. The hallway outside was empty. The cloaked figure closed the door and turned to the wall.

He removed from its nail a mirror which hung between two doors, and disclosed the circular front of a safe. His black hand twirled the combination dial. He turned his moon head, listening alertly. He heard faint clicks. When he drew up, he turned the handle of the safe door and opened it.

Locks meant little to him.

Into the safe he thrust a black-gloved hand, and brought out a sheaf of banknotes. He drew them inside his cape. He closed the safe and twirled the combination.

Suddenly a loud snap! . . . A flood of light drenched the room.

The figure whirled.

In the doorway stood a woman, her eyes widened with fright. She was forty and fat. She was wearing a spangled gown. Her one bejewelled hand dropped limply from the lightswitch. She stood transfixed, staring at the figure with the silver head, and gasped:

"Martin!"

She had no need to call. Her husband was at her back. He stared over her shoulder, as startled as she.

"The Moon Man!" he exclaimed.

The man in the silver mask whirled toward the open French door.

Martin Richmond, clubman, broker, man of position, was wiry and athletic. He leaped past his wife with one bound. He sprang toward the French windows with the intention of blocking the way of the grotesque thief. The Moon Man reached it at the same instant.

Richmond flung up his arms to grapple with the intruder. He groped through empty air. An ebony hand, clenched into a fist, cracked against the point of Richmond's chin.

Richmond staggered, making a desperate attempt to clasp the man with the spherical head. His hand clutched a black one. Another thrust tumbled him backward. Something soft remained in his fingers as he sprawled. The Moon Man darted through the door, slamming it shut behind him.

The door opened on a balcony. Beneath it was twenty feet of empty space. The Moon Man leaped over the railing of the balcony, throwing himself into the void.

Martin Richmond scrambled up. From below came a quick, smooth purr. He rushed onto the balcony and looked down. He saw nothing. The Moon Man was gone.

"Call the police!" Richmond gasped as he sprang back into the room.

He jerked to a stop and looked at the thing he had in his hand. It was a black silk glove.

"We've been robbed!"

The words came ringing over the wire into the ear of Detective Lieutenant Gil McEwen. He was perched at his desk, in his tiny office in headquarters. He clamped the receiver tightly to his ear.

"Who's talking?"

"Martin Richmond, Morning Drive. The Moon Man robbed me. He got away!"

"Coming right out!" snapped McEwen.

He slammed the receiver on its hook and whirled in his chair to face a young man who was standing by the window. McEwen's face was hard and wrinkled as old leather; the young man's was smooth-skinned and clean-cut. McEwen's eyes were gray and glittering; the young man's were blue and warm. McEwen was fifty, hardened, by twenty years on the force; the young man was half his age, and had just been made a detective sergeant.

He was Stephen Thatcher, son of Peter Thatcher, the chief of police.

"Steve, it's the Moon Man again!" the veteran detective snapped. "Come on!"

"I'll be damned!" said Steve Thatcher. "Can't we do anything to stop his robberies?"

"I'll stop him!" McEwen vowed as he grabbed for the knob. "I'll stop him if it's the last thing I ever do!"

He went out the office on a run. Steve Thatcher ran after him with long legs flexing lithely. They thumped down the wooden steps. They rushed into the adjoining garage. A moment later they swerved a police-car into the street and dashed away with the speedometer flickering around sixty.

Martin Richmond's residence on Morning Drive was five miles away. Gil McEwen made it in less than five minutes. With Steve Thatcher at his side he hurried to the front door and knocked very urgently. Martin Richmond himself opened it.

The party was still going on. Couples were still dancing in the large room at the right. McEwen saw them through closed French doors, and followed Richmond into the library opposite. Richmond wasted no time.

"My wife found the Moon Man in our room. He'd just finished robbing our safe. It was almost an hour ago."

"An hour ago? Why didn't you call me sooner?" McEwen snapped. "By this time he's crawled into a hole somewhere."

"I found that our phone wires were cut. I stopped to see how much had been stolen. Then I had to find a phone. It took some time to get my neighbors to get up and let me in. I called you as soon as I could."

"Let me see the bedroom," McEwen ordered.

He trod up the stairs with Steve Thatcher at his heels. Thatcher could well understand the veteran detective's anger. The Moon Man had done this sort of thing repeatedly. He had committed robberies without number in his characteristic daring, grotesque way.

The papers had been filled with his exploits. The police department had been absolutely unable to find a single clue pointing to his identity. He appeared like magic, robbed, and vanished.

The papers and the police commissioners were howling for an arrest. The public was demanding protection against the mysterious thief. And the police were helpless. Steve Thatcher could well understand why Gil McEwen was in no amiable mood.

McEwen paced about the bedroom. He examined the safe. He looked out the balcony. He ran downstairs and inspected the ground below. He came back red-faced and puffing.

"He used a car. Driveway right below. Stopped the car under the balcony, climbed on the top of it, then swung himself up. Beat it the same way. Not a tire-mark or a footprint! Not one damn' thing to tell who—"

"Look at this!" said Martin Richmond quickly.

He thrust the black silk glove toward McEwen. McEwen took it slowly, narrowed his eyes at it, and passed it to Steve Thatcher.

"I pulled it off his hand as he was rushing out the door," Richmond explained. "He—"

"It's a right glove," McEwen interrupted. "The chances are he's right-handed. Then he had to use his bare hand to open the door and make a getaway. That means he's probably left a fingerprint on the knob!"

He examined the knob. He could see nothing. Raising, he turned sharply on Steve Thatcher.

"Beat it to a phone and get Kenton up. Tell him we've got to dust this knob right away—can't wait. Get him up here quick!"

Hours later Gil McEwen hunched over his desk in Headquarters peering at a photograph. It was a photograph of a door knob. On the knob was a clearly defined impression of a thumb. It was not the thumb-print of Martin Richmond, nor of Mrs. Richmond, nor of any one else in the burglarized house. McEwen had made sure of that.

It was the thumb-print of the Moon Man!

McEwen settled back in his chair exhaustedly, and peered into the face of Kenton, the fingerprint expert.

"You're absolutely sure that this print doesn't match any in the files?"

"Absolutely sure," Kenton answered. "The thumb that made that print has never been recorded by any police department in the United States."

"Hell!" grunted McEwen. "Then it can't tell us who the Moon Man is—

yet. But when I find a guy whose thumb-print matches up with this one,—I'll collar him hard!"

Kenton went out. Steve Thatcher settled into a chair.

"We know, anyway, that the Moon Man is somebody who has no criminal record."

"Yeah, but he'll soon have! The time's coming when that guy's going to make a slip. When I grab him, he's going up the river on so many counts of robbery that he'll never live to come out of prison. And I'll grab him, all right—I'll do it!"

They looked toward an older man seated beside the desk. He was portly, with a kindly face and curly white hair. He was Chief Peter Thatcher. His were the keen eyes of a born law officer. His was the straight, stern mouth of a strict disciplinarian. He was a good chief, and at present he was a very worried one.

"We've *got* to get the Moon Man, Gil," he declared. "We've got to stop at nothing to get him."

"Listen!" McEwen said sharply. "I've been on the force twenty years. I've got a reputation. No crook has ever succeeded in getting away from me once I set out on his trail. I went to Brazil to get Doak, didn't I—and I got him. I went to India to get Stephano, and I got him. I'm not going to let any smart aleck Moon Man make a fool out of me. I've sworn to get him, and I will!"

Chief Thatcher nodded slowly. "The Police Board is clamoring for that bird's hide. So are all the papers. We've got to grab the Moon Man some-how, Gil—and quick."

"Chief, you've got my promise. I'm not going to stop trying till I've grabbed him. Nothing's going to keep me from it. And when I make a promise, I live up to my word."

"I know you do," the chief said soberly. "I'm depending on you, Gil. It's your case. It's entirely in your hands."

Steve Thatcher looked solemn.

"I haven't been a detective long enough to be of much help," he said quietly. "I wish to gosh I could do more. But you know you can count on me, Gil, for—"

The door opened. A girl came in. She was twenty-two, pretty, animated. Her face resembled Gil McEwen's strongly; she was his daughter. She greeted her father cheerfully, nodded to Chief Thatcher, and went quickly to Steve. She kissed him.

On Sue McEwen's third left finger glittered a solitaire. Steve had put it there. The wedding was not far off.

"Baffled!" she exclaimed, surveying the disgruntled expressions of the three. "Aren't the papers awful? You'd think the Moon Man was the greatest criminal of the age, the way—"

"He is, as far as I'm concerned!" her father snapped. "Sue, we're trying to get at the bottom of this thing. We'll see you later."

"Why chase me out?" Sue asked with a smile. "Maybe I can help. Perhaps the thing you need is a little womanly intuition."

"Huh!" said her father. "You're too eager to mix yourself up in police matters, Sue. I don't think you can be of any help."

"Don't be so sure," Sue insisted. "I would say, for instance, that the Moon Man must be someone far above the level of an ordinary crook. He has more intelligence. He plans his moves cleverly. So far, he has always succeeded in getting what he wants, and making a clean getaway. Going through the Rogue's Gallery would be only a waste of time. The man you want is well-bred, with a fine mind, good manners, and a broad social background."

"Trying to make a hero of him—a thief?" her father asked skeptically.

"Not at all. After all, he is a thief, and stealing, besides being illegal, is revolting to anyone of sound character. The man deserves all the punishment you want to give him, Dad. I'm only suggesting the kind of a man he is —one whose character has been despoiled by the dishonorable business of robbery. There—have I helped?"

"Not much. Now—"

"How much did he steal this time?"

"Six hundred and fifty dollars."

"Only six hundred and fifty?" Sue McEwen repeated in surprise. "Why, that pushes him even lower in the scale of thieves. He's nothing but a petty pilferer!"

The parsonage of the Congregational Church of Great City was located not far from the business district. The Reverend Edward Parker lived there alone. At nine o'clock on the night following the Moon Man's latest exploit he heard a knock at his door. He opened it.

A short, squatty man stood on the step. He had a twisted nose that evidently had once been broken in a fistfight. He had a cauliflower ear. He had scarcely any neck. He nodded, and handed through the door a sealed envelope.

"From a friend, for the needy of the parish," he said.

Immediately the Rev. Mr. Parker accepted the envelope, the pugilistic gentleman turned and walked away. The darkness swallowed him up. Dr. Parker opened the envelope. Inside it he found a bundle of banknotes. They were bound by a single band of silver paper, and they amounted to $250.

Maude Betts was a widow with no work and three children. She lived in a tenement in the warehouse district of Great City. The stove in the kitchen was cold. There was no food in or on it. Her cupboard was bare. She was about to be evicted by a landlord who declared that the four months' rent, past due, must be paid him at once. She was facing the county poor farm.

A knock sounded at her door. She dried her eyes, opened the door, and found a tough-looking young chap handing her an envelope. She took it as he said: "From a friend."

He went away. Mrs. Betts opened the envelope and gasped with joy. From it she removed a pack of banknotes held together by a band of silver paper. They totalled just $200.

Ethel Knapp, twenty and not bad to look at, stood in her furnished room and peered at the gas jet. For ten minutes she had been peering at it, trying to summon the courage necessary to turn it on—without a lighted match above it. She had no money. She had come to Great City from her home in Ohio to work. She had no work. She had no way of returning to her mother and father. But she did have a way of saving herself from further hunger and humiliation. The gas jet.

She raised her hand toward it. Startled, she paused. A faint rustling sound came into the room. Looking down, she saw an envelope creeping under the door. She took it up, bewildered, and opened it. Inside lay money—currency held together by a band of silver paper—banknotes totalling $200!

She jerked open the door. The hall was empty. She ran down the steps. She saw a few persons on the street, and paused bewildered. She had no way of knowing that the money had been left her by the squatty, combative-looking young man who was just vanishing around the corner. But that money meant life and happiness to Ethel Knapp. . . .

> For the Rev. Edward Parker, $250.
> For Maude Betts, $200.
> For Ethel Knapp, $200.
> Just $650 in all! . . .

II

The Moon Man Speaks

In their delight, neither Dr. Parker, nor Mrs. Betts, nor Miss Knapp noticed the oddity of the silver band which encircled the money that had so mysteriously come to them. None of them thought to associate it with the Moon Man.

Had they suspected, they might have thought the stocky chap to be the Moon Man. They would have been wrong.

Ned Dargan, ex-lightweight—he of the broken nose and cauliflower ear—walked along a dark street in a shabby section of the city. He glanced neither right nor left; he walked steadily; he knew where he was going. When he reached the black doorway of an abandoned tenement building—a structure condemned by the city but not yet demolished—he paused.

Making sure he was not observed, he entered the lightless hallway. He closed the door carefully and tightly behind him and trod up a flight of broken, uncarpeted stairs. Plaster littered them. Dust lay everywhere. The air was musty and close. Dargan walked along the upper hall to another door.

As he reached for the knob a voice called:

"Come in, Angel."

Dargan went in, smiling. The room beyond was dark. A moment passed before his eyes became accustomed to the gloom. Gradually he was able to see a form standing behind a table, a figure that blended out of the blackness like a materializing ghost. The figure was swathed in a black cape. Its head was a smooth globe of silver.

"Evenin', boss," said Dargan.

A chuckle came from the silverheaded man. "You've distributed the money, Angel?"

"Yeah. Got it out right away. And it certainly was badly needed, boss."

"I know. . . . You realize why I selected Martin Richmond as a victim, Angel?"

"I've got an idea he ain't all he seems to be."

"Not quite that," answered the voice that came from the silver head. "He's quite respectable, you know. Social position, wealth, all that. But there's one think I don't like about him, Angel. He's made millions by playing the market short, forcing prices down."

"Nothin' wrong in that, is there?" Dargan asked.

"Not according to our standards, Angel; but the fact remains that short-selling had contributed to the suffering of those we are trying to help. I've taken little enough from Richmond's kind, Angel. I must have more—later."

Dargan peered. "I don't quite get you, boss. You're takin' an awful chance—and you don't keep any of the money for yourself."

A chuckle came from the silver globe. "I don't want the money for myself. I want it for those who are perishing for want of the barest necessities of life. What would you do if you saw a child about to be crushed under a truck? You'd snatch her away, even at the risk of your own life.

"I can't bear to see suffering, Angel. I can no more help trying to alleviate it than I can help breathing. If there were any other way of taking money from those who hoard it, and giving it to those who desperately need it—if there were any other way than stealing, I'd take that way. But there isn't."

"Don't think I'm questioning you, boss." Dargan hastened to explain. "I'm with you all the way, and you know it."

"Yes, Angel," said the Moon Man gently, "I know it. You're the only man in the world I trust. You know what it is to suffer; that's why you're with me. Well, you've been scouting today. What's the result?"

Dargan wagged his head. "Things are pretty bad, boss. The regular charities ain't reaching all the folks they should, and they're pretty slow. I don't know what some of these folks would do without your help.

"There's a steamfitter out of a job named Ernest Miller. He's got a daughter, Agnes, who's sick with consumption. The kid's goin' to die if she ain't sent to Arizona. Miller can't send her—he hasn't got any money, boss."

The Moon Man nodded his silver head. "Miller shall have money, Angel —all he needs."

"Then there's the guy named Frank Lauder, I told you about."

"Lauder will be compensated, Angel."

"Then there're two kids—Bill and Betty Anderson—a couple of sweet kids they are. Their mother just died. They ain't got nowhere to go but to their aunt and uncle, named Anderson. The Andersons are barely gettin' along as it is, and can't take the kids in. So they'll have to go to an orphanage if somethin' ain't done for 'em."

"They won't go to the orphanage, Angel. You've done your work well. I'll have money for all of them tomorrow."

"Tomorrow?" Dargan peered again at the small moon which was the head of the man in the black cape. "Boss, ain't you takin' an awful chance, followin' up so close? Last night—and now tonight! Ain't it gettin' dangerous?"

There was a pause. "Yes, Angel, it is getting dangerous. The police now have my thumb-print."

"Your thumb-print! Holy cripes! Now if they ever catch you they'll be able to prove you—"

"I don't think it will occur to Gil McEwen to look in the right place for me, Angel," the Moon Man interrupted with a soft laugh. "Still, as you suggest, I've got to be very careful. At any time McEwen might accidently find a print which matches the one he found on the Richmond bedroom door-knob last night—and when he does—"

"Cripes, boss!" gasped Dargan.

* * *

The Moon Man straightened. "Don't worry, Angel. Keep an eye on yourself. Report back to me tomorrow night, half an hour after midnight, here. All clear?"

"Sure, boss."

Ned Dargan turned from the room. He closed the door tightly on the Moon Man. He peered at the panel, as though trying to penetrate it with his gaze and read the secret of the man in the room—a secret even he did not know. He walked down the stairs slowly, and eased out the front door.

"I can't figure out *who* that guy is!" he told himself wonderingly. "But, cripes! I know he's the swellest guy that ever lived!"

Ned Dargan had a solid reason for feeling as he did about the man whose face he had never seen—the Moon Man. He'd gone bad in the ring. A weakened arm made further fighting impossible. He found it just as impossible to find work. He'd drifted downward and outward; he'd become a bum, sleeping in alleys, begging food. Until, mysteriously a message had come to him from the Moon Man.

Some day Ned Dargan was going to fight again. Some day he was going to get into the ring, knock some palooka for a row, and become champ. And if he ever did, he'd have the Moon Man to thank for it. . . .

The Moon Man stood in the center of the dismal room. He watched Dargan close the door. He listened, and in a moment heard a creak, then another. He knew those sounds the stairs made. The first was pitched at A Flat and the second at B in the musical scale. When B sounded before A Flat, someone was coming up. The Moon Man heard B follow A Flat and knew that Dargan was gone.

He turned away, opened a connecting door, and stepped into an adjoining room. He turned a key in the lock. The air was pitch black. The Moon Man made motions which divested himself of his cape. He pulled off his black gloves—luckily he had provided himself with more than one pair. He removed from his head that silver sphere, and he put all his secret regalia in a closet. The closet door he also locked.

Turning again, he silently opened a window, and eased out onto a rusted fire-escape. Rung by rung he let himself down into the alleyway behind. He paused, listening and looking around. Then he stepped forth. . . .

The street-light's glow fell into the face of Stephen Thatcher!

Steve Thatcher thought of things as he walked away from the house he had made the Moon Man's rendezvous. In his mind's ear he heard Gil McEwen saying: "I've sworn to get the Moon Man, and I will!" McEwen, the toughest detective on the force, who never failed to bag his man!

And he heard the voice of the girl he loved: "He's nothing but a petty pilferer!"

Steve Thatcher lowered his head as though stubbornly to butt an obstacle. A wild scheme—his! He knew it. But, also, he knew the world—cruel
and relentless—and he could not stand by and do nothing to save those
who were suffering. The mere thought of letting others perish, while nothing was done to save them, was unendurable.

He was a cop's son—revolt against injustice was in his blood—and not
even the law could keep him from trying to right the wrongs he knew
existed. Beyond the written law was a higher one to which Steve Thatcher
had dedicated himself—the law of humanity.

And if he were caught? Would he find leniency at the hands of Gil
McEwen and Chief Thatcher? No. He was certain of that. Even if McEwen
and the chief might wish to deal kindly with him, they would be unable to.
The Moon Man now was a public enemy—his fate was in the hands of the
multitude. Steve Thatcher would be dealt with like any common crook—if
he were caught.

He remembered Ernest Miller's daughter, who must go to Arizona or die;
he remembered Frank Lauder, who must be cared for; he remembered Bill
and Betty Anderson, who must have help.

"It's got to be done!" he said through closed teeth. "Damn, it's *got* to be
done!"

He walked swiftly through the night.

III

Another Victim!

Detective Lieutenant Gil McEwen's phone clattered. He took it up. He
glared at a photograph he was holding—a photograph of the Moon Man's
fingerprint—and grunted: "Hello!"

"Detective McEwen? Listen carefully. I'm calling—"

"Speak louder!" McEwen snapped. "I can't hear you."

"My name is Kent Atwell, Mr. McEwen," the voice came more plainly.
"I'm phoning you from a pay-station downtown because I don't dare phone
you from my home. I've been threatened—by the Moon Man."

"What!" barked McEwen. He knew the name of Kent Atwell. Atwell was
one of Great City's most prominent citizens. His home was one of the finest.
His influence went far. And here he was, huddling in a booth downtown like
a rabbit in a hole, using a public phone because a threat of the Moon Man
had filled him with fright! "The devil!" McEwen said.

"I've got to see you, Mr. McEwen—immediately. The Moon Man has threatened to rob me tonight. I don't dare let you come to my home, or my office. Can I meet you somewhere?"

"Where are you?"

"In a drug store at State and Main streets."

"You're close to the Palace Theatre," McEwen said briskly. "Buy a ticket and go in. Go down into the men's room—be there in ten minutes. I'm coming right along, and I'll meet you there."

"Certainly. Thank you!"

McEwen pushed the phone back and scowled. He tramped out of his office into Chief Thatcher's. He found the chief absent, but Steve Thatcher was sitting in his father's old padded chair. The young man looked up.

"You come with me, Steve!" McEwen snapped. "This thing is getting worse and worse! The Moon Man's going to stage another robbery—and this time he's saying so ahead of time!"

"I'll be damned!" said Steve Thatcher. "Listen, Gil. I've just found out—"

"Never mind! Come with me!"

McEwen went out the door. Steve Thatcher frowned; but he followed. He loped down the steps, crowded into a police-car beside McEwen, and said nothing until the car was whizzing down the street.

"Of all the damned gall!" the veteran detective blurted. "Sending a warning ahead of time! He must think he's living a charmed life—that we can never touch him. I'll show him where he's wrong—then, by damn, he'll wish he was on the moon!"

Steve Thatcher sighed. "I was about to tell you, Gil, that I think I've found out about this mask the Moon Man wears. You've wondered how he could see his way about, with a silver globe on his head. Well, evidently he can, because the thing isn't silver at all, but glass."

"Glass?" McEwen repeated. "How do you know?"

"It must be. That mask of the Moon Man's has made us all curious, and I began trying to figure out how he could manage to move about with his head completely enclosed in a metal ball. Well, he can't, of course. I browsed around the library today, and found the answer—Argus glass."

"What's Argus glass?"

Steve Thatcher smiled. "If you were a frequenter of speakeasies in New York, you'd know. Argus glass is named for the son of the mythological god, Zeus. Argus had a countless number of eyes, and some of them were always open and watching, so the legend goes. Argus glass is a mirror when you look at it from one side, and a perfectly clear piece of glass when you see it from the other."

"Didn't know there was any such thing!" McEwen snapped, sending the car swerving around a corner.

"Nor I, until I read about it. A big French jeweller's store has in it several pillars of the glass. They look like mirrors to the customers, but they're not. They're hollow, and inside them sit detectives on revolving chairs. They can see everything that goes on in the store, but no one can see them. It wasn't so long ago that speakeasy proprietors found out about the glass. They use it in their doors now instead of peep-holes. Nobody can see in, but they can see out."

"Say! Maybe we can learn who the Moon Man is by tracing that glass globe!" McEwen exclaimed. "Who makes the glass?"

"The Saint Gobain Company of France. Argus glass is the answer, Gil. The Moon Man can see as clearly as though he wasn't masked at all, but nobody can see his face. His mask must be split down the middle so he can get his head into it, and he's evidently painted the mirror surface to look like a moon."

"By damn!" McEwen declared. "Just let me get within reach of that guy and I'll take a whack at that glass mask. It'll turn into splinters and then we'll see who the Moon Man is!"

Stephen Thatcher smiled. He had not thought of that likelihood. A sharp blow would shatter the globe that masked the face of the Moon Man! . . . His smile faded. He was almost sorry now that he had divulged the secret. He had told McEwen this only because he was supposed to be working on the case and, to safeguard himself from suspicion, had decided that he had better make some discovery about himself.

"No kidding, Gil," he said quietly. "Aren't you keeping something back? Haven't you some idea who the Moon Man is?"

"Not a damn' notion!" McEwen declared. "How about you, Steve? Who do you think he is?"

"I," said Steve Thatcher with a sigh, "couldn't say."

McEwen parked the police car a block from the Palace Theatre. He strode to the ticket-booth with Steve Thatcher; they bought tickets and went in. Immediately they turned toward the downstairs men's room. They entered it to find Kent Atwell waiting.

Atwell was thin, dapper; his eyes were dark and deep-set. And at the moment he was visibly agitated. When McEwen identified himself, he immediately launched into a frightened, indignant explanation of the Moon Man's threat.

"Here!" he exclaimed, pushing a sheet of crumpled paper toward McEwen. "Read that! The incredible presumption of it!"

The bit of paper was torn irregularly at the bottom. It was typewritten—done, McEwen could not dream, on a machine in police headquarters! Its message was terse:

DEAR MR. ATWELL:
    Withdraw from your bank today the sum of five thousand dollars. Place it in a safe in your home. I intend to call for it tonight. Let me warn you that if you notify the police of my intentions, you will suffer worse punishment than death. That is my promise to you.

McEwen looked blank. "How do you know this is from the Moon Man?" he asked sharply. "Where's the rest of it—the part that is torn off?"

Atwell turned pale. "It's of no importance—just the typewritten signature. I accidentally tore it off and lost the piece, so—"

McEwen gestured impatiently. "Mr. Atwell, I beg your pardon, but it is my business to know when men are telling the truth. You are not being frank with me. There was more of this message—and if I'm to help you, I've got to have it."

"Really, there—"

"Unless you produce it right now, Mr. Atwell, you can count on no help from me," McEwen snapped.

Atwell sighed. He fumbled in his pocket. McEwen quickly took the bit of paper he produced—the lower half of the sheet he had already read. And he scanned a second paragraph:

    What do I mean by a "worse punishment than death"? I mean disgrace and humiliation, the loss of your friends and position, becoming a pariah. I know that, while you were handling the drive for money under the United Charities, you as the treasurer of the organization helped yourself to five thousand dollars of the funds. I can and will produce proof of my statement if circumstances demand it. It is that stolen five thousand I want. You will leave it for me in your safe, as I direct, and make no move to interfere with my taking it—or I will give the facts to the newspapers.

                                       MM

McEwen peered at Kent Atwell. "Is this true?" he demanded sharply.

"Certainly not! There is not a particle of fact in what is written there. I preferred not to let you see that paragraph, because it is all so preposterous. I refuse to be mulcted out of money that is rightfully mine, and I'm asking you to do something to protect me from this maniac who calls himself the Moon Man."

"I can't do a damned thing until he shows up and tries to rob you," McEwen answered. "He says he'll come tonight. Is there some way of my getting into your house without being seen?"

"Yes. I can tell you how. But am I to deliberately wait for him to come and—"

"If I may suggest it, Mr. Atwell," Steve Thatcher spoke up quietly, "you had better follow the Moon Man's directions to the letter. Get the money from the bank and put it in your safe as he directs. If he suspects that you're laying a trap for him, he may not show up; but if you appear to be acting in good faith, we may stand a chance of grabbing him."

"Exactly. He seems to know everything and be everywhere," McEwen agreed. "If he learns, somehow, that you haven't been at your bank today to withdraw that sum, he may stay in hiding. Our only chance of getting him is to have that money in the house—as bait."

Steve Thatcher smiled.

"But what," said Kent Atwell, "but what if your precautions fail, and the money is stolen regardless and—"

"You'll have to take that chance. This is an opportunity to grab the Moon Man tonight. If we don't make the most of it, he'll get you in some other way, and you'll be helpless." Gil McEwen fixed the gentleman with a stern eye. "If you have no faith in what I'm suggesting, you shouldn't have come to the police, Mr. Atwell."

"Yes, yes—I agree!" Atwell answered. "I will go to the bank immediately. I'll take the money home and put it in the safe. And you—"

"We'll come to your house tonight, after dark. I'll have enough men with me so that there'll be no chance of the Moon Man's escaping if he comes after that money. I'll phone you beforehand, to make arrangements."

"I'll follow your instructions to the letter."

Kent Atwell fumbled with his gloves and left. McEwen and Steve Thatcher waited a few minutes, then hurried from the theatre. McEwen's face was twisted into a grimace of distaste.

"I half believe that what the Moon Man wrote about Atwell is the truth," he said. "Damn—who is that crook, anyway? How can he know so much?" He started along the street at a stiff pace. "Tonight, Steve—tonight, unless something goes very wrong—I'll grab him!"

"Where're you heading, Gil?" Steve Thatcher asked quickly.

"I'm going to send a cable to the Saint Gobain factory in France. I'm going to find out who they made that glass mask for!"

Steve Thatcher's eyes twinkled. Again—unseen by the veteran detective —he smiled.

Outside the windows of Police Chief Thatcher's office hung veils of darkness. Inside, lights burned brilliantly. Detective Lieutenant Gil McEwen stood in the center of the room, facing a group of six men who had just entered in answer to his call. Each of the six was a plainclothes man.

"I've just made arrangements with Atwell," McEwen was saying, crisply. "We're going to slip into his house so we won't be seen, in case someone is watching. We're going to be damned careful about that. You're to follow my orders strictly, and be ready to leave here as soon as I say the word."

McEwen had chosen his men well. Each of the six was an old-timer on the force. Each had demonstrated, in the headquarters target gallery, that he was a dead shot. Each possessed a record of courage and daring.

As McEwen talked to them, the door of the chief's office opened quietly. Sue McEwen sidled in, stood aside, and listened with intense interest. His eyes strayed to those of Steve Thatcher, who was standing beside his father's desk; they exchanged a smile.

"This is our chance," McEwen declared to his men. "We've got to make it good. If the Moon Man gets away from us tonight, God only knows if we'll ever grab him. Wait downstairs."

The six men turned and filed from the office. McEwen paced across the rug. Steve Thatcher looked thoughtful. The chief of police sighed and wagged his head.

"You're all set, Gil?" Chief Thatcher asked.

"Yeah. You wait right by that phone, chief, in case of an emergency. And I hope when I phone you it will be to say we've got our man."

Sue McEwen stepped toward her father eagerly. "How soon are you leaving, dad? I wouldn't miss this for anything."

McEwen stared at her. "You're not getting in on this, young lady!"

"Why not?" Sue asked. "If I go to the house with you it won't do any harm, and I may be able to help. As long as I'm a detective's daughter, I want to make the most of it."

"How many times have I got to tell you, Sue," her father sighed, "that this sort of thing is not for you? We've argued about it a thousand times. I won't let you mix yourself up in police matters."

"You forget," Sue answered, smiling, "that I gave you the tip that helped send John Hirch, the forger, to prison. And didn't I figure out where Mike Opple was hiding after he killed his woman? I don't think I'm so bad at this. If you'll give me a chance tonight—"

"Nothing doing!" Gil McEwen snapped. "You go home and go to bed!"

"Dad," said Sue indignantly, "I'm not a child. I'm perfectly able to take care of myself. This Moon Man fascinates me, and I'm going to—"

"I think your dad's right, Sue," Steve Thatcher interrupted gently. "You'd better leave this to us. There's no telling what will happen."

Sue raised her chin defiantly. "It's going to take more than an argument to stop me this time. I—"

The telephone jangled. Gil McEwen snatched the instrument off the chief's desk. A voice twanged into his ear:

"This is Preston, downstairs, McEwen. You told me to let you know if a message came for you. There's one coming in now."

"Be right down!" McEwen answered quickly. He dropped the telephone and hurried to the door. "Answer to my cable coming in over the teletype!" he exclaimed as he hurried out.

Steve Thatcher's eyes brightened. He hastened out the door after McEwen. They jumped down the stairs side by side, paced along the brick corridor, and squeezed into a little room. Inside it was a sergeant, a battery of telephones, a short-wave radio receiving set, and a teletype machine. The teletype was clicking and spinning out its yellow ribbon.

McEwen leaned over it and read the words as they formed:

Police Headquarters Great City—Argus Glass Sphere Shipped to Gilbert McEwen General Delivery Great City—St. Gobain.

"By damn!" gasped McEwen.

He tore the strip out of the machine. He glared at it. He said unprintable things.

"By damn! He ordered that mask under *my name!*"

Steve Thatcher's eyes were twinkling. He had known what this cable would say. He had planned for this exigency. And he was enjoying the veteran detective's discomfiture.

"Looks suspicious, Gil," he remarked. "*You're* not the Moon Man, are you?"

"Yah!" snarled McEwen. "He's smart, isn't he? He's clever! Pulling a stunt like that—getting his damn' glass mask made under my name! Wait'll I get my hands on that guy!"

Steve Thatcher chuckled in spite of himself.

McEwen squeezed out of the teletype room. He hurried down the corridor to a door which opened into a larger room. His six detectives were there, perched on and around a table usually devoted to pinochle.

"Come on!" he snapped. "We're going!"

The six men began trooping after McEwen. Steve Thatcher followed the veteran detective a few steps.

"You've got all your car will carry, Gil. I'd better follow you in mine. I'll be along in a minute."

McEwen nodded his agreement and pushed through a big door into the adjoining garage, with the six following him. Steve Thatcher looked up and saw Sue McEwen coming down the stairs. He turned to her.

"I want to come with you, Steve," she said.

"Darling, I'm sorry. I'll phone you as soon as there's news."

"But, Steve—"

He did not wait to listen. He did not like this insistence of Sue's. It emphasized in his mind the painful disaster that would surely follow if it were ever learned that he, Steve Thatcher, son of the chief of police, was the Moon Man. He hurried out the entrance, turned sharply, and went into a drug store on the corner.

He slipped into a phone-booth and called a number which was unlisted in the directory, unobtainable by anyone, known to none save him and one other.

Two miles away, in the maze of the city, a phone rang. A stocky, broken-nosed young man picked it up. He heard a voice say over the wire:

"Hello, Angel."

"Hello, boss."

"Listen carefully. I want you to leave the car in front of the home of Kent Atwell at exactly five minutes before midnight tonight."

"Sure, boss."

"Don't wait. Take a taxi back. Leave the car right in front of the house, and make sure nobody sees you do it. I'll meet you at the usual place thirty-five minutes later."

"Right, Boss."

"Wish me luck, Angel."

Then the line went dead.

IV
The Trap Is Set

Nine o'clock. A sedan buzzed past the front of the home of Kent Atwell. It rolled on smoothly and turned at the next corner. Halfway down the block it turned again, swinging into the driveway of a dark house. It paused in front of the garage; and out of it climbed Gil McEwen and his six detectives.

Standing silent in the darkness, they waited. A moment later another car turned from the street and crept into the driveway. It braked behind the sedan. Steve Thatcher climbed out of it and walked to Gil McEwen's side.

No one spoke. Leading the way, McEwen strode past the garage and pushed his way through a high hedge. Steve Thatcher followed, and the six men. They walked silently across the rear of an adjoining estate, and paused at a gate in the hedge. They listened a moment, then eased through.

They drifted like shadows to the rear of the home of Kent Atwell. McEwen knocked softly at the door. It opened; no light came out. McEwen, Thatcher and the six men entered. Kent Atwell closed the door, turned, and led them into a spacious library.

"Okay," said McEwen without formality. "You alone, Atwell?"

"Yes," said the gentleman. "My wife is away, and I've given the servants the night off."

"Place all locked up?"

"Every door except the front, and every window. All the blinds are drawn."

"Money in the safe?"

"Yes."

Atwell crossed the room to a stack of bookshelves. From one the height of his head he removed a unit of four thick volumes. In the wall behind shone the front of a circular safe.

"Locked?" McEwen asked.

"No," Kent answered as he replaced the books.

"Good. Now." The detective turned. "We're all going to keep out of sight and wait. First thing, I want to make sure there's only one way for the Moon Man to get in—the front door. Steve, take a quick look around, will you— upstairs and down."

Steve Thatcher circled the library, and made sure every window was locked. Stepping into the rear hallway, he determined that the bolt was in place. In the other rear rooms he repeated his examination; then he climbed the steps to the second floor and entered, in turn, each of the bedrooms. McEwen, listening, heard him moving about. In a moment Steve returned.

"All set," he announced.

"Good. Where in this room can I keep out of sight, Atwell?"

Again Atwell crossed the room. He opened a door and disclosed a closet space behind. It offered a large, comfortable hiding-place to McEwen. The detective nodded.

"Mr. Atwell, I want you to go upstairs and prepare for bed. Pretend that you are alone. I'm going to put a man in every room upstairs and down. Every window will be watched, and every door, in case the Moon Man tries something tricky. I'm going to stay here in the library and watch the safe. Understand?"

They understood.

McEwen signalled two of his men. He conducted them across the vestibule and into the two rooms on the opposite side of the house. Stationing one man in each, he closed the doors and went up the stairs with the others following. He waited until Kent Atwell went into the master bedroom, then assigned one man to each of the remaining rooms on the second floor.

Five doors opened. Five doors closed. Behind each of them a detective began to wait. Behind one of them Steve Thatcher listened.

He heard Gil McEwen go downstairs.

McEwen stepped into the library. He closed its doors. He strode to the safe, opened it, reached inside, and removed a thick pack of banknotes. He counted them—five thousand dollars. He put them back and closed the safe.

From his pocket he removed his service automatic. He examined it very intently. Crossing the room, he opened the closet door, moved a chair inside. Stepping in, he swung the door until it was within an inch of being closed. He sat, with his automatic in his hand, and waited.

The house was utterly silent.

The vigil had begun.

An hour passed.

Another.

Silently an automobile turned the corner of the street on which the Atwell mansion sat. Its lights were dimmed. It drew to the curb near the corner and its lights went out. A hand reached for the ignition switch and clicked it off. The hand was that lovely one of Miss Sue McEwen.

The young lady settled down in the cushions and looked reprovingly at the Atwell residence. Its windows were dark, save for a few chinks of light shining through the draperies on one side of the lower floor. Inside, Sue McEwen knew, were her father and her fiancé and six detectives and an intended victim of the Moon Man. Inside, she knew, interesting things were almost sure to happen. She said to herself in a whisper:

"I *won't* be left out!"

She opened her handbag. From it she removed a tiny automatic. It was a fancy little thing, with handle of mother-of-pearl; but it was deadly. In the hand of an expert shot it could spout death. Sue McEwen, by dint of long and arduous practice in her own back yard, under the guidance of her father, was by way of being an expert shot.

The minutes crept past.

A quarter of twelve.

The determined young lady looked and listened and waited.

Five minutes of twelve.

A soft whirr came from behind Sue McEwen's parked roadster. She did not stir, but through the corners of her eyes she saw a coupe swing into the street. Its lights were out. It rolled along without a sound. And that, thought Miss McEwen, was strange.

The lightless car eased to a stop directly in front of the Kent Atwell home. One of its doors opened. A black figure stepped out of it and began to walk toward the farther corner. When it was halfway there another sound came from behind Sue McEwen. A second car—this time with its headlamps on and making no attempt to be quiet—purred past her. It was a taxi. It spurted toward the far corner and stopped.

The squatty young man climbed into it. The cab started up again. It swung around the corner and disappeared.

"I," said Sue McEwen to herself suddenly, "am going to see what that's all about!"

She started her engine. She spurted away from the curb—her tiny automatic lying in her lap—and eased past the dark car parked in front of the Atwell home. Should she get out and look it over? No; that would take time, and she wanted to follow that taxi; it might get away from her if she stopped now. She stepped on the gas.

At the next corner she swung left. And there, two blocks ahead, she saw the red tail-light of the taxi gleaming.

She followed it. It drove straight on. It was going toward the central business district of Great City. Just this side of the main thoroughfare it turned. When she reached that corner Sue McEwen also turned. For a moment the taxi was out of sight, but she picked it up again immediately. She was keeping well behind it. She was taking no chances.

"Something," she thought, "is up."

The taxi went on. Sue McEwen went on. The two cars, separated by two blocks, turned into a route that took them around the nocturnally popular section of the city. Presently the taxi was rolling into a region that gave Sue McEwen some uneasiness. It was dark, lonely, dangerous; and, after all, she was alone.

But she kept following that taxi. And suddenly she saw it stop.

It paused just past an intersection. The young, chunky fare got out and paid the driver. Sue McEwen could not see his face. A moment later the taxi spurted off and, at the next corner, swung out of sight. The young man walked along the black street, turned and entered a "dog cart" in the middle of the block.

From the tower of the City Hall came the reverberations of a striking gong. The town clock was striking. It tolled twelve.

What, Sue McEwen wondered, was happening back in the Kent Atwell house? She could not guess. She wanted to keep an eye on that strange young man.

She drew to the curb, cut the ignition, and blinked off her dimmers. She waited. For twenty minutes she waited. At the end of that time her quarry came out of the lunch cart and began walking away.

She started after him, cautiously. She saw him turn the corner. As she rounded the corner, she saw the young man make a quick move and disappear.

She saw that he had gone into the black doorway of an empty tenement.

She stopped. She got out of the car and, keeping in the deep darkness which flanked the buildings, slowly worked her way toward that doorway. It was empty now. The young man had gone inside. She listened and heard nothing. With the utmost care she eased the door open an inch and peered through. She saw nothing.

Then, taking a tight grip on her little automatic, she crept in.

The house was a black tomb—silent. She stood still until her eyes became accustomed to the darkness. Gradually she saw the details of a staircase leading to the second floor. She moved toward it. She went up the steps, one after another. And suddenly she stopped.

A board creaked under her foot.

Ned Dargan stood stock still in the darkness of the room which was the rendezvous of the Moon Man. He had heard that creak. A second later he heard another. His hand slipped into his coat pocket and came out grasping a gun. He turned slowly.

Stealing toward the closed door which communicated with the hallway, he listened. He heard no sound now. He wondered if the creaks had been caused by the loose boards warping back into place after being strained by his own weight. He decided he had better make sure. He opened the door stealthily, and stepped into the hallway.

Every nerve alert, he walked to the head of the stairs. He went down them slowly. The boards creaked again as he crossed them. He went on.

Again those sounds served as a signal. Sue McEwen heard them. She was hidden behind the door of a room directly across from that which Ned Dargan had just left. Realizing that the creaking of the board under her feet might have been heard, she had hastened along the hallway and slipped into the front room just as Dargan had opened the rear one. Now, seeing the way clear, she crept back into the hall.

She crossed it. She opened the door of the room which Dargan had left— the hidden headquarters of the Moon Man. She slipped inside and looked around. It was bare. It was musty. It looked unpromising; but Sue McEwen was tantalized by the mystery of what was happening.

She gasped. From the hallway again came creaks. The man she had seen enter the house was returning to the upper hallway. Even as she turned, Sue McEwen heard his step toward the door she had just entered.

She turned quickly away from that door. She hurried across to another, which apparently communicated with a room beyond; but it balked her. It was locked. She whirled again. In a corner she saw a closet. She jerked open its door. It was empty. She sidled inside and closed the door upon herself.

At that instant she heard a step in the room. The man had come back. He was standing within a few yards of her now—unaware of her presence. She stood straight, her tiny automatic leveled. She was determined to wait—and listen—and learn.

Now she was going to see what connection all this had with the Moon Man. Now, perhaps, she might even learn who the Moon Man was.

V

In Dead of Night

Faintly the sound of a tolling gong came into the library of Kent Atwell. Twelve slow strikes—midnight.

Gil McEwen, hidden in the closet, heard the trembling beats. Steve Thatcher, in a room directly above, listened to them and smiled.

He silently opened the door of the bedroom which had been assigned to him. He stepped into the hallway and closed the door behind him. Along each wall of the hall was a row of such doors, all closed. Behind one of them was Kent Atwell himself. Behind the others were detectives.

Steve Thatcher crept to the nearest door. Beneath its knob the handle of a key protruded—outward. Very slowly he turned it—without a sound. And he smiled. While making the rounds of the house he had carefully removed the keys from the inside of all the bedroom doors and placed them on the outside. He passed up and down the hallway silently as a ghost. At each door he turned a key.

Now one millionaire and four detectives were securely locked in their rooms—and did not know it!

Steve Thatcher crept down the front stairs into the vestibule. Again he locked a door and imprisoned another detective. He crept to the rear hallway and made a captive of another sleuth. So far he had contrived to imprison every man save Gil McEwen.

Steve Thatcher drew the bolt of the rear entrance, slipped outside, and hurried toward the street. At the car left by Gargan he stopped. He unocked the rumble compartment and from it removed a black bundle. Then, quickly, he returned to the rear door of the house.

Pausing, he drew on his long, black cloak and pulled on his black silk gloves. He placed on his head the glass mask modeled as a moon. It was padded inside so that it sat firmly on his head. A deflecting plate, which came into position over his nose and mouth, sent his breath downward and out, so that it would not fog the glass and blind him. He was ready.

He stealthily opened the rear door and let himself in. Through the glass he could see as clearly as though there was nothing on his head. He trod up the rear stairs, along the hallway, then down the front flight into the vestibule. Outside the unlocked door of the library he paused.

Gil McEwen, he knew, was inside—waiting.

The Moon Man laid his black hand on the knob of the library door. He twisted it. He eased the door open and peered through the narrow crack. Within six feet of him, though unseen, sat Gil McEwen.

McEwen's closet door was partly open, but he could see only the wall opposite, the wall in which the safe was set. He could not see the door opening slowly under pressure of the Moon Man's hand. He heard not the slightest sound. The Moon Man drifted into the room.

The black-cloaked figure flattened itself against the wall. It moved toward the closet door with one arm outstretched. The other arm also moved— toward a light chair. The Moon Man picked it up. His body tensed.

Suddenly he sprang. He struck the closet door and slammed it shut. Instantly he braced the chair under the knob. A startled cry came from behind the door. The knob rattled. From inside McEwen pushed—hard. The door would not open. The tilted chair wedged it firmly in place.

"By damn!" rang through the panels.

The Moon Man turned away quickly as the door shook. McEwen was throwing himself against it. From the black space within came another muffled cry:

"Get him! Carter! Landon! Winninger! Carpen! Go after him!"

The sound of McEwen's furious voice carried through the walls. Quick movements sounded upstairs. Knobs rattled. Across the lower hallway two more knobs rattled. Upstairs and down six imprisoned detectives and one imprisoned millionaire cursed.

And the Moon Man chuckled.

Suddenly the report of a gun blasted with a hollow sound. Splinters flew from a panel of McEwen's closet. A bullet hissed across the room and shattered a window pane on the opposite side. The shattered glass fell very close to the position of the wall-safe.

"No use, McEwen!" the man in the silver mask exclaimed. "I've already got it!"

McEwen snarled; and he did not fire again. He flung himself against the door. It literally bulged under the impact of his body. The Moon Man heard the wood of the chair crack. He hurried to the wall-safe.

He grasped the four books and flung them away. He snapped open the door of the safe. He snatched out the sheaf of banknotes. They disappeared through a slit in the side of his cape.

The closet door thumped again. This time it gave a little more. Upstairs men were pounding and cursing. Bedlam filled the house. And once more McEwen crashed against the inside of the closet door.

The Moon Man hurried into the vestibule. He jerked open the front door and sped along the walk to the street. He ducked behind the car and with quick movements divested himself of his costume. Cloak, gloves and glass mask went into the rumble compartment. The next instant Steve Thatcher's hands went to the wheel.

A shot rang sharply near the house. A bullet whizzed through the air. Steve Thatcher jerked a glance backward to see one of the lower windows opening, and a plainclothes man leaping through—after him. Steve's motor roared. He slammed into gear and spurted away.

Another shot. Another. Then Steve Thatcher sent the coupe swerving around the corner—and he was out of range.

In the library a splintering crash sounded. A panel of the closet door cracked out under the terrific impact of Gil McEwen's hard shoulder. He reached through the opening, snatched the chair away, slammed out.

He heard the shots outside the house. He went out the front door at almost a single leap. The plainclothes man with the smoking gun saw him and shouted:

"He's getting away in that car!"

McEwen whirled like a top. He sped toward the edge of the Atwell grounds and crashed through the hedge with a flying leap. As fast as his legs could swing he ran toward the driveway in which the police-cars had been left. There he stopped short and cursed.

The sedan was farthest back in the driveway. Steve Thatcher's roadster was behind it, blocking the way out! McEwen hurried to it—and saw that the ignition was locked! He spun back furiously, slipped behind the wheel of the sedan, and started the motor. With an utter disregard for law and garden, he spurted off around the opposite side of the house, jounced off the curb, twisted the wheel madly, and pressed the gas pedal against the floorboards.

The tires whined as he wrenched the car around the corner. Far away he saw a gleam of red—the tail-light of another car traveling at high speed. McEwen's eyes narrowed shrewdly. At the next corner he turned again; at the next, again. Running then along a street parallel with the fleeing coupe, he let the motor out.

He did not slow for intersections. He slowed for nothing. With the car traveling at its fastest, he plunged along the street. McEwen knew the fleeing coupe could not long keep up its break-neck speed. It must surely slow down to pass through the streets near the business center, or suffer the shots of a traffic policeman. Moreover, the city narrowed like a bottle's neck toward the river. If the fugitive coupe went on, it must soon reach the bridge.

McEwen had the advantage. No traffic officer would try to stop or shoot at his police-car. Deliberately he sent the sedan catapulting through the very center of Great City, its horn blaring. Lights flashed past. Other cars scurried for the curb. Pedestrians fled to the sidewalks. In a matter of seconds McEwen had put the congested district behind him and was racing toward the bridge.

Within a block of it, where two streets intersected in a V, he turned back. He knew that he was ahead of the coupe now. He shot to the next intersection and looked up and down the cross street. The same at the next, and the next. There was no place the coupe could escape him now if it stayed in the open. Sooner or later he was sure to see it.

Soon he did!

Glancing along a dark street lined by warehouses and shabby tenements, he saw a pair of headlights blink out. Instantly McEwen shut off his own, and stopped. He saw a coupe, two blocks ahead. He saw a dark figure climb out of it, turn, and hurry back along the street. He watched with eyes as keen as an eagle's—and saw the dark figure slip into an alleyway.

McEwen got out of his car. He gripped his automatic tightly and began running through the shadows toward the alleyway. When he reached it he paused.

One second before Gil McEwen glanced down the dark alleyway, Steve Thatcher lowered the rear window on the second floor of the abandoned tenement. A quick climb up the rusty fire escape had brought him to it. In the darkness of the bare room he turned, lowering a dark bundle to the floor.

A moment later Steve Thatcher had vanished; the Moon Man had appeared.

He stepped to the closet and opened it. By the glow of a flashlight he worked quickly. He separated the sheaf of banknotes into three parcels.

Each he fastened together with a band of silver paper. He snapped off the flash and turned to the connecting door.

He unlocked it. Slowly he went into the room. Ned Dargan turned at his approach. The Moon Man moved toward the table. From his one black-gloved hand dropped the four packets of currency.

"There you are, Angel."

Dargan silently took up the money. He blinked; he thrust it into his pocket.

"Boss," he said, "I'm worried."

"Why?"

"Just after I came into this place a little while ago, somebody followed me."

"Who?"

"I don't know. I heard the stairs creak. I went down to look around but I didn't find anybody. Cripes, boss, I don't like it!"

"Nor I, Angel. I've an idea that in future we must be more careful. You had better stop delivering the money personally—send it by messenger. And we'd better change our headquarters. I'll phone you, Angel—about a new place."

The muffled voice broke off. The silver-masked head came up. Ned Dargan's breath went sibilantly into his lungs.

From the hallway came a creak!

Then another!

"Somebody's comin' up!" gasped Dargan.

The Moon Man moved. He rounded the table, crossed to the door. With a quick motion he shot a bolt in place.

"Out the rear window, Angel—quick!"

Ned Dargan hesitated. "Say, listen! I ain't goin' to skip and leave you to face the music alone! I'm in this as much as you are, boss!"

"Angel, yours is a true heart. But get out that window right now! I'll take care of myself."

The Moon Man's voice rang commandingly. Dargan did not hesitate again. He hurried into the adjoining room. He slid up the window and ducked through.

"Make it snappy, Angel! Take the car. And if you don't hear from me again —bless you."

"Boss—"

"Snappy, I said!"

Dargan moved. He disappeared downward in the blackness.

The closet door opened silently. Sue McEwen slipped into the room without a sound. She hesitated, peering through the open communicating door. In there, beyond the threshold, was a vague black figure.

It was turning—turning to close the connecting door.

Sue McEwen raised her tiny automatic.

"Please," she said sharply, "throw up your hands!"

The Moon Man stood frozen. Through the glass that masked his face he could see the girl, standing in the glow of the moonlight that was shafting through a window. He could see the glittering gun in her hand—aimed squarely at him.

If she learned—

"Take off your mask!" she commanded.

The Moon Man could not move.

Then a sound—the rattle of a door-knob. The door connecting with the hallway opened. The girl glanced toward it, catching her breath. Then, in a sob—a sob of relief—she exclaimed:

"Dad!"

Gil McEwen came through the door. He stared at his daughter. He turned and stared into the adjoining room, at the black-cloaked figure standing there—the thing with the silver head.

"By damn!" he said.

He sprang toward the Moon Man.

Instantly Steve Thatcher leaped forward. With one movement he slammed the door shut and twisted the key. He leaped back as a gun roared, as a bullet crashed through the wood. He whirled toward the window. He ducked out—cloak and mask and all—and began dropping down the fire escape.

Gil McEwen raised his gun to fire again through the door. But he did not fire. He spun on his heel, sprang into the hallway, leaped down the stairs. He burst out the front door, and whirled into the alley.

He peered at the window above. It was open. He peered at the fire-escape. It was empty. He peered down the black alley. The Moon Man was not in sight.

McEwen sped through the shadows behind the buildings, but soon he paused. Useless to hunt here! As he came back his eyes turned to a row of wooden boxes, each fitted with wooden lids, which sat at the base of the tenement rear wall. They were coal-bins; each of them was large enough to hold a man. With gun leveled he moved toward them.

McEwen paused, grumbling with disappointment. On each bin-cover was a rusty hasp, and on each hasp was a closed padlock, corroded and useless, untouched for perhaps years. He turned away.

McEwen hurried toward the police-car with his daughter following close. A moment later the quiet of that dismal district was broken by the snarling of a motor and the whining of tires as the car spurted away.

After that, for a long time, the alley behind the deserted tenement was silent.

Then, at last, a faint movement. The cover of one of the coal-bins shifted. One edge of it raised—not the front edge, which was fastened by the padlock, but the rear edge, from which the hinges had been removed. Like a Jack-in-the-box, a man came out of it.

"I'll get him! Don't worry—the day's comin' when I'm going to grab that crook!"

So said Gil McEwen as he paced back and forth across the office of Chief of Police Thatcher while bright sunlight streamed into the room—the sunlight of the morning after.

Chief Thatcher sighed and looked worried. His son looked at Gil McEwen solemnly.

"He's got us all buffaloed, that's all. A swell detective I am! The way I climbed out of Atwell's bedroom window, then went chasing an innocent man for blocks, thinking he might be the Moon Man!" In this way Steve Thatcher had explained his absence from the Atwell home immediately following the Moon Man's escape. "Gil, I guess if he's ever caught, you'll have to do it."

"I will do it," said McEwen. "That's my promise. I'm never going to stop until I grab that guy!"

And McEwen, Steve Thatcher knew, meant exactly that.

The chief's son looked at his watch. Inside its cover was a photograph. It was a portrait of Sue McEwen.

"If you only knew what you almost did!" he addressed the picture in silent thought. "If you only knew!"

THE LADY IS A CORPSE!

John D. MacDonald

I

The Buildup

Park Falkner took a deep breath, exhaled half of it, squeezed the trigger slowly. The rifle spat, a sound as vicious as an angry wasp. Far out across the dancing blue water of the gulf the glint of the can jerked, disappeared.

"Enough," he said. He stood the rifle in the corner of the private terrace that opened off his bedroom, the highest terrace of the vast gleaming-white fortress that dominated the two-mile sand spit called Grouper Island, and sometimes Falkner Island.

He stretched and yawned. He was a tall, spare, rock-hard man in his mid-thirties. A tropical disease had eliminated, forever, hair, eyebrows, lashes. His eyes were a startling pale shade against the sun-glossed mahogany of skin. There was a touch of cruelty in the beaked nose and set of the mouth, and humor as well. He wore a faded Singhalese sarong, knotted at the waist.

"I should think it is enough," Taffy Angus said, in her hoarse gamin's voice.

She stood on her hands, her heels against the wall of the house, her white hair hanging in fluid lines to the terrace tiles. She wore a bandanna as a halter, and the jeans, salt-faded to powder blue, were hacked off raggedly at knee length. The position brought a flush under her tan.

"Does that make you a junior leaguer?" Falkner asked.

"Don't be nasty, darling," she said. She dropped onto hands and toes, came gracefully up onto her feet. "I'm an old, old gal, as you well know, and a daily hand-stand has therapeutic values."

Falkner looked at her admiringly. "Bless you! You're my favorite neighbor. When I forget you're forty-two I feel like a cradle snatcher."

"In my prime I came a little after the Gibson Girl, Park. But just to change the subject, how about those people who are coming?"

Park looked at his watch. "The cocktail hour approacheth. Go prettify thyself, wench."

She bowed low. "Sire!" she breathed. Her lips thinned a little. "Park, just for the record—couldn't we drop the Mussolini edict about living dangerously and grow fat and happy in the sunshine on your money? These people you ask here . . ."

They had walked to the hallway door. He opened it and gently shoved her through.

"Okay, okay," she sighed. "I never opened my fool mouth."

Falkner shut the door. His smile faded. Taffy knew as well as he did what had happened those times he had tried stagnation. He had grown restless, irritable. There was no point in trying to add to the fund which was more than he could possibly spend in his lifetime. The company of the equally affluent brought a sickening boredom. And so life had to be spiced by the house parties. An amateur cop or a god of vengeance. Take your choice. Flip a coin. When there's guilt in the air it can be scented, as an animal scents the odor of fear. He looked along the beach to the spot where one of his house guests, Carl Branneck, had killed Laura Hale. For a moment there was revulsion in him and he wanted to call this newest house party off. Then he remembered the report from the New York agency and his interest began to quicken.

He crossed the big room to the built-in record player. He pondered. Atonal stuff would probably help tension along better than anything traditional. He selected two hours of Milhaud, Schonberg and Anthiel, stacked them on the spindle, cut in the amplifiers of the sea-level terrace where they would have cocktails and the amplifiers in the east gardens, and then adjusted the volume down for background.

The only thing in the big room not suitable to a practising Sybarite was the hard, narrow cot on which he slept. There were deep couches, a massive grey-stone fireplace, paintings of a certain freedom in deep niches, softly lighted.

He untied the sarong, dropped it, stepped out of it. The shower stall was big enough to hold a seven-handed poker game. The dressing room adjoined the bath. As he was toweling himself he heard the descending roar of the amphib. That would be Lew Cherezack flying in the ladies, right on schedule.

He selected a grey casual shirt, trousers of a deeper shade of grey. As he walked from the dressing room into the bedroom he heard Lew's knock at the door.

Lew came in, his boxer pup's face slyly wrinkled. He turned with an expansive gesture. "Look what I got!"

A blonde and a brunette. Both tall and grave, with knowing eyes, sweet, wise mouths. "The blonde," Lew said, "is Georgie Wane. Blackie is called June Luce. Say hello to the boss, girls."

"How do you do, Mr. Falkner," they said gravely, almost in unison.

"Nice to see you. You know what the job is?"

Georgie, the blonde, turned spokesman. "If the job includes anything over and above what Mr. Empiro stated, Mr. Falkner, the deal is off. I want that understood."

Park grinned. "I left out a few details, but nothing either of you will balk at. Four young men are coming to visit me. They should be along any minute now. You are each being paid fifty dollars a day. I want you to be as charming as possible to my guests, and I insist that they be kept in ignorance of the fact that I'm paying you. Now here's the additional instruction. There are two of you and four young men. Both of you are lovely enough to have learned how to handle men. I want them played off against each other. I want their beautiful friendship split up in any way you can manage it. Each night, at twelve, you go off duty, as far as I am concerned. Lew will show you your rooms right now. The doors lock. You have the freedom of the place. We're well equipped for amusement here. Tennis, badminton, swimming—in the gulf and in the pool. There is only one restriction. I do not want either of you to leave the island until, in my opinion, the job is done."

"Fair enough," June Luce said. "But who are we supposed to be?"

Park grinned. "Call yourselves nieces of mine. That ought to spice their imaginations a little."

When Lew took them out, Falkner went down two flights to the kitchens. Mrs. Mick Rogers, cook and wife of the battered ex-pug who was Park's man of all work, smiled at him. Francie, the doughy little maid, was at one of the work tables finishing the construction of a tray of canapés.

"Set for the deluge, Mrs. Mick?" Falkner asked.

"What's eight people, counting yourself? A nothing. Practise, yet."

Just then Mick drove in across the private causeway from the mainland with the station wagon. Park walked out the side door of the smaller kitchen and across to the parking space. Mick slid neatly to a stop.

The first one got out, looked hesitantly at Falkner. "I—I'm Bill Hewett. Are you the host?"

Hewett was tall, frail, gangly. Physically he seemed barely out of his adolescence, but his pale-blue eyes were knowing and there was a downward sardonic twist about his wide mouth.

"Glad to see you, Hewett. Let me see. You're the copywriter, aren't you?"

"Right. With Lanteen, Saran and Howliss. I write deathless prose for TV commercials. And this is Prine Smith, our newspaperman."

Prine was dark, stocky, muscular, with a square strong jaw and an aggressive handshake. He said, "We're pretty much in the dark about all this, Falkner, and—"

Park smiled. "Let's talk about it over cocktails."

Hewett broke in. "And this is the actor in the group. Guy Darana."

Guy was tall, with a superb body, classic profile, brown, tightly curled hair. But there was a vacant docility about his expression, an aimless, childlike amiability in his eyes.

"Howya," he said softly in the richest of baritones.

The fourth and last was a wiry redhead with pointed features, a jittery hyperthyroid manner. "You hear that?" he said. "The actor in the group he calls Darana. What about me? What about Stacey Brian? I make with the voice on the radio. Character parts. I work at it. All that hunk has to do is revolve slowly to give them a look at both sides of the profile."

"Radio is a dying medium," Darana said languidly.

Falkner sensed that it was an old argument. He shook hands with Stacey Brian. Mick Rogers was taking the luggage from the tailgate.

"We'll take our own stuff up. Don't bother," Hewett said.

"Mick, you show them their rooms," Park said. "As soon as you all freshen up, find your way down to that front terrace. You can see it from here."

Falkner went back up to his room, started the music, went back down to the front terrace. Mick had already changed to white jacket and he was putting the small terrace bar in order.

"Jittery as hell," Mick said. "All of them. And seven thousand questions. I didn't know nothing."

"Make the drinks heavy on the boys, Mick. And lay off our two hired tootsies."

"Festivities about to begin?" Taffy said, close behind him. Park turned. She wore a white blouse pulled down off her deeply tanned shoulders. The gay skirt swung as she walked. A hammered-silver Aztec bracelet looked impossibly heavy on her slim wrist. Her white hair was a purer form of silver, heavy, thick, molten, alive.

"Jezebel," he whispered. "Lillith! Krithna of the purple seas."

"Don't mind me," Mick said.

"This," said Taffy, "is what you get for inviting little girls who could be my daughters. I have to keep up my morale."

There was no more time for talk then because Stacey Brian came out onto the terrace. The sun was slipping toward the grey-blue gulf. The others came, were introduced. Mick was chanting, "Step up and name it and I can make it. They go down like honey and then kick you behind the ear." Taffy sat on the wall and looked smug. She made Georgie and June look awkward, young, and she made the others look. She winked solemnly at Park Falkner.

Conversation was general, polite, aimless. Georgie Wane had inconspicuously drifted to the side of Guy Darana. He looked at her with mild, sleepy approval.

June Luce said in a silky soft voice, "Miss Angus, I *must* tell you. My mother took me to see you in *Time for Play*, oh, ages ago! I think I was six at the time. That was before you became such a successful model, wasn't it?"

Park concealed his grin by taking a drink. June looked with rapt interest at Taffy. Taffy looked puzzled. She said, "My goodness! Now I *know* I'm ancient! I've just forgotten how to make kitty-talk. Why, if you'd said anything like that to me five years ago I'd have thought of some nasty-nice way to call attention to the way you're letting yourself get . . ." She stopped. "Oh, I mustn't be rude. I'm sorry." She beamed at June.

June's eyes narrowed. "What's wrong with me?"

"Nothing, sister," Mick said. "You're a nice dish. You just ain't bright. You challenged the champ. Now shut up or she'll make you so mad you'll be sick to your stomach and she'll just sit here grinning at you."

Taffy pouted. "He never lets me have any fun."

Prine Smith walked scowling over to Park, planted his feet, his stocky legs spread, his square hand holding the cocktail glass. "Look!" he said. "I don't go for cat-and-mouse games. Maybe I'm not properly civilized. So you're a big enough shot to get strings pulled to get us all off at the same time. So you play on curiosity in a smart enough way to get us all down here, expenses paid. You're out after laughs, Falkner. Let's blow away the smoke screen and talk sense for a minute."

"Glad to," Park said "I guess I'm just a nosy type. I like mysteries. Nine months ago the four of you lived in a big apartment in the Village, two blocks from Sheridan Square. You've split up now, but that was the status quo. Hewett had a girl friend, lovely from all reports, named Lisa Mann. On a hot afternoon, June fourth to be exact, Lisa Mann, using a key that Hewett had given her, let herself into the apartment. A girl named Alicia French happened to see her. Alicia lived in the next apartment down the hall. All four of you were able to prove that you were out that afternoon. The first one to get back to the apartment was Guy Darana. He returned a little after eleven that night. No one has seen Lisa Mann since. Apparently she never returned to her own apartment. There was an investigation. Her parents are well-to-do. I asked you four down here because things like that intrigue me. I hope that during your stay here one of you will, directly or indirectly, admit to his guilt in the death of Miss Mann. Does that blow away the smoke, Smith?"

Prine Smith stared at him. "Are you crazy?"

Hewett said softly, "I know she's dead. I know it. She would have come back."

"Young girls disappear every day," Stacey Brian said. "That she happened to come to our place was coincidental."

June and Georgie listened with great intentness, their mouths open a bit.

"Are you serious, Falkner?" Prine Smith asked, still scowling. "Do you actually think that just by having us down here you can break open a case that the metropolitan police haven't been able to unravel?"

Park shrugged. "It might work that way."

"I don't get it. If one of us should be guilty, which is silly even to think of, wouldn't you have given him warning by now?"

"Of course."

Prine Smith sighed. "Okay. Have your fun. It's your money and I guess you know what you want to do with it. Me, I'm going to relax and enjoy myself."

"That's what you're all supposed to do," Park said amiably.

Hewett had been drinking steadily and with purpose. He said, "Her eyes were tilted a little, and the black lashes were so long they were absurd. She came up to my shoulder and when she laughed she laughed deep in her throat."

"Knock it off," the red-headed Stacey Brian said sharply. "Drop it, Bill."

"Sure," Bill Hewett said. "Sure."

The dusk was upon them and the music was a wry dirge. Taffy's face was shadowed. A gull swung by, tilting in the wind, laughing with disdain. The soft waves were the tired breath of the water. Death whispered in the thin jacaranda leaves.

Hewett laughed with excessive harshness. "Sure," he said again. "Forget her. We're all nice clean young men, we four. Our best friends don't have to tell us, because we've bought the right products. We have built-in value, four-way virtue. Remember the brand name. Go to your nearest crematory and ash for our product. That's a joke, son. But forget little dead girls because little dead girls have nothing in common with these four upright, sterling, time-tested, young men of market-proven value. You can't write a commercial about a dead girl. The product will never sell."

"Shut up, Bill," Guy said.

June hugged her elbows though the dusk was warm. Mick's face, behind the bar, was carved of dark stone. Over on the mainland a diesel train bellowed, a distant creature of swamps and prehistory.

"You people can eat any time," Mrs. Mick said.

II

The Decoy

Taffy lay on her face in the sun by the pool. Falkner sat crosslegged beside her, rubbing the oil into the long, clean lines of her back.

"Mmmm," she said, with sleepy appreciation.

June came to the edge of the pool, her dark hair plastered wet to her head. She hung on and said, "Hello, people."

"How goes the war of the sexes?" Falkner asked.

June pursed her lips. "Georgie has attracted the big handsome hunk, Guy Darana, and also Mr. Muscles, the newspaper guy. I am left with the agile little redhead, who can sling passes from any off-balance position. Hewett is not interested."

"How is Georgie doing?"

"Reasonable. Guy and Prine Smith are now on the beach showing off."

"Back to the battle, June," Park directed. "Take Stacey Brian down there and see if you can confuse things."

June swam away. Taffy yawned. "Legs," she said.

Park moved down a bit, filled his palm with oil. Taffy sat up suddenly. "No, dearie. I think I do this myself," she said. She took the bottle from him. "An aged creature like me has to be well smeared with this glop or the wrinkles pop out like waste land erosion."

As she worked she looked over at him. "Falkner, my man, this little house party makes me feel physically ill. Why don't you break it up?"

"Just when everybody's having so much fun?"

"Fun! They've all got the jumps."

"Sure they have. Right from the beginning each of them, the three un-guilty ones, whoever they might be, have had a dirty little suspicion. They were trying to forget it. Now I've reawakened the whole thing. They're drinking too much and laughing too loudly and they're all wound up like a three-dollar watch. We just wait and see."

Her brown eyes were suddenly very level, very grave. "But you usually add another ingredient, Park."

"This time, too. Maybe tonight."

"Do you really think one of them killed that girl?"

"I do."

"But why?" Taffy wailed.

"Why do people kill people? Love, money, position, hate, envy, passion, jealousy. Lots of reasons."

"Please be careful, Park. Don't let anything happen to you."

"Am I that valuable?"

"With you gone, what would I do for laughs?"

He leaned his hand tenderly against her bare shoulder and pushed her into the pool.

He had gone apart from the others and now he sat on the sand with his hands locked around his knees and he thought of the small thin sound she had made as he struck her and how he had caught her as she fell and listened, hearing the pulse thud in his ears, the hard rasp of his own breathing. She had felt so heavy as he had carried her quickly to where he had planned. She was really a small girl. There was no blood.

Again the dusk, and the music and the cocktails. And Mick behind the bar and Taffy in pale green and all of them sun-stunned by the long hot day, tingling from the showers, ravenous, bright eyed.

"I don't want to be a bore, Park," Prine Smith said, "but what are you accomplishing?"

Falkner shrugged. "Nothing, I guess. Maybe we ought to talk. That is, if nobody objects."

"Talk," Bill Hewett said tonelessly.

"Objectivity," Park said, "is often easier at a distance. The police concentrated on the apartment. That, I feel, was a mistake. The fact that the body has not appeared indicates to me that it was a crime carefully planned. Too carefully planned to assume that the murderer would select a city apartment as the scene of the crime and hope to get away with it, to walk out with the body. She was seen going into the apartment. She was not seen coming out. The apartment had a phone. All four of you were able to prove that you could not possibly have gotten back to the apartment before eleven. But you couldn't prove, had you been asked to do so, that Lisa Mann had not come to you. She could have been summoned by phone to the place where she was murdered and where the body was disposed of so successfully."

"Just how do you dispose of a body successfully?" Prine Smith asked.

"Fire, the sea, chemicals. But, best of all, legally. Death certificate and a funeral."

Something deep inside him laughed. The forest floor had been thick with loam under the needles. He had scraped away the needles, and the edge of the new spade had bitten deeply, easily. The hole was not long enough for her and so he put her in it, curled, on her side, her knees against her chest. Later, after he had patted the earth down, replaced the needles of the pines, he burned the new shovel handle and the old coveralls. He kicked the hot shovel blade over into the brush. No trace. None.

"Why would anyone kill her?" Hewett asked. "Why? She was my girl. There wasn't any question of that. What good would she do anyone dead?"

"Sometimes a man kills," Falkner said, "for the very simple reason that the act of killing gives him pleasure."

"It would be nice to meet him," Hewett said. "Nice." He looked hard, first at Guy, then Prine Smith, then Stacey Brian.

"Off it!" Prine said harshly. "We were over that. You know the three of us, kid. You know we aren't capable of anything like that."

Hewett continued to stare and there was a trace of madness in his eyes. Slowly it faded. He walked over to the bar. Mick filled his glass.

"Hell," said Stacey, "Lisa may be wandering around right now. Amnesia. You can't tell about things like that."

"Sure," Hewett said. "Sure. It could be that." He didn't speak as though he believed it.

On the way to dinner Georgie Wane took Park aside. "Fifty a day," she said, "is nice. I like it. You've got a nice place here. But how about this, Uncle? One of these boys maybe clobbered a girl. It leads one to think. Maybe it's a habit yet."

"Not a habit. Not quite that. Call it a tendency."

"I thought maybe you could tell by looking at hands. I've been looking. No dice, Uncle. I would say Hewett didn't. Beyond that I cannot go. Shouldn't a murderer look like a murderer?"

"I knew one once who could have been your twin, Georgie."

"I can see now how she got in the killing mood," Georgie said.

At three in the morning Falkner awoke at the sound of the first tap on his door. He came completely awake in a fraction of a second. He pulled his robe on as he went to the door. It was Taffy.

She looked small, young, wan in the lamplight.

"You can't sleep either, eh?" she said.

"What's got you down, Taff?" he asked. "Come on in."

They walked out onto the terrace. The wind was directly out of the west. It had sea fragrance.

She said, "You hear about something like this. I mean it's a problem like filling in a nine-letter blank beginning with G meaning a South African herb. Then you meet the people and it's something else again. Gee, they're nice kids. I don't want it to be one of them."

He put his arm around her. "Old Taff, the world mother. She loves everybody. Maybe I'm wrong this time. The agency checked it out pretty carefully, though. Lisa Mann was one of those rare people who make no enemies. No one profited by her death. She was exceptionally striking. Emotions can get wound up pretty tightly."

"If one of them did it," she said softly, "I wonder if he is sleeping right now. I don't see how he could be, knowing that all this is supposed to make him give himself away. I've been watching them so carefully. It's not Hewett, of course. Darana seems like a big sleepy animal. But he *did* come alive when he did that part out of his last play for us. Stacey Brian is an awful nice little guy. Prine Smith is a little quarrelsome, but you sense a certain amount of integrity in him. I can't see him murdering anybody. Park, you *must* be wrong. You *must!*"

"The tension is building, Taff. You can feel it."   ·

She moved out of his arm. "And you love it, don't you? It's bread and wine to you. Park, there's a faint streak of evil in you."

"Man is a predatory animal," he said happily.

She sighed. "Too late to change you now. I should have adopted you when you were a baby."

"Foster mother at the age of seven?"

"I matured early."

He lay rigid in the darkness, remembering, remembering. It was Lisa's fault. No one could get around that. He had told her he loved her. He had told her this affair with Hewett had to stop at once. But she laughed, even when he told her she would be very sorry if she continued to torture him this way. He cried and she laughed again and again. Sin must be punished, whenever it is found. There is no wrong in that, and this great clown, Falkner, can do nothing because there will never be any clue. He knew from the way Hewett acted that Lisa had never told him about the scene.

When Falkner came down, Taffy, Georgie, Guy and Stacey Brian were breakfasting on the patio, shielded from the brisk morning wind. He heard them laughing before he saw them. They made room for him. He had touched his bell a few minutes before coming down. Mrs. Mick brought him his breakfast tray.

Georgie said, "I was telling them about home in Scranton when I had a crush on a guy who drove a hearse. We didn't have any place to be alone so we used to go and neck in the room where they stored the coffins. Well this one time Joey heard the boss coming back unexpected, so what does he do but pop me in a box and shut the lid and then make like he's taking an inventory. My God, I was petrified. It's dusty. I sneeze. The boss says, 'Whassat?' He opens the lid and says, 'Girl, you ain't dead!' Joey, the dope, says, 'Her aunt died. She was looking for a box.' Next time I see Joey, he's driving a bread truck. Terrible kind of breakfast talk, isn't it? But on this house party maybe it isn't so far out of line after all."

"You say you and this Joey had a place where you could be alone," Guy Darana said. "That isn't a question. I'm just thinking out loud."

"Stop making like a detective," Stacey Brian said.

"He's working on our little problem," Taffy said. "Can't you see the look of the hunter?"

"What kind of a detective you want?" Stacey Brian said. "A Jimmy Stewart type? Like this? Wal, I guess all you . . . uh . . . nice people need a . . . uh . . . little detectin' done around here. Or how about an Edward G. Robinson? Like so. Listen to me, sugar. You got to lay it right on the line, see? You're not talking to no small town copper, see? This is the big time, sugar. See?"

They laughed and applauded. The imitations had been uncannily accurate. Hewett came onto the patio and the look of him quenched the high spirits. His eyes appeared to have receded back into his head. His mouth was a thin, bitter line.

"Good-morning, all," he said. "Fun and games?"

"You look rocky, honey," Georgie said.

He smiled coldly. "Bad dreams. Copywriter's dreams. I could see Lisa with her eyes bulging and hands around her throat, but I couldn't tell whose hands."

"Ugh!" Georgie said.

"By the way, Bill," Park said, "I'm assuming that you would like to find out whether or not one of your friends killed her. I'm assuming you'll help by answering questions. Did you and Lisa have a place where you used to go to be alone?"

"It's not any of your business," Hewett snapped.

"Blunt and to the point."

"We did have. A farmhouse so broken down you couldn't go into it. Just the foundation where the barn had been. But you could drive in there and not be seen from the road. She used to pack lunches and we'd picnic there."

"Did you ever go separately?"

"Sure. We'd meet there. She had a car. You know that already. It was in the newspapers. They found the car five days later in a big parking lot on West Forty-first Street. Nobody could say who'd driven it in there. Maybe she did. I used to take a bus out to Alden Village and walk to the farm."

"Did you tell the police that?" Park asked.

"Why should I? She never went there except when we went together, or when we were going to meet there."

"Her body might be there, Hewett. She could have been decoyed there."

"How do you mean?"

"A faked message from you. It wouldn't be hard. Any of your apartment mates could get their hands on your handwriting."

Bill Hewett looked down at his plate. Suddenly he looked no longer young, as though he had donned the mask he would wear in middle age. "I went back once. Alone. It was like visiting some damnable cemetery. The wind whined. She could be there, all right."

"I'll wire the New York police. Tell me the name of the farm or how to direct them to it."

"About a mile and a half north of the village on the left on a curve. Route 8. They call it the Harmon place."

III

Confession

He sent the wire after breakfast. At 11:30 they were all out by the pool. Park was nursing a purpling bruise high on his cheek where Mick Rogers had tagged him heavily during the usual morning workout. Mick hummed as he made drinks. He seemed well pleased with himself.

"Gotta remember to keep that left hand higher, boss," he said, grinning.

Taffy swam effortless lengths of the pool, her brown arms lifting slowly from the pale-green water. Stacey Brian, in deference to his red-headed lack of skin pigmentation was the only one in the shade. Stocky Prine Smith was whispering to June Luce. He was propped up on his elbows. She lay on her back with plastic linked cups on her eyes to protect them from the sunglare. From time to time she giggled in a throaty way. Stacey glared over at them. Georgie Wane was trying to teach big Guy Darana how to make a racing turn against the end of the pool.

From the amplifier came muted music, jazz piano by Errol Garner and Mary Lou Williams and Art Tatum. The last record, one by Garner, had played twice. Park thought of sending Mick up to reverse the stack, but suddenly an idea came to him. He went up himself, walking slowly, planning it in detail. It was based on the sensitive mike he had hooked into the set. Once, when it had been left turned on quite inadvertently, during a party, one couple who had sneaked away from the crowd came back to find that every word, every sound, had blared out above the noise of the music. He had had the mike installed to simplify some of the problems of running the household.

He reversed the stack of records, waited for the music to start, clicked on the mike at the point of a loud remembered chord in the music, hoping that it wouldn't be heard. He picked the table mike up gingerly and carried it away from the set. He set it on the bedside table, picked up the phone and dialed the number of the hotel. Before anyone could answer, he pushed the receiver down with his fingers.

"Give me Mr. Norris' room please. 412 I think it is. . . . Hello. Lieutenant Norris? This is Falkner. I guess your trip hasn't been a waste after all. Yes, I think I know who our man is. Right. He'll crack under the strain and we'll have something definite to go on. Yes, I'll call you just as soon as—"

The door burst open and Mick came running in, panting from the run up the stairs. "Hey, the mike's on! Every word is coming over the—"

Park reached out quickly and clicked the mike off.

He grinned. "Thanks, Mick." He hung up the phone.

Mick's eyes widened with comprehension. "So! A fake, is it?"

"Did you hear what I said?"

"No. I started running when I heard you dial."

Park repeated the conversation. "What do you think?" he asked.

Mick scrubbed his heavy jaw with his knuckles. "It ought to make the guy pretty uneasy. I can't figure which one it could be. Maybe it isn't any one of the three."

"I'm placing my bet that it is one of them."

They went back down. The atmosphere had changed. Hewett was the color of watery milk under his two-day tan. He stood with his fists clenched, staring at his friends, one by one. June had sat up, moved a bit away from Prine Smith. Taffy stood near the diving tower, toweling herself. Georgie sat alone on the edge of the pool, her feet in the water. Guy Darana stood behind her, his eyes slitted against the sunlight, looking half asleep. Stacey Brian looked at Hewett and said, "Easy, boy. Easy."

"I'm terribly sorry that happened," Park said. "It shouldn't have happened. Like a fool I forgot the mike was on. I'm afraid I've forewarned the man who killed Lisa Mann."

Hewett walked over to Park. "Who is it?" he said. "Tell me who it is."

"Not quite yet, Bill," Park said soothingly.

"Tell me, damn you!"

"I don't think I'm wrong, but there's always that chance. I'm not ready to tell you. You're in no emotional condition to handle yourself properly if I should tell you."

Hewett threw his fist full at Falkner's face with an almost girlish ineptitude. Park caught the fist in the palm of his hand and squeezed down on it. Hewett's mouth changed with the impact of the sudden pain.

"Don't try that again," Park said.

Hewett yanked his hand free, turned without a word and walked across to the house.

Everyone started to make bright, shallow conversation to cover the awkwardness. Taffy came over to Park and lowered her voice so that only he could hear her. "Dirty pool, friend," she said. "Very dirty pool."

"I don't understand, Taff."

"The music suddenly got louder and then faded back again. The mike stands near the set. You should have carried it over to the phone before turning it on."

"You know, you'd be a very difficult type to be married to."

"I don't think I can quite class that as a proposal. You and your mythical lieutenants!"

He grinned with a flash of white teeth against the deep brown of his face. "That's where I got you, Taff. There is a Lieutenant Norris and he is registered at the hotel and he is from New York. But he's on an extradition case. If I can't give him something to get his teeth into by tomorrow night, he has to start back with his man."

He fell silent and the talk around him was meaningless. It had to be a clever trap. There was nothing Falkner could know. Nothing. But the man was clever. It took cleverness to locate a body sixteen hundred miles away, a body that had been searched for by experts. They might not find it. Probably they would. He hadn't risked going back to see if the dirt had settled. The laboratories would go to work on the body. He had carried the body a short distance. Could some microscopic bit of evidence have been left?

Dusk broke up the badminton doubles. The last set had been Guy Darana and June Luce against Georgie and Stacey Brian. Everyone had played in their swim suits. Brian's wiry quickness had made up for Darana's advantage in height. Georgie was nursing a swollen underlip which, in some strange fashion, she had managed to club with her own racket.

All four were winded. Mick had wheeled the rolling bar out onto the edge of the court, plugging in the ice compartment at the outlet near the tennis court floodlights.

"Sometimes," Stacey said, "it's good to become bushed. When the infantry reluctantly let me go, I swore I'd never get physically tired again for the rest of my life. Here I am, running around in the sun and beating on a cork with feathers sticking out of it."

"Infantry!" Darana said with heavy disgust. "Why didn't you pick yourself a branch?"

"Don't tell me what you were, Guy," Georgie said. "Let me guess. A fly boy. A hot pilot. A tired hat and nine rows of ribbons."

"Not a hot pilot," Guy said. "I pushed tired old C-40's and 47's around for the ATC. I was too big to fit into a fighter with any comfort. But old Prine here had the real deal. Warm food, good bed. All the luxuries. Of course they sank a couple ships under him, but that Navy was it."

"How about Bill?" June asked. "What was he?"

"OWI. Hell, I wish he'd come down out of his room and stop sulking."

Taffy giggled. "You know what our jolly host did for his country?"

"Whatever it was, I bet it was a job smarter than the one Stace picked," Guy said.

Before she could reply Hewett came walking out of the grey darkness. "Sorry I blew my top," he murmured.

"Quite all right," Park said.

"You see," Hewett continued, "if I lose my head I won't get my cracks at whoever killed Lisa. I've got to stay calm. I have it all figured out. As soon as you know for sure, you'll tell that lieutenant. But maybe I can find out for sure before you do, Falkner. And if I do, he might not stand trial, whoever he is. I'm beginning to get an idea."

Stacey Brian stood up and shivered. "That wind's getting cooler. Or have I got a chill just because there's a murderer in the house? Good-bye, you people. I'm off for a shower."

The group slowly split up until only Prine Smith and Park Falkner were left. Mick wheeled the bar inside. Prine Smith's face was in shadow.

He said, "I can almost see your point. A dilettante in crime. Gives you a purpose in life, maybe." His tone was speculative. "But human beings aren't puppets, Falkner. They take over the strings. They make up their own lines. I've done some checking. You've had considerable violence here on your Grouper Island. Do you sleep well at night?"

"Like a baby."

"I've been in the newspaper game longer than you'd think to look at me, Falkner. I can smell violence in the air. Something is going to bust open here."

"It's possible."

"What precautions are you taking?"

"I think that would be pretty valuable information to someone."

"Don't be a fool! You can't possibly suspect me."

Falkner was surprised at the trace of anger in his own voice. "Don't try to judge me or my methods, Smith. Don't set yourself up as an arbiter of my moral codes or lack of same. A girl died. There's the justification."

In the darkness he could sense Prine Smith's grin as he stood up. "Glad to know you sometimes doubt yourself, Falkner. Maybe I like you better."

He went off to the house. Falkner stayed a few minutes more.

Sometimes there is safety in inaction, he thought. And sometimes it is wise to move quickly. He locked the door, opened the toilet-article kit, took out the small bottle of white powder. It was cool against his palm. They said that later the lips smelled of almonds. He wondered.

Bill Hewett looked full into the eyes of his friend. The others were by the beach fire. Hewett knew that he had drunk too much. Falkner's room wavered dizzily. He struggled for soberness. He said thickly, "You said you could tell me who killed Lisa."

"I can."

"What's that you've got? A record? What have you been doing here? It seems to be a funny place to meet, the host's room."

"Yes, this is a record. I got here first. I made a record on his machine."

"You mean you say on the record who killed her?" Hewett asked.

"That's right. Here. Have a drink. Then we'll listen to it. Together."

"Can't you just tell me?" Hewett asked plaintively. He tilted the glass high, drained it.

"Now I can tell you. I'll put this record on the spindle. Like this."

"Who is it? Who killed her?"

"You did, Hewett. You killed her. Can't you remember?"

"What kind of a damn fool joke is this?"

His friend went quickly toward the door, opened it, glanced out into the hall. He turned. "Good-bye, Bill. Give my regards to Lisa. My very best regards. I think you might live another ten seconds—after that drink I gave you."

The door shut softly. Hewett stared at the empty glass. It slipped from his hands to the rug, bounced, didn't break. He put both hands to his throat and turned dizzily. The moon was bright on the small private terrace. He saw a brown arm, almost black in the moonlight, reach over the terrace wall, saw a man pull himself up quickly.

Hewett fell to his knees.

* * *

They were all near the fire, the ember glow reddening their faces. Mick was telling them how the lights went out in Round 5 during his bout with John Henry Lewis.

Park came close to them. Mick looked over and stopped talking.

"What is it?" Taffy asked quickly.

"I've just told Norris to come over. The local police will be here too. Our little house party is over, I'm afraid."

Georgie Wane looked around the circle. "Where's Bill?" she demanded.

"Bill is in my room. He's very dead, and not at all pretty. Poison."

He heard the hard intake of breath. Taffy said, "Oh, no!"

"Before he did it he left his confession. I think you might like to hear it. Mick, go on up and play the record that's on the spindle right now. Pipe it onto the front terrace. We'll walk over there to listen."

Mick went across the sand and into the darkness. They stood up slowly, full of the embarrassed gravity with which any group meets the death of one of their number. Taffy came next to Park in the darkness as they walked, her fingers chill on his wrist.

"No, Park. I can't . . . believe it."

They stood on the front terrace, close to the sea. The amplifier made a scratching sound. The voice that came was thin, taut with emotion. There was no need for the voice to identify itself.

"I can't pretend any more. She said she was through with me. She told me she was fed up with neurotics. I had her meet me at the farm. Falkner trapped me about that. I took a shovel and coveralls. I came up behind her, struck her with the flat of the shovel blade. I carried her fifty feet into the woodlot and buried her there. I burned the shovel handle and the coveralls. I drove her car back and put it in the busiest lot I could find and tore up the check. I couldn't face the thought of her going to someone else, someone else's arms around her and lips on hers. I'm not sorry. Not sorry at all. . . ."

There was a dry, rasping sound of needle on empty grooves and then silence as Mick lifted the arm.

"Crazy," June Luce said softly. "Plain crazy. Gee, the poor guy."

Sirens shrilled through the distant night, coming closer. Park said quickly, "Go on into the front living room, all of you. They'll take the body out and then Norris will probably want to talk to you. I see no reason why it might not be simple routine."

IV
The Man from the Dead

It was a full forty-five minutes after the cars had swung across the private causeway and parked that Lieutenant Norris came into the front living room. He was a tall, stooped, sick-looking man, with a face that showed the lean fragility of the bone structure underneath. He wore an incongruous dark suit and his eyes were remote, disinterested.

"Let's get it over," he said. "You're Smith? No? Oh, Darana. And you're Brian. Okay, I got you all straight now, I guess. I can question you all at once. Did Hewett seem depressed since you've been here?"

Several people said yes at the same moment.

Georgie said, "The guy was pretty antisocial. I thought it was because his gal had disappeared. I've been wrong before."

"Now," said Norris, "about this beach party tonight. Anybody see him leave?"

There was silence. Park said, "The sea was warm. About half the group were swimming from time to time. You couldn't really keep track of any individual. I guess that at one time or another every one of us wandered off. I found Hewett, as I told you, when I went up to my room to change to dry clothes. It was getting just a little chilly."

Prine Smith crossed his arms. "Let's drop this patty-cake routine, shall we?"

Norris stared coldly at him. "What's on your mind?"

"Hewett was drinking too much. That record sounds too sober to me. And I knew Hewett inside and out. I say nuts to this suicide angle. Lisa was his gal and she meant every look she gave him. I'm the only one outside of Bill and Lisa that knew the wedding date was set. I thought Falkner's idea was a bust for a time, but I've felt the tension growing here. And now I think I know the angle." He spun and took two steps toward Stacey Brian. "Come on, kid. Make imitations for the people. Show 'em how you can be Jimmy Stewart, or Edward G. Robinson—or Bill Hewett. Maybe you were Bill Hewett over the phone when you got Lisa to go out there to that farm. Bill never killed himself. He had more guts than any of you know. For my money, Stacey, you got him up there to Falkner's room, made the record yourself and slipped him a drink with the stuff in it."

Stacey Brian turned as white as a human being can turn. He came out of the chair like a coiled spring suddenly released. His fist spatted off Prine Smith's mouth before Smith could lift his arms. Park leaped in and grabbed Brian from behind. He struggled and then gave it up.

"Will you be good?" Park asked.

Stacey Brian nodded. Park released him.

Stacey said in a level monotone, "Any guy who can think up that kind of an angle probably did it himself. He was on the make for Lisa ever since the first time Bill brought her around. We all knew that. We didn't tell the cops because we didn't think he was a guy to kill anybody. Sure I make imitations. But if any of you think I did a thing like that, you can all go to hell in a basket."

Norris drawled, "You guys can slap each other around until you're tired. It doesn't make no never mind to me. I got my case solved and I like the solution. Hewett smeared his gal and covered it nice. I got the dope today they found the body just like he said in the record."

"But, damn it, man," Prine said, "can't you see that Brian could put that same dope on the record and make it sound just like Hewett?"

Stacey said, "Smith, I don't want to ever see you or talk to you or hear your name again as long as I live. I'm going back to New York just as fast as I can get there and I'm packing my stuff and moving out of that apartment we got two months ago."

"Good!" Smith said.

"You sound like a couple of babies," Guy Darana said.

"He's a slick one, he is," Prine said. "He even did his imitations here for us, because he knew that if he didn't do them somebody would wonder why he'd given up his pet party trick."

Norris sighed. "I'm tired. You people are trying to foul up my case. Sleep on it, will you? Nobody leaves the island. I'll be back in the morning. They've taken the body to town." He looked around with a sudden, surprising, wry amusement. "Have fun," he said. He turned and left the room.

Guy whispered to Georgie and then said to the room at large, "We're taking a walk. The air is fresh out there."

"Be back in half an hour," Park said. "We'll all meet at the enclosed patio at the rear of the house. I think that by then we'll be able to talk calmly and iron out this trouble."

"Never!" Stacey Brian said calmly.

"But you'll give it a try."

"If it'll amuse you. It's your party."

Park walked off the terrace out into the night and sat in the sand, his back against the concrete sea wall. He heard a sound and looked up over his right shoulder. Taffy stood with her elbows on the wall, her head bent, her thick white hair falling toward him, a sheen in the pale moonlight behind her.

"He's right, you know. Smith," she said. There was utter sadness in her voice.

"Don't fret, Taff."

"The poor lost man. Poor Bill. This is a night for losing things. We're lost too, you know."

"How do you mean that?"

"I could go along in your plans before this happened, Park. I told myself you were doing good. But I really didn't believe it. Now a boy is dead, Park. And boys stay dead a long time. It's been nice."

He found her hand. "Trust me."

"I want to. But I can't. Not any more. Because this thing that happened is wrong. Norris is a fool. You're being a fool too."

"I don't want to lose you, Taff."

"But you did. When Bill died you lost me."

"Old Taff. The world mother, the open warm heart for lost dogs and children."

"Don't make bright talk. Just kiss me and say good-bye like a little man."

"You can't go now."

"I'll stay until morning, but this is a good time for good-bye."

When he came in with Taff they were all in the enclosed patio. The wall lights were on, the bulbs of that odd orange that repels insects.

"Post mortem," June Luce said. "A post mortem by my generous uncle who pays me fifty bucks a day to grace his lovely home." She laughed. There was liquor in her laugh.

"Please shut up, dear," Georgie said.

"Well," Park said, "it all seems to be over. And I, for one, am satisfied with Norris' conclusion."

"I'm happy for you," Prine Smith said. "You're easily satisfied."

Guy Darana stood with his big arm around Georgie's slim waist. He rubbed his chin against her sleek golden head.

Taffy wore the look of a lost child. Mick, by the corner bar, was glum.

"He didn't die easy," Park said. "It was quick, but from the look of his face there wasn't anything easy about it."

"Is this discussion necessary?" June asked. "Even at fifty a day there's a limit."

"I'm switching to bourbon, Mick," Stacey said.

June glanced beyond Falkner to the stone arch that led out into the side garden. She made a sound. It was not a scream. It was harsh and long and came from the deepest part of her lungs.

Park moved to one side.

Guy Darana had his arm around Georgie Wane's waist. With one heave of his shoulders he flung her to the side. She spun, tripped and fell hard.

Bill Hewett, ghastly pale in the archway, his mouth twisting so that lips were pale worms entwining, said, "I left some unfinished business behind, I think."

Prine Smith stood without a movement, with no expression at all on his face. Stacey Brian stood with the glass in his hand. His hand shut and the glass made a brittle sound. A clot of blood dropped and spattered on the stone.

Guy Darana stood with his hands flattened against the wall behind him. "No," he whispered. "No!"

His big pale hand flickered in the light, disappeared, reappeared with the glint of metal. Bill Hewett took a slow step toward Guy. The gun spoke, a slapping, stick-breaking sound, metallic in the enclosed patio. He fired pointblank at Bill Hewett. He fired six times. The hammer clicked three more times. The gun dropped onto the stone. Hewett took another slow step toward Darana, grinning now, grinning in a ghastly fashion.

Darana's big, handsome face lost its human look. The features seemed to grow loose and fluid. Knee bones thudded against the stone. It was as though he were at prayer, worshiping some new and inhuman god. His lips moved and he made sounds, muted little growlings and gobblings that were zoo sounds.

Norris came in from the garden, as though walking into a drugstore for a pack of cigarettes. "Okay," he said, "print that. It ought to do it. On your feet, Darana."

Guy looked up at him and said, the words pasted stickily together, "There's nothing you can do to me because it is part of me to avenge and destroy. There is sin and weakness in the world. Weakness and sin. They have to be punished. I'm an instrument of death. The garden and the word. The time is now. All the rich orchard time of turning and no man is known who can unbend the others." He glared around at them, then slipped down onto his haunches and began idly patting the stone with the palm of his hand, cooing softly, crooning to himself.

"Ain't it the way," Norris said with disgust. "You go to all this trouble and what do you get? He flips the wig just as you grab him. Well, maybe we piled it on a little strong. Help me, you guys. If he's violent he'll be tough to handle."

But Guy Darana let himself be led out placidly. He looked vacantly at Georgie on the way out. She put the back of her hand to her lips and her eyes were wide and terrified.

*   *   *

They gathered in Falkner's room. It was two in the morning. The fireplace fire drove back the night chill.

Georgie's burned knee and elbow had been bandaged. She had lost almost all her casual flippancy.

"What *can* you believe about people?" Prine Smith asked. "I had Darana pretty well evaluated in my own mind. A big handsome hunk with more of a spark of acting talent than he was willing to admit. I had him pegged to go a long way. Hollywood had nibbled once but he didn't like the offer. How do you figure it, Park?"

Falkner shrugged. "Women came running to him. He must have alternated between thinking he was a minor god and feeling a strong sense of guilt, probably the result of a strict childhood home life. Guilt can do odd things. He must have been on the edge when he made a play for Lisa. She turned him down. That was something new. He brooded over it. The one woman he wanted he couldn't have, and Hewett's happiness with her was like a blow in the face. He was an actor. He could do tricks with that voice of his. We'll never know for sure, probably, but I think he phoned her pretending to be you, Bill. I guess you can fill out the rest of the details. He justified himself by saying to himself that he was punishing her for a sin."

Park turned to Prine again. "Our precautions were very simple. Lew and Nick took turns going through your rooms deactivating anything that looked lethal. Lew was the one who found the gun while Guy was swimming. He reloaded it with frangible blanks that look like the McCoy. Mick found the unlabeled bottle. He emptied it on a hunch, washed it, refilled it in the kitchen. While we swam at night, Lew was out beyond the breaker line in the *Nancy* watching with night glasses to see that nothing funny happened. I saw Darana talk to Bill and then leave in the direction of the house. In a little while Bill followed along. I followed him. When I saw him go into my room I went down onto the terrace below mine and climbed up. Guy left the room as I came over the wall. Poor Bill thought he'd really been poisoned. When I convinced him that he hadn't he was shaken enough to be willing to play ball with us. I called Norris and explained it to him. We needed a little more on Darana than Bill's naked word. Well . . . we got it."

Hewett said, "It's over now, I guess. I knew all along she must be dead. But because I didn't know who or how, I couldn't relax. Now I can start rebuilding."

"Can you use any help?" June asked, smiling.

Hewett grinned. "I'll consider it."

The group broke up. Park promised transportation after breakfast. Taffy and Georgie Wane lingered behind. Georgie gave Taffy a quick look and then she smiled at Park, saying, "Here I am, wounded. Look, does a girl get a chance to stay here for a few days? Recuperation, we could call it, and it won't cost you fifty a day. Only what I can eat."

Park looked expressionlessly at Taffy. "Why, I suppose that it would be—"

Taffy gave Georgie the warmest smile in her book. "Darling, Mr. Falkner intends to give you a little bonus to take care of the scraped knee and elbow. I really think it would be best for all concerned if you went with the others."

Georgie shrugged. "Sorry, boss. I didn't see any sandwich signs on him. 'Night, all."

Taffy shut the door firmly. She turned, her hands on her hips. "If you think for one minute I'd let you keep that—that *female* here after the others go . . ."

Park gave her a look of outraged innocence. "But you told me we were through!"

"Well, we aren't. Any argument?"

He didn't give her an argument. He was too busy.

THE LUNATIC PLAGUE

Donald Wandrei

The big black police limousine nosed toward the curb, stopped in front of 13 State Street. From it emerged a man of slender stature, scarcely more than five feet six, whose truculence and erect bearing suggested former military service. He was reddish of face, with graying hair, but carried his forties like twenties.

Inspector Frick, in charge of the homicide bureau, ran a large white handkerchief across his forehead as he walked toward the stone mansion.

In the smoky haze that passed as atmosphere, the outlines of buildings shimmered. The tall apartment houses lining Riverside Drive seemed outlined in flame against the sun and shaken by tremors of earth. New York was suffering one of the annual heat waves that made seven million people wonder why they'd ever arrived at or stayed in that infernal congestion of dirt, detestable odors, torrid humidity, and air, street, and harbor pollution.

Inspector Frick punched the bell under a brass plate, green with verdigris that almost concealed the name: I. V. Frost.

He heard no bell ring, no sound, but after perhaps ten seconds the door opened magically and Frick walked in. He had made many visits to Frost in the past, but he never failed to be impressed by the quiet efficiency of the different inventions and scientific discoveries that Frost utilized.

The door closed behind the inspector. He cocked an eye resentfully at the Buddha that squatted in a niche at the end of the hallway. He disliked the inhumanly human eye that turned in mid-air with a slow, unpleasant motion. He could not imagine why any one would collect artificial eyes as a hobby. Frost may have been serious or sardonic when he once remarked, "The eyes I place around me are a constant reminder of the steady vigilance needed for all emergencies."

Frick sighed when he entered the library.

The professor's streamlined assistant, Jean Moray, looked up from the desk at which she sat, and waved him to the laboratory.

Some men snub the fates that favor them. Frost, an eagle in his solitude, lived purely for the thrill of the man hunt, the pursuit of knowledge, the application of logic and science to the solution of crime. At no time had he shown awareness that one of the most desirable of unattached sirens served him. Jean Moray's exotic style of beauty and alert mind made her a distinct asset.

He entered the laboratory. Frost sat on a stool at one of the tables. With his great height and thinness, his ascetic face in profile against a window, he looked like a specter or the incarnation of a bird of prey.

A low hum, persistent, steady, droned from the table. Approaching closer, Frick saw a mass of steel, armor casing around what resembled a dynamo.

Frost, engrossed in it, drawled, "What's the difficult problem now? I'll listen while you talk. Unfortunately, the centrifuge will require my attention for a few minutes."

The inspector asked in a slightly nettled tone, "What makes you think I'm not just paying a social call? You haven't even looked at me."

"Your own reply, if nothing else. I might remark that one does not necessarily scrutinize perfume in order to detect its scent, or peer at an egg to ascertain its taste, or stare at a radio set to determine its tonal qualities."

"True enough. Also, I can look at your machine without getting any idea what it's for."

"The centrifuge? This particular specimen, an improved model, which I started two hours ago, has reached a speed of 300,000 r.p.m. It works somewhat on the principle of a cream separator. There's a quartz observation piece and a light-beam reflector to watch what happens. At present the cell contains several drops of blood from which the red coloring matter, hemoglobin, has filtered out."

"What good is it?"

"It permits the measurement of molecular structures, and the separation of a liquid into the components. It may lead to new discoveries or processes; it may prove of help in crime detection. Thus far I've tried it out on blood, alcohol beverages, saline solutions, and cellulose compounds.

"You haven't yet stated the purpose of your visit."

"Confound it, Frost, you always have some new gadget or curiosity that takes other people's minds off their business, and then you complain because they forget what they came for," the inspector protested. He added with seeming irrelevance, "Did you ever hear of a plague of lunacy? Is there such a thing as an epidemic of insanity, or contagious madness?"

While the inspector spoke, Frost's right hand had been moving toward the control of the centrifuge, but it stopped before reaching its objective and darted toward a pocket of his leather jacket. It came out with a long cigarette. When lighted, the cylinder sent up fumes of pungent aroma. So far as the inspector knew, that gesture was Frost's only invariable habit. He never smoked, unless a knotty problem aroused his interest, and he never smoked anything but the excessively long cylinders which he manufactured himself.

Frost stated, "Insanity as such is not communicable in the sense that various diseases are. However, some infections result in mental derangement, and the person contracting an infection of that kind could loosely be said to have caught insanity as a secondary product of a primary disease.

"Mob hysteria, war fever, lynch-gang fury, and other mass demonstrations have been considered proof by several psychologists that mental disorders can be contagious, but other authorities have challenged the conclusions. In meanings rather than words, there has not yet appeared the slightest evidence that lunacy can be epidemic, or that a normal person can catch it from a victim of insanity."

"I was afraid so. Just the same, the whole town's gone crazy in the past week. A couple of queer cases started me thinking yesterday afternoon; I spent all of to-day on an investigation, and now I've got a collection that reads like the records of a lunatic asylum. Listen to these:

"About a week ago, on August 3rd, the riot squad had a call to Fifth Avenue and Sixteenth Street during the noon hour. A jam of hundreds surrounded an elderly chap who was pushing a peanut up the sidewalk with his nose. The crowd, of course, jeered and kidded him.

"He refused to call off the act. The police arrested him on charges of disturbing the peace. Then we found we had dynamite on our hands, or a lemon, depending on how you look at it. The man turned out to be Harmin, president of the big White Trust Co. Nobody in the crowd or the riot squad had recognized him, fortunately, and we squashed charges. A couple of evening papers carried the story, but they didn't know Harmin's identity.

"Do you know what he said when we asked him why he pushed a peanut up the street with his nose? Harmin made the silly answer, 'Oh, I thought it was a jelly bean.' " Inspector Frick snorted.

"On August 5th, the homicide squad had a run in Queens. A girl went up in her private plane, and jumped overboard—without a parachute. Her plane crashed a mile away. If you remember the headlines, she was Paula Van Wyke, heiress to the Van Wyke coffee millions. She had everything she wanted, everything to live for. A host of activities took up all her time. Popular and attractive, with plenty of dates, she had fallen in love recently and set the wedding for next month. There simply wasn't any reason for her to commit suicide by diving out of a plane, but she did."

II

The inspector continued: "Before nine a.m. on August 6th, radio cruisers answered a call to the main offices of the Oil Products Co. When the first of the clerical staff arrived that morning, they found the rooms littered with frogs—hundreds of them—hopping all over the place. Nobody would admit anything about how the frogs got there. Nothing was stolen and no other damage done. We decided that some disgruntled employee had caused the trouble, but to-day I learned that the office manager, a fellow named Gildreth, received an order to take a compulsory three months' leave of absence to recover from a nervous breakdown. He's already at sea. Though other officials won't talk, they evidently consider him to blame for the frogs.

"On the day following, at about two o'clock in the afternoon, the next incident happened. Suspicious actions by a well-dressed, distinguished-looking man attracted the attention of a patrolman on duty in Central Park. The man carried a dazzling lamp—in spite of the bright sunshine. He walked along slowly with the lamp aimed at his feet. The patrolman went up to question him.

"He said he was looking for a million dollars.

"The patrolman didn't believe him and asked if he'd lost cash or securities.

"The man blurted, 'Oh, I didn't lose anything. I was just looking to see if I could find a million dollars.' Then he said the darkness made it impossible for him to see without the torch. He claimed to be the society sportsman, Elerton, but had nothing to prove it. The officer arrested him for observation.

"At headquarters, they allowed the man to make a phone call. His secretary came down soon after and identified him as Elerton. Elerton refused to explain his goofy stunt. He wouldn't commit himself one way or another when they offered him an easy 'out' by asking if he'd paid off one of those freak bets you sometimes hear about."

Frost lighted a new cigarette from the butt of the former as the inspector turned another page.

"The evening of August 8th, a Saturday, saw a good crowd at the Plaisir, one of the Broadway night clubs. Most of them don't do much business on week-ends in summer, because the people with money go to the country or travel abroad, but the Plaisir picks up what's left, besides the out-of-town buyers and tourist traffic. It's a theater, made into a restaurant with the usual stuff—cover charge, extras, floor show, etc.

"It's one of the places we keep a plain-clothes detective on duty.

"That night he watched arrivals in the lobby for a while, and talked a little with the hat-check girl at 11:30. Her name is Loy Loris, or at least that's what she calls herself. The detective then gave the rest of the premises a looking over and drifted back to the entrance around midnight. Then he stood by a palm plant and kept an eye on the hat-check booth.

"This girl, Loy Loris, is a black-haired beauty who probably just missed being a featured entertainer. She wears a costume: white satin trousers and a scarlet silk blouse with a gold heart on it. She looks stunning in it.

"Well, she had taken the blouse off. She wore a circlet around her throat. Tied to it by a piece of thread, an oversized fishhook hung at her breast. The detective figured it for a new stunt by the management—until he saw her search all the stuff that had been checked.

"He walked over to make the arrest.

"She asked on what grounds.

"For larceny, he explained.

"Loy Loris protested, 'Oh, I didn't steal anything. I put a dollar bill in each of the hats!'

"The detective investigated, though he didn't believe her, and by the shades below, that's exactly what she had been up to! While they chewed the rag, a man came in alone, a fellow who'd been there often, a ward politician named Mike Hoolan.

"Hoolan said to the girl, 'I didn't wear a hat so I'll check this two-dollar bill, but I want some change.'

"The girl took the bill. She unfastened the fishhook and gave it to him. She said, 'Here's your change.'

"Hoolan's hands started trembling. He pricked his thumb, but finally managed to put the fishhook in his pocket. He turned around and went out. Loy Loris picked up her blouse and got into it.

"The goggle-eyed detective couldn't drag a word out of her. Before and after that one incident, she acted normal. The management didn't like it. They almost fired her, but after raising a fuss they let her stay on."

Frick turned to another page. "Yesterday afternoon, August 11th, the last of these things happened—but first I'll have to go back a little. The night before, a radio cruiser, drifting along Greenwich in the produce-market district, spotted a man fidgeting on a street corner. He loitered around, seemingly ill at ease. The cruiser circled the block.

"As the two patrolmen drew near him a second time, ready to question him, a thin, swarthy figure popped out of the shadows and blasted away three times. The first man died before he hit the sidewalk. The officers got the killer, but couldn't find the gun. They combed the vicinity, and later squads of police searched every inch within blocks. They didn't locate the weapon.

"During the half-block chase to catch the killer, he either tossed the gun to an accomplice hidden in one of the dark store entrances he passed, or he slung the gun away and it landed on one of the trucks going by.

"The murderer was Gus Berber, a gangster and racketeer whose power has been growing recently. But here's the fantastic part: The pockets of the dead man contained nothing except two wet, dead goldfish. Berber claimed he had never laid eyes on the man before, couldn't identify him, happened to stroll by through pure chance and tough luck, and had no connection whatever with the murder.

"We identified the dead man later through an appeal to the missing persons bureau from his wife.

"She told us he received a telephone call about nine that night; it seemed to upset him. He went out a while after, for an hour's walk, so he explained. She grew worried when he failed to return by midnight. She couldn't account for the goldfish. It developed that he had gone to his room before leaving the apartment. He removed everything in his pockets and took two goldfish out of a bowl.

"I know; I know it sounds crazy, but that's the way it happened," the inspector insisted as Frost sat up straighter with an expression of what he mistook to be skepticism. "The murdered man was Fitzroyd, the orchestra conductor. So far as we've learned, Berber and Fitzroyd actually were complete strangers to each other.

"We quizzed Berber the rest of that night and all the next morning, without making a dent in his story.

"His lawyer went to Judge Hagerman in the afternoon for a habeas corpus writ. Judge Hagerman made an astounding ruling. He ordered Berber's release on the ground of lack of evidence. Two police officers eyewitnessed the murder. They didn't lose sight of the killer for a second during the chase. They caught him cold. But, said Judge Hagerman, they couldn't show a motive and they hadn't found a weapon. By their own admission, Berber must have had a gun; but, since he didn't have a gun, he couldn't be the killer. We couldn't charge him or hold him for trial until we found the gun and linked it by fingerprints or serial numbers to Berber."

Frick unconsciously tightened his right fist and beat the knuckles against his left palm after he laid the portfolio aside.

"There they are, Ivy. If you can make sense out of them or throw light on them you'll do us a favor that I, in particular, won't forget. It's a mess. The very fact that we are the police hampers us badly here. We can't file charges against most of the persons involved. We can't use pressure to make them talk. They obstinately refuse to admit anything.

"I spent all of to-day gathering these reports. I've personally seen a few of the people concerned. I got exactly nothing out of them. I've an idea the episodes are all linked together, but how and for what purpose I don't know. Of course, it's possible that there's no connection between them, but if there isn't, they're the most incredible set of coincidences in my experience. Otherwise, it looks to me like a plague of lunacy."

"Neither coincidence nor lunacy." Frost glanced at a clock. "Five minutes of six. By to-morrow morning at this hour, and perhaps sooner, I'll have the mystery solved."

An air of doubt crossed the inspector's face. "Aren't you stretching your optimism quite a bit? How could you even begin to get around to all these people in twelve hours?"

Frost lifted his eyebrows. "I have not the slightest intention of bothering myself with the individuals concerned."

"But damn it all, how can you say that?" Frick checked the names off on his fingers. "There's the financier, Harmin, who pushed the peanut with his nose. Paula Van Wyke, the heiress, dived out of a plane. The business executive, Gildreth, specialized in frogs. The society sportsman, Elerton, used a high-powered torch to hunt for a million dollars in broad daylight. The hat-check girl, Loy Loris, wore a fishhook for a necklace and gave it away as change to a politician named Hoolan who checked a two-dollar bill because he didn't have a hat. The orchestra conductor, Fitzroyd, kept a couple of dead goldfish in his pockets when shot and killed by a gangster, Gus Berber, who didn't even know the victim, and whom Judge Hagerman freed on a phony technicality.

"For all I know, a lot of other queer things that don't figure in these reports may have happened. What more could you ask? Where the dickens can you start if not with the facts?"

"What results did the police achieve when they started with the facts?" Frost asked pointedly.

Inspector Frick came as close to flushing as he ever could, but he made no answer.

The professor continued, "No, the difficulty is that your portfolio does not involve enough people. The lunatic plague must spread, or be made to spread, even farther." He opened the switch of the centrifuge, but the drone continued. It would run for hours under momentum.

Frick began, "If you manage to clear up any part of the mystery that—"

"The whole sequence is perfectly clear already, but the most important detail remains to be filled in."

"If deduction took you that far, why not all the way? Why don't you just think a while longer and tell me everything?"

"You credit logic with the powers of magic, but in pique, I suspect, rather than from belief," Frost retorted. "Deduction is only one of many faculties and resources necessary for the solution of crime problems. To the best of my knowledge no murder case has ever been solved without the use of deductive processes.

"On the other hand, I am not acquainted with any homicide that pure deduction alone has solved, not excepting Poe's celebrated story about the Marie Roget case. I have heard it called a masterpiece of pure deduction. It's nothing of the sort. Analysis, synthesis, logic, the examination of evidence and evaluating it, the obtaining of material data and suggested courses of action are all in the narrative.

"I dislike the term, 'the scientific method,' for there are several scientific methods and the phrase only lends itself to confusion, but it serves for a guiding description to the modern technique. Deduction may identify a murderer, but it will never catch him. Fast action must bring the killer to justice."

"What do you propose to do?"

"Visit the Grand Central Terminal, and possibly the Pennsylvania Station."

"The Grand Central! Are you pulling my leg? What on earth can the Grand Central possibly have to do with an epidemic of lunacy?"

"Gold lies where you find it," Frost murmured.

The inspector looked bewildered when he departed. Frost walked out of the laboratory with him, while Frick's glance lingered for a moment on the highly interesting facial beguilment and enticing contours of Jean Moray's topography. A visit to Frost had this one redeeming feature. When the professor's meaning eluded him, he could always feast his eyes upon Frost's charming assistant.

III

Did you record the conversation?" Frost asked.

"It's on the dictaphone roll." Jean Moray looked too ravishing to be human, but her beauty was wasted, she saw with resentment. She eyed him, a malignant hope nestling inside her that some day she would pierce his impregnable armor.

The moment that Inspector Frick left, the professor's bearing changed in a subtle, indefinable manner. His figure somehow radiated a flow of invisible power, of will thrusting toward a definite though unexplained goal.

He ordered crisply, "Call police headquarters and give the desk sergeant this message to be placed as a memorandum on Frick's schedule. Say that I. V. Frost will see him tomorrow at ten with important developments pertaining to the lunatic plague."

"But he was just here. Why didn't you tell him then?"

"I've no intention of seeing him at ten with regard to anything."

Jean lifted the phone receiver. She had long ago found it futile to ask questions when Frost chose to speak in contradictions. While she carried out his instructions, she noticed him flip the pages of the telephone directory.

He jotted down numbers, went into the laboratory, returned with a device like a small microphone that he handed her together with the list of numbers. "Now call these and in each case say, 'The job was well done. That's all. There won't be any more.' "

"What's the mike for?"

"Speak through it. It's a voice filter. The listener will be unable to determine whether you are male or female, young or old."

"And the numbers?"

"Are those of the surviving members of what we may call the lunatic band. Repeat to them only the message I gave you, and ring off immediately."

Frost vanished into the laboratory again.

A half hour later, after Jean finished the last call and the last of the Arabic scrawls that formed her special preference in shorthand, Frost reappeared as though she had made an audible signal.

She reported, "The telephone laid some eggs. Naturally, I didn't have time to find out anything, since I wasn't supposed to talk. If you want the illuminating answers, they include, 'Say that over again,' and 'Huh?' and 'Who are you?' and 'Thanks, but—' and 'Oh, yeah? What the—' "

"Ah!" Frost exclaimed. "That's sufficient."

"For what? Scrambled eggs? Or am I supposed to rest in the dark like a sort of incubator tray?" Jean flared.

"If you could achieve it, that would be a fate not without strong merits," Frost said with enthusiasm. "I refer, of course, not so much to the tray itself as to the contents thereof which, in darkness and warmth, under controlled temperatures, commence the cycle of generation that produces—"

Hot argument hovered on Jean's lips, but before she could interrupt or Frost finish, the doorbell rang. Frost broke off his discourse abruptly.

"Handle the interview. When it's over, get to the basement garage as fast as you can, take the Demon, trail him or her, as the case may be. If you work at top speed you should manage it with seconds to spare. Keep your eyes open. You're going to race with death but you'll be safe inside the car. If anything causes you to lose sight of the quarry, stay in that vicinity, wherever it is, and tune in on the short-wave micro-set. Its four-mile range ought to be ample. If you don't hear from me by nine o'clock, return here."

He hiked off, his long legs carrying him out at a pace that would have meant a brisk trot for the average man.

Jean walked to the front door. When she opened it, utter astonishment stilled her for an instant. The visitor brushed past her and into the reception room. Jean recovered from her amazement and followed close behind.

The visitor, a young woman in her early twenties, wore a costume the like of which Jean at first thought she had not seen since college days when sororities pledged and hazed the annual crop of yearlings. On second thought, Jean decided she'd never seen the like of that costume anywhere.

The caller stood a couple of inches shorter than Jean, with a fuller figure and a face attractive in a sort of pointed fashion—a thin, pointed nose, a chin that ended with a tiny, pyramid tip, a mouth with a distinct point on the upper lip.

The girl wore a mule with a white pompon on her left foot, an alligator-skin sandal on her right. One stocking was sheer and flesh-colored; the other open meshwork and black. For a hot, muggy evening, she chose to wear a fur coat, unbuttoned. Underneath it lay exposed generous areas of skin around her only other garments. Upon her head, however, perched a monstrously ugly hat, festooned with a long feather—a hat so hideous and unsightly that it must have survived from the 1890s.

Her left hand clenched an object. She had shoved her right loosely into a pocket of the fur coat.

This bizarre apparition said, her voice toneless, "I'd like to see Professor I. V. Frost."

"I'm sorry, he's not in," Jean lied with perfectly convincing innocence. "I'm his assistant, Miss Moray. You can speak freely, and I'll give him your message when he comes back. What is your name?"

"It doesn't matter. He doesn't know me. I won't be here again. I only wanted to give him a present."

"A present?" Jean instantly became suspicious, watched every gesture the woman made. "What for?"

"I don't know. I was told to get it and deliver it to him in person, but if he's absent— How long will he be gone?"

"I've no idea. Perhaps hours."

"I can't wait that long. Then I might as well leave it with you. You'll be sure to give it to him?"

"Of course. What is it?"

"A goose egg."

The woman opened her fist, handed Jean a big white goose egg, turned around, and walked out.

IV

Jean took the egg by automatic response. The outer door closed before the spell upon her broke and she remembered Frost's instructions. She had no time to waste on the bewildering visit and the preposterous present. Fleet-footed as a faun, she sped to the basement garage and dived inside the Demon. It purred up the ramp. The car that had brought the woman already rolled well on its way down the street. Jean almost lost it at the corner. She watched for the immense bonnet, then picked out the characteristics of the sedan with a keen eye, and thereafter had no trouble keeping it in sight.

Traffic was fairly heavy. The hour of dusk had come, with the sun just set and the street lights going on. Jean noticed another occupant in the front seat of the car ahead. A man, but so far as she could tell from the back of their heads, they did not talk to each other.

The sedan rolled down Broadway, past Times Square, and on all the way to Union Square. At Fourteenth Street, the woman stopped and got out. She pulled the fur coat tightly around her. Oblivious to the stares of pedestrians, she hurried into a tobacco shop where she entered one of the telephone booths.

She emerged a minute later, returned to the driver's seat, and drove off just before a policeman reached her. The officer hesitated, with the air of investigating nonsense afoot, shrugged his shoulders, and moved away as Jean picked up the trail again.

It led uptown back the route it had previously followed. It continued toward the uppermost regions of Manhattan.

The towers and skyscrapers of the midtown area, and the tall apartment buildings of the residential section on the upper west side faded into the dusk behind. Houses began to appear, then vacant lots, as the trail cut in toward the Bronx.

They traveled along Culver Avenue now. Jean flashed by an intersection where a parked auto had its wheels almost flush with the avenue. By the rear-view mirror she saw the headlights that swung around in her wake.

Her heart grew tight. Her glance flicked alternately between the sedan ahead and the car behind, until she confirmed her fears. She had ceased to be the hunter, had become the hunted, and the pursuers drove hot after her, the headlights looming ever larger as they closed the gap.

She pressed her foot on the accelerator. The Demon hummed a song of vast power and sailed away like a rocket. The feel of the magnificent machine in that swift pickup restored her courage. The vehicle was a masterpiece of engineering, specially designed and built for Frost after gangster bombs destroyed his previous model. A mobile fortress with punctureproof tires, steel armor, incased motor and gasoline tank, bulletproof glass, the Demon possessed many other features built in to Frost's specifications. She had once seen the speedometer touch 120 on a ten-mile straightaway before deceleration for a curve became necessary.

These thoughts flooded her for the few seconds that the Demon gathered momentum. The sedan seemed to stand still as she bore down on it. She lifted her foot.

The jaws of a trap threatened her. If she outran the pursuit, she must also race away from the sedan. If she kept her distance behind the sedan, she would be overhauled.

She put her faith in the Demon and in Frost. Tight-lipped, she held her relative position.

The dark limousine came on like a thunderbolt, swung out to the center of the road, drew abreast of her. A sudden gasp burst from her throat. She vaguely realized she had stopped breathing these last tense seconds.

The sinister snout of a gun, the barrel of a gun with a double grip and a drum that resembled a canister for motion-picture films, poked through the narrow, rear ventilation window. It spewed flame in spurts and flashes.

Even the completely closed Demon was not soundproof enough to conceal the vicious *ta-ta-ta-ta-ta-ta* of the submachine gun, though it sounded deceptively faint and far away. Fractures like dimes and quarters bloomed on the windows. Jean ducked her head. The crackle of lead against glass tortured her ears. She heard the whine of slugs that smote steel.

The firing ceased. She watched the limousine, saw the gun withdrawn. The Demon had come through, she thought, but as she exulted, the other car forged ahead and edged in. Pressed toward the curb and a crack-up, she stepped on the brake.

The limousine cut over more sharply.

Her gray-green eyes acquired the glint of ice. She pushed the accelerator violently. The Demon leaped as though sprung from a catapult, hit the limousine with the power of a pile driver. The jolt flung Jean against the steering wheel. The limousine slued, wabbled crazily, smashed a wheel against the curb across the road.

The Demon itself swerved, not because the impact had deflected its ponderous weight, but because Jean's grip slackened from the letdown. The car angled away from the roadbed. She straightened it out, scanned the avenue ahead.

The sedan had disappeared.

Her ribs ached. A glance at the rear-view mirror showed figures piling out of the limousine. Jean turned at the next corner. She crisscrossed the neighborhood in a futile search. She switched the short-wave set on but heard nothing. Finally she drove back toward the scene of collision and parked a few blocks away.

Of all the events crowding the past hour, she remembered most vividly the moment when the limousine drew parallel with her and the snout of a submachine gun slanted toward her, while the faces of three painted, grotesquely grinning clowns pressed against the windows.

V

Frost closed the laboratory door at 13 State Street after ordering Jean Moray to interview the unknown client who had just rung the bell. He left the house and strode to the sedan parked in front.

He entered as casually as if he owned it, but sprawled down on the front seat. A woman's bag rested there. He scrutinized the contents, which consisted of currency, a handkerchief, and female stuff such as the inevitable lipstick. The dashboard compartment contained nothing. One side pocket yielded a .28 automatic. He found an old shopping receipt wadded down in a corner of the other pocket, below a hunk of waste and some road maps.

Frost had barely finished the swift survey when the door handle turned and a fantastically garbed young woman climbed in. Her eyes narrowed. Frost sat upright.

"What are you doing here? Get out of my car!"

"Good evening, Miss Kelsey; allow me to introduce myself. I am Professor I. V. Frost. I suggest that you drive away from here instantly."

"Of all the nerve! What do you mean by—"

"Get started."

She slammed the door, produced and turned the ignition key, and whipped out the automatic.

"A pretty thing," Frost murmured. "Tear-gas pens are useful, too, when they are loaded."

Her finger quivered on the trigger.

"Fire if you wish. Perhaps the gesture will relieve your nervous tension. I assure you that I'm in no danger since I took the liberty, and the pleasure, of removing the clip."

She jerked the trigger. Empty clicks sounded. She swung the barrel toward him. His fingers stopped it—fingers whose long and tapered beauty suggested the hand of an artist or feminine grace but the force of that grip reminded her of nothing so much as steel cable.

"Drive on!" Frost commanded.

She set her head forward, her eyes smoldering in her pale, pointed face. "Are you going to get out?"

"Eventually, yes; certainly not now."

"I left a present in the house for you. Why don't you go look at it?"

"Later."

"It's a goose egg."

"I'll counter with a cross."

Her brows wrinkled. The statement puzzled her. She glanced at him from the corners of her eyes, then threw the car in gear.

No word passed between them on the way down Broadway to Union Square nor did she volunteer information. If she noticed the auto that trailed her, she paid no attention to it.

Frost did not attempt to follow her when she stopped and used the telephone booth of a tobacco shop.

She resumed driving. Miles slipped behind them. They cut across upper Manhattan toward the Bronx. As Patricia Kelsey turned off Culver Avenue to a cross street, the mirror reflected spurts of flame from an auto that had swept alongside the big car keeping pace with them.

"There ought to be a law against people shooting off fireworks," Pat Kelsey stated indignantly as she reached another corner and turned again. Her knuckles whitened from her clench on the steering wheel; her mouth trembled.

"There is. There's also a law against shooting off firearms, but it has not prevented a good many thousands of marble slabs from being erected over the recipients of successful target practice."

Patricia ran the car up a private driveway and into a garage adjoining a large house surrounded by well-trimmed lawn and shrubbery.

She went around to the front of the house, Frost at her side, and found the door locked. She looked surprised, hesitated with indecision, then rang the bell.

A middle-aged man of substantial and prosperous appearance answered it. His pointed chin gave him a vague facial resemblance to Patricia.

His eyes gaped astonishment. He stared at the pair confronting him. "Pat!" he exclaimed. "Why are you running around in that—that— Words fail me. Is it some costume party you didn't tell me about—"

The girl ran past him without a word. He whirled, cried "Pat!" again, but she did not reply. He watched her flight until the bang of a door told that she had locked herself in a room.

He seemed on the point of following her but finally turned his attention to Frost. He glanced up the five inches that separated him from the professor's gaunt and towering length. "I don't recall having seen you with my niece before, Mr.—er—er—"

Frost introduced himself.

"Indeed?" exclaimed the other. "A private investigator? Did Pat request your services? Or has she been up to mischief? I don't understand this. Will you come in? I am Dr. Kelsey—Dr. Herbert Kelsey."

In the living room, Frost declined the offer of a drink but lighted one of his own aromatic cigarettes. "At what time did your niece leave this house?"

"I've no idea. She was not here when I arrived from my office downtown. That must have been at six thirty or so. Why do you ask? What significance does it have?"

Frost gave a scant outline of the circumstances under which Patricia had come to him.

Dr. Kelsey shook his head. "A goose egg, you say? Strange, to say the least. I confess I'm baffled. To the best of my knowledge she's never before done anything like it. When she's calmer I'll try to find out what she means by such absurd behavior."

"You may succeed where the police must fail, though I doubt whether you can elicit the slightest information from her. Let me know immediately if you do."

"Why should I succeed? Oh, I see. Because I'm a physician and, like lawyers and ministers, entitled to confidences. As it happens, medical men rarely treat members of their family, except for minor ailments and emergencies. They summon other physicians as a rule. I am no exception. I feel certain that Pat's case will simmer down to a mere prank or a feminine emotional explosion. In that event I will notify you. If a serious nervous disorder or mental disturbance indicates its presence, it would need therapeutic treatment, not the police."

"But why the police? I understood you to be a private investigator. Surely the police would not interest themselves to any extent in the case of a young woman who chose to wear unconventional clothing while making a visit. Granted that she brought a goose egg to you, a stranger. If you won't take offense, you yourself are just as unconventional in your tobacconary preferences. What it all amounts to—"

The ringing of a bell interrupted him. He crossed the room and lifted a telephone receiver. "Dr. Kelsey speaking."

He listened for a full half minute. His face grew perplexed. A knot of muscle collected on each jawbone. "But good Heavens, think of my practice, my reputation! Why, I can't possibly—"

After another pause, he answered slowly, "Oh, I see." He dabbed a handkerchief at his forehead.

He listened again and ended with, "Very well, then, I'll expect the call."

Grim wrinkles lined his face. He put the phone down. Oblivious to Frost, preoccupation with other thoughts making his eyes vacant, he picked up a decanter of sherry. He poured out a glass which he drank in rapid sips. He twirled the glass and murmured, "I must prepare for an urgent case. Suppose you phone me to-morrow."

Frost, already on the way out, flung a terse acknowledgment over his shoulder.

VI

In the shadow of a retaining wall at the nearest intersection to the Kelsey residence, Frost took the mouthpiece of the micro-set from his pocket. "J. M.," he broadcast softly.

The voice of Jean Moray instantly replied. He sent her directions to meet him. A couple of minutes later the Demon rolled along and Frost slipped from his concealment.

Seated beside his assistant, he listened to her narrative, asked, "Did you recognize any of the three clowns?"

Jean sniffed. "You wouldn't recognize even your best friend if he painted his face up. How could you? But I can identify one of them by something else. The machine gunner had the thumb and little finger missing from his left hand. There can't be many men in the city with that special deformity; the only one I know of is Three-fingered Lefty, who's supposed to get paid by Gus Berber. How did you get here so quickly?"

Frost drawled, "I rode in the car that you trailed."

Her eyes glinted sparks. "And you just kept on riding while three killers did their hardest to put lots of nice cozy bullets inside me? That was sweet of you, so thoughtful and considerate. Or maybe you think I'd look better if I was ventilated like a Swiss cheese?"

"Your escape proves that you kept your wits. The Demon protected you from serious danger," Frost said nonchalantly. From a compartment at the base of the seat he took out two bundles, one of which he handed to her. "Slip into this bulletproof cloak. You'll need it later. Leave the hood off while you're driving, but put it on when you get out. Keep your pistol ready.

"While I talked with Dr. Kelsey, he received a telephone call. He will become another victim of the lunatic series during the next hour. Follow him if he goes away from the house. If he doesn't, and if he receives a visitor who seems eccentric for any reason, follow the visitor instead. Whichever it is, don't let him out of your sight. Notice particularly other persons that you may encounter.

"There's a miniature camera here that takes clear pictures, even by moonlight. If the subject does anything that attracts attention, photograph the crowd.

"I'm going to Grand Central Station now on another line of investigation."

"What a life!" Jean sighed, and turned the full force of her glance upon Frost. "Here it's a beautiful summer evening, and I broke a date with one of my favorite scoundrels in order to chase all over town and get shot at, where as we would have been dancing on a roof garden now, and later he'd have made love to me and—"

Frost eased himself out and closed the door. Jean smiled a contented smile, hoping she had irked him. His inscrutable expression, as he vanished around the corner, did not leave her a single clue.

She lolled behind the wheel of the Demon after Frost's exit. Nothing happened for the first half hour. Minutes passed until, at 9:15, a long, sleek roadster slid up to the Kelsey residence. The driver, its sole occupant, stepped out.

Jean's eyes bulged for the third time that evening. She instantly recognized the newcomer as April Holley, one of the most talented of rising screen actresses. April defied classification because she changed her personality, her make-up, her style, and her appearance for every role. She radiated in abundance that indefinable magnetic quality which separates the creative from the imitative artist.

The darkness and the distance at which Jean sat made it impossible for her to determine more than that April, in real life, seemed about five feet four and possessed a marvelous figure. She walked with a sinuous glide that floated her along. She wore a one-piece bathing suit of some pastel shade that caused Jean trouble in deciding where the fabric began and ended.

April merged with the shadows of the porch.

She came down the steps a few minutes later clinging to an arm of Dr. Kelsey. She said something. He appeared ill at ease. In startling contrast to her scanty raiment, he had donned full dress, including top hat and gloves. Not until they reached the roadster did Jean discover the reason for his nervousness. He walked barefoot. He had omitted shoes, socks, and spats. The unadorned feet obviously caused him extreme self-consciousness.

The roadster picked up speed. Power aplenty lay under its hood. It rivaled Frost's Demon.

April drove expertly but at reckless velocity toward Brooklyn. She jumped traffic signals, careened around corners, shot along thoroughfares. Jean found herself pressed to keep pace with the queerly dressed pair who streaked away. She dropped a dangerous distance behind on occasions; at other times she followed in their exhaust.

The flight continued to Coney Island. The roadster turned along the ocean-front drive and halted beyond the board walk's limits.

Dr. Kelsey stepped out of one side, April from the other. The screen actress carried a bucket. The doctor balanced a long-handled fork of close-set tines on his shoulder. They marched across the beach. They waded until the water reached their waists.

April held the bucket while her companion began digging for clams.

A few late fugitives from the metropolitan heat wave watched the performance with growing curiosity. New arrivals strolled over. A knot of spectators assembled.

Jean, parked a few dozen yards behind the roadster, lowered a window. The faintest of stars flecked the misty darkness. She heard the pounding surge and retreat of the Atlantic. The salt wetness of ocean filled the air. With Frost's camera, she took a dozen pictures of the spectators.

When the pair emerged, April looked fresh from the dip, but Kelsey's ruined outfit clung to him soggily. He dripped pools of water.

They met the law as they started up the sands. A member of the beach patrol dispersed the crowd. Another confronted April and her companion. The tone of his voice indicating that he recognized the screen star, he spoke, "You'll have to dump those clams back."

"Why?"

"It's against health regulations, Miss Holley. You can't eat 'em. The water's polluted and they're bad. What's the idea, anyway? Is this a publicity stunt?"

"We're on a scavenger hunt. It's a sort of game," Kelsey volunteered.

"I don't know anything about that, mister."

April said, "Take the clams. Throw them back. Eat them. Do what you want with them."

A hysterical edge suddenly altered her liquid accents. She thrust the bucket at the surprised officer and unceremoniously fled to her roadster like a frightened nymph from the sea. Kelsey pattered after her. He barely had time to jump on the running board before the roadster leaped away.

Instead of returning to the city, April followed the South Shore road and sped up Long Island. The congested sections and suburbs slipped behind. She drove at her former reckless speed and again Jean found it a hard task to keep the roadster in view.

An hour passed. April was still streaking northeast and had reached a lonely, deserted stretch when headlights of a distinctly bluish tinge winked from far ahead. At this spot several hundred yards of flat, sandy soil covered with low bushes and clusters of weeds separated the road from the ocean. Hilly ground sloped on the landward side.

April braked the roadster to a violent stop.

An eighth of a mile behind, Jean slowed down. By the faint farthermost glow of her headlights she saw Kelsey descend and slam the door shut.

The roadster swept onward, went into high gear, made a right-angle turn. Jean took a sharp breath. Things happened so fast she couldn't comprehend them.

April drove straight for the ocean. The roadster bumped and jerked; its velocity mounted, it became a blur that tunneled the moonless darkness.

Kelsey whirled, stared, started to run after it. He shouted again and again, then hesitated and looked toward the bluish lights of the auto bearing down on him.

Jean stepped on the gas, switched her lights to flood, and angled toward the sea. The long beam picked out the sleek roadster, April's face, wild and desperate, unwaveringly awaiting the ocean. Her car must have been hurtling above sixty miles an hour when it smote the Atlantic with a hiss and a great splash. The waters closed over it.

April did not come to the surface.

Frost's Demon hummed a song of thirsting power as Jean shot it across the waste land. The Demon's weight and reserves kept it under control. She flung it true to the mark. She was dimly aware that the blue headlights had outlined Kelsey and that he held his hands high. The lights blinked off.

"Watch him; watch him!" Frost's words echoed through her mind.

"Let him be killed," her instincts commanded. One or the other—the man or the trapped, drowning girl—she couldn't manage both. Her nerves screamed to the rasp of rubber on sand as she swung the Demon broadside to the sea.

"Come up, come up, you've got to come up!" Jean implored aloud.

April did not rise to the surface.

Jean leaped out. Tongues of evil flame blossomed on the road. "They're killing him; they're killing him," she thought feverishly. Then hornet buzzes filled the air and slugs screeched off the Demon. Two stinging blows hit her through the bulletproof cloak as she darted around the Demon. She realized all at once that she—and not Kelsey—was the target. The shock sobered her. She had no time for battle or rage or anything but rescue of the drowning girl.

She reached the seaward side of the Demon, its body protecting her from the bullets. The extended burst of machine-gun fire, the spray of lead, ceased as she tore the cloak off. She kicked her shoes away, slipped out of her dress with a lithe motion at hectic speed, and flashed to the water.

A good swimmer, she shattered all her past records. A long crawl stroke cleft the surface, carried her beyond the spot where the roadster had submerged. She dived, came up a minute later for a gulp of fresh air, dived again. In eighteen feet of water she found April slumped over the roadster's wheel. She hauled the girl free, pushed for the surface.

She couldn't tell if April still lived. She used her right arm to keep the unconscious head above water, stroked out with her left arm.

The blue lights winked on, pointing toward the Demon. They began to cross the waste land, faster and faster. The vicious flames spurted anew. Jean went under. Her heart thundered. She swam until exhausted, came up for air, found she could touch bottom. The red flashes had ceased, and no bullets clipped the water around her, but the bluish headlights raced closer.

"Come out of it; wake up; hurry, you've got to help me make it!" she pleaded to the limp girl, but there came only a horrible gurgling rattle for answer.

Dismay filled Jean; she remembered that the nearest doors of the Demon were locked from the inside. It would do her no good to reach it ahead of the bluish lights. She would have to run into the open, face their murderous glare.

Splashing for shore, towing the inert figure, Jean stared frantically at the onrushing lights that brought death.

VII

After Frost had told his assistant to watch the Kelsey residence, he walked several blocks before he found a cab.

It dropped him at Grand Central Station. Frost joined the usual small rush of commuters who spent the evening in town and began an exodus around nine o'clock. The hands of the station clock stood at twenty minutes past the hour.

Frost went directly to the office of the station master.

A bent old wisp of a man with the gloomy face of a chronic hypochondriac sat back in a chair with his feet on the table. He had to spread them to see who came in.

He looked even more woebegone after he sighted Frost. "No, I'm not glad to see you." His voice rasped thin and shrill. "A fine friend you are. I don't see you for months on end, only when you got something you want to get out of me. The answer is no! Why don't you throw away that old leather jacket? I bet it would stand up if you threw it in a corner. I bet it's got so many acid stains on it now that you could boil it and get enough stuff out of it to win a war."

"Glad to find you in such good spirits, Mac," Frost greeted him cheerfully. "As a matter of fact, you're looking worse. You've probably convinced yourself that you've added arteriosclerosis, gout, and neuritis to your long list of fancied ailments since I last saw you."

"They aren't fancy ailments and anyway you're wrong. It's my hearing that ain't what it used to be. I'll be deaf in another—"

"Perhaps, but that will require six months to prove, whereas I cannot devote even sixty minutes to what I'm here for.

"On each side of the station there's a bank of steel lockers."

"Oh, sure, you mean the parcel locks. You interested in them?" MacDonald took his feet off the desk and perked up his ears, his face a little less mournful. "They're quite a gadget—automatic, you know. You open the locker, put your parcel in, and chuck a dime through the slot so you can get the key out. Then you lock the door and walk away. The key is your check, but you have to use it inside of twenty-four hours. What about it? Is this for one of your cases?"

"Yes, and a tough one. Is the mechanism such that a depositor could return within the time limit every day, insert another dime, and thus retain exclusive occupancy for as long as he wished?"

"Sure."

"Do you keep duplicate keys?"

"We don't have anything to do with them. The lockers are made by an outfit called Locker-Tite. It owns them and rents the station space. It has its own service man who comes around every morning to collect the dimes and see that the empties work O.K. They know me. Want me to call them? There's a man on all night."

"Find out if they list the individual receipts; if so, whether any lockers have yielded daily payments for the last two weeks. Get the numbers."

MacDonald lifted the telephone receiver and dialed. He absentmindedly toyed with a pencil while seeking the information. His thoughts kept straying back to a period two years ago when, as a locomotive engineer, he had driven his passenger express around a curve and piled it into a line of freight empties that were being sidetracked. He received critical injuries, but survived to find himself fired, then tried and convicted on charges of criminal negligence, involving manslaughter. He testified that the signal light showed green. The company experts found it in perfect working order.

The freight crew testified it had been set for red. MacDonald's stoker couldn't testify about anything because he died in the wreck. Frost read a full account of the circumstances, stepped in, and demonstrated how the light values could have been deliberately reversed by either of two methods. He found a few clues on the site and suggested a new line of investigation that produced the real criminal and exonerated MacDonald. Incapacitated for heavy work, the pilot asked for, at Frost's suggestion, and received the job of station master.

MacDonald hung up. "Here are your numbers. The first three boxes in the top row of each bank have been used every day. No. 27 is the only other locker that collected dimes the past two weeks. Hey, wait a jiff—"

Frost, disappearing through the door, called over his shoulder, "I'll be back in a minute."

He scanned the lockers as he strode past them to No. 27. Before he reached it, he took out several flat, blank keys which were coated with wax, and selected one. He inserted it, twisted it gently, and withdrew it. The action required scarcely more than a second.

He returned to MacDonald's office and, over the station master's voluble protests, perched himself on the desk. He studied the marks on the wax coating of the key, clipped the soft metal with a scissors that had nippers as tiny as a line on an oyster fork and thin like a razor blade, then used a small file to polish the edges.

MacDonald complained morosely, "There goes my job. Before my eyes he makes a key to open a box in my station with hundreds of witnesses. It isn't enough that I'm going deaf; he makes me a party to a larceny. And the jails are so drafty I'll probably catch pneumonia."

"You'll live to be a hundred," Frost prophesied.

"I'll live to be hunted? Who's responsible for that?" he cackled and launched a dissertation on deafness that never caught up with Frost's ears or his heels.

Frost inserted the key in Locker 27 and opened the door.

Inside lay a miscellany that would have supported the yellow tabloids for years. The nest could spawn blackmail, extortion, breach of promise, fraud, scandal, and murder. It included incendiary letters, forged checks, a pistol, IOUs, memoranda, pawnshop tickets, records of crooked business deals, proof of bribery, wax disks, clinical case histories, a diary in feminine script, and other items.

The documentary group, though not large, involved famous names, some in lesser ranks of society, others of unknowns. But the extensive photographic collection made it seem anaemic.

The picture studies comprised at least fifty, a miniature camera, equipped with telephoto lens, had obviously taken most of them from a distance. Many were of a nature to make the orbs bulge on even a veteran censor. The back of each snapshot bore the name of the subject. Single letters cut out of newspaper print and pasted together spelled the names.

Harmin, who pushed the peanut with his nose, had once written an angry letter that read like a threat of violent physical assault, and which could still bring him a prison sentence. A photograph of Kelsey and a woman could more than wreck his career. Gus Berber, before he had a police record, killed a man of whose murder he was never suspected. Gus later wrote the full details to a woman companion in a burst of incomparable stupidity and boastfulness. That confession, in police hands, would enable them to send him on the long road, perhaps even the last mile.

All the persons whom Frick had mentioned a few hours earlier appeared in the data by name or by photograph.

"Thanks for finding us the evidence. We'll take it now," ordered a voice at Frost's elbow.

He turned around. Seven plainclothes detectives, whom he did not recognize, ringed him in; at least a dozen more streamed toward him from all directions, the wail of a police siren rose outside, and a wild uproar swept through the station as the passenger traffic diverted to the scene of disturbance.

VIII

Jean, hampered by the dead weight of April Holley, struggled through the shallows to reach shore ahead of the blue lights. She breathed convulsive gasps. Her pulse hammered in her throat, temples and ears. She staggered out of the water, trembling and flushed from her exertions. She hauled the relaxed form to the running board, snatched up the bulletproof cloak.

There was no time to don it. She held it in front of her as a loose shield and darted around the rear of Frost's Demon. The long garment protected all but her legs below the knees as it flapped against her body. Then the machine gun snarled its savage chatter again; messengers of death winged the air. She didn't know how many bruises she received—half a dozen at least—from the impact of pellets that flattened on the fabric. Her ribs started aching once more.

She twisted the door handle. The cloak slipped, and her heart gave a great bound. It stopped entirely during the fractional instant that the headlights mercilessly flooded her. Then the door swung and slammed, and the bitter pills screamed off Frost's fortress.

Jean's heart raced wildly now, uncontrollably. She slid across the seat, snapped the opposite door open, tugged at April's body. She didn't look to see what the blue lights did. She couldn't look. She had to get that inert weight inside.

"Frost!" her lips whistled his name, and more loudly, "Frost!" Always before the professor had materialized like a magician, a phantom, at her moments of greatest need, but he was not here to help her now. She dragged April's head and torso into the car, worked madly to bring up the trailing legs.

Wraithlike figures slid around the Demon, one at each end; cold-eyed killers with pistols rising. Their faces made only a blur on her consciousness as they sped toward her. She stuffed the girl's ankles and feet toward the foot rest, yanked the door fast and clicked the lock. Her hands flew to the wheel.

Both men leaped on the running board. She put the Demon into high instantly, with the last drain upon its reserves which Frost had ordered her never to attempt except under fear of death.

The Demon took a mighty leap, like a plane catapulted on its way. The men grabbed with flailing arms, but no human strength could have resisted that prodigious thrust. The Demon drove forward with the power of a battering-ram. They bowled off into darkness, both of them, and Jean fought to head the Demon away from the sea. It purred across the sand, turned, streaked for the road.

Only then did she permit herself a glance at the rear-view mirror. She saw the blue lights crawl toward the pair. They picked themselves up and jumped into the car. It gathered speed. The blue lights circled toward the road, but away from the Demon, heading northeast.

Jean stopped at the pavement. She felt the actress' heart, found a faint, perceptible beat. Jean pulled, panted, shoved, and toiled with a heroic determination. She got April's head down on the front upholstery and her legs dangling on the back floor so that her body made a jackknife. Jean kneaded the girl's lungs. Water purled from the bloodless lips. April's breathing grew regular between spasms of coughing.

Jean scanned the road. Far ahead crawled red tail lights, preceded by a milky glow. No other vehicle intervened. Jean threw the Demon into gear and started overhauling those far lights. It might be a wild-goose chase, but blue paper can color white light, and blue filters can be torn off white lights by a moment's work.

She swiftly narrowed the distance from the far tail lamp. She didn't know if it was the right car or if it contained Kelsey. She had lost track of Kelsey. The flying tail lamp offered the only action she could take.

April no longer needed emergency treatment. She ought to have hospitalization to guard against pneumonia, but Jean counted on finding aid at one of the towns ahead long before the time it would take to drive back to New York.

April trembled, began to push her hands against the seat. When she regained consciousness she climbed weakly in front and relaxed. The exertion brought a fit of coughing.

"Take it easy," Jean advised. "You're safe now."

"Why did you do it?" Despair undertoned the question.

"That's what I ought to ask," Jean retorted. "Why did *you* do it?"

April caught a corner of her lower lip between her teeth, made no reply.

Jean, after a sidelong glance, confessed herself unable to pigeonhole the character of the young actress. She sensed a personality complex, changeable, elusive. April Holley, in real life, proved the same enigma that had made her screen portrayals fascinating. She presented a problem, difficult to analyze, not because of pose but because of her genuine self. Even her eloquent violet eyes told little. Terror, curiosity, resentment, any of a dozen reasons might have caused their expression.

Jean changed the subject. "Somebody's going to pay for a perfectly good dress and practically brand-new shoes I left back there on the beach."

"I'm sorry. I'll—"

"Forget it. I didn't mean it that way. Driving barefoot doesn't exactly soothe my soles. Can you reach the pocket behind you? It ought to hold a pair of sneakers."

April turned and rummaged, brought them forth. Jean put them on with difficulty. With equal difficulty, April helped and tied the laces. "Do you carry extras of everything?"

Jean smiled. "Hardly. The sneakers are handy in summer time. The cloak will have to do for a dress when I get out.

"You'll find cigarettes in my pocketbook, but I don't think you ought to smoke now."

"Thanks." April drew one out and lighted it. After a minute she asked, "Where are you driving?"

"Frankly, I don't know." Jean introduced herself, added, "I know your name, of course. As far as tonight's concerned, don't worry. It won't reach print. And you'll see the end of the lunatic plague."

April looked puzzled.

Jean explained, "Ivy Frost will stop it. I can't say how, but he will. If you don't happen to know about Frost, he's a scientist who taught at universities for a good many years until academic life bored him. He had done research for crime detection laboratories among other things. When he resigned his professorship, he returned to private life as a specialist. Now he's one of the best. He won't touch run-of-the-mill stuff. Most of his cases spell murder. Even then it takes a strange mix-up or something bizarre to get his interest."

April, who had turned her head while Jean spoke, said irrelevantly, "You've got a strong personality of your own. Unusual. And looks enough. Have you ever tried Hollywood? If you want to come out some time—"

Jean shook her head. "Definitely no. Right now I hold about the most exciting position in the country. Maybe I won't live long at it but it produces more danger and thrills in a week than Hollywood could in a year. It makes living intense, hectic. It's packed full of hazards, but they're worth it."

Jean abruptly suppressed further comments she intended to make and silently called herself names. She wasn't getting information; she was giving it. True, she had idly chattered to put the girl at ease but she saw now that no one could control April. When the actress' nerves exploded and she wanted to drown herself, she instantly went ahead. Rescued, she had already forgotten the incident. Ill from exposure though she might be, she had certainly nursed Jean into admission of facts.

April Holley smiled wanly, her large purple eyes cherishing a secretive glow. Perhaps she had guessed what thoughts upset Frost's assistant.

Jean's answer died on her lips. Her attention jumped past April. It shifted because the car ahead turned off the road and ran up a short driveway to a bungalow that loomed dark against the sea beyond.

Jean continued driving, saw other isolated cottages, and around the next bend encountered the main cluster of a summer colony. No lights showed. The clock on the dashboard indicated 12:45. She parked off the road under a clump of poplars.

A quandary stumped her. She couldn't take April along. She feared that the actress might grow inquisitive about the Demon, or cause damage, or give way to an unpredictable whim if left behind in Frost's car. Every second's delay reduced her chances of learning what went on at the bungalow, if the occupants of the car were what she expected.

She took the ignition key, a pistol, flashlight, the cloak and hood. "Wait here," she told April. "I'll only be gone a few minutes."

April curled down on the seat. "Wake me when you get back." She closed her eyes.

Jean didn't know how to take the gesture and didn't stop to watch. The long cloak over her, she returned to the cottage.

It stood five or six hundred feet from the sea, with a ragged lawn that rolled down to the beach sands. The shadowy outlines of bushes, saplings, and young trees loomed against the ocean and sweep of sky. The mild, rhythmic wash of waves whispered upon the air. The sea was the calmest she had ever seen. That she could observe so much surprised her. A strange darkness prevailed. Without moon, and with the stars hazed out, the night held a mysterious, impalpable glow. She saw masses but not details. The warm, wet air made her uncomfortable.

The car, all lights off, rested at the road front of the cottage. A single square of illumination streamed from a window on the seaside. She heard clinking, hammering sounds. She was cautiously moving forward when the noise ceased. The light vanished.

Jean stopped dead still. A few seconds later came the thud of feet on the stoop, the click of doors opened and closed. The headlights beamed; the engine caught, and away rolled the auto.

Jean sped to the darkened window, swept the room with her beam.

Kelsey lay on the floor, spread-eagled, each arm and leg handcuffed to a spike. A big bruise welted his forehead.

Summer cottages seldom have doors or windows locked. Jean pulled the hood over her head, then raised the window and listened. She heard nothing.

Once inside, she knelt over Kelsey. His heart beat strongly. His captors had probably donated the bump on his head just to make him manageable. And when he wakened, he could die slowly, with no chance whatever of freeing himself.

She tested a spike, found it solidly embedded. She couldn't do much by her unaided efforts. She stood up.

"Hold it!" a harsh voice grated at the window.

She snapped the flashlight out, jumped for the door. At the same instant, the overhead light flooded the room.

"Stop where you are!" came a husky bark from the doorway.

Jean half turned to bring both in view, her mind racing, desperate. The two killers who had been bowled off the running board of the Demon had caught up with her.

The one at the window started coming in.

"Back or I'll shoot!" Jean ran for the window.

He came through. Two spurts exploded from her pistol. She saw him jerk. The effect was astounding. Feet on the sill, he leaped toward her, arms outflung. Too late, too bitterly, she realized that his powerful build represented not muscle but a bulletproof jacket. Her third shot hit the ceiling as the weapon flew out of her hand.

Pinioned from behind, she saw the second man pick up her pistol. His left hand lacked thumb and little finger.

"Nice work, boys."

Gus Berber drifted through the door jauntily. Gus looked like half weasel, half eel. He ripped the hood off Jean, cooed, "I thought so. When you lam from a joint, you don't have to keep on going. So we came back to see the pretty mouse. It's curtains."

Three-fingered Lefty scowled. "You mean it?"

"I mean it."

"Here?"

"Naw, down the road. Leave the guy to wiggle loose all by himself. Take her for a ride. Then tie up what's left and dump it in the sea."

"What's against the dame? Listen, Gus, you losin' your mind? You gave us screwy orders early this evenin'. Put paint on our faces and go some place and shoot a certain party if they tailed a certain party." Lefty snarled, "I didn't know who she was then. Next you give us screwy orders to put blue lights on our car and go to hell-and-gone and pick up a guy and bring him here. Sure, you were with us, so what? So here we are and the dame's such a knock-out I been wonderin' where I saw her. Now I know. She works for Frost."

"What of it?"

"What of it!" squawked Lefty. "Remember what he did to the Blake mob? And cleaned out the ROPA? And a lot of others? Gee, that guy's poison. Bump off the dame? We'd never even get a chance at court! He'd pick us off in just about the time it takes to tell!"

"The order stands," said Gus, softly—very softly. "It's the works, unless you want—" He left the sentence unfinished.

Lefty glowered, took a nasal breath, subsided. "O.K."

"That's better. I'm still running this show."

Jean's eyes widened.

A bluish muzzle crept over the window sill. Violet eyes and a flushed, reckless face bobbed up. "Drop your guns! I'll shoot the runt first! Turn her loose!"

"April!" Jean screamed. "Bulletproof vests! Shoot at heads!"

A fist clapped over her mouth.
Lefty spun for the window, his finger taut on the trigger.

IX

Frost smiled at the host of detectives who thronged around him in the Grand Central Terminal. A beatific expression lighted his features, as with secret, supreme appreciation of some cosmic jest. He drawled, "Life is sometimes inspiredly lunatic. One detective can catch twenty killers, but it takes twenty detectives to catch one detective. Get Inspector Frick down here."

"Any minute now," said the nearest man. "He left orders. We notified him the second you barged into the station."

The siren stopped wailing. The detective squad went to work to disperse the mob. Inspector Frick bustled through the hurrying commuters. He seemed both uneasy and self-satisfied as he approached the professor.

Frick ventured, with a half apology, "We caught up with you this time, Ivy. When I left you this afternoon I ordered twenty detectives placed here and another twenty on duty at the Pennsylvania Station. What have you got there?"

He glanced at the cache hastily, whistled, "Phew! We ought to clear the mystery up in short order after we work on this stuff and the experts go over it."

"They'll never see it!" Frost snapped tersely. He shut and locked the door.

"See here, Ivy—"

"Let's settle it outside, in your official limousine."

Frost strode off. The inspector issued a rapid order to the captain of the detective squad, then chased after the retreating figure.

Inside the automobile, Frost explained, "Headquarters will never see the material in that locker because I'm going to destroy it!"

"You can't do that!"

"I can and will. That assortment merely accounts for the lunatic plague. I could have told you as much this afternoon. I located the horde partly to verify my deductions, and partly in the hope that it might supply a lead. It doesn't. It offers not the slightest clue of any value to capture or identify the criminal.

"With twenty detectives and control of the station you can forcibly transport the stuff to police headquarters over my objections. If you do, I withdraw from the case and I can assure you it will never be solved. If you don't, I'll make the identification before to-morrow noon. I'll guarantee unquestionable proof of his guilt."

"We can reach the same result by analyzing the stuff."

"You won't get anywhere by analyzing the whole lot!" Frost answered impatiently. "There's a phrase that's lost its meaning from overuse, but it certainly applies here. We're up against a fiendish mind. You won't find one single fingerprint in all that pile. You won't obtain a solitary clue though you examine the letters and photographs from now till doomsday. You can question all the individuals concerned, threaten them, prosecute them, and you'll draw an absolute blank for all your efforts. Why? Because even they haven't the faintest idea who's guilty, and if they did they'd never talk because they'd face worse ruin."

"They'll face it and like it. They'll talk!"

"Why wreck the lives of a hundred in a futile search for one? They're no better and no worse than any average assortment of humanity. I've never met the individual, male or female, who didn't possess a flaw or a skeleton somewhere in the closet.

"Hasn't it occurred to you that the locker contains numerous prints, but no films? Where are the negatives from which those prints were made? On the basis of your recital this afternoon, logic at once told me that too many of the lunatic cases existed even for coincidence, therefore, they must be purposive, a common link must unite them; yet the persons involved in each scene had no personal acquaintance with those connected to other cases. Nor did fantastic behavior form their point of similarity."

"I told you they didn't connect."

"Ah, but they did. All the victims proved alike in their refusal to talk, their failure to offer any explanation whatsoever for the performances.

"Why did they refuse? Because they must have been commanded to silence. Why would they indulge in humiliating or even murderous actions and offer no defense? Because they acted under compulsion and possessed a deeper fear of the consequences if they failed in the least detail.

"What could account for such an intense fear? A combination of two reasons, and two reasons only. Each individual had a skeleton in his closet, some past offense against society or some folly committed, of which evidence existed. Some one owned that evidence, but the victims did not know his or her identity.

"Starting from those premises, deduction solved a little more than the basic pattern of the mystery. Many persons of prominence were already involved. The sword unquestionably hung over the heads of others. It would be physically impossible for the criminal to obtain overnight a wide variety of evidence that damns a large group. Therefore, he must have accumulated it over a period of time. Unlike the average blackmailer, he did not strike immediately, or strike for cash. The passage of years would make it still harder for the victims to trace his identity."

* * *

Frost emphasized. "He bided his time and struck. Now do you see the full magnitude of his scheme? What a terrific menace he is? He's cunning, ruthless, infinitely resourceful. No suspicion would fall on him, but if it did, no evidence proving his guilt must be found. Therefore, he would not keep the material on his premises. Yet he needed access to it day and night during his campaign of terror. Therefore, he would not store it in a bank safety-deposit box. Where could he put it? In a public lock box. From available sites he would choose the railroad terminal because of its size and traffic, with less likelihood of any one noticing him. But if the police found that box, they would get no clue to his identity, and he would preserve a sub-stantial part of his power by storing the films elsewhere.

"They are his reserve. They lie in a safe-deposit vault rented under an assumed name at a bank."

"I'll put a hundred detectives to work! I'll have them comb every box in town if it takes months!"

"And he'll know every step you take! There's a leak in your own office. I found that out before I laid eyes on the locker. My assistant phoned a memorandum for your desk. Within an hour the lunatic plague—in the shape of a weirdly costumed woman—made its appearance at my residence. If you didn't announce your purpose at your office, no one could have foreseen your visit to me. Therefore, the memorandum. Through his hold over one police official, the criminal would learn the contents of the note. He would either stop his activities then or issue a thumb-at-his-nose ges-ture."

"A police official could trace the call!"

"Not the way this crook works. The official goes to a specified public pay booth at a specified time every day. There he receives a call from another pay booth and makes his report. He is then given the number and location of another booth, and the time to be there the following day, and at the hour is called from still a different public booth. Each booth is one of a large group at a busy place.

"Frick, the preparation of years went into this mess. Ordinary methods won't smash the plan overnight. Bank authorities won't coöperate with you on such a wholesale scale for a search based on a hypothesis. In any event, by the time you located the vault, the safety box would be empty and the films stored somewhere else. You'd only get a fictitious name and perhaps a vague, useless description from the guard."

"There must be a way! We've got to run him down!"

Frost drawled, "How? There are seven million suspects in this area, and no tangible clues. Any person already involved, living or dead, and any name or person figuring in the locker contents may be guilty of the lunatic plague."

"What!" The inspector gasped incredulously.

"Perhaps that's the most brilliant stroke. I'm convinced, for reasons too long to detail, that he deliberately included evidence which incriminated himself, so that he would automatically be eliminated from suspicion."

"Well, I'll be damned!" Frick exploded, his red face redder still from the flare of anger. "Does he think he's going to make a monkey out of us?"

"My dear inspector," Frost snapped, "that is exactly what he's doing. He had the insufferable egotism to compel one of his victims to bring me a goose egg, he's so supremely confident that the combined results of our work will total precisely zero." Frost glanced at the dashboard clock.

"When they bring him in," Frick threatened, "I'll tell the boys to work on him all they please if it costs me my job!"

"And if they never bring him in?"

Frick made no answer.

The professor continued: "Furthermore, some of that evidence came into his hands by a method that either deliberately framed innocent persons, or made it impossible for victims to know until now that it existed. The picture of a doctor and a woman patient could ruin them both, but you won't learn anything by quizzing them. Why? Because the criminal could have picked his name at random from a directory, rented an office across from his in another building, and waited days or weeks to get that one snap with a telephoto lens. As a matter of fact, it's only a routine physical examination such as any doctor makes hundreds of times, but it looks bad, very bad.

"You might locate the office used by the photographer. Later tenants would have obscured all trace of his occupancy, years back, under an assumed name. The rental agent at this date could hardly give much useful information. The guilty one may even be dead already."

"How the deuce can you figure that?"

"Fitzroyd, the orchestra leader, if responsible for the plague, could have issued a whole series of orders to different victims for them to carry out at future dates. He could have made the appointment at which Gus Berber shot him. Berber, on suspicion, may have determined to kill whomever he met on the chance that he was dealing directly with the man in whose power he lay. Fitzroyd, in advance, would order Judge Hagerman to free any suspect accused of a murder to occur that night at a certain locality. Fitzroyd may have planned to kill Berber, and the tables turned."

"Fitzroyd didn't have any gun on him," Frick protested.

"Neither did Berber. I believe that Berber planted one of his own men in a darkened doorway as an extra precaution. When he fled, he tossed the gun to his accomplice. And while the police chased Berber, the accomplice had ample time to frisk the dead man's pockets. The fact that Fitzroyd had a couple of fish in his pockets when taken to the morgue is no proof at all that they did not contain other items at the moment he fell.

"In that case, Berber's gang would have the key to the locker, would discover the contents, and be able to force his release even if Fitzroyd hadn't given instructions to the judge. I leave you to imagine how the lunatic plague would sweep on under the loving hands of Berber's gangsters.

"Gus Berber may be the criminal we seek. He could have accumulated much of the material in the locker through his various racketeering and vice connections.

"And neither Berber nor Fitzroyd may afford the answer. Consider then the dilemma that faced Berber. If he didn't kill Fitzroyd as ordered, he would go to the electric chair when the terrorist sent the incriminating record of a past murder to the police. If Berber did slay Fitzroyd, he would face the chair for that crime."

Frick insisted stubbornly, though with less conviction, "The dragnet will get him sooner or later. We'll make people testify. We'll salt him away for the rest of his life."

"Will you? On what charges? Blackmail? So far it does not appear that he's exacted a dollar of tribute. As the mystery stands, I see no grounds to convict him. A good defense attorney could demolish the prosecution's case because of its tenuous and hypothetical nature.

"Yet he killed Paula Van Wyke, Fitzroyd, and perhaps others as surely as if he drove a dagger into their hearts. His crimes are the more monstrous because he compelled others to accomplish the act and assume the burden of guilt. He's perfected his method and technique to such a degree that he enjoys virtual immunity from the law. In some respects he has originated a new kind of crime."

"There aren't any new kinds of crime." Frick scowled.

"Aren't there? I'd call this compulsory lunacy, or forcible performance, or murder by remote control. Libel and slander are on the statutes, but what law covers personal damage to yourself by your own crazy behavior? If we don't stop him and trap him fast, he'll establish a secret, one-man rule of terror over a hundred or more persons in all walks of life. He'll have the power of a dictator. He'll be an invisible god, controlling puppets. What he will do then is limited only by the wildest imagination. Anything; everything; wholesale homicide; blackmail on a scale of millions; whatever he wants to do." Frost looked at the clock again.

The inspector was silent for a moment. He didn't doubt any longer. Frost had painted a deadly picture. "Frost, you can do things we can't. Red tape and politics don't bother you. This thing has got to be stopped. Pass me the word and I'll get all the men and equipment you can use. If there's a way I can help you—"

"There is. Lend me this auto."

"Hm?" Frick exclaimed.

"That's all. I need power, speed, and perhaps the siren now. My own Demon is, unfortunately, in use."

Frick opened the door. "Want the chauffeur? He's inside."

"No. Be at your office after two a.m."

The limousine swung out and away.

X

At the cottage on Long Island, Lefty spun toward the window, his automatic pointing.

"Hold it!" drawled a cold, implacable voice from the doorway behind Gus Berber.

The instant that Frost spoke, Gus screeched. Whatever his words were, the roaring fury that swept the room drowned them.

Lefty continued swinging toward the window; his gun spat flame; but the explosion sounded like the echo of Frost's shot. Lefty swayed. His eyes peered stupidly at the spot on the wall where his bullet had plowed. He pitched over, a hole through his temple.

Gus Berber yammered and twitched as the window unloosed a spray of red flashes. April's wild shooting smacked his vest, thudded on Frost's cloak, took Gus once at the skull. Gus leaned against the wall, a curious look of surprise entering his face. His body sagged, and his face sagged into idiotic vacancy.

The third gunman released an arm to fire, tried to hold Jean for a shield with the other. She twisted, flung herself aside, stumbled sprawling over Kelsey. The second and final blast from the long-barreled pistol that Frost carried punched a piece of the gunman's face through the back of his head. By some oddity of reflex, his finger tightened and two more bursts spewed from his automatic. The slugs flattened at the level of Frost's knees. The gunman toppled.

Frost mourned dryly, without regret, "Not quite as I planned. However, the young woman's intrusion did not alter the results. I would suggest that she indulge in extensive target practice for the future, and wear more adequate protection."

April sprang across the sill, shivered from reaction. "I've never had so much excitement!" she cried hysterically. "That's why I became an actress! Nothing ever happened to me; I had to pretend all the adventures I wanted! I couldn't wait at the car. I found the gun there and came here, just hoping that—" She slumped in a complete faint.

Jean got up. "Ivy! If you'd reached us a minute later!"

Frost corrected her. "I was here before they arrived."

"But what—how could you have guessed?"

"I didn't guess; I knew. It's Kelsey's cottage. He had a picture of the place in the living room of his home. Give me the outline of what happened to you."

He listened to her résumé. His eyes suddenly glinted. "Splendid! That clears everything. Get the Demon and drive it here. Frick's limousine brought me but it's safely hidden where he can send for it to-morrow."

Frost went to work. By the time Jean returned he had freed Kelsey and restored both Kelsey and April.

Jean drove the Demon, April again at her side. As it gathered momentum Jean asked, "Where shall I stop first? Hospital or 13 State Street?"

"Neither. Police headquarters," was Frost's laconic answer.

Dr. Kelsey frowned. "Is that necessary?"

"It is, to stop you and the lunatic plague."

"Are you serious? I've no idea what you're talking about. You've killed the men who assaulted me. Is it something to do with them?"

"They died because I don't care for professional killers, and I particularly dislike individuals who try their marksmanship on my valuable assistant. I settled one score there. But they weren't acting on their own initiative. Berber had received orders from the nameless voice, the invisible threat— which was you! Now I am going to settle that score."

"Great Scott, man, look at what they did to me! I would have died if you hadn't rescued me!"

"What they did was also at your order and for the sole purpose of exonerating yourself from suspicion. You wouldn't have died or even suffered severely. When you remained missing, your niece would look here first of all. Or you may have left orders with some other victim to come to this cottage to-morrow."

"You're building mountains out of pure moonshine and utter nonsense!"

"By no means. You committed two errors—one trifling and one serious. The first consisted of including your niece among your victims. You did it because of the relationship. Knowing her habits and whereabouts, you could always use her for an emergency, as you did to-night. The weakness lay in ostensibly putting two members of one family under the same menace. If innocent, they, alone, of the victims would best be able by comparing notes to identify the criminal. If not innocent, one must be the criminal himself.

"The second error damns you. Miss Moray noticed it and by truly brilliant deduction, without my aid, arrived at the identical conclusion which I had also reached. When she entered the cottage, she did so not to free you but to bring you to justice.

"You put on an act at Coney Island to prove yourself caught by the lunatic plague. When you emerged from the water with Miss Holley, a policeman stopped you. Farther up the island waited a car with blue headlights to carry out the rest of your commands. You could not risk arrest because then Miss Holley could not keep the appointment.

"You volunteered the explanation that the pair of you were on a scavenger hunt. It meant nothing to Miss Holley. It meant everything to Miss Moray. All other victims gave no explanation for their behavior. They were under threat. No threat hung over you. Only you and you alone could offer a reasonable account of a fantastic performance."

"Bah!" Kelsey replied. "I'm perfectly willing to go to a police station. I'll not only face your foolish charges, I'll collect a nice fat sum for false arrest."

"You're not going to be charged," Frost stated.

"It's about time you changed your mind. Besides, you saw and heard for yourself the telephone call I received in your presence. I'll have to admit now that I'm one of the victims and you've seen how the voice works. If you don't catch him fast I'll be ruined."

"You mistake me," Frost answered dryly. "That telephone call was not a coincidence. There are no coincidences in your plan. I can explain every detail and show how each came about through your deliberate plotting. You took the incriminating photograph of yourself and a patient. You put the camera on the window sill of your office and snapped the shutter by pulling a thread.

"I repeat, I am taking you to police headquarters, but you will not be arrested, or charged, or tried." Frost's voice took on a hint of scorn and sardonic approval. "Inspector Frick is waiting for me. He will instantly commit you to the psychopathic ward at Bellevue for observation. Alienists will examine you. Within a month, you will leave to spend the rest of your life in an insane asylum."

A tense, protracted silence seemed only to deepen as Kelsey's breathing grew audibly hoarser.

Frost drawled, "I could tell you now most of your method, what started you off, how you operated, where you obtained some of the incriminating evidence, how you even forced some victims to bring you others. I shall leave that for the alienists."

Kelsey shouted, "You can't; you can't; you can't do that to me! I demand that I be arrested! You've got to place charges against me!"

Frost shook his head. "You're not a criminal genius, Kelsey. You're not a superbrain. You're nothing but a superlunatic, a dangerous maniac.

"What the alienists find when they are finished with you will be of interest to abnormal psychology, but not to the police. Your cell will be padded. There you can keep your delusions of grandeur and power to yourself. You can dream of terrorizing cities and nations. Your delusions won't annoy any one. You can pretend that you hold under your control every one who is stronger or more powerful or more important than your own warped little self. Your ego has already carried you from irresponsibility to madness. Possibly the alienists themselves will not be able to predict the final stages of your dementia."

Kelsey whipped a handkerchief from his breast pocket, patted his face. Something passed between his lips, and his teeth crunched. The odor of bitter almond drifted off on the currents of air washing through the car. His body twitched with almost instantaneous death.

"The easiest way out, for him." Frost shrugged, to April's horrified gasp. To Jean he said, "You can turn off the dictaphone now."

Her hand clicked a switch that she had touched when she started the Demon at the cottage.

Frost murmured, "I promised I would counter with a cross."

"What do you mean by that?" Jean asked.

"When he sent me a goose egg, I remarked that I would counter with a cross. And X marks the spot—

"Make it the morgue!"

SLACK WIRES

Arthur J. Burks

The face of Nick Mechem was grimly set, as he watched the way of Harlan Dyce on the wires. There was something almost diabolical about Dyce in his confidence in himself—a confidence which could be found in few men.

"It's nothing, Nick, really," Dyce had said. "I hadn't anything else to do, lots of times, in the Big Show, so I took it up as a hobby."

Nick stared out the open window, into the black, windy night. It was icy cold out there, and Dyce wore no coat—as though that lack were what disturbed Mechem!

Fifty feet above the grounds of the Durban place—over which late fall had spilled the whispering brown of fallen leaves—with the howling wind tugging at his sixty-pound body, Harlan Dyce was flirting with death. So Nick thought. Dyce had laughed at the idea.

"I wouldn't be safer on the ground, Nick. You'll see!"

And Nick was seeing.

Dyce used a pole perhaps twelve feet long. Nick had gone to some pains to find it. Dyce had been explicit as to weight and length. Dyce couldn't use the same kind other wire walkers might.

Slowly, carefully, Dyce was feeling his way along the slack wire, with his tiny, rubber-soled shoes.

"There's enough juice in the wire," thought Mechem, "to turn a man twice his size to a cinder."

There were wires to the right and left of Dyce. If he fell, and struck one or the other—Mechem had a swift inner vision of a flash of spluttering blue flame, out there in the dark. He didn't know too much about the ways of electricity.

Nor did he like Norwalk, and the strange idea that had brought Harlan Dyce into Connecticut.

"It's horrible," Dyce had said, "but so obvious I wonder nobody ever thought of it before."

Blackmail on a huge scale! And after Norwalk, other Connecticut cities and towns, where lived commuting New Yorkers, who made the neighboring State their "bedroom." And the outfit back of it was shrewdly captained, ruthless, without mercy.

What could that little man, out there on the wire, possibly do to thwart the ring?

"He'll do something, that's sure," Nick Mechem told himself. "He'll always do something—something eminently successful."

Nick caught his breath. A swift rush of wind—that had bathed Mechem's face like ice water—caught Dyce squarely. For a moment he swayed perilously, manipulating the short pole wildly to keep his balance. Then he was in command again. Mechem had to grin. Dyce, as though it, too, were necessary, had put a scarf around his slight waist! Yellow and red, it stood out from Dyce's body now, straight in the wind.

"An actor," Mechem thought, "and a good one."

He liked his midget employer.

But would Dyce ever reach his objective? Even if he did, what would he accomplish? To reach the wall of that black house now looked to be a certainty for Dyce, but after that? He had to get inside, then, on the spur of the moment, find out how to handle a given situation.

On his own part, Dyce was having a good time. He liked to walk high wires, especially slack ones. And if they were charged with high voltage, so much the better. It added to the excitement.

He was scarcely giving a thought to the people he intended contacting in that house. He would take care of that when the right time came. Now, he put one foot exactly ahead of the other, balanced himself, with a scarcely perceptible movement of the pole, took another step.

"Cinch!" said Dyce into the wind. "I could turn a back flip on this wire, even in the wind."

Now the house was close, so close that the shadow of it hovered over him. Out of the corner of his eye he saw a man on the street below, staggering. A gust of wind spun the man half around, throwing him against a picket fence, twisting his head. The man looked up. He saw Dyce, but did not, obviously, believe in what he saw. For he screamed, wildly, drunkenly, and ran down the sidewalk.

Dyce chuckled. The man would come back, but not until to-morrow, when he would wish to make sure; by which time Dyce would, he hoped, have long since been gone.

Now the wall of the house was very close, and Dyce was planning the next step. For a minute or so he'd have to balance on the wire without the pole. He couldn't, very well, take it into the house with him. And he hoped the window would be unlocked. People in Connecticut did not need locks as they did in New York City.

The window was three or four feet to one side of the wires.

Carefully, Dyce turned, backed against the cold brick wall, and placed the pole across the three wires. He gauged the distance to that window, grinning as he knew that Nick Mechem held his breath, waiting, hoping.

Then Dyce jumped easily across, taking a chance that the room beyond the window was vacant. He landed on the sill, pressing his body close against the glass. For a moment he teetered. Then he slid slowly down to his knees, fumbled for a way in. The window was not locked. He heard a whispering on the wire and knew, without looking, what caused it. His pole was sliding slowly down the curve of the slack wire.

"I'll have to walk down to it, going back," he thought, "without a pole." The window, above his tiny finger tips—which were surprisingly strong—began to rise. Finally there was space enough through which to crawl. Harlan Dyce sprawled on the window sill, to go through quickly. Inside a dark room, which had been warm, but was cooling because of the open window and the icy wind, Dyce did something that was as natural with him as breathing. He smoothed down his hair with his palms. The wind, on the wires, had flung it awry. Dyce was always meticulous in matters of dress and general appearance.

He closed the window behind him.

He moved swiftly about the room, searching for a door. Nick Mechem, in that window across the way, would grow cold in the wind, waiting for him. Nick was a faithful watchdog, immensely useful in his way, and a master in crises.

Dyce opened the door. Light streamed up a stairway from below.

He caught the murmur of voices.

And he sensed undercurrents in them.

"John, you're behaving strangely of late. The last two weeks. Has anything gone wrong at the office?"

"No, Kitty." Low and rumbling, but worried, came the voice of Durban. "Nothing is wrong."

"But you're so strange."

"Maybe I'm getting tired of riding two hours every day with the same faces around me, the same voices in my ears."

"Not tired," said Dyce to himself, "but terrified! And only I, in this house —besides yourself, John—knows why."

He reconnoitered the stairs carefully before going down. The speakers were not in sight. He started down the steps, testing each as he went.

"We've been so happy, John," said the woman's voice. "If anything ever happened to our happiness—"

Durban's voice was harsh. "What in the world could happen?" he asked.

"If I lost you—"

"What diabolical imp of Satan," Dyce asked himself, "made her say that? The very worst thing she could have said. Women's intuition gets me down sometimes. Subconsciously she knows that her happiness is in danger; maybe, even, her subjective mind gives her a distorted picture of what it is."

Dyce went on down.

Nobody saw him. The door of a room was ajar, and from it the voices came. He went and looked through the crack, and his heart almost stopped. There, he knew, were a man and wife who adored each other, worshiped each other—

"And the cur that would spoil it deserves killing," thought Dyce. "Why *will* men stand for it?"

John Durban was sitting in a vast easy-chair before a fireplace. His wife was sitting on his lap, her cheek against his neck. Dyce had a twinge of jealousy. He'd never experience anything like that, he knew. Once there had been a girl, of Dyce's own size—but a circus elephant had stepped on her, accidentally. That had been a long time ago.

"If Martha had been a grown woman," thought Dyce, "she'd have looked like John's Kitty."

All the more reason, he thought, for helping these two out of their dreadful predicament.

He must get some message to Durban, but not when Kitty was around, or where she could see or hear him, Dyce. So Harlan Dyce waited for the breaks.

The first was a long time coming.

"Better go see how Dede is making out," said John Durban. "She kicks the covers off, and it's a cold night."

Obediently, Kitty Durban rose from the knees of her stalwart, gray-haired husband, moved toward the door. Dyce flung himself swiftly into a hall, among the shadows, where he stood to watch the wife of John Durban mount the stairs. His eyes glowed as he watched. She was so lovely, so fine.

It made him hate the unseen enemies even more.

Kitty was gone. He'd have to move fast.

Dyce went back to the door. Durban had his head turned away, and lowered against his chest. Dyce knew that his thoughts were terrifying. Dyce stepped in, snapping out the light.

"Take it easy, Mr. Durban," said Dyce. "I'm a friend."

"What sort of friend," came the strained voice, as Dyce heard Durban jump to his feet, "comes in the night, and turns off the lights?"

"I have my reason for not showing myself, but I am a friend. Listen, John Durban. You must not pay, understand? Tell your wife everything! Everything, understand? She is a woman of wisdom, of knowledge—and you know in your heart that you have nothing to hide."

There was a long pause. Dyce could sense Durban testing his voice, trying to guess what manner of man spoke out of the dark to him. Dyce could see Durban against the fireplace; Durban could not see Dyce in the shadows.

"How do I know?" asked Durban grimly. "I've been in town, going in every day, coming back every night, for years. I have every opportunity. Kitty knows that—and she used to be jealous. There is nothing, thank Heaven, for me to be ashamed of. But I'm afraid to start Kitty wondering!"

"And so, you're going to play into their hands? In so doing you will make it easier for them with everybody else on their list. How much do they want?"

"Fifty dollars a week, indefinitely."

"And your salary is?"

"A hundred and twenty-five."

"Your wife handles your money? Hurry, before she comes back."

"Yes."

"And when she misses the fifty, as she must? What, *then*, will she think? You'll have paid and built up more cause for wondering than if you told everything, *now*."

Durban's voice was harsh. "Who are you? If you come from them you—"

"Would I urge you not to pay? To tell the whole story to your Kitty? Promise me you will. I am a detective. I'm after the blackmailers. You must help."

"But what will they do to Kitty? To Dede? They've threatened—"

"They may not do anything. Better some trouble now, though, than trouble, and ever-increasing demands, the rest of your life. Think it over. You are a sensible man."

Durban groaned in agony of spirit. Dyce heard Kitty coming back down the stairs. He slid out of the door like a wraith, hoping she would not see him. Then he was gone, back into the shadows again. He saw the light go on in the room. Mrs. Durban passed through the door. Dyce slipped back to it, glad that Durban, so harassed by trouble, was not coming out to search for the strange intruder who was Dyce.

Dyce grinned when he heard Durban say, "Kitty, there is something I must tell you—"

Dyce went swiftly up the stairs. Out of curiosity, he went into the room where Dede slept, looked down at her flaxen curls, her sweet mouth twisted a little in a smile, as though her dream were pleasant.

"You're worth fighting for, Dede," whispered Dyce. Dede stirred, mumbled in her sleep.

Dyce went back to his window, slipped out, back against the now-lowered glass. Then he jumped, landing on the wire, while over across Nick Mechem held his breath. The pole was fifteen or twenty feet away, down the slant of the wire. Dyce walked to it steadily, without faltering, stooped, gathered it up, finished the precarious walk to Nick Mechem's coign of vantage.

"That, Nick," said Dyce, "is that. Now, for a night's sleep. To-morrow Nick Mechem takes his little boy for a train ride!"

II

I told you she was just the right size to be smart!"

That was when Helene Kocsis, Dyce's little secretary, had reported the weird undercurrent of terror she had detected in the morning train from South Norwalk. Helene lived in Connecticut herself.

"A lot of the men are scared," she had reported. "They don't even trust one another—not even men who've been commuting, and playing bridge together, for years on end."

"Find out more," Dyce had told her.

She had. She'd brought him names and addresses—and a story one harassed man had told her, because he had to tell some one or go mad.

"Some one, unknown to any of them, knows all about most of them, especially those who make any salary to speak of," her report had said, "and is systematically—"

"I know," said Dyce. "He, or they, is or are, making use of the fact that the wives of those men trust them, but don't know exactly what they do while they're in the city. It would be a cinch, and men are such fools. Some of them, perhaps, aren't to be trusted away from home. Most are. But so many wives can never be sure of that. Nick, we've got a job! We're going to make those trains safe for commuters. And if we can put the enemy behind bars—"

Nick hadn't liked it. He didn't believe in deliberately looking for trouble. Neither did he even think of opposing Dyce.

The walk across the wires, into the house of Durban, had been the first move.

"It's the one method of ingress nobody will notice," Dyce explained. "Nor will it leave footprints in the dew or frost. Besides, I like the idea."

And the first step had been taken.

But somewhat dubiously, Nick Mechem had agreed to take the next step.

"I believe the enemy keeps close watch over his or her victims," said Dyce.

So, Mechem, following Dyce's instructions exactly, and feeling like a fool —as any old-time bachelor might well feel—had outfitted Dyce with a boy's clothes.

Now, next morning after John Durban—Dyce hoped—had told his wife everything, Mechem and Dyce were taking the morning train out of South Norwalk. Mechem stared at Dyce, almost unbelieving. Dyce was a small boy, and he could play the part to perfection, as during his circus days he had often played small-boy parts. Dyce grinned.

"How do I look, Nick?" asked Dyce.

"Like a nasty little brat," said Nick promptly.

"Good! That's just how I wish to look. And it gives me an idea of how to go about things. You'll hold my hand, and look worried, like the properly harassed father."

"One thing you'll have to remember, chief," said Nick Mechem grimly.

"What?"

"No cigars!"

"That's a thought. I might have shoved one into my face without thinking about it. You're really valuable to me, Nick."

It sounded queer to say "Thank you, sir," to that small boy, but Nick Mechem said it. Harlan Dyce practiced a mincing walk for a few minutes, to get back the hang of it, he said. Then they were ready.

When the train pulled out of South Norwalk that morning, Nick Mechem and his small "son" were in the smoking car. Nick looked around. Helene Kocsis hadn't exaggerated; he knew that right away. He had never seen so many harassed faces, all together at one time, in his life.

"They've got to plenty of them, already," thought Nick Mechem.

"Have you ever thought," said Dyce, out of the corner of his mouth, "what a hundred times fifty dollars a week would be?"

"Yeah."

"And plenty get more money, and so pay more heavily. It's a great racket, Nick—and I'd bet my bottom dollar that some spy of the gang is here right now, gloating over his or her victims."

There were, Nick noted, six women in the smoking car. Women, it seemed, invaded every privacy of man.

Three bridge games were in progress. Nick Mechem studied the twelve men who were playing. Not one, he thought, was really interested in his game, or had his mind on it.

"Be ready," said Dyce softly, "to lose patience with your little son! But be belligerent about it, and in no hurry to yank my arm out by the roots. I've got ideas."

Dyce slid from the seat, stepped over Mechem's feet, scampered into the aisle. He headed straight for one of the bridge boards set by a porter. Nick watched him. Dyce could never have looked quite so much like a mischievous small boy.

Dyce leaned against one of the boards. It tilted, and several cards slid into the aisle. Dyce grinned engagingly from under his cap.

"Go on back to your dad," said one of the men.

"Gimme a nickel," said Dyce, "and I'll go!"

"You need," the man said, "a good thrashing. If I were your dad, you'd get it."

Dyce promptly flung himself into a tantrum. His small hands shot out to the cards on the table. They all went into the aisle as though struck by a wind. The train smashed its way toward New York City. The four men stood up. Two were scowling. Harlan Dyce was screaming and kicking.

"I wanta nickel! I wanta nickel!"

Nick Mechem, watching, was astounded. There was a small boy who had been spoiled beyond all redemption. There wasn't a man in the car—and all were looking now, and some of them, even the most harassed-looking, were grinning slightly—who suspected that Dyce was other than he pretended to be. Nick held his breath, wondering what in the world Dyce hoped to accomplish by his absurd antics.

One of the men caught Dyce by the wrist.

"Where's your father, little man?" he asked.

"I don't want to go back to him, and I'm no little man!" shrieked Dyce.

But the man started along the aisle with Dyce, and Mechem noticed that, exasperated though he was, the man did not squeeze Dyce's wrist too harshly. He had, Mechem thought, plenty of experience with kids. Dyce started kicking at the man's ankles, and squalling as though he were being murdered. The man swore, lifted his foot.

Dyce jerked away, started running along the aisle.

He stopped running, and stopped squalling, almost as suddenly as he had started. It was as though he had accomplished whatever he had had in mind with his tantrum, and were already thinking of something else.

A man leaned over the back of Mechem's seat.

"Better take charge of the kid or somebody will call the conductor. You can't let him annoy the passengers like this."

Nick turned. His face got savage.

"Who's annoying who?" he demanded. "And what the hell business is it of your's?"

The fellow's face went white. Nick grinned to himself, beginning now to guess what Dyce was driving at. In this strange way Dyce was sizing up the men in the car, segregating the courageous from the cowardly, the rats from the men. Whatever else the man behind Mechem might be, he hadn't the courage required to put over the vast coup Dyce hoped to smell out. And Mechem had studied the four men at the table Dyce had disarranged. All had been exasperated by Dyce, but none more than he would have been with a child of his own who did the same thing. Five men, Mechem thought, were thus eliminated from suspicion.

But how would Dyce go about judging, testing the others?

Dyce changed tactics. He went to a seat occupied by one man, crawled up beside him, sat down. The man glanced from his paper at Dyce, grinned briefly, went on with his reading. Dyce studied the man—apparently a small boy gravely regarding a stranger. But Mechem knew that Dyce missed no item of the man's apparel, that, when he had finished, he had taken as complete an inventory—almost of the man's soul—as any man could have taken.

Dyce got down, went to another seat occupied by two men. They were discussing politics and blowing great clouds of smoke. Dyce kicked the nearer on the shins, hard. The man whirled, caught Dyce by the shoulders, pushed him away.

"Here, here! Don't do that."

Dyce studied this man, and the one beyond him. So did Nick Mechem— wondering all the time how the men could fail to understand the weird thing that was being done in this car. Mechem himself could sense odd undercurrents—murderous hatred, terror, misery, guilt. Others must sense the same thing, or know it of their own experience. How, then, did no one guess that there was anything queer about the ornery kid in the aisle?

Dyce went on. He walked to another seat where two men were talking, leaned against it, listened to their words. A child could do this; a man would have been ordered about his business. The man nearer to Dyce shifted uncomfortably, frowned at Dyce and at Mechem, but said nothing to either, though the thread of his discourse was interfered with, because he was so conscious of the staring "small boy."

Mechem did not go to his rescue.

At one time or another every man and woman in the car stared at Harlan Dyce. A woman tried to take him onto her lap. He kicked at her, screamed, and her face was fiery red as she gave over the attempt.

"A blackmailer," thought Mechem, "wouldn't have touched him with a ten-foot pole—unless there were a lash on it! That lets *that* woman out."

Thirty minutes to go. Dyce had to work fast. For ten more minutes he went from seat to seat, listening to conversation, sometimes butting into it with childish prattle. Once the conductor came through; nobody made a complaint about Dyce. But the conductor asked whose kid he was. Mechem claimed him, and the conductor said, "Kids aren't allowed to play in the aisles."

Dyce had sat down beside Mechem until the conductor had passed through, when he had gone on with his strange examination of faces, his eavesdropping on conversations, his odd cataloguing of men and women.

He had, Mechem noted, in one way or another, eliminated all of the women but one, and most of the men. That no guilty persons were here was possible. That one or more might be in other cars was likely. It was like looking for a needle in a haystack, requiring infinite patience—possessed by both Mechem and Dyce in plenty.

In fifteen minutes they would be in Grand Central Station, and the commuters would scatter to the four winds, en route to their offices all over the city. Yet no sign of anything suspicious had come to Mechem from "the brat."

Dyce did not stop.

There were still a dozen men with whom he had had no contact. The train was crawling through the underground dark before anything worthy of note transpired.

Dyce spoke to a man. "Gimme a nickel!"

"I've been wanting to do this for almost an hour," snarled the man. "I've been wishing somebody else would do it. And if your dad wants to make anything out of it—"

He slapped Harlan Dyce on the mouth with the back of his hand. Dyce slid along the aisle, cracking his head against a seat. Mechem, at a glance from Dyce, rose to his feet, hurled himself at the attacker. But the man was hurrying for the door. Dyce's mouth was bleeding.

Mechem flung himself after the man who had slapped Dyce.

Dyce got up, started for the door.

Somebody said loudly, "Somebody ought to keep an eye on that blasted kid—"

A hand reached for Dyce, who was running.

"Keep your hands off me!" snarled Dyce.

His voice, now, wasn't a boy's voice. It was Dyce's voice, but Dyce didn't care. The man would never guess the truth. He'd only know that something queer had happened, and wonder about it until his brain got all twisted up.

Dyce looked back. The fellow, mouth open, was staring at him. Dyce raced out to Forty-second Street, opened the door of a taxi-cab.

"Here, sonny, what are you doing?"

"Take me to—" and Dyce gave the address of his own office.

"But listen, kid—" the cabby began again.

Dyce leaned forward, his face twisted, looking strangely old through the dribbling blood. "Get going, blast you!" he snapped. He showed the man a five-dollar bill, and the cab got started.

"And step on it, molasses!" said Dyce.

"Gee!" said the cabby. "Gee!"

In his own office, Dyce said to Helene Kocsis, "Any of my own clothes here?"

"In the closet, Mr. Dyce," said efficient Helene, with never a hint of a smile. Wise girl, Helene Kocsis; a smile at that moment would have cost her her job.

"I'm expecting a call from Nick," said Dyce. "Put it right through."

"Yes, sir."

"And listen, Kocsis!"

"Yes?"

"You had the right dope about those Connecticut commuters. Now you're a junior partner in the Dyce Detective Agency!"

"I know. I've got the papers all made out!"

Dyce stopped, stared at her.

"Read my mind, eh? Smart girl! Have you also raised your own pay?"

Still no smile. "Yes, twenty dollars a week, to start."

Dyce grinned. "Good! I've been wondering how to collect from all those commuting clients you brought me. *You'll* do it!"

III

Dyce had learned a great deal more on the morning train than Nick Mechem could have guessed. He had spent so many years studying the people who studied him that he would have been a master psychologist had he wished. As it was, he knew almost the complete story of those who had been in the car.

A man named Michael Heber, for example, was wondering whether or not to pay two hundred dollars a week—and Dyce knew that Heber lied; that he had never earned that much money in his life. He knew that one man, who had nothing to say whatever about mysterious blackmail, paid almost twice that amount, had paid two installments of the endless grind Dyce knew blackmail invariably was. It was useless to pay blackmailers, for they always came back for more and had less sympathy than murdering kidnapers.

By this word and that, a name here and there, Dyce had checked pretty thoroughly the report Helene Kocsis had made to him. And it was almost, even this soon after the beginning of operations, as though he had visited each family concerned, in turn, and listened to their confessions.

John Durban had been on the train, too, with a look of peace on his face. "He's told her, all right," Dyce had thought—and Durban, smiling, had bent forward and patted Dyce on the head. "But if he knew I'm the spoiled brat back of his decision he—"

Dyce, nattily dressed now, as usual, sat impatiently behind his desk, waiting for the call from Nick Mechem. Had Nick lost that man, who had slapped Dyce, in the shuffle, the race through pedestrians at the station? Had he lost him—apparently—and then discreetly tailed him?

The telephone rang.

"Nick, chief," came the excited voice. "I think you picked your man, all right, or at least one of 'em, and it's big stuff."

"Big?"

"Yeah. I think the blackmail business on the train is nothing compared to all they do! There's murder in it—and other commuter trains from all points of the compass, not only coming into New York City, but into many other big cities. This angle of it is just part of the general attempt to run everything that has money in it—even bridge games."

"I'd suspected that, Nick," said Dyce impatiently. "But where's your man?"

"In an apartment house, in the best part of Greenwich Village. But I can't get in."

"Can't get in?"

"No, and that's what makes it queer, chief. Nobody answers buzzers at the door—and a cop drove me away when I kept pushing one of 'em. Just the same, the fellow I was after didn't hesitate, though I wasn't close enough to find out whether he had a key or not."

"You mean the place is a fort?"

"Yes. And a torture chamber, maybe lots of chambers—"

"I'll be right there. Meet me on a corner—"

Dyce, clicking down the receiver, regarded, with distaste, the child's clothing he had just taken off. Always, he knew, he would be hard pressed to get around and do his work without giving it away, or attracting attention to his midgetism.

Reluctantly, he slipped back into the boy's clothing, which he had grown to hate. A small boy could do so many things without attracting attention.

"But that fellow who smacked me will wonder, if he sees me," thought Dyce. "So, I mustn't let him."

Outside Dyce glanced at Helene Kocsis.

"How much should we charge 'em, chief?" she asked.

"Charge who?"

"Those commuters you're trying to get out of the hands of blackmailers?"

"*Trying* to get out? I'm going, actually, to get them out."

"Yes, I know. But how much?"

"Ten per cent of whatever their first blackmail payments were to have been. They won't object to that."

"That was my estimate, too. But I wished to check with your judgment."

Still she didn't smile at the way he looked. Nor, after he had left, did she smile. Instead, she stopped the clattering of her typewriter and stared at the closed door for a long time, with a rapt look in her eyes. Then she stirred.

"Stop it, Helene," she said to nobody. "You're nothing to him but a junior partner, and even if you weren't, so what?"

Meanwhile, Dyce paid off another amazed cabby two blocks from his destination, and then hurried to meet Nick Mechem, who pointed out the apartment house to which he had referred. Dyce studied it for a long time.

"Did you think of trying the top, Nick?" asked Dyce.

"What good would that be? Look at the windows?"

There were bars on all the windows they could see, and the building, twelve stories tall, would have withstood the battering of a big naval gun.

"There's always a way into any house," said Dyce. "And your hunch is right. That's probably the stronghold of one of the biggest mobs in history, right in the city, the building bought and paid for from murder and robbery, and occupied by murderers and bandits—every one knowing his place against the inevitable day when it must withstand attack from all sides by coppers, sailors, maybe, and soldiers. But we're just guessing, and scaring ourselves. We've got to get inside."

"I'll try anything, chief, but I'm sure of one thing: that no man who isn't welcome there ever gets out if, by some miracle, he gets in in the first place."

"They'd be fools to let such a person out. But if he, or she, is smart enough to get in, he should be smart enough to get out. Nick?"

"Yes?"

"I want a hundred feet of clothesline."

"Listen, chief. Walking hot wires fifty feet above the ground may be all right, but walking slack rope, twelve stories up—"

"This isn't the place for that, Nick. I've got something else on my mind. Get that rope!"

But, after spending the entire day, looking the place over, Dyce was not ready to go in until dark. A man on a roof during the day was too noticeable, he said. Nick covered two sides of the building; Dyce covered two. Nobody went in or out.

"There's a way in and out, maybe several of them," Dyce said, "that doesn't touch the street at all. Any number of the adjoining houses may mask entrances and exits—"

But, after dark, they got into one building, almost a block away, and worked their way to the roof. Mechem had the rope about his middle, to leave his hands free. In the dark of many stairs he followed the lead of Harlan Dyce, who still persisted in his boy's clothing, because a boy could get away with things impossible to a midget with a man's intelligence.

On the roof they worked their way carefully, taking plenty of time, almost without sound, to a building adjacent to that which they must enter —to find themselves one story short of their goal, and the wall of that building as smooth as ice.

Mechem, at Dyce's soft command, heaved the rope at the high coping, understanding now why Dyce had insisted on a small, four-pronged hook on the rope's end. The hook caught. Dyce went swiftly up. Mechem whispered.

"They'll have a guard up there."

"I've got to take that chance."

Dyce made easy-going of it. Presently, he looked down.

"It'll hold you, Nick," he called softly, "if you hold your breath!"

Nick swore, but started climbing. Soon, amid shadows, they stood on the roof of the suspected enemy hangout. Dyce was chuckling.

"What's eating you, chief?" asked Mechem.

"I was just wondering what their faces would look like if they spotted me, after I got inside—"

"How are you going in? I mean, how are *we* going in?"

"*We* aren't; I am. You're too big. There's no skylight, no stairs to the roof from below—which explains why they don't have a guard up here. I've already looked. But see there, Nick!"

"A fireplace chimney, I'd guess," said Nick. "But what good—"

And then, realizing the intention of the indomitable midget, Nick gasped.

"Listen, chief," he protested. "You might get in that way, but if there isn't another way out, what then? You can't fly up a chimney!"

Dyce's voice grated as he replied. "I can look out for myself, Mechem. Just do what I tell you!"

There was a big man's determination in Dyce's voice. He led the way to the chimney, which rose five feet or so from the roof.

"Boost me, Mechem!" snapped Dyce. Nick did so. Dyce lay on the chimney, peering down, listening.

"No light," he said finally, turning his head. "I hear a mumble of voices. And the opening is big enough, if I lift my arms straight over my head."

"Chief," said Mechem, "on your way down you'll start soot to moving, right into the room where they're mumbling! All they'll have to do is shoot—"

"Nick," said Dyce again, grimmer than before, "I won't tell you again that I won't be coddled. Do what I tell you, or hunt another job."

Mechem subsided, his face grim in the dark, his lips a straight line. Carefully, looking up, he checked operations as Dyce looped the rope about his chest, just below the arms. He noticed that Dyce had unfastened the four-pronged hook, retaining it in his right hand. It was, Mechem knew, a formidable weapon, even in the little hands of Harlan Dyce.

Dyce twisted, got his feet and legs into the black opening.

"Take it easy, Nick," he whispered down. "I'm going into this place!"

The small head disappeared. Nick Mechem wiped the sweat from his face. He didn't believe he—had the situation been reversed—would have had the courage of Harlan Dyce, in the face of the menacing, weird unknown.

Slowly, the rope paid through his hands.

Inside the chimney, Dyce was gripped by the four brick sides of the sooty trap, which closed so tightly about him that he could not take a full, deep breath.

He hadn't the slightest idea what he was going into, only that he was going and that no one could dissuade him. He would have to use his wits, every second, that was all. An army couldn't have fought its way out if this place were habited—as he was sure it was—by the grimmest denizens of the underworld.

The soot curled about him, out of the cracks between the bricks. It bit into his nostrils. Perspiration dripped from his every pore, before he had gone three feet into the narrow, black pit. He knew that clouds of soot were going down ahead of him, that it couldn't be otherwise—and that if any one saw it, pouring out of the fireplace below—

But he allowed Nick Mechem to keep on lowering. Above him now was a tiny square of sky, with two stars set in it like blinking diamonds—and he saw even that, oddly, through the four prongs of the hook, his only weapon aside from his wits.

Then, as he went farther down, the swirling soot above him blotted out even the sky. He fought to keep from sneezing, and to keep as little of the soot as humanly possible out of his lungs.

He was beginning to wonder whether the chimney ran clear to the ground floor, when he felt greater space below his feet, around his ankles, almost to his knees.

More than that!

Hands were fumbling at his ankles!

IV

Dyce's brain worked at lightning speed. He couldn't get away from those hands, so he must cope with them. He couldn't fight them off, or kick them off, so he must try to figure out about them. It was a weird feeling, though, and it made his wits work even faster than they were accustomed. First, he decided that the hands were fearful, fumbling. An ordinary man, seeing tiny legs dangling down into his fireplace, might have grabbed and jerked. These hands merely fumbled, as though their owner were unable to decide that what he saw was really there.

Dyce called: "Drop me, Nick! Fast!"

But his words went straight up, as though shot from a mortar, and he knew by the still gradual letting out of the rope that Nick hadn't been able to hear. He should have posted the man atop the chimney, against just such a contingency, though it was too late for that now.

Slowly, ever so slowly, he was lowered to the fireplace. Those hands fumbled with him as he lowered. He heard labored breathing.

His feet touched. Instantly, he slipped the rope from about his shoulders. He stared out into a brightly lighted room, and into a heavy, scarred face. Beyond the face of the man, who was on hands and knees before the fireplace, was a table. On it were empty bottles, and one that was not quite empty.

The man, too drunk to stand erect, was mumbling. Dyce realized it had been his mumbling he had heard aloft. This was the sentry—whose job was so lacking in importance that he was allowed all the liquor he could drink.

"It's there," said the voice. "I saw it, felt it. I can still see it. But why doesn't it talk?"

Dyce scarcely breathed. He didn't know whether to speak or not. The drunken man was frightened, unbelieving. He licked parched lips. His eyes were very big and round.

Dyce was warned by the man's right hand, which turned on the floor so that its edge touched the board and the fingers could curl. Dyce had seen men curl their fingers like that to catch flies. The drunkard was intent.

"If it's real," he mumbled, "then I'm—I'm—"

Dyce jumped as the man's right hand flung at him—flung out with the speed of a striking rattlesnake. Had it struck him, even a glancing blow, it would have broken him in two.

Then the big man noted the four-pronged hook, and there was a miraculous change in him. It wasn't the first time Dyce had seen a man change from drunk to sober in the batting of an eye. The big man was on his feet.

"I don't know what you are," he said, "but coming in here, like this, making me think I've got 'em again and—"

The big fellow started stalking Dyce. Dyce had no time for that. It was a losing game. And he couldn't get out of the room until the big man was taken care of. The big fellow lunged. Dyce darted aside. Then he came in, swift as light. He raked with the prongs—a side swipe at the back of the big man's leg.

A piercing scream rang through the room. The big mouth was open, drooling, and the fellow sank down like a wolf-worried stag.

But he reached for Dyce, and Dyce gave him the prongs again, in the hand.

"How do I get out?" snapped Dyce. The deep voice from a figure so small must have startled the wounded man half out of his already addled wits. "Tell me, or get this hook across the face, or in the eyes. And I won't mind doing it. You've done it to plenty here, I'll bet."

The wounded man snarled. "That we have, whatever imp of Satan you are, as you'll find out before you ever get out of here again!"

"Just out of this room," said Dyce quietly.

"I'd be sent to the 'Auditorium.' "

"Auditorium?"

"Yes, where our friends scream, and we listen. By friends I mean *not* friends."

The fellow was edging forward. There was murder in his eyes now—his eyes that were so bloodshot and hellish. Dyce watched as he would have watched the coiling of a rattler whose range he might have misguessed. He had to get the fellow on the head, next time, put him entirely out of the running. Then, when he came around, he might think he had imagined it all.

"But if nobody else sees me, and he tries to explain," thought Dyce, "they'll say he had D. T.'s—unless that fellow from the train remembers."

The big man struck. So did Dyce. The big man, his forehead bleeding as though he had just taken a bullet between the eyes, fell forward, groaning, on his face. Dyce went through his pockets, appropriating his ring of keys. Some of them had small metal tags on them, bearing tiny words: Cloister, Abbey, Auditorium, Rectory, Cathedral. All the names sounded sinister, blasphemously so. One key's tag said "Belfry." That, he thought, would be this room.

And there were letters addressed to "Hebe" Strawn. Probably this chap's name, Dyce figured. En route to the door, with the Belfry key, Dyce saw himself in a mirror. He was coal-black, save where sweat had etched white streaks on his face. And his hair was black, and all awry. For the first time, he didn't pat it down.

"If I were a giant," he thought, "I'd scare the wits out of anybody who saw me."

He turned the key in the lock, opened the door. A rich building, this. No doors standing open in the hallway, though. The inhabitants, if any, must all be asleep, or—

Dyce couldn't go beyond the "or," because there was a suggestion of beastly, unmentionable rites in it. But in the hallway, he understood why nobody had heard the screams of Strawn. There were other screams, faint with distance, ringing through the place. Two or three stories down, he judged. This place was soundproof, though, for neither he nor Mechem had heard any sounds on the roof.

He kept thinking of Strawn's leer when he had spoken of the Auditorium. That would be—would be—what?

"One of the things I came to find out," thought Dyce. "But I wish Nick was here."

He started swiftly down the hallway, seeking a door to a stairs. He didn't dare use the elevators, though he noted a bank of them. A busy place, this, luxurious—had cost plenty of money. He wondered how much misery, how many women's tears, had been built into the stone walls, the steel beams, the mortar between the rocks—and thought how small he was to seek payment for the least of them.

He drew back in a corner when he heard the elevator door open. Then, swiftly, he stepped through a door leading to stairs. A man dashed out of the elevator, entered the room he had just left. Dyce could have gained the elevator, gone down in it. But he might not know how to run it. He had a hunch that any one bold enough to erect an apartment to crime in the heart of New York would foresee emergencies like that, and that the elevator would be one some one would have to be trained to operate.

The man came rushing out again. His face was white. His mouth hung open. He was screaming, "Geke! Geke!"

What in the world, Dyce thought, did "Geke" mean? A name, maybe, but he couldn't be sure. The name of the master of all this? No way of telling.

Dyce went down to the next landing, where the screams, heartbreaking, ghastly, were louder. But they were still a floor below.

Dyce went down another. The stairs, he knew, were seldom used, as stairs seldom are where there are elevators. There was little to fear in them. Now he opened a door, and the screams were very clear.

The elevator stopped again, with the operator rushing from it, still yelling, "Geke! Geke!" Then he dashed through a door, which closed behind him—shutting off his screams and the others Dyce had heard.

Dyce hurried, looked through the keyhole—straight into Hell. He saw an almost-nude man on a dais, spread-eagled against what looked to be a heavy oak desk.

The man was John Durban.

Standing over him, with a cat-o'-nine-tails in his hand, its ends crimson with Durban's blood, was another man—the same one who had slapped Dyce on the train.

The gory lash fell; but Durban did not scream. His head fell forward on his chest. All eyes were on that tableau, Dyce knew. All ears attuned to Durban's sounds. Dyce set the key in the lock, opened the door, entered.

The only light was that which showered down over Durban and the man with the lash—as though the desk which held Durban prisoner had been a ring, the two actors fighters for a ghastly championship.

Scores of shadowy forms sat back from those lights, arms folded—grimly watching, as though the tableau were both a prize ring and a grim drama of the screen.

The fellow who had dashed into, and out of, the Belfry was moving toward one of the shadows. Dyce watched, saw him bend over a seated man in the midst of the other men.

"That, I'll bet," thought Dyce, "is the man I'm really after."

Dyce saw that man jump to his feet, knew that the lights all over the Auditorium would go on at once. They did, but when they did Dyce was down, crawling under the rows of seats, heading straight for the man who had risen, whose voice now spoke softly—yet so that every ear could hear its cold, crystallike notes—utterly without excitement.

"There's an enemy in the place," said the voice, "unless both Strawn and Glockner have D. T.'s! Look about you!"

V

Harlan Dyce had no fear of this sort of search. There wasn't one chance in a thousand that any one would think of looking for a midget.

Dyce could actually feel them looking into one another's faces.

"See if your neighbor is known to you!" went on the crystal-sharp voice.

Dyce could almost hear their necks swivel, right and left, as they looked. From the whipping post came the raucous breathing of John Durban. Dyce was not too greatly concerned about him. He was a strong man, could take the punishment—and this was more to be preferred than years of harassment at the hands of blackmailers.

"Simes!" said the crystal-hard voice.

"Yes, Geke?"

"Go to the door and note every one who goes out, make sure of their faces. Understand?"

Simes, it developed, was the man who had slapped Dyce. Dyce listened, almost without breathing. Simes went to the door. The other men rose in their seats—and the feet of several were close enough for Dyce to have touched them—and stood for the word of command, like soldiers rising from table, or prisoners in a disciplined mess hall.

Simes stood, waiting.

"By rows, beginning nearest the door," said the voice of Geke, "go out the door. Then each of you knows what his territory is in this building. You will search every nook and cranny, and bring to me any one you may find."

They began to march, with a shuffling of feet indicative, Dyce thought, of their servitude to Geke. Dyce had a certain grim respect for the man. He got what he went after, even obedience to the slightest whim. Dyce could crane his neck and look up at the man. Geke was under thirty, with a face like a white, pasty mask, and eyes that were deep and black and utterly without mercy. There, Dyce knew, was a man who must have committed, or procured the committing of, many murders. Men did not gather vast sums of money, outside the law, without bloodshed. And Dyce had studied many rogues' galleries in his time, and many of these faces he remembered. There was no crooked job conceivable that Geke could not have procured if he wished.

And this great apartment house—always, of course, "filled"—was a master stroke. Not even coppers on the beat would question it. Its denizens never bothered anybody, apparently, came and went without disturbance.

And squealers? Well, if they would punish John Durban as they had been punishing him, merely because he had refused to give them fifty dollars a week, what would they do, at Geke's command, to squealers?

Dyce shuddered, just to think, and wondered how many bodies had gone out of here, to oblivion, with none save Geke the wiser.

One by one, the men filed out of the Auditorium. One by one, they paused before Simes, turned their faces this way and that for him to make a careful study. One by one, Simes nodded to them, and they were gone. Dyce grinned.

None of *them* would find him, anyhow!

John Durban was twisting, writhing in his bonds, trying to return to consciousness. Geke looked at him.

"Strange what some men will suffer for the sake of fifty dollars a week, Simes," said Geke. "That was a good racket you worked out, Simes. We can extend it to Philly and Chicago trains, you know. It might even pay out well if we developed it. But, Simes—"

"Yes, sir."

"Don't get ideas, just because you doped out this one by yourself. I'm still the boss of this outfit."

Dyce could feel Simes cringe.

"I know," said Simes.

"And if you led a dick here today—"

"I lost him, I tell you, chief!"

"I know you said so, but if you didn't—it's the Rectory for you!"

"The Rectory?" Simes almost screamed.

"I won't have men about me who make mistakes."

"I just slapped a nasty kid, boss, and his dad chased me. That's all. His dad wanted to knock my block off."

"But you wouldn't have told me that if Rosie hadn't been on the train and seen it."

"Probably not, for it didn't seem important."

"You were ordered to report everything!"

"I know. Now, chief, you said that an enemy had got in. How could that be possible?"

"Strawn may have imagined things, but he never cut himself up the way he was found. Somebody, or something, got to him. It, or he, or she, is still inside, and"—grim and horrible was the voice now—"will stay inside until found!"

Dyce couldn't prevent a cold shudder from racing along his spine. It wasn't just murder he read in that voice, but complete annihilation. Geke would stamp him out, or any one else, as an ordinary man would step on a bug.

"Go on out now, Simes," said Geke, "and help the boys search. Turn the place upside down. Listen to what Strawn has to say, no matter how wild it is—"

"Right, Geke. And you?"

"I've a few words to say to John Durban here, words he is to take to his friends on the morning train—if he doesn't want something to happen to his wife, Kitty, or his daughter, Dede!"

His words struck horror to Dyce's heart. For now he could see, through the seats, that Durban had regained consciousness.

Simes departed.

Geke strode to Durban. Geke was meticulously dressed. Dyce, studying him, knew that he was of the mold which is received in the highest society, might even by his own right be in the social register. Men sometimes had strange motives for doing horrible things.

Geke stared at Durban.

"How does it happen that you have the courage to refuse to contribute, Durban?"

"Payment of blackmail," came Durban's agonized voice, "won't free me of trouble at home. My wife handles the money and will miss it. I'll pay, and payment will accomplish nothing."

"You should not flirt with strange women in the city!"

"I do not. I never have. You know it, too. Curse you, you know everything!"

"It is my business to know everything. Yes, I know you are a faithful husband; but can your wife, during the hours you are not in Norwalk, be sure of that, as sure as you are, or I am?"

"No—and payment won't make any difference. So I still refuse to pay."

"Did the lash hurt?"

"Of course."

"It would hurt worse, would it not, Durban, if it fell on the soft skin of Kitty or Dede?"

"Damn you! Don't dare mention their names!"

Geke slapped Durban across the face.

"Don't tell me what to do, what not to do. I dare anything. And I tell you that you will pay—or either or both of your loved ones will be here, perhaps enduring even worse than you have had. I have beasts among my men!"

Dyce gritted his teeth. Durban groaned.

"Who," went on Geke, "advised you not to pay?"

Dyce held his breath, awaiting the answer.

"No one," lied Durban.

Dyce sighed his relief. He had been afraid Durban might remember, and recall that the voice he had heard in the dark had come from abnormally close to the floor. Then this Geke, a genius of his kind, would put two and two together—Durban's story, and Simes' story of the kid he had slapped—and come close to the right answer.

Dyce almost prayed: "If only I can still do it. I haven't tried for years, and if I fail—"

His words suddenly died away in his throat, but his throat continued moving—and a voice came from somewhere behind Durban: "You're through, Geke," said that voice. "You have committed your last major crime!"

Dyce's face was red with effort, as his voice seemed to come from beyond Durban. He couldn't keep up his ventriloquial effort very long, for he had never practiced long or often, and not at all for years.

"What's that, Durban?" asked Geke.

"I said nothing."

"But that voice—"

Was there the faintest hint of terror in Geke's voice? Geke stood like a statue for a minute or more, staring at the shadows behind Durban.

Then he moved, swiftly. A gat darted into his hand. He passed Durban like a streak, got behind the dais. And Harlan Dyce, a small black shadow, shot out from under the chairs, slid between Durban's legs, vanished under the desk against which Durban was tied, where the shadows would hide him. There he watched the swift-moving legs of Geke.

"Damn strange!" said Geke, hoarsely. "Durban, are you a ventriloquist?"

"No."

"Did you hear that voice?"

"Yes."

There was something odd in Durban's voice, and Dyce knew that the tortured eyes of the prisoner had seen him, scuttling like a crab from the shadows of the seats.

There was hope in the voice of Durban—and terror, too; lest the hope that grew in him should not pan out.

Dyce still held the four-pronged hook in his hand. Geke came back to face Durban.

"What," he rasped, "is going on here, Durban? I think you know."

Durban did not answer. Geke struck him twice across the face with the muzzle of his gat—and John Durban laughed, as though he didn't mind at all! And fear was growing in the voice of the man called Geke.

"Durban, were you on that train this morning, when Simes was on it?"

"Yes, only I did not know him then."

"I take care my men do not show themselves often enough in a given place to be remembered. But tell me what happened."

"I remember little, except that a spoiled brat had the whole smoking car in a turmoil—and Simes finally slapped him. The kid's dad chased Simes through Grand Central Station."

"A spoiled brat, you say?"

"Yes, a boy of seven or eight."

Geke would have the answer soon, Dyce knew. When he got it he might bend over the desk itself, look under it and say, with an air of triumph: "I've got the answer, midget! Come on out!"

Dyce watched Geke's legs. The backs of them were now turned to Durban. Geke, Dyce knew was searching the empty seats—for something. Yes, Geke had a suspicion, already.

It was time for Dyce to make his move. His small, muscular hand gripped the four-pronged hook stoutly. He dared not miss, for if he missed, he died. So did Nick, up on the cold roof, and John Durban—and many others.

And many already dead would not be atoned for to the law.

Dyce struck. Two of the hooks went into and behind the great tendon above Geke's right heel. The man's leg quivered with the shock. Geke was still. Dyce had not expected a scream, at least for a few seconds, while the man tried to guess what had struck him.

"Make a sound, Geke," said Dyce softly, "and I'll jerk it out by the roots! And when you're down I'll jerk out the left one, too. Then, Geke, your own wolves will turn on you!"

Geke made no sound. There was only the quivering of the leg into which Dyce had sunk the steel hooks so deeply.

"Turn slowly, and carefully, Geke," said Dyce, "and unfasten Durban's bonds!"

VI

Dyce thought, "If the situation were reversed, I'd let the other fellow rip me apart before I'd give in."

But Geke didn't see it that way. Apparently he could not stand the pain that he was so willing to administer to his victims.

"I'll rip if you scream," warned Dyce again. "I'll give you until I count five to twist and unfasten Durban. I'll twist with you, so as not to increase the pain."

Geke hesitated.

"One!" snapped Dyce.

Geke quivered in every muscle. Dyce knew he was trying from somewhere deep within him to find the courage to scream. But Dyce had made a shrewd guess about Geke and his men. If Geke went down, they would jump him, literally, like so many wolves. So Geke did not yell.

"Two!" said Dyce, bringing the slightest additional pressure to bear on Geke.

"Three!" said Dyce.

Then Geke turned, carefully, as though holding his very breath against the pain.

"Is he unfastening you, Durban?" asked Dyce.

"Yes," Durban seemed to be panting with eagerness. "I'd like just one good punch at him—"

"Let the law handle him, Durban!"

"Whatever you say goes, whoever you are," said Durban.

But Geke was slow, torturous, and Dyce had to twist again, just once. He heard a low groan of anguish come from the lips of Geke.

Durban said: "You can hand it out, can't you, Geke, but when it comes to taking some of your own medicine—"

"Does he hand it out like this, Durban?" asked Dyce.

"Worse. Chinese torturers are no more expert. And the Rectory!"

"What about the Rectory?"

"That's where men and women disappear. They never show up again. They are weighted and dropped at sea, ten miles and more offshore—after going through hideous things."

"How do you know?"

"I was told, when I was slated for the same thing, if I didn't recant!"

Dyce, careful not to move his body, was unfastening the belt of his boy's trousers. He couldn't, he decided, stay here all night, until Durban got out and brought help—for Durban might never get out at all. And there was Nick Mechem to be considered, too. The belt came free.

Dyce grinned to himself, then said: "Can you stand up and walk, Durban?"

"To get these murderers and blackmailers I could walk on the raw stumps of my legs!"

"Good. Go turn out the lights in this Auditorium. I've got some nice things yet to do to Geke. I plan that he shall tell me things about this place of his. First, Geke, are the police your allies?"

"No. They're too dumb—and too honest!"

"I wonder if, an hour from now, you will repeat that to their faces! I hope so, for it will keep people from claiming the police are in with you. Ready, Durban?"

"Yes."

"Then, the lights! Good! Now, Geke, I'm going to give you fifteen minutes in which to plan your story, while I figure out how I'm going to get out of here with you."

Geke did not answer.

"Durban," said Dyce, "in one way or another, and one at a time, you are to get Geke's men in here, crown them as they come through the door, and bind them with their own belts or suspenders. Can you do it?"

"*Can* I? I wouldn't wish for anything nicer."

"But you may be trapped again, not get out at all."

"I'll be no worse off than I have been. I'll take the chance, gladly, for the sake of my friends. You know, whoever you are, the total this man and his men wanted from us ran to over ten thousand a week, from near-by Connecticut towns alone."

Dyce whistled.

Dyce had removed his shoes. And now, making no sound, he slid out into the dark, holding his breath lest Geke realize what was happening, lest Geke understand that merely by slacking his own muscles he could free himself of the steel trap into which he had stepped. For only Dyce's belt held him now, run through the ring of the hook and fastened to a leg of the desk.

Dyce caught at Durban's hand, as the tortured man, breathing heavily because he had been so badly tortured and his wounds were agony, moved toward the door.

"Look out first," he whispered, "and see if the coast is clear. Then, do me a favor, will you?"

"Anything."

"Stand with your legs close together, so I can get out past you without being seen. Then, don't watch me go. There are reasons now, as there were reasons last night in your home, why I don't wish to be seen—by any one."

"All right."

Bare whispers, threads of sound. No sound came from Geke, there by his own dais of torture.

Durban looked out. "Nobody out there," he whispered.

Durban stood with his legs close together. Dyce scurried out, knowing that Durban had turned his head, looked back into the room. Dyce gained the door leading to the stairs, went through it, listened for a moment. The stairs were not being used. Ticklish business now, for Dyce, because he had no weapon whatever—save his wits. But, thank Heaven, they seemed to work at lightning speed.

Up the stairs, two flights of them, still fingering the keys in his pocket, keeping both hands in his pockets to hold up his trousers.

The door of the Belfry—and whatever might lurk beyond it. He applied his ear to the panel. No sound came out. Either they had taken Strawn out of there to question him, or the murderous big man was unconscious. Dyce opened the door and went in.

The room seemed to be empty at first. Then he saw Strawn, a bundle like a small mountain, behind the table that was bottle-covered. Now every bottle was empty. There was blood on the floor around Strawn. Dyce shuddered. There was something obscene about the man—and Dyce had drawn that blood.

Dyce stepped into the fireplace, looked up. The soot had settled again. The rope he found by fumbling, where it hung against the black side of the narrow shaft.

Now he called out, softly.

"Nick!"

A great shadow hovered over the top of the chimney, and Dyce knew that Nick had climbed to the chimney top, to be in position to haul him out when the word came.

"Yes, chief," came Nick's answer.

"Heave away, son, and fast!"

It was easier going up, for Dyce clung to the rope and Nick pulled him so that Dyce's own weight narrowed his shoulders, brought his arms straighter above his head. Even so, the soot started again, and Dyce was choking by the time his head shot, like a black bullet, out at the top.

Nick lowered him to the roof without a word, dropped down beside him, walked with him to the edge, lowered him over. He knew without being told that speed was paramount.

Then Nick fastened one end of the rope to the chimney and let himself down, using a hitch that could be jiggled loose when Nick stood on the roof below.

The rope came over into Nick's hands.

"Well, chief, what now?" he asked.

"Plenty!" said Dyce. "That place is worse even than you guessed, or than I guessed. Murders have been going on in it without discovery since it was built. Men and women have screamed in it, unheard. And Durban is in there now, getting revenge!"

"What do we do?"

"You call the police, all the prowl cars you can get. Tell them anything, so long as they agree to force an entrance to the place!"

"Right! And you?"

"Who, save to order him to scat, will pay any attention to a curious colored boy?"

And Dyce laughed. Obviously he was pleased with himself. On the way down to the street he told Nick Mechem what had happened to him, and Nick laughed, too—not because it was funny, but because he was so relieved that Dyce, having gone through so much, had returned to him safely. If anything ever happened to Dyce—

"First," said Dyce, "the prowl cars are to come without sounding their sirens. They are to cover every possible exit from the place, which means all adjoining buildings. Then, they go in at the front—and it will be a battle to the death!"

They reached the street, Nick Mechem, tall, grim, a grown man—with a disheveled "colored boy" at his side—who remained on the sidewalk, however, while Nick entered a cigar store to start wheels grinding that would shock a nation.

"I want a policeman!" Nick told the operator.

He got his man, told his story—and more policemen, on the strength of that story, started moving into Greenwich Village than had moved on any major crime objective since "Two-gun" Cross had defied any, or all, to take him.

Prowl cars came, absolutely without sound. Dyce, holding his breath, wished he could guess what was transpiring inside the grim structure.

"In your hands, Nick," said Dyce briefly. "Nobody would take *me* seriously."

"*I* would!" said Nick, with deep feeling.

"Don't get sentimental!" snapped Harlan Dyce. "I'm not, really, you know, your little boy! Tell them what's what, while I make myself small to watch!"

VII

Men poured out of prowl cars. Harness bulls seemed to come from everywhere, giving Dyce his first deep appreciation of the efficiency of the police. Some officers carried riot guns; some carried tommies; some carried police positives; some tear-gas bombs. There were no smiles among them. They meant business. If thoughts of their own death were uppermost in their minds it was not evident. Facing death was part of their daily job. Dyce felt that the climax of the job he had undertaken was in the very best of hands.

Mechem spoke softly and swiftly to sergeants and lieutenants, as they came to him. They spoke to their men, in turn, who wheeled to obey commands like soldiers on parade. They went into adjoining houses with their weapons poised, ready. And that no sounds of warning came from the occupants of those houses was proof of the police efficiency which kept them silent.

Dyce's heart glowed. Here was life, activity to delight the normal man— and he was part of it, though not a single officer knew. All thought Nick Mechem, private detective, had worked up all this, and all due credit was given him.

"Take it yourself, boys, when the newspaper lads ask questions," said Nick.

Later, he said to Dyce, "I only wish you could get the credit you deserve."

Dyce grinned. "Just knowing, myself, is enough for me! How do you think they'll do?"

"No crooks ever successfully stayed out of their hands, even the toughest of 'em."

Swiftly, in silence, the coppers were deployed. No sound came from the grim, sinister building, though there might be plenty inside. Simple sound-proofing had kept the secret of this building since it had been erected—

"Probably done by architects and contractors owned and operated by Geke himself," thought Dyce.

The attack was to start with a whistle by Mechem. Nick now held the whistle.

Dyce watched, listened. Several officers had snapped at him, said, "Keep clear, sonny!" And Dyce had tried to look properly impressed, as a colored boy might.

"Now!" said Dyce. "They've had time to make all their dispositions."

"Then," said Mechem, "blow the whistle! It's your right."

He extended the whistle to Dyce. Dyce's heart hammered with excite-ment. It was like playing soldiers in earnest. But from the police whistle, instantly, went skirling the signal—and a dozen men hurled themselves from a dark doorway, heading straight for the door of the sinister apart-ment.

Dyce raced down the street to watch more closely.

The twelve darted into the areaway. Two knelt, busying themselves with fuse and nitro. Then they raced back, ducking to right and left, to get the walls between them and—

A dull, rocketing explosion immediately followed, which Dyce escaped by darting around a corner of another building—a corner that shook like a leaf in the wind.

The coppers rushed back. Two now held the canisters and nozzles of acetylene torches; for the door, though scarred and twisted, had not gone down. Flames began to eat into the metal door.

"Take it easy!" shouted Mechem. "There'll be men behind that door with gats and tommies!"

But that did not deter the cops. The flames bored into the metal of the great doors.

A hole appeared. Out of it, almost instantly, came a stream of lead. A copper went down, with his stomach full of lead. But right afterward two other coppers closed in, tommies chattering in their hands, etching leaden patterns about that hole, spilling bullets through on the men behind.

"Geke," Dyce thought, "must have figured it out, or they wouldn't be ready."

Dull booms were coming from other places, as officers forced their way into the objective building. They were moving forward with the surety of a many-wheeled, monstrous Juggernaut.

The outer door did not go down, but it twisted and bent under the assaults of the law, and the law streamed in—to be met by a hail of lead from two directions. Dyce saw men fall and could stand it no longer.

He raced across the street, got through, watched the coppers at work. A sergeant saw him, grabbed him in a big hand, masked him with his own body. Dyce kicked him, hard. The sergeant flung Dyce into a corner and then forgot him.

Stubbornly, grimly, the attacked gave way before the converging forces of the law. The officers jammed the elevator on the ground floor, shot the operator. Then, floor by floor, with Dyce among them, watching everything he could, they moved up.

There was blood on the stone steps.

There were dead men, lawless and of the law, sprawled on the steps and in the hallways. But Dyce did not count the cost too great. If he had had nothing to do with it, the cost might have been higher—certainly would have been if Geke and his ilk had never been checked.

One floor after the other was cleared of the bandit-murderer blackmailers. Dyce watched each clearing and pronounced it good. If anybody thought of Dyce's presence as odd now, no one gave a sign. Maybe everybody thought somebody else was looking after him.

Bullets came close to Dyce, but none touched him.

Nick Mechem was in the thick of things, too, with kicking gats in his two fists—and Dyce watched him with a glow about his heart. There, he thought, was a man to tie to.

Women belonging to the attacked were taken alive—fighting wildcats they were, too, with more courage than their men; but the law would not shoot them down, though three policemen died at the hands of women.

Higher and higher the fight mounted.

Then, Dyce spoke to Mechem: "Take these keys, and get into these rooms, where all the evidence you could possibly wish for—including clues to many murders—will surely be found. But first, this, the Auditorium!"

Nick went in. Durban was in there, and Geke, and Durban was taunting the master mind. There were a dozen men scattered around the room, struggling against the bonds Durban had fastened on them.

He looked everywhere, but to Dyce as he said, "If I'd had time, I'd have got the lot of them."

Nobody else seemed to notice Dyce, which suited him perfectly.

Coached by Dyce, Nick addressed Geke, "What's the idea of standing there like that? Why didn't you lead your men?"

"I'm a prisoner. Something has me hooked, fast."

Nick knelt, lifted the curtain which hid the "trap."

"Look, Geke," he said.

Geke looked. His face went white. Durban had taken his gat away from him, and he had only his bare hands. But he went berserk. He did what he had not been able to bring himself to do in time to save his stronghold. He surged forward, pulling himself free. Blood dyed his trousers leg. He fell on his face, rolled to his back—and out of his clothing came another gat.

Nick Mechem was on top of him, with a swift, well-aimed kick. The gat went spinning.

Dyce made himself small during what followed. Men were being herded in from everywhere—dozens, scores of them. Grim-faced lieutenants of the law spoke, and their voices quivered as they told of things they had found in the Rectory, the Belfry, the Cloister—

"Enough to send you and your men, Jed Sacs, to the chair a dozen times over."

"Jed Sacs!" snapped Nick Mechem. "Not *the* Jed Sacs, of Palm Beach, Newport, Palm Springs and—"

"The same!" said a lieutenant, while Dyce fought to keep from saying that he had long since known that Geke belonged high in society, by reason of which his operations could not have failed to succeed.

"No," spoke up Simes, "not *all* of us will burn! Geke was behind everything. We had to obey—"

A gat spoke. Some prisoner had managed to fool those who had searched him. Simes went down with a bullet in his brain.

But he had started something; he had started to talk.

And others talked, telling a tale the world would know by morning—a tale of world-wide blackmail, mixed with murder when the victim defied the blackmailers; a tale of vanished bodies, lost in the depths of the sea. A complete, mighty clean-up.

The police were jubilant, and Nick and Dyce slipped away unnoticed, drove back to the offices of the Dyce Detective Agency.

In the inner office, passing Helene Kocsis, who had stayed at her desk to await developments, Dyce sat back with a sigh of relief—and Nick Mechem burst out laughing for the first time since Dyce had known him.

"What are you laughing at, you hyena?" asked Dyce.

"Your face!" said Nick. "You look like—like— But look at yourself in a mirror."

There was no mirror, so Dyce sent for Helene Kocsis, who held her own small one for him, taken from her vanity. Helene did not smile. Nor did Dyce when he saw himself.

Finally, Dyce looked over the mirror at Helene.

"Do you wish to make yourself completely happy, Kocsis?" he asked.

She didn't answer. Her lip trembled a little.

"Then go get a wet rag," said Dyce softly, "and give yourself the extreme, maternal pleasure of washing your boss' face!"

And Helene went, as though her heels had been winged—and Nick Mechem stopped smiling.

Homicide Hunch
Robert Leslie Bellem

I was slightly plastered that evening or I might not have fallen for the gag. But the Scotch had lulled my suspicious nature; so I answered right away when somebody knocked on the front door of my apartment stash and said: "Telegram for Dan Turner."

The instant I opened the portal I realized I'd made a bad mistake. Instead of a messenger boy, my visitor was a swarthy creep named Pedro Romelo—a tall, lanky Latin who played minor villain roles in Cosmotone horse operas and carried his villainy around with him in private life.

He had a narrow, mulish puss with black sideburns running down past his ears to emphasize the glitter in his slitted glims, and he affected a costume that belonged only on a studio set—velvet pants flaring at the cuffs, high heeled boots, a Spanish jacket over a pink silk shirt open at the throat to show how hairy his chest was. As soon as I tabbed him, I knew I was in for trouble in copious quantities. He and I had crossed swords in the past, and he bore little love for me. In fact, what he bore for me at the moment was a pearl-handled .28 automatic.

He grinned as he thrust the roscoe against my favorite vest. "Want a hole in your tweeds, snoop?"

"No, thanks. The noise might disturb the neighbors." I glued the measuring glimpse on him; wondered how much chance I had of swatting his rod aside and planting a set of fives on his sneery panorama. I concluded he was too close to me for that kind of risk. I didn't have enough room to swing.

He seemed to guess my thoughts. "Make a move for your shoulder holster and I let you have it," he warned me.

"You needn't bother, bub. What cooks?"

"Wait and see. I got a taxi waiting. Let's go for a ride. If you whistle copper even once, you'll be minus a kidney. Savvy?"

I said: "Yeah. So I won't whistle copper."

He reached under my coat, frisked me for the .32 I always tote in an armpit rig. Then he pocketed both heaters, mine and his own; kept his mitt on the little .28 so its muzzle made a bulge in my direction through the cloth. "Get going."

We went down to his Yellow and it ferried us out to the Tower Arms on Sunset. Presently Romelo prodded me into a lavish layout on the seventh floor; closed the door after us. I set fire to a gasper; took a hinge around the joint.

The blue carpet must have cost a peck of kopecks, its thick pile seething up around your ankles when you walked on it. All the furniture was modernistic: glass-and-chromium tables, blue drapes, metal-and-leather chairs. A screwy floor lamp cast indirect light against the ceiling and the glow bounced back down around a blue leather divan. When I piped this divan, I widened my peepers and choked: "What the—?"

There was a blonde quail stretched out on the glossy cushions, trussed hand and hoof with knotted ropes. Her piquant pan would have been gorgeous even without its heavy makeup.

It wasn't her she-male beauty that floored me, though. It was the way she greeted me. "Dan, d-darling!" she moaned.

I gave vent to strangled noises, because I wasn't her Dan darling. As a matter of fact I'd never seen her before in my life—and I've got an address book as wide as your wrist. Evidently I'd been overlooking a bet somewhere.

Then, while I was struggling to cope with this screwball situation, the Romelo rodent maced me over the head with his cannon.

When consciousness rejoined me, I was slumped in a chair with my wrists and ankles tied like a Christmas goose. There was a lump on my thatch the size of Grant's Tomb and I had a headache built for an elephant.

The wren on the divan twisted around to hang the gander on me, being careful not to disarrange her golden coiffure. "Poor Dan," she whimpered. "I'm so sorry, honey."

Pedro Romelo sneered down at me. "Ready to spill, gumshoe?"

I said: "Yeah. Ready to spill your clockworks all over the precinct as soon as I get loose from these ropes."

"Don't be that way, pal. The only thing it'll buy you is some more lumps. I want Mort Pollak's key."

I twitched as if I'd been jabbed with a lighted cigar. Until recently, Mort Pollak had been a .22 caliber talent agent in Hollywood—a crooked heel who used his offices on the Sunset Strip to mask any number of illegal shenanigans. Mort had made the serious error of committing first degree killery on one of his lady friends during a blackmailing operation, and I'd pinned it on him. As a result, the State convicted him and rendered him defunct in the gas house at San Quentin.

I had no regrets about this. Pollack was guilty, he took the rap, and that was that. But I didn't know anything about his keys and I said so, emphatically. I'd have used gestures but my dukes were too well tied.

Romelo leaned down, breathed in my kisser. "You lie, Sherlock. You've got it and I want it."

"Maybe you'd better explain what key you mean." I tried to spar him away.

He said: "Look. Pollak stashed ten grand in a safety deposit box somewhere in town just before you sent him over the road. I think you've been waiting all these weeks for the heat to die before you open the box and glom that cabbage. But you waited too long, see? I found out about it and I'm cutting in for the whole wad. Pollak owed me about that much, anyhow. So this is where I collect—when you give me the key."

"Nuts to you," I grunted. "You're as haywire as snowballs in San Diego."

"You think you can dummy up on me, hunh?" He took mincing steps across the room. "So okay. Start belching or I get rough with your sweetie, here." He meant the doll on the couch.

I said: "She's not my sweetie, so go ahead. I don't even know her name."

That drew a sobbing protest from the golden-haired jane, together with a reproachful stare. "Dan, darling, how c-can you say such a thing when we've meant so much to each other?"

"How much have we meant to each other, babe?"

"Oh-h-h, p-please, don't try to keep up the pretense. There's no use lying to Romelo. I've already t-told him you and I are engaged. He . . . f-forced me to. I tried to k-keep it a secret, but he beat me w-with his fists."

I said: "So that's why he nudged me up here."

"Yes." Then she began whimpering as the Latin louse bent over her, and started slapping. First his right hand would smack her cheek; then his left would jolt her the other way. She couldn't stop him on account of the ropes that bound her helplessly.

The guy was thoroughly business-like, I'll say that much for him. I strained at my own bonds, but all I drew were some chafed places on my wrists and an assortment of blisters on my disposition.

"Dan . . . !" the gazelle wailed faintly. "Don't let him . . . I can't st-stand it . . . !"

"I guess you'll have to, hon. What can I do?"

"Tell him wh-where the k-key is. Please!"

For an instant this didn't make any more sense to me than six aces in a poker deck. Then, suddenly, I caught hep to what she was driving at. "Okay, skunk," I yelled to Romelo. "Lay off her. I'll spill."

He bent his narrow puss in a smile. "That's much better. Now—give!"

"I haven't got it on me. You know that. You probably frisked me while I was unconscious."

"Sure I did. So just tell me where to find it."

I fished a quick lie out of my think-tank. "It's in the lower left desk drawer of my office downtown, in a small envelope. Know where my office is?"

"Yeah. And if this is on the level I'll come back, turn you and your sweetie loose. Otherwise, it's going to be just too bad." He went to the door; powdered.

As soon as I couldn't hear his footfalls in the corridor any longer, I copped an irate hinge at the yellow-haired dish on the divan. "A fine kettle of herring," I growled.

"I know. Please d-don't blame m-me. I was at my wits' end or I wouldn't have d-dragged you into the mess, Mr. Turner." At least she had quit calling me darling, I noticed.

I said: "How's for spooning me the lowdown? Who are you, and what's the score?"

"My n-name is June Dawne. I was Mort Pollak's g-girl friend once upon a time; long before you fastened that m-murder on him."

"Oh. And you held it against me, eh?"

"Not at all," she said swiftly. "He got what was coming to him. That's not the p-point."

"What is the point, then?"

She drew a deep breath. "Pedro Romelo k-kidnaped me because he knew I used to be friendly with Pollak. Pedro figured I'd know about the key to Pollak's strongbox."

"Well?"

"But I didn't know any m-more about it than you do. No matter how hard Pedro b-beat me, I couldn't t-tell him anything. He wouldn't believe me, though. He thought I was holding out."

I said sarcastically: "So you issued me an invitation to your troubles."

"Yes," she blushed through the admission. "I needed help; and I knew of your reputation as a clever detective. I f-fibbed to Romelo; told him you were my fiance. I also told him you had Pollak's k-key."

"Mighty nice of you. What was the idea?"

"Isn't it rather obvious? I figured Romelo would b-bring you here, which he did. And I figured you'd help me."

"Which I didn't," I said sourly.

Her glims widened. "Oh, but you *have* helped me! You've chased Romelo off on a f-false trail. He'll be gone at least an hour or so."

"And when he comes back without the key, he'll convert me into undertaker bait." I made a bitter mouth.

"He won't even f-find you here. Me either. I've been w-working on these ropes for quite a while. My wrists are just about loose." She tugged, and her mitts slipped out of the knots.

I glued the flabbergasted gaze on her as she sat up and started working on her ankle fetters. Presently they fell away and she drifted toward me. She dredged a penknife out of my pants pocket; hacked me free of the cords that trussed me. When I finally stood upright, I spent a full minute trying to get the circulation back into my arms and legs.

The chick watched me sympathetically. She piped: "Isn't there anything I can do to make up for pulling you into danger?"

"You can do this, babe," I grunted. Then I slid my arms around her; helped myself to a kiss.

She didn't object, apparently. At least she didn't struggle.

I sank my mitts in her shoulders, held her at arm's length and shook the daylights out of her. "Okay, tramp. Now come clean or I'll take you apart from your beauty!" I snarled.

"Wh-what do you m-mean?"

"I mean you've been feeding me a lot of horse-radish. To start with, Pedro Romelo didn't slug you with his fists. Your hair isn't even mussed."

"But—b-but—"

I rasped: "In the second place, it would be impossible for you to loosen any of Romelo's knots. I tried it without making so much as a dent in them."

A scared look slithered into her optics. "You—"

"And in the third place, Mort Pollak never had any ten grand stashed in a safety deposit box," I said. "If he'd had that amount of geetus, he'd have hired a mouthpiece to defend him at his murder trial to keep him from going to the gas chamber."

"Wait. Listen—"

"Quiet!" I growled. "This whole thing smells like a plant of some sort. A frame. You and Pedro Romelo ran a whizzer on me; and I yearn to know why."

Her pan went three shades paler than adulterated milk. "You've g-got to trust me, Mr. Turner . . . D-Dan. . . ." Then her arms coiled around my neck.

I was a sucker, of course. A guy in his right mind would have laid a haymaker on her dimple and scrammed. But this golden-haired honey was a lovely bowl of cherries, and I never could resist natural blondes, anyhow. I remembered later she seemed to be listening for something. Suddenly she tightened her grip 'round my neck; pulled me close. "Dan darling . . . kiss me . . . my sweet . . ." she begged loudly.

From the doorway a voice raged: "You dirty bum!"

I bounced three feet straight up in the ozone; landed upright and squinted stupidly at the party who'd just ankled in. He was a bald, middle aged bozo with a puss like a full moon and glims that blazed like bonfires. Oddly enough, I recognized him. He was a Cosmotone director by the name of Maxie Shannon, an expert on cheapie westerns. He directed most of the horse operas in which Pedro Romelo played minor villains.

Now he lurched toward me, frothing at the yap. "So you're the dirty louse who's been stealing my wife!"

I said: "Hey, wait. Is this jessie your wife?"

"She's not yours, anyway. Although anybody'd think so. I've got a good notion to—"

Even as he swung on me, a roscoe sneezed: *"Ka-Chow!"* from the kitchenette doorway. Baldy toppled forward on his profile, slugged a dent in the carpet with his trumpet. He was deceased before he stopped bouncing.

Then the concealed heater blasted again, and a hornet stung me over the ear; put another crease in my haircut. The impact short-circuited my fuses. I went bye-bye.

When I snapped out of my trance, Maxie Shannon's remainders lay sprawled in front of me. The only thing new about him was an automatic in his wilted right duke and a scrap of paper in his left—neither of which had been there when he got creamed.

I dragged myself closer to his carcass; took a blurry hinge at the scrap of paper. It was an anonymous note telling him that his ever-loving frau was playing around with another man, and giving the address of this blue-and-chrome tepee. Which explained why the poor slob had busted in, accused me of playing fast and loose with his home life.

But who had shot him from the kitchenette and then tried to push a pill through my skull? Who had planted a gun and a note in Shannon's defunct clutch? I couldn't ask anybody, because there was nobody in the joint to talk to. The blonde doll had taken it on the lam while I was senseless; I was all alone with the bald bozo's remnants.

I staggered to my pins, stuck a gasper in my face, set it on fire. The smoke helped, but not much. There was a cellarette in one corner, though, and I found some first aid in it. Ordinarily I never guzzle gin, but gin was all I could see. I sloshed about a pint of it past my tonsils; waited for it to do its work. Presently I began to feel normal.

With normalcy came another discovery. I lamped a .32 automatic on the floor; recognized it as mine—the one Pedro Romelo had lifted out of my armpit rig when he first put the snatch on me at my own apartment stash. It had been fired recently. You could smell the burned cordite in the muzzle.

Then I caught hep to the setup. Romelo was the rodent who had drilled his director, Maxie Shannon. And he'd pulled the kill with my personal rod.

But how had he got back into this igloo? I knew he hadn't come in through the front doorway or I'd have spotted him entering, since I hadn't been out of the room at any time. There was no back door, either; I checked on that. Moreover, none of the apartment windows opened on a fire escape, so that theory was nixed.

In brief, the front door was the only possibility; yet the Latin louse hadn't returned that way. To make it worse, this front portal was now locked and bolted *on the inside!*

Which meant Romelo and the blonde cupcake hadn't departed by the doorway route after Shannon was chilled. And a seventh floor stash was too high for them to have jumped out the window without serious damage to their complexions. Yet they were gone, leaving my guilty roscoe behind them.

So there I was with a guy who'd been croaked with some of my private bullets—and suddenly I heard a pounding on the door. A voice said: "Open up in there. The law."

I could guess what had happened. Some nosey neighbor had reported the sounds of gunfire; put in a bleat to the bulls. Now I stood a good chance of being jerked to the bastile on a homicide beef—and the frame might stick, too, when you considered how the set had been dressed. I was alone with a corpse in a locked room, my cannon was responsible for the killery, and I had no witnesses to substantiate the screwy truth.

I prodded my mental machinery into high gear while the cop out in the corridor renewed his pounding. There had to be another way out of this wikiup; otherwise Pedro Romelo and the golden-haired tomato would still be in my midst. The question was, which way had they powdered?

Then I tumbled. There was a dumb waiter in the kitchenette—one of those pint-size elevators they use in the swankier joints to lower the garbage and bring up the morning milk. So that was how the Romelo polecat had returned to blast his director and frame me. It was also how he and Shannon's blonde widow made their subsequent getaway.

I went into action. I scooped up my automatic, holstered it. I also grabbed the other gun—the one in Shannon's defunct fist. I put this in my pocket, and then I dragged the murdered guy into the kitchenette; crammed him into the dumb waiter. I lowered him until I felt the cage touch bottom; slid my own heft down the cable just as the cop smashed his way into the living room.

I wasn't in the clear, though. Not by a long distance. A basement is no place to find yourself with a cadaver on your hands when the law is on the prowl. Luckily enough, I piped an empty galvanized trash can nearby; a big one with a lid on it. I lifted the lid, stuffed Maxie Shannon inside, covered him. Two minutes later I ankled into the rear alley and ran.

I pelted once around the block and then skulked toward my parked jalopy. No other bulls were in evidence, so I slid under the wheel and drove off as if nothing had happened. It was like shooting fish.

Now I was in the clear; and the sensible thing to do was go home, forget all about the Shannon bump-off. Nobody could possibly finger me, the way things stood. I'd been lucky enough to bust myself out of a nasty spot.

But I wasn't satisfied to dismiss the frame Pedro Romelo had tried to drape on me. I craved large slices of vengeance, and there was just one way to collect. That would be to put Pedro's sideburns in the cooler. Maybe the blonde tessie, too.

I stopped at a druggery, bought some adhesive tape for my damaged dome and thumbed the phone book; got Maxie Shannon's address. It was on a swanky street just this side of the Beverly Hills line. I rolled there in a hurry.

A cute little French maid opened up to my ring. "I am sorree, *monsieur.* My mistress is not at home. Neither is *Monsieur* Shannon. I do not know when they will return."

I could have told her Shannon never would, except in a mahogany box. But I kept it to myself and said: "Okay, sweets. I'd just as soon talk to you another time. What are you doing next Thursday night?"

She blushed. "*Madame* does not give me any time off. Besides, I do not know you, *monsieur.*"

"You will, in time. Meanwhile I'd like some questions answered." I gave her a squint at my special badge.

Her dark peepers popped. "You are a policeman, no?"

"No, I am a policeman, yes. Just a private snoop looking for some inside dope."

"Concerning my employers? *Mais non, monsieur.* It is not ethical for a servant to repeat gossip."

I grabbed her gently but firmly; pulled her close to me. "Now look, Frenchie. I like you, see? Your glims are like stars. Your stems belong behind footlights."

"I think I comprehend, *monsieur,*" she giggled.

"Good. Now are we going to be pals, or do I have to slap the ears off you?"

"But—but this is fantastic, *monsieur!*"

"It'll be catastrophic unless you tell me what I want to know. We'll start with Mrs. Shannon. What was her maiden name?"

"Wh-why, Pollak. June Pollak."

"Does she love her hubby?"

"I—I do not think so."

"Has she any boy friends?"

"*Oui.* But I shall not give you his name. Hit me if you wish." I kissed her instead; then I barged back to my bucket, fed it a ration of ethyl.

After a while I anchored in the alley behind the Tower Arms on Sunset; gumshoed down to the basement. It was no job at all to lift Maxie Shannon's shell out of the trash can where I'd left him; but when I began probing at his bald spot with the long blade of my pocket knife, it wasn't so easy. Surgery isn't in my line.

I kept at it, though, and presently I had the slug that had joined him with the angels. I lugged him out to my coupe and propped him in it. Then, on a hunch, I went back down the steps to hunt for a janitor's phone.

Sure enough, I located one. In a trice I was connected with the chromium-and-blue apartment on the seventh floor, which by now was apparently infested with homicide dicks called from headquarters by the copper who'd busted in. A familiar voice answered my ring.

I said, "Lieutenant Donaldson, please."

"This is Donaldson."

"Turner talking," I said. "How would you like to put the arm on Maxie Shannon's murderer?"

Dave yowled: "Shannon? So that's where all this gore came from! But how did you know about it? How do you know he's been bumped? How did you figure I'd be here investigating a case without a corpus delicti—?"

"Stow the questions, cousin. Listen." I gave him some hurried suggestions;

rang off before he could demand details. Then I went out to my iron; headed for La-Brea. I had to drive with one hand and hold Shannon's corpse with the other.

Pedro Romelo's wigwam was a cheap cottage in a bungalow court. I toted the late Maxie Shannon onto the front porch, braced him before me as a shield; rang the bell.

Romelo's voice filtered through the thin woodwork. "Who is it and I don't want any."

"Telegram for Mr. Romelo, sir." I hooked him with the same gag he'd used on me.

He opened up. I thrust Shannon at him like a ventriloquist's dummy and disguised my tone: "You thought you killed me but you made a mistake, you stinking skunk."

The lanky Latin let out a yeep you could have heard from Wyoming to Woonsocket. Then he pulled his little .28 and began blasting.

I felt the bald director's husk jerking in my grasp as the slugs bunted him in the chest. Then I let him topple as Romelo's roscoe clicked empty. Romelo got his first gander at me, and his peepers bulged like squeezed grapes. "Y-you—!"

"Yeah," I said, and handcuffed him.

Then a wildcat hit me in the shape of Maxie Shannon's blonde widow. She tried to claw my optics out of their sockets, but I objected to this. How could I appreciate her gorgeousness without my glims? And she *was* gorgeous; no doubt about it.

I swatted her with my open duke; put everything I had behind the poke. It almost tore her profile off. She sat down on the rug, glassy-eyed as a ten day drunk.

Romelo rattled the nippers on his wrists. "Wh-what's the idea of—?"

I gave him a pleasant smile. "You're under arrest for croaking Maxie Shannon. You were smitten with his wife, but Maxie probably refused her a divorce. So the two of you decided to fix him up with a nice resting place in some graveyard."

"You—you can't—"

I said: "You also decided to make a double-barreled job while you were at it. Oddly enough, Mrs. Shannon happens to be the late unlamented Mort Pollak's sister; so naturally she harbored a thick grudge against me for sending him to the smoke chamber a few months back. Therefore the scheme was to murder Shannon and pin it on me."

"Prove it!"

"Okay. You rented that Tower Arms apartment temporarily, as a scene of operations. You lured me there; fed me a silly story about a missing strong box key—which was a lot of nonsense. In a little while, you left; but you sneaked right back in again by the dumb waiter."

"And?"

"The jane staged a little act with me. Meanwhile, you had sent Shannon a note telling him his wife was at that address with another man. Shannon walked in, spotted her in my arms; whereupon you corpsed him from the kitchenette with my rod."

"Do tell," he sneered politely.

I said: "Yeah. Next, you tried to cream me with a second gun. The slug notched me on the noggin but failed to render me defunct. You didn't know this, though. You figured I was dead. So you put the second cannon in Maxie's mitt, tossed mine on the floor; made it look as if we'd burned each other down in a pistol duel. You locked up the wigwam from inside; and finally you took your girl friend down the dumb waiter."

Romelo bared his grinders. "A very clever song, Hawkshaw. The only trouble is, you can't make it stick."

"Sure I can. Or anyhow enough of it to make you sniff cyanide. You just emptied a whole clip of pills into Maxie, which inserts your nose in a wringer."

"They can't execute me for shooting holes in corpses. He was dead when you shoved him at me. The bullet that killed him came out of your automatic."

"How would you know that?"

"Because I—" All of a sudden he turned gray around the edges. "Oh, my God!" he moaned.

I stepped aside so he could see Dave Donaldson standing on the porch getting an earful. "A nice confession, eh, Dave?"

Dave grunted: "Yeah," and used his own cuffs to nipper the yellow-haired Shannon widow. "Up on your tootsies, sis. Let's all go down to the jug."

So I didn't have to wait until Thursday night for my date with the French maid, after all. Her employer was deceased and her mistress was pinched for it, so she had her evenings free.

POWER OF THE PUPPETS
Fritz Leiber

I

A Plot Afoot?

Look at the ugly little thing for yourself then, and tell me if it's an ordinary puppet!" said Delia, her voice rising.

Curiously I examined the limp figure she had jerked out of her handbag and tossed on my desk. The blue-white dollface grinned at me, revealing yellowish fangs. A tiny wig of black horse hair hung down as far as the empty eye-sockets. The cheeks were sunken. It was a gruesome piece of workmanship, with a strong flavor of the Middle Ages. The maker had evidently made a close study of stone gargoyles and strained-glass devils.

Attached to the hollow papier-mâché head was the black garment that gave the figure its appearance of limpness. Something after the fashion of a monk's robe, it had a little cowl that could be tucked over the head, but now hung down in back.

I know something about puppets, even though my line is a far cry from puppeteering. I am a private detective. But I knew that this was not a marionette, controlled by strings, but a hand puppet. It was made so that the operator's hand could be slipped up through the empty garment until his fingers were in a position to animate the head and arms. During an exhibition the operator would be concealed beneath the stage, which had no floor, and only the puppet would be visible above the footlights.

I drew the robe over my hand and fitted my index finger up into the head, my second finger into the right sleeve, and my thumb into the left sleeve of the puppet. That, as I recalled, was the usual technique. Now the figure was no longer limp. My wrist and forearm filled out the robe.

I wiggled finger and thumb, and the manikin waved his arms wildly, though somewhat awkwardly, for I have seldom manipulated a puppet. I crooked my first finger and the little head gave a vigorous nod.

"Good morning, Jack Ketch," I said, making the manikin bow, as if acknowledging my salutation.

"Don't!" cried Delia, and turned her head away.

Delia was puzzling me. I had always thought her a particularly level-headed woman and, up to three years ago, I had seen a great deal of her and had had a chance to judge.

Three years ago she had married the distinguished puppeteer, Jock Lathrop, with whom I was also acquainted. Then our paths had separated. But I'd had no inkling of anything being amiss until she had appeared this morning in my New York office and poured out a series of vague hints and incredible suspicions so strange that anything resembling them did not often come a private detective's way, though I hear many odd and bizarre stories during the course of a year's work.

I looked at her closely. She was, if anything, more beautiful than ever, and considerably more exotic, as might be expected now that she was moving in artistic circles. Her thick, golden hair fell straight to her shoulders, where it was waved under. Her gray suit was smartly tailored, and her gray suede shoes trim. At her throat was a barbaric-looking brooch of hammered gold. A long golden pin kept a sketchy little hat and a handful of veil in place.

But she was still the old Delia, still the "softie Viking," as we sometimes used to call her. Except that anxiety was twisting her lips, and fear showed in her big gray eyes.

"What really is the matter, Delia?" I said, sitting down beside her. "Has Jock been getting out of hand?"

"Oh, don't be foolish, George!" she replied sharply. "It's nothing like that. I'm not afraid of Jock, and I'm not looking for a detective to get any evidence for me. I've come to you because I'm afraid for him. It's those horrible puppets. They're trying . . . Oh, how can I explain it! Everything was all right until he accepted that engagement in London you must remember about, and began prying into his family history, his genealogy. Now there are things he won't discuss with me, things he won't let me see. He avoids me. And, George, I'm certain that, deep in his heart, he's afraid too. Terribly afraid."

"Listen, Delia," I said. "I don't know what you mean by all this talk about the puppets, but I do know one thing. You're married to a genius. And geniuses, Delia, are sometimes hard to live with. They're notoriously inconsiderate, without meaning to be. Just read their biographies! Half the time they go around in a state of abstraction, in love with their latest ideas, and fly off the handle at the slightest provocation. Jock's fanatically devoted to his puppets, and he should be! All the critics who know anything about the subject say he's the best in the world, better even than Franetti. And they're raving about his new show as the best of his career!"

Delia's gray suede fist beat her knee.

"I know, George. I know all about that! But it has nothing to do with what I'm trying to tell you. You don't suppose I'm the sort of wife who would whine just because her husband is wrapped up in his work? Why, for a year I was his assistant, helped him make the costumes, even operated some of the less important puppets. Now he won't even let me in his workshop. He won't let me come backstage. He does everything himself. But I wouldn't mind even that, if it weren't that I'm afraid. It's the puppets themselves, George! They—they're trying to hurt him. They're trying to hurt me too."

I searched for a reply. I felt thoroughly uncomfortable. It is not pleasant to hear an old friend talking like a lunatic. I lifted my head and frowned at the malevolent dollface of Jack Ketch, blue as that of a drowned man. Jack Ketch is the hangman in the traditional puppet play *Punch and Judy*. He takes his name from a Seventeenth Century executioner who officiated with rope and red-hot irons at Tyburn in London.

"But Delia," I said, "I don't see what you're driving at. How can an ordinary puppet—"

"But it isn't an ordinary puppet!" Delia broke in vehemently. "That's why I brought it for you to see. Look at it closely. Look at the details. *Is* it an ordinary puppet?"

Then I saw what she meant.

"There are some superficial differences," I admitted.

"What are they?" she pressed.

"Well, this puppet has no hands. Puppets usually have papier-mâché or stuffed muslin hands attached to the ends of the sleeves."

"That's right. Go on."

"Then the head," I continued unwillingly. "There are no eyes painted on it —just eyeholes. And it's much thinner than most I've seen. More like a—a mask."

Delia gripped my arm, dug her fingers in.

"You've said the word, George!" she cried. "Like a mask! Now do you see what I mean? Jock doesn't operate his own puppets any more. He has some horrible little creatures like rats that do it for him. They wear the puppets' robes and heads. That's why he won't allow me or anyone else to come backstage during a performance. And they're trying to hurt him, kill him! I know. I've heard them threaten him."

"Delia," I said, gently taking hold of her arms, "you don't know what

you're saying. You're nervous, over-wrought. Just because your husband in-
vents a new type of puppet—why, it explains itself. It's because of his work
on these new-type puppets that he's become secretive."

She jerked away from me.

"Won't you try to understand, George? I know how mad it sounds, but I'm
not mad. At night, when Jock has thought I was asleep I've heard them
threaten him with their high little voices like whistles. 'Let us go—let us go
or we'll kill you!' they cry, and I'm so weak with fear I can't move. They're so
tiny they can creep about everywhere."

"Have you seen them?" I asked quickly.

"No, but I *know* they're real! Last night one of them tried to scratch my
eyes out while I was asleep. Look!"

She swept back the thick hair from her temple, and at that moment I also
felt as if the needle-touch of fear had been transmitted to me. There in the
creamy skin, an inch from the eye, were five little scratches that looked as if
they might have been made by a miniature human hand. For a moment I
could almost see the ratlike little creature Delia had described, its clawed
hand upraised. . . .

Then the image faded and I was realizing that such grotesque happenings
were impossible. But oddly I felt as if I no longer could attribute everything
Delia had told me to her neurotic fancies. *I* feared, also—but my fear was
that there was a plot afoot, one meant to terrify her, to work on her superstitious fears, and delude her.

"Would you like me to visit Jock?" I asked quietly.

Some of the weight seemed to drop from her shoulders.

"I was hoping you'd say that," she said, with relief. . . .

The exquisitely lettered sign read:

LATHROP'S PUPPETS—2nd Floor

Outside, Forty-second Street muttered and mumbled. Inside, a wooden
stair with worn brass fittings led up into a realm of dimness and comparative
silence.

"Wait a minute, Delia," I said. "There are a couple of questions I'd like you
to answer. I want to get this whole thing straight before I see Jock."

She stopped and nodded, but before I could speak again our attention was
attracted by a strange series of sounds from the second floor. Heavy stamp-
ing, then what seemed to be an explosion of curses in a foreign language,
then rapid pacing up and down, another explosion of curses, and more
pacing. It sounded as if a high-class tantrum were in progress.

Suddenly the noises ceased. I could visualize a person "pausing and swelling up in silent rage." With equal suddenness they recommenced, this time ending in a swift and jarring *clump-clump* of footsteps down the stairs. Delia shrank back against the railing as a fattish man with gray eyebrows, glaring eyes, and a mouth that was going through wordless but vituperative contortions neared us. He was wearing an expensive checked suit and a white silk shirt open at the neck. He was crumpling a soft felt hat.

He paused a few steps above us and pointed at Delia dramatically. His other hand was crumpling a soft felt hat.

"You, madam, are the wife of that lunatic, are you not?" he demanded accusingly.

"I'm Jock Lathrop's wife, if that's what you mean, Mr. Franetti," Delia said coolly. "What's the matter?"

I recognized Luigi Franetti then. He was often referred to by the press as the "Dean of Puppeteers." I remembered that Jock had been in his workshop and studied under him several years ago.

"You ask me what is the matter with me?" Franetti ranted. "You ask me that, Madam Lathrop? Bah!" Here he crumpled his hat again. "Very well—I will tell you! Your husband is not only a lunatic. He is also an ingrate! I come here to congratulate him on his recent success, to take him to my arms. After all, he is my pupil. Everything he learned from me. And what is his gratitude? What, I ask you? He will not let me touch him! He will not even shake hands! He will not let me into his workshop! Me! Franetti, who taught him everything!"

He swelled up with silent rage, just as I'd visualized it. But only for a moment. Then he was off again.

"But I tell you he is a madman!" he shouted, shaking his finger at Delia. "Last night I attended, unannounced and uninvited, a performance of his puppets. They do things that are impossible—impossible without Black Magic. I am Luigi Franetti, and I know! Nevertheless, I thought he might be able to explain it to me today. But no, he shuts me out! He has the evil eye and the devil's fingers, I tell you. In Sicily people would understand such things. In Sicily he would be shot! Bah! Never will I so much as touch him with my eyes again. Let me pass!"

He hurried down the rest of the stairs, Delia squeezing back and turning her head. In the doorway he turned for a parting shot.

"And tell me, Madam Lathrop," he cried, "what a puppeteer wants with rats!"

With a final "Bah!" he rushed out.

II
Strange Actions

I didn't stop laughing until I saw Delia's face. Then it occurred to me that Franetti's accusations, ludicrous as they were, might seem to her to fit with her own suspicions.

"You can't take seriously what a man like Franetti says," I remonstrated. "He's jealous because Jock won't bow down to him and make a complete revelation of all his new technical discoveries and inventions."

Delia did not reply. She was staring after Franetti, absentmindedly pulling at the corner of a tiny handkerchief with her teeth. Watching her, I knew again the fear she felt, as if again she were feeling a little creature gouging at her temple.

"Anything to that last remark of Franetti's?" I asked lightly. "Jock doesn't keep white rats for pets by any chance?"

"I don't know," Delia said abstractedly. "I told you he never lets me in his workroom." Then she looked at me. "You said you wanted to ask me some more questions?"

I nodded. On the way here I had been revolving in my mind an unpleasant hypothesis. If Jock no longer loved Delia and had some reason for wanting to be rid of her he might be responsible for her supicions. He had every chance to trick her.

"You said the change in Jock began to show while you were in London," I said. "Tell me the precise circumstances."

"He'd always been interested in old books and in genealogy, you see, but never to the same extent," she said, after a thoughtful pause. "In a way it was chance that began it. An accident to his hands. A rather serious one, too. A window fell on them, mashing the fingers badly. Of course a puppeteer's no good without hands, and so Jock had to lay off for three weeks. To help pass the time, he took to visiting the British Museum and the library there. Later he made many visits to other libraries to occupy his time, since he's apt to be very nervous when anything prevents him from working. When the war started we came back, and the London dates were abandoned. He did not work here, either, for a quite long time, but kept up his studies.

"Then when he was finally ready to start work again he told me he'd decided to work the puppets alone. I pointed out that one man couldn't give a puppet show, since he could only manage two characters at a time. He told me that he was going to confine himself to puppet plays like *Punch and Judy*, in which there are almost never more than two characters in sight at one time.

"That was three months ago. From that day he's avoided me. George—" her voice broke "—it's almost driven me crazy. I've had the craziest suspicions. I've even thought that he lost both his hands in the accident and refused to tell!"

"What?" I shouted. "Do you mean to tell me you don't know?"

"Do you begin to see how secretive he is?" she said with a wan and rather pitiful smile.

"No. Seems strange, doesn't it? But I can't swear even to that. He never lets me come near, and he wears gloves, except in the dark."

"But the puppet shows—"

"That's just it. That's the question I keep asking myself when I sit in the audience and watch the puppets. *Who* is manipulating them? What's inside them?"

At that moment I determined to do everything I could to battle Delia's fear.

"You're not crazy," I said harshly. "But Jock is!"

She rubbed her hand across her forehead, as if it itched.

"No," she said softly, "it's the puppets. Just as I told you."

As we went on upstairs then I could tell that Delia was anxious to get my interview with Jock started. She had had to nerve herself up to it, and delays were not improving her state of mind. But apparently we were fated to have a hard time getting up that flight of stairs.

This time the interruption came when a slim man in a blue business suit tried to slip in the semi-darkness unnoticed. But Delia recognized him.

"Why, hello, Dick!" she said. "Don't you know old friends?"

I made out prim, regular features and a head of thinning, neutral-colored hair.

"Dick, this is George Clayton," Delia was saying. "George, this is Dick Wilkinson. Dick handles my husband's insurance."

Wilkinson's "Howdya do?" sounded embarrassed and constrained. He wanted to get away.

"What did Jock want to see you about?" asked Delia, and Wilkinson's apparent embarrassment increased. He coughed, then seemed to make a sudden decision.

"Jock's been pretty temperamental lately, hasn't he?" he asked Delia.

She nodded slowly.

"I thought so," he said. "Frankly, I don't know why he wanted to see me this morning. I thought perhaps it was something in connection with the accident to his hands. He has never done anything about collecting any of the five-thousand-dollar insurance he took out on them two years ago. But whether that was it or not I can't tell you. He kept me waiting the best part of half an hour. I could not help hearing Mr. Franetti's display of temper. Perhaps that upset Jock. Anyhow when Franetti went away, fuming, five minutes later Jock leaned out of his workshop door and curtly informed me that he had changed his mind—he didn't say about what—and told me to leave."

"I'm so sorry, Dick," murmured Delia. "That was rude of him." Then her voice took on a strangely eager note. "Did he leave the door of his workshop open?"

Dick Wilkinson wrinkled his brow. "Why yes, I—I believe he did. At least, that was my impression. But, Delia—"

Delia had already slipped on ahead, running swiftly up the steps. Hastily I said good-by to the perplexed insurance agent and followed her.

When I reached the second floor I went into a short hall. Through an open door I glimpsed the closely-ranked seats of the puppet theater. Delia was vanishing through another door down the hall. I followed her.

Just as I came into a small reception room, I heard her scream.

"George! George! He's whipping the puppet!"

With that bewildering statement ringing in my ears, I darted into what I took to be Jock Lathrop's workshop, then pulled up short. It too was dim, but not as dim as the hall. I could see tables and racks of various kinds, and other paraphernalia.

Delia was cowering back against a wall, stark fear in her eyes. But my attention was riveted on the small, stocky man in the center of the room— Delia's husband. On, or *in*, his left hand was a puppet. His gloved right hand held a miniature cat-o'-nine-tails and he was lashing the puppet. And the little manikin was writhing and flailing its arms protectively in a manner so realistic that it took my breath away. In that strange setting I could almost imagine I heard a squeaking, protesting voice. Indeed, the realism was such and the grin on Lathrop's face so malign that I heard myself saying:

"Stop it, Jock! Stop it!"

He looked up, saw me, and burst into peals of laughter. His snub-nosed, sallow face was contorted into a mask of comedy. I had expected anything but that.

"So even the skeptical George Clayton, hard-boiled sleuth, is taken in by my cheap illusions!" he finally managed to say.

Then he stopped chuckling and drew himself up nonchalantly, like a magician about to perform a feat of sleight of hand. He tossed the whip onto a nearby table, seized the puppet with his right hand and, to all appearances, wiggled his left hand out of it. Then he quickly flipped me the limp form, thrust both hands into his pockets, and began to whistle.

Delia gave a low, whimpering cry and ran out of the room. If it had been easy for me to imagine a tiny, nude creature scuttling away behind Jock, half concealed by his left hand, what must it have been for her, in her tortured, superstitious state?

"Examine the thing, George," Lathrop directed coolly. "Is it a puppet, or isn't it?"

I looked down at the bundle of cloth and papier-mâché I had caught instinctively. It was a puppet all right, and in general workmanship precisely similar to the one Delia had shown me at my office. Its garments, however, were a gay, motley patchwork. I recognized the long nose and sardonic, impudent features of Punch.

I was fascinated by the delicate craftsmanship. The face lacked the brutishness of Jack Ketch, but it had a cunning, hair-trigger villainy all its own. Somehow it looked like a composite of all the famous criminals and murderers I had ever read about. As the murderous hero of *Punch and Judy*, it was magnificent.

But I had not come here to admire puppets.

"Look here, Jock," I said, "what the devil have you been doing to Delia? The poor girl's frightened to death."

He regarded me quizzically.

"You're taking a lot for granted, aren't you?" he said quietly. "I imagine she hunted you up as a friend, not in your capacity as a detective, but don't you think it would have been wiser to hear both sides of the case before forming judgment? I can imagine what sort of wild stories Delia's been telling you. She says I'm avoiding her, doesn't she? She says there's something queer about the puppets. In fact, she says they're alive, doesn't she?"

I heard a furtive scuffling under the work table, and was startled in spite of myself. Jock Lathrop grinned, then whistled shrilly between his teeth. A white rat crept hesitatingly into view from behind a pile of odds and ends.

"A pet," he announced mockingly. "Is it Delia's belief that I have trained rats to animate my puppets?"

"Forget Delia's beliefs for the present!" I said angrily. "Whatever they are, you're responsible for them! You've no excuse in the world for mystifying her, terrifying her."

"Are you so sure I haven't?" he said enigmatically.

"Good Lord, she's your wife, Jock!" I flung at him.

His face became serious and his words took on a deeper quality.

"I know she's my wife," he said, "and I love her dearly. But George, hasn't the obvious explanation of all this occurred to you? I hate to say it, but the truth is that Delia is bothered by—er—neurotic fancies. For some crazy reason, without the slightest foundation she has become obsessed with some sort of deep-seated—and thoroughly unreasonable—jealousy, and she's directing it at the puppets. I can't tell you why. I wish I knew."

"Even admitting that," I countered quickly, "why do you persist in mystifying her?"

"I don't," he flatly denied. "If sometimes I keep her out of the workshop, it's for her own good."

His argument was beginning to make sense. Jock Lathrop's voice had a compelling matter-of-fact quality. I was beginning to feel slightly ridiculous. Then I remembered something.

"Those scratches on her face—" I began.

"I've seen them," said Jock. "Again I hate to say it, but the only rational explanation I can see is that they were self-inflicted with the idea of bolstering up her accusations, or perhaps she scratched herself in her sleep. At any rate, people with delusions have been known to do drastic things. They'll go to any lengths rather than discard their queer beliefs. That's honestly what I think."

Pondering this quiet statement, I was looking around. Here were all the tools of the expert puppet-maker. Molds, paints, varnishes, clay models of heads, unformed papier-mâché, paper clippings, and glue. A sewing machine littered with odds and ends of gay-colored cloth.

Tacked above a desk were a number of sketches of puppets, some in pencil, some in colors. On a table were two half-painted heads, each atop a stick so that the brush could get at them more easily. Along the opposite wall hung a long array of puppets—princesses and Cinderellas, witches and wizards, peasants, oafs, bearded old men, devils, priests, doctors, kings. It almost made me feel as if a whole doll-world was staring at me and choking back raucous laughter.

"Why haven't you sent Delia to a doctor?" I asked suddenly.

"Because she refuses to go. For some time I've been trying to persuade her to consult a psychoanalyst."

I didn't know what to say. The white rat moved into my line of vision. It occurred to me that a rat could be used to explain the scuffling sounds made by anything else, but I put such an irrational thought out of my mind. More and more I found myself being forced into complete agreement with Lathrop. Delia's suspicions were preposterous. Lathrop must be right.

"Look here," I continued feebly, "Delia keeps talking about something that happened to you in London. A change. A sudden interest in genealogy."

"I'm afraid the change was in Delia," he said bitterly. "As for the genealogy business, that's quite correct. I did find out some startling things about a man whom I believe to be an ancestor of mine."

As he spoke, eagerly now, I was surprised to note how his features lost their tight, hard appearance. The look of impudence was gone.

"I *do* love Delia very much," he said, his voice vibrant, low. "What would she think of me, George, if it turned out that her accusations were partly true? Of course, that's nonsense. But you can see that we are in trouble, George—bad trouble, that is considerably out of the line of work a private detective follows. Your work is concrete, though in your criminal investigations you must have learned that the mind and body of man are sometimes subject to brutal powers. Not supernatural—no. But things—hard to talk about.

"George, would you do something for me? Come to the performance tonight. Afterward we can discuss this whole matter more fully. And another thing. See that old pamphlet over there? I have good reason for thinking it concerns an ancestor of mine. Take it with you. Read it. But for heaven's sake don't let Delia see it. You see, George—"

He broke off uncertainly. He seemed about to take me into his confidence about something, but then the hard, self-contained look returned to his face.

"Leave me now," he said abruptly. "This talk, and that business with the old fool, Franetti, has made me nervous."

I walked over to the table, carefully laid down Punch, and picked up the yellow-paged, ancient pamphlet he had indicated.

"I'll see you tonight after the show," I said.

III

Punch and Judy

As I closed the door behind me, I thought I saw in Lathrop's eyes that same look of fear I had seen in Delia's. But it was deeper, much deeper. And only then did I remember that not once during our interview had Jock Lathrop taken his hands out of his pockets.

Delia rushed up to me. I could tell she had been crying.

"What will we do, George—what will we do? What did he say to you? What did he tell you?"

I had to admit that her hectic manner was consistent with Jock's theory of neurotic fancies.

"Is it true, Delia," I asked abruptly, "that he's been urging you to see a psychoanalyst?"

"Why, yes." Then I saw her stiffen. "Jock's been telling you it's only my imagination, and you've been believing him," she accused.

"No, that's not it," I lied, "but I want to have time to think it all over. I'm coming to the performance tonight. I'll talk with you then."

"He *has* persuaded you!" she insisted, clinging to my sleeve. "But you mustn't believe him, George. He's afraid of them! He's in worse trouble than I am."

"I agree with you partly," I said, not knowing this time whether I was lying or not, "and after the performance we'll talk it over."

She suddenly drew away. Her face had lost something of its helpless look.

"If you won't help me," she said, breathing heavily, "I know a way of finding out whether I'm right or wrong. A sure way."

"What do you mean, Delia?"

"Tonight," she said huskily, "you may find out."

More than that she wouldn't say, although I pressed her. I took away with me a vision of her distraught gray eyes, contrasted oddly with the thick sweep of golden hair. I hurried through the hall, down the stairs. The measured pandemonium of Forty-second Street was welcome. It was good to see so many people, walk with them, be jostled by them and forget the fantastic fears of Delia and Jock Lathrop.

I glanced at the pamphlet in my hand. The type was ancient and irregular. The paper was crumbly at the edges. I read the lengthy title:

A TRUE ACCOUNT, as related by a Notable Personage to a Trustworthy Gentleman, of the CIRCUMSTANCES attending the Life and DEATH of JOCKEY LOWTHROPE, an Englishman who gave PUPPET SHEWS; telling how many surmised that his Death was encompassed by these same PUPPETS.

Night was sliding in over New York. My office was a mass of shadows. From where I was sitting I could see the mammoth Empire State Building topping the irregular skyline.

I rubbed my eyes wearily. But that did not keep my thoughts from their endless circling. Who was I to believe? Delia or Jock? Was there a disordered mind at work, fabricating monstrous suspicions? And if so, whose mind was it? They were questions outside the usual province of a private detective.

I tilted the pamphlet to catch the failing light and re-read two passages that had particularly impressed me.

At this Time it was rumored that Jockey Lowthrope had made a Pact with the Devil, with a view to acquiring greater Skill in his Trade. There were many who testified privately that his Puppets acted and moved with a Cunning beyond the ability of

Christian Man to accomplish. For Jockey took no assistants and would explain to no one how his Manikins were activated. . . .

Some say that Moll Squires and the French Doctor did not tell all they saw when they first viewed Jockey's Corpse. Certain it was that a long, thin Needle pierced his Heart and that both Hands were hacked off at the Wrists. Jockey's wife Lucy would have been held for Trial for Murder at the Assizes, only that she was never seen afterwards. Moll Squires averred that the Devil had come to fetch Jockey's hands, to which he had previous granted an unholy Skill. But many maintain that he was slain by his own Puppets, who chose the Needle as being a Weapon suitable to their Size and Dexterity. These recall how the Clergyman Penrose inveighed against Jockey, saying "Those are not Puppets, but Imps of Satan, and whosoever views them is in Danger of Damnation."

I pushed the pamphlet to one side. What could one make of events that had happened one hundred and fifty years ago—faint reverberations from the Eighteenth Century fear-world that had underlaid the proud Age of Reason? Especially when one read of them in an account obviously written for the sake of sensation-mongering?

True, the names were oddly similar. Lowthrope and Lathrop were undoubtedly alternate spellings. And from what Jock Lathrop had said he had further evidence of a blood relationship.

The pamphlet angered me, made me feel as if someone were trying to frighten me with nursery tales of ghosts and goblins.

I switched on the light and blinked at the electric clock. It was seven-forty-five. . . .

When I reached the puppet theater it was buzzing with conversation and the hall outside was already blue with cigarette smoke. Just as I was getting my ticket from the sad-eyed girl at the door, someone called my name. I looked up and saw Dr. Grendal. I could tell that the garrulous old man had something on his mind besides his shiny, bald pate. After a few aimless remarks he asked his question.

"Seen Jock since he got back from London?"

"Just to say hello to," I answered cautiously.

"How'd he impress you, hey?" The doctor's eyes glanced sharply from behind their silver-rimmed spectacles.

"A little uneasy," I admitted. "Temperamental."

"I thought you might say something like that," he commented, as he led me over to an empty corner. "Fact is," he continued, "I think he's definitely queer. Between ourselves, of course. He called me in. I thought he needed me in a professional capacity. But it turned out he wanted to talk about pygmies."

He couldn't have surprised me more.

"Pygmies?" I repeated.

"Just so. Pygmies. Surprised you, didn't it? Did me, too. Well, Jock was especially curious about the lower limits of possible size of mature human beings. Kept asking if there were any cases in which they were as small as puppets. I told him it was impossible, except for infants and embryos.

"Then he began shifting the conversation. Wanted to know a lot about blood relationship and the inheritance of certain traits. Wanted to know all about identical twins and triplets and so on. Evidently thought I'd be a mine of data because of the monographs I've scribbled about medical oddities. I answered as best I could, but some of his questions were queer. Power of mind over matter, and that sort of stuff. I got the impression his nerves were about to crack. Told him as much. Whereupon he told me to get out. Peculiar, hey?"

I could not answer. Dr. Grendal's information put new life into the disturbing notions I had been trying to get out of my mind. I wondered how much I dared tell the old physician, or whether it would be unwise to confide in him at all.

The people in the hall were moving into the theater. I made a noncommittal remark to Grendal and we followed. A rotund figure pushed in ahead of us, muttering—Luigi Franetti. Evidently he had not been able to resist the temptation presented by his former student's puppets. He threw down the price of the ticket contemptuously, as if it were the thirty pieces of silver due Judas Iscariot. Then he stamped in, sat down, folded his arms, and glared at the curtain.

There must have been two hundred people present, almost a full house. I noticed quite a splash of evening dresses and dress suits. I didn't see Delia, but I noted the prim features of Dick Wilkinson, the insurance agent.

From behind the curtain came the reedy tinkle of a music box—tones suggestive of a doll orchestra. The seats Grendal and I had were near the front, but considerably to one side.

The little theater grew dim. A soft illumination flowed up the square of red silk curtain. The melody from the music box ended on a note so high it sounded as though something in the mechanism had snapped. A pause. The deep, somber reverberation of a gong. Another pause. Then a voice, which I recognized as Lathrop's pitched in falsetto.

"Ladies and gentlemen, for your entertainment Lathrop's Puppets present —*Punch and Judy!*"

From behind me I heard Franetti's "Bah!"

Then the curtain parted and slid rustling to the sides. Punch popped up like a jack-in-the-box, chuckled throatily, and began to antic around the stage and make bitingly witty remarks, some of them at the expense of the spectators.

It was the same puppet Jock had let me examine in the workshop. But was Jock's hand inside? After a few seconds I quit worrying about that. This, I told myself, was only an ordinary puppet show, as clever as the manipulations were. The voice was Jock Lathrop's, pitched in puppeteer's falsetto.

It is ironic that *Punch and Judy* is associated with children and the nursery, for few plays are more fundamentally sordid. Modern child educators are apt to fling up their hands at mention of it. It is unlike any fairy tale or phantasy, but springs from forthright, realistic crime.

Punch is the prototype of the egotistical, brutish criminal—the type who today figures as an axefiend or sashweight slayer. He kills his squalling baby and nagging wife, Judy, merely because they annoy him. He kills the doctor because he doesn't like the medicine. He kills the policeman who comes to arrest him. Finally, after he is thrown into jail and sentenced to death, he manages to outwit and murder the fearsome executioner Jack Ketch.

Only in the end does the devil come to fetch him, and in some versions Punch kills the devil. During all these crimes Punch seldom loses his grim and trenchant sense of humor.

Punch and Judy has long been one of the most popular puppet plays. Perhaps the reason children like it is that they have fewer moral inhibitions than grown-ups to prevent them from openly sympathizing with Punch's primal selfishness. For Punch is as thoughtlessly selfish and cruel as a spoiled child.

These thoughts passed rapidly through my mind, as they always do when I see or think of *Punch and Judy*. This time they brought with them a vivid memory of Jock Lathrop whipping the puppet.

I have said that the beginning of the play reassured me. But as it progressed, my thoughts crept back. The movements of the puppets were too smooth and clever for my liking. They handled things too naturally.

There is a great deal of clubbing in *Punch and Judy*, and the puppets always hold on to their clubs by hugging them between their arms—the thumb and second finger of the puppeteer. But Jock Lathrop had made a startling innovation. His puppets held their weapons as a man normally does. I wondered if this could be due to some special device.

Hurriedly I got out my opera glasses and turned them on the stage. It was some time before I could focus one of the puppets; they jerked about too much. Finally I got a clear view of Punch's arms. As far as I could make out, they ended in tiny hands—hands that could shift on the club, clenching and unclenching in an uncannily natural way.

Grendal mistook my smothered exclamation for one of admiration.

"Pretty clever," he said, nodding.

After that I sat still. Of course the tiny hands were only some sort of mechanical attachment to Lathrop's fingertips. And here, I thought, was the reason for Delia's fears. She had been taken in by the astonishing realism of the puppets.

But then how to explain Jock's actions, the strange questions he had put to Dr. Grendal? Merely an attempt to create publicity?

It was hard for a "hard-boiled sleuth" to admit, even to himself, that he did have an odd feeling that those manikins were alive. But I did, and I fought against this feeling, turning my eyes from the stage.

Then I saw Delia. She was sitting in the row behind and two chairs further to the side. There was nothing of the "softie Viking" about her now, despite the glimmering, curving lines of her silver lamé evening dress. In the ghostly illumination from the stage, her lovely face was cold, stony, with a set determination that made me apprehensive.

I heard a familiar mutter and turned to see Franetti moving down the far aisle as if the stage were drawing him like a magnet. He was glaring at the puppets and talking to himself.

Twice I heard him mutter, "Impossible!" Patrons gave him irritated looks as he passed or murmured complainingly. He took no notice. He reached the end of the aisle and disappeared through the black-curtained doorway that led backstage.

IV
Dark Heritage

Rapidly the play was drawing toward its climax. Punch, in a dark and dismal prison, was whining and wailing in self-pity. Jack Ketch was approaching from one side, his face and black hair hideous in the dim light. In one hand he carried a noose; in the other, a needlelike sword about five inches long. He brandished both dexterously.

I could no longer view the scene in a matter-of-fact way. This was a doll-world, where all the dolls were brutes and murderers. The stage was reality, viewed through the wrong end of a telescope.

Then came an ominous rustle behind me. I turned. Delia had risen to her feet. Something was gleaming in her upraised hand. There was a sharp crack, like a whip. Before anyone could stop her she emptied the chambers of a small revolver at the stage.

On the fourth shot I saw a black hole appear in Punch's mask.

Delia did not struggle against the bewildered men who had risen to pinion her hands. She was staring fixedly at the stage. So was I. For I knew what she hoped to prove by those shots.

Punch had disappeared, but not Jack Ketch. He seemed to be staring back at Delia, as if the shots had been an expected part of the performance. Then the high tuning voice, screamed, a reedy scream of hate. And it was not Jock Lathrop's falsetto voice that screamed. Then Jack Ketch raised his needlelike sword and plunged down out of sight.

The scream that followed was a full-voiced cry of desperate agony that silenced and froze the milling audience. And this time it was Jock's voice.

Hurriedly I pushed my way toward the curtained door. Old Grendal was close behind me. The first thing that caught my eye in the backstage confusion was the trembling form of Luigi Franetti. His face was like wax. He was on his knees, murmuring garbled prayers.

Then, sprawled on his back beneath the puppet-stage, I saw Lathrop.

Hysterical questions gave way to shocked whispers, which mounted to a chorus as others swarmed backstage.

"Look! He's dead—the man that works the puppets!"

"She got him all right! Fired through the curtains underneath!"

"I saw her do it myself. She shot him a dozen times."

"Somebody said she's his wife."

"She got him on the last shot. I heard him scream. She's crazy."

I understood the mistake they were making, for I knew that everyone of Delia's shots had hit above stage level. I walked over to Jock Lathrop's body. And it was with the shock of my life that I saw that Jack Ketch's pygmy sword had been driven to the hilt in Lathrop's right eyeball. And on Jock Lathrop's right and left hands were the garments and papier-mâché heads of Punch and Jack Ketch.

Grendal hastened forward and knelt at Lathrop's side. The chorus of frightened whispers behind us kept rising and falling in a kind of mob rhythm. The drab insurance agent Wilkinson stepped up and peered over Grendal's shoulders. Indrawn breath whistled between his teeth. He turned around slowly and pointed at Franetti.

"Mr. Lathrop was not shot, but stabbed," he said in a curiously calm voice that caught the crowd's ear. "I saw that man sneak back here. He murdered Mr. Lathrop. He was the only one who could have done it. Get hold of him, some of you, and take him out front."

Franetti offered no resistance. He looked utterly dazed and helpless.

"The rest of you had better wait out front too," Wilkinson continued. "I shall telephone the police. See to it that Mrs. Lathrop is not troubled or annoyed. She is hysterical. Do not allow her to come back here."

There was a rustle of hushed interjections and questions, but the crowd flowed back into the theater. Wilkinson, Grendal, and myself were left alone.

"There's no hope, is there?" I managed to say.

Grendal shook his head.

"He's dead as a nail. The tiny instrument penetrated the eyesocket and deep into the brain. Happened to be driven in exactly the proper direction."

I looked down at Lathrop's twisted body. Even now I could hardly repress a shudder at the sight of the puppets. The vindictive expressions on their masks looked so purposeful. I regarded the bullet hole in Punch's mask. A little blood was welling from it. The bullet must have nicked Lathrop's finger.

At that moment I became aware of a confused surge of footsteps outside, and of the crowd's whispering, muffled by the intervening hangings, rising to a new crescendo.

"Look out, she's getting away!"

"She's running! Stop her."

"Has she still got the gun?"

"She's going back there. Grab her, somebody!"

The black draperies eddied wildly as Delia spun through the door, jerking loose from a hand that had sought to restrain her. In a swirl of golden hair and shimmering silver lamé she came in. I glimpsed her wild gray eyes, white-circled.

"*They* killed him, I tell you, *they* killed him!" she screamed. "Not me. Not Franetti. *They!* I killed one. Oh, Jock, Jock, are you dead?"

She ran toward the corpse. Then came the final nightmare.

The arms of blue-faced Jack Ketch began to writhe, and from the puppet-mask came squealing, malevolent laughter.

Delia, about to fling her arms around her dead husband, slid to the floor on her knees. A sigh of horror issued from her throat. The silver lamé billowed down around her. And still the puppet tittered and squealed, as if mocking her and triumphing over her.

"Pull those blasted things off his hands!" I heard myself crying. "Pull them off!"

It was Wilkinson who did it, not the feebly pawing Dr. Grendal. Wilkinson didn't realize what was happening.

He was still convinced that Franetti was the murderer. He obeyed automatically. He seized the papier-mâché heads roughly, and jerked.

Then I knew how Jock Lathrop had died. I knew why he had been so secretive, why the ancient pamphlet had affected him so profoundly. I realized that Delia's suspicions had been correct, though not what she had believed. I knew why Jock Lathrop had asked Grendal those peculiar questions. I knew why the puppets had been so realistic. I knew why Jockey Lowthrope had had his hands hacked off. I knew why Jock Lathrop had never let anyone see his own ungloved hands, after that "change" had begun in London.

The little finger and ring finger on each of his hands were normal. The others—the ones used in motivating a puppet—were not. Replacing the thumb and second finger were tiny muscular arms. The first finger was in each case a tiny, wormlike body, of the general shape of a finger, but with a tiny sphincterlike mouth and two diminutive, malformed eyes that were all black pupil. One was dead by Delia's bullet. The other was not. I crushed it under my heel. . . .

Among Jock Lathrop's papers was found the following note, penned in longhand, and evidently written within a few days of the end:

> If I die, *they* have killed me. For I am sure they hate me. I have tried to confide in various people, but have been unable to go through with it. I feel compelled to secrecy. Perhaps that is *their* desire, for *their* power over my actions is growing greater every day. Delia would loathe me if she knew. And she suspects.
>
> I thought I would go mad in London, when my injured fingers began to heal with a *new* growth. A monstrous growth—that were my brothers who were engulfed in my flesh at the time of my birth and did not begin to develop until now! Had they been developed and born at the proper time, we would have been triplets. But the *mode* of that development now!
>
> Human flesh is subject to horrible perversions. Can my thoughts and activities as a puppeteer have had a determining influence? Have I influenced their minds until those minds are really those of Punch and Jack Ketch?
>
> And what I read in that old pamphlet. Hands hacked off. . . . Could my ancestor's pact with the devil have given him his fiendish skill? Given him the monstrous growth which led to his ruin? Could this physical characteristic have been inherited, lying dormant until such time as another Lathrop, another puppeteer, summoned it forth by his ambitious desires?
>
> I don't know. What I do know is that as long as I live I am the world's greatest puppeteer—but at what cost! I hate *them*, and *they* hate me. I can hardly control them. Last night one of them clawed Delia while I slept. Even now, when my mind wandered for a moment, the *one* turned the pen and tried to drive it into my wrist. . . .

I did not scoff at the questions that Jock Lathrop had asked himself. I might have at one time. But I had seen *them*, and I had seen the tiny sword driven into Lathrop's eye. No, I'm not going to spend any more time trying to figure out the black mystery behind the amazing skill of Jock Lathrop. I'm going to spend it trying to make Delia forget.

Death is a Vampire
Robert Bloch

I

Won't You Walk into My Parlor?

The gate handle was rusty. I didn't want to touch it. But that was the only way of getting in, unless I wanted to climb the high walls and leave part of my trousers on the iron spikes studding the top.

I grabbed the handle, pushed the gate open and walked down the flagstone path to the house.

If I were a botanist, I'd have been interested in the weeds growing along that path. As it was, they were only something to stumble over. I ignored them and stared at the mansion ahead.

The Petroff house was not quite as big as a castle and not quite as old as Noah's Ark. It looked like the kind of a place the Phantom of the Opera would pick for a summer home.

As far as I was concerned, it was something to donate to the next scrap drive.

But that was none of my business. My business was to sneak inside and wangle old Petroff into giving me an interview about his art treasures. The Sunday supplement needed a feature yarn.

I walked up to the big porch, climbed the stairs, and jangled the old-fashioned door pull. Nothing happened, so I did it again. Same result. It looked as though the Butler's Union had pulled its man off this job.

Just for fun I edged over and turned the door-knob. As I did, I noticed a garland hanging down from the metal projection. It was a wreath of smelly leaves. Not a funeral wreath—just leaves.

That was none of my business, either. I was interested in whether or not the door was unlocked.

It was. So I walked in.

Why not? When Lenehan gave me the assignment, he told me it was a tough one. He had talked to old Petroff over the phone, and Petroff had refused to meet the press or drool over his art treasures.

I expected to be met at the door by a bouncer with a shotgun. But this was easy, and I took advantage of it. It wasn't polite, but newspaper reporting isn't a polite occupation.

The door swung shut behind me, and I stood in a long hallway. It was hard to see anything specific in the afternoon twilight, but I got a musty whiff of stale air, mothballs, and just plain age and decay.

It made me cough. I coughed louder, hoping to rouse my host.

No results. I started down the hallway, still coughing from time to time. An open door led into a deserted library. I ignored it, passed a staircase, walked on.

Behind the stairs was another door. I halted there, for a faint light gleamed from underneath it. I groped for the handle and coughed again. Once more the cough was genuine—for hanging on the door-knob was another garland of those leaves.

Inside here the smell was terrific. Like a Bohemian picnic. Suddenly I recognized the odor. Garlic.

According to the stories going around, old Petroff was a bit of a screwball. But it couldn't be that he had turned the house into a delicatessen.

There was only one way to find out. I opened the door and walked into the parlor where the lamp burned.

It was quiet inside—quiet enough to hear a pin drop. In fact, you could tell which end hit the floor first: the head or the point.

But a pin had not hit the floor in this room. Petroff had.

He looked like his photo, all right. He was tall, thin, with black hair, curled and gray at the temples. A beaked nose and thick lips dominated his face.

He lay there on the floor, his nose pointing up at the ceiling. I got to his side in a hurry, and the floor creaked as I bent over him.

It didn't matter. The noise wouldn't bother him. Nothing would ever bother Igor Petroff again.

His hand was icy. His face was paper-white. I looked around for a mirror but didn't spot any. I pulled my cigarette case out and put it against his lips. The shiny metal clouded slightly. He was still breathing, at any rate.

Probably he'd had a stroke. I lifted his head and stared into his bloodless face. His collar was open. I felt for a pulse in his neck, then took my hand away, quick.

I stared down at his throat, stared down and saw the two tiny punctures in his neck, shook my head and stared again.

They looked like the marks of human teeth!

There was no use asking if there was a doctor in the house. I got up and dashed out into the hall to get to the phone. I got to it. I jiggled the receiver for nearly a minute before I noticed the dangling cord trailing on the floor. Whoever had bitten Petroff had also bitten through the cord.

That was enough for me. I made the two miles back to town in about ten minutes and five hundred gasps. I still had a gasp left in me when I ran into Sheriff Luther Shea's office at Centerville and knocked his feet off the desk.

"Accident out at the Petroff place!" I wheezed. "Get a doctor, quick!"

Sheriff Luther Shea was a fat little bald-headed man who seemed to enjoy keeping his feet on the desk. He put them right back up and scowled at me over his Number Elevens.

"What'sa big idea of bustin' in here? Who are you, anyhow?"

I faced my genial quiz-master without a thought of winning the sixty-four-dollar question.

"Can't you hear?" I yelled. "Call a doctor! Mr. Petroff has been injured."

"Ain't no doctor in this town," he told me. "Now state your business, fella."

I stated it, but loud. He perked up his ears a little when I told him about Petroff, but he didn't take his feet off the desk until I flashed my press badge. That did it.

"No sense trying to find a doctor—nearest one's back in L.A.," he decided. "I'm pretty handy at first-aid. I'll get the car and we'll go out and pick him up."

Sheriff Shea banged the office door behind him, and I grabbed a phone. I got hold of Calloway right away and he promised to send the ambulance out to Centerville. Somehow, after having had a good look at Petroff, I didn't have much confidence in Sheriff Shea's "first-aid."

Then I put through a call to the paper.

Lenehan growled at me, and I barked right back.

"Somebody bit his throat? Say, Kirby—you drunk?"

I breathed into the phone. "Smell that," I said. "I'm cold sober. I found him lying on the floor with two holes in his neck. I'm still not sure he wasn't dead."

"Well, find out. Keep on this story and give me all you've got. We can hold three hours for the morning edition. Looks like murder, you say?"

"I didn't say a blamed thing about murder!" I yelled.

"Come on, quit stalling!" Lenehan yelled back. "What's your angle on this?"

I lowered my voice to a whisper. "Confidentially," I said, "my theory is that old Petroff bit himself in the throat just for the publicity."

Lenehan apparently didn't believe me, because he launched off into a discussion of my ancestry that was cut short when Sheriff Shea appeared in the doorway. He wore a rancher's black Stetson and a shoulder holster. On him it didn't look good.

"Come on, fella," he said, and I hung up.

His rattletrap Chevvy didn't deserve a C card, but we made time down Centerville's single street and chugged out along the highway.

"From the L.A. papers, huh?" he grunted. "Whatcha doing up at Petroff's?"

"My editor gave me an assignment to write a feature story about the art treasures of the Irene Colby Petroff estate. Do you know anything about them?"

"Don't know nothing, fella. When old man Colby was alive, he and the missus would come into town and do a little trading once in a while. Then he died and she married this foreign gigolo, Petroff, and that's the last we seen of them in town. Then she died, and since then the place has gone to pot. This business don't surprise me none. Hear some mighty funny gossip about what goes on out at Petroff's place. All fenced off and locked up tighter'n a drum. Ask me, he's hiding something."

"I got in without any trouble."

"What about the guards? What about the dogs? What about the locks on the gate?" I sat up. "No guards, no dogs, no locks," I told him. "Just Petroff. Petroff lying there on the floor with the holes in his throat."

We rounded a bend in the highway and approached the walls of the Petroff estate. The setting sun gleamed on the jagged spikes surmounting the walls. And it gleamed on something else.

"Who's that?" I yelled, grabbing Sheriff Shea's arm.

"Don't do that!" he grunted. "Nearly made me go off the road."

"Look!" I shouted. "There's a man climbing up the wall."

Sheriff Shea glanced across the road and saw the figure at the top of the wall. The car ground to a halt and we went into action. Shea tugged at his shoulder holster.

"Stop or I'll shoot!" he bawled.

The man on the wall considered the proposition and rejected it. He turned and jumped. It was a ten-foot drop but he landed catlike and was scuttling across the road by the time we reached the base of the wall.

"After him!" Shea grunted.

The man ran along the other side of the road, making for a clump of trees

ahead. I dashed along behind. The fugitive reached the grove a few steps
ahead of me and I decided on a little football practice.

It was a rather ragged flying tackle, but it brought him down. We rolled
over and over, and on the second roll he got on top. He didn't waste time. I
felt powerful fingers dig into my throat. I tore at his wrists. He growled and
twisted his neck. I felt his mouth graze my cheek. He was trying to bite me.

I got his hands loose and aimed a punch at his chin, but he ducked and
pressed his thumbs in my eyes. That hurt. I aimed another punch, but that
wasn't good either. By this time he had those hands around my neck again,
and things began to turn red. The red turned black. I heard him growling
and snarling deep in his throat, and his fingers squeezed and squeezed.

This was no time for Queensbury rules. I kicked him in the tummy. With
a grunt of appreciation he slumped back, clutching his solar plexus.

II

They Fly by Night

Sheriff Shea arrived, wheezing, and together we collared our prisoner and
dragged him to his feet.

He was not pretty. He wore one of those one-piece overall outfits, and
between the spikes on the wall and the tussle, he'd managed to destroy its
integrity. Patches of his skin showed through, advertising the need of a
bath. His yellow hair was matted and hung down over his eyes, which was
just as well. They were as blue as a baby-doll's—and just as vacant. His lips
hung slackly, and he was drooling. A prominent goitre completed the en-
semble.

"Why, it's Tommy!" said the Sheriff. "He's a little touched," he whispered,
"but harmless."

He didn't have to tell me the kid was touched. That I could easily believe.
But the "harmless" part I doubted. I rubbed my aching eyes and neck while
Shea patted Tommy on the back.

"What were you doing on the wall, Tommy?" he asked.

Tommy lifted a sullen face. "I was looking at the bats."

"What bats?"

"The bats that fly at twilight. They fly out of the windows and you can
hear them squeaking at each other."

I glanced at Sheriff Shea. He shrugged.

"Ain't no bats around here except the ones in Tommy's belfry."

I took over. "What else were you looking at, Tommy?" I inquired.

He turned away. "I don't like you. You tried to hurt me. Maybe you're one of them! One of the bad people."

"Bad people?"

"Yes. They come here at night. Sometimes they come as men, wearing black cloaks. Sometimes they fly—that's when they're bats. They only come at night, because they sleep in the daytime."

Tommy was in full cry, now. I didn't try to stop him.

"I know all about it," he whispered. "They don't suspect me, and they'd kill me if they thought I knew. Well, I do know. I know why Petroff doesn't have any mirrors on the walls. I heard Charlie Owens, the butcher, tell about the liver he sends out every day—the raw liver, pounds of it. I know what flies by night."

"That's enough," said Sheriff Shea. "Whatever you know, you can tell us inside."

"Inside? You aren't going in there, are you? You can't take me in there! I won't let you! You want to give me to him. You'll let him kill me!"

Again, Shea cut him off. Grasping his arm, he guided the half-wit across the road. I followed. We made straight for the gate.

Shea halted. "Push it open," I said.

"It's locked."

I looked. A shiny new padlock hung from the rusty handle.

"It was open half an hour ago," I said.

"He always keeps it locked," Shea told me. "Usually has a man out here, too—a guard. And dogs in the kennels back of the house." He eyed me suspiciously. "You sure you were up here, Mr. Kirby?"

"Listen," I advised him. "I was up here a little over half an hour ago. The gate was open. I went in and found Petroff on the floor. He had two holes in his throat and I'm not sure whether he was still breathing or not. I'll give you every explanation you want later, but let's go inside, quick. He may be dead."

Shea shrugged. He stood back and drew his revolver. The shot resounded, the lock shattered. I held Tommy tightly and pushed him through the gateway.

After that I took the lead. Up the steps, through the door, down the hall. It was slow going in the gathering twilight. We stumbled along toward the room behind the staircase.

"Here," I said. "Here's where I found him." I opened the door. The light was still on. I pointed to the floor. "Here," I said.

"Yeah?" grunted Shea. "Where is he?"

The room was empty. The rug was on the floor, but Petroff was not. I stared, and the room began to whirl. I took a deep breath and inhaled fresh air.

It was coming from the open French windows at the end of the room.

Of course! The windows were open. I had made some kind of a mistake. Petroff had been breathing. He had fainted, or something. After I left he recovered, went for a stroll on the porch beyond the open windows, and locked his gate. The holes in his throat. Maybe he'd cut himself while shaving.

I was a fool. A glance at Sheriff Shea confirmed the suspicion. He grinned at me.

But Tommy was not grinning.

"You were here before," he murmured. "You saw him lying here with holes in his throat."

"I—I made a mistake," I mumbled.

"No. When you were here it was still daylight. Now it's dusk. When you were here he was still asleep. But he comes alive at night."

"What do you mean? Who comes alive at night?"

"The vampire," he whispered. "He comes alive. And at night he flies. Look!"

Tommy screamed. His finger stabbed at the dusk beyond the opened windows.

We stared out into the night and saw the black shadow of a bat skimming off into the darkness, a mocking squeak rising from its throat.

In just a little while there was the devil of a lot of activity. The ambulance I had sent for finally arrived, and Shea had to stall them off with a trumped-up excuse about a fainting fit. Then Shea wanted to play detective and go over the place. Personally, I think he was dying to case the joint merely to collect some gossip.

I won't bother remembering the bawling-out he handed me. I had to take it, too. After all, my story sounded pretty phony now.

Tommy was the only one who believed me. And his support was not much help. A half-wit's comments on vampires doesn't make good testimony.

While Shea handled the ambulance men, Tommy kept talking.

"Look at the garlic wreaths on the doors," he said. "He must have been trying to keep them out. They can't bear garlic."

"Neither can I," I answered. "And I'm no vampire."

"Look at the books," Tommy exclaimed. "Magic."

I stepped over to the built-in bookshelves. This time Tommy really had something. There were rows of blackbound volumes; musty, crumbling treatises in Latin and German. I read the titles. It was indeed a library of demonology. Where there's smoke there's fire.

But what did that prove? Occultism isn't a rare hobby on the Coast. I knew half a hundred crackpots who belonged to "secret cults," and down Laguna way there was a whole colony of them.

Still, I ran my eyes and fingers along the rows. One of the books on the lower shelf protruded a bit more than was necessary. It offended my sense of neatness. As I reached in to push it back, a card slipped out from between yellowed pages. I palmed it, turned around just as Sheriff Shea reentered the room.

"Come on," he sighed. "Let's get out of here."

Driving back to town, with Tommy wedged between us on the front seat, Shea gave me another going over.

"I don't understand all this monkey business," he declared. "I don't know what you were doing in that house in the first place. Least I can do is hold you on suspicion of illegal entry. As for Tommy here, he's liable to get booked on the same charges. I'm gonna see his folks about this. But what I want to know is—where's Petroff?"

"I shot him." I grinned. "But the bats flew off with his body."

"Never mind that," Shea snapped. "You smart-aleck reporters aren't tampering with the law down here. I'd like to get the D.A. in on this, but there's nothing to go on, yet. Maybe after I hold you on suspicion a few days you'll be ready to talk. I want to know how you cut those telephone wires, too."

"Now listen," I said. "I've got work to do. I'm willing to play ball on this thing and help straighten matters out. If Igor Petroff has disappeared and I'm the last man who saw him alive—or dead—that's important to me, too. The paper'll want the story. But I'm down here on an assignment. I've got to move around."

"No, you don't. Case I didn't mention it, you're under arrest right now, Mr. Kirby."

"That," I sighed, "is all I want to know."

I eased the car door open gently and swiftly. We were going thirty, but I took my chances. I jumped and hit the road.

Shea swore. He brought the rattling Chevvy to a halt, but by that time I was running along the ditch on the other side of the road. It was good and dark.

Shea bawled and waved his revolver, but he couldn't spot me. Then he turned the car around and zoomed back up the road. I went into the field, kept going. In a few minutes the road was far behind me, and I headed across to the other side of the field and another dirt road running parallel.

Here I found the truck that took me back to L.A. I hopped off downtown, found a drug store, and called Lenehan at the office.

"Where in thunder are you?" he greeted me. "Just had this hick sheriff on the wire. He's bawling you're a fugitive from justice. And what's all this business about a disappearing body? Give."

I gave. "Hold the yarn," I pleaded. "I've got a new angle."

"Hold it?" yelled Lenehan. "I'm tearing it up! You and your disappearing Dracula! Petroff was drunk on the floor when you found him and you were drunk on your feet. He had the decency to wander off and sober up, but you're still drunk!"

I hung up.

Then I fished around in my pocket and pulled out the card I had snatched from the book in Petroff's library.

It was nicely engraved:

HAMMOND KING
Attorney at Law

I turned it over. A man's heavy scrawl spidered across the back read:

> You may be interested in this volume on vampirism.
>
> H. K.

The plot was thickening. Hammond King? I knew the name. A downtown boy. Wealthy attorney. What was the connection?

I called Maizie at the office.

"Hammond King," I said. "Check the morgue."

She got me the dope. I listened until she came to an item announcing that Hammond King was attorney for the Irene Colby Petroff estate. I stopped her and hung up.

It was eight o'clock. Not likely that Hammond King would still be at his office, but it was a chance worth taking. The phone book got me the number and I deposited my third nickel.

The phone rang for a long time. Perhaps he was going over a tort or something. Then a deep voice came over the wire.

"Hammond King speaking."

"Mr. King—this is Dave Kirby, of the Leader. I'd like to come over there and talk to you."

"Sorry young man. If you'll phone my office tomorrow for a more definite appointment—"

"I thought we might have a little chat about vampires."

"Oh."

That stopped him.

"I'll be right over," I said. "So long."

He didn't answer. I whistled my way out of the phone booth, ordered a ham sandwich and a malted milk, disposed of same, and took a cab downtown.

The night elevator brought me to Hammond King's office. The door was open and I walked into one of those lavish layouts so typical of wealthy attorneys and impecunious booking agents.

I ignored the outer office and made for the big door marked "Private."

King was examining a bottle of Scotch with phony nonchalance.

My nonchalance was just as phony as I examined him.

He was a short, stocky man of about fifty-five. Gray hair and mustache to match. His eyes slanted behind unusually thick bifocals. He wore an expensive gray suit, and I admired his taste in ties. He looked like a hundred other guys, but he sent books on vampirism to his friends. You never know these days.

"Mr. Kirby?" he inquired, getting up and extending his hand. "To what do I owe this pleasure?"

"I told you over the phone," I said. "I'd like to have a little chat with you about vampires."

"Oh."

The phony nonchalance faded away and the hand dropped to his side.

"I'd rather have talked to Mr. Petroff about it," I continued. "Matter of fact, I dropped in on him this afternoon. But he wasn't there. That is, he was there, and then he wasn't. You know how vampires get restless about twilight."

"What do you mean?"

"You know what I mean, King," I said. "I just thought I'd warn you. In case anybody tries to bite you in the throat, it's your old client, Igor Petroff."

"How'd you know he was my client?"

"I know a lot of things," I told him, wishing it were true. "And what I don't know you'd better tell me, but fast. Unless, of course, you want it splashed all over the front page of the Leader."

"Let's be reasonable," Hammond King pleaded. "I'll be glad to help you all I can. Anything involving my client—"

The phone rang. King reached for the receiver, then drew his hand back.

"Pardon me, please," he said.

He got up and went into the outer office and shut the door.

III

The Bat's Kiss

I would have given my left arm to know who King was talking to. But I didn't have to give my left arm. All I needed to do was reach out with it and gently pick up the receiver. Call it eavesdropping, if you wish. You do a lot of things in this business.

"Mr. King?" a girl's voice came over the wire. "This is Lorna Colby. I'm at the Eastmore Hotel, Room Nine-nineteen. . . . No, Igor sent for me. He wanted to talk about a settlement on the will."

"Have you seen Petroff?" Hammond King barked into the phone at this end.

"No, not yet."

"Well, I'll be around in the morning, at ten. We've got to work fast, you understand? Something's happening that I don't like."

"What is it?" asked Lorna Colby.

"I can't talk now. See you tomorrow. Good night."

He hung up. I hung up. It was my turn to look at the Scotch bottle as he came in.

"Where were we?" he asked.

"You were just going to spill the beans," I said.

Hammond King smiled. "Was I? Lucky for me I got called away. I'm afraid I can't talk this matter over with you just at present. That call was from a client in Pasadena. I've got to take the train tonight."

I rose. One of his desk drawers was half opened. I reached in and scooped up a handful of garlic leaves.

"You had these left over from decorating the Petroff house, I presume," I told him. "Too bad you didn't think to put these on the French windows."

I slipped the garlic wreath into his hand and left the room. He stood there with his mouth open, giving a poor imitation of a stuffed moose.

I rode downstairs and walked around the corner and across the block to the Eastmore Hotel. I didn't bother to send my name up, but rode in person to the ninth floor. Nine-nineteen was down the hall to my left. I found the room and knocked on Lorna Colby's door.

There was no answer—except a sudden, ear-shattering scream.

I jerked the door-knob. The door opened on a tableau of frozen horror.

A blond girl lay slumped on the bed. Crouching above her was a shadowy figure out of a nightmare. Its head was bending toward her neck. I saw lean, outstretched fingers claw down, saw the mouth descend—then the shadow straightened, turned, swooped across the room and out through the open window.

Lorna Colby lay there, clutching her throat and staring in wide-eyed terror. I stared, too. For the intruder had been Igor Petroff.

When I reached the window, the fire-escape outside was empty. Perhaps it had never held a figure. Perhaps I'd have done better to look for something flying in the sky.

I turned back to the bed. Lorna Colby was sitting up. There was still fear in her hazel eyes as she looked at me.

"Who are you?" she demanded.

I introduced myself. "Dave Kirby, of the Leader. You're Lorna Colby, of course?"

She nodded. "Yes. But how did you know? And what made you come here?"

"Hammond King sent me," I lied.

It was the right hunch.

"Then maybe you can tell me," she said, "what's wrong with my uncle? He sent me a wire to come down and talk about the estate. I waited to hear from him tonight. I was getting sleepy and lay down on the bed. When I opened my eyes again, he was in the room."

"Petroff?"

"Yes. You recognized him, too?"

I nodded.

"He must have come through the window some way. He just crouched over me, staring, and there was something wrong with his face. It was so white, but his eyes glared, and I couldn't look away. Then I felt his hands come down toward my neck, and I screamed, and then—"

I shook her, not gently. It was fun, but this was no time for amusement.

"Stop it!" I snapped. "Relax."

She cried a little. Then she sat up and fished around for her make-up. I took the opportunity to study her more closely.

Lorna Colby was tall, blond, and about twenty-two. She had a good face and a better figure. All in all, the kind of a girl worth whistling after.

That noise like a ton of bricks was me, falling. She didn't notice it. After a while she patted her hair back and smiled.

"Your uncle is—ill," I said. "That's what Hammond King asked me to tell you. We're trying to keep things quiet until we can take him away for a rest."

"You mean he's crazy?"

I shrugged.

"I've always thought so," Lorna declared. "Even when Aunt Irene was alive, I knew there was something wrong with him. He led her an awful life."

She halted, bit her lower lip, and continued.

"After she died, he got worse. He kept dogs at the house, guarding it. He wanted to guard her tomb, he said. I haven't seen him now for almost a year. Nobody has seen him since the day she died. She had a heart attack, you know. He buried her in the private vaults on the estate. He wouldn't even let me see her or come to the funeral.

"I knew he hated me, and it came as a surprise when I got his wire yesterday, asking me to come down from Frisco to talk about the will. That didn't make sense, either. After all, Aunt Irene left him the whole estate, even though he can't touch the money for a year."

Something clicked into place. I decided to follow it up.

"By the way, who was your aunt's physician?" I asked.

"Dr. Kelring."

"I'd like to talk to him," I told her. "It's important."

"You think he might know what's wrong with Uncle Igor?"

"That's right." I nodded. "He must know."

I looked him up in the book. Dr. Roger Kelring. I called his downtown office, not hoping for much of anything. Still, this gang seemed to work late. Hammond King was on the job, and Igor Petroff was a regular night-owl. Or was he? "They fly by night."

The phone gave off that irritating sound known as a busy signal. That was enough for me.

"Come on, Miss Colby," I said. "We're going over to Dr. Kelring's office."

"But you didn't talk to him," she objected.

"Busy signal," I explained. "On second thought, I'd just as soon not say anything to him in advance."

"What do you mean? Do you think he's mixed up in all this?"

"Definitely," I assured her. "I wouldn't be a bit surprised if your uncle was up there with him now."

Lorna put on her coat and we went downstairs. In the lobby, she halted indecisively.

"Wait a minute, Mr. Kirby. Aren't we going to report seeing Uncle Igor in my room? After all, if he's sick somebody should be looking after him. He may be—"

"Dangerous? Perhaps. But let's not start something we can't finish. It's my hunch that he's over at Dr. Kelring's office. Don't ask me why, but I've got reasons. Besides, you don't want to get mixed up in a lot of cross-questioning, do you?"

She agreed. I was relieved. What could I do if we called some Law? Tell them that a suspected vampire was running around attacking girls in hotel rooms?

Besides, I didn't think Igor Petroff was "running around." He might be flying around. Or he might be working according to a plan. Dr. Kelring would know the plan.

We took a cab to Kelring's office, in a building off Pershing Square.

"What's the doctor like?" I asked Lorna.

"He's a rich woman's doctor," she told me. "You know—smooth, quiet, genial. He's about fifty, I guess. Bald-headed, with a little goatee. I only saw him once, at Aunt Irene's, a few months before she died. He was pleasant, but I didn't like him."

Lorna's voice betrayed her inner tension. I understood. It's not every night that a girl is attacked by a vampire, even if he's a member of the family.

Partly for that reason and partly for personal pleasure, I held her arm as we took the elevator up to Kelring's office. A light burned behind the outer door. I opened it and stepped in. I had no gun, but if there was anything doing, I counted on the surprise element.

There was one.

Seated at the desk in the reception room was a man of about fifty, bald-headed, and wearing a small goatee. His hand rested on the telephone as though he were going to pick it up and make another call.

But Dr. Kelring would never make another call. He sat there staring off into space, and when I touched his shoulder his neck wobbled off at an angle so that his goatee almost touched the spot between his shoulder-blades. Roger Kelring was quite, was definitely, was unmistakably dead.

I was patting Lorna's shoulder and making with the reassurement when the phone rang. Its sharp note cut the air, and I jumped. For a moment I stared at Dr. Kelring, wondering why his dead hand didn't lift the receiver and hold it to his ear.

Then I got around the desk, fast, and pried his cold fingers from the receiver.

"Lorna," I said, "how did—he—talk?"

"You mean Dr. Kelring?" She shuddered.

"Yes."

"Oh, I don't remember. . . . Yes, I think I do. He had a soft voice. Very soft."

"Good."

I whipped out my handkerchief and covered the mouthpiece. Just a hunch.

"Hello," I said lifting the receiver.

"Hello. That you, Kelring?"

I jumped as I recognized the voice. Hammond King!

"What is it?" I said, softly.

"Kelring, I must talk to you." He sounded frightened. Too frightened to analyze my voice.

"Go ahead. What's on your mind?"

"Did you ever read 'The Fall of the House of Usher'?"

"What?"

"You know what I'm talking about, Kelring. She's alive out there. I know it!"

"Who's alive?"

"Mrs. Petroff. Don't stall me, Kelring. I'm desperate."

"What makes you think so, man?"

"It happened two months ago. I was out there at the house with Petroff, arguing about the will. You know he's been trying to get me to turn over the estate before the time stipulated. I won't bother with details, but I heard a noise. A woman's voice, coming from behind the wall. It came from the private staircase behind the bookshelves—the one leading down to the family burial vaults in the hillside."

"Get to the point, King," I said.

"He tried to hold me off, but I made him take me down there. I don't know how to tell you this—but beyond the iron grille entrance, in the vaults, I caught a glimpse of Irene Colby Petroff. Alive."

"But I pronounced her dead of heart failure," I said, remembering what I'd been told.

"She was alive, I tell you! She ran into one of the passages, but I recognized her face. I tried to get Petroff to open the grille and go in, but he dragged me back upstairs. Then he told me the story."

"What story?"

"You know, all right, Kelring. That's why I didn't call before. I wanted to investigate on my own. Now I need your help."

"Better tell me all you know, then."

"I know that she's a—vampire."

I held my breath. King didn't wait for any comment.

"Petroff broke down and confessed. Said he knew it and you knew it. She'd been mixed up in some kind of Black Magic cult in Europe when he met her. And when she died, she didn't really die. She lived on, after sundown, as a vampire."

"Preposterous!"

"I wasn't sure myself, then. I wanted to call in the police. But Petroff pleaded with me. Said he had the guard and the dogs and kept people away.

He had her locked up down there, fed her raw liver. Because you were trying to work on a cure. He asked for a little more time. And he explained it all. Gave me books on demonology to read. I didn't know what to believe, but I promised to wait. Then, three nights ago, he called and told me that she had tried to attack him. He asked me to come out this afternoon and talk things over.

"I went out there about four today. Maybe I was a fool, but I took some garlic with me. The books say garlic wards them off. When I arrived, I found Petroff lying on the floor. There were two holes in his throat—the marks of a vampire's teeth. So he has become a vampire now!

"I got frightened and ran. I knew he had sent for his niece, Lorna Colby. I wanted to talk to her before I did anything. Then, tonight, a young man called on me. Said he was from the newspapers. He knows something, too.

"Kelring, I've made up my mind to act. I won't call the police. I—I can't. They'd laugh at me. But there's a monster loose tonight, and I can't stand waiting any longer. I'm going out to the Petroff place now."

"Wait!" I said.

His voice was shrill as he replied. "Do you know what I've been doing, Kelring? I've been sitting here molding silver bullets. Silver bullets for my gun. And I'm leaving now. I'm going out there to get him!"

"Don't be a fool!" I yelled, in my natural voice.

But he had hung up.

"Come on," I snapped at Lorna. "I'll call the police and report on Kelring now. But we're getting out before they come."

"Where are we going?"

"To Petroff's house," I answered.

She nodded. I moved around the table. As I did, I saw something on the floor. It was a spectacle-case. I picked it up, turned it over. It was an expensive case, with an engraved name. The silver signature read:

Hammond King

IV
Vampire's Teeth

As the cab driver grumbled about the long haul, I told Lorna what I thought was wise.

I was too groggy to think clearly. Lenehan thought I was drunk, I'd jumped arrest, I'd eavesdropped, and impersonated, and messed up a murder. And it looked like an even busier day tomorrow unless I could straighten this tangle out tonight.

That's my only excuse, I guess. I was a punch-drunk fool to take Lorna to that house, with only a crazy hunch to guide us, and armed with nothing but my suspicions.

But I did it. We rolled up to the black, forbidding portals of the Petroff place. We walked up the porch of the Petroff mansion and the cab waited in the driveway. I didn't see Hammond King's car, and I was glad we had arrived first.

He was wrong, I thought. Petroff was not here. And if he wasn't, we could find that staircase, take a look into the vault, and see for ourselves whether Irene Colby Petroff walked or slept forever.

Never mind the details. The garlic odor choked us in the creaky hall. It flooded the parlor as I lit the lamp, tapped bookcases, and found the button that opened a section of the wall. Lorna shivered at my side. The setup looked like something out of "The Cat and the Canary."

I kept listening for sounds. All quiet on the Western Front. With the light streaming from the parlor behind us, we took the secret staircase in stride. Down below was another panel in the wall. I switched on the light and walked down a long corridor. It was damp. King had said the private vaults of the family were out under the hillside.

We rounded a turn and came to the iron grille barring the hall. A perpetual light burned behind it. I tried the door. It was open. It squeaked as I pushed.

The squeak was drowned in a scream.

I turned.

Something black scuttled around the corner of the passageway. Something swooped down on Lorna, engulfed her in a sable cloud. I saw glaring eyes, red lips—Igor Petroff was here!

I made a dive for him. Petroff didn't dodge. He stood there, and as I came on, his arm lashed out. The blow caught me off balance and as I wavered, his hand moved out. Something flashed down, and then I fell.

There was a blurred impression of movement, screaming, and scuffling. Petroff had dragged Lorna through the grille, down into the vaults.

I lurched to my feet as another figure raced around the bend. More blamed traffic down here, I thought, dazedly.

It was Hammond King.

He didn't see me. He stared, glassy-eyed, as he ran past into the gloom of the corridor beyond. He was carrying a gun. Silver bullets!

I dashed after him. As we took another flight of stairs, I gazed over his shoulder at the family vaults beyond.

Lorna stood in a corner, crouching against a wall. The cloaked figure of Igor Petroff glided towards her, and I thought of Dracula, and of childhood terrors, and of nightmares men still whisper about.

Hammond King didn't think. He began pumping shots from his gun, firing in maniac fury.

Petroff turned, across the room. And then, he smiled. He didn't fall down. He smiled. He smiled, and started to run toward Hammond King with his arms extended, and Hammond King gave a little choking gurgle and fell down.

I didn't fall. As Petroff advanced, I ran to meet him. This time I was not off-balance. I let him have one right on the point of his white chin. He grunted, but his arms swept up and then I felt the cold embrace as he clawed at me. I hammered into his ribs, but he was hard, rigid. Rigor mortis is like that, I thought madly.

He smelled of dampness and mold and ancient earth. His arms were strong and he was squeezing me. I dropped to the floor and he began to reach for my throat. He chuckled, then, deep in his throat; an animal growl. A growl of hunger, the growl of a carnivore that scents blood.

He had me by the neck, and I reached out with one hand and scrabbled frantically against the floor until I felt the cold steel of the gun Hammond King had dropped.

Petroff wrenched my arm back, trying to tear the gun from my fingers. I wanted to fight him off, but his other hand was at my neck, squeezing. I felt myself falling back, and I pulled my arm free and brought the gun-butt up against his head, once, twice, three times.

Igor Petroff wobbled like a rundown mechanical doll and dropped with a dull thud.

I got up and slapped Lorna's face. She came out of her trance, crying. Then I went over to Hammond King and slapped him around. Just a one-man rescue squad.

"Go upstairs, you two," I said. "The cab-driver's waiting outside. Tell him to go into Centerville and bring back Sheriff Shea. I'll meet you in a moment."

They left.

I went through the vault until I came to what I wanted to find. When I was quite finished with my inspection I went back upstairs.

Lorna and Hammond King were waiting in the parlor. She had fixed her hair again, and he looked well enough to smoke a cigarette.

"The police should be here in five minutes," King said.

"Good."

"Perhaps I'd better look outside," he suggested. "I'm expecting Dr. Kelring."

"Kelring isn't coming," I said, gently. "He's dead."

"But I talked to him over the phone."

I told him who he'd talked to. And then I decided to tell him a few other things.

"You should have gone to the police the night you saw Mrs. Petroff here," I said. "Then all this wouldn't have happened."

"But I saw her. She was alive."

"Right. But she wasn't a vampire. Too bad you believed that crazy story Petroff concocted. When you stumbled onto her existence, he had to think of something and the vampire story just popped out. After you half-swallowed it, he planned the rest. He had to convince you completely, and he was good at planning."

"What do you mean?"

"It all started, I think, when Petroff and Dr. Kelring decided to fake Mrs. Petroff's death. They were in on it together, to split the inheritance. They didn't have the nerve to kill her outright but drugged her, held a private funeral, and faked the death certificate. Then Petroff kept her a prisoner down here in the vaults. That's why he had dogs and a guard. She was alive until about three days ago."

"How do you know?"

"I just found her body in the vault," I explained. "And I've seen her living quarters—a room beyond. She's dead now, all right, and I'd say she died of starvation."

"I don't understand," Lorna sighed.

"Simple. When her fake death was accepted, Petroff and Dr. Kelring were all set to divide the spoils. But there were no spoils—not for a year, according to the terms of her will. They hadn't counted on that. So Petroff was trying to get King, here, to advance money against the inheritance.

"King, being a smart attorney, would do no such thing. But after he saw Mrs. Petroff alive and heard this vampire line, he began to weaken. Petroff took advantage of it, showing him books on demonology, and telling wild stories about secret cults."

Hammond King nodded miserably. "He was wearing me down," he admitted. "But I wouldn't release any money. I couldn't, legally."

I took over again. "Then, three days ago, Mrs. Petroff actually died. Perhaps he deliberately starved her, perhaps not. In any event, she was dead, and his extortion plot and fake death was now actually murder. He wanted that money at once, needed it desperately.

"So he phoned you, King, and asked you to come out today, planning to show himself lying on the floor as the victim of a vampire attack. He had it figured that you'd be too shocked to call the police at once. Then, after dark, he would call upon you as a supposed vampire, threaten you with his bite, and get you to advance personal funds against the estate."

King was looking bewildered.

"But I'd never do that," he protested. "He must have been mad!"

"He was—and desperate, too." I grinned. "Here's where I come into the story. Dave Kirby, the Boy Reporter. I got here today just after you left in the afternoon. I blundered in before Petroff could escape, so he lay there on the floor, hoping to fool me. When I left for the sheriff, he took a powder.

"Now the jig was up, but Petroff decided to carry the plan through. If he worked fast, he might still succeed. He'd called Lorna, asked her to come to town. He had only one idea—to appear before her as a supposed vampire and thus further bolster his story when he saw King and demanded money. This he was doing as I arrived at Lorna's room. He fled, and undertook his next step in the plan—the murder of Dr. Kelring."

"But why would he murder Kelring?" King asked.

I shrugged. "There were several reasons. The first is the one that led me to the scene. You remember, I came out to the house for an interview on the Petroff estate art treasures, an interview Petroff had already refused to grant."

"Yes?"

"There was a reason for my coming and a reason for his refusal. You see, my editor had a tip that several valuable vases recognized as part of the Petroff collection had been offered for sale at private auction. Get it?

"Petroff was already raising money by illegally disposing of art treasures belonging to the estate. Kelring must have just discovered this and demanded his cut. Otherwise, he would squeal about the fake death certificate. So Petroff had to kill him. Just as an added touch, he left a little souvenir after strangling him in his office."

I handed King his spectacle case.

"You nearly had credit for that piece of work," I said. "I'm sure he would have threatened to turn you in had you refused him money when he demanded it this evening. So it's lucky I had you on the phone and can support an alibi."

King blinked.

"After killing Dr. Kelring he scooted out here to wait for you. He knew you'd be out to check up. He hadn't counted on Lorna and me arriving, but when we showed up first, he was ready. After that you dashed in, made your bang-bang with the silver bullets, and passed out. You aren't a good shot,

King. Those bullets are in the walls, not in his body. But it wouldn't have mattered much. He wore a bullet-proof vest under the cloak. Felt it when I tackled him."

Lorna looked at me.

"You tackled him," she whispered. "That was wonderful. Even if he might be a vampire, you took the chance."

"But he wasn't a vampire. I knew that."

"Didn't you find him with holes in his throat?"

"Right. But he made them himself. Shallow cuts with a paper-knife, no doubt. You see, a vampire's bite will drain all blood. And there was no blood. I know something about superstitions myself, Lorna."

Sirens punctuated my sentence. The law was arriving in full force.

Suddenly I was very tired and very contented. Lenehan would get a story after all. And I'd get some sleep.

Lorna kissed me.

"What's that for?" I asked.

"For being brave. I don't care what you say, he might have been a vampire."

"Not a chance." I grinned. "I knew that from the beginning. When I looked at him on the floor this afternoon, his mouth was open. That was the tip-off."

"What do you mean?"

"He couldn't be a vampire because he couldn't bite anyone. After all, darling, who ever heard of a big, bad vampire with false teeth?"

DEATH AT THE MAIN

Frank Gruber

Oliver Quade had perused both the *Social Register* and *Bradstreet's Journal* on a number of occasions and he calculated mentally that there was easily a billion dollars worth of blue blood here tonight in this big renovated barn. Reggie Ragsdale, the host, was worth a hundred million if he was worth a cent; the average fortune of the two hundred-odd other men could be estimated conservatively at five million.

Long Island didn't see many cocking mains. Cocking wasn't a gentleman's sport like horse racing and fox hunting. In fact, many of Long Island's blue-bloods had shaken their heads when Young Ragsdale took up cock fighting. But they had eagerly accepted invitations to the Ragsdale estate to witness the great cocking main between Ragsdale's birds and the best of the Old South, the feathered warriors of George Treadwell.

Ragsdale had cleared out this large barn, had built tiers of seats in the form of a big bowl surrounding the cockpit. The place was ablaze with lights, and servants in uniforms scampered about with liquid refreshments for the guests.

Oliver Quade had crashed the gate and was enjoying himself immensely. He'd heard of the cocking main quite by accident; and being a Southerner by birth and a cocking enthusiast, he'd "crashed." He'd brought along a bagful of books, too. After a long and varied career he never knew when the opportunity might present itself to dispose of a few volumes and he wanted to be prepared for any contingency.

He chuckled at the thought of it. Two hundred millionaires protected daily by business managers, secretaries and servants; few of them had ever been compelled—or privileged, depending upon your viewpoint—to listen to a really good book salesman. And Quade *was* a good book salesman, the best in the country. Oliver Quade, the Human Encyclopedia, who traveled the country from coast to coast, selling books and salting away twenty thousand dollars every year.

The fights had already been started when Quade bluffed the doorkeeper into letting him into the Ragsdale barn. For an hour he rubbed elbows with the Long Island aristocrats, talked with them and cheered with them while the feathered warriors in the pit fought and bled and died.

The score stood at eight-all now, with the seventeenth and last bout of the evening to come up, which would decide the superiority of Ragsdale's Jungle Shawls and the Whitehackles of George Treadwell. Ragsdale rose to make an announcement as the handlers carried out the birds after the sixteenth fight.

"There'll be a short intermission of ten minutes before the final bout, gentlemen."

Quade's eyes sparkled. This was his golden chance, the one he'd waited for all evening. Perhaps they'd throw him out, but Quade had been thrown out of places before. Chuckling, he climbed upon a bench. He held out his hands in a supplicating gesture.

"Gentlemen," he cried out suddenly in a booming voice that surprised people who heard it issue from such a lean body, "give me your attention for a minute. I'm going to entertain you—something entirely new and different."

A couple of attendants looked with surprised eyes at Quade. Reggie Ragsdale, on the other side of the pit, frowned. Quade knew that he'd have to talk fast—catch the interest of the audience before Ragsdale tried to stop him. He had confidence in his oratorical powers.

"Gentlemen," he continued in his rich, penetrating voice. "I'm Oliver Quade, the Human Encyclopedia. I have the greatest brain in the United States, probably the greatest in the world. I know the answers to all questions: what came first, the chicken or the egg; the population of Sydney, Australia; the dates of every battle from the beginning of history; the founders of your family fortunes. Try me out, gentlemen. Any question at all—any! History, science, mathematics, general interest. You, sir, ask me a question!"

Quade, knowing the hesitation of any audience to get started, pointed to a man close to him, whose mouth was agape.

The man flushed, stammered. "Why, uh—I don't know anything I want to ask—Yes, I do! At what price did N.T.&T. close today?"

"Easy!" cried Quade. "You could read that in today's newspaper. National Telephone and Telegraph closed today at 187½. A year ago today it was 153. Ask me something harder. You, sir," he pointed. "A question; history, science, mathematics—"

"What is the distance to the moon?"

"From the center of the earth to the center of the moon the distance is approximately 238,857 miles. Next question!"

The game was catching on. Quade didn't have to point at anyone now. The audience had gathered its wits and the next question came promptly.

"What is ambergris?"

"Ambergris is a greasy substance spewed up by sick whales and is used in the manufacture of perfumes. It comes in lumps and is extremely valuable, a chunk of approximately thirty pounds recently found in the North Atlantic bringing $5,200. Next!"

"How do you measure the thickness of leather?" That was evidently a wealthy shoe manufacturer, but his question didn't phase Quade in the least.

"By irons," he shot back. "An iron is one seventy-second of an inch. The ordinary shoe sole is eight irons thick, although some run as thick as twelve irons and those on dancing pumps as thin as four irons—And now—"

Quade stooped, snapped open his suitcase and extracted a thick volume from it. He held it aloft. "And now I'm going to give each and every gentleman here tonight an opportunity to learn the answers *themselves* to any question that may arise, today, tomorrow or any time during the year. This book has the answers to ALL questions. *The Compendium of Human Knowledge,* the knowledge of the ages crammed into one volume, two thousand pages. Classified, condensed and abbreviated."

Quade paused for a brief breath and shot a glance at Reggie Ragsdale. The young millionaire, who had assumed a tolerant, amused expression a few moments ago when he saw that Quade's game was catching on with the guests, was frowning again. Entertaining the guests was all right, but selling something to them, that was different! Quade knew that he'd have to work even faster.

He launched again into his sales talk, exhorting in a vibrant, penetrating voice that was famous throughout the country. "The price of this magnificent volume is not twenty-five dollars as you might expect, not even fifteen or ten dollars, but a paltry two ninety-five. It sounds preposterous, I know, but it's really true. The knowledge of the ages for only two ninety-five! Yes, Mr. Ragsdale, you want to ask a question before you purchase one of these marvelous books?"

"I don't want to buy your confounded book!" cried Ragsdale. "I want to know how you got in here."

Quade chuckled. "Why, your doorkeeper let me in. I told him I was a book salesman and thought this gathering would be ideal for selling books. Really, Mr. Ragsdale, that's exactly what I told him and he let me in. Of course, if he didn't believe me, that's not my fault."

A roar of laughter swept the audience. None doubted that Quade had actually made his entrance in that manner. His audacity appealed to the thrill-jaded aristocrats. Even Ragsdale grinned.

"All right, you can stay. But put up your books now; they're coming in with the birds for the last fight. After it, you can sell your books. I'll even buy one myself."

Quade was disappointed. He'd made his pitch, built up his audience to the selling point and he didn't like to quit before collecting. But he couldn't very well cross Ragsdale—and sight of the handlers coming in with the birds was making the sportsmen turn to the pit. The best book in the world couldn't compete against a couple of fighting roosters.

Quade closed his sample case, walked down to Reggie Ragsdale's ringside seat and prepared to watch the last fight of the evening. Ragsdale grinned at him.

The handlers were down in the pit now. Ragsdale's handler, Tom Dodd, carried a huge, red Jungle Shawl and Treadwell's handler, Cleve Storm, a fierce-looking Whitehackle.

"Treadwell must have a lot of confidence in that Whitehackle," Quade remarked. "He's battle scarred. Been in at least four professional fights."

Ragsdale looked at Quade in surprise. "Ah, you know that cocks are at their best in their first fight?"

"Of course," said Quade. "I was raised down in Alabama and fought a few cocks of my own. That Whitehackle must be one of those rare ones that's improved with every fight instead of deteriorated. Ah!"

The referee had finished giving the handlers their instructions and Storm and Dodd retired to opposite sides of the sand-covered pit.

The referee looked at first one handler, then another. He hesitated a moment, then cried, "Time!"

Both handlers released their birds. There was a fluttering of wings, a rushing of air from both directions and a sudden rumbling of voices from the audience. For the Jungle Shawl faltered in his charge, turned yellow. An unforgivable weakness in a fighting bird.

It cost the Shawl his life, for with a squawk and flutter of wings the Whitehackle hurtled through the air and pounced on his opponent. His vicious beak hooked into the hackle of the Shawl and for a second he straddled the bird, then the two-inch steel gaffe slashed down and the Jungle Shawl was dead!

"Hung!" cried Tom Dodd.

Both handlers rushed forward. Quade looked at Reggie Ragsdale. The young millionaire was rising to his feet, his lips twisted into a wry grin. Quade looked across the cockpit at George Treadwell and gasped.

Treadwell was still seated, but his arms and head hung over the top of the pit and even as Quade looked, his hat fell from his head and dropped to the sandy floor. At the distance Quade could see that Treadwell's eyes were glassy.

"Treadwell!" Reggie Ragsdale exclaimed. He, too, had glanced across the pit.

Ragsdale brushed past Quade and hurried around the pit to Treadwell's side, Quade following. Other spectators saw Treadwell then and a bedlam of noise went up.

"Don't anyone leave!" thundered Ragsdale, his bored manner gone. "Treadwell is dead!"

"He's been murdered!"

The three words rang out above the rumble of noise. Quade looked down into the pit at the awe-stricken face of Cleve Storm, Treadwell's handler.

"Don't be a fool, man!" he cautioned. "You can't make an accusation like that! Mr. Treadwell probably died of heart failure."

"He's been murdered, I tell you!" cried Storm. "There wasn't nothin' the matter with his heart."

Ragsdale straightened beside Quade. "Doctor Pardley!" he called.

A middle-aged man with a grey-flecked Vandyke came up. He made a quick examination of George Treadwell, without touching the body. Then he frowned at Ragsdale. "Hard to say, Reggie. Might have been apoplexy except that he's not the type."

Ragsdale blinked. "He was a dead game sportsman. I'll see that his widow receives my check at once."

"That ain't gonna bring him back to life!" cried Cleve Storm. "I-I warned him not to come up here."

"Why?" snapped Ragsdale testily.

Cleve Storm looked around the circle of hostile faces, for most of the men here were personal friends of Ragsdale. He gulped. "Because he didn't have a chance, not against your money. You you always win."

Ragsdale winced. It was the deadliest insult any man could have hurled at him: to accuse him of not being a real sportsman. His lips tightened.

Quade came to Ragsdale's assistance. "I'd advise you to keep your opinions for the cops."

Ragsdale flashed him a wan smile of thanks. "That's right, we've got to call the police. And when the newspapers hear of this!"

Quade knew what he meant. Cock fighting was an undercover sport. A murder on the Ragsdale estate—cock fighting. The tabloids would have a scoop.

Ragsdale signaled to a steward. "Telephone for the Charlton police, Louis," he ordered. "Tell them someone died here—might possibly be a murder." He did not spare himself.

Quade looked at his leather case full of books and shook his head. Well, this shattered his hopes of making sales. The prospective customers wouldn't be in the mood now for buying books, even if Quade had the bad taste to try selling them with a corpse just a few feet away.

Wait—a thought struck Quade. The police! They'd be here in a few minutes. This might be a murder after all and everyone here knew everyone else—except Quade. He was a gate-crasher—and he was *not* a millionaire. Why—why, he might even have some very bad moments trying to explain his presence here.

The police came, four of them, led by Chief Kells. With them came the county medical examiner. There was deference in the chief's manner as he approached Ragsdale.

"Cock fighting, sir? It's going to make quite a stir in town. It's—it's against the law!"

"I know," replied Ragsdale wearily. "Go ahead, do your duty."

The chief looked importantly at the medical examiner who was already going over the body of George Treadwell. "Very well, sir, you might begin by telling me just what happened."

Ragsdale sighed. "Our birds were fighting in the pit—the last bout. My bird lost. When I looked across the pit, there was Treadwell, head hanging over the railing, dead."

"Who was beside him?" asked the chief.

Ragsdale shook his head. "I don't know, several of my guests, I suppose. I know only that I was directly opposite him across the width of the pit. But no one—excepting myself—had any motive for wishing his death."

"And why yourself?" The chief pounced on Ragsdale's self-accusal.

"Because I had a bet with Treadwell and lost."

The chief looked worried, but just then the medical examiner came up. He, too, was frowning. "Not a mark on him," he said. "Yet I'd swear that it wasn't apoplexy or heart failure. Symptoms indicate he's been poisoned, but I can't find anything on him. I'll have to do a post-mortem."

Cleve Storm, who had released his Whitehackle in the pit and come up, sprang forward. "I knew he was poisoned. I knew it."

"How did you know it?" asked Chief Kells sharply. "And who are you anyway?"

"He was Treadwell's trainer," explained Ragsdale. "A loyal employee."

Kells shrugged his shoulders hopelessly. "It would have to be murder. All right, Mr. Ragsdale. I've got to do some questioning. How much money did you have bet on the final outcome of these cock fights?"

"Ten thousand—no, wait. Thirty-five thousand altogether. Ten thousand with Treadwell and twenty-five thousand with a man down in the South."

"Who? Is he here?"

"No, and I really don't know the man except by reputation. The bet was made through correspondence. A cocking enthusiast who lives in Nashville; C. Pitts is the name."

The chief's eyes narrowed. "That sounds screwy. You mean this Pitts guy just up and sent you twenty-five thousand as a bet?"

"Not exactly. Pitts sent the money to the editor of the *Feathered Fighter*," explained Ragsdale. "I gave my own check to Mr. Morgan when he arrived here."

"That's true," said a heavy-set man, stepping forward. "I have both checks in my pocket right now."

Kells bit his lip. "You know this Pitts fellow?"

"Not personally," said the magazine man, "but by reputation. He bets on many of the cocking mains and I've held stakes for him before. The arrangements have always been made by mail."

Kells grunted. "How long you been raising roosters, Mr. Ragsdale? I thought horses was your game."

"They are, but a few months ago Treadwell got me interested in game cocks. To tell you the truth, I've only raised a few birds and they're still too young to fight. All the cocks I fought here tonight were purchased specially for the occasion. It's quite ethical, I assure you."

Quade perked up his ears. This was ironical indeed. Ragsdale with millions at his command and intensely interested in winning in everything he did, had probably spent an enormous sum for his fighting birds—and yet they'd lost, against ordinary fighting birds raised by Treadwell himself. Quade began to take a more serious interest in the situation. There might be something here yet that would prove interesting, perhaps afford Quade an opportunity to use that marvelous brain of his.

"From whom did you buy your roosters?" Kells again.

"Terence Walcott, who lives in the state of Oregon. Tom Dodd brought the birds East and handled them for me, during the fights. Dodd!"

Tom Dodd came forward. He was a little bandy-legged man of about forty.

"You the chap who raises these roosters?" questioned the chief.

"Yes, I work for Mr. Terence Walcott of Corvallis, Oregon. I been working around game cocks all my life."

"Where were you when Treadwell was kil—died?"

"In the pit, of course."

Kells looked at Ragsdale for confirmation. The latter nodded. "That's right. He was down in the pit. In the opposite corner from Treadwell. Treadwell's handler, Cleve Storm, was in the other corner, just under Tread-well's seat. Federle, the referee, was all around the pit."

"And everybody was watching them? That sorta lets those three out. Well, who was close by Treadwell at the moment?"

"I was," a lean, middle-aged man spoke up. "I was right beside him on his left. I was so excited over the fights down in the pit, however, that I didn't even know anything had happened to poor George Treadwell until Ragsdale came dashing around."

The chief looked at the man with suspicion-laden eyes. "What's your name?"

"Ralph Wilcoxson. Treadwell was my business partner. Treadwell & Wilcoxson, Lumber."

The chief looked even more hostile than before. "And who was on the other side of him?"

"I was," said Morgan, the editor of the *Feathered Fighter*.

The chief snorted in disgust. "Hell, everyone here is a friend of someone and respectable as a deacon. What chance have I got?"

Louis, the steward, who was standing behind his master, coughed. "Pardon, sir, everyone here isn't a friend. I—I let the gentlemen in at the door—and one of them didn't have a card."

Quade swore softly. Ragsdale, the sportsman, hadn't seen fit to betray him, but the servant, who'd been the butt of Quade's harmless joke awhile ago, couldn't take it. This was his revenge.

"He means me, Chief," he said, beating the traitorous steward to the punch.

The chief's shoulders hunched, and his teeth bared. Here was someone who didn't belong. "Who are you?" he asked, in a voice that almost shook the rafters.

Quade grinned impudently. "Oliver Quade, the Human Encyclopedia, the man who knows the answers to all questions." The introduction rolled glibly off Quade's tongue. It was part of his showmanship.

The chief's mouth dropped open. "Human Encyclopedia! What the hell you talkin' about?"

"Just what I said. I'm the Human Encyclopedia who knows everything."

"Ask him who killed Treadwell," called out a wag in the crowd.

Quade winced. His wits had been wool-gathering, otherwise he'd never have left himself open for that. The chief pounced on it, too. "All right, Mr. Encyclopedia—who and what killed Treadwell?"

Quade gulped. "Ah, now, Chief, you're not playing fair! Even Human Encyclopedias have a code of professional ethics. We don't go into competition with other professions. You wouldn't think it fair for cops to take in laundry on the side or sell moth tabs from door to door?"

Chief Kells tried to look stern but made a failure of it. "So you're not so smart after all."

"Well," said Quade, "it's against union rules, but I'll help out a bit." He pointed at the body of Treadwell. "Notice how the arms are hanging over the pit. I suggest you look at the hands!"

The medical examiner sprang forward, reached down and picked up Treadwell's limp arms. He exclaimed almost immediately. "He's right. There's a tiny spot of blood right in the palm of his right hand. And it's inflamed. Looks like he's been struck with a hypodermic!"

The chief whirled and leveled a finger at Cleve Storm. "You—you're the man!"

The cock handler's jaw dropped and his eyes threatened to pop from his head. "Me!" he cried.

"Yes, you! You been doing all the hollering about murder around here and you're the only one *could* have done it!"

"I could not!" screamed Storm, suddenly panic-stricken that the tables had been turned on him. "I was down in the pit when he was killed."

The chief nodded grimly. "That's why I'm accusing you. Look," he pointed at the body of Treadwell. "He's hanging over the pit right over the side where you was waiting while the roosters were fighting. Dodd was over on Ragsdale's side, so it couldn't have been him. And the referee was moving all around, which lets him out."

The chief's reasoning was sound, but the expression on Cleve Storm's face caused Quade to pucker up his brow. Storm didn't act like a murderer—and if he really was, he'd been damned dumb awhile ago to insist on murder when everyone else was willing to let it go as heart failure.

He looked down into the cockpit. The Whitehackle was still down there and was now quietly scratching away in the sand, hopefully trying to find a worm or bug. But where was the Jungle Shawl's carcass?

Chief Kells spat out a stream of tobacco juice. "I'm arresting you, Storm. If I find a hypodermic anywhere around here you're as good as burned right now. Oscar!" He signaled to one of his policemen. "Go over that pit down there, inch by inch. Look for a needle or hypodermic. You, Myers and Coons, you go over this place with a fine-tooth comb!"

Kells turned to Reggie Ragsdale. "I don't believe there'll be any more now, Mr. Ragsdale. Of course you know I got to bring charges about the cock fighting. That'll mean maybe a small fine or suspended sentence. You'll be notified when to appear in court."

Ragsdale nodded. "Of course, Chief, and thanks for the way you've handled things here. I'll speak to the board of councilmen about you."

The chief's eyes glowed. He rubbed his hands together and began shouting orders. Men bustled around. The body of Treadwell was carried out on a stretcher. Cleve Storm, still protesting his innocence, was led out. Guests began to leave.

Quade gathered up his bagful of books and topcoat. He walked over to Ragsdale. "Sorry about the trouble. Hope everything will work out all right."

"Thanks." The young sportsman smiled wanly.

Quade nodded and swung around. His topcoat caught on the top of the railing. He gave it a jerk and it came away with a slight ripping sound. Quade swore softly. The coat was only about a year old. He reached out to touch a nail on which the coat had caught.

He stopped his fingers an inch from the point and his eyes narrowed suddenly. It wasn't a nail on which the coat had caught, but a needle. It stuck up about a sixteenth of an inch from the top of the flat railing. This was the exact spot behind which Treadwell had sat.

At that moment one of the policemen down in the pit yelled. "I've found it!" He held aloft a shiny hypodermic needle. The medical examiner hurried down into the pit and took the needle from the policeman's hand. He sniffed at it. "Not sure," he said, "but it smells like *curare*, that stuff the South American Indians put on their blow-gun arrows. Kills instantly. Figured it was something like this that killed Treadwell," he said triumphantly.

Quade shook his head. *Curare* at a cock fight! Things were getting complicated. A scrap of information in the back of Quade's head bothered him. He had a habit of filing away odd bits of information in his encyclopedic brain, and when he had time, marshaling them together like the pieces of a crossword puzzle. A marvelous memory and this faculty of fitting together apparently irrelevant bits of information was largely responsible for his nickname —the Human Encyclopedia.

Quade deserved that name. Fifteen years ago he'd come into possession of a set of the *Encyclopedia Americana*, twenty-five large volumes. Quade read all the volumes from A to Z and then when he had finished, began at A again. He was now at *PU* on the fifth trip through the volumes. Fifteen years of reading the encyclopedias, plus extensive reading of other books had given him a truly encyclopedic brain.

What was this odd bit of information that puzzled him? It had something to do with the mix-up here tonight—something he'd observed or heard. Storm? No, because Quade was quite sure Storm was innocent. Something about the birds?

He hesitated for a moment, then sauntered over to the rear door of the barn. He slipped out quietly.

The yard was pitch dark. In the front of the building he could hear voices and automobiles, but back here it was as still and dark as the inside of a pocket. There was no moon or stars. A long black shadow loomed up ahead. Quade made his way toward it.

As he approached the building he recognized it for a Cornell type laying house. There was a door at one end of the building. Quade set down his bag and tried it. It was unlocked. He pushed it open. He stepped inside and struck a match. By the light of it he saw a light switch beside the door. He turned it and electric lights sprang on.

Quade saw that the building was evidently used as a conditioning room for poultry. Wire coops, sacks of feed, a bench on which stood cans of oil, remedies, tonics and other paraphernalia. Quade examined the objects and grinned. There was even a box of face rouge. Having raised birds himself he knew that breeders often used rouge to touch up the ear lobes of the birds. Baking soda was used to bring out the color of the red Jungle Shawl birds. The oil was for slicking up the feathers.

A large gunny sack on the floor caught his eye. There was a small pool of dark liquid beside the sack. Quade stooped and picked up the sack. He dumped out the contents—four Jungle Shawl cocks—dead.

Four? Nine of Ragsdale's birds had met defeat. Quade hadn't seen all the bouts, but he'd been informed by other spectators that six of the losing Shawls had been killed, three merely wounded. Well, where were the other two carcasses? The bag was large enough to have held all of them. That didn't make sense. If Tom Dodd had brought the carcasses here why hadn't he brought them all? Or hadn't Dodd brought them here?

A sound behind him caused Quade to whirl. He was just in time to see the door push open and a couple of hairy arms reach in. The hands held a huge, red fighting cock. Even as Quade looked, the cock was dropped to the floor and the door slammed shut. Quade heard the hasp rattle outside and knew that the person who had thrown in the Jungle Shawl had locked the door on the outside.

Quade's eyes were focused on the fighting cock. The bird was ruffling up his hackles and uttering warning squawks. Quade gasped. He'd known game

cocks down in the South to kill full-grown sheep with their naked spurs—
and those were ordinary games. These Jungle Shawls were only one generation removed from the wild ancestors of the Malay jungles.

This particular cock was well equipped for fighting. It had needle-pointed
steel gaffs on his spurs which seemed to Quade longer than those the birds
in the pits had used. They were at least three inches long.

One slash of those powerful legs and the needles would rip through
clothing, skin and flesh. They would lay open a thigh to the bone.

Quade was given no time for thought. With a sudden vicious squawk the
Jungle Shawl hurled himself at Quade, half running, half flying. Quade
sprang backward and collided with a sack of egg-mash. He stumbled on it
and tripped to the floor. He rolled over on his side as quickly as he could
and just missed the attack of the angry rooster. One wing brushed his face.
He sprang to his feet and put a safe distance between himself and the bird.

The cock whirled and uttered a defiant screech. Then it charged again.
Quade sidestepped and began stripping off his topcoat which he'd donned
before leaving the big barn. He held the coat a foot or so before him and
waited.

The bird charged. Quade flicked out the coat like a bull fighter teasing a
bull and lashed out with his foot at the same time. The bird hit the coat and
there was the ripping sound of cloth. At the same moment Quade's foot
caught something solid and a sharp streak of pain shot through his leg.

The kick hurled the bird several feet backward and Quade looked down.
The steel gaffs had slashed the topcoat clean through, pierced Quade's
trouser leg and the skin underneath. Quade felt the warm blood course
down his shin and cursed aloud.

He was fighting a losing fight, he knew. The bird seemed hurt by the kick
but was preparing for another charge. Quade tossed his coat aside and
sprang across the room for a heavy broom that stood against the wall.

Glass tinkled as Quade hefted the broom. His eyes shot to the little
window beside the door. A red galvanized pail appeared in the opening and
its liquid contents poured onto the floor with a tremendous splash. The
fumes of gasoline hit Quade's nostrils and he gasped. The distraction fortunately had also attracted the attention of the fighting cock, for if it had
charged just then it would have been too bad for Quade.

The hair on Quade's neck bristled. He had a feeling that he was in the
most dangerous spot of his entire life. In front of him a fighting cock—and
on the side—?

The rooster was cackling again. Quade took the fight to the bird now. He
rushed across the room and met him in full charge. The smack of the broom
as it hit the rooster could have been heard a hundred yards away. The cock

screeched as it was lifted off its feet and hurled against the wall. Quade followed up his attack, smashed the bird again as it hit the floor.

Then—then the entire room shot up in one terrific blaze of fire. The attacker outside the shed had tossed a blazing piece of newspaper into the gasoline. One entire side of the room was a sheet of flame, from floor to ceiling. Quade rushed back from the crippled bird and stared, panic-stricken, at the fire.

The door was locked on the outside. The windows were small and had wire mesh nailed outside of the glass. He could never get through one of them—not in time at least. This building was made of dry spruce boards. It would be in ashes inside of ten minutes.

Quade was trapped.

Heat from the huge flames scorched Quade's face. Fire! Of what use now was his encyclopedia knowledge when he was trapped in a burning building? Was there anything in the *Encyclopedia Americana* that would tell him how to get out of such a predicament?

Fire—what would extinguish a fire? Water. There was none in here. Chemicals. There were none—Wait!

Chemicals—no—but baking soda! Why, there were three large cartons of it right here behind him on the bench. Baking soda, one of the finest dry fire extinguishers in the world. Quade had read about it in his encyclopedias and had tried it out—as he had many other things that particularly interested him. He'd built a fire of charcoal wood and paper, had let it blaze fiercely. Then with an ordinary carton of baking soda he'd put out the fire in an instant. That had been an experiment on a small scale, however; would it work on a large scale—when it was an absolute necessity?

Quade reached behind him and snatched up a five-pound carton of baking soda. He reached in, drew out a handful and hurled it into the midst of the big blaze. A flash of white leaped high and was followed by greyish smoke. Quade's eyes, looking sharply at the floor where the soda fell, saw that the fire burned less fiercely there.

He advanced on the fire then. It seared his face and hands, but he threw the baking soda full into the flames, handful after handful. Then, finally, with a desperate gesture, he emptied the box. He whirled his back on the fire and started back for the second box. He caught it up, ripped open the cover and turned it on the fire.

A wild surge of joy rose in him. Why, there was a wide swath of black-ened flooring now leading to the door. The fire still blazed around the edges but the heart was cut out of it. Quade attacked the fire with renewed effort. He hurled soda right and left. His eyes smarted, his lungs choked and his skin was scorched, but he persisted. The second box of soda went and now the fire was but a few flickering flames around the edges. It required only a few handfuls from the third box to put out the last little flame.

Quade surveyed the fire-blackened wreckage and let out a tremendous sigh of relief. A stench of burnt flesh penetrated his nostrils. A mass of smoking flesh and feathers told of the fate of the fighting cock that had attacked him.

Five minutes later Quade leaned against the doorbell of the big Ragsdale residence. A butler opened the door, gasped and tried to close the door again, but Quade shoved it open smartly and stepped into the hallway.

"Mr. Ragsdale in?"

The butler rolled his eyes wildly. "Why—uh—I don't think so."

Quade heard voices and the tinkling of glasses ahead. He brushed past the butler. A wide door opened off the hallway into a luxuriously furnished room, containing about twenty men. Ragsdale, standing just inside the door, caught sight of Quade and cried out in astonishment. "Why—it's Oliver Quade. Good Lord, man, what happened to you?"

Quade walked into the room. His eyes searched the crowd, picking out familiar faces—Morgan, Wilcoxson, the medical examiner, even Tom Dodd. Then his eyes came back to Ragsdale. "One of your hen houses caught on fire and I put it out," he explained.

"Good for you!" exclaimed Ragsdale. "We all left the barn right after the police found the hypodermic which pinned Treadwell's murder on Cleve Storm."

"Storm didn't kill Treadwell," Quade said buntly. "The murderer is right here in this room. He's the same man who poisoned your Jungle Shawls and made you lose the cocking main."

"He's a liar!" Tom Dodd, face black as a thundercloud, came forward. "Your birds weren't poisoned, Mr. Ragsdale. I handled them myself and examined each one before I pitted them."

Quade looked insolently at the furious handler. "I didn't see all the bouts, but I did see four Shawls in a row get killed—and each one of them was killed because he apparently turned yellow—and faltered. But they didn't really falter. They were poisoned—"

"That's a lie!" screamed Tom Dodd. "The Shawls lost because they were up against better birds."

Quade grinned wolfishly. "Say—whose side are *you* on?" he asked. "You brought those Shawls here and claimed they were the best in the world."

"That's right!" snapped Ragsdale. "I paid Walcott a fancy price for those birds and he guaranteed them to beat the best in the country."

"I think they would have," Quade assured him. "They were real fighters. One of them almost killed me—but let that pass for the moment. Mr.

Ragsdale, just to prove my point, pick up that phone there and call Mr. Terence Walcott, of Corvallis, Oregon."

"Why should he call up the boss?" cried Dodd. "I'm the handler. I've raised fighting cocks all my life!"

"Have you?" Quade didn't seem impressed. "I've raised a few birds myself. By the way, have you gentlemen noticed that we Southerners use different cocking terms than Northerners? For example, up here you say 'stuck' when a bird is wounded. Down South we say 'hung.' Am I right, Mr. Morgan?"

"That's right, Mr. Quade," the editor replied. "There's quite a difference in the terminology of the South and North. I've published articles on the subject in my magazines."

"Well, did any of you notice that every time a Jungle Shawl was hung, Tom Dodd cried out, 'Hung'? Yet Mr. Dodd says he comes from the *North!*"

The silence in the room was suddenly so profound that Tom Dodd's hoarse breathing sounded like a rasping cough. Quade broke the silence. "By the way, Dodd, that's a peculiar ring you're wearing. Mind letting me take a look at it?"

Tom Dodd looked down at the ring on his left hand. His lips moved silently for a moment, then he looked at Quade. "No—I don't mind. Here—"

He started toward Quade, who, to the surprise of everyone in the room, suddenly lashed out with his right fist. He put everything into the blow, the pent-up emotion and anger he'd accumulated in the burning poultry house. The fist caught Dodd on the point of the jaw, smashed him back into a couple of the guests. They made no move to catch him and Dodd slid off them to the floor. He lay in a huddle, quiet.

"There's your murderer!" cried Quade, blowing on his fist.

That broke the spell. Men began shouting questions. Quade stooped down, slipped the ornate ring from Dodd's finger. He held it up for all to see. "See this little needle that shoots out on the inside of the ring?" Heads craned forward.

"That's why those birds of yours died without fighting, Mr. Ragsdale," Quade explained. "Just as Dodd would let them go, he'd prick them with this needle. There's poison on it, which took effect almost instantly."

Ragsdale shook his head in bewilderment. "But Treadwell—"

"Was killed in a similar fashion, but not with the ring. Remember there was an intermission before the last fight—during which I tried to sell you men a few books," Quade grinned. "That's when Dodd stuck a little poisoned needle into the flat top of the railing where Treadwell sat. Perhaps he'd noticed Treadwell eyeing him with suspicion. Suspecting that he was poisoning the cocks. Dodd worked out the whole thing pretty cleverly.

Took no chances. Witness the hypodermic which he tossed into the sand. That was for a blind.

"He'd figured out that when Treadwell's bird won the last and deciding bout that Treadwell would probably smack the railing in his excitement— maybe he'd watched him doing it after other bouts. Well, that's exactly what Treadwell did. The needle's still in the railing. I ripped my coat on it when I started to leave."

"But what made you suspect Dodd?" asked Ragsdale.

Quade grinned. "My encyclopedic brain, I guess. In the excitement of learning that Treadwell was murdered, Dodd was still cool enough to remove the carcass of the Shawl. That was the first thing that got me to thinking. Then the matter of terminology stuck in my mind. I didn't catch it at first. Dodd cried out 'hung' every time. Well, that's a Southern term and Dodd was supposed to have come from Oregon: claimed he'd lived there all his life."

"You mean to say that Dodd does not actually come from Oregon?" exclaimed Ragsdale. "Why—that would mean that he isn't really Dodd at all?"

"Right," said Quade. "And Treadwell must have known that. He'd probably met the right Dodd at some time or other. I suspect you'll learn after talking to Walcott on the phone that the real Dodd doesn't look like this one at all. Where he is, I don't know. This chap may have bought him off, murdered him perhaps. That isn't so important because he'll burn for the murder of Treadwell anyway. It's enough that we know this chap took the real Dodd's place somewhere between Oregon and here."

"Yes—but who is he?" asked Ragsdale.

Quade screwed up his lips. "I think you'll find that he sometimes uses the name of C. Pitts. In fact, I'm willing to lay odds that a handwriting expert will declare the signature on that check Morgan has, was made by this chap. Twenty-five thousand is a lot of money and Mr. Pitts wanted to make sure he won."

"I'll be damned!" said Ragsdale. "You've certainly figured everything out. And—I believe you. I can understand now why they call you the Human Encyclopedia."

Quade's eyes lit up. "That reminds me—I didn't get finished out there in the barn. So if you have no objections, I'll continue with my little talk about the *Compendium of Human Knowledge.* 'All the knowledge of the ages condensed into one volume.'"

I Feel Bad Killing You

Leigh Brackett

I

Dead End Town

Los Angeles, Apr. 21.—The death of Henry Channing, 24, policeman attached to the Surfside Division and brother of the once-prominent detective Paul Channing, central figure in the Padway gang-torture case, has been termed a suicide following investigation by local authorities. Young Channing's battered body was found in the surf under Sunset Pier in the beach community three days ago. It was first thought that Channing might have fallen or been thrown from the end of the pier, where his cap was found, but there is no evidence of violence and a high guard rail precludes the accident theory. Sunset Pier was part of his regular beat.

Police Captain Max Gandara made the following statement: "We have reliable testimony that Channing had been nervous and despondent following a beating by *pachucos* two months ago." He then cited the case of the brother, Paul Channing, who quit the force and vanished into obscurity following his mistreatment at the hands of the once-powerful Padway gang in 1934. "They were both good cops," Gandara said, "but they lost their nerve."

Paul Channing stood for a moment at the corner. The crossing-light, half a block along the highway, showed him only as a gaunt shadow among shadows. He looked down the short street in somber hesitation. Small tired houses crouched patiently under the wind. Somewhere a rusted screen door slammed with the protesting futility of a dying bird beating its wing. At the end of the deserted pavement was the grey pallor of sand and, beyond it, the sea.

He stood listening to the boom and hiss of the waves, thinking of them rushing black and foam-streaked through the pilings of Sunset Pier, the long weeds streaming out and the barnacles pink and fluted and razor sharp behind it. He hoped that Hank had struck his head at once against a timber.

He lifted his head, his body shaken briefly by a tremor. *This is it*, he thought. *This is the deadline.*

He began to walk, neither slowly nor fast, scraping sand under his feet. The rhythm of the scraping was uneven, a slight dragging, off-beat. He went to the last house on the right, mounted three sagging steps to a wooden porch, and rapped with his knuckles on a door blistered and greasy with the salt sweat of the sea. There was a light behind drawn blinds, and a sound of voices. The voices stopped, sliced cleanly by the knocking.

Someone walked heavily through the silence. The door opened, spilling yellow light around the shadow of a thick-set, powerful man in shirtsleeves. He let his breath out in what was not quite a laugh and relaxed against the jamb.

"So you did turn up," he said. He was well into middle age, hard-eyed, obstinate. His name was Max Gandara, Police Captain, Surfside Division, L.A.P.D. He studied the man on the porch with slow, deliberate insolence.

The man on the porch seemed not to mind. He seemed not to be in any hurry. His dark eyes looked, unmoved, at the big man, at him and through him. His face was a mask of thin sinewy flesh, laid close over ruthless bone, expressionless. And yet, in spite of his face and his lean erect body, there was a shadow on him. He was like a man who has drawn away, beyond the edge of life.

"Did you think I wouldn't come?" he asked.

Gandara shrugged. "They're all here. Come on in and get it over with."

Channing nodded and stepped inside. He removed his hat. His dark hair was shot with grey. He turned to lay the hat on a table and the movement brought into focus a scar that ran up from his shirt collar on the right side of his neck, back of the ear. Then he followed Gandara into the living room.

There were three people there, and the silence. Three people watching the door. A red-haired, green-eyed girl with a smouldering, angry glow deep inside her. A red-haired, green-eyed boy with a sullen, guarded face. And a man, a neat, lean, swarthy man with aggressive features that seemed always to be on the edge of laughter and eyes that kept all their emotion on the surface.

"Folks," said Gandara, "this is Paul Channing." He indicated them, in order. "Marge Krist, Rudy Krist, Jack Flavin."

Hate crawled into the green eyes of Rudy Krist, brilliant and poisonous, fixed on Channing.

* * *

Out in the kitchen a woman screamed. The swing door burst open. A chubby pink man came through in a tottering rush, followed by a large, bleached blonde with an ice pick. Her dress was torn slightly at the shoulder and her mouth was smeared. Her incongruously black eyes were owlish and mad.

Gandara yelled. The sound of his voice got through to the blonde. She slowed down and said sulkily, to no one in particular, "He better keep his fat paws off or I'll fix him." She went back to the kitchen.

The chubby pink man staggered to a halt, swayed, caught hold of Channing's arm and looked up at him, smiling foolishly. The smile faded, leaving his mouth open like a baby's. His eyes, magnified behind rimless lenses, widened and fixed.

"Chan," he said. "My God. Chan."

He sat down on the floor and began to cry, the tears running quietly down his cheeks.

"Hello, Budge." Channing stooped and touched his shoulder.

"Take it easy." Gandara pulled Channing's arms. "Let the little lush alone. Him and—that." He made a jerky gesture at the girl, flung himself heavily into a chair and glowered at Channing. "All right, we're all curious—tell us why we're here."

Channing sat down. He seemed in no hurry to begin. A thin film of sweat made the tight pattern of muscles very plain under his skin.

"We're here to talk about a lot of things," he said. "Who murdered Henry?" No one seemed particularly moved except Budge Hanna, who stopped crying and stared at Channing. Rudy Krist made a small derisive noise in his throat. Gandara laughed.

"That ain't such a bombshell, Chan. I guess we all had an idea of what you was driving at, from the letters you wrote us. What we want to know is what makes you think you got a right to holler murder."

Channing drew a thick envelope from his inside pocket, laying it on his knee to conceal the fact that his hands trembled. He said, not looking at anybody, "I haven't seen my brother for several years, but we've been in fairly close touch through letters. I've kept most of his. Hank was good at writing letters, good at saying things. He's had a lot to say since he was transferred to Surfside—and not one word of it points to suicide."

Max Gandara's face had grown rocky. "Oh, he had a lot to say, did he?"

Channing nodded. Marge Krist was leaning forward, watching him intently. Jack Flavin's terrier face was interested, but unreadable. He had been smoking nervously when Channing entered. The nervousness seemed to be habitual, part of his wiry personality. Now he lighted another cigarette, his hands moving with a swiftness that seemed jerky but was not. The match flared and spat. Paul Channing started involuntarily. The flame seemed to have a terrible fascination for him. He dropped his gaze. Beads of sweat came out along his hairline. Once again, harshly, Gandara laughed.

"Go on," he said. "Go on."

"Hank told me about that brush with the *pachucos*. They didn't hurt him much. They sure as hell didn't break him."

"Flavin, here, says different. Rudy says different. Marge says different."

"That's why I wanted to talk to them—and you, Max. Hank mentioned you all in his letters." He was talking to the whole room now. "Max I knew from the old days. You, Miss Krist, I know because Hank went with you—not seriously, I guess, but you liked each other. He liked your brother, too."

The kid stared at him, his eyes blank and bright. Channing said, "Hank talked a lot about you, Rudy. He said you were a smart kid, a good kid but headed for trouble. He said some ways you were so smart you were downright stupid."

Rudy and Marge both started to speak, but Channing was going on. "I guess he was right, Rudy. You've got it on you already—a sort of greyness that comes from prison walls, or the shadow of them. You've got that look on your face, like a closed door."

Rudy got halfway to his feet, looking nasty. Flavin said quietly, "Shut up." Rudy sat down again. Flavin seemed relaxed. His brown eyes held only a hard glitter from the light. "Hank seems to have been a great talker. What did he say about me?"

"He said you smell of stripes."

Flavin laid his cigarette carefully in a tray. He got up, very light and easy. He went over to Channing and took a handful of his shirt, drawing him up slightly, and said with gentle kindness, "I don't think I like that remark."

Marge Krist cried, "Stop it! Jack, don't you dare start trouble."

"Maybe you didn't understand what he meant, Marge." Flavin still did not sound angry. "He's accusing me of having a record, a prison record. He didn't pick a very nice way of saying it."

"Take it easy, Jack," Gandara said. "Don't you get what he's doing? He's trying to wangle himself a little publicity and stir up a little trouble, so that maybe the public will think maybe Hank didn't do the Dutch after all." He pointed at Budge Hanna. "Even the press is here." He rose and took hold of Flavin's shoulder. "He's just making a noise with his mouth, because a long time ago people used to listen when he did it and he hasn't forgotten how good that felt."

Flavin shrugged and returned to his chair. Gandara lighted a cigarette, holding the match deliberately close to Channing's sweaty face. "Listen, Chan.

Jack Flavin is a good citizen of Surfside. He owns a store, legitimate, and Rudy works for him, legitimate. I don't like people coming into my town and making cracks about the citizens. If they step out of line, I'll take care of them. If they don't, I'll see they're let alone."

He sat down again, comfortably. "All right, Chan. Let's get this all out of your system. What did little brother have to say about me?"

Channing's dark eyes flickered with what might have been malice. "What everybody's always said about you, Max. That you were too goddam dumb even to be crooked."

Gandara turned purple. He moved and Jack Flavin laughed. "No fair, Max. You wouldn't let me."

Budge Hanna giggled with startling shrillness. The blonde had come in and sat down beside him. Her eyes were half closed but she seemed somehow less drunk than she had been. Gandara settled back. He said ominously, "Go on."

"All right. Hank said that Surfside was a dirty town, dirty from the gutters up. He said any man with the brains of a sick flea would know that most of the liquor places were run illegally, and most of the hotels, too, and that two-thirds of the police force was paid to have bad eyesight. He said it wasn't any use trying to do a good job as a decent cop. He said every report he turned in was thrown away for lack of evidence, and he was sick of it."

Marge Krist said, "Then maybe that's what he was worried about."

"He wasn't afraid," said Channing. "All his letters were angry, and an angry man doesn't commit suicide."

Budge Hanna said shrilly, "Look out."

Max Gandara was on his feet. He was standing over Channing. His lips had a white line around them.

"Listen," he said. "I been pretty patient with you. Now I'll tell you something. Your brother committed suicide. All these three people testified at the inquest. You can read the transcript. They all said Hank was worried; he wasn't happy about things. There was no sign of violence on Hank, or the pier."

"How could there be?" said Channing. "Hard asphalt paving doesn't show much. And Hank's body wouldn't show much, either."

"Shut up. I'm telling you. There's no evidence of murder, no reason to think it's murder. Hank was like you, Channing. He couldn't take punishment. He got chicken walking a dark beat down here, and he jumped, and that's all."

Channing said slowly, "Only two kinds of people come to Surfside—the ones that are starting at the bottom, going up, and the ones that are finished, coming down. It's either a beginning or an end, and I guess we all know where we stand on that scale."

He got up, tossing the packet of letters into Budge Hanna's lap. "Those are photostats. The originals are already with police headquarters in L.A. I don't think you have to worry much, Max. There's nothing definite in them. Just a green young harness cop griping at the system, making a few personal remarks. He hasn't even accused you of being dishonest, Max. Only dumb —and the powers-that-be already know that. That's why you're here in Surfside, waiting for the age of retirement."

Gandara struck him in the mouth. Channing took three steps backward, caught himself, swayed, and was steady again. Blood ran from the corner of his mouth down his chin. Marge Krist was on her feet, her eyes blazing, but something about Channing kept her from speaking. He seemed not to care about the blood, about Gandara, or about anything but what he was saying.

"You used to be a good reporter, Budge, before you drank yourself onto the scrapheap. I thought maybe you'd like to be in at the beginning on this story. Because there's going to be a story, if it's only the story of my death.

"I knew Hank. There was no yellow in him. Whether there's yellow in me or not, doesn't matter. Hank didn't jump off that pier. Somebody threw him off, and I'm going to find out who, and why. I used to be a pretty good dick once. I've got a reason now for remembering all I learned."

Max Gandara said, "Oh, God," in a disgusted voice. "Take that somewhere else, Chan. It smells." He pushed him roughly toward the door, and Rudy Krist laughed.

"Yellow," he said. "Yellower than four Japs. Both of 'em, all talk and no guts. Get him out, Max. He stinks up the room."

Flavin said, "Shut up, Rudy." He grinned at Marge. "You're getting your sister sore."

"You bet I'm sore!" she flared. "I think Mr. Channing is right. I knew Hank pretty well, and I think you ought to be ashamed to push him around like this."

Flavin said, "Who? Hank or Mr. Channing?"

Marge snapped, "Oh, go to hell." She turned and went out. Gandara shoved Channing into the hall after her. "You know where the door is, Chan. Stay away from me, and if I was you I'd stay away from Surfside." He turned around, reached down and got a handful of Budge Hanna's coat collar and slung him out bodily. "You, too, rumdum. *And* you." He made a grab for the blonde, but she was already out. He followed the four of them down the hall and closed the door hard behind them.

* * *

Paul Channing said, "Miss Krist—and you too, Budge." The wind felt ice cold on his skin. His shirt stuck to his back. It turned clammy and he began to shiver. "I want to talk to you."

The blonde said, "Is this private?"

"I don't think so. Maybe you can help." Channing walked slowly toward the beach front and the boardwalk. "Miss Krist, if you didn't think Hank committed suicide, why did you testify as you did at the inquest?"

"Because I didn't know." She sounded rather angry, with him and possibly herself. "They asked me how he acted, and I had to say he'd been worried and depressed, because he had been. I told them I didn't think he was the type for suicide, but they didn't care."

"Did Hank ever hint that he knew something—anything that might have been dangerous to him?" Channing's eyes were alert, watchful in the darkness.

"No. Hank pounded a beat. He wasn't a detective."

"He was pretty friendly with your brother, wasn't he?"

"I thought for a while it might bring Rudy back to his senses. He took a liking to Hank, they weren't so far apart in years, and Hank was doing him good. Now, of course—"

"What's wrong with Rudy? What's he doing?"

"That's just it, I don't know. He's 4-F in the draft, and that hurts him, and he's always been restless, never could hold a job. Then he met Jack Flavin, and since then he's been working steady, but he—he's changed. I can't put my finger on it, I don't know of anything wrong he's done, but he's hardened and drawn into himself, as though he had secrets and didn't trust anybody. You saw how he acted. He's turned mean. I've done my best to bring him up right."

Channing said, "Kids go that way sometimes. Know anything about him, Budge?"

The reporter said, "Nuh-uh. He's never been picked up for anything, and as far as anybody knows even Flavin is straight. He owns a haberdashery and pays his taxes."

"Well," said Channing, "I guess that's all for now."

"No." Marge Krist stopped and faced him. He could see her eyes in the pale reflection of the water, dark and intense. The wind blew her hair, pressed her light coat against the long lifting planes of her body. "I want to warn you. Maybe you're a brilliant, nervy man and you know what you're doing, and if you do it's all right. But if you really are what you acted like in there, you'd better go home and forget about it. Surfside is a bad town. You can't insult people and get away with it." She paused. "For Hank's sake, I hope you know what you're doing. I'm in the phone book if you want me. Good night."

"Good night." Channing watched her go. She had a lovely way of moving. Absently, he began to wipe the blood off his face. His lip had begun to swell.

Budge Hanna said, "Chan."

"Yeah."

"I want to say thanks, and I'm with you. I'll give you the biggest break I can in the paper."

"We used to work pretty well together, before I got mine and you found yours, in a bottle."

"Yeah. And now I'm in Surfside with the rest of the scrap. If this turns out a big enough story, I might—oh, well." He paused, rubbing a pudgy cheek with his forefinger.

Channing said, "Go ahead, Budge. Say it."

"All right. Every crook in the Western states knows that the Padway mob took you to the wall. They know what was done to you, with fire. They know you broke. The minute they find out you're back, even unofficially, you know what'll happen. You sent up a lot of guys in your time. You sent a lot of 'em down, too—down to the morgue. You were a tough dick, Chan, and a square one, and you know how they love you."

"I guess I know all that, Budge."

"Chan—" he looked up, squinting earnestly through the gloom, his spectacles shining—"how is it? I mean, can you—"

Channing put a hand on his shoulder, pushing him around slightly. "You watch your step, kid, and try to stay sober. I don't know what I may be getting into. If you want out—"

"Hell, no. Just—well, good luck, Chan."

"Thanks."

The blonde said, "Ain't you going to ask me something?"

"Sure," said Channing. "What do you know?"

"I know who killed your brother."

II

Badge of Carnage

The blood swelled and thickened in Channing's veins. It made a hard pain over his eyes and pressed against the stiff scar tissue on his neck. No one spoke. No one moved.

The wind blew sand in riffles across the empty beach. The waves rushed and broke their backs in thunder and slipped out again, sighing. Up ahead Sunset Pier thrust its black bulk against the night. Beyond it was the huge amusement pier. Here and there a single light was burning, swaying with the wind, and the reaching skeletons of the roller coaster and the giant slide were desolate in the pre-season quiet. Vacant lots and a single unlighted house were as deserted as the moon.

Paul Channing looked at the woman with eyes as dark and lonely as the night. "We're not playing a game," he said. "This is murder."

The blonde's teeth glittered white between moist lips.

Budge Hanna whispered, "She's crazy. She couldn't know."

"Oh, couldn't I!" The blonde's whisper was throatily venomous. "Young Channing was thrown off the pier about midnight, wasn't he? Okay. Well, you stood me up on a date that evening, remember, Budgie dear? And my room is on the same floor as yours, remember? And I can hear every pair of hoofs clumping up and down those damn stairs right outside, remember?"

"Listen," Budge said, "I told you I got stewed and—"

"And got in a fight. I know. Sure, you told me. But how can you prove it? I heard your fairy footsteps. They didn't sound very stewed to me. So I looked out, and you were hitting it for your room like your pants were on fire. Your shirt was torn, and so was your coat, and you didn't look so good other ways. I could hear you heaving clear out in the hall. And it was just nineteen minutes after twelve."

Budge Hanna's voice had risen to a squeak. "Damn you, Millie, I—Chan, she's crazy! She's just trying—"

"Sure," said Millie. She thrust her face close to his. "I been shoved around enough. I been called enough funny names. I been stood up enough times. I loaned you enough money I'll never get back. And I ain't so dumb I don't know you got dirt on your hands from somewhere. Me, I'm quitting you right now and—"

"Shut up. Shut up!"

"And I got a few things to say that'll interest some people!" Millie was screeching now. "You killed that Channing kid, or you know who did!"

Budge Hanna slapped her hard across the mouth.

Millie reeled back. Then she screamed like a cat. Her hands flashed up, curved and wicked, long red nails gleaming. She went for Budge Hanna.

Channing stepped between them. He was instantly involved in a whirlwind of angry flailing hands. While he was trying to quiet them the men came up behind him.

There were four of them. They had come quietly from the shadows beside the vacant house. They worked quickly, with deadly efficiency. Channing got his hand inside his coat, and after that he didn't know anything for a long time.

Things came back to Channing in disconnected pieces. His head hurt. He was in something that moved. He was hot. He was covered with something, lying flat on his back, and he could hardly breathe. There was another person jammed against him. There were somebody's feet on his chest, and somebody else's feet on his thighs. Presently he found that his mouth was covered with adhesive, that his eyes were taped shut, and that his hands and feet were bound, probably also with tape. The moving thing was an automobile, taking its time.

The stale, stifling air under the blanket covering him was heavy with the scent of powder and cheap perfume. He guessed that the woman was Millie. From time to time she stirred and whimpered.

A man's voice said, "Here is okay."

The car stopped. Doors were opened. The blanket was pulled away. Cold salt air rushed over Channing, mixed with the heavy sulphurous reek of sewage. He knew they were somewhere on the road above Hyperion, where there was nothing but miles of empty dunes.

Hands grabbed him, hauled him bodily out of the car. Somebody said, "Got the Thompson ready?"

"Yeah." The speaker laughed gleefully, like a child with a bass voice. "Just like old times, ain't it? Good ole Dolly. She ain't had a chansta sing in a long time. Come on, honey. Loosen up the pipes."

A rattling staccato burst out, and was silent.

"For cripesake, Joe! That stuff ain't so plentiful. Doncha know there's a war on? We gotta conserve. C'mon, help me with this guy." He kicked Channing. "On your feet, you."

He was hauled erect and leaned against a post. Joe said, "What about the dame?"

The other man laughed. "Her turn comes later. Much later."

A fourth voice, one that had not spoken before, said, "Okay, boys. Get away from him now." It was a slow, inflectionless and yet strangely forceful voice, with a hint of a lisp. The lisp was not in the least effeminate or funny. It had the effect of a knife blade whetted on oilstone. The man who owned it put his hands on Channing's shoulders.

"You know me," he said.

Channing nodded. The uncovered parts of his face were greasy with sweat. It had soaked loose the corners of the adhesive. The man said,

"You knew I'd catch up with you some day."

The man struck him, deliberately and with force, twice across the face with his open palms.

"I'm sorry you lost your guts, Channing. This makes me feel like I'm shooting a kitten. Why didn't you do the Dutch years ago, like your brother?"

Channing brought his bound fists up, slammed them into the man's face, striking at the sound of his voice. The man grunted and fell, making a heavy soft thump in the sand. Somebody yelled, "Hey!" and the man with the quiet lisping voice said, "Shut up. Let him alone."

Channing heard him scramble up and the voice came near again. "Do that again."

Channing did.

The man avoided his blow this time. He laughed softly. "So you still have insides, Chan. That makes it better. Much better."

Joe said, "Look, somebody may come along—"

"Shut up." The man brought something from his pocket, held his hand close to Channing's ear, and shook it. "You know what that is?"

Channing stiffened. He nodded.

There was a light thin rattling sound, and then a scratching of emery and the quick spitting of a match-head rubbed to flame.

The man said softly, "How are your guts now?"

The little sharp tongue of heat touched Channing's chin. He drew his head back. His mouth worked under the adhesive. Cords stood out in his throat. The flame followed. Channing began to shake. His knees gave. He braced them, braced his body against the post. Sweat ran down his face and the scar on his neck turned dark and livid.

The man laughed. He threw the match down and stepped away. He said, "Okay, Joe."

Somebody said, sharply, "There's a car coming. Two cars."

The man swore. "Bunch of sailors up from Long Beach. Okay, we'll get out of here. Back in the car, Joe. Can't use the chopper, they'd hear it." Joe cursed unhappily. Feet scruffed hurriedly in the sand. Leather squeaked, the small familiar sound of metal clearing a shoulder clip. The safety snicked open.

The man said, "So long, Channing."

Channing was already falling sideways when the shot came. There was a second one close behind it. Channing dropped into the ditch and lay perfectly still, hidden from the road. The car roared off. Presently the two other cars shot by, loaded with sailors. They were singing and shouting and not worrying about what somebody might have left at the side of the road.

* * *

Sometime later Channing began to move, at first in uncoordinated jerks and then with reasonable steadiness. He was conscious that he had been hit in two places. The right side of his head was stiff and numb clear down to his neck. Somebody had shoved a red-hot spike through the flesh over his heart-ribs and forgotten to take it out. He could feel blood oozing, sticky with sand.

He rolled over slowly and started to peel the adhesive from his face, fumbling awkwardly with his bound hands. When that was done he used his teeth on his wrist bonds. It took a long time. After that the ankles were easy.

It was no use trying to see how much damage had been done. He decided it couldn't be as bad as it felt. He smiled, a crooked and humorless grimace, and swore and laughed shortly. He wadded the clean handkerchief from his hip pocket into the gash under his arm and tightened the holster strap to hold it there. The display handkerchief in his breast pocket went around his head. He found that after he got started he could walk quite well. His gun had not been removed. Channing laughed again, quietly. He did not touch nor in any way notice the burn on his chin.

It took him nearly three hours to get back to Surfside, crouching in the ditch twice to let cars go by.

He passed Gandara's street, and the one beyond where Marge and Rudy Krist lived. He came to the ocean front and the dark loom of the pier and the vacant house from behind which the men had come. He found Budge Hanna doubled up under a clump of Monterrey cypress. The cold spring wind blew sand into Hanna's wide-open eyes, but he didn't seem to mind it. He had bled from the nose and ears—not much.

Channing went through Hanna's pockets, examining things swiftly by the light of a tiny pocket flash shielded in his hand. There was just the usual clutter of articles. Channing took the key ring. Then, tucked into the watch pocket, he found a receipt from Flavin's Men's Shop for three pairs of socks. The date was April 22. Channing frowned. April 21 was the day on which Hank Channing's death had been declared a suicide. April 21 was a Saturday.

Channing rose slowly and walked on down the front to Surfside Avenue. It was hours past midnight. The bars were closed. The only lights on the street were those of the police station and the lobby of the Surfside Hotel, which was locked and deserted. Channing let himself in with Budge Hanna's key and walked up dirty marble steps to the second floor and found Budge Hanna's number. He leaned against the jamb, his knees sagging, managed to force the key around and get inside. He switched on the lights, locked the door again, and braced his back against it. The first thing he saw was a bottle on the bedside table.

He drank straight from the neck. It was scotch, good scotch. In a few minutes he felt much better. He stared at the label, turning the bottle around in his hands, frowning at it. Then, very quietly, he began to search the room.

He found nothing until, in the bottom drawer of the dresser, he discovered a brand new shirt wrapped in cheap green paper. The receipt was from Flavin's Men's Shop. Channing looked at the date. It was for the day which had just begun, Monday.

Channing studied the shirt, poking his fingers into the folds. Between the tail and the cardboard he found an envelope. It was unaddressed, unsealed, and contained six one hundred dollar bills.

Channing's mouth twisted. He replaced the money and the shirt and sat down on the bed. He scowled at the wall, not seeing it, and drank some more of Budge Hanna's scotch. He thought Budge wouldn't mind. It would take more even than good scotch to warm him now.

A picture on the wall impressed itself gradually upon Channing's mind.

He looked at it more closely. It was a professional photograph of a beautiful woman in a white evening gown. She had a magnificent figure and a strong, provocative, heart-shaped face. Her gown and hairdress were of the late twenties. The picture was autographed in faded ink, "Lots of Luck, Skinny, from your pal Dorothy Balf."

"Skinny" had been crossed out and "Budge" written above.

Channing took the frame down and slid the picture out. It had been wiped off, but both frame and picture showed the ravages of time, dust and stains and faded places, as though they had hung a long time with only each other for company. On the back of the picture was stamped:

SKINNY CRAIL'S
Surfside at Culver
"Between the Devil and the Deep"

Memories came back to Channing. Skinny Crail, that bad-luck boy of Hollywood, plunging his last dime on a night club that flurried into success and then faded gradually to a pathetically mediocre doom, a white elephant rotting hugely in the empty flats between Culver City and the beach. Dorothy Balf had been the leading feminine star of that day, and Budge Hanna's idol. Channing glanced again at the scrawled "Budge." He sighed and replaced the picture carefully. Then he turned out the lights and sat a long while in the dark, thinking.

Presently he sighed again and ran his hand over his face, wincing. He rose and went out, locking the door carefully behind him. He moved slowly, his limp accentuated by weakness and a slight unsteadiness from the scotch. His expression was that of a man who hopes for nothing and is therefore immune to blows.

There was a phone booth in the lobby. Channing called Max Gandara. He talked for a long time. When he came out his face was chalk-colored and damp, utterly without expression. He left the hotel and walked slowly down the beach.

The shapeless, colorless little house was dark and silent, with two empty lots to seaward and a cheap brick apartment house on its right. No lights showed anywhere. Channing set his finger on the rusted bell.

He could hear it buzzing somewhere inside. After a long time lights went on behind heavy crash draperies, drawn close. Channing turned suddenly sick. Sweat came out on his wrists and his ears rang. Through the ringing he heard Marge Krist's clear voice asking who was there.

He told her. "I'm hurt," he said. "Let me in."

The door opened. Channing walked through it. He seemed to be walking through dark water that swirled around him, very cold, very heavy. He decided not to fight it.

When he opened his eyes again he was stretched out on a studio couch. Apparently he had been out only a moment or two. Marge and Rudy Krist were arguing fiercely.

"I tell you he's got to have a doctor!"

"All right, tell him to go get one. You don't want to get in trouble."

"Trouble? Why would I get in trouble?"

"The guy's been shot. That means cops. They'll be trampling all over, asking you why he should have come here. How do you know what the little rat's been doing? If he's square, why didn't he go to the cops himself? Maybe it's a frame, or maybe he shot himself."

"Maybe," said Marge slowly, "you're afraid to be questioned."

Rudy swore. He looked almost as white and hollow as Channing felt. Channing laughed. It was not a pleasant sound.

He said, "Sure he's scared. Start an investigation now and that messes up everything for tonight."

Marge and Rudy both started at the sound of his voice. Rudy's face went hard and blank as a pine slab. He walked over toward the couch.

"What does that crack mean?"

"It means you better call Flavin quick and tell him to get his new shirt out of Budge Hanna's room. Budge Hanna won't be needing it now, and the cops are going to be very interested in the accessories."

Rudy's lips had a curious stiffness. "What's wrong with Hanna?"

"Nothing much. Only one of Dave's boys hit him a little too hard. He's dead."

"Dead?" Rudy shaped the word carefully and studied it as though he had never heard it before. Then he said, "Who's Dave? What are you talking about?"

Channing studied him. "Flavin's still keeping you in the nursery, is he?"

"That kind of talk don't go with me, Channing."

"That's tough, because it'll go with the cops. You'll sound kind of silly, won't you, bleating how you didn't know what was going on because papa never told you."

Rudy moved toward Channing. Marge yelled and caught him. Channing grinned and drew his gun. His head was propped fairly high on pillows, so he could see what he was doing without making any disastrous attempt to sit up.

"Fine hood you are, Rudy. Didn't even frisk me. Listen, punk. Budge Hanna's dead, murdered. His Millie is dead, too, by now. I'm supposed to be dead, in a ditch above Hyperion, but Dave Padway always was a lousy shot. Where do you think you come in on this?"

Rudy's skin had a sickly greenish tinge, but his jaw was hard. "You're a liar, Channing. I never heard of Dave Padway. I don't know anything about Budge Hanna or that dame. I don't know anything about you. Now get the hell out."

"You make a good Charlie McCarthy, Rudy. Maybe Flavin will hold you on his knee in the death-chair at San Quentin."

Marge stopped Rudy again. She said quietly, "What happened, Mr. Channing?"

Channing told her, keeping his eyes on Rudy. "Flavin's heading a racket," he said finally. "His store is just a front, useful for background and a way to make pay-offs and pass on information. He doesn't keep the store open on Sunday, does he, Rudy?"

Rudy didn't answer. Marge said, "No."

"Okay. Budge Hanna worked for Flavin. I'll make a guess. I'll say Flavin is engineering liquor robberies, hijacking, and so forth. Budge Hanna was a well-known lush. He could go into any bar and make a deal for bootleg whiskey, and nobody would suspect him. Trouble with Budge was, he couldn't handle his women. Millie got sore, and suspicious and began to yell out loud. I guess Dave Padway's boys overheard her. Dave never did trust women and drunks."

Channing stared narrow-eyed at Rudy. His blood-caked face was twisted into a cruel grin. "Dave never liked punks, either. There's going to be trouble between Dave and your pal Flavin, and I don't see where you're

going to come in, except maybe on a morgue slab, like the others. Like
Hank."

"Oh, cripes," said Rudy, "we're back to Hank again."

"Yeah. Always back to Hank. You know what happened, Rudy. You kind
of liked Hank. You're a smart kid, Rudy. You've probably got a better brain
than Flavin, and if you're going to be a successful crook these days you need
brains. So Flavin pushed Hank off the pier and called it suicide, so you'd
think he was yellow."

Rudy laughed. "That's good. That's very good. Marge was out with Jack
Flavin that night." His green eyes were dangerous.

Marge nodded, dropping her gaze. "I was."

Channing shrugged. "So what? He hired it done. Just like he hired this
tonight. Only Dave Padway isn't a boy you can hire for long. He used to be
big time, and ten years in clink won't slow him up too much. You better call
Flavin, Rudy. They're liable to find Budge Hanna any time and start searching his room." He laughed. "Flavin wasn't so smart to pay off on Saturday,
too late for the banks."

Marge said, "Why haven't you called the police?"

"With what I have to tell them I'd only scare off the birds. Let 'em find out
for themselves."

She looked at him with level, calculating eyes. "Then you're planning to
do it all by yourself?"

"I've got the whip hand right now. Only you two know I'm alive. But I
know about Budge Hanna's shirt, and the cops will too, pretty soon. Somebody's got to get busy, and the minute he does I'll know for sure who's who
in this little tinpot crime combine."

Marge rose. "That's ridiculous. You're in no condition to handle anyone.
And even if you were—" She left that hanging and crossed to the telephone.

Channing said, "Even if I were, I'm still yellow, is that it? Sure. Stand still,
Rudy. I'm not too yellow or too weak to shoot your ankle off." His face was
grey, gaunt, infinitely tired. He touched the burn on his chin. His cheek
muscles tightened.

He lay still and listened to Marge Krist talking to Max Gandara.

When she was through she went out into the kitchen. Rudy sat down,
glowering sullenly at Channing. He began to tremble, a shallow nervous
vibration. Channing laughed.

"How do you like crime now, kiddie? Fun, isn't it?"

Rudy gave him a lurid and prophetic direction.

Marge came back with hot water and a clean cloth. She wiped Channing's
face, not touching the handkerchief. The wound had stopped bleeding, but

the gash in his side was still oozing. The pad had slipped. Marge took his coat off, waiting while he changed hands with the gun, and then his shoulder clip and shirt. When she saw his body she let the shirt drop and put her hand to her mouth. Channing, sitting up now on the couch, glanced from her to Rudy's slack pale face, and said quietly,

"You see why I don't like fire."

Marge was working gently on his side when the bell rang. "That's the police," she said, and went to the front door. Channing held Rudy with the gun. He heard nothing behind him, but quite suddenly there was a cold object pressing the back of his neck and a voice said quietly,

"Drop it, bud."

It was Joe's voice. He had come in through the kitchen. Channing dropped his gun. The men coming in the front door were not policemen. They were Dave Padway and Jack Flavin.

Flavin closed the door and locked it. Channing nodded, smiling faintly. Dave Padway nodded back. He was a tall, shambling man with white eyes and a long face, like a pinto horse.

"I see I'm still a bum shot," he said.

"Ten years in the can doesn't help your eye, Dave." Channing seemed relaxed and unemotional. "Well, now we're all here we can talk. We can talk about murder."

Marge and Rudy were both staring at Padway. Flavin grinned. "My new business partner, Dave Padway. Dave, meet Marge Krist and Rudy."

Padway glanced at them briefly. His pale eyes were empty of expression. He said, in his soft way, "It's Channing that interests me right now. How much has he told, and who has he told it to?"

Channing laughed, with insolent mockery.

"Fine time to worry about that," Flavin grunted. "Who was it messed up the kill in the first place?"

Padway's eyelids drooped. "Everyone makes mistakes, Jack," he said mildly. Flavin struck a match. The flame trembled slightly.

Rudy said, "Jack. Listen, Jack, this guy says Budge Hanna and his girl were killed. Did you—"

"No. That was Dave's idea."

Padway said, "Any objections to it?"

"Hanna was a good man. He was my contact with all the bars."

"He was a bum. Him and that floozie between them were laying the whole thing in Channing's lap. I heard 'em."

"Okay, okay! I'm just sorry, that's all."

Rudy said, "Jack, honest to God, I don't want to be messed up in killing. I don't mind slugging a watchman, that's okay, and if you had to shoot it out with the cops, well, that's okay too, I guess. But murder, Jack!" He glanced at Channing's scarred body. "Murder, and things like that—" He shook.

Padway muttered, "My God, he's still in diapers."

"Take it easy, kid," Flavin said. "You're in big time now. It's worth getting sick at your stomach a couple times." He looked at Channing, grinning his hard white grin. "You were right when you said Surfside was either an end or a beginning. Dave and I both needed a place to begin again. Start small and grow, like any other business."

Channing nodded. He looked at Rudy. "Hank told you it would be like this, didn't he? You believe him now?"

Rudy repeated his suggestion. His skin was greenish. He sat down and lighted a cigarette. Marge leaned against the wall, watching with bright, narrow-lidded eyes. She was pale. She had said nothing.

Channing said, "Flavin, you were out with Marge the night Hank was killed."

"So what?"

"Did you leave her at all?"

"A couple of times. Not long enough to get out on the pier to kill your brother."

Marge said quietly, "He's right, Mr. Channing."

Channing said, "Where did you go?"

"Ship Cafe, a bunch of bars, dancing. So what?" Flavin gestured impatiently.

Channing said, "How about you, Dave? Did you kill Hank to pay for your brother, and then wait for me to come?"

"If I had," Padway said, "I'd have told you. I'd have made sure you'd come." He stepped closer, looking down. "You don't seem very surprised to see us."

"I'm not surprised at anything any more."

"Yeah." Padway's gun came smoothly into his hand. "At this range I ought to be able to hit you, Chan." Marge Krist caught her breath sharply. Padway said, "No, not here, unless he makes me. Go ahead, Joe."

Joe got busy with the adhesive tape again. This time he did a better job. They wrapped his trussed body in a blanket. Joe picked up the feet. Flavin motioned Rudy to take hold. Rudy hesitated. Padway flicked the muzzle of his gun. Rudy picked up Channing's shoulders. They turned out the lights and carried Channing out to a waiting car. Marge and Rudy Krist walked ahead of Padway, who had forgotten to put away his gun.

III
"I Feel Bad Killin' You . . ."

The room was enormous in the flashlight beams. There were still recognizable signs of its former occupation—dust-blackened, tawdry bunting dangling ragged from the ceiling, a floor worn by the scraping of many feet, a few forgotten tables and chairs, the curling fly-specked photographs of bygone celebrities autographed to "Dear Skinny," an empty, dusty band platform.

One of Padway's men lighted a coal-oil lamp. The boarded windows were carefully reinforced with tarpaper. In one end of the ballroom were stacks of liquor cases built into a huge square mountain. Doors opened into other rooms, black and disused. The place was utterly silent, odorous with the dust and rot of years.

Padway said, "Put him over there." He indicated a camp cot beside a table and a group of chairs. The men carrying Channing dropped him there. The rest straggled in and sat down, lighting cigarettes. Padway said, "Joe, take the Thompson and go upstairs. Yell if anybody looks this way."

Jack Flavin swore briefly. "I told you we weren't tailed, Dave. Cripes, we've driven all over this goddam town to make sure. Can't you relax?"

"Sure, when I'm ready to. You may have hair on your chest, Jack, but it's no bulletproof vest." He went over to the cot and pulled the blanket off Channing. Channing looked up at him, his eyes sunk deep under hooded lids. He was naked to the waist. Padway inspected the two gashes.

"I didn't miss you by much, Chan," he said slowly.

"Enough."

"Yeah." Padway pulled a cigarette slowly out of the pack. "Who did you talk to, Chan, besides Marge Krist? What did you say?"

Channing bared his teeth. It might have been meant for a smile. It was undoubtedly malicious.

Padway put the cigarette in his mouth and got a match out. It was a large kitchen match with a blue head. "You got me puzzled, Chan. You sure have. And it worries me. I can smell copper, but I can't see any. I don't like that, Channing."

"That's tough," Channing said.

"Yeah. It may be." Padway struck the match.

Rudy Krist rose abruptly and went off into the shadows. No one else moved. Marge Krist was hunched up on a blanket near Flavin. Her eyes were brilliant green under her tumbled red hair.

Dave Padway held the match low over Channing's eyes. There was no draft, no tremor in his hand. The flame was a perfect triangle, gold and blue. Padway said somberly,

"I don't trust you, Chan. You were a good cop. You were good enough to take me once, and you were good enough to take my brother, and he was a better man than me. I don't trust this setup, Chan. I don't trust you."

Flavin said impatiently, "Why didn't you for godsake kill him the first time? You're to blame for this mess, Dave. If you hadn't loused it up—okay, okay! The guy's crazy afraid of fire. Look at him now. Put it to him, Dave. He'll talk."

"Will he?" said Padway. "Will he?" He lowered the match. Channing screamed. Padway lighted his cigarette and blew out the match. "Will you talk, Chan?"

Channing said hoarsely, "Offer me the right coin, Dave. Give me the man who killed my brother, and I'll tell you where you stand."

Padway stared at him with blank light eyes, and then he began to laugh, quietly, with a terrible humor.

"Tie him down, Mack," he said, "and bring the matches over here."

The room was quiet, except for Channing's breathing. Rudy Krist sat apart from the others, smoking steadily, his hands never still. The three gunsels bent with scowling concentration over a game of blackjack. Marge Krist had not moved since she sat down. Perhaps twenty minutes had passed. Channing's corded body was spotted with small vicious marks.

Dave Padway dropped the empty matchbox. He sighed and leaned over, slapping Channing lightly on the cheek. Channing opened his eyes.

"You going to talk, Chan?"

Channing's head moved, not much, from right to left.

Jack Flavin swore. "Dave, the guy's crazy afraid of fire. If he'd had anything to tell he'd have told it." His shirt was open, the space around his feet littered with cigarette ends. His harsh terrier face had no laughter in it now. He watched Padway obliquely, his lids hooded.

"Maybe," said Padway. "Maybe not. We got a big deal on tonight, Jack. It's our first step toward the top. Channing read your receipt, remember. He knows about that. He knows a lot of people out here. Maybe he has a deal on, and maybe it isn't with the cops. Maybe it isn't supposed to break until tonight. Maybe it'll break us when it does."

Channing laughed, a dry husky mockery.

Flavin got up, scraping his chair angrily. "Listen, Dave, you getting chicken or something? Looks to me like you've got a fixation on this bird."

"Looks to me, Jack, like nobody ever taught you manners."

The room became perfectly still. The men at the table put their cards down slowly, like men playing cards in a dream. Marge Krist rose silently and moved towards the cot.

Channing whispered, "Take it easy, boys. There's no percentage in a shroud." He watched them, his eyes holding a deep, cruel glint. It was something new, something born within the last quarter of an hour. It changed, subtly, his whole face, the lines of it, the shape of it. "You've got a business here, a going concern. Or maybe you haven't. Maybe you're bait for the meat wagon. I talked, boys, oh yes, I talked. Give me Hank's killer, and I'll tell you who."

Flavin said, "Can't you forget that? The guy jumped."

Channing shook his head.

Padway said softly, "Suppose you're right, Chan. Suppose you get the killer. What good does that do you?"

"I'm not a cop any more. I don't care how much booze you run. All I want is the guy that killed Hank."

Jack Flavin laughed. It was not a nice sound.

"Dave knows I keep a promise. Besides, you can always shoot me in the back."

Flavin said, "This is crazy. You haven't really hurt the guy, Dave. Put it to him. He'll talk."

"His heart would quit first." Padway smiled almost fondly at Channing. "He's got his guts back in. That's good to know, huh, Chan?"

"Yeah."

"But bad, too. For both of us."

"Go ahead and kill me, Dave, if you think it would help any."

Flavin said, with elaborate patience, "Dave, the man is crazy. Maybe he wants publicity. Maybe he's trying to chisel himself back on the force. Maybe he's a masochist. But he's nuts. I don't believe he talked to anybody. Either make him talk, or shoot him. Or I will."

"Will you, now?" Padway asked.

Channing said, "What are you so scared of, Flavin?"

Flavin snarled and swung his hand. Padway caught it, pulling Flavin around. He said, "Seems to me whoever killed Hank has made us all a lot of trouble. He's maybe busted us wide open. I'd kind of like to know who did it, and why. We were working together then, Jack, remember? And nobody told me about any cop named Channing."

Flavin shook him off. "The kid committed suicide. And don't try manhandling me, Dave. It was my racket, remember. I let you in."

"Why," said Padway mildly, "that's so, ain't it?" He hit Flavin in the mouth so quickly that his fist made a blur in the air. Flavin fell, clawing automatically at his armpit. Padway's men rose from the table and covered him. Flavin dropped his hand. He lay still, his eyes slitted and deadly.

Marge Krist slid down silently beside Channing's cot. She might have been fainting, leaning forward against it, her hands out of sight. She was not fainting. Channing felt her working at his wrists.

Flavin said, "Rudy. Come here."

Rudy Krist came into the circle of lamplight. He looked like a small boy dreaming a nightmare and knowing he can't wake up.

Flavin said, "All right, Dave. You're boss. Go ahead and give Channing his killer." He looked at Rudy, and everybody else looked, too, except the men covering Flavin.

Rudy Krist's eyes widened, until white showed all around the green. He stopped, staring at the hard, impassive faces turned toward him.

Flavin said contemptuously, "He turned you soft, Rudy. You spilled over and then you didn't have the nerve to go through with it. You knew what would happen to you. So you shoved Hank off the pier to save your own hide."

Rudy made a stifled, catlike noise. He leaped suddenly down onto Flavin. Padway motioned to his boys to hold it. Channing cried out desperately, "Don't do anything. Wait! Dave, drag him off."

Rudy had Flavin by the throat. He was frothing slightly. Flavin writhed, jerking his heels against the floor. Suddenly there was a sharp slamming noise from underneath Rudy's body. Rudy bent his back, as though he were trying to double over backwards. He let go of Flavin. He relaxed, his head falling sleepily against Flavin's shoulder.

Channing rolled off the cot, scrambling toward Flavin.

Flavin fired again, twice, so rapidly the shots sounded like one. One of Padway's boys knelt down and bowed forward over his knees like a praying Jap. Another of Padway's men fell. The second shot clipped Padway, tearing the shoulder pad of his suit.

Channing grabbed Flavin's wrist from behind.

"Okay," said Padway grimly. "Hold it, everybody."

Before he got the words out a small sharp crack came from behind the cot. Flavin relaxed. He lay looking up into Channing's face with an expression of great surprise, as though the third eye just opened in his forehead gave him a completely new perspective.

Marge Krist stood green-eyed and deadly with a little pearl-handled revolver smoking in her hand.

Padway turned toward her slowly. Channing's mouth twitched dourly. He hardly glanced at the girl, but rolled the boy's body over carefully.

Channing said, "Did you kill Hank?"

Rudy whispered, "Honest to God, no."

"Did Flavin kill him?"

"I don't know . . ." Tears came in Rudy's eyes. "Hank," he whispered, "I wish . . ." The tears kept running out of his eyes for several seconds after he was dead.

By that time the police had come into the room, from the dark disused doorways, from behind the stacked liquor. Max Gandara said,

"Everybody hold still."

Dave Padway put his hands up slowly, his eyes at first wide with surprise and then narrow and ice-hard. His gunboy did the same, first dropping his rod with a heavy clatter on the bare floor.

Padway said, "They've been here all the time."

Channing sat up stiffly. "I hoped they were. I didn't know whether Max would play with me or not."

"You dirty double-crossing louse."

"I feel bad, crossing up an ape like you, Dave. You treated me so square, up there by Hyperion." Channing raised his voice. "Max, look out for the boy with the chopper."

Gandara said, "I had three men up there. They took him when he went up, real quiet."

Marge Krist had come like a sleepwalker around the cot. She was close to Padway. Quite suddenly she fainted. Padway caught her, so that she shielded his body, and his gun snapped into his hand.

Max Gandara said, "Don't shoot. Don't anybody shoot."

"That's sensible," said Padway softly.

Channing's hand, on the floor, slid over the gun Flavin wasn't using any more. Then, very quickly, he threw himself forward into the table with the lamp on it.

A bullet slammed into the wood, through it, and past his ear, and then Channing fired twice, deliberately, through the flames.

Channing rose and walked past the fire. He moved stiffly, limping, but there was a difference in him. Padway was down on one knee, eyes shut and teeth clenched against the pain of a shattered wrist. Marge Krist was still standing. She was staring with stricken eyes at the hole in her white forearm and the pattern of brilliant red threads spreading from it.

Max Gandara caught Channing. "You crazy—"

Channing hit him, hard and square. His face didn't change expression. "I owe you that one, Max. And before you start preaching the sanctity of womanhood, you better pry out a couple of those slugs that just missed me. You'll find they came from Miss Krist's pretty little popgun—the same one that killed her boy friend, Jack Flavin." He went over and tilted Marge Krist's face to his, quite gently. "You came out of your faint in a hurry, didn't you, sweetheart?"

She brought up her good hand and tried to claw his eye out.

Channing laughed. He pushed her into the arms of a policeman. "It'll all come out in the wash. Meantime, there are the bullets from Marge's gun. The fact that she had a gun at all proves she was in on the gang. They'd have searched her, if all that pious stuff about poor Rudy's evil ways had been on the level. She was a little surprised about Padway and sore because Flavin had kept it from her. But she knew which was the better man, all right. She was going along with Padway, and she shot Flavin to keep his mouth shut about Hank, and to make sure he didn't get Padway by accident. Flavin was a gutty little guy, and he came close to doing just that. Marge untied me because she hoped I'd get shot in the confusion, or start trouble on my own account. If you hadn't come in, Max, she'd probably have shot me herself. She didn't want any more fussing about Hank Channing, and with me and Flavin dead she was in the clear."

Gandara said with ugly stubbornness, "Sounded to me like Flavin made a pretty good case against Rudy."

"Sure, sure. He was down on the ground with half his teeth out and three guys holding guns on him."

Marge Krist was sitting now on the cot, while somebody worked over her with a first aid kit. Channing stood in front of her.

"You've done a good night's work, Marge. You killed Rudy just as much as you did Flavin, or Hank. Rudy had decent stuff in him. You forced him into the game, but Hank was turning him soft. You killed Hank."

Channing moved closer to her. She looked up at him, her green eyes meeting his dark ones, both of them passionate and cruel.

"You're a smart girl, Marge. You and your mealy-mouthed hypocrisy. I know now what you meant when you accused Rudy of being afraid to be questioned. Flavin couldn't kill Hank by himself. He wasn't big enough, and Hank wasn't that dumb. He didn't trust Flavin. But you, Marge, sure, he trusted you. He'd stand on a dark pier at midnight and talk to you, and never notice who was sneaking up behind with a blackjack." He bent over her. "A smart girl, Marge, and a pretty one. I don't think I'll want to stand outside the window while you die."

"I wish I'd killed you, too," she whispered. "By God, I wish I'd killed you too!"

Channing nodded. He went over and sat down wearily. He looked exhausted and weak, but his eyes were alive.

"Somebody give me a cigarette," he said. He struck the match himself. The smoke tasted good.

It was his first smoke in ten years.

The Case
of the Frozen Corpses

Ray Cummings

I

Hell's Refrigerator

My name is George Roberts. I'm senior partner—senior by four years in age and about eight inches of height—of the firm of Roberts & Co., Investigators. My sister Dorothy is the "Co." That's the legal side of it, anyway. But of actuality this dynamic sister of mine is anything but a second fiddle. No man—in this or any other line of business—ever had a better partner. I am twenty-six. A big blond fellow. Slow-witted, Dot says. Maybe so; but it seems to me I use a man's method of thinking logically. Dot doesn't exactly think—she just acts by feminine intuition or something. She's a small girl; slim, black-haired, clever, quick-witted. And I'm telling you, she can be a mighty hard customer when anyone angles her into a tough spot. She's about as gentle as an angry lion when she really gets mad.

Well, that's us. Now for the weird and gruesome case of the Frozen Corpses. It began, actually, about a week before Dot and I got into it. A man named Bob Allen—chief chemist of the Houghton Chemical Company, here in New York City—had been murdered. Stabbed in the back; found, one night, in the laboratory of the company's plant, where he had been doing some experimenting.

The police went to work on it, but they got nowhere. Then one afternoon, Dot and I got a telephone call from Ralph J. Houghton, owner of the Houghton Chemical Company. "I understand Allen met your sister socially, a few months ago," Houghton told me over the phone. "He remembered her very well. He told me about her—well, under rather peculiar circumstances, just before he was murdered. Will you come up? I want to talk to you about it."

That decided us. We grabbed our little roadster and drove from our downtown office, up the West Side ramp to Houghton's home on lower Riverside Drive. It was about six o'clock—a late summer afternoon, sultry, oppressively hot. The butler admitted us into the somber, luxurious library. We found Ralph Houghton pacing the room nervously. He had summoned his company lawyer, John Tremaine—a large, handsome man of forty-odd —there to meet us. Houghton was a middle-aged, very distinguished look- ing man. Fifty perhaps, with iron-grey hair and a neat black mustache, solid black, suggesting that he dyed it to make him look younger. All his appear- ance gave one that impression. He was clad in an immaculate white linen suit; his neat bow tie was youthfully red and blue and above his sport shoes you could see red and blue clocks on his socks.

"Thanks for your promptness," Houghton greeted. He introduced us to Tremaine, his lawyer. Then we all sat down.

"It's quite possible that Mr. Roberts and his sister are not familiar with the case," Tremaine said. "Are you, Mr. Roberts?"

I shook my head. "No. Not particularly. We've been pretty busy—"

Then Tremaine began sketching, with a most admirable legal succinct- ness, just what the police were known to be doing. Which was just about nothing—no need anyway, for me to go into details. Bob Allen's murder, as it turned out, was only a sideline.

"What was it Bob Allen so mysteriously said about me?" Dot put in sud- denly.

"I was coming to that," Tremaine said. "You tell them, Mr. Houghton. You have the first-hand knowledge."

The portly, white-clad manufacturing chemist was still pacing the room. "At eleven o'clock the night that Allen was found murdered at the plant," Houghton told us, "he telephoned me. He seemed tense, excited. 'I've found something,' he said. Or words to that effect."

"He was phoning from the company laboratory?" Dot asked.

"Yes," Houghton agreed. "And then he said: 'I've just worked it out—on a small scale, of course. And only in theory. It could be dastardly—in prac- tice—murderous. As the start of a double chemical reaction—there are two salts—' The telephone clicked, with an interrupted connection. That, I think now, was just a normal coincidence. A few seconds later, I heard him again. During the brief interruption, he had evidently changed his mind. 'No need telling you now,' he said hurriedly. 'I'll be right up.' And then he mentioned having met a girl detective. That's you, Miss Roberts. He said we might need you and your brother." Houghton smiled faintly. "Now that I've met you," he added, "I think maybe he was right. But, with the tragedy—so many police interviews—I forgot you until today. Then I told Tremaine, and we agreed . . ."

"That reference to you, Miss Roberts," the lawyer interrupted, "could well have been Allen's last words. He didn't arrive here that night. Mr. Houghton phoned him at midnight. The laboratory phone didn't answer—then later in the night we went there and found him."

It made the murder of Allen at least seem understandable. He had discovered—in theory at least—some mysterious chemical process. Something with two salts that had murderous potentialities. And he had been killed, doubtless, to prevent his telling what he had found.

Was it some impending plot against Houghton? The chemical manufacturer quite evidently feared so. I had a premonition then that he was right—though Heaven knows none of us could imagine that the damnable thing would strike so quickly.

A woman's voice interrupted us: "Oh—excuse me, gentlemen. Ralph, I thought we were going to the Country Club for dinner."

Houghton's young wife, Gloria, stood in the library doorway. And the reason for Houghton's obvious desire to look young was instantly apparent. Gloria Houghton—as we found out later—had been an actress. Her name had been Gloria Zorn—and she had married Houghton about a year ago. We saw her now as a tall blonde woman of about thirty. Expensively dressed; lavishly jeweled, a flawless, baby-doll face that didn't seem particularly characterful; a figure full, rounded, voluptuous—beauty of a purely physical quality that one could well imagine would enthrall the rich, middle-aged Houghton.

As I regarded her now while she advanced, graciously acknowledging her husband's introduction of us, a figure appeared behind her. Involuntarily I gasped. Here, behind the youthful, beautiful Gloria Houghton was a man so weirdly gruesome in aspect that it made me suck in my breath. It was Leo Zorn, Gloria's brother. He was a squat, thick-set barrel-chested hunchback —a man of perhaps thirty. He had been employed as a chemist in Houghton's plant, as we later learned. And through his contact with some obscure, malevolent chemicals, disease had attacked him. What had perhaps been a rugged, handsome face, now was dead-white, with pinched bluish lips and puffed, diseased-looking flesh, in which moist blackish sores lay like little pits of horror.

At the doorway, as though he seemed surprised at so many of us there, without waiting for introduction, he retreated; to stand like a massive, diseased ape, out in the foyer, peering in at us, grimly.

The portly Houghton was closing off our conversation; assuring his wife that he would start for the Country Club in a moment. Dot was saying something to Tremaine, the lawyer. And then the horror burst upon us.

An exclamation from Houghton made us all stare at him. It was a startled gasp; and in the middle of a sentence he checked himself. For a second or two he stood as though numbed by surprise. Then terror swept his face. And suddenly I saw that he was livid, blue-lipped. His teeth were chattering. From head to foot he was shaking, as though with a chill.

Heaven knows I find it difficult to describe the weird thing. Certainly no more than thirty seconds were involved. The stricken Houghton had a moment before becoming red-faced, perspiring in the oppressive heat of the room. But he was blue-white, shaking with chill now.

And we all felt it—a wave of coldness, as though a huge refrigerator door had been opened, and its cold interior air blasted at us. Coldness, like an explosive blast, coming from Houghton!

There were a few more seconds while he tottered on his feet, his hands wildly fumbling. Then he fell; twitched feebly; seemed to stiffen. . . .

On the floor before our horrified gaze the blue-white body of the dead Ralph Houghton lay frozen as though it had been packed in ice! And from it a wisp of vapor momentarily rose—a white vaporlike steam that briefly streamed up, condensed in the warm air of the room and was gone!

II
Bridge of Death

It was nearly seven-thirty that evening when Dot and I had grabbed a bit of supper and gotten back to our office. I needn't describe the scene of turmoil—the arrival of the police—up there at Houghton's home. We stayed for a while, and then we got away—came back to the office to get our automatics which we hadn't taken with us.

Dot's theory is always to keep away from the police; not even for her and I to talk much—but always to act quickly. She remembered now that the murdered Bob Allen had mentioned that he had a girl cousin who was a bookkeeper in a laundry. A girl named Anne Johnson.

"I think we ought to go see her," Dot declared. "Allen wasn't a fellow who cared much for girls—I doped that out pretty quick the one time I met him. He discovered something—probably after a lot of secret research—found it at last, that night in the laboratory. When a man has anything that really worries him on his mind, he's just got to tell it to some woman. Allen didn't have any girl, except this cousin—"

There's feminine logic for you!

"And you think his cousin Anne Johnson will of course know all about it?" I retorted. "She wouldn't have told the police by now, would she? Just waiting for you—"

Dot grinned. "Well, I think we ought to go to that laundry anyhow. You were looking at the laundry mark on Houghton's linen coat, up there a while ago? Well, so was I. This girl Anne Johnson works in a laundry—"

She had something there. I had been interested to know what laundry Houghton's white linen suit and other clothes might have come from. But you couldn't tell that from a laundry mark. It tells the laundry to which customer the garment belongs, but that's all. And most certainly I didn't want to ask such questions from the Houghton household—not with that Gloria and her diseased brother to find out that I was probing such an angle.

And then, as often, my little sister astonished me. She was rummaging in the pocket of her sport jacket. "Take a look at this, George. Didn't want to show you before—just in case we were being followed." Even now in the seclusion of our office, she cast a furtive look around and instinctively lowered her voice. "I ducked up to Houghton's bedroom," she added, "while the police had everybody downstairs. Nobody saw me—and look what I found in the waste basket."

She displayed a torn bit of wrapping paper on which was a pasted label: *From the Bridge Hand Laundry.* Followed by the laundry's address.

"And that," Dot said, "is where the Johnson girl works."

A clear connection! What it meant I could only imagine. But I knew a bit more about it than Dot did, at that, because I was present when the frozen corpse of Houghton was disrobed by the police—I saw his linen suit, stiffened by cold; his underwear, limp now and moist, with strange little flakes of melting ice just vanishing in the heat of the room. . . .

We drove down to the Bridge Hand Laundry, parked our car a few blocks away, and went forward on foot. It was now nearly eight-thirty. The laundry seemed to occupy the whole of a big wooden structure, in what is certainly a disheveled, dilapidated part of the city—that tangle of low-lying streets of slums, with the streams of traffic on the Brooklyn Bridge roaring close over the rooftops.

The darkness of a hot, sullen night was just gathering. The shabby streets were heavy with smells; crowded and noisy with children, pushcarts and

pedestrians. This was Saturday night. The laundry evidently had been working late; girls were pouring out now as Dot and I approached. Then we had
a bit of luck. A man passed us and accosted a group of the laundry girls—a
young fellow, sort of weak-chinned.

"Has Anne come out yet?" we heard him ask.

"Anne who?" one of the girls retorted.

"Anne Johnson—the bookkeeper."

She hadn't; and all we had to do was keep the young fellow in sight to
locate her. It was easy. He met her at the door, put his arm briefly around
her, and they started off together. Whether we would have accosted them
or not, I don't know. We didn't; because as they passed us, we heard him
say:

". . . something I've just got to tell you, Anne."

He certainly looked worried, apprehensive. More than that—furtive. I can
tell a crook when I see him. This fellow might be on the level with this girl
—but he wasn't apt to be on the level with anything else. That's about the
way I doped it out. He began telling her something as they walked along. It
was damnably tantalizing because we didn't dare get close enough to try and
hear it. But whatever it was, it frightened Anne Johnson.

We followed them back toward City Hall, and up on the pedestrian walk
of the bridge. It's easy to follow anyone when you've got a girl with you.
Nobody figures a detective will take his girl along. We sauntered fairly close
behind them. On this hot summer night there were quite a few pedestrians
walking between New York and Brooklyn. Anne Johnson and the young
man were walking swiftly. I recall now that the girl looked hot.

We had about reached the middle of the central span, high over the dark,
sullen river where, far down, the lights of passing boats showed, when
suddenly we saw the girl's companion seize her and force her to a bench.
Dot and I, at the moment were a good two hundred feet behind them. And
abruptly we realized that they were struggling with each other. That was
what it looked like at first; then the girl jumped to her feet, with the man
plucking at her clothes, tearing at her filmy summer dress! A fiend suddenly
crazed, so that he would attack a girl here in this public place? It looked so.
She screamed. Then we saw that he had thrown her down; and he crouched
over her, with pawing hands stripping her garments from her so that in a
moment she lay nude beside him.

It was dim, there on the pedestrian walk close under the bridge parapet.
Dot and I were dashing forward. Other pedestrians were coming. By chance
a group of young girls were nearest. They rushed forward; then scattered in
terror, screaming.

In a second it was a scene of turmoil. The nude girl was lying on the bridge. We had a vague glimpse of the man as he suddenly gathered up her clothes and cast them over the parapet. They fluttered; went down into the darkness of the river. . . .

In the dim chaos of milling people, Anne Johnson lay naked. She was only half conscious; her face livid, blue-lipped; her teeth chattering with a suddering chill that shook all her virginal little body as though by a convulsion!

"Where's a policeman?" someone shouted. "Don't they have policemen on this damn bridge?"

They didn't. There was no one here in the confused, excited group to exercise authority, save Dot and I. We shoved the people back; got to the naked girl; bent over her.

"Your coat," Dot gasped. "Good Lord, look at her—she's freezing!"

Her flesh, from shoulder to knee, was moist. Pallid flesh, with all the blood gone from its surface.

"Coat wouldn't do any good," I murmured. I knelt; began rubbing her flesh, and Dot helped me, while the crowd, increasing every moment, stood gasping with awed silence. Moist flesh, icy to the touch—numbed by cold. She didn't seem quite unconscious. In a moment her eyelids fluttered up; her blue, quivering lips seemed gratefully trying to smile at our efforts. Then she drifted off again—numbed into a daze of semi-consciousness.

"If we only had some whiskey," I murmured. And Dot jumped to her feet. "Whiskey," she called at the crowd. "She needs a drink—who's got a drink?"

A man produced a flask. We forced some of the whiskey down the girl's throat. She gulped at it gratefully, and it seemed to revive her a little. And then from the crowd somebody shouted:

"Where the hell is the damned fiend who attacked her? Where is he?"

Hindsight is very easy! It's simple enough to look back and see what you might have done, that would have been better than what you did!

Vehemently Dot and I would have liked to have our hands on that young fellow. But in the excitement—our horror, because we knew so much more about this thing than did the crowd—we had thought only of emergency first aid to the girl who might be dying. The crowd considered the man a fiend who had attacked her. But we knew why he had stripped the girl.

He was gone now. In the turmoil, the excitement, the dimness, I can realize how easily he got away. The passing streams of automobiles had stopped and tangled the traffic. People rushed to them, shouting that the police were needed. And an ambulance must be summoned. . . . Almost everyone was trying to get closer to the naked girl who was lying in the crowd. But there were others, on foot and in vehicles, who were going shoreward; and nobody paid much attention to them.

Anne Johnson did not die. Within half an hour she had revived. Obviously there was no need of an ambulance—nothing the matter with her save terror and a deadly chill from which now, this hot summer night, she was recovering. The police came. An ambulance came and went away. There was complete confusion. . . .

"I'll beat it," I murmured to Dot presently. "You're going to stay with her?"

"Yes. She's agreed to let me take her home in a taxi, when we get through answering police questions." Dot lowered her voice still further. "I can drag a lot of things out of her when I get her alone."

Anne was huddled now in a sheet and blanket which the ambulance had left. A taxi had been sent for.

"We'll contact at home," I told Dot. "Some time around midnight?"

"Okay," Dot murmured. As always when we part, I tweaked her nose. There's an affection between me and my little sister which, Heaven knows, in our line of business, doesn't get much chance for expression. I'm always a bit apprehensive over Dot when we're working separately on a case. It may have been premonition this time. A little sinking sensation plucked at my middle when I left her there in the turmoil of the bridge.

Clues get cold very quickly. That's an axiom that Dot and I always follow. We had already had plenty of clues from the stricken Anne Johnson. The police would be after those clues later in the night; but I went after them now, heading back for the Bridge Hand Laundry. It wasn't much of a walk; but enough so that I had time to sort in my mind what we had learned. . . .

The young fellow who had just escaped us was named Peter Duffy. He was Anne Johnson's fiance. Whatever this Duffy might know of the gruesome affair, certainly it seemed that Anne knew very little. She had met Duffy tonight. He had told her he was going away. Where, or why, so far under Dot's questions, she had maintained that she did not know. Walking on the bridge tonight, the girl had been hot. Perspiring from the exercise. Then suddenly she had felt unaccountably cold. Her undergarments, dank against her, abruptly were so cold that they had seemed sticking to her numbed flesh. That was about all she remembered, except that Duffy had torn off her clothes.

Why had he done it? The answer to that was easy: to save her from death. And to have done that so promptly, so effectively, I figured he must have had guilty knowledge of the real deadliness of whatever it was which was attacking this girl he loved. And then he had thrown her garments into the river. Why? To keep them from remaining as evidence of what had occurred!

As I pondered the weird circumstances, I was walking swiftly shoreward. In the sodden heat of the oppressive night, I found myself freely perspiring —my underwear dank and cold against my flesh. Against all reason, the damnable thought set my heart pounding. And then another thought stabbed at me. I recalled that a week ago, Dot had been annoyed at our uptown laundry for overcharging us. She had said that Norah, our maid, recommended that the big downtown laundries were cheaper. Where had Norah sent our laundry, this last time? I did not know. And probably, Dot did not know either. And then I pondered—what did we know of Norah, this maid we had so recently hired?

The thoughts were vaguely terrifying. The heat of my perspiring body suddenly was horrible. And I thought of Dot, there on the bridge, with her filmy chemise wet from perspiration. . . .

III
Fire that Freezes

The big wooden building which housed the Bridge Hand Laundry was dark when I got there now, with only a small light burning in one of its lower rooms at the side and back. Far more than when Dot and I came here before, I was interested in this laundry now. The thing was beginning to hook together. Peter Duffy—so Anne Johnson had told us—was a solicitor for the laundry. His job was to get new accounts. And he had gotten the family of Ralph J. Houghton for customers only a few days ago. The first bundle of the finished work had been delivered to the Houghton residence just this afternoon!

For a moment I stood across the street, gazing at the big wooden structure which housed the laundry. Then I crossed; tried the small lower front door. It was locked. There was a bell, and I rang. After an interval, I rang again. It happened, as I was standing there, that my gaze went toward the back of the dark side yard. There seemed a blob back there in the shadows of the building. A man watching me? It seemed so, for suddenly as I turned to move toward him, the figure ducked and ran. Had he decamped, or gone into a back door from which he had emerged to see who was ringing?

I rang again. Then presently I heard footsteps. The door opened, disclosing a small, palish thin man; the proprietor, as he told me, who was working alone here tonight on his accounts. I'm a pretty good judge of character. I was convinced within a minute or two that this fellow—his name was Franklin—was on the level. He went into a panic when I told him bluntly that I was a detective working on a murder case. But that was nothing compared to the horror that shook him when he realized from my questions that it was the gruesome "Frozen Corpse"—as the radio was already calling it—death of Ralph J. Houghton; and that his laundry was involved.

We were in his small back office, dim with just a spot of hooded light over his desk. The door here into the dark backyard was open for air, this hot summer night. Another door opened to the main ironing room. It was dark in there, with the white ironing rolls, the steam tables and the white padded ironing boards eerie blobs, like ghosts in the darkness.

To me the damn place was weird, and I wasn't at all sure but what there was a danger here. That figure lurking in the yard—someone watching me? I believed so now. It hadn't been Franklin, but a much thicker-set figure. I don't get the jitters very easily, but I kept my hand in the general proximity of my underarm holster, just the same.

I can't say either that my automatic gave me much comfort. The close air here was moist and heavy with the smell of laundered garments. And as I stared at the pale little proprietor who was sweating with nervousness under my questions, I couldn't help feeling that the thing might strike again . . . a wave of frigid coldness, with Franklin turning into a frozen corpse before my eyes . . . and again I was conscious of my own perspiration, with my undershirt sticking dankly to my chest and back.

"Peter Duffy?" Franklin was saying. "Well, I only hired him a week ago. But he seems like a nice young fellow. Got me several new accounts—a real hustler. I'm a humanitarian, Mr. Roberts. Just because a lad's in trouble—"

"In trouble?" I prompted.

The complete answer to that was startling. Peter Duffy had been brought here by Anne Johnson, trying to get him a job.

"They told me the truth," Franklin was saying. "I liked that. Duffy said right away—when I questioned him—that he'd been fired from the Houghton Chemical Company. He certainly changed his line of business. He's a chemist, Anne says."

No argument but what that was startling! Then presently Franklin showed me Duffy's clothes locker, in a corner of the big ironing room. The locker was open, with one of Duffy's jackets hanging there. I searched it.

"What—what's that?" Franklin tremblingly demanded as I brought out a crumpled slip of paper. The laundry proprietor was getting the drift of things now. "My God, you don't mean murder has been planned, here in my place by one of my employees?"

In the litter of Duffy's pockets I had found the crumpled paper. It was partly torn—a fragment of penciled memorandum:

NH_4Cl plus KNO_3 Then at minus 28° F. CO_2 by—

The diagonal tear down the middle had amputated the rest of it. But lower down, where the diagonal widened, there was another fragment:

. . . . *thus without usual needed pressure, minus* 28° *F. freezes the* CO_2 *with resultant at least minus* 200° *F. for a brief*—

That was all. "What's it mean?" Franklin murmured in terrified awe.

"Is this in Duffy's handwriting?" I countered.

He inspected it. "Why yes—looks so. What—"

To him it was a cryptogram, but it wasn't exactly so to me. I'm far from a professional chemist; but I had a lot of chemistry in college. NH_4Cl—that's ammonium chloride; mixed, in this case, with KNO_3, which is potassium nitrate, commonly called saltpeter. When mixed in the presence of moisture —you get a reaction so suddenly absorbing heat that the mixture will freeze! Your receptacle will freeze to the table on which it stands!

Two salts! Young Bob Allen, just before he was murdered, had mentioned two salts that could be dastardly—murderous!

But that was only a reaction to produce a sub-freezing temperature. And then Duffy's memorandum said: CO_2 freezing without pressure, giving minus 200°! Here was the murderous process which Duffy so evidently had perfected. CO_2—that's carbon dioxide. When it freezes under pressure it produces what now as a trade term is called "dry ice," a mysterious substance of such a deadly cold that one may not touch it without danger of freezing the flesh!

Dimly I could envisage now the diabolic process, not to produce dry ice, but something chemically akin to it. . . . Undergarments impregnated with those two salts and with CO_2 and God knows what other ingredients. The moisture of perspiration . . . a sudden chemical reaction to produce a sub-freezing temperature. And this freezing, instantly to progress to the second reaction with the CO_2. A drop to minus 200°! A momentary drop— but enough to freeze human flesh and organs into gruesome, sudden death, with the heart stopping from the shock, even before the blood stream was fully chilled. . . .

"But what is it?" Franklin demanded again. "Is that a formula?"

"A formula for murder," I said.

Where had Duffy worked upon his diabolical lethal scheme? Not here in the laundry; that would hardly be practical.

"Queer thing," Franklin said suddenly, "we were late delivering that bundle of laundry to Houghton's home today. It was finished and ready to go out last evening, but it got mislaid . . . I'm trying to help you, Mr. Roberts. My God, I—to think that my laundry—"

"You are helping me very much," I assured him. . . . Duffy, I could imagine now, had taken the bundle of clothes out of here last night, and returned

THE CASE OF THE FROZEN CORPSES

it today, with Houghton's undergarments prepared for his death. . . . Duffy, who had been fired from the chemical company, and had a grudge against Houghton? Maybe that. But it didn't seem enough. For money then —money from the real fiend planning and executing this damnable thing? But what of Anne Johnson, who had so narrowly escaped being another victim? Why did they try to murder her?

Then I found what seemed still another clue. On the floor of Duffy's locker there was a bit of paper ash—a tiny bit of paper which he had evidently burned and dropped here. The writing on it still was dimly visible —a few words of an address in upper New York City—not obliterated because the graphite used in pencil leads is a mineral and will not burn. Duffy should have remembered that and crumpled the ashes!

I think that perhaps in another moment or two I would have left the laundry. I was eager to investigate this address. And even more eager to contact Dot. She was on the main trail—through Anne Johnson we might be able to nab Duffy.

I was just saying goodbye to Franklin, when in a momentary silence between us, distinctly we heard a sound. A thumping, bumping scrape, as though some heavy object had fallen. It was in the cellar underneath us. The cellar door was beside us, standing partly open. Automatic in hand, with a gestured warning to the petrified Franklin, I went down the stairs on a run— down into the dimness of a big littered cellar. It was an empty barrel which had fallen and rolled—fallen from a big pile of barrels, boxes and rubbish.

And what the fallen barrel had disclosed struck me numb so that I stood gasping. Another frozen corpse! Within the pile of rubbish the nude body of a woman was buried! The ghastly grey-black face stared up at me. A woman I had never seen before—a beautiful face, framed by flowing dark hair. Her torso was visible, but the legs were hidden by the rubbish. Voluptuous breasts, shoulders, abdomen—flesh blackened by the horrible sub-zero cold!

I had no more than a second or two to gaze at the ghastly thing. Then, from down in the litter of rubbish that still partly concealed the nude corpse, there was a flash. A sizzling, hissing, burning, sustained flash, as of a train and a pile of gunpowder suddenly ignited. And now I was aware of the smell of gasoline. . . .

That gasoline-soaked pile of rubbish went up into a sheet of flame. I staggered back, jumped for the stairs. The whole cellar was a glare of blinding lurid flame and blurring smoke. But through it I had a glimpse of a moving figure. A man who had been hiding here—a man who like myself was almost trapped, and who was climbing to the safety of a window near him. I had no chance to shoot at him. I was staggering backward at the stairs. And I turned and stumbled wildly up them, with a roaring inferno of flame and smoke following me.

But with that fleeting glimpse I had recognized the other figure. Not Peter Duffy! It was a squat, massive misshapen form. Humped shoulders. A face of bloated, diseased flesh!

Gloria Houghton's brother! The diseased Leo Zorn!

I had come staggering from the cellar. Franklin was standing confused in the center of the room. From the opened cellar door, smoke and flame were pouring. I jumped for the door; tried to close it, but the smoke and fire drove me back.

"My—my records," Franklin gasped. "My cash—I've got money in the drawer there."

He stumbled for it; but I seized him. "Come on, you fool—no time now—"

I was pulling him toward the door; and for a moment, in his confused panic, he resisted me. And suddenly, while we were still near the center of the room, the sprinkling system went off! Pipes holding water under pressure were threaded along the low ceiling. The heat from the cellar doorway had melted the soft metal fuses of their vents.

It was impotent protection in this inflammable wooden structure, against such a fire as this! But it did its best. From a dozen vents overhead, sprays of water descended upon us—a drenching torrent through which in the heat and smoke and licking flames, we staggered for the door.

Heat? In those weird seconds as I gripped the drenched terrified Franklin, suddenly a wave of cold from him struck at me. In horror I cast him loose, and for another second or two, I stood staring as he tottered and fell, with ghastly white face and blue chattering lips. Then his twitching body stiffened. At my feet he lay, another of the ghastly frozen corpses, with the water from the overhead sprinklers freezing upon him!

Choking in the smoke, with licking hissing flames from the cellar driving me back, I staggered from the room.

IV

Dot Stalks Terror

At about eleven o'clock that same evening, Dot stood on a street of the lower West Side—the west Twenties over by the Hudson River. There was little traffic; hardly a passing vehicle and only a few pedestrians. The street was dim; overhead the sky was grey-black with threatening clouds, and the hot summer night was more oppressive than ever.

Dot was watching the house in which Anne Johnson lived—a big dilapidated structure, in a solid row which stood well back from the street. It was a boarding house. Anne was in there now; but Dot had every reason to think that she might come out.

It was not quite as easy for a girl, as for a man, to stand loitering in a public place without attracting attention. But Dot, Heaven knows, was experienced. My sister is a trig little figure. She generally wears very unobtrusive sports clothes. She's a small, dark girl, not in the slightest sense beautiful. But she's pretty, with an alert personality which makes her immensely attractive.

Dot was tense now; she had been waiting here in the block more than half an hour. Would Anne come out . . . ? Dot, as planned, had taken the stricken girl home, had sat with her awhile until she fully recovered. But Dot's persuasive, careful questions had only yielded disappointment. Whatever this girl bookkeeper might really know of the grisly affair, Dot could not guess. Resolutely Anne had parried every question.

But she had seen that Anne was tense; frightened, with an apprehension which was akin to terror. And as the evening grew later, it had become evident that Anne wanted to get rid of her solicitous visitor. My little sister, as I have indicated, is a good guesser rather than a logician. Her guess was that just before the weird affair on the bridge, Duffy had arranged something with Anne—something with which Dot's presence was interfering. So Dot had left. . . .

Her guess was right. At about quarter past eleven, Anne came out. From quite a distance down the block, Dot followed her as she headed east. Modern disguise for a detective hardly includes the traditional big mustache and chin whiskers. It is, instead, more often a question of minor details. In that line, a woman has a big advantage—especially in dealing with another woman. Dot's cloth sport hat was designed to permit instant and radical alteration of shape. That, in itself, worked wonders in her aspect. Her jacket was reversible, from a quiet grey on one side, to a somewhat sporty plaid on the other. She was sure that from a little distance, Anne would not recognize her.

At Seventh Avenue, Anne went into an uptown subway kiosk. That sort of thing requires a quick cleverness when you're tailing. Dot boarded the Van Cortlandt Express just a bit after the other girl—and into an adjacent car. It was a long but quick ride. At Dykeman Street Anne disembarked; and Dot followed her west, down into that queerly wild and lonely wooded region where the Spuyten Duyvil Creek flows into the Hudson River and terminates Manhattan Island. There are patches of woods here on the side, with the railroad trestle winding high over the ancient Dutch-named creek. It is still New York City, but one would hardly guess it.

Anne walked swiftly, though sometimes seeming uncertain as to her direction. The house which Dot finally realized Anne sought stood on a small but rugged hillside, facing the shabby creek and the Hudson River. The encroaching city was close; but here on the descending slope, the shadowed grounds of the huge old house were solidly dark. Dot had a vague idea of the place—one of those old Dutch mansions which still are standing. A place of ornate gabled roofs—a very typical old haunted house, somber and black, apparently deserted now, with great black trees clustered around it.

At the gate, Anne hesitated for a moment, as though in fear. Then she moved forward through the dark garden. Dot was outside on the winding driveway. On the verandah a brief flashlight beam showed. A man had come out to meet the girl; and at once they went into the front door, which closed after them.

Was it Peter Duffy she had met? Dot could not be sure. . . . My sister can break into anything but a bank vault without much difficulty. After a minute or two of prowling she found a window not too securely fastened. And like a cat, she went in.

The room in which she found herself was furnished—a sort of old-fashioned parlor. The padded furniture looked ghostly with its white summer slip covers. The place was heavy with brooding silence. Then Dot heard a murmur of voices. More than ever like a cat, with her automatic in hand, she moved into a dim hall. Another room showed a vague spot of light—the flickering light of a candle.

Through an opened doorway, Dot peered presently into what seemed a big old-fashioned den. Trophies were on the wall; the place was crowded with mounted specimens of fish and animals. An ornate onyx-top table held an array of Oriental curiosities. To one side, in a shadowed recess, there was a suit of armor—trappings of a knight of the Middle Ages, while on a taboret beside it—curious anachronism—stood a modern telephone. The big, littered room had only this hall door, and a single window, shrouded by drawn shade and portier.

All this Dot saw at her first swift glance. The lighted candle was on the taboret by the telephone. Its flickering beams showed Peter Duffy and Anne Johnson on a small couch nearby. The girl's arms were around him as she sat pleading, her face white and her eyes wide with terror.

"Oh Pete—what have you done?"

"Stop it!" he growled. "Good God, don't snivel. Are you going to stand by

me or aren't you? I'm not as bad as he is, anyway. And I've got the money—
we'll be rich. What the hell more do you want?"

He was reaching into his pocket. "Here, take this." He shoved a roll of
bills at her. "That'll hold you—I'm going to beat it. We'll get together—it
won't be long, Anne. You got to get out of here now—an' when I get the rest
of the money from him, I'll scram."

He kissed her as she clung to him. So many otherwise good girls have
clung like this to a murderer! Dot's heart went out to her.

"Oh Pete—dear God—they'll catch you. This—"

"Quit it!" he growled again. "What's done is done. That damn Houghton
deserved it anyhow—"

"We'll talk more about that later," Dot said suddenly from the doorway.
"Put your hands up. You're going out of here without any fuss."

She advanced through the doorway, with her automatic leveled at them.
There's nothing about Dot, when she holds a gun on you, that would give
the impression you can trifle with her. Anne gave a startled scream and
jumped to her feet, clutching at Duffy. He also leaped up. His jaw dropped,
terror swept him, but obediently his arms went over his head.

"Thanks," Dot said as she slowly advanced. "Break away there—turn him
loose, Anne. I want to see if he's got any weapon on him. Is that telephone
working?"

"I—I don't know," Duffy gasped.

Still eyeing him, Dot started for the 'phone—to summon me, if possible—
or to call the police. She didn't reach that telephone.

Across the room, something struck the candle. The light went out, plunging the place into blackness.

Even now, Dot is not a bit sure just what happened. The ghastly thing
was so utterly beyond what anyone could have expected that it struck her
into a horrified chaos. That's not like my sister, but Heaven knows, in this
grisly case you couldn't blame her. The candle fell to the floor. The plate on
which it had been standing, crashed. Mingled with Duffy's terrified oath and
Anne's hysterical scream, Dot was aware of a queer hissing sound—like air
or steam escaping under pressure. It was mingled with the tinkling of breaking glass. Something had been thrown. It had struck Duffy. Dot heard his
cry. And a second later there was more breaking glass and a scream from
Anne. . . .

Dot had whirled; jumped backward. She was alert to a new antagonist,
but in the blackness she could see nothing. And then she recoiled as though
struck by a physical blow. Like a wall, a great wave of frigidity surged over
the black room. Before its advance, Dot staggered back into the hall. From
the room there was the thud of a body falling . . . then another. . . .

In the silence there was nothing to see; nothing now to hear. For a moment the cold air poured out into the hot hall—a low, heavy current that numbed Dot's legs and feet. But it eased presently, and she darted into the chilled room, with a wave of warm air, high up, following her. God knows she should not have been so incautious, but horror for what she knew she would find, impelled her. She snapped on her flashlight. On the floor Peter Duffy and Anne Johnson lay dead—two more of the ghastly frozen corpses, with stiffened clothing moist with melting iceflakes. Frozen heads and faces this time . . . ghastly faces, with flesh dark-grey.

Dot in that second was shivering with cold, shuddering with horror. And behind her there was a sudden sound. She had no time to whirl. Her automatic was struck from her hand. She tried to turn and hurl her flashlight; but a man's arms went around her. Big powerful arms jerking her slight figure backward with an encircling arm pressing her breasts, and a hand clapped upon her mouth!

V

"The Fiend's Got Me!"

That big ramshackle frame building which housed the Bridge Hand Laundry went up in flames like a tinder box. Neither Franklin's body, nor the body of the nude woman in the cellar were recovered. And a short while later, from the midst of police, firemen and all the chaos of that East Side neighborhood, I summarily decamped.

Dot and I live in an apartment up near Columbia University. I grabbed our parked car, which was near the laundry, and went home. Dot would be there, I hoped. But she wasn't. We have a little phonograph-recording gadget rigged on our private telephone. But there was no message on it.

Apprehensive, I sat down to wait, wondering how Dot was making out with Anne Johnson. Vehemently I wanted to connect with Dot, before I started off on a new trail. And there seemed plenty of new trails. The weird case appeared to have clarified a bit. Duffy's diabolic chemistry was plain now. But Duffy, I reasoned, was just a tool of the sinister, diseased Leo Zorn. I could begin to see the motive. A mentality warped—a brooding, depressive mind. Lord knows, I had seen that in the aspect of Leo Zorn, up there in Houghton's library, just before Houghton so gruesomely turned into the first of the frozen corpses. The brooding Zorn, doubtlessly with an incurable disease eating into him, had come to hate Houghton, his erstwhile employer. He had been stricken through working with chemicals in Houghton's plant, and felt that Houghton personally was to blame.

All this was pretty clear. And there could be still other motives in Zorn's unbalanced mind. Houghton's young wife was Zorn's sister. Houghton was rich. With his sister inheriting wealth, Zorn of course could profit by it. Was Gloria Houghton in the plot? On that point I could not be sure. I recalled that she had seemed an imperious, headstrong young woman. Not very brainy—the exact type who so often uses her physical beauty for her own selfish advancement. A woman perhaps of loose morals. But a murderess? I doubted it. I thought rather that she was the unwitting cause of a portion of Zorn's motive.

All that was very simple. But why had Anne Johnson been an intended victim? The fear that Duffy had told her too much? On the other hand, I had a sneaking suspicion that maybe Anne's near-death on the bridge had been an accident. Through some mistake—the details of which, for a fact we never have learned—Anne put on those garments, that evening in the laundry to go out with Duffy. She thought they were hers. But they weren't. They had been prepared with chemicals by Duffy—prepared perhaps for the murder of that other woman whose corpse now was burned to ashes in the inferno of the laundry cellar. And Anne got them by mistake.

I think I was right in that reasoning concerning Anne Johnson. But who was the gruesome nude woman in the cellar? I could not guess. So far, quite obviously, she had not previously come into the case. But I could imagine what Zorn was doing there: laying a powder train for an incendiary fire to burn the laundry, that nude corpse—and any chemical evidence that Duffy had left around. . . . And why had Franklin been killed? That of course was obvious—to prevent him from telling me the very things about Duffy which he had told!

Midnight came as I sat there at home alone, pondering, waiting for Dot. Still no word from her. That address which Duffy had burned and I had read on the ashes in his locker, was the old Stuyvesant Mansion, up in the Dykeman section. I had heard that the rich young Charlie Stuyvesant, sportsman and world traveler, was in the Orient; and his three maiden aunts, all that was left of the famous old Dutch-New York family, were in England for a month of the summer. . . . Why was the Stuyvesant place of interest to Duffy? . . . Life is sometimes very ironical. I was worried about Dot; and I was sitting inactive, wondering if I ought to go up and investigate that old Dykeman house, and in reality, at this moment Dot was in deadly danger, in that house!

Then suddenly my telephone rang. I hadn't realized quite how apprehensive I was over Dot; my hand was shaking as I reached for the receiver.

"George? Listen—don't talk—" I stiffened at the swift intensity of Dot's low, furtive voice. "The fiend's got me! Stuyvesant Mansion—Dykeman

Parkway. Got me locked in a room—ground floor, west. He's gone down-stairs—to destroy chemical apparatus. Oh George—come alone! Don't tell anyone—no police! If he's warned of attack, he'll kill me! You'll have a better chance getting in here alone—Here he comes now. Oh George, George!"

The 'phone clicked as the connection broke. Numbly I hung up. Maybe you can imagine how I felt. Anyway, when in a minute or two I came out of my numbed fog, I grabbed my cap, went down to my car, I guess I broke about every rule against reckless driving in that dash up to Dykeman Street. . . .

The weird, haunted-looking old house was solid black when I crept upon it. Not a glimpse of light; and nothing but a somber brooding silence. Ground floor west—back. Dot's furtive words whirled in my head. I don't know how to describe the combination within me of quivering confused terror, mingled with the realization that I had to put this job over now. . . . *The fiend's got me!* In all our years together, my little sister had never had occasion before to say such words. They pounded in my head like a horrible knell. . . . Was I too late? Would I find her, like those others, a ghastly frozen corpse?

I located a dark window only a few feet above ground, which seemed as though it were the west, back room Dot had meant. It was locked; but the old lock yielded when I pried it, with only a little rasp of sound. Slowly, cautiously inch by inch, I raised the sash. There was no sound from within the room. With the utmost care I raised the blind. Still there was only blackness, and my groping hand found a dark portier inside, close against the window. I shoved it slowly aside.

The air of the room was chill and dank. I saw a faint flickering glow of light that drifted in through an opened opposite doorway—light from a candle in an outside hall. The faint reflected radiance showed me a room crowded with trophies. And on a small couch, Dot was lying! My racing heart thumped with triumph and relief. I saw that she was bound and gagged—but not a frozen corpse. Thank God for that. She was alive; appar-ently unharmed. She had heard the light noise I made at the window—her eyes were turned my way as she mutely stared.

Weapon in hand, I climbed through the window. "Dot—thank God—" I whispered. Her body twitched as she strained at her bonds to answer me. As I bent over her, reaching for the cloth gag that was tied into her mouth, she tried to mumble. And her eyes were imploring me.

Imploring me. God knows—since that telephone call from her that so struck me with terror—I was anything but normal. And now the rush of my thank-fulness so swept me that I did not interpret her imploring eyes. And her words in my memory, as I had heard them over the 'phone—"Come alone, George—don't bring the police—" Surely I should have realized. . . .

I was reaching for her gag, when from the dimly candlelit hall a groan sounded. A choked gurgling groan—and then a sudden oncoming tread! It snapped me into alertness. I jumped sidewise from Dot, whirled up my automatic as the candlelit doorway was blotted by a squat hunchbacked figure!

Leo Zorn!

My finger was pressing the trigger of my gun. But I didn't fire. Zorn was a silhouette for a second. Then he took a staggering step, not forward, but backward from the doorway. And the light fell on the front of him. His ghastly, bloated, diseased face was blood-smeared! In his barrel chest a horrible wound was oozing crimson upon his shirt! In that second as I withheld my shot, he tottered on buckling legs, half twisted around and crumpled to the hall floor.

"Dot! Good God—" I gasped as I jumped for Zorn. There was a choked mumble from Dot. And another sound, behind me! All I saw as I whirled was a crouching dark blob of figure, partly behind the voluminous black portiers near the window. A crouching man, with his arm going up and back, his hand clutching a white ball on which the faint light glistened as he was in the act of throwing it.

My shot rang out. Then another, and another, as fast as I could fire. Heaven knows, I was taking no chances this time. There was a tinkling crash of glass—the white ball shattered above his head by my first bullet. Then there was a thud as he fell forward. I was running at him; but through the acid smoke of my shots, a wave of cold struck at me—a blast from the fiend's crumpled body so that I staggered back, rushed to Dot and with her in my arms, dashed from the room. As I untied her, with cold air blasting out at us, I saw that Zorn—lying here in the hall—was not dead. He was lying with his gaze on us; and I caught his faint, blood-choked words:

"You got him? I tried—but he—got me instead—"

We were back in the room in a moment—staring at the crumpled body of John Tremaine, Houghton's lawyer, where he lay with one of my bullets in his shoulder! It hadn't been my bullet that killed him, but the shattered glass ball which he had been about to throw at me! Wisps of white vapor were rising from him now—vapor like liquid air volatilizing into the infinitely warmer air of the room. The handsome, stalwart Tremaine, with the frozen flesh of his face ghastly grey-white; and his frozen eyeballs congealed with the look of terror still in them. The last of the frozen corpses.

Zorn did not die. From him—and from Gloria Houghton's full confession on which the D.A. agreed not to prosecute her—we were able to piece together the main points of John Tremaine's grisly murder plot. His motive, queerly enough, I had doped out fairly well, though I had thought Zorn was the fiend. Gloria Zorn had had an affair with the handsome, unscrupulous Tremaine before she married the rich, middle-aged Houghton. And after her marriage, Tremaine came at her again—with love-making, and threats of telling her husband of their former relations. She had again yielded; and his hold over her was complete. Tremaine, it seems, was always in money trouble—a spendthrift; and a gambler, always losing. From Gloria he had forced considerable sums of money. And then he conceived a bigger stake: the murder of her husband. He knew that as a rich widow, she would gladly marry him, and it would be no trouble to get the Houghton fortune away from her. But Tremaine was also entangled with another woman—the woman whose corpse I had seen in the cellar of the laundry. He included her in his gruesome killings, to get rid of her and clear the way for Gloria. It was Tremaine who had set that time-fuse and caused the fire—for just the reasons I had thought.

The horrible method of murder was, to Tremaine, undoubtedly a brilliant stroke of cleverness, which would divert all possible suspicion from him. Weird frozen corpses—that chain of murders could so easily be imagined the work of the diseased, brooding Zorn! Tremaine had lured Zorn to that old Stuyvesant house; stabbed him. And was planning to leave him with the bodies of no less than four frozen corpses—Anne and Duffy, Dot and myself. Zorn would be considered a mad fiend, wholly crazed at last so that he had committed suicide among his victims. It had all worked out just as Tremaine planned. Almost. But Zorn had been a sudden obstacle. Tremaine hated Gloria's deformed brother, and the hatred was mutual. Zorn knew of his sister's helpless infatuation. And when Bob Allen was murdered, and then Houghton, Zorn suspected Tremaine. But he wanted to settle it himself. He was afraid to tell the police, afraid that his sister would be involved as an accomplice. Zorn had seen Tremaine and Duffy go to the laundry the previous night. Tonight Zorn had prowled in the cellar, just before the fire, and had discovered the nude corpse. And he was just as surprised as I was when the blast went off and almost got us both.

That fellow Allen—you've got to admit he had all the makings of a genius. They tell me now that police chemists have worked out Allen's full process, as completed by Duffy. The basic chemistry of it is, in broad principle, just about what I conceived, from Duffy's formula. Not the manufacture of dry ice—not exactly liquid air. Something, I gather, midway, chemically, between them. The chemists say that they have impregnated fabrics, and gotten a brief temperature of more than minus two hundred degrees, when moisture was added. And they've constructed some of the diabolic little glass balls—bombs of coldness, as you might luridly call them. The exact same chemical reactions—the dry chemicals held separate from the moisture within the glass ball—mixing when the glass is shattered. It's a neat chemical formula, they say. But it's a formula for murder—I don't want any more of it. Not as long as I live.

Tremaine, we have learned, knew the Stuyvesant family, and thus he and Duffy had access to the old mansion. When he caught Dot there, instead of killing her at once, he used her to trap me. He was standing at her side, with a knife pressed against her breast, when she 'phoned that decoy message to me.

I think that's about all I need recount of the case of the frozen corpses. It was a weird, ghastly affair. The damned thing sets me shuddering, even now. And most particularly, God knows, I don't ever want my little sister to telephone me again and have to say, "The fiend's got me!" Those terrible words give me the creeps, every time I think of them.

Names in the Black Book

Robert E. Howard

Three unsolved murders in a week are not so unusual—for River Street," grunted Steve Harrison, shifting his muscular bulk restlessly in his chair.

His companion lighted a cigarette and Harrison observed that her slim hand was none too steady. She was exotically beautiful, a dark, supple figure, with the rich colors of purple Eastern nights and crimson dawns in her dusky hair and red lips. But in her dark eyes Harrison glimpsed the shadow of fear. Only once before had he seen fear in those marvelous eyes, and the memory made him vaguely uneasy.

"It's your business to solve murders," she said.

"Give me a little time. You can't rush things, when you're dealing with the people of the Oriental quarter."

"You have less time than you think," she answered cryptically. "If you do not listen to me, you'll never solve these killings."

"I'm listening."

"But you won't believe. You'll say I'm hysterical—seeing ghosts and shying at shadows."

"Look here, Joan," he exclaimed impatiently. "Come to the point. You called me to your apartment and I came because you said you were in deadly danger. But now you're talking riddles about three men who were killed last week. Spill it plain, won't you?"

"Do you remember Erlik Khan?" she asked abruptly.

Involuntarily his hand sought his face, where a thin scar ran from temple to jaw-rim.

"I'm not likely to forget him," he said. "A Mongol who called himself Lord of the Dead. His idea was to combine all the Oriental criminal societies in America in one big organization, with himself at the head. He might have done it, too, if his own men hadn't turned on him."

"Erlik Khan has returned," she said.

"What!" His head jerked up and he glared at her incredulously. "What are you talking about? I saw him die, and so did you!"

"I saw his hood fall apart as Ali ibn Suleyman struck with his keen-edged scimitar," she answered. "I saw him roll to the floor and lie still. And then the house went up in flames, and the roof fell in, and only charred bones were ever found among the ashes. Nevertheless, Erlik Khan has returned."

Harrison did not reply, but sat waiting for further disclosures, sure they would come in an indirect way. Joan La Tour was half Oriental, and partook of many of the characteristics of her subtle kin.

"How did those three men die?" she asked, though he was aware that she knew as well as he.

"Li-crin, the Chinese merchant, fell from his own roof," he grunted. "People on the street heard him scream and then saw him come hurtling down. Might have been an accident—but middle-aged Chinese merchants don't go climbing around on roofs at midnight.

"Ibrahim ibn Achmet, the Syrian curio dealer, was bitten by a cobra. That might have been an accident too, only I know somebody dropped the snake on him through the skylight.

"Jacob Kossova, the Levantine exporter, was simply knifed in a back alley. Dirty jobs, all of them, and no apparent motive on the surface. But motives are hidden deep, in River Street. When I find the guilty parties I'll uncover the motives."

"And those murders suggest nothing to you?" exclaimed the girl, tense with suppressed excitement. "You do not see the link that connects them? You do not grasp the point they all have in common? Listen—all these men were formerly associated in one way or another with Erlik Khan!"

"Well?" he demanded. "That doesn't mean that Erlik Khan's spook killed them! We found plenty of bones in the ashes of the house, but there were members of his gang in other parts of the city. His gigantic organization went to pieces, after his death for lack of a leader, but the survivors were never uncovered. Some of these might be paying off old grudges."

"Then why did they wait so long to strike? It's been a year since we saw Erlik Khan die. I tell you, the Lord of the Dead himself, alive or dead, has returned and is striking down these men for one reason or another. Perhaps they refuse to do his bidding once more. Five were marked for death. Three have fallen."

"How do you know that?" said he.

"Look!" From beneath the cushions of the divan on which she sat she drew something, and rising, came and bent beside him while she unfolded it.

It was a square piece of parchment-like substance, black and glossy. On it were written five names, one below the other, in a bold flowing hand—and in crimson, like spilled blood. Through the first three names a crimson bar had been drawn. They were the names of Li-chin, Ibrahim ibn Achmet, and Jacob Kossova. Harrison grunted explosively. The last two names, as yet unmarred, were those of Joan La Tour and Stephen Harrison.

"Where did you get this?" he demanded.

"It was shoved under my door last night, while I slept. If all the doors and windows had not been locked, the police would have found it pinned to my corpse this morning."

"But still I don't see what connection—"

"It is a page from the Black Book of Erlik Khan!" she cried. "The book of the dead! I have seen it, when I was a subject of his in the old days. There he kept accounts of his enemies, alive and dead. I saw that book, open, the very day of the night Ali ibn Suleyman killed him—a big book with jade-hinged ebony covers and glossy black parchment pages. Those names were not in it then; they have been written in since Erlik Khan died—and that is Erlik Khan's handwriting!"

If Harrison was impressed he failed to show it.

"Does he keep his books in English?"

"No, in a Mongolian script. This is for our benefit. And I know we are hopelessly doomed. Erlik Khan never warned his victims unless he was sure of them."

"Might be a forgery," grunted the detective.

"No! No man could imitate Erlik Khan's hand. He wrote those names himself. He has come back from the dead! Hell could not hold a devil as black as he!" Joan was losing some of her poise in her fear and excitement. She ground out the half-consumed cigarette and broke the cover of a fresh carton. She drew forth a slim white cylinder and tossed the package on the table. Harrison took it up and absently extracted one for himself.

"Our names are in the Black Book! It is a sentence of death from which there is no appeal!" She struck a match and was lifting it, when Harrison struck the cigarette from her with a startled oath. She fell back on the divan, bewildered at the violence of his action, and he caught up the package and began gingerly to remove the contents.

"Where'd you get these things?"

"Why, down at the corner drug store, I guess," she stammered. "That's where I usually—"

"Not these you didn't," he grunted. "These fags have been specially treated. I don't know what it is, but I've seen one puff of the stuff knock a man stone dead. Some kind of a hellish Oriental drug mixed with the tobacco. You were out of your apartment while you were phoning me—"

"I was afraid my wire was tapped," she answered. "I went to a public booth down the street."

"And it's my guess somebody entered your apartment while you were gone and switched cigarettes on you. I only got a faint whiff of the stuff when I started to put that fag in my mouth, but it's unmistakable. Smell it yourself. Don't be afraid. It's deadly only when ignited."

She obeyed, and turned pale.

"I told you! We were the direct cause of Erlik Khan's overthrow! If you hadn't smelt that drug, we'd both be dead now, as he intended!"

"Well," he grunted, "it's a cinch somebody's after you, anyway. I still say it can't be Erlik Khan, because nobody could live after the lick on the head I saw Ali ibn Suleyman hand him, and I don't believe in ghosts. But you've got to be protected until I run down whoever is being so free with his poisoned cigarettes."

"What about yourself? Your name's in his book too."

"Never mind me," Harrison growled pugnaciously. "I reckon I can take care of myself." He looked capable enough, with his cold blue eyes, and the muscles bulging in his coat. He had shoulders like a bull.

"This wing's practically isolated from the rest of the building," he said, "and you've got the third floor to yourself?"

"Not only the third floor of the wing," she answered. "There's no one else on the third floor anywhere in the building at present."

"That makes it fine!" he exclaimed irritably. "Somebody could sneak in and cut your throat without disturbing anyone. That's what they'll try, too, when they realize the cigarettes didn't finish you. You'd better move to a hotel."

"That wouldn't make any difference," she answered, trembling. Her nerves obviously were in a bad way. "Erlik Khan would find me, anywhere. In a hotel, with people coming and going all the time, and the rotten locks they have on the doors, with transoms and fire escapes and everything, it would just be that much easier for him."

"Well, then, I'll plant a bunch of cops around here."

"That wouldn't do any good, either. Erlik Khan has killed again and again in spite of the police. They do not understand his ways."

"That's right," he muttered uncomfortably aware of a conviction that to summon men from headquarters would surely be signing those men's death warrants, without accomplishing anything else. It was absurd to suppose that the dead Mongol fiend was behind these murderous attacks, yet—Harrison's flesh crawled along his spine at the memory of things that had taken place in River Street—things he had never reported, because he did not wish to be thought either a liar or a madman. The dead do not return—but what seems absurd on Thirty-ninth Boulevard takes on a different aspect among the haunted labyrinths of the Oriental quarter.

"Stay with me!" Joan's eyes were dilated, and she caught Harrison's arm with hands that shook violently. "We can defend these rooms! While one sleeps the other can watch! Do not call the police; their blunders would doom us. You have worked in the quarter for years, and are worth more than the whole police force. The mysterious instincts that are a part of my Eastern heritage are alert to danger. I feel peril for us both, near, creeping closer, gliding around us like serpents in the darkness!"

"But I can't stay here," he scowled worriedly. "We can't barricade ourselves and wait for them to starve us out. I've got to hit back—find out who's behind all this. The best defense is a good offense. But I can't leave you here unguarded, either. Damn!" He clenched his big fists and shook his head like a baffled bull in his perplexity.

"There is one man in the city besides yourself I could trust," she said suddenly. "One worth more than all the police. With him guarding me, I could sleep safely."

"Who is he?"

"Khoda Khan."

"That fellow? Why, I thought he'd skipped months ago."

"No; he's been hiding in Levant Street."

"But he's a confounded killer himself!"

"No, he isn't; not according to his standards, which means as much to him as yours do to you. He's an Afghan who was raised in a code of blood-feud and vengeance. He's as honorable according to his creed of life as you or I. And he's my friend. He'd die for me."

"I reckon that means you've been hiding him from the law," said Harrison with a searching glance which she did not seek to evade. He made no further comment. River Street is not South Park Avenue. Harrison's own methods were not always orthodox, but they generally got results.

"Can you reach him?" he asked abruptly. She nodded.

"Alright. Call him and tell him to beat it up here. Tell him he won't be molested by the police, and after the brawl's over, he can go back into hiding. But after that it's open season if I catch him. Use your phone. Wire may be tapped, but we'll have to take the chance. I'll go downstairs and use the booth in the office. Lock the door, and don't open it to anybody until I get back."

When the bolts clicked behind him, Harrison turned down the corridor toward the stairs. The apartment house boasted no elevator. He watched all sides warily as he went. A peculiarity of architecture had, indeed, practically isolated that wing. The wall opposite Joan's doors was blank. The only way to reach the other suites on that floor was to descend the stair and ascend another on the other side of the building.

As he reached the stair he swore softly; his heel had crunched a small vial on the first step. With some vague suspicion of a planted poison trap he stooped and gingerly investigated the splintered bits and the spilled contents. There was a small pool of colorless liquid which gave off a pungent, musky odor, but there seemed nothing lethal about it.

"Some damned Oriental perfume Joan dropped, I reckon," he decided. He descended the twisting stair without further delay and was presently in the booth in the office which opened on the street; a sleepy clerk dozed behind the desk.

Harrison got the chief of police on the wire and began abruptly.

"Say, Hoolihan, you remember that Afghan, Khoda Khan, who knifed a Chinaman about three months ago? Yes, that's the one. Well, listen: I'm using him on a job for a while, so tell your men to lay off, if they see him. Pass the word along *pronto.* Yes, I know it's very irregular; so's the job I hold down. In this case it's the choice of using a fugitive from the law, or seeing a law-abiding citizen murdered. Never mind what it's all about. This is my job, and I've got to handle it my own way. All right; thanks."

He hung up the receiver, thought vigorously for a few minutes, and then dialed another number that was definitely not related to the police station. In place of the chief's booming voice there sounded at the other end of the wire a squeaky whine framed in the argot of the underworld.

"Listen, Johnny," said Harrison with his customary abruptness, "you told me you thought you had a lead on the Kossova murder. What about it?"

"It wasn't no lie, boss!" The voice at the other end trembled with excitement. "I got a tip, and it's big!—*big!* I can't spill it over the phone, and I don't dare stir out. But if you'll meet me at Shan Yang's hop joint, I'll give you the dope. It'll knock you loose from your props, believe me it will!"

"I'll be there in an hour," promised the detective. He left the booth and glanced briefly out into the street. It was a misty night, as so many River Street nights are. Traffic was only a dim echo from some distant, busier section. Drifting fog dimmed the street lamps, shrouding the forms of occasional passers-by. The stage was set for murder; it only awaited the appearance of the actors in the dark drama.

Harrison mounted the stairs again. They wound up out of the office and up into the third story wing without opening upon the second floor at all. The architecture, like much of it in or near the Oriental section, was rather unusual. People of the quarter were notoriously fond of privacy, and even apartment houses were built with this passion in mind. His feet made no sound on the thickly carpeted stairs, though a slight crunching at the top step reminded him of the broken vial again momentarily. He had stepped on the splinters.

He knocked at the locked door, answered Joan's tense challenge and was admitted. He found the girl more self-possessed.

"I talked with Khoda Khan. He's on his way here now. I warned him that the wire might be tapped—that our enemies might know as soon as I called him, and try to stop him on his way here."

"Good," grunted the detective. "While I'm waiting for him I'll have a look at your suite."

There were four rooms, drawing room in front, with a large bedroom behind it, and behind that two smaller rooms, the maid's bedroom and the bathroom. The maid was not there, because Joan had sent her away at the first intimation of danger threatening. The corridor ran parallel with the suite, and the drawing room, large bedroom and bathroom opened upon it. That made three doors to consider. The drawing room had one big east window, overlooking the street, and one on the south. The big bedroom had one south window, and the maid's room one south and one west window. The bathroom had one window, a small one in the west wall, overlooking a small court bounded by a tangle of alleys and board-fenced backyards.

"Three outside doors and six windows to be watched, and this the top story," muttered the detective. "I still think I ought to get some cops here." But he spoke without conviction. He was investigating the bathroom when Joan called him cautiously from the drawing room, telling him that she thought she had heard a faint scratching outside the door. Gun in hand he opened the bathroom door and peered out into the corridor. It was empty. No shape of horror stood before the drawing room door. He closed the door, called reassuringly to the girl, and completed his inspection, grunting approval. Joan La Tour was a daughter of the Oriental quarter. Long ago she had provided against secret enemies as far as special locks and bolts could provide. The windows were guarded with heavy iron-braced shutters, and there was no trapdoor, dumb waiter nor skylight anywhere in the suite.

"Looks like you're ready for a siege," he commented.

"I am. I have canned goods laid away to last for weeks. With Khoda Khan I can hold the fort indefinitely. If things get too hot for you, you'd better come back here yourself—if you can. It's safer than the police station—unless they burn the house down."

A soft rap on the door brought them both round.

"Who is it?" called Joan warily.

"I, Khoda Khan, *sahiba*," came the answer in a low-pitched, but strong and resonant voice. Joan sighed deeply and unlocked the door. A tall figure bowed with a stately gesture and entered.

Khoda Khan was taller than Harrison, and though he lacked something of the American's sheer bulk, his shoulders were equally broad, and his garments could not conceal the hard lines of his limbs, the tigerish suppleness of his motions. His garb was a curious combination of costume, which is common in River Street. He wore a turban which well set off his hawk nose and black beard, and a long silk coat hung nearly to his knees. His trousers were conventional, but a silk sash girdled his lean waist, and his foot-gear was Turkish slippers.

In any costume it would have been equally evident that there was something wild and untamable about the man. His eyes blazed as no civilized man's ever did, and his sinews were like coiled springs under his coat. Harrison felt much as he would have felt if a panther had padded into the room, for the moment placid but ready at an instant's notice to go flying into flaming-eyed, red-taloned action.

"I thought you'd left the country," he said.

The Afghan smiled, a glimmer of white amidst the dark tangle of his beard.

"Nay, *sahib*. That son of a dog I knifed did not die."

"You're lucky he didn't," commented Harrison. "If you kill him you'll hang, sure."

"*Inshallah*," agreed Khoda Khan cheerfully. "But it was a matter of *izzat*—honor. The dog fed me swine's flesh. But no matter. The *memsahib* called me and I came."

"Alright. As long as she needs your protection the police won't arrest you. But when the matter's finished, things stand as they were. I'll give you time to hide again, if you wish, and then I'll try to catch you as I have in the past. Or if you want to surrender and stand trial, I'll promise you as much leniency as possible."

"You speak fairly," answered Khoda Khan. "I will protect the *memsahib*, and when our enemies are dead, you and I will begin our feud anew."

"Do you know anything about these murders?"

"Nay, *sahib*. The *memsahib* called me, saying Mongol dogs threatened her. I came swiftly, over the roofs, lest they seek to ambush me. None molested me. But here is something I found outside the door."

He opened his hand and exhibited a bit of silk, evidently torn from his sash. On it lay a crushed object that Harrison did not recognize. But Joan recoiled with a low cry.

"God! A black scorpion of Assam!"

"Aye—whose sting is death. I saw it running up and down before the door, seeking entrance. Another man might have stepped upon it without seeing it, but I was on my guard, for I smelled the Flower of Death as I came up the stairs. I saw the thing at the door and crushed it before it could sting me."

"What do you mean by the Flower of Death?" demanded Harrison.

"It grows in the jungles where these vermin abide. Its scent attracts them as wine draws a drunkard. A trail of the juice had somehow been laid to this door. Had the door been opened before I slew it, it would have darted in and struck whoever happened to be in its way."

Harrison swore under his breath, remembering the faint scratching noise Joan had heard outside the door.

"I get it now! They put a bottle of that juice on the stairs where it was sure to be stepped on. I did step on it, and broke it, and got the liquid on my shoe. Then I tracked down the stairs, leaving the scent wherever I stepped. Came back upstairs, stepped in the stuff again and tracked it on through the door. Then somebody downstairs turned that scorpion loose—the devil! That means they've been in this house since I was downstairs!—may be hiding somewhere here now! But somebody had to come into the office to put the scorpion on the trail—I'll ask the clerk—"

"He sleeps like the dead," said Khoda Khan. "He did not waken when I entered and mounted the stairs. What matters if the house is full of Mongols? These doors are strong, and I am alert!" From beneath his coat he drew the terrible Khyber knife—a yard long, with an edge like a razor. "I have slain *men* with this," he announced, grinning like a bearded mountain devil. "Pathans, Indians, a Russian or so. These Mongols are dogs on whom the good steel will be shamed."

"Well," grunted Harrison. "I've got an appointment that's overdue now. I feel queer walking out and leaving you two to fight these devils alone. But there'll be no safety for us until I've smashed this gang at its root, and that's what I'm out to do."

"They'll kill you as you leave the building," said Joan with conviction.

"Well, I've got to risk it. If you're attacked call the police anyway, and call me, at Shan Yang's joint. I'll come back here some time before dawn. But I'm hoping the tip I expect to get will enable me to hit straight at whoever's after us."

He went down the hallway with an eery feeling of being watched and scanned the stairs as if he expected to see it swarming with black scorpions, and he shied wide of the broken glass on the step. He had an uncomfortable sensation of duty ignored, in spite of himself, though he knew that his two companions did not want the police, and that in dealing with the East it is better to heed the advice of the East.

The clerk still sagged behind his desk. Harrison shook him without avail. The man was not asleep; he was drugged. But his heartbeat was regular, and the detective believed he was in no danger. Anyway, Harrison had no more time to waste. If he kept Johnny Kleck waiting too long, the fellow might become panicky and bolt, to hide in some rat-run for weeks.

He went into the street, where the lamps gleamed luridly through the drifting river mist, half expecting a knife to be thrown at him, or to find a cobra coiled on the seat of his automobile. But he found nothing his suspicion anticipated, even though he lifted the hood and the rumble-seat to see if a bomb had been planted. Satisfying himself at last, he climbed in and the girl watching him through the slits of a third-story shutter sighed relievedly to see him roar away unmolested.

Khoda Khan had gone through the rooms, giving approval in his beard of the locks, and having extinguished the lights in the other chambers he returned to the drawing room, where he turned out all lights except one small desk lamp. It shed a pool of light in the center of the room, leaving the rest in shadowy vagueness.

"Darkness baffles rogues as well as honest men," he said sagely, "and I see like a cat in the dark."

He sat cross-legged near the door that let into the bedroom, which he left partly open. He merged with the shadows so that all of him Joan could make out with any distinctness was his turban and the glimmer of his eyes as he turned his head.

"We will remain in this room, sahiba," he said. "Having failed with poison and reptile, it is certain that men will next be sent. Lie down on that divan and sleep, if you can. I will keep watch."

Joan obeyed, but she did not sleep. Her nerves seemed to thrum with tautness. The silence of the house oppressed her, and the few noises of the street made her start.

Khoda Khan sat motionless as a statue, imbued with the savage patience and immobility of the hills that bred him. Grown to manhood on the raw barbaric edge of the world, where survival depended on personal ability, his senses were whetted keener than is possible for civilized men. Even Harrison's trained faculties were blunt in comparison. Khoda Khan could still smell the faint aroma of the Flower of Death, mingled with the acrid odor of the crushed scorpion. He heard and identified every sound in or outside the house—knew which were natural, and which were not.

He heard the sounds on the roof long before his warning hiss brought Joan upright on the divan. The Afghan's eyes glowed like phosphorus in the shadows and his teeth glimmered dimly in a savage grin. Joan looked at him inquiringly. Her civilized ears heard nothing. But he heard and with his ears followed the sounds accurately and located the place where they halted. Joan heard something then, a faint scratching somewhere in the building, but she did not identify it—as Khoda Khan did—as the forcing of the shutters on the bathroom window.

With a quick reassuring gesture to her, Khoda Khan rose and melted like a slinking leopard into the darkness of the bedroom. She took up a blunt-nosed automatic, with no great conviction of reliance upon it, and groped on the table for a bottle of wine, feeling an intense need of stimulants. She was shaking in every limb and cold sweat was gathering on her flesh. She remembered the cigarettes, but the unbroken seal on the bottle reassured her. Even the wisest have their thoughtless moments. It was not until she had begun to drink that the peculiar flavor made her realize that the man who had shifted the cigarettes might just as easily have taken a bottle of wine and left another in its place, a facsimile that included an unbroken seal. She fell back on the divan, gagging.

Khoda Khan wasted no time, because he heard other sounds, out in the hall. His ears told him, as he crouched by the bathroom door, that the shutters had been forced—done almost in silence a job that a white man would have made sound like an explosion in an iron foundry—and now the window was being jimmied. Then he heard something stealthy and bulky drop into the room. Then it was that he threw open the door and charged in like a typhoon, his long knife held low.

Enough light filtered into the room from outside to limn a powerful, crouching figure, with dim snarling yellow features. The intruder yelped explosively, started a motion—and then the long Khyber knife, driven by an arm nerved to the fury of the Himalayas, ripped him open from groin to breastbone.

Khoda Khan did not pause. He knew there was only one man in the room, but through the open window he saw a thick rope dangling from above. He sprang forward, grasped it with both hands and heaved backward like a bull. The men on the roof holding it released it to keep from being jerked headlong over the edge, and he tumbled backward, sprawling over the corpse, the loose rope in his hands. He yelped exultantly, then sprang up and glided to the door that opened into the corridor. Unless they had another rope, which was unlikely, the men on the roof were temporarily out of the fight.

He flung open the door and ducked deeply. A hatchet cut a great chip out of the jamb, and he stabbed upward once, then sprang over a writhing body in the corridor, jerking a big pistol from its hidden scabbard.

The bright light of the corridor did not blind him. He saw a second hatchet-man crouching by the bedroom door, and a man in the silk robes of a mandarin working at the lock of the drawing room door. He was between them and the stairs. As they wheeled toward him he shot the hatchet-man in the belly. An automatic spat in the hand of the mandarin, and Khoda Khan felt the wind of the bullet. The next instant his own gun roared again and the Manchu staggered, the pistol flying from a hand that was suddenly a dripping red pulp. Then he whipped a long knife from his robes with his left hand and came along the corridor like a hurricane, his eyes glaring and his silk garments whipping about him.

Khoda Khan shot him through the head and the mandarin fell so near his feet that the long knife stuck into the floor and quivered a matter of inches from the Afghan's slipper.

But Khoda Khan paused only long enough to pass his knife through the hatchet-man he had shot in the belly—for his fighting ethics were those of the savage Hills—and then he turned and ran back into the bathroom. He fired a shot through the window, though the men on the roof were making no further demonstration, and then ran through the bedroom, snapping on lights as he went.

"I have slain the dogs, *sahiba!*" he exclaimed. "By Allah, they have tasted lead and steel! Others are on the roof but they are helpless for the moment. But men will come to investigate the shots, that being the custom of the *sahibs*, so it is expedient that we decide on our further actions, and the proper lies to tell—*Allah!*"

Joan LaTour stood bolt upright, clutching the back of the divan. Her face was the color of marble, and the expression was rigid too, like a mask of horror carved in stone. Her dilated eyes blazed like weird black fire.

"Allah shield us against Shaitan the Damned!" ejaculated Khoda Khan, making a sign with his fingers that antedated Islam by some thousands of years. "What has happened to you, *sahiba?*"

He moved toward her, to be met by a scream that sent him cowering back, cold sweat starting out on his flesh.

"Keep back!" she cried in a voice he did not recognize. "You are a demon! You are all demons! I see you! I hear your cloven feet padding in the night! I

see your eyes blazing from the shadows! Keep your taloned hands from me!
Aie!" Foam flecked her lips as she screamed blasphemies in English and
Arabic that made Khoda Khan's hair stand stiffly on end.

"*Sahiba!*" he begged, trembling like a leaf. "I am no demon! I am Khoda
Khan! I—" His outstretched hand touched her, and with an awful shriek she
turned and darted for the door, tearing at the bolts. He sprang to stop her,
but in her frenzy she was even quicker than he. She whipped the door open,
eluded his grasping hand and flew down the corridor, deaf to his anguished
yells.

When Harrison left Joan's house, he drove straight to Shan Yang's dive,
which, in the heart of River Street, masqueraded as a low-grade drinking
joint. It was late. Only a few derelicts huddled about the bar, and he noticed
that the barman was a Chinaman that he had never seen before. He stared
impassively at Harrison, but jerked a thumb toward the back door, masked
by dingy curtains, when the detective asked abruptly: "Johnny Kleck here?"

Harrison passed through the door, traversed a short dimly-lighted hallway and rapped authoritatively on the door at the other end. In the silence
he heard rats scampering. A steel disk in the center of the door shifted and a
slanted black eye glittered in the opening.

"Open the door, Shan Yang," ordered Harrison impatiently, and the eye
was withdrawn, accompanied by the rattling of bolts and chains.

He pushed open the door and entered the room whose illumination was
scarcely better than that of the corridor. It was a large, dingy, drab affair,
lined with bunks. Fires sputtered in braziers, and Shan Yang was making his
way to his accustomed seat behind a low counter near the wall. Harrison
spent but a single casual glance on the familiar figure, the known dingy silk
jacket worked in gilt dragons. Then he strode across the room to a door in
the wall opposite the counter to which Shan Yang was making his way. This
was an opium joint and Harrison knew it—knew those figures in the bunks
were Chinamen sleeping the sleep of the smoke. Why he had not raided it,
as he had raided and destroyed other opium-dens, only Harrison could have
said. But law-enforcement on River Street is not the orthodox routine it is
on Baskerville Avenue, for instance. Harrison's reasons were those of expedi-
ency and necessity. Sometimes certain conventions have to be sacrificed for
the sake of more important gains—especially when the law-enforcement of
a whole district (and in the Oriental quarter) rests on one's shoulders.

A characteristic smell pervaded the dense atmosphere, in spite of the reek
of dope and unwashed bodies—the dank odor of the river, which hangs
over the River Street dives or wells up from their floors like the black
intangible spirit of the quarter itself. Shan Yang's dive, like many others, was

built on the very bank of the river. The back room projected out over the water on rotting piles, at which the black river lapped hungrily.

Harrison opened the door, entered and pushed it to behind him, his lips framing a greeting that was never uttered. He stood dumbly, glaring.

He was in a small dingy room, bare except for a crude table and some chairs. An oil lamp on the table cast a smoky light. And in that light he saw Johnny Kleck. The man stood bolt upright against the far wall, his arms spread like a crucifix, rigid, his eyes glassy and staring, his mean, ratty features twisted in a frozen grin. He did not speak, and Harrison's gaze, traveling down him, halted with a shock. Johnny's feet did not touch the floor by several inches—

Harrison's big blue pistol jumped into his hand. Johnny Kleck was dead, that grin was a contortion of horror and agony. He was crucified to the wall by skewer-like dagger blades through his wrists and ankles, his ears spiked to the wall to keep his head upright. But that was not what had killed him. The bosom of Johnny's shirt was charred, and there was a round, blackened hole.

Feeling suddenly sick the detective wheeled, opened the door and stepped back into the larger room. The light seemed dimmer, the smoke thicker than ever. No mumblings came from the bunks; the fires in the braziers burned blue, with weird sputterings. Shan Yang crouched behind the counter. His shoulders moved as if he were tallying beads on an abacus.

"Shan Yang!" the detective's voice grated harshly in the murky silence. "Who's been in that room tonight besides Johnny Kleck?"

The man behind the counter straightened and looked full at him, and Harrison felt his skin crawl. Above the gilt-worked jacket an unfamiliar face returned his gaze. That was no Shan Yang; it was a man he had never seen— it was a Mongol. He started and stared about him as the men in the bunks rose with supple ease. They were not Chinese; they were Mongols to a man, and their slanted black eyes were not clouded by drugs.

With a curse Harrison sprang toward the outer door and with a rush they were on him. His gun crashed and a man staggered in mid-stride. Then the lights went out, the braziers were overturned, and in the stygian blackness hard bodies caromed against the detective. Long-nailed fingers clawed at his throat, thick arms locked about his waist and legs. Somewhere a sibilant voice was hissing orders.

Harrison's mauling left worked like a piston, crushing flesh and bone; his right wielded the gun barrel like a club. He forged toward the unseen door blindly, dragging his assailants by sheer strength. He seemed to be wading through a solid mass, as if the darkness had turned to bone and muscle about him. A knife licked through his coat, stinging his skin, and then he gasped as a silk cord looped about his neck, shutting off his wind, sinking deeper and deeper into the straining flesh. Blindly he jammed the muzzle against the nearest body and pulled the trigger. At the muffled concussion something fell away from him and the strangling agony lessened. Gasping for breath he groped and tore the cord away—then he was borne down under a rush of heavy bodies and something smashed savagely against his head. The darkness exploded in a shower of sparks that were instantly quenched in stygian blackness.

The smell of the river was in Steve Harrison's nostrils as he regained his addled senses, river-scent mingled with the odor of stale blood. The blood, he realized, when he had enough sense to realize anything, was clotted on his own scalp. His head swam and he tried to raise a hand to it, thereby discovering that he was bound hand and foot with cords that cut into the flesh. A candle was dazzling his eyes, and for awhile he could see nothing else. Then things began to assume their proper proportions, and objects grew out of nothing and became identifiable.

He was lying on a bare floor of new, unpainted wood, in a large square chamber, the walls of which were of stone, without paint or plaster. The ceiling was likewise of stone, with heavy, bare beams, and there was an open trap door almost directly above him, through which, in spite of the candle, he got a glimpse of stars. Fresh air flowed through that trap, bearing with it the river-smell stronger than ever. The chamber was bare of furniture, the candle stuck in a niche in the wall. Harrison swore, wondering if he was delirious. This was like an experience in a dream, with everything unreal and distorted.

He tried to struggle to a sitting position, but that made his head swim, so that he lay back and swore fervently. He yelled wrathfully, and a face peered down at him through the trap—a square, yellow face with beady slanted eyes. He cursed the face and it mocked him and was withdrawn. The noise of the door softly opening checked Harrison's profanity and he wriggled around to glare at the intruder.

And he glared in silence, feeling an icy prickling up and down his spine. Once before he had lain bound and helpless, staring up at a tall black-robed figure whose yellow eyes glimmered from the shadow of a dusky hood. But that man was dead; Harrison had seen him cut down by the scimitar of a maddened Druse.

"Erlik Khan!" The words were forced out of him. He licked lips suddenly dry.

"*Aie!*" It was the same ghostly, hollow voice that had chilled him in the old days. "Erlik Khan, the Lord of the Dead."

"Are you a man or a ghost?" demanded Harrison.

"I live."

"But I saw Ali ibn Suleyman kill you!" exclaimed the detective. "He slashed you across the head with a heavy sword that was sharp as a razor. He was a stronger man than I am. He struck with the full power of his arm. Your hood fell in two pieces—"

"And I fell like a dead man in my own blood," finished Erlik Khan. "But the steel cap I wore—as I wear now—under my hood, saved my life as it has more than once. The terrible stroke cracked it across the top and cut my scalp, fracturing my skull and causing concussion of the brain. But I lived, and some of my faithful followers, who escaped the sword of the Druse, carried me down through the subterranean tunnels which led from my house, and so I escaped the burning building. But I lay like a dead man for weeks, and it was not until a very wise man was brought from Mongolia that I recovered my senses, and sanity.

"But now I am ready to take up my work where I left off, though I must rebuild much. Many of my former followers had forgotten my authority. Some required to be taught anew who was master."

"And you've been teaching them," grunted Harrison, recovering his pugnacious composure.

"True. Some examples had to be made. One man fell off a roof, a snake bit another, yet another ran into knives in a dark alley. Then there was another matter. Joan La Tour betrayed me in the old days. She knows too many secrets. She had to die. So that she might taste agony in anticipation, I sent her a page from my book of the dead."

"Your devils killed Kleck," accused Harrison.

"Of course. All wires leading from the girl's apartment house are tapped. I myself heard your conversation with Kleck. That is why you were not attacked when you left the building. I saw that you were playing into my hands. I sent my men to take possession of Shan Yang's dive. He had no more use for his jacket, presently, so one donned it to deceive you. Kleck had somehow learned of my return; these stool pigeons are clever. But he had time to regret. A man dies hard with a white-hot point of iron bored through his breast."

Harrison said nothing and presently the Mongol continued.

"I wrote your name in my book because I recognized you as my most dangerous opponent. It was because of you that Ali ibn Suleyman turned against me.

"I am rebuilding my empire again, but more solidly. First I shall consolidate River Street, and create a political machine to rule the city. The men in office now do not suspect my existence. If all were to die, it would not be hard to find others to fill their places—men who are not indifferent to the clink of gold."

"You're mad," growled Harrison. "Control a whole city government from a dive in River Street?"

"It has been done," answered the Mongol tranquilly. "I will strike like a cobra from the dark. Only the men who obey my agent will live. He will be a white man, a figure-head whom men will think the real power, while I remain unseen. You might have been he, if you had a little more intelligence."

He took a bulky object from under his arm, a thick book with glossy black covers—ebony with green jade hinges. He riffled the night-hued pages and Harrison saw they were covered with crimson characters.

"My book of the dead," said Erlik Khan. "Many names have been crossed out. Many more have been added since I recovered my sanity. Some of them would interest you; they include names of the mayor, the chief of police, district attorney, a number of aldermen."

"That lick must have addled your brains permanently," snarled Harrison. "Do you think you can substitute a whole city government and get away with it?"

"I can and will. These men will die in various ways, and men of my own choice will succeed them in office. Within a year I will hold this city in the palm of my hand, and there will be none to interfere with me."

Lying staring up at the bizarre figure, whose features were, as always, shadowed beyond recognition by the hood, Harrison's flesh crawled with the conviction that the Mongol was indeed mad. His crimson dreams, always ghastly, were too grotesque and incredible for the visions of a wholly sane man. Yet he was dangerous as a maddened cobra. His monstrous plot must ultimately fail, yet he held the lives of many men in his hand. And Harrison, on whom the city relied for protection from whatever menace the Oriental quarter might spawn, lay bound and helpless before him. The detective cursed in fury.

"Always the man of violence," mocked Erlik Khan, with the suggestion of scorn in his voice. "Barbarian! Who lays his trust in guns and blades, who would check the stride of imperial power with blows of the naked fists! Brainless arm striking blind blows! Well, you have struck your last. Smell the river damp that creeps in through the ceiling? Soon it shall enfold you utterly and your dreams and aspirations will be one with the mist of the river."

"Where are we?" demanded Harrison.

"On an island below the city, where the marshes begin. Once there were warehouses here, and a factory, but they were abandoned as the city grew in the other direction, and have been crumbling into ruin for twenty years. I purchased the entire island through one of my agents, and am rebuilding to suit my own purposes an old stone mansion which stood here before the factory was built. None notices, because my own henchmen are the workmen, and no one ever comes to this marshy island. The house is invisible from the river, hidden as it is among the tangle of old rotting warehouses. You came here in a motor boat which was anchored beneath the rotting wharves behind Shan Yang's dive. Another boat will presently fetch my men who were sent to dispose of Joan La Tour."

"They may not find that so easy," commented the detective.

"Never fear. I know she summoned that hairy wolf, Khoda Khan, to her aid, and it's true that my men failed to slay him before he reached her. But I suppose it was a false sense of trust in the Afghan that caused you to make your appointment with Kleck. I rather expected you to remain with the foolish girl and try to protect her in your way."

Somewhere below them a gong sounded. Erlik Khan did not start, but there was a surprise in the lift of his head. He closed the black book.

"I have wasted enough time on you," he said. "Once before I bade you farewell in one of my dungeons. Then the fanaticism of a crazy Druse saved you. This time there will be no upset of my plans. The only men in this house are Mongols, who know no law but my will. I go, but you will not be lonely. Soon one will come to you."

And with a low, chilling laugh the phantom-like figure moved through the door and disappeared. Outside a lock clicked, and then there was stillness.

The silence was broken suddenly by a muffled scream. It came from somewhere below and was repeated half a dozen times. Harrison shuddered. No one who has ever visited an insane asylum could fail to recognize that sound. It was the shrieking of a mad woman. After these cries the silence seemed even more stifling and menacing.

Harrison swore to quiet his feelings, and again the velvet-capped head of the Mongol leered down at him through the trap.

"Grin, you yellow-bellied ape!" roared Harrison, tugging at his cords until the veins stood out on his temples. "If I could break these damned ropes I'd knock that grin around where your pigtail ought to be, you—" he went into minute details of the Mongol's ancestry, dwelling at length on the more scandalous phases of it, and in the midst of his noisy tirade he saw the leer change suddenly to a startled snarl. The head vanished from the trap and there came a sound like the blow of a butcher's cleaver.

Then another face was poked into the trap—a wild, bearded face, with blazing, bloodshot eyes, and surmounted by a disheveled turban.

"Sahib!" hissed the apparition.

"Khoda Khan!" ejaculated the detective, galvanized. "What the devil are you doing here?"

"Softly!" muttered the Afghan. "Let not the accursed ones hear!"

He tossed the loose end of a rope ladder down through the trap and came down in a rush, his bare feet making no sound as he hit the floor. He held his long knife in his teeth, and blood dripped from the point.

Squatting beside the detective he cut him free with reckless slashes that threatened to slice flesh as well as hemp. The Afghan was quivering with half-controlled passion. His teeth gleamed like a wolf's fangs amidst the tangle of his beard.

Harrison sat up, chafing his swollen wrists.

"Where's Joan? Quick, man, where is she?"

"Here! In this accursed den!"

"But—"

"That was she screaming a few minutes ago," broke in the Afghan, and Harrison's flesh crawled with a vague monstrous premonition.

"But that was a mad woman!" he almost whispered.

"The *sahiba* is mad," said Khoda Khan somberly. "Hearken, *sahib,* and then judge if the fault is altogether mine.

"After you left, the accursed ones let down a man from the roof on a rope. Him I knifed, and I slew three more who sought to force the doors. But when I returned to the *sahiba,* she knew me not. She fled from me into the street, and other devils must have been lurking nearby, because as she ran shrieking along the sidewalk, a big automobile loomed out of the fog and a Mongol stretched forth an arm and dragged her into the car, from under my very fingers. I saw his accursed yellow face by the light of a street lamp.

"Knowing she were better dead by a bullet than in their hands, I emptied my pistol after the car, but it fled like Shaitan the Damned from the face of Allah, and if I hit anyone in it, I know not. Then as I rent my garments and cursed the day of my birth—for I could not pursue it on foot—Allah willed that another automobile should appear. It was driven by a young man in evening clothes, returning from a revel, no doubt, and being cursed with curiosity he slowed down near the curb to observe my grief.

"So, praising Allah, I sprang in beside him and placing my knife point against his ribs bade him go with speed and he obeyed in great fear. The car of the damned ones was out of sight, but presently I glimpsed it again, and exhorted the youth to greater speed, so the machine seemed to fly like the steed of the Prophet. So, presently I saw the car halt at the river bank. I made the youth halt likewise, and he sprang out and fled in the other direction in terror.

"I ran through the darkness, hot for the blood of the accursed ones, but before I could reach the bank I saw the Mongols leave the car, carrying the *memsahib* who was bound and gagged, and they entered a motor-boat and headed out into the river toward an island which lay on the breast of the water like a dark cloud.

"I cast up and down on the shore like a madman, and was about to leap in and swim, though the distance was great, when I came upon a boat chained to a pile, but one driven by oars. I gave praise to Allah and cut the chain with my knife—see the nick in the edge?—and rowed after the accursed ones with great speed.

"They were far ahead of me, but Allah willed it that their engine should sputter and cease when they had almost reached the island. So I took heart, hearing them cursing in their heathen tongue, and hoped to draw along side and slay them all before they were aware of me. They saw me not in the darkness, nor heard my oars because of their own noises, but before I could reach them the accursed engine began again. So they reached a wharf on the marshy shore ahead of me, but they lingered to make the boat fast, so I was not too far behind them as they bore the *memsahib* through the shadows of the crumbling shacks which stood all about.

"Then I was hot to overtake and slay them, but before I could come up with them they had reached the door of a great stone house—this one, *sahib* —set in a tangle of rotting buildings. A steel fence surrounded it, with razor-edged spearheads set along the top but by Allah, that could not hinder a *lifter* of the Khyber! I went over it without so much as tearing my garments. Inside was a second wall of stone, but it stood in ruins.

"I crouched in the shadows near the house and saw that the windows were heavily barred and the doors strong. Moreover, the lower part of the house is full of armed men. So I climbed a corner of the wall, and it was not easy, but presently I reached the roof which at that part is flat, with a parapet. I expected a watcher, and so there was, but he was too busy taunting his captive to see or hear me until my knife sent him to hell. Here is his dagger; he bore no gun."

Harrison mechanically took the wicked, lean-bladed poniard.

"But what caused Joan to go mad?"

"*Sahib*, there was a broken wine bottle on the floor, and a goblet. I had no time to investigate it, but I know that wine must have been poisoned with the juice of the fruit called the black pomegranate. She can not have drunk much, or she would have died frothing and champing like a mad dog. But only a little will rob one of sanity. It grows in the jungles of Indo-China, and white men say it is a lie. But it is no lie; thrice I have seen men die after having drunk its juice, and more than once I have seen men, and women too, turn mad because of it. I have traveled in that hellish country where it grows."

"God!" Harrison's foundations were shaken by nausea. Then his big hands clenched into chunks of iron and baleful fire glimmered in his savage blue eyes. The weakness of horror and revulsion was followed by cold fury dangerous as the blood-hunger of a timber wolf.

"She may be already dead," he muttered thickly. "But dead or alive we'll send Erlik Khan to hell. Try that door."

It was of heavy teak, braced with bronze straps.

"It is locked," muttered the Afghan. "We will burst it."

He was about to launch his shoulder against it when he stopped short, the long Khyber knife jumping into his fist like a beam of light.

"Someone approaches!" he whispered, and a second later Harrison's more civilized—and therefore duller—ears caught a cat-like tread.

Instantly he acted. He shoved the Afghan behind the door and sat down quickly in the center of the room, wrapped a piece of rope about his ankles and then lay full length, his arms behind and under him. He was lying on the other pieces of severed cord, concealing them, and to the casual glance he resembled a man lying bound hand and foot. The Afghan understood and grinned hugely.

Harrison worked with the celerity of trained mind and muscles that eliminates fumbling delay and bungling. He accomplished his purpose in a matter of seconds and without undue noise. A key grated in the lock as he settled himself, and then the door swung open. A giant Mongol stood limned in the opening. His head was shaven, his square features passionless as the face of a copper idol. In one hand he carried a curiously shaped ebony block, in the other a mace such as was borne by the horsemen of Ghengis Khan—a straight-hafted iron bludgeon with a round head covered with steel points, and a knob on the other end to keep the hand from slipping.

He did not see Khoda Khan because when he threw back the door, the Afghan was hidden behind it. Khoda Khan did not stab him as he entered because the Afghan could not see into the outer corridor, and had no way of knowing how many men were following the first. But the Mongol was alone, and he did not bother to shut the door. He went straight to the man lying on the floor, scowling slightly to see the rope ladder hanging down through the trap, as if it was not usual to leave it that way, but he did not show any suspicion or call to the man on the roof.

He did not examine Harrison's cords. The detective presented the appearance the Mongol had expected, and this fact blunted his faculties as anything taken for granted is likely to do. As he bent down, over his shoulder

Harrison saw Khoda Khan glide from behind the door as silently as a panther.

Leaning his mace against his leg, spiked head on the floor, the Mongol grasped Harrison's shirt bosom with one hand, lifted his head and shoulders clear of the floor, while he shoved the block under his head. Like twin striking snakes the detective's hands whipped from behind him and locked on the Mongol's bull throat.

There was no cry; instantly the Mongol's slant eyes distended and his lips parted in a grin of strangulation. With a terrific heave he reared upright, dragging Harrison with him, but not breaking his hold, and the weight of the big American pulled them both down again. Both yellow hands tore frantically at Harrison's iron wrists; then the giant stiffened convulsively and brief agony reddened his black eyes. Khoda Khan had driven his knife between the Mongol's shoulders so that the point cut through the silk over the man's breastbone.

Harrison caught up the mace, grunting with savage satisfaction. It was a weapon more suited to his temperament than the dagger Khoda Khan had given him. No need to ask its use; if he had been bound and alone when the executioner entered, his brains would now have been clotting its spiked ball and the hollowed ebon block which so nicely accommodated a human head. Erlik Khan's executions varied along the whole gamut from the exquisitely subtle to the crudely bestial.

"The door's open," said Harrison. "Let's go!"

There were no keys on the body. Harrison doubted if the key in the door would fit any other in the building, but he locked the door and pocketed the key, hoping that would prevent the body from being soon discovered.

They emerged into a dim-lit corridor which presented the same unfinished appearance as the room they had just left. At the other end stairs wound down into shadowy gloom, and they descended warily, Harrison feeling along the wall to guide his steps. Khoda Khan seemed to see like a cat in the dark; he went down silently and surely. But it was Harrison who discovered the door. His hand, moving along the convex surface, felt the smooth stone give way to wood—a short narrow panel, through which a man could just squeeze. When the wall was covered with tapestry—as he knew it would be when Erlik Khan completed his house—it would be sufficiently hidden for a secret entrance.

Khoda Khan, behind him, was growing impatient at the delay, when somewhere below them both heard a noise simultaneously. It might have been a man ascending the winding stairs and it might not, but Harrison acted instinctively. He pushed and the door opened inward on noiseless oiled springs. A groping foot discovered narrow steps inside. With a whispered word to the Afghan he stepped through and Khoda Khan followed. He pulled the door shut again and they stood in total blackness with a curving wall on either hand. Harrison struck a match and a narrow stairs was revealed, winding down.

"This place must be built like a castle," Harrison muttered, wondering at the thickness of the walls. The match went out and they groped down in darkness too thick for even the Afghan to pierce. And suddenly both halted in their tracks. Harrison estimated that they had reached the level of the second floor, and through the inner wall came the mutter of voices. Harrison groped for another door, or a peep-hole for spying, but he found nothing of the sort. But straining his ear close to the stone, he began to understand what was being said beyond the wall, and a long-drawn hiss between clenched teeth told him that Khoda Khan likewise understood.

The first voice was Erlik Khan's; there was no mistaking that hollow reverberance. It was answered by a piteous, incoherent whimpering that brought sweat suddenly out on Harrison's flesh.

"No," the Mongol was saying. "I have come back, not from hell as your barbarian superstitions suggest, but from a refuge unknown to your stupid police. I was saved from death by the steel cap I always wear beneath my coif. You are at a loss as to how you got here?"

"I don't understand!" It was the voice of Joan La Tour, half-hysterical but undeniably sane. "I remember opening a bottle of wine, and as soon as I drank I knew it was drugged. Then everything faded out—I don't remember anything except great black walls, and awful shapes skulking in the darkness. I ran through gigantic shadowy halls for a thousand years—"

"They were hallucinations of madness, of the juice of the black pomegranate," answered Erlik Khan. Khoda Khan was muttering blasphemously in his beard until Harrison admonished him to silence with a fierce dig of his elbow. "If you had drunk more you would have died like a rabid dog. As it was, you went insane. But I knew the antidote—possessed the drug that restored your sanity."

"Why?" the girl whimpered bewilderedly.

"Because I did not wish you to die like a candle blown out in the dark, my beautiful white orchid. I wish you to be fully sane so as to taste to the last dregs the shame and agony of death, subtle and prolonged. For the exquisite, an exquisite death. For the coarse-fibered, the death of an ox, such as I have decreed for your friend Harrison."

"That will be more easily decreed than executed," she retorted with a flash of spirit.

"It is already accomplished," the Mongol asserted imperturbably. "The executioner has gone to him, and by this time Mr. Harrison's head resembles a crushed egg."

"Oh, God!" At the sick grief and pain in that moan Harrison winced and fought a frantic desire to shout out denial and reassurance.

Then she remembered something else to torture her.

"Khoda Khan! What have you done with Khoda Khan?"

The Afghan's fingers clamped like iron on Harrison's arm at the sound of his name.

"When my men brought you away they did not take time to deal with him," replied the Mongol. "They had not expected to take you alive, and when fate cast you into their hands, they came away in haste. He matters little. True, he killed four of my best men, but that was merely the deed of a wolf. He has no mentality. He and the detective are much alike—mere masses of brawn, brainless, helpless against intellect like mine. Presently I shall attend to him. His corpse shall be thrown on a dung-heap with a dead pig."

"Allah!" Harrison felt Khoda Khan trembling with fury. "Liar! I will feed his yellow guts to the rats!"

Only Harrison's grip on his arm kept the maddened Moslem from attacking the stone wall in an effort to burst through to his enemy. The detective was running his hand over the surface, seeking a door, but only blank stone rewarded him. Erlik Khan had not had time to provide his unfinished house with as many secrets as his rat-runs usually possessed.

They heard the Mongol clap his hands authoritatively, and they sensed the entrance of men into the room. Staccato commands followed in Mongolian, there was a sharp cry of pain or fear, and then silence followed the soft closing of a door. Though they could not see, both men knew instinctively that the chamber on the other side of the wall was empty. Harrison almost strangled with a panic of helpless rage. He was penned in these infernal walls and Joan La Tour was being borne away to some abominable doom.

"*Wallah!*" the Afghan was raving. "They have taken her away to slay her! Her life and our *izzat* is at stake! By the Prophet's beard and my feet! I will burn this accursed house! I will slake the fire with Mongol blood! In Allah's name, *sahib*, let us do something!"

"Come on!" snarled Harrison. "There must be another door somewhere!"

Recklessly they plunged down the winding stair, and about the time they had reached the first floor level, Harrison's groping hand felt a door. Even as he found the catch, it moved under his fingers. Their noise must have been heard through the wall, for the panel opened, and a shaven head was poked in, framed in the square of light. The Mongol blinked in the darkness, and

Harrison brought the mace down on his head, experiencing a vengeful satisfaction as he felt the skull give way beneath the iron spikes. The man fell face down in the narrow opening and Harrison sprang over his body into the outer room before he took time to learn if there were others. But the chamber was untenanted. It was thickly carpeted, the walls hung with black velvet tapestries. The doors were of bronze-bound teak, with gilt-worked arches. Khoda Khan presented an incongruous contrast, bare-footed, with draggled turban and red-smeared knife.

But Harrison did not pause to philosophise. Ignorant as he was of the house, one way was as good as another. He chose a door at random and flung it open, revealing a wide corridor carpeted and tapestried like the chamber. At the other end, through wide satin curtains that hung from roof to floor, a file of men was just disappearing—tall, black-silk clad Mongols, heads bent somberly, like a train of dusky ghosts. They did not look back.

"Follow them!" snapped Harrison. "They must be headed for the execution—"

Khoda Khan was already sweeping down the corridor like a vengeful whirlwind. The thick carpet deadened their footfalls, so even Harrison's big shoes made no noise. There was a distinct feeling of unreality, running silently down that fantastic hall—it was like a dream in which natural laws are suspended. Even in that moment Harrison had time to reflect that this whole night had been like a nightmare, possible only in the Oriental quarter, its violence and bloodshed like an evil dream. Erlik Khan had loosed the forces of chaos and insanity; murder had gone mad, and its frenzy was imparted to all actions and men caught in its maelstrom.

Khoda Khan would have burst headlong through the curtains—he was already drawing breath for a yell, and lifting his knife—if Harrison had not seized him. The Afghan's sinews were like cords under the detective's hands, and Harrison doubted his own ability to restrain him forcibly, but a vestige of sanity remained to the hillman.

Pushing him back, Harrison gazed between the curtains. There was a great double-valved door there, but it was partly open, and he looked into the room beyond. Khoda Khan's beard was jammed hard against his neck as the Afghan glared over his shoulder.

It was a large chamber, hung like the others with black velvet on which golden dragons writhed. There were thick rugs, and lanterns hanging from the ivory-inlaid ceiling cast a red glow that made for illusion. Black-robed men ranged along the wall might have been shadows but for their glittering eyes.

On a throne-like chair of ebony sat a grim figure, motionless as an image except when its loose robes stirred in the faintly moving air. Harrison felt the short hairs prickle at the back of his neck, just as a dog's hackles rise at the sight of an enemy. Khoda Khan muttered some incoherent blasphemy.

The Mongol's throne was set against a side wall. No one stood near him as he sat in solitary magnificence, like an idol brooding on human doom. In the center of the room stood what looked uncomfortably like a sacrificial altar—a curiously carved block of stone that might have come out of the heart of the Gobi. On that stone lay Joan La Tour, white as a marble statue, her arms outstretched like a crucifix, her hands and feet extending over the edges of the block. Her dilated eyes stared upward as one lost to hope, aware of doom and eager only for death to put an end to agony. The physical torture had not yet begun, but a gaunt half-naked brute squatted on his haunches at the end of the altar, heating the point of a bronze rod in a dish full of glowing coals.

"Damn!" It was half curse, half sob of fury bursting from Harrison's lips. Then he was hurled aside and Khoda Khan burst into the room like a flying dervish, bristling beard, blazing eyes, knife and all. Erlik Khan came erect with a startled guttural as the Afghan came tearing down the room like a headlong hurricane of destruction. The torturer sprang up just in time to meet the yard-long knife lashing down, and it split his skull down through the teeth.

"Aie!" It was a howl from a score of Mongol throats.

"Allaho akabar!" yelled Khoda Khan, whirling the red knife about his head. He threw himself on the altar, slashing at Joan's bonds with a frenzy that threatened to dismember the girl.

Then from all sides the black-robed figures swarmed in, not noticing in their confusion that the Afghan had been followed by another grim figure who came with less abandon but with equal ferocity.

They were aware of Harrison only when he dealt a prodigious sweep of his mace, right and left, bowling men over like ten-pins, and reached the altar through the gap made in the bewildered throng. Khoda Khan had freed the girl and he wheeled, spitting like a cat, his bared teeth gleaming and each hair of his beard stiffly on end.

"Allah!" he yelled—spat in the faces of the oncoming Mongols—crouched as if to spring into the midst of them—then whirled and rushed headlong at the ebony throne.

The speed and unexpectedness of the move were stunning. With a choked cry Erlik Khan fired and missed at point-blank range—and then the breath burst from Khoda Khan in an ear-splitting yell as his knife plunged into the Mongol's breast and the point sprang a hand's breadth out of his black-clad back.

The impetus of his rush unchecked, Khoda Khan hurtled into the falling figure, crashing it back on to the ebony throne which splintered under the impact of the two heavy bodies. Bounding up, wrenching his dripping knife free, Khoda Khan whirled it high and howled like a wolf.

"Ya Allah! Wearer of steel caps! Carry the taste of my knife in your guts— to hell with you!"

There was a long hissing intake of breath as the Mongols stared wide-eyed at the black-robed, red-smeared figure crumpled grotesquely among the ruins of the broken throne, and in the instant that they stood like frozen men, Harrison caught up Joan and ran for the nearest door, bellowing: "Khoda Khan! This way! Quick!"

With a howl and a whickering of blades the Mongols were at his heels. Fear of steel in his back winged Harrison's big feet, and Khoda Khan ran slantingly across the room to meet him at the door.

"Haste, sahib! Down the corridor! I will cover your retreat!"

"No! Take Joan and run!" Harrison literally threw her into the Afghan's arms and wheeled back in the doorway, lifting the mace. He was as berserk in his own way as was Khoda Khan, frantic with the madness that some-times inspired men in the midst of combat.

The Mongols came on as if they, too, were blood-mad. They jammed the door with square snarling faces and squat silk-clad bodies before he could slam it shut. Knives licked at him, and gripping the mace with both hands, he wielded it like a flail, working awful havoc among the shapes that strove in the doorway, wedged by the pressure from behind. The lights, the up-turned snarling faces that dissolved in crimson ruin beneath his flailing, all swam in a red mist. He was not aware of his individual identity. He was only a man with a club, transported back fifty thousand years, a hairy-breasted, red-eyed primitive, wholly possessed by the crimson instinct for slaughter.

He felt like howling his incoherent exultation with each swing of his bludgeon that crushed skulls and splattered blood into his face. He did not feel the knives that found him, hardly realizing it when the men facing him gave back, daunted at the havoc he was wreaking. He did not close the door then; it was blocked and choked by a ghastly mass of crushed and red-dripping flesh.

He found himself running down the corridor, his breath coming in great gulping gasps, following some dim instinct of preservation or realization of duty that made itself heard amidst the red dizzy urge to grip his foes and strike, strike, strike, until he was himself engulfed in the crimson waves of death. In such moments the passion to die—die fighting—is almost equal to the will to live.

In a daze, staggering, bumping into walls and caroming off them, he reached the further end of the corridor where Khoda Khan was struggling with a lock. Joan was standing now, though she reeled on her feet, and seemed on the point of collapse. The mob was coming down the long corridor full cry behind him. Drunkenly Harrison thrust Khoda Khan aside and whirling the blood-fouled mace around his head, struck a stupendous blow that shattered the lock, burst the bolts out of their sockets and caved in the heavy panels as if they had been cardboard. The next instant they were through and Khoda Khan slammed the ruins of the door which sagged on its hinges, but somehow held together. There were heavy metal brackets on each jamb, and Khoda Khan found and dropped an iron bar in place just as the mob surged against it.

Through the shattered panels they howled and thrust their knives, but Harrison knew until they hewed away enough wood to enable them to reach in and dislodge it, the bar across the door would hold the splintered barrier in place. Recovering some of his wits, and feeling rather sick, he herded his companions ahead of him with desperate haste. He noticed, briefly, that he was stabbed in the calf, thigh, arm and shoulder. Blood soaked his ribboned shirt and ran down his limbs in streams. The Mongols were hacking at the door, snarling like jackals over carrion.

The apertures were widening, and through them he saw other Mongols running down the corridor with rifles; just as he wondered why they did not shoot through the door, then saw the reason. They were in a chamber which had been converted into a magazine. Cartridge cases were piled high along the wall, and there was at least one box of dynamite. But he looked in vain for rifles or pistols. Evidently they were stored in another part of the building.

Khoda Khan was jerking the bolts on an opposite door, but he paused to glare about and yelping "Allah!" he pounced on an open case, snatched something out—wheeled, yelled a curse and threw back his arm, but Harrison grabbed his wrist.

"Don't throw that, you idiot! You'll blow us all to hell! They're afraid to shoot into this room, but they'll have that door down in a second or so, and finish us with their knives. Help Joan!"

It was a hand grenade Khoda Khan had found—the only one in an otherwise empty case, as a glance assured Harrison. The detective threw the door open, slammed it shut behind them as they plunged out into the starlight, Joan reeling, half carried by the Afghan. They seemed to have emerged at the back of the house. They ran across an open space, hunted creatures looking for a refuge. There was a crumbling stone wall, about breast-high to a man, and they ran through a wide gap in it, only to halt; a groan burst from Harrison's lips. Thirty steps behind the ruined wall rose the steel fence of which Khoda Khan had spoken, a barrier ten feet high, topped with keen points. The door crashed open behind them and a gun spat venomously. They were in a trap. If they tried to climb the fence the Mongols had but to pick them off like monkeys shot off a ladder.

"Down behind the wall!" snarled Harrison, forcing Joan behind an un-crumbled section of the stone barrier. "We'll make 'em pay for it, before they take us!"

The door was crowded with snarling faces, now leering in triumph. There were rifles in the hands of a dozen. They knew their victims had no fire-arms, and could not escape, and they themselves could use rifles without fear. Bullets began to splatter on the stone, then with a long-drawn yell Khoda Khan bounded to the top of the wall, ripping out the pin of the hand grenade with his teeth.

"*La illaha illulah; Muhammad rassoul ullah!*" he yelled, and hurled the bomb—not at the group which howled and ducked, but over their heads, into the magazine!

The next instant a rending crash tore the guts out of the night and a blinding blaze of fire ripped the darkness apart. In that glare Harrison had a glimpse of Khoda Khan, etched against the flame, hurtling backward, arms out-thrown—then there was utter blackness in which roared the thunder of the fall of the house of Erlik Khan as the shattered walls buckled, the beams splintered, the roof fell in and story after story came crashing down on the crumpled foundations.

How long Harrison lay like dead he never knew, blinded, deafened and paralyzed; covered by falling debris. His first realization was that there was something soft under him, something that writhed and whimpered. He had a vague feeling he ought not to hurt this soft something, so he began to shove the broken stones and mortar off him. His arm seemed dead, but eventually he excavated himself and staggered up, looking like a scarecrow in his rags. He groped among the rubble, grasped the girl and pulled her up.

"Joan!" His own voice seemed to come to him from a great distance; he had to shout to make her hear him. Their eardrums had been almost split by the concussion.

"Are you hurt?" He ran his one good hand over her to make sure.

"I don't think so," she faltered dazedly. "What—what happened?"

"Khoda Khan's bomb exploded the dynamite. The house fell in on the Mongols. We were sheltered by that wall; that's all that saved us."

The wall was a shattered heap of broken stone, half covered by rubble—a waste of shattered masonry with broken beams thrust up through the litter, and shards of walls reeling drunkenly. Harrison fingered his broken arm and tried to think, his head swimming.

"Where is Khoda Khan?" cried Joan, seeming finally to shake off her daze.

"I'll look for him." Harrison dreaded what he expected to find. "He was blown off the wall like a straw in a wind."

Stumbling over broken stones and bits of timber, he found the Afghan huddled grotesquely against the steel fence. His fumbling fingers told him of broken bones—but the man was still breathing. Joan came stumbling toward him, to fall beside Khoda Khan and flutter her quick fingers over him, sobbing hysterically.

"He's not like civilized man!" she exclaimed, tears running down her stained, scratched face. "Afghans are harder than cats to kill. If we could get him medical attention he'll live. Listen!" She caught Harrison's arm with galvanized fingers; but he had heard it too—the sputter of a motor that was probably a police launch, coming to investigate the explosion.

Joan was tearing her scanty garments to pieces to staunch the blood that seeped from the Afghan's wounds, when miraculously Khoda Khan's pulped lips moved. Harrison, bending close, caught fragments of words: "The curse of Allah—Chinese dog—swine's flesh—my *izzat.*"

"You needn't worry about your *izzat,*" grunted Harrison, glancing at the ruins which hid the mangled figures that had been Mongolian terrorists. "After this night's work you'll not go to jail—not for all the Chinamen in River Street."